D0620927

A
Garland Series

VICTORIAN

FICTION

NOVELS OF FAITH
AND DOUBT

A collection of 121 novels
in 92 volumes, selected by
Professor Robert Lee Wolff,
Harvard University,
with a separate introductory volume
written by him
especially for this series.

HAWKSTONE

William Sewell

Two volumes in one

Garland Publishing, Inc., New York & London

1976

Bibliographical note:

this facsimile has been made from a copy in the
British Museum
(1362.c.2)

Library of Congress Cataloging in Publication Data

Sewell, William, 1804-1874.
    Hawkstone.

    (Victorian fiction : Novels of faith and doubt)
    Reprint of the 1845 ed. published by J. Murray,
London.
    I. Title. II. Series.
PZ3.S5177Haw15 [PR5349.S65]   823   75-446
ISBN 0-8240-1526-6

Printed in the United States of America

HAWKSTONE.

VOL. I.

LONDON:
Printed by A. SPOTTISWOODE,
New-Street-Square.

HAWKSTONE:

A TALE OF AND FOR ENGLAND

IN 184–.

IN TWO VOLUMES.

VOL. I.

LONDON:

JOHN MURRAY, ALBEMARLE STREET.

1845.

TO

LORD JOHN MANNERS,

AND OTHERS,

THE PROMISE AND FORERUNNERS OF A NEW
AND BETTER GENERATION,

𝕿𝖍𝖊 𝖋𝖔𝖑𝖑𝖔𝖜𝖎𝖓𝖌 𝕻𝖆𝖌𝖊𝖘 𝖆𝖗𝖊 𝕴𝖓𝖘𝖈𝖗𝖎𝖇𝖊𝖉

BY A HAND UNKNOWN TO THEM,

WITH THE RESPECT

DUE TO EARNESTNESS OF MIND, AND LOFTINESS OF PURPOSE ;

AND WITH THE PRAYER,

THAT AS THEY ALREADY CHERISH

FAR HIGHER ASPIRATIONS THAN THE WORLD AROUND THEM,

SO THEY MAY SOON ACQUIRE

SUCH CLEAR AND DEFINITE VIEWS OF PRACTICAL DUTY,

AS MAY RENDER THEM

AN EXAMPLE AND A BLESSING TO

DISTRACTED AND DEGRADED

ENGLAND.

PREFACE.

"NEITHER was this in use only with the Hebrews, but it is generally to be found in the wisdom of the more ancient times — that as men found out any observation that they thought was good for life, they would gather and express it in parable, or aphorism, or fable. But for fables, they were vicegerents and supplies, where examples failed: now that the times abound with history, the aim is better when the mark is alive. And therefore the form of writing, which of all others is the fittest for this variable argument of negotiation and occasions, is that which Machiavel chose wisely and aptly for government, namely, discourse upon histories or examples; for knowledge drawn freshly, and, in our view, out of particulars, knoweth the way best to particulars again; and it hath much greater life for practice when the discourse attendeth upon the example than when the example attendeth upon the discourse: for this is no point of order, as it seemeth at first, but of substance;

for when the example is the ground, being set down in a history at large, it is set down with all circumstances which may sometimes control the discourse thereupon made, and sometimes supply it as a very pattern for action; whereas the examples alleged for the discourse's sake are cited succinctly and without particularity, and carry a servile aspect towards the discourse which they are brought in to make good.

" But this difference is not amiss to be remembered, that as history of times is the best ground for discourse of government, such as Machiavel handleth, so history of lives is the most proper for discourse of business, because it is more consonant with private actions."— BACON'S *Advancement of Learning*.

December 23, 1844.

HAWKSTONE.

CHAPTER I.

It was a dark stormy night, and the wind was sweeping in gusts down the deserted streets of the town of Hawkstone, when Mr. Bentley, the young curate, was startled as he was sinking into his first sleep by a strange distant sound, mingling confusedly in the pauses of the wind, and growing louder and louder. He rose up on his elbow, and, after listening for a few moments, sprung from his bed, threw open the window, and through the trampling of feet, and the hoarse, broken clamour of a crowd, he caught distinctly the cry of fire. In a few moments, a man, breathless and half dressed, ran down the street, knocking and ringing at the doors. Windows were thrown open, and anxious terrified faces were thrust out, calling for information to the watchmen who were hurrying by. The fire-bell rang. The hollow iron rattle of the engine was heard, as it galloped past amidst the cracking of whips and the cries of the men and boys who had seated themselves about it; and on going to another part of the house Bentley saw at once a red, lurid glare, which showed him where the calamity had occurred.

Bentley was neither a cool nor a courageous man;

but he was a man of warm sensibility, and the curate
of the parish; and he lost no time in flinging on his
clothes and hastening to the spot. As he was
running down the steps of his house, Mrs. Alsop,
the old woman who managed his little household,
cried after him to give him his hat, and inquire if
she should make up the blue bed, in case it should
be wanted by any of the sufferers. "Yes, yes,"
was the reply, and "get mine ready too. Any thing
you can think of for them poor souls." And the
next minute he was out of sight.

A fireman who was running for more help told
him, as he passed, that the fire was in Barton Row;
and Bentley soon made his way to the spot, through
a labyrinth of dark courts, and filthy alleys, which
few persons knew of in Hawkstone, but himself, and
the miserable beings whom he visited there. As he
turned into one of these narrow passages, a strong
red light at the end fell on a crowd of terrified faces,
who were gazing on the scene of destruction; and
the cries of "More water!" "More hose!" "Move
the ladders!" "Pump away!" mingled with oaths,
and screams, and the roaring of the flames, and the
howling of the wind, struck a cold chill upon him,
and almost broke his resolution to go nearer; for
Bentley, as we said before, was a man of feeling,
rather than a man of courage. But as he stopped,
and leaned for a moment against the wall, a wild
piercing shriek was heard; the flames shot up suddenly above the roofs, and as a cry of terror and
anguish burst from the crowd, Bentley found himself,
he scarcely knew how, standing in sight of the
burning building. And the sight was sickening.
The house which was on fire itself was one of a
dingy red brick row, such as grow up in the suburbs
of manufacturing towns, and, having been originally
intended for decent occupants, become, by degrees,

the abode of numerous poor families, who each
tenant a single room, and hide, under an exterior of
some pretension, a degree of poverty, misery, and
vice, greater, perhaps, than exists in huts and hovels.
The fire had begun in the ground room, and had
been discovered in time to permit the escape of a
crowd of wretched, haggard men and women, bearing
naked children in their arms, and endeavouring to
save as treasures the little bedding, the clothes,
stools, kettles, and rugs, which formed all their property in the world. All were supposed to have
escaped; and they had gathered in little groups at
a distance from the fire, the children cowering round
their parents, and the parents endeavouring to wrap
them from the cold, and to place them as guards
over the little property they had saved; while, as the
flames made their way from room to room, they
looked on with a face almost of desperate unconcern,
as if, for beings so destitute and wretched, it mattered little what fate awaited them, the fire or the
famine.

The first floor had already fallen in; the lower
part of the staircase was destroyed, and the firemen,
hopeless of saving the house, were beginning to play
on the adjoining buildings, when, to the horror of
the crowd, a boy, about 14 years old, was seen shrieking for help at one of the garret windows. At the
same moment a man and woman half clad rushed to
the house, and, but for the interposition of the firemen, would have thrown themselves into the flames.
"My child! my child! save my child! O God! save
my child! save him! save him! O God! O God!"
were the sounds that reached Bentley's ear just as
he gained the spot. The man, a strong muscular
swarthy ruffian, struggled with the desperation of a
maniac to escape from the policeman, who held him
back from rushing into certain destruction. The

woman, held back likewise, fell down upon her knees
before Bentley, saying, "Save him! save him! let me
go! I have a right to go! he is my child! save him!
save him! my child! my child!" till Bentley, in an
agony of distress, burst from her, and she sunk down
in a fit. "Ten guineas! twenty guineas! a hundred
guineas!" he cried (his whole stipend was scarcely
more), any thing, only save the boy." No one answered.

"Is it impossible?"

"Yes, sir," said the man, with a dead hollow
voice, who was working at the engine, "it is impossible; no one could get up the ladder through the
flames. It is quite out of the question; God help it!"

And the poor man, who had children of his own,
fairly burst into tears.

"Try—make an effort," returned Bentley.

"Can't be," said the man; "we must submit to
God's will; God have mercy on it! Look at the
ladder, sir; look there!"

And Bentley saw a burst of fire from the windows
wrap it round and round like a whirlwind, just as
the father, who, by one gigantic effort, had cast off
his detainers, had mounted a few yards from the
ground, and fell back as if blasted.

"Take the ladder away! take it away," cried the
firemen. "It's no use : the next house has caught.
More water! more water!"

And with that sturdy sense of command which
Englishmen even in the lowest post of authority
exercise over their feelings when engaged in official duties, he was proceeding to push aside Bentley,
who was even thinking of making the attempt
himself, and to remove the ladder, when a stranger
made his way through the crowd. He was a man
tall, vigorously formed, and with all those marks
of high birth and commanding mind which the
lower orders so instinctively recognise and obey.

There was a quietness and steadiness in his movements which contrasted strongly with the tumult
about him; and even Bentley, a man of education
and religion, felt himself in the presence of a superior, and was unconsciously abashed at his own
agitated state of feeling.

"Let the ladder stay, my good fellow," said the
stranger gently; "let it stay. I have a protection
here against the flames; hold it fast at the bottom,
and let me mount." And the words were uttered
in a tone of command which threw the firemen back.
He stopped to put on a pair of thick gloves and a
mask of wire over his face; knelt down for a moment as in prayer, folded his hands over his cheeks,
and those who stood near asserted that he made the
sign of the cross on his forehead, and then sprung up
the ladder before the by-standers had recovered
themselves to interfere. He had seized the moment,
when a fall of one of the inner walls had lulled the
flames, which were bursting round him; and the
crowd, who were looking on with intense anxiety,
hailed him with a loud cheer as he reached the
window. The boy had already disappeared, having
sunk down stupified with the smoke, and with terror.
The window was closed and fastened within; but
the glass was broken, and the stranger, with all his
strength, tore away sufficient of the woodwork to
obtain an entrance. As he disappeared within
the room, another volley of flame and smoke broke
forth from the floor beneath, and cries of "Make
haste! make haste! the floor is falling! for God's
sake, make haste! save yourself!" burst from the
people, followed by a tremendous cheer as he appeared on the sill of the window with the boy wrapt
up in a blanket. Another moment, and it had been
too late. A frightful crush behind him announced
the falling of the floor. A heavy chimney at the

side staggered, bowed, and fell upon the ruins; and before the flames could shoot out again, the stranger and his burden had slided down the ladder. Scorched and nearly stifled as he was, his first act on reaching the ground was once more to kneel down, and bury his face in his hands in silent prayer. Then giving the boy to Bentley, whose enthusiasm of admiration now was only equal to his agony of anxiety before, he quietly fell back into the crowd; and as they pressed about him with cries of " God bless him ! There's a fine man ! Bless your honour ! " cheering him and thrusting their hands into his, and waving their hats, he simply answered, " Thank ye, thank ye ! Will you allow me to pass ? " And turning down the same alley through which Bentley had come upon the spot, he was lost to sight.

" Do you know who the gentleman is ? " asked Bentley, of many of the by-standers who had gathered round the poor man and woman, as they sat with the boy in their arms, and watched him gradually returning to life.

" No, sir," was the general answer. " We never saw him before. He is a stranger in the town."

" But he's a real gentleman," said a poor labourer to another. " Yes, that he is," cried they all, " a real gentleman, and that's a fine thing to say. God bless him ! say I." " God bless him !" cried another. " God bless him !" murmured the poor mother, as the boy's eyes began to open. Even the ruffian father relaxed his surly, gloomy look, and, though he did not say " God bless him," he muttered something about thanks, and, bidding his wife look to the things, took up the boy in his arms, and followed a poor neighbour, who had offered a part of her hovel as their refuge for the remainder of the night.

CHAP. II.

On the Monday afternoon, in the week after the fire, a sensation (to use the fashionable term) was caused in the principal street of Hawkstone, by symptoms of an approaching festivity in the apartments of Miss Mabel Brook, who occupied the first-floor bow window in the very respectable house of Messrs. Silkem the linen-drapers. Mrs. Crump, the lame old lady who occupied a similar bow window on the opposite side of the way, and who, having a strong desire to know what was passing in the world, could yet command only that portion of the world which came within the focus of the above-mentioned window, had observed, as she informed her maid, that the little girl from the Grey school who waited on Miss Brook had gone out no less than three times that morning, and returned on each occasion with a something (Mrs. Crump could not tell what), but she had her suspicions. On the first sally, Mrs. Crump had traced her as far as her eye could stretch to the end of the street, when she turned a corner abruptly; but in a few minutes she came back again, and Mrs. Crump's ingenuity immediately called to mind that there was a pastry-cook's shop just at the distance required to account for this temporary disappearance. On the second occasion, there had been an open visit to Mallam's the grocer before Mrs. Crump's own eyes; and a return with a packet of tea, whether it was green or souchong, Mrs. Crump had been unable to ascertain. But as she knew Miss Brook three days before had sent for a pound of tea to the same shop, Mrs. Crump inferred that it could not yet be exhausted, and that the new importation was probably green tea for company. The third expedition, at about four o'clock P. M. baffled Mrs. Crump completely. The little grey-clad abigail vanished at the end of the street, and when she returned she was accompanied by two other abigails clad in the same uniform, and bearing prodigious packages of some mysterious article wrapt up in white linen. In vain the old lady rubbed her spectacles, wiped the window, moved from one pane to the other; the contents of these portentous packages were impervious to her eyes. The Grey girls and the packages both disappeared at the side door of Messrs. Silkem's premises; the door closed upon them, and, in a fit of desperation, Mrs. Crump returned to her elbow-chair, pulled the bell rope, which was tied to it, and desired her maid immediately to go over, with her love to Miss Brook, and inquire how she did this evening.

"You can find out," she said, "from her servant, by the by, whether Miss Brook has company to tea."

No distressed lady in Mrs. Crump's predicament was ever blessed with an Iris more anxious to fulfil a task, which involved an occasional gossip, than Mrs. Crump's Martha, and, after a little delay, which provoked no little irritation in her impatient mistress, she returned with the announcement that Miss Brook had company to tea, and that she was expecting no less than ten ladies.

"Ten!" interrupted Mrs. Crump; "why, where is she to put them?"

Martha, who was out of breath, proceeded. "It was the great monthly meeting of the Hawkstone Dorcas or Benevolent Lying-in Union Society, of which Miss Mabel was the honoured secretary, and most active supporter; and there was to be Mrs. Thompson, and the Miss Macdougalls, and Mrs. and young Miss Maddox; and muffins, and tea-cake, and wine and water afterwards. And the sofa had been uncovered, and the window curtains put up. And Mr. Peachit, the gardener, had sent some flowers for the chimney-piece, and Miss Brook was so busy, with her table covered with flannel, and nightcaps, and gingham, and all sorts of things; — and the company were expected almost directly." To all this, to the great disappointment of Martha, Mrs. Crump only answered "pish," and the "pish" was repeated at the close; accompanied, however, it must be confessed, with a rubbing of the spectacles and an advancement of the wheeled chair to the window, for the purpose, it may be presumed, of obtaining ocular demonstration of the arrival of the visiters. But the "pish" implied much. It implied, first, that Mrs. Crump was not a member of the Dorcas or Benevolent Lying-in Union Society ; secondly, that she was no friend to it; thirdly, that she was, as she delighted to say, one of the old school. She did not think that any good ever came from such societies. She did not like mixing with Dissenters; the Miss Macdougalls were Presbyterians, and the Maddoxes Unitarians; she liked the good old way, and kept to the church, as her father and mother had done before her; and if dozing regularly every morning over the psalms and lessons, attending regularly in her pew at church every Sunday, and even on Wednesdays, and Fridays, and Saints' days, and giving her annual mite to the National Schools, and, we may add, playing her nightly rubber with Dr. Grant, the old paralytic rector, constituted a friend to the Church, no one could be relied on for more determined support than Mrs. Crump. And yet on the "pish" there followed

something like a sigh ; and as the old lady sat
watching for the first arrival, she fell into a soliloquy
on the evils of a solitary old age, when there were
no children to repay the care of their youth, and
society treated her as a burthen, and weak health
and advancing infirmities prevented her from engaging in any active occupation either of business
or amusement. There was, indeed, to relieve the
heavy days which dragged on without change and
without hope, an occasional morning call (few they
were, and far between), from Miss Mabel Brook, and
the other dowagers of the town. And at times, one
or two of the younger ladies charitably reminded
each other that they ought to call on poor Mrs.
Crump. And once or twice in the month, Martha,
who knew how her mistress required some relief to
her monotonous existence, would entrap a stray
nursery maid with Mrs. Thompson's little girls, or
Mrs. Jones' baby ; and, as the old lady crawled to
her cupboard for the slice of sweet cake, or made
them sit down at her feet to show them the wonders
of her worsted work, a tear would stand in her eyes
at the thought of what had been denied to herself, — a
child, a grandchild, any being whom she might look
to for support, and love and watch over, and think
on as a second self, instead of hanging upon a cold
neglectful world, without interest, and without affection, until the grave closed over her head. And
another thought sometimes struck her, little as her
mind was formed to deeper reflection, that God
could not have intended such things to be; that if he
were, as she devoutly believed, a god of love, and
Christianity were designed by him to be a blessing to
all mankind, there might be somewhere in its system,
when rightly brought out, a provision for destitution
like hers, and that something might be deficient in
a church, which left her the widow, the labouring

with sickness, the desolate, the all but oppressed —
whom it prayed for, as one of its especial objects of
care, — with no consolation but a Bible, as little understood as it was monotonously perused; and no
fixed task of duty but her worsted work, and the
feeding of her cat; no one bound to attend on her
but the hired Martha ; and, saving one day in seven,
no aid or comfort to her devotion, but once or twice
a hurried service in a cold and desolate church,
with no one, perhaps, but the children in the grey-
school gallery, and poor Betty Foyle the blind old
woman from the almshouse, to join in offering
praises and thanksgiving, for a population of thousands.

Whether or not the old lady's soliloquy would
have terminated thus, we cannot presume to say ;
for it was interrupted by the first arrival at Miss
Mabel Brook's soirée, in the person of the two Miss
Morgans, the pretty daughters of the principal
surgeon in the town of Hawkstone.

And here we must apologise once for all for our
inability to amuse our readers, and especially that
privileged class who dwell in parks and villas,
places, halls, and courts, at a distance from the
vulgar town, for our inability to supply them with
the usual facetious catalogue of odd characters, and
still odder names with which modern art has loaded
the population of our country towns. Hawkstone,
indeed, like all other places of human resort, had its
characters; and those characters had names. But
we lament, for the sake of our readers, that they
were little remarkable in any way. If they could
not boast of Fitz's, and Ville's, and Saints, and De's,
neither were they afflicted with the unseemly appel-
latives of Hobbs and Dobbs, Simkins or Scroggins.
They were, in fact, fair, ordinary specimens of the
middle class of English people; neither very clever

nor very stupid, very vulgar nor very polished, very
enlarged in their notions nor very narrow.   In one
point they resembled all English people alike.
They acknowledged an implicit submission for the
little world in which they moved; anxiously aspiring
to the notice of its leaders, and condescendingly
patronizing all who came beneath themselves; and
measuring the whole fate and character of the vast
terra incognita beyond them, by the opinions, acts,
and vicissitudes of their own little *coterie.*   Perhaps,
indeed, the Dorcas Society could not pretend to in-
clude exactly the élite of Hawkstone; for there were
several little suburban villas in the neighbourhood,
which being uncontaminated by pavement and gas
lamps, aspired to a claim to rurality, and held somewhat aloof from the decidedly town population.
But still it was composed of "respectables," in that
sense of the word, which perhaps might be properly
rendered "without a shop."   Besides the Miss
Morgans, the surgeon's daughters, there was Mrs.
Lomax, the banker's wife, who officiated as president; the Miss Macdougalls, who tenanted the
large brick house with five windows in front, and
a coach-house and garden, at the north entrance
of the town; Mrs. and Miss James, who had
recently retired from the superintendence of a
very respectable seminary for young ladies; Mrs.
Hancock, the wife of Capt. Hancock, an officer on
half pay, who continued to vegetate in a neat little
verandaed cottage in the outskirts of the town; and
the Maddoxes, whom their father's success in trade
had placed in easy circumstances, and left them
abundance, both of time and money, to devote to
the charities of Hawkstone.   And one after another
they arrived at Miss Mabel's door; and though Mrs.
Crump, who was by no means a favourable critic,
did detect about them all a little bustle of serious

importance, more than the occasion required; and Miss James had put into her cap rather a gayer display of flowers than suited the sobriety of her age; and the Miss Macdougalls looked somewhat prim; and Mrs. Lomax was guilty of a little ostentation in making her footboy follow her with a work-basket and cloak; still there was little to censure in their appearance, and nothing to ridicule. And any one who could have seen the hearty welcome with which Miss Mabel received them, and the kind mutual greetings of the party, and the cheerfulness with which they produced work-boxes and baskets, scissors and needles, and ranged them on the green cloth of Miss Mabel's largest table, would think it a very ill-placed satire which attempted to caricature such a charitable meeting, assembled, as modern philanthropy delights to express it, without distinction of sect or party, to promote the comfort and relieve the wants of their fellow-creatures.

Of the whole party no one was so pleased as Miss Mabel herself. It was the first time that she had been enabled, by a removal into a new lodging, to entertain the Dorcas Society in her single room. And earnest were her pains to make her guests comfortable and happy; and visible the satisfaction, notwithstanding all her pains to suppress it, with which she received the congratulations of the Miss Morgans on her cheerful view of the High Street, so close to the Crown Inn, where she might see every day no less than three coaches stop and change horses; and Mrs. Lomax's panegyric on the prettiness of her sofa coverings; and Miss James's admiration of the silver tea-pot, the only relic saved from the wreck of her father's little property; and the praise which all bestowed on the delicious tea-cakes, and excellent cream. Every one seemed anxious to say some-

thing which would please and flatter her; for Miss
Mabel was a general favourite.

She was the only daughter of an officer in the
navy who had died at an advanced age, leaving Miss
Mabel, neither young nor beautiful, with his blessing
and a very small annuity, to make the remainder of
her way through the troubles of the world by her
own exertions. By dint of the strictest economy,
she contrived soon to bring her wants and wishes
within the compass of sixty pounds a year. High
spirits and active habits engaged her in a variety of
occupations which filled up her time, and absorbed
both past and future, so far as anxiety or sorrow
was concerned, in the interests of the present; and
an inexhaustible fund of good humour and good
nature made her invaluable to the little society of
Hawkstone. It was Miss Mabel who undertook the
management of the national schools; Miss Mabel
who was secretary and chief mover, not only of the
Dorcas Society, but of all the ladies' societies which
flourished with a mushroom growth at Hawkstone;
the Ladies' Branch Bible Society, the Ladies' Anti-
Cruelty-to-Animals Society, the Ladies' Book Society, the Ladies' Association for the Conversion of
the Jews, the Ladies' District-Visiting Society, the
Ladies' Penitentiary, the Ladies' Female Orphan,
and Deaf and Dumb, and Pastoral Aid, and General-
Religious-Purpose Society. None could flourish,
and few had originated, without Miss Mabel; her
whole soul was in doing good. And if there mixed
with this ardour of sincere benevolence some little
bustle and over-zeal, and no little ignorance as to the
right mode of doing good, it was the fault not so
much of Miss Mabel herself, as of the age in which
she was born; and which her own warmth of feeling
and delight at the excitement of charity in which
she had involved herself, represented to her as a

model of wisdom, and a Paradise of newly discovered
virtues. Nor was her benevolence confined to
public life. How she contrived to do so much no
one could understand; but scarcely a *respectable*
family in Hawkstone was ignorant of the value of
her services. If Mrs. Jones was ill, Miss Mabel
would come and spend the day and take care of the
children. If a death occurred in a family, Miss
Mabel was the first looked to for assistance in those
melancholy moments; if a wedding, Miss Mabel
assisted in distributing the bride cake; if a children's
dance, at Mrs. Lomax's, Miss Mabel was the first who
arrived to help in putting the young ones in motion,
and the last who remained to see the candles put
out, when the wearied hostess had retired to bed,
and Mr. Lomax had shaken both her hands with a
hearty wish that every one could be so useful. And
in all this, there was neither conceit nor pretension;
simply the overflowing of a kindly-disposed heart,
which could not rest without doing something, and
happily was most pleased when that something contributed, as she hoped, to the comfort of her kind
friends and neighbours.

And having arrived at this point, it is high time
to relieve the apprehensions which our fair readers,
who care nothing for a story not strewed thick with
lords and ladies, Almack's and diamonds, will feel,
when our talk seems likely to be of market towns,
and Mrs. Crumps, Dorcas Societies, and flannels.
They need be under no alarm lest Miss Mabel Brook,
much as we have enlarged her merits, should be the
intended heroine of our tale; or lest we should
already have destined her to pair off, after trials and
temptations, with either Mr. Bentley or the unknown stranger of the fire. Miss Mabel is by no
means an unimportant personage; but she is not
the most important.

And they will be rejoiced to learn at once that our heroine will be a real lady, such as a heroine should be. Not as if the middle walks of life were contemptible, and had no joys or sorrows, duties or virtues, to excite our sympathies and interest ; but because, where goodness does exist accompanied with rank and birth, it exists in a higher and nobler form than in a humbler station. It is a grievous mistake to think that the highest ranks of society are the only objects worth attention, or to under-value the middle classes. But it is an equal mistake to make society rest on the foundation of the middle classes, or to suppose that leading minds, minds fitted to command and rule, will be found, except by some extraordinary accident, in any but men, whom nature, from their birth, has placed on an eminence, and accustomed them to receive the homage of the world as their birthright, without either vanity to court, or affectation to disclaim it. To Miss Mabel, however, we must return. And cheerful as she seemed, laughing with one, and arranging flannel with another, and pressing another cup of tea upon a third, it might be remarked that her eye glanced often to the door, and then to an old easy chair, stationed in the warmest corner of the room, and provided with a cushion and a foot-stool, which no one yet had presumed to occupy. She was evidently anxious for another arrival.

" We shall see Mrs. Bevan, I hope, to-night," said Mrs. Lomax, with a tone of sincerity.

"I trust she is coming," subjoined Miss Macdougall, in a voice which implied no regret if she were to remain away.

" What can make her so late ?" continued Mrs. Maddox, with something of censoriousness in her manner.

And even Mabel began to wonder at her absence,

not without some secret misgivings as to the desirableness of her presence. And yet, if there was one person in the world whom Mabel venerated, it was Mrs. Bevan; who on the death of Captain Brook had offered her the shelter of Brookfield Parsonage; had accustomed her to the active duties of charity, to which she had subsequently devoted herself, and had been to her almost a mother. She had seen this friend pass through trial after trial with a quiet fortitude, an undisturbed piety, and a sweetness of temper almost angelic. Two children had been taken from her in early life. Her husband, the Rector of Hurst, after a life of zealous devotion to his duty, had followed them to the grave; and she herself was now established in Hawkstone, dividing her time between reading and charity, and in both continuing to follow the principles which her excellent husband had taught her in the management of his parish. On the dispersion of his little property at his death, she had contrived, at some sacrifice, to retain the greater part of his small but well selected library, composed chiefly, like most others belonging to parochial clergymen of a former generation, of the English divines of the seventeenth century. To these occasional additions were made by her son, who was resident at Oxford, as a fellow of——college. And Mrs. Bevan, having little taste for the trash of the circulating library, was content to read through and through her little store, and gradually became something of a sound divine, sufficient at least to excite the wonder of the Hawkstone ladies at her learning, and even, though with no intention on her own part, to perplex Dr. Grant, and still more Mr. Bentley, with an accidental reference or question. One thing we must do Mrs. Bevan the justice to add; she was no writer. She had never thought herself competent to undertake to direct the religious world by means of periodical papers. If she heard of erroneous opinions rising up in the Church, she did not write letters to the newspapers, warning her beloved countrymen against the encroaching heresy. She left this task in the hands where God had placed it—to his own ministers. Neither did she dare to frame prayers and meditations for others, however much she might think they were wanted. Still less did she relish the idea of unbosoming herself to the public, laying bare her movements, and feelings, and fancies, and sympathies in a memoir, or a tour, or an auto-biography, or any other similar form, in which young ladies as well as young gentlemen now delight to come forward on the stage, uncalled for and un-wished for, in the hope of obtaining some random applause. She had her notions of domestic economy, and very good notions they were; but political economy she left to Mr. Malthus. And she spent no little portion of her time in the school of Hawk-stone, and had suggested many sensible improvements in the management of it; but if it had been pro-posed to her to enlighten the world on the subject of education, she would probably have smiled with surprise, that any one who professed to know what education was, should think of its being discussed by one who had never studied the deep principles of philosophy, on which it must be based, and without which it becomes mere quackery. In short, Mrs. Bevan, though in her own little circle of study she was a very well-read lady, was by no means a literary lady. And so much the better for herself and for those around her.

Her only compositions were her letters to her son at Oxford; and regularly once a week Charles Bevan, on his return from morning chapel, found to his great delight a little folio on his table, containing

the news of Hawkstone; how the school was
flourishing, how the church was attended, how
opinions were improving. And when the vacation
arrived, and they were once more seated together
in the evening—Charles, with his folio, and his paper
and pencil, and his mother making his tea, or engaged in the mysteries of her work-box—she was
able to enter with him into the subject nearest his
thoughts, and to talk of his dear Oxford, and the
struggle which was then commencing there against
the follies of the day, and to follow him in his plans
and conjectures, and his observations on the works
which it was sending forth. If, indeed, at first,
she was startled by the earnestness and depth of his
views, her alarms were soon quieted by observing
that they were quiet, diffident, and discriminating.
Many of them, new to him, were old to herself.
She could recollect the time when, every morning
and evening, there was a regular service in Hawkstone church; when, on saints' days, a sermon had
been preached, in compliance with an old benefaction
—when the very name of a dissenter would have
been sufficient to set the populace in commotion—
when the grammar school, now sunk into neglect,
had educated the sons of all the tradesmen and
farmers around, and every day the boys might have
been seen following the master to church, to take
part in the regular service. She had known Hawkstone in its simple unsophisticated state, before Lord
Claremont had been obliged to leave his estate at
nurse in the hands of trustees, and retire himself
to the Continent—and General Villiers had deserted
the Priory—and Mr. Smith had discovered the capacities of Hawkstone stream, and raised on its
banks the enormous hundred-windowed factory,
with its steam-engines, and spinning-jennies, and
smoking chimney, and haggard mob of occupants,

c 2

which now shocked the eye of the traveller, on his quitting the park paling and woods of the Priory, and entering the metamorphosed town. And she could sigh with Charles over the change which had taken place—on the empty church—the crowded meeting-houses—the squalid, vitiated, turbulent population—the distracted political parties—the absence of any man of birth, and property, and sound principles, to keep the town in order, and devise means for bringing it once more into "unity of spirit, into the bond of peace, and into righteousness of life." With these feelings, Mrs. Bevan could easily sympathise with her son, when he spoke of reviving again the right moral influence of the Church; of giving it new strength and additional arms to grasp and bring back to its bosom the thousands whom it had permitted to wander—when he talked with enthusiasm of the men by whom the thought and hope of such a consummation had been roused—when he described the purity of their lives, the depth of their learning, the quiet, unobtrusive way in which they practised what they taught, and then, almost with tears in his eyes, blessed God, who even in this wilful age had kept from destruction those noble institutions in which the spirit that animated them had been preserved alive, burning under a heap of ruins.

"And so, then," some of our readers will exclaim, "Mrs. Bevan was a Puseyite." Mrs. Bevan was a lady—a lady by birth, education, habits of society, and refinement of mind. And no one could practise better that quiet, dignified, but severe, castigation, which such ladies are able to bestow on impertinence and flippancy. And the young person (for old persons do not indulge in such vulgarities) who had once presumed to apply to her, within hearing, such a silly and mischievous nickname, would undoubtedly never have ventured to repeat it a second time. "But she had studied the 'Tracts for the Times,' then?" We rather believe not. Some portions her son had read out to her; and she admired the eloquence of some, hesitated as to expressions in others, perhaps did not quite like the tone of speaking here and there. But with the principles, which her late husband had inculcated and practised, and the habitual perusal of the great standard works of the English Church, Mrs. Bevan found little novelty in the "Tracts for the Times," and other works of the same authors, and preferred, as the Tracts themselves recommended, her own course of old divinity, to any modern teaching, on one side or the other. And she gladly agreed with Charles, (who, at one time, she feared, might be led away by his personal respect for the leaders in the new movement,) when he congratulated her that sound doctrines were now reviving independently in several parts of the Church, and less necessity would exist for the guidance of individual men.

All this time we are detaining our readers (we would fain hope they are impatient readers) from Miss Brook and the Dorcas Society. And we must return in time to find Miss Brook, with some disappointment in her countenance, perusing a little twisted note which has just arrived to announce that Mrs. Bevan was unable to attend.

"Is Mrs. Bevan unwell?" said Miss Macdougall, with rather an offended look.

"She has no engagement, I know," said the younger Miss Maddox, in a tone bordering on reproach.

"We must do as well as we can without her," subjoined Mrs. Maddox, with a sigh in which she intended to convey more of sorrow than of anger.

"Does Mrs. Bevan mention any reason?" asked Mrs Lomax, pacifically.

Miss Mabel looked again at the note, but no reason appeared, only there was a postscript hoping to see Miss Mabel to-morrow. The whole party sympathetically said, "Well!" and then proceeded to commence the business of the evening.

This has been a longer chapter than we antici-pated. And as we know that, with most of our readers, reading is an uphill work, and their own powers of attention not a little asthmatic, — that they are either lolling in an easy chair after eating a full dinner, or lying on a sofa in their club-room; or, if they are young ladies, that one is tired with reading us out, while the others are yawning over their work-boxes and worsted frames; for all these reasons we think it better to give them and ourselves a respite, and to postpone the business of the Dorcas Society till another chapter.

CHAP. III.

'AND they proceeded to the business of the evening.'

This business was opened by Miss Mabel Brook, who brought before the society the case of Mrs. Connell. Mrs. Connell was one of the poor women who had been burnt out by the late fire, and whose boy had been saved from the flames. She was in great poverty. Her husband was a drunken, worthless profligate; she herself near her confinement. And Miss Jane Morgan, who had accidentally found her in great distress both of mind and body, had promised to apply for relief to the Society in her approaching illness. All voices were unanimous in her favour. And while the bag was making up, Miss Jane proceeded to describe her interview with the poor woman. She had given her some money, and added a ticket for the Dispensary, and recommended a plaster for the face of the boy who had been scorched in escaping from the fire. Nothing could be better. She had also spoken to her generally on the subject of religion, on the state of her husband, and the duty of prayer. And she had given her a Prayer-Book, with the service of the visitation of the sick, and promised to mention her state to Mr. Bentley the curate. But at these words, Miss Brook was alarmed to see the colour rising in Mrs. Maddox's face.

"I must really beg your pardon, Miss Jane," exclaimed the matronly lady, "but you must know that doing any thing of the kind is contrary to the fifth rule

of the Society, which expressly says, that we are
not to attempt making proselytes."

"Proselytes!" replied Miss Jane, slightly confused,
"I really never thought of such a thing; she told me
she had been baptized in our Church."

"Indeed!" rejoined Mrs. Maddox: "it happens
that poor Mrs. Connell has nothing to do with your
Church. She used at one time to wash for me; and
ever since that, I know that she has attended our
chapel; for every Sunday that she goes to chapel, I
told her, you know," addressing her daughters,
"that she was to have her dinner with our servants."

"Oh, yes," cried the young ladies, "I assure you
she belongs to us." And poor Miss Jane was
obliged to apologise for having given the Prayer-
Book, and mentioned Mr. Bentley, to the poor sufferer.

"Religion, indeed," subjoined Mrs. Maddox, in a
forgiving and placable tone, "we must all inculcate
in our visits. But peculiar doctrines," she added
with a bland smile, "you know, my dear Miss Jane,
we have agreed, shall never disturb our charitable purposes." Miss Jane, who knew nothing of religion
but what she had learned from her Prayer-Book
and Catechism, and the Bible as explained from
the pulpit of Hawkstone church, made at once a
resolution to set aside those prejudiced associations,
and to form a religion for herself, without any peculiar doctrines, and which she might speak of to
the poor and afflicted without incurring Mrs. Maddox's censures.

"I will go myself," said Mrs. Maddox, "and see
the poor woman, and will not trouble you, my dear
Miss Jane, as she is one of us. And I have no doubt
the Society will be glad to give her some relief
from the money which Mr. Bentley has placed at our
disposal. I will take it to her to-morrow." And

though some slight misgiving came across Miss Mabel at the appropriation of Mr. Bentley's donation from the Offertory money, to the evident purpose of keeping Mrs. Connell to the Unitarian chapel, all had before their eyes the fear of being suspected of a desire to make proselytes, and the grant was proposed and carried.

The next motion related to Betsy Trotter, and Miss Mabel evidently laboured under some embarrassment in alluding to it. Betsy Trotter, like Mrs. Connell, was a poor woman; five children; husband earning eight shillings a week; an honest man, — every thing to recommend the case. But the application for assistance had been made to Miss Mabel, as secretary; and she begged to transfer the task of conveying the Society's grant to the applicant to the hand of Miss Macdougall.

" I suppose," said that lady to Miss Mabel, " you feel some little difficulty about Jenny?"

And Miss Mabel owned the impeachment. It appeared that Jenny Trotter had belonged to the Grey School, one of those old-fashioned charities, which the benevolent but illiberal founders saddled with the express condition of their being extended only to children in communion with the Church. Now John Trotter the father worked regularly in Miss Macdougall's garden. And Miss Macdougall, with a laudable zeal for the spiritual welfare of all her dependants, had recommended him one Wednesday evening to go and hear Mr. Bryant at the Presbyterian chapel. She had also, with the same laudable zeal, lent him a number of tracts, in which, perhaps without the lender's knowledge, the Church of England, (in which, by-the-by, poor John had been baptized,) was spoken of in no very respectful terms ; its bishops were called tyrants and oppressors — why and wherefore John did not know ; but never having seen a bishop himself, he could not contradict the statement. Then the Liturgy was mere popery; and John, who knew the history of Guy Faux by heart, was naturally alarmed at having so long been an accomplice with that wicked papist. The surplice also, which he had seen Dr. Grant and Mr. Bentley wear every Sunday, was called a filthy rag. And though the word seeméd rather strong, John could not help acknowledging that very often it was not so clean as it should be. And having no other place to go to on a Wednesday evening after he had finished his work, and being naturally of a religious frame of mind, John went again and again to the chapel. And again and again he heard Mr. Bryant say pretty much the same as Miss Macdougall's tracts. And a good deal of what he used to be told by Mr. Bentley, about faith and love, and going by the Bible only, and the worthlessness of forms and the sufficiency of prayer to obtain the aid of God,—all this he heard from Mr. Bryant; only Mr. Bryant said a great deal more on points on which Mr. Bentley had never uttered a word, and on which therefore poor John was wholly at a loss,— such as the duty of obedience to the Church, the authority of bishops, the necessity of the Sacraments, and the like. And unhappily all that Mr. Bryant said made John look on these points as absurd and even wicked. Then one day while he was digging a border, Mr. Bryant, who had been paying a congregational visit to Miss Macdougall, came by accident into the garden, and after asking for his wife and children, told him he was glad to see him so often at church, and slipped half-a-crown into his hand to buy him a Bible. And another time he called in at John's cottage to inquire how he did; and after talking with a sad and grieved countenance of the spiritual destitution of Hawkstone,—

only Mr. Bentley to do all the duty, and Dr. Grant
rolling in wealth, and paying him only 90*l.* a year. —
Mr. Bryant shook his head in a melancholy way,
and took his leave with a soliloquy, which John was
evidently intended to overhear: "Alas! poor
Church of England! it ruins more souls than it
saves!" In short, we need not follow up the steps
by which John shifted his place on Sunday from the
cold wet pavement and narrow bench in the aisle
under the pulpit of Hawkstone church, and where his
face had been seen for years, to a warm comfortable
seat, provided for him by Mr. Bryant himself, in the
Presbyterian chapel. And once there, he was soon
taught to feel as much aversion for the church as
he had before felt love. And conscientious and
honest as he was, he was resolved not merely to
save his own soul by quitting an evil church, governed by those enemies to the Gospel, bishops and
archbishops, but to save his children also. Jenny,
therefore, was ordered to attend him on Sundays to
Mr. Bryant's meeting. In vain Miss Mabel, to
whom was confided the chief superintendence of
the Grey School, condemned Jenny for her first
absence from church, and even threatened to punish
her. It was her father's order; and Miss Mabel
felt it impossible to inculcate disobedience to parents. In vain, when the offence was repeated, Miss
Mabel paid a visit to John's cottage, to remonstrate
on the secession; John was inexorable. And as
Mr. Bryant had taken care to provide his inquiring mind with texts from Scripture respecting
preaching the Gospel, and sundry difficulties about
the use of the word bishop in the epistles, besides
the unanswerable question whether St. Paul had
50,000*l.* a year, like the Archbishop of Canterbury,
Miss Mabel, who knew little more of a bishop than
that he wore a wig, and sat in parliament, and was

called my lord, and travelled about the country on
rare occasions of confirmation, was compelled to
beat a retreat for fear of being discomfited in argument. One more attempt she made, and then John,
encouraged by success, launched out in such violent
invectives on the Church, and every one that belonged to it, and especially on young Mr. Bentley,
whom she had taken under her especial patronage,
that, unable to suppress her indignation, she pronounced on him a formal anathema; and at an extraordinary meeting of the Grey committee, Jenny
was dismissed from the school.

It was this which caused her present difficulty.
"How can I," as she justly remarked, "do kindnesses to persons whom I believe to be doing wrong,
who are attacking and abusing what I most value,
without leading them to suppose that I do not think
them in the wrong, or do not reverence what they
abuse? I can repay with kindness a personal injury;
this is only the duty of a Christian: but the Trot-
ters I believe to be in commission of a sin. And I
cannot show them any mark of favour without
compromising my own conscience, and misleading
theirs. I do not find fault with them, remember,
for leaving the Church—that is a question between
them and their Maker; and every one should act
according to his conscience: but I do blame them
highly for abusing the Church, Mr. Bentley, and
myself, and the ladies of the school, after their
daughter had been in it so long, and Mr. Bentley
had been so kind to them." And Miss Mabel,
having stated the difficulty, was silent. To this
difficulty, Miss Macdougall, though she did not
exactly see the sin of abusing the Church, willingly
assented, and undertook to act as almoner of the society in place of Miss Mabel; for the society, in its
corporate capacity, being precluded from entertain-

ing any peculiar attachment to the Church, was quite insensible to the crime of abusing it; and, indeed, being raised wholly above any distinctions of right or wrong in religious matters, looked only on John's small wages and his wife's large family; and the question was easily decided, — so easily, indeed, that several of the young ladies could not help remarking to themselves how troublesome it was to have a conscience; and how easily all these difficulties might have been removed if Alderman Brown had not insisted on the children of the Grey School going to church, or if Miss Mabel would allow every one to have their own opinion on religion. Mrs. Maddox, indeed, could not help saying that she hoped the new charity commissioners would do away with these persecuting restrictions of the Grey School; and that the children of all sects might partake together of the bounties of Alderman Brown, and of a sound religious education, without any peculiar doctrines to disturb their mutual affection.

"And now, my dear Mabel," she continued, with a peculiar complacency of voice which indicated a consciousness of success, "what is to become of the bazaar? You are always at the bottom of these things, you know you are — so active — so liberal — such enlarged views." And she turned to Miss Mabel, who, with a little confusion of conscious importance, protested that she was not in the secret — she had nothing to do with it. Only Mr. Bentley had been describing the sad destitution of the sufferers by the fire, and she had just mentioned it accidentally; and Lady Thompson at Rosewood Villa had thought it would be a good thing; and Mrs. Lomax had promised to hold a stall. Mrs. Lomax bowed a grave acquiescence.

"And whom else will you have?" said Mrs. Maddox, unconsciously glancing at her daughters.

"Why," said Miss Mabel, equally unconsciously betraying the secret that she had been engaged in active correspondence on the subject, "there is some hope that the Dowager Lady Sudborn will help us; and then Lady Thompson has promised to invite Miss O'Neill to stay with her, and keep her stall,—the beautiful Miss O'Neill, you know, who sold such a number of things at the Fairfield bazaar."

"Miss O'Neill!" cried a little voice from the bottom of the table; "what! the beautiful Miss O'Neill?"

And Miss Martha Beadon, who was a niece of Mrs. Lomax', and was then staying on a visit to her aunt, immediately entered into a low laughing communication with two other young ladies who were sitting next her. In vain Mrs. Lomax looked, and frowned, and nodded. Little Martha's high spirits carried her away; and even Miss Mabel, at the other end of the table, busied as she was in cutting out a baby's frock, and discussing its proper length with Mrs. Maddox, could overhear the words "Fairfield" — "Miss O'Neill" — "two officers" — "three guineas" — "pair of gloves" — "handsome girl," and other stray passages, which, when put together, seemed to imply some anecdote of the bazaar not quite conformable to the notions which Miss Mabel maintained of strict feminine delicacy. After a few sentences, Miss Martha's voice sunk into a whisper; and "oh! oh, fy! hush!" — and the gravity suddenly assumed by the young hearers confirmed her suspicions, and very nearly overturned all her plans for a Hawkstone bazaar, together with a design for a splendid kettle-holder, which she had intended to work herself, and devote to the purposes of the charity.

"Lady Thompson," she said in a hurry, in order to stop farther tittle-tattle at the bottom of the table, "was proposing a ball. She thought many persons

who would not give any thing to the poor persons, or
buy at the bazaar, would willingly show their charity
by coming to the ball."

The Miss Macdougalls both looked prim, and
seemed suddenly immersed in the perplexity of some
plaited calico before them.

"We should all like a ball," said Mrs. Lomax,
looking to Martha, at the bottom of the table, and
thinking that she should probably be asked to be one
of the patronesses.

"Yes," said Miss Lomax, "and we might all make
parties from the country. If you remember the last
time we asked the Vincents and the St. Barbes, and
the Grahams, and they stayed with us three days;
and it was so agreeable; only I remember papa
quarrelled at the expense of so many dinners. But
then it was all for charity; and the St. Barbes
would never have come if we had not asked them."

"How well," whispered Miss Maddox, "I remember that ball. You must know papa gave us
all new dresses, white satin timmed with blond; and
only think, that awkward waiter at the Bell threw a
cup of coffee over mine, and spoiled it for ever : mine
alone cost six guineas."

"What a pity!" exclaimed the little knot of young
ladies.

"And do you remember, too, how silly it was of
Mary Vincent: she would not go at all; and the
only reason was, that she had been to see the poor
people in the morning, and could not get their
distress out of her head. She said she really
could not dance with any pleasure while thinking
of them."

"How very odd!" exclaimed the young ladies at
the bottom of the table.

And just at this time Miss Mabel, at the top, who
had been searching for some papers in an account-
book, read out the sums of money raised for the last

misfortune of a similar kind : — Sermon at church,
5*l.* 10*s.* 4½*d.*   Private subscriptions, 26*l.* 7*s.* 10*d.*
Balance of ball, deducting expenses, lights, music,
rooms, and refreshments, 6*l.* 9*s.* 6*d.*

"My own notion," she added, "was an oratorio
in the church.   It is so much more solemn ; and
sacred music is so delightful.   Is it not, my dear
Miss Macdougall?"   But that lady again looked
prim, and, muttering something indistinctly, was
again perplexed with her calico.

"Oh, do let us have an oratorio!" cried Miss
Martha.   "I shall never forget going to one at
Worcester Cathedral.   It was the most beautiful
thing I ever saw ; all the famous opera-singers were
there, and Signor Bellini, and Signora Strozzi.   I
remember I was so surprised ; for the last time I
heard them it was at the theatre, and I could not
help expecting to see them come dressed in the same
way, with helmets and plumes of feathers, and velvet
cloaks, and shields and swords, and all that ; but
they were dressed just like common people.   It
was quite disappointing."

"Do you remember, Anne," said Mrs. Lomax to
her youngest daughter, who was the musician of the
family, "how admirably Strozzi sang those sweet
things from The Messiah ?   She had the finest voice
I ever heard.   It was quite pathetic.   Only"—
and here Mrs. Lomax fell into a *sotto voce* remark
to her next neighbour, of which nothing was
audible but "sad character ! — poor thing ! — quite
dissolute, I assure you."

"And how well," interposed Miss Anne, "they
had arranged the seats !   All the upper part of the
choir was boarded over ; and as we had some interest with the stewards, we had the most comfortable place you can conceive, just over the altar ;
I do believe I was exactly in the centre, just upon
it.   And we heard so well!"   Just at this moment

something made Miss Macdougall look up from her work with a rather surprised air, and Mrs. Maddox and Miss Catherine exchanged little glances accompanied with the slightest curl of a smile on their lips.

"It would take a long time," said Miss Mabel, thoughtfully, "to fit up the church."

"Yes, I think they told us at Worcester they had been obliged to suspend the service for six weeks or more. And I shall never forget the clattering, and hammering, and the swearing of the workmen, while they were pulling down the scaffolding. It sounded quite strange in the cathedral."

"What we should want," said Miss Mabel, thoughtfully again, "would be stewards. It generally costs the stewards a tolerably round sum. At Worcester, I believe, they usually lose about 800*l.* between them."

"But then," said Mrs. Lomax, "they gain four or five hundred for the charity; and that, you know, is a great thing."

"If we have a bazaar," said Miss Mabel, thoughtfully as before, "we must work for it."

"Oh! we will all work," exclaimed a number of voices, in which the Misses Macdougall did not join.

"And it must not be any thing useful," added Miss Mabel, — "I mean any thing one really wants; for, you know, persons always buy such things best at the shops: and it would throw the poor workmen out of employment, if we set up a rival establishment."

"Oh no, certainly not," was the answer. And each began to consider in what she could best employ her time without producing any thing which should be really useful. One would paint a pair of screens; another could ornament a card-box with paste and paper, so as to make it look like real wood; another had learned the art of stuffing little

D

figures of birds, and covering them with real feathers; a fourth had already commenced the cover of an ottoman, which was to consume four or five guineas' worth of wool and silk, besides six weeks' uninterrupted labour, morning and evening, and which, when it was finished, with the border of yellow and crimson, and St. George and the Dragon, in deep blues and reds, in the centre, and the framework, and the tassels, no one thought would be dearly priced at five pounds.

Mrs. Lomax promised to give up the children to their governess for a week or two, and contribute a little model of a farmyard (a papyreum it was called), in which were to be cows and pigs, and a haystack, two ploughmen, and one milkmaid, besides barns and outhouses, all constructed by some ingenious process which she kept a profound secret, out of silver paper, and which, under a glass case, would look beautiful on a table in a drawing-room. And Miss Mabel once more reverted to her kettle-holder, and almost engaged, in addition, for a patch-work counterpane, provided all present would engage to furnish her with fragments from their wardrobes.

"And what progress has been made in the subscription," said Miss Catherine Macdougall, at length folding up her work, and looking as if she wished to go home.

"Tolerable," replied Miss Brook. "Mr. Lomax very liberally headed it with two pounds; and most of the tradespeople have given their five and ten shillings."

"I assure you," said Mrs. Lomax, in a melancholy tone, "these subscriptions are ruinous. Mr. Lomax declared to me, solemnly, that last year they had cost him no less than twenty guineas, besides what he gives in charity at the door. With his family, and situated as we are, obliged to keep so much company, and with our establishment, I cannot bear to see him asked for any thing which is not absolutely necessary. But this is a case—no less than four families without a home. Is it not, my dear Miss Mabel?"

"Five!" said Miss Mabel. "The only odd thing that I have heard yet is the refusal of the stranger at the Bell—the gentleman, you know, who saved the child—our hero, as we call him."

"He refuse!" cried the whole party.

"How very handsome he is!" whispered Miss Maddox. "Do not you think so?" And little Martha, to whom the question was addressed, coloured up as taken by surprise, and answered, "Yes—no—I cannot tell," though ever since the night of the fire her whole fancy was running on the mysterious stranger, whom she had caught sight of in the street the next morning, and at once had set down as a prince, or at least a count, in disguise, who might possibly fall in love with herself and make her a countess.

"The fact is," said Mrs. Maddox, significantly, "I know more about the circumstances than any one else. And I must say, they struck me as very strange—I might even say suspicious." And she looked round for some mark of approbation of her great sagacity. "You know how well it was arranged that the subscription should be set on foot without any distinction of sects or parties." This was uttered with another bland smile on the amiable Mabel. "So Mr. Maddox and Mr. Lomax took one part of the town, and Mr. Bentley and our excellent friend Mr. Bryant"—a smile at Miss Macdougall —"took the other. Well, when Mr. Maddox and Mr. Lomax called on the stranger at the Bell; they were shown up into his room—the best room in the house, I assure you, over the coffee-room. And the

waiter seemed so civil, and indeed to be quite afraid
of him.   And Mr. Maddox said that he observed
several travelling-cases, and an imperial, and every
thing, in fact, like a man of fortune.   Nothing could
be more polite.   Evidently quite a man of the
world.   But on learning the object of the visit, he
regretted that he could not do any thing, as he
always gave his contributions through the hands of
the clergyman of the parish."

"How odd!" cried the young ladies.

"Not very liberal, I must say," said Miss
Catherine Macdougall.

"But," continued Mrs. Maddox, nearly out of
breath, and afraid lest any one should seize the end
of the story without her, "the strangest thing is to
come.   When Mr. Bentley and Mr. Bryant called in
consequence, he was very civil to Mr. Bentley, and
very cold and stiff indeed to poor Mr. Bryant; and
after all, on some foolish excuse or another, he would
not give them any thing.

"How extremely shabby!" was the exclamation,
in which the voice of Miss Catherine, who could
not help feeling for Mr. Bryant, was heard with
peculiar sharpness.

"But this is not all," continued Mrs. Maddox,
rising from the table and becoming agitated.   "You
know," she said, looking to Miss Catherine, who was
leaning forward to catch any thing which might
avenge the slight offered to her favourite preacher,—
"you know this gentleman," (and there was a
bitterness mingled in the expression this 'gentleman,') "though he did behave very well in saving
the child, was seen by fifty persons crossing himself, actually crossing himself.   He must be a Papist!"
and her voice became louder, as she reached the
climax.

"Certainly!" said Miss Catherine and Miss

Macdougall both, with a firm, decisive, judicial, condemnation of the unhappy criminal. "And you know Lord Claremont is erecting a Catholic" (if Mrs. Bevan had been here she would have insisted on its being called a Roman) "Catholic chapel. And parliament is just going to be dissolved. And now I think I need say no more : you can guess who this gentleman is, and what he is doing in Hawkstone ; I have not a doubt he intends to be the new member."

Why Mrs. Maddox should leap so rapidly to her conclusion, and feel so much interest, and speak with such evident exasperation on the subject, was a problem to the Dorcas Society at large ; and much pondering was proceeding in secret, when the diffident Sarah Morgan, from the bottom of the table, with a very faltering voice, which she had not trusted herself to utter during the whole evening, except to her nearest neighbour, and colouring at thus coming forward in public, ventured to say that she had heard something also which clearly proved that the incognito was a Papist. Mr. Morgan's housemaid was sister-in-law to the first cousin of Robert, the head waiter at the Bell ; and thus Miss Morgan, whose curiosity, in common with all the other inhabitants of Hawkstone, had been wonderfully excited by the handsome stranger, was put in possession of many little facts, not known to the common world. It appeared that one morning Mary the chambermaid had found in arranging his bedroom a little gold cross with a hair chain attached to it, which he received from her without any confusion, and put round his neck. Moreover, on Friday last when Robert after breakfast brought him the bill of fare, Robert's observant eye detected that nothing had been touched but a crust of bread, and, to his still greater surprise, nothing was ordered

for dinner but a poached egg: this was evidently
fasting. And to crown all, Mr. Bryant, when
making his visit of charity, having been shown
into the room before the stranger appeared, had
turned over several books on the table, and two of
them were Greek folios, which Mr. Bryant did not
understand, and a third was mixed up with red
letters, and the fourth Mr. Bryant had seen by the
lettering was a breviary. What a breviary was, the
ladies of the Dorcas Society did not exactly understand, but they had met with the word in several
romances connected with monks and beads, nuns
and crosses, and they could not doubt it was something bad.

We must not dwell on the ejaculations, partly of
pity and partly of grave condemnation, with which
these facts were received. The notion that a Papist
should ever come forward as member for Hawkstone, on which notion Mrs. Maddox seemed strangely
bent, was deemed an absurdity. "And after all, my
dear Mrs. Maddox," said Miss Mabel, "we know
nothing of the stranger, not even his name; he had
no directions on his trunks." (How Miss Mabel had
learned this fact was a mystery.) "He has received no
letters, he has never given his name to the waiter;
and there is something so commanding about him,
that the people at the Bell are afraid to ask him.
All I can hope," continued she, "is that Mr.
Bentley may find some opportunity of speaking to
him; and if any one can convert him, it must be Mr.
Bentley. What a beautiful sermon he preached
against popery last Sunday!—so very impressive!"

"Oh, it was beautiful! Did you not like it?" said
little Martha, looking up in the face of Miss Catherine Macdougall, who had left her chair for some
work, and was leaning over Martha's shoulder.

Mrs. Lomax coughed significantly.

"Was it not beautiful, Miss Macdougall?"

Two more coughs from Mrs. Lomax; but Martha heeded not. "I do hope," she continued, "you like Mr. Bentley? I never heard such a delightful preacher."

"Martha, my dear, lend me your scissors," cried Mrs. Lomax from the other end of the table; and as Martha took up the scissors she met a look and a frown which plainly told her she was making some mistake.

"We always go to our own church," replied Miss Catherine, very coldly.

"But I thought you lived in Hawkstone?" asked the innocent Martha, who, as a stranger, was not enlightened on the polemical statistics of the place.

"So we do," said Miss Catherine.

"But where do you go to church, then?" continued Martha, warned in vain by a friendly foot touching her under the table. "There is only one church in the town, is there?"

Here Jane Lomax took the opportunity of some little movement to whisper, "They are Presbyterians."

"Oh, she meant the chapel, then," whispered Martha.

"No, my dear," said Miss Catherine, colouring, who had no wish to avoid the discussion, "I meant the church. Our place of worship is a church as well as yours."

"But I thought," again asked Martha, "that there was only one Church? Does not the Bible say there is only one Church, aunt?" Mrs. Lomax had no wish to reply, and was busy with her work-basket.

"You know," continued Miss Catherine, "we are the Church in Scotland, and you are Dissenters; and we are Dissenters here, and you are the Church."

D 4

"But then there must be two Churches," said
Martha; "and the Bible says there is but one. Is
not that strange?"

"My love," said Mrs. Lomax, impatiently, "we
should not talk of things which we do not understand.
So put up your work, for it is getting quite late—half
past nine, I declare." And Martha proceeded to arrange her work-basket, pondering in her mind how
Miss Macdougall could call her chapel a church, when
the Bible said there was but one Church, and resolved
to ascertain as soon as possible what the meaning
of a Church was, and whether, which she strongly
doubted, it meant any thing at all.

Mrs. Lomax's move seemed gladly seconded by
Mrs. Maddox, who had evinced for some time a little
fidgetty impatience, implying that she wished the
evening at a close. And the party had soon partaken of Miss Mabel's wine-and-water, adjusted their
cloaks, put on their clogs, and galoshes, and Glou-
cester boots, and wishing each other a kind, good
night, they made their way down Mabel's narrow
staircase, into the gas-lighted street. Mrs. Maddox
alone found a singular difficulty in fastening her
cloak. And after allowing the others to depart, and
telling her daughter that the servant might come
again for her, she no sooner saw that all were gone,
than closing the door, she seated herself once more
by the fire, and announced that she had something
to impart of consequence. Mabel took the opposite
seat, and assumed the air of an attentive listener;
and Mrs. Maddox proceeded.

"I want you very much, my dear Mabel, to come
and dine with us to-morrow—quite quietly—scarcely
any one but ourselves."

Mabel wondered at this being a matter of such
importance. But she saw evidently there was some-

thing beyond. Mrs. Maddox paused, for she knew that she was on delicate ground.

"I will tell you candidly why I wish it so much," she continued. "Now, do not be angry. You won't be angry, will you? But your cousin Marmaduke" (here Mabel started, coloured deeply, and drew herself up with every mark of indignation), "your cousin Marmaduke," proceeded Mrs. Maddox, affecting not to notice these symptoms, "is coming to us for some days. And I should be so glad, so very glad, if I could see you meet him on friendly terms, and forget all the unpleasantness between you. He is such a clever man, and so agreeable. And he is making his way in the world, rising, I assure you, very rapidly. Mr. Lomax assured me that he had been asked several times to Lord Germain's, Germain House, you know, where all the clever men are invited. And the government have made him one of the new commissioners for inspecting the gutters, with 1500*l.* a year. And he writes in the *Westminster Review*. The very best article in the last number, I am told, was his. And, indeed, I should not be surprised," (here her voice became mysteriously low,) "if he were to get into parliament in case of a dissolution. It is such a pity that you cannot meet him in a friendly way."

Mabel had heard, or rather she might have heard, all this, for she sat perfectly unmoved, drawn up in a rigid posture, with a very high colour in her cheeks, and a look of which Mrs. Maddox had caught a sidelong view, and which she did not venture fairly to face. But Mrs. Maddox's eulogium had no sooner ceased than her answer was ready. She expressed no little surprise that Mrs. Maddox, an old friend, one for whom she felt the most cordial esteem, with whom she was more intimate than any one in the world, should have thought of making a proposal to her so painful and unreasonable. She had no ill-will to Marmaduke. She was glad to hear of his rising in the world. She could meet him, if absolutely necessary, as she would any other person; but for any thing like cordiality or friendship, such a feeling as she had to the Maddoxes for instance, and the Macdougalls, it was quite impossible.

"You know well, my dear Mrs. Maddox," she added, "the principal circumstances of his conduct. You remember my poor brother Charles" (and here Mabel's voice faultered, for it was her only brother, whom she had doted on, of whom she was speaking). "You know he sacrificed himself, I may say he lost his life, in extricating Marmaduke from that disgraceful affair at Gibraltar. Charles never recovered it; and the very first thing which Marmaduke did, as soon as he was released from prison, while Charles was lying dead, was to vilify him, to impugn his word, to prevent his brother officers from showing any respect to his memory, and to endeavour to overturn all the plans which Charles had been all his life contriving for the welfare of his family. When he came to England, his first business was to sow dissension between all the branches of the family; to dispute my father's will; to try to deprive me of the little pittance I possess: and all this with a show of kindness and profession of liberality, which common sense must see to be hypocrisy. The very last words my poor father said to me on his death-bed was a caution against Marmaduke; he almost prophesied what he would do, knowing his cold selfish unprincipled sneering nature. And he intreated me, or rather, I should say, he laid his solemn injunctions on me, to abstain from any communication with him. I owe it to the memory both of my father and my brother, to have no further association with him than is absolutely necessary. I should com-

promise my own feelings and sense of right, and lose
myself in public opinion, and, as far as an humble person like myself can do, lower the standard of public
morals, if I overlooked these acts as if they had
never been, and could feel or affect to feel to such a
man the same as to a friend. You will see this, I am
sure, my dearest friend, in the same light with myself, and will not urge me to place myself in a
position where I could not with propriety show
what I really feel, and yet by concealment I should
disgrace myself in my own eyes, and the eyes of
others, and only harden him in his shamelessness."

Mabel ceased—and Mrs. Maddox was silent, for
she felt rather ashamed of herself ; at last she took
courage to hope that Mabel would not be offended, that
she could quite understand the feeling; and on the
whole she agreed that it was better for persons
who could not cordially sympathise with and respect
each other to associate together as little as possible.

"I am not offended at all," was Mabel's reply. "It
would take a great deal to make me quarrel with
you, whom I have known so long, and so intimately,
and love very dearly ; indeed, there is no one in
Hawkstone whom I live with more than yourself,
and I hope it always will be so,"—

"Though we do differ in religious notions," said
Mrs. Maddox, recovering her spirits and smiling
playfully.

"Yes," said Mabel, "though you are a Unitarian,
I do not think religious opinions should ever interfere
with our social friendship. Thank God, we are not
bigots in Hawkstone, and there is no one, except
indeed" (she checked herself) "a Papist, with whom
I could not live on the most affectionate terms."

"God bless you, my dear, God bless you!" was
the answer ; and with a hearty and mutual kiss Mrs.
Maddox retreated to the door, and Mabel put out
her candles and "retired to her couch."

CHAP. IV.

MABEL was roused the next morning from a disturbed dream, in which Mr. Marmaduke Brook, assisted by Mrs. Maddox, was in the act of seizing her splendid kettle-holder, and plunging it in the gutter, by a merry peal of bells from the tower of Hawkstone church. Nothing could sound more light and cheerful. Bell took up the sound from bell, and each seemed to rival the other in ringing out some glad intelligence to the whole country round. The sun shone brightly into Mabel's room; and again the peals rang round and round, and up and down, now swelling out in full chorus, and now dying gently down, only to resume the happy clamour with renewed life and vigour. What could be the reason? A marriage? No! Miss Mabel was the sworn confidant of all the Hawkstone young ladies, and could not be taken by surprise on such a subject. Some victory, or a naval battle, perhaps? No! Though Mabel did not devote much study to the newspapers, she knew that at that time we happened to be in a profound peace, and not even to have an ally to conquer untowardly, or a fleet of his to destroy. What could be the matter? On looking from her window, to her still greater surprise, she discerned, waving on the dark grey tower, a splendid pale blue banner. Mabel rang her bell; and little Connor, the Grey girl, was sent to ascertain the news, while Mabel herself pursued her toilet. Connor had not far to go; for Mabel, with a truly liberal and charitable spirit, was in the habit of maintaining that politics, as well as religion, ought not to be con-

sidered in the friendly associations of life, and that
every one should be allowed to follow his own
conscience, whether in obeying or disobeying laws.
She had, therefore, felt no scruple in establishing
her quarters in the house of Messrs. Silkem, the
radical linendrapers. And Messrs. Silkem willingly
sent up to Mabel the Morning Chronicle, which had
just arrived, containing all the news. The first
words which caught Mabel's eye, in large letters,
were " Glorious Triumph of Dissenters!" The next
were something about "inevitable downfal of a
tyrannical and priest-ridden Church!" and, without
much difficulty, Mabel found that the bells were
ringing and the flag flying on the grey tower of the
old church to announce that a liberal measure had
just been carried in parliament, by the hands of a
conservative ministry; a measure on which she had
heard both Mrs. and Charles Bevan declare turned
virtually the whole question of an established religion in this country. It seemed strange: but then
there was at Hawkstone, as in other towns, a
radical and unitarian churchwarden; and poor
old Dr. Grant was too infirm to enter into the
dispute on the right of ringing the bells, and
Mr. Bentley, of course, could not move. And so
Mabel, a warm Conservative at heart, and whose
errors were only overflowings of real benevolence
and piety ill instructed, was compelled to dress herself to the sound of the tuneful church bells, ringing out merrily the downfal of the Church, and
with nearly a darkened room, lest she should have
before her eyes the spectacle of that odious pale
blue banner, floating over the grey pinnacles of that
ancient tower.

Her toilet was soon over, and her breakfast
despatched; but the latter not without many movements from the table, and searchings among heaps

of papers and references to drawers, in order for
Mabel to lose no time, but to arrange her business for
the day while she was eating her meals.   For this
day, like every other day in the week, was a day of
business.   And sometimes Mabel sighed, and sometimes she asked for pity and sympathy ; but at all
times she felt a little excitement and sense of importance, which might (such is the frailty of our
nature) rise occasionally into something like vain-
gloriousness, as she thought how many things could
not be done without her.   And to-day there was
the Grey School committee, and the National School
to be visited.   And Mr. Bentley's new plans for the
Sunday School to be talked over with four or five
other ladies, and the last private meeting with three
or four others to originate a new ladies' association
for the discouragement of drunkenness, and the
accounts of the Tract Society to be audited, and the
report of the Ladies' District Visiting Club to be
drawn up ; and, greatest of all, the first meeting of
the Ladies' Society for the Conversion of the Irish,
which was to be held in the great ball-room at the
Bell, and where Mr. Bentley and Mr. Bryant would
each make a speech, and perhaps pay a compliment
to her "laborious and energetic offices as secretary,"
amidst cries of "hear!" and "hear!" and the amiable congratulations of female friends to cover her
natural confusion.   The day was filled up to the
brim.   Still there was another object on which she
resolved, not without some misgivings, to bestow the first hour of the morning.   Why did not
Mrs. Bevan come to the last night's meeting ?   Was
there, as she feared, an anticipation of withdrawing
from it ?   Did Mrs. Bevan disapprove of any thing
that had been done ?   And Mabel could not rest till
these questions were solved.

Attired, as she always was attired, in her respect-

able economical black silk cloak, and her respectable never-wearing-out black velvet bonnet, and,
sole relic of wealthier days, her handsome boa,
Mabel sallied forth—for in novels distinguished
persons always move in that way—into the High
Street of Hawkstone. There was seemingly a little
bustle. Two or three persons were congregated here,
one or two there. Mr. Brown the grocer was holding
a confabulation with Mr. More the chemist and Mr.
Alley the shoemaker, at the shoemaker's door. A
little knot had gathered round the stable entrance of
the Bell, waiting for the arrival of the Highflyer coach
from London. And at the corner of Westgate Street,
turning down to the Bank, Mr. Morgan was in close
conversation with Mr. Lomax, and evidently on
some deep subject, for one of Mr. M.'s hands had
seized Mr. L.'s button, and the other was busily
employed in laying down the law and dictating some
line of conduct, with a half-patronising and half-
reverential air, to which Mr. L. was listening condescendingly submissive, and not without gratification, though at the same time importantly grave.
As she passes the other little groups, they make
way for her with more than ordinary deference.
Mr. Brown takes off his hat; Mr. More smiles significantly, and retreats within the shop to avoid
touching her dress. The hostlers at the Bell look
respectful and admiring. But both the gentlemen
at the corner are cool—cooler than usual; and a
hasty good morning is all that they vouchsafe. "But
then they are evidently talking on business," thought
Mabel, who was not used to cool looks, and by no
means liked them.

But what makes Mabel on a sudden start, and
look in wonder at that long dead brick wall which
runs at the back of Mr. Aspland's garden? Why
does the colour come to her cheek, and her heart

begin to flutter, and she looks out to see if any one is behind her? Mabel's eyes were arrested, as well they might be, by her own name, in large white letters, three feet high, and half a foot broad, painted with artistic skill on the whole length of that red brick wall, "Brook for ever!" Mabel rubbed her eyes, but it was no delusion. There was the wall, and there her name; and there, what struck her most, the magic words "for ever!" She was greatly touched, flattered, surprised; but still modestly, and with a deep sense how little she deserved such a testimony of popular approbation. She knew, indeed, that she was of some little use to the town; that the poor people always liked to see her at their cottages; that the school could not do without her; that she was secretary to no less than a dozen societies; that her whole time was spent in doing good. Still, like the gentleman from Oxford who went up to London the day after he had obtained his first class, and entered the Opera-house just as the whole house rose up to thunder out their applause on the entrance of the king, she was not prepared for such a public manifestation of popular feeling. It was too much. She preferred being left in retirement, doing good by stealth: and, afraid lest persons should gather round her, she put her parasol before her face, and, casting a side glance on the gratifying inscription, she passed on. But for Mabel's modesty there was no escape; she had scarcely turned the corner of King Street, going down Prince's Lane, than once more, on the front of Mr. Russel's old malt-house, there stood the same letters—the letters of her own name; not quite so large, indeed, and this time in black paint instead of white, but coupled with a longer suffix, "Brook and Religious Liberty!" Quite overcome, she thought of those charitable sentiments, which she had so often ap-

plauded, and professed, and with which she had endeavoured to hold together the sisterly societies of
Hawkstone, " without distinction of sect or party ; "
and could not but confess that, humble as she was,
her heart indeed did merit this tribute to her Christian benevolence. A little bewildered at finding
herself thus the marked object of popular gratitude
and admiration, before she saw clearly where she
was going, a rough " by-your-leave" compelled her
to make way for a dirty, fustian-clad, ragged-haired
man, with a short ladder on one shoulder, a mass of
paper hanging over one arm, and a black paste-pot,
with a huge brush sticking in it, in his other hand.
She had just time to save her silk cloak from the
paste-pot, and to cast a look of reproachful wonder
on a rude man, who showed so little deference for a
person so extensively and deservedly beloved, when
the bill-sticker proceeded to fix his ladder against
the wall, to smear his paste over it, to transfer a
long sheet of paper from his arm to the surface, to
descend his ladder, and vanish in a minute. Mabel
looked up as she passed ; — and once again,—conceive
her astonishment, — her own name, M. Brook, in
large letters, at the foot of some copious printing.
What to think she knew not. Short-sighted as she
was, it took a little time to find her glass, and examine the singular phenomenon. And then, alas !
the mystery was dispelled. She read at the top of
the paper, " To the free and independent Electors
of the Borough of Hawkstone." She read one sentence, which showed her that the address proceeded
from her amiable cousin Marmaduke, who solicited
the honour of their votes at the approaching parliamentary election. Mabel passed on hastily, very
much surprised, a little ashamed, a little disappointed, half laughing at herself for suffering such
silly thoughts in her head, more than half angry

E

at her cousin for presuming to come forward on the
radical interest and disturb the peace of Hawkstone, after having behaved so ill to herself: and
yet the thought flitted past—it is a respectable
thing to be cousin to a member of parliament! And
before the thought had passed by there was a
friendly hand placed within her own, and a pair of
laughing eyes were looking up in her face, with an
ironical congratulation. It was Anne Morgan, who
had just returned from one of her district visits, in
which she had been reading to a poor sick man, and
endeavouring to show him the necessity of coming
to church, but without being exactly able to explain
to him why he might not just as well go to chapel;
and Anne was not sorry to escape from her difficult
task of enlightening ignorance with ignorance.
There were kind allusions to last evening's agreeable meeting—kind hopes that Mabel was not tired
with her gaiety — and kind hopes from Mabel herself, that Mr. and Mrs. Morgan and all the children
were well.

Yes, all well; Mr. Morgan tolerable. " But," said
Anne, sinking down into seriousness, " you must have
heard of his being called up last night. Poor Mary
Vincent — extremely ill, they say, with the typhus
fever. And my father was obliged to go there
again this morning. But we hope she is a little
better." Poor Mary Vincent! she, who would not
go to the ball because she could not dance with the
misery of her fellow-creatures in her mind. And
she, it might be added, the simple, retired, pure-
minded, sensible girl, who was growing up in the
village of Hurst to be a blessing to her parents, and
a pearl beyond price to any clergyman who could
win her affections, and associate her with him in the
manifold duties of his parish. And now she was
lying on a bed of sickness — perhaps never to rise

from it again. And many hearts, as Mabel knew,
were wrapt up in her as in a precious treasure;
and one, above all, whom Mabel thought, with comfort, that she was not likely to meet where she was
now going, for she believed Charles Bevan to be in
Oxford.

It was, therefore, with no little dismay that in
Mrs. Bevan's passage she observed a hat and stick
on the table; and, on entering the little drawing-
room, which served also for a library, she found
himself, as usual, with his large book before him,
and his pencil in his hand, and his note-book at his
side. His mother's chair and her work-table showed
she had not left the room long. And Charles was
sitting with his back to the door, with his head
resting on his hand, but not reading; for Mabel observed afterwards that the leaves of his book were
blistered with tears. But Charles had been brought
up in a school which did not encourage scenes —
which looked on human feelings — real feelings,
that is, and innocent — too reverently to tolerate
display of them. If there was one thing which he
despised, it was theatrical sensibility. And thus
the sight of Mabel quieted him at once; and he
could enter into the common topics of a visit
without betraying himself. He had come down, he
said, from London unexpectedly last night, and took
to himself the blame of his mother's absence from
the Dorcas Society. And his mother soon appeared to answer for herself; — her usual quietness
of manner, shaded over by evident sorrow, and her
eye glancing unobservedly on her son with an expression of affectionate compassion, which went to
Mabel's heart.

"A note from Mr. Morgan, ma'am," said the
servant, following his mistress into the room. And
Mabel saw Charles take up his pencil, and begin

writing hurriedly, as if not daring to look up. His
mother's hand shook violently as she attempted to
open it ; but, to Mabel's great delight, her face relaxed as she read it; and, putting it before her son,
with a slight pressure of the hand, returned, Oh!
how warmly! she turned to Mabel to inform her that
it was a line from Mr. Morgan, who had just returned from Hurst, to say that things were going
on well, and all danger was over. Mabel only saw
that Charles's eyes were turned up for one moment
with an expression of thankfulness and piety such as
she had never seen before; and then, while the two
ladies were in conversation, he folded up his papers,
and without being observed left the room.

Nearly half an hour had elapsed before he returned, with a composed and cheerful countenance,
— so much so, that Mabel was emboldened to look
him full in the face, and even to appeal to him as
arbiter on the discussion which she was then holding with his mother. " I am explaining to Miss
Brook," said Mrs. Bevan, " the reasons which we
were talking over last night, and which have induced me to think of leaving the Dorcas Society.
But I would rather she should hear them from you ;
for I am not quite sure that it is not an evil sign
where ladies undertake to be teachers, and to lead
instead of following."

Charles smiled, with something of an affirmative
in his smile which Mabel did not like. Besides
this, she was not a little afraid of him, for their
opinions often differed ; and she was conscious of
something defective in her own system, what it was
precisely she could not tell, which made her uncomfortable in his superiority.

" Are you aware, my dear mother," he said,
" what you are doing, — proposing to me to undertake a war with all the ladies' societies in Hawkstone,

with Miss Brook at their head, and all the liberality
and charity in the country to come to their rescue,
myself almost single handed? I must expect to
have my eyes torn out with the points of buckles,
as the Athenian ladies destroyed their rebel, or to
be pricked to death with scissors, like poor L'Escuyer,
in the church at Avignon, by the ladies of the
French revolution. For, whenever there is a revolution there you will certainly find that ladies, like
other members of society, fall out of their proper
places, and that they are the cause of the greatest
mischief. In the Lord George Gordon riots," he
continued, affecting to look grave, "it is a well-
known fact, that the lower ranks of London ladies
formed the most troublesome and destructive portion
of the mobs — burning houses, and bursting open
prisons. And I need not remind you of the pois-
sardes of Paris, who stormed Versailles and overawed the convention, or of the more genteel Parisian
ladies, who subsequently petitioned the Assembly,
that they might be allowed to trail a pike in the
Champ de Mars, and who used to take their work
and sit every morning under the guillotine."

"What do you mean?" exclaimed Mabel, half-
offended and half-perplexed. "Do you seriously
mean to compare us with those horrible wretches?
Are these your new Oxford notions?"

Charles smiled at her warmth. "No, my dear
Miss Brook, far be it from me to make any such
comparison; and far be it from you to lay upon
poor Oxford all the strange notions which strange
men belonging to it may take into their heads.
Poor Oxford has enough to answer for already, has
it not?" he asked, laughingly. And Mabel looked
grave; for, though she had not found time to learn
what Oxford notions really were, Mr. Bentley had

preached a most powerful sermon against the new
heresy, as he called it, and always shook his head
with a profoundly melancholy expression whenever
the subject was mentioned, as it often was mentioned in the little Hawkstone coteries. Nor must
we forget that she had more than once seen the
Record newspaper, which distinctly charged the
whole University with popery; and the statement
being in print, and moreover in a religious newspaper, who could hesitate to believe it?

" But you look with such contempt," she said,
plaintively, " on us poor women, as if we were
wholly useless, mere slaves, fit only to talk scandal
or sew silk."

" Ask my mother," said Charles, " if I speak
contemptuously of women." And his voice softened
as he spoke, and his eye became graver, and Mabel
thought moistened, for his thoughts just then had
turned on Mr. Morgan's note. " Be assured," he
continued, " no man ever spoke contemptuously of
women without having a bad heart as well as a bad
head. I believe that God made them to be a help-
meet for man, — to be his great earthly support, his
comfort, his encouragement in trials, his nurse, his
earliest teacher, his last friend, his mother, and
sister, and wife. And without mother, and sister,
and wife, what would man be? And yet," he added,
" there may be a peculiar sphere in which only they
ought to act; and they may overstep their duties,
and be too active, too zealous, too enlightened, as it
is called. And they may want guidance and control
even in their best of actions, their charities, and
devotions, — may they not?"

" Certainly," said Mabel; " and yet what would
you do in this town of Hawkstone, for instance, if
it were not for ladies? Dr. Grant paralytic; poor

Mr. Bentley fagged to death with his three services
on the Sunday, and all the weekly duty, and a population of thousands to take care of, with only 150*l.*
a year. How can he attend to the schools, or visit
the poor, or manage the hundred things which are
implied in the care of a parish — much more now the
manufactories have brought here such a number of
poor, and there is so much sickness among them?
No gentleman can attend to these things; they
cannot teach in the schools, or attend to the sick, or
have any thing to do with cutting out flannels, and
distributing tracts. What is to become of the town
if the ladies are not to be active ?"

" And you may add," subjoined Charles, "what
is to become of the whole country if the towns are
not taken care of — if the ladies are not active
—if such masses of population are brought together
as we see throughout England, to ferment and rot
in heaps, without any one to give them religion, or
to stand over them constantly with a high and
parental authority, acting on them like the eye of
a parent on a headstrong child, not by force, which
soon must fail, but by gratitude, kindness, shame,
advice, assistance, admonition — the ten thousand
secret influences which regulate the human heart,
and which no books, no teaching, can create, nothing
but personal, close, constant, minute, affectionate
association with a power above them."

" And this, then," said Mabel, triumphantly,
"must be done by ladies ?"

" Much of it, undoubtedly. I fear my fingers
would move but clumsily, if I took my mother's
needle out of her hand, and set to work on that
white lily which she is embroidering. And I fear
also, my dear Miss Brook, that you would be a
little puzzled at these strange hieroglyphics," (and

he pointed to his Greek folio). "Each of us to his natural vocation. Educating young children, nursing the sick, regulating families—above all, exhibiting without your knowing it a spectacle of purity, gentleness, and affection to us whose hearts are so often seared and tainted by the rough commerce of the world, — these are the tasks which nature has assigned to you, and with which we are not to interfere. And in these you can do incalculable service, both to the Church and to the country. No Church can be perfect without you. And how highly the Church and churchmen value you, you may learn even from the simple fact, that the Church itself has been named with your name, and delights in assuming your relations as a mother and a spouse. Therefore never charge me with speaking contemptuously of women."

Mabel listened, and certainly felt flattered. But why Mr. Bevan should have spoken of services *to the Church* — why he did not say, in disseminating the Gospel, or in making men Christians, or doing them good generally, she did not exactly see. It was one of his strange Oxford notions; and she felt sorry that he was so bigoted.

"Shall I tell you," continued Charles, as he stood before her, and perceived what was passing in her mind, by her not venturing to look up, — " shall I tell you, why I laid so much stress on the word Church ? Or are you afraid lest I should convert you to popery ? "

" No, not exactly," said Mabel, half-peeping from under her bonnet, and yet a little afraid.

" I spoke of the Church," said Charles, " because if we are to engage either in serving God or in blessing his creatures, — that is, if we are to undertake any work of any description either from piety or charity, — we must undertake it as the servants

of God, according as he wills, in submission to that
authority which he has placed in the world for that
purpose. What would you say if some active clever
boy in the National School, wishing to benefit his
schoolfellows and do good, were to put himself at
the head of a class and insist on teaching them their
lessons, instead of the master, or without consulting
the master, or when the master forbade it,— would
you think the excuse sufficient that he was most
zealous in doing good? Whether he did good or not,
would be another question. But the very attempt
would be an act of insubordination, would it not?
and as such you would punish it. The children are
placed under the governors of the school, are they
not? and no one has a right to interfere with them
but the governors themselves, or persons authorised
by them."

"Certainly," said Mabel, for she was one of the
most active governors herself, and no one was
more ready to vindicate their claim to an implicit
obedience. Not two days before Patty Sykes had
been sent away at her suggestion, because Patty's
mother had come to the school and interfered with
some regulations of the committee, that no parent
should speak with the children during school-time.

"Think also," continued Charles, "that to do
good to man is not an easy task. To make them wise
and virtuous, and religious, happy upon earth, and
fit for happiness in heaven,—this is not a light thing.
We must be sure that what we teach them is true—
sure that what we would have them do is really
good—sure that God's blessing is upon us, that he is
not against us, frustrating our empty efforts to do
good without him, or against him: and unless there
is God's own voice confirming us in all these things,
what do we know of them?"

" Nothing," said Mabel, " certainly."

" And how can we hear this voice," he continued, " unless we hear it from his ministers, from those whom he has sent himself, and specially commissioned to deliver his message to mankind ? "

" We hear it from the Bible," said Mabel, reproachfully.

" We hear it from the Bible, assuredly," said Charles. " But the Bible is but a document put into our hands by the ministers to whom it is entrusted by God himself. If I sent to you a message by a friend, and that friend gave you a paper containing the message, but containing also an injunction that you should attend to the explanation of that friend, ask his advice, consult his opinion, respect him as my own representative, would you say that the document alone, whether you understood it or not, doubted about it or not, was all that you would look to,—that you would listen to no further information from that friend himself of the interpretation I put upon the document ? "

Mabel was silent, for she had heard so often from Mr. Bentley of " the Bible and the Bible alone," and of the attempts of the Oxford heretics to supersede the Bible by tradition, that she knew, as she afterwards declared, that something was wrong in the argument, though what it was she could not discover : and as Mr. Bentley had never explained to her that there was a considerable difference between a power in human hands to decree articles of faith beyond and opposed to the Bible, and a power in the same hands to convey down, under suitable checks against corruption, the same truths which are contained in the Bible, Mabel stumbled, as other persons less ignorant and not more well intentioned do, on the fatal word " tradition," and already lamented that she had ever come within such a popish atmosphere.

"But what has this to do with the Dorcas Society?" she ventured to ask, in hope of escaping from her difficulties.

"I wished," said Charles, as he smiled good-naturedly at the sight of her perplexities (for Mabel, with all her little ignorances, had too much goodness of character not to be a favourite with him)—"I wished to suggest that when ladies, like other persons, do undertake missions of piety or offices of charity, they should place themselves under the guidance of the Church, that is, of God's own appointed ministers of piety and charity, and act as a part of that body, according to its rules, with a constant reference to its welfare and principles."

"Surely," said Mabel; "but where is the Church? Are not all who preach the Gospel ministers of God?"

"Not exactly," answered Charles. "If the letter I send you by the messenger is stolen from him, and presented to you by another person, that person does not become by the mere fact of such a presentation my representative and minister, does he?"

"No," said Mabel.

"And if persons not appointed by God do happily preach the word of God, does this make them ambassadors of God?"

"No, certainly."

"But who are appointed? How am I, a poor ignorant person, with none of those great books within my reach, and if they were in my reach, without means to understand them,—how am I to decide who are the true ministers of God, when they

all put into my hands the same Bible, and each
claims to be such himself?"

What Charles's answer would have been to this
problem it is difficult to say; for at this moment the
door opened, a morning visitor from the country
was announced; and Mabel, gathering up her black
silk pelisse and adjusting her boa, shook hands with
both Charles and his mother, whether cordially or
not she could not exactly decide, and took her
leave with a promise that her question should be
put again at some more favourable time.

CHAP. V.

AND who is the lady with the green silk cloak and red-ribboned bonnet, who has seized Mr. Bentley's arm at the corner of King Street, close by that large house with the little house fastened on at its side, and bearing on its brass plate the name of Mr. Atkinson, solicitor?

It is Mrs. Maddox; and she is busily repeating to Mr. Bentley, who, as chairman of the Ladies' Branch Bible Society, cannot but listen attentively to one of the chief members of the committee, all the information which had been collected respecting the mysterious stranger at the Bell.

" He is a Papist," said Mrs. Maddox; and Mr. Bentley's face assumed a rueful look.

" He wears a cross," said Mrs. Maddox; and Mr. Bentley might have pointed at the cross over the church porch, but by chance he did not think of it.

" He fasts," continued Mrs. Maddox. And Mr. Bentley might have informed her that in one of the pages of the Church of England Prayer Book there were especial injunctions for fasting. But the fact was, that Bentley's studies had not lain in the rubric, and he never thought of it.

" He has a breviary," continued Mrs. Maddox. And here again, as Bentley had never read a breviary, he could only answer,

" You do not say so?"

" He would give nothing to the subscription for the fire," said Mrs. Maddox. And she had intended

to conclude with a request, that if he should come
forward on Lord Claremont's interest for the borough of Hawkstone, Mr. Bentley would refuse him
his vote, and give it to Mr. Marmaduke Brook, the
clever young man, who was then staying in her own
house ; but Bentley was obliged to interrupt her by
explaining, that the stranger had given something
— a very large sum — one hundred guineas ; that
he had given it last Sunday among the alms offered
at the Holy Communion, and Bentley had found it
in a small packet folded up with a note to himself,
expressing a wish that it might be appropriated, if
the clergyman and churchwardens thought fit, to
the relief of the sufferers by the fire. Mrs. Maddox
was thrown back surprised — even dismayed ; for
what chance could Mr. Marmaduke Brook, with his
1500*l.* commissionership, have against such means
and such liberality ?

"Mere bribery," she said. But Bentley checked
her observation. He did not think it necessary to
add, that in the same slip of paper there was a request
that eighty of the hundred should be appropriated to
such sufferers as were members of the Church, and
the other twenty only given to Dissenters in case
they were in considerable distress, and could not
obtain assistance from the frequenters of their several chapels.

"Strange !" thought Bentley — "very illiberal :"
but so it was. And Bentley forgot just at that moment
the injunction of the Apostle "to do good unto all
men, but especially unto those that are of the household of faith."

For more reasons than a mere love of gossip,
which, as Aristotle tells us, is natural to all men, Mrs.
Maddox would probably have hastened away at once
to carry this intelligence to Mr. Marmaduke's committee, then sitting in secret conference in her own

drawing-room. But just as she was wishing Bentley
good-morning, who should issue out from Mr. Atkinson's brass-knockered brass-plated door, and escorted to the door with very deferential politeness
by the grave Mr. Atkinson in person, but the mysterious stranger himself! He passed Mr. Bentley
with a gentlemanly bow of recognition, but found
considerable difficulty in executing the same manœuvre with Mrs. Maddox; for what with the surprise, and the notion of being so close to a Papist,
and the indignation at his standing against Mr.
Brook, and at the same time a little awe inspired
by his great dignity of manner, and a little confusion at the consciousness of her own thoughts,
besides a doubt whether she ought to notice him,
and a resolution to toss up her head as he passed —
all these things so embarrassed poor Mrs. Maddox,
that shifting backwards and forwards from side to
side, she ended in very nearly pushing her parasol
into his eye, and compelled him, with an apology for
his awkwardness, to step out into the road. But the
apology was gracious, the voice refined, the manner
noble. And Mrs. Maddox, after achieving her evo-
lution, could not help looking back at his tall commanding figure. She then recollected (it is singular
how recollections of the kind do come upon us) that
it was her duty, a duty which she reproached herself much for having so long neglected, to call on
Mrs. Atkinson to inquire after the health of little
Jesse Atkinson, the youngest but four of Mrs. Atkinson's ten children, and who had pricked herself with a
thorn a full fortnight back, and had been suffering
from a swelled finger. She moved to the door, rang
the bell, and to her great delight Mrs. Atkinson was
at home. But Mrs. Atkinson, a plain, sensible,
domestic person, little stirred by curiosity, little disposed to communicate her husband's secrets, and

caring for little in the world but her own family duties, and Mr. Atkinson's comfort, and her ten children's health and happiness, was not the person from whom much information could be extracted on the subject of the mysterious stranger. She was surprised at the call, for there were political reasons why Mrs. Maddox did not call often, — Mr. Atkinson was a Conservative, Mr. Maddox a Radical, — she was surprised at the tender inquiry after Jesse's finger, for Jesse's finger had been quite well ten days ago. And when Mrs. Maddox's careless well-managed "by-the-by" (for Mrs. Maddox was rather an intriguer, and understood diplomacy) had brought forward the subject of the stranger, Mrs. Atkinson knew nothing about him. She believed he had some business with Mr. Atkinson—he had been often to the house, closeted with Mr. A. in the library — was fond of children.

" Oh, yes," cried little Willy, who was in the room playing ; " and do you know, yesterday, when I was in the library, he came in and took me on his knee and asked me my name, and told me such a pretty story ! "

" How artful and electioneering ! " thought Mrs. Maddox.

" What was his name ? "

Mrs. Atkinson did not know.

" Was he rich ? "

She could not tell.

" How long would he stay in Hawkstone ? "

She had not heard.

" Had Mrs. Atkinson seen him ? "

Yes, for a minute, but only for a minute, except at church, when he sat in Mr. Atkinson's pew.

" At church ! " exclaimed Mrs. Maddox. " Why, he is a Papist ! "

" I should think not," observed Miss Simpson,

the governess, who had been sitting by in silence; for every time that I have been to eleven o'clock prayers on Wednesdays and Fridays, he has been at church, and also on the last Saint's day."

" How singular," thought Mrs. Maddox, and also Mrs. Atkinson.

" What can a gentleman have to do at church on a week day? He is not a clergyman, is he?"

" No :" the eldest Miss Atkinson had remarked one day that he wore a light-coloured waistcoat.

" Any relation to Lord Claremont?"

No one knew.

" Had he been asked to dinner?"

It was a bold question, and Mrs. Atkinson felt offended. But Mrs. Maddox's patience was exhausted.

" Yes; Mr. Atkinson, she believed, without mentioning it to her, had asked him to dine last Friday, which he had declined on the ground that he never dined out on Fridays."

" He has been very liberal in an odd way about the poor people at the fire," observed Mrs. Maddox, severely.

" Has he?" said Mrs. Atkinson.

And Mrs. Maddox in despair rose up and took her leave, ejaculating mentally, or, as it has been correctly defined, not ejaculating at all, but keeping close within her own breast, the exclamation, " Oh, that impracticable woman!"

And in the mean time what had become of the stranger? He had turned into the high street, not unfollowed by curious eyes, had crossed over the bridge, passed by the huge, hideous manufactory with its hundred windows, and its tall, smoke-vomiting chimney; from whence he had pursued the high road, until he reached the old lodge gate of the Priory, and here he entered, without asking leave.

"Please, sir, be you going to the house?" cried an old grey-headed man, endeavouring to pursue him, and warn him from trespassing.

"Yes, my good friend," said the stranger, returning, and seeming to recollect himself. "Pray, is it shown?"

"Yes, sir," answered the old man.

"Is any one there?"

"No one, sir, and has not been for many a long year since Lady Esther's death, — all gone away to foreign parts."

The stranger said nothing, but walked on — and he walked with folded arms, slowly, and stopping at times, as if oppressed by a multitude of recollections. And then he looked up and round with a searching eye, as if to see if any thing was missing from an old and much-loved picture. And as the road, winding under its dark masses of wood, rose gradually along the side of a steep declivity, he stopped here and there as at well-known resting-places, and seemed to search in the blue landscape, now nearly obscured by trees, for a distant spire, the gleam of the river beneath, the grey smoke of Hawkstone, as for old familiar objects which he longed to behold again. At one point he struck off from the road into the tangled thicket, until he reached a knoll projecting over the river, and commanding one of its fairest reaches. And the old bench which he found there, decayed and fallen from its support, and furred with fungi and moss, he took up reverentially, and replaced, as if it were something that he valued. And further on he stopped to examine an old beech tree, under which some deer had been reposing; and the grey silvery bark still bore on it the traces of initials which the stranger stooped down to examine, and was obliged to lean against the trunk and unbutton his coat, as

if to recover breath from some internal pressure.
His walk was soon resumed. And yet his object
was not the house; for on reaching the summit of
the hill the road turned down again between two
bold swelling downs tufted with beech and oak, and
matted in parts with brown fern and thickets of
holly and thorn. The deer were lying in groupes on
the sides of the valley: and nearly at the bottom,
on a gentle eminence, rose the grey, gabled, deep-
windowed mansion, with its avenue of cedar and
chestnut stretching out into the lower park, and,
close by it, a small churchyard and church nearly
hidden in overgrown plantations of evergreens.
Even under a grey October sky, with the damp
dews upon the grass, and the sere leaf dropping from
the trees, it was a scene which might well attract a
passer-by to pause. But now all was bright and
summer-like, and the old windows of the mansion
were lighted up with a bright afternoon sun, and
the very air was sweet and gladsome. And the
stranger did pause, but only for a minute; and then,
instead of descending to the house, he diverged
across the turf, following a narrow sheep-path almost
buried in moss, and threading a wild forest brake
which crowned the top of the park.

" Are you going to the ruins, sir?" said a shep-
herd boy who met him. "You won't be able to
find your way by yourself, sir. Can I show you,
sir?"

" No, I thank you," said the stranger; and he
plunged into the wood, and made his way as if he
knew each step, through brake and briar, and
matted wood and coppice, till he reached the green
sward again, and below him, embosomed in that
quiet solitary dell, with the oak and the beech
clustered round it, and the yew trees and junipers
studding every knoll, and the little stream fretting

and chafing under its rocky bank, there stood the ruin.

And as it broke upon him, once more the stranger stopped, and sat, or almost sank down, on the trunk of an old uprooted oak tree, gazing on those grey relics with thoughts far deeper than mere admiration of their beauty.

And yet they were beautiful indeed. Few monastic buildings had escaped the plunder and desecration of Henry the Eighth's times so well as Hawkstone Priory. Much of the outer wall, with its gateway overhung with ivy, was still standing. One gable of the refectory and part of its oriel window hung together, but almost in the air : the prior's garden could yet be traced, though a slim ash had shot up by the tall chimney of the prior's lodgings : and two arches of the cloisters, exquisitely wrought and wreathed with ivy, had been spared in the general devastation, as if to show what the church had raised, and the state had destroyed. But the chapel was the principal feature. The roof, indeed, had fallen in, but one whole row of windows, with tracery almost running wild in its richness, and even fragments of painted glass still discernible in the upper compartments, showed that Hawkstone Priory had been the work of no mean hand. Two clustered pillars still rose up from the green turf, where the antechapel had stood. The great east window, nearly gutted, retained only one slender shaft, supporting a hanging fragment of masonry, which threatened every moment to fall. But through it was seen the bright eastern sky and the bank beyond the river, with its grey rock and gnarled trunks and brake of gorse, melted down into a hazy softness. And the stranger's eye wandered over it, not without thought, and then fixed on a little projecting oratory still perfect in all its parts, and of which the battlements and pinnacles had been even recently repaired, which was attached to the eastern extremity. At last he seemed to summon up resolution, descended into the dell, and as he entered within the walls of the chapel, roofless as it was, he reverently uncovered his head, for he stood on consecrated ground, ground which no act of robbery or tyranny could ever render common.

Without stopping to examine the masses of carving, grotesque and luxuriant, with which the ground was cumbered, he advanced at once to the east end, paused before the place where the altar had stood, and inclined his head, and then approached a strong iron-grated door, fixed in the wall, and fastened with chains and padlocks, long since covered with rust. Twenty years had elapsed since that door had been opened; and when last it had been opened the stranger remembered well how he had stood as a boy beside it, drest out with the trappings of woe, and had watched with a cold awe that nearly dried up tears a long funereal train lower through it into its deep dark resting place the coffin of the being whom he loved best in the world. How many things had passed over his head since that melancholy hour! How many things were yet to come, if it should please God to enable him to accomplish the plans which were forming in his breast! How much must he sacrifice, how much had he given up for ever, if he was to abide by their execution! Should he have strength to do it? And that tall, commanding, noble form turned away from the iron grate, and fell upon his face before the altar, with his lip quivering and the tears streaming down his cheeks, praying God in the hour of temptation to be his guide and defender, and even now in the day of peril to save his holy Church.

F 3

CHAP. VI.

But the stranger is leaving the ruins hastily, and looks back as he ascends the side of the valley to listen to some merry light-hearted music — a fife and flute, and even a drum, which, mingled with approaching voices and the murmur of a cheerful crowd, is approaching through the wood below. They issue from the trees in gay procession; first the band, then a body of respectable looking men in blue coats with white wands, then, four and four in lengthened line, men, and women, and children, all drest in holiday clothes, gay and smiling, and each bearing teacups in their hands, and some of them teakettles. It is the Hawkstone Temperance Society, met to celebrate their third anniversary by a merry and innocent tea-drinking amidst the ruins of the priory. And the rubbish in the chapel is soon cleared sufficiently to arrange the deal tables on their tressels; and no place so convenient as the altar to light three or four fires, each with their simmering kettle. And the cakes are produced from the baskets, and the young persons are all seated in rows with their clean cups before them, so decent and quiet, so very respectable. Who shall complain of the progress of society, or of the state of our manufacturing population? The signal is given; and Mr. Bowler, a neighbouring squire, with his bald shining head and good-natured face, is pressed by Mr. Bentley, and Mr. Bryant, and Mr. Armstrong the Baptist minister, and Mr. Howell the Independent minister, and Mr. Mason the

Quaker, and Mr. Priestley the Unitarian, all of them pressing him (he having consented ten days ago to submit to being pressed) to take the chair. For who more fit to preside over a moral and religious social meeting than Mr. Bowler? a good, kind man, a justice of the peace, and, above all (it made it so respectable, so free from party or sectarian spirit), a layman. And Mr. Bowler therefore is moved into the chair, and Mr. Bentley, and Mr. Bryant, and Mr. Armstrong, and Mr. Howell, and Mr. Mason, and Mr. Priestley, range themselves by his side. There is a grace to be said, and Mr. Bowler looks round deferentially to ask which of *the clergymen* is to say it; and the other clergymen look deferentially to Mr. Bentley, as if anxious to pay him a compliment, and therefore Mr. Bentley says grace. But, as one of the children belonging to the National School remarked to the child sitting next her, it was not the same grace which Mr. Bentley said when the National School children had roast beef and plum pudding at the coronation, for then he had ended it in the same form in which the prayers in the Prayer Book ended; now he left this out. They did not know that Mr. Priestley, the Unitarian minister, was now sitting opposite him, and that Mr. Bentley had too much delicacy to hurt his feelings by introducing any allusion to peculiar doctrines. The tea was drank, the cake eaten, with hearty relish, but temperately, as became the occasion; and as they emptied cup after cup, there was a conscious gravity about the process, and little side glancings of eyes to see if others were looking; and the generality seemed to sit uneasy on the benches, as if they did not exactly know what to do with their hands. And the conversation was rather forced, with long pauses between, except when some bolder spirit, anxious to enliven the meeting cried aloud for more tea, and ostentatiously swallowed it, with many self-congratulations that it could not get into his head. But then the Temperance Society was a voluntary meeting assembled to do that of themselves which neither God commanded nor man enforced; and, somehow or another, voluntary acts of this kind cannot be done without persons thinking of themselves, and therefore at times feeling awkward. But the awkwardness all vanished when a loud rapping on the table was heard at the upper end, and Mr. Bowler's bald head and sleek good-humoured face, with all eyes upturned to it, was seen rising to address the meeting. Unhappily the exact address itself has been lost to posterity by the loss of the reporter's notes, but as Mr. Bowler will make nearly the same speech at the next anniversary, and indeed at every other religious meeting in which he will be asked to take the chair, those who are curious to hear it may still hope for a chance of success. It began, we know, with "ladies and gentlemen," at which the little boys and girls, and the young men from the factory made loud demonstrations of applause. It then proceeded to enlarge on the incapacity of Mr. Bowler himself for the high and distinguished office which he had been invited to fill, with many humble protestations of his want of talents, and learning, and eloquence, in which the meeting seemed contentedly to acquiesce, and did not make against them such decided remonstrances and denials as Mr. Bowler had expected: Mr. Bentley, indeed, said "no, no," but it was uttered with a faint voice, and did not reach farther than Mr. Bowler himself, who bowed gratefully and modestly, but still as conscious that Mr. Bentley was right and he himself was wrong.

A sentence followed in a different strain, begin-

ning with a "But;" and when Mr. Bowler had
enlarged in the most glowing and pathetic terms on
his devotion to the welfare of his fellow-creatures,
and especially of the Temperance Society, "an institution which formed an æra in the world, and on
which the safety of the world depended," all his
hearers felt their own importance rise into enthusiasm, and the tables echoed with hammerings, and
the ivy wreaths hanging round the mullions of the
windows actually waved with the commotion.
Another congratulatory remark on the harmony of
these social meetings — on the delight of seeing
around him so many *clergymen* of different per-
suasions, all agreeing to sink sectarian distinctions
and to unite in the common good of the people committed to their care,—was loudly cheered by the
dissenters. And Mr. Bryant, and Mr. Mason, and
Mr. Priestley, took the opportunity of stretching
their hands across to Mr. Bentley in the sight of the
meeting; at which proof of fraternal charity the
uproar became general. And Bentley gave his
hand in return, though he felt somewhat embarrassed at this cordial assumption of equality; and as
he looked up, his eye caught on one of the delicately
carved corbels — a bishop's face, quiet, but firm
and severe, which seemed to frown on him reproachfully. But the fancy was soon dispelled, for
the pith of Mr. Bowler's speech was coming; and,
as with honest cheerful face he told two ludicrous
stories, illustrating the advantages of temperance,
every body laughed with him; and every body
in good humour followed him as he subsided into
his chair with loud applause, and "one cheer
more."

And now the chairman, having wiped his face and
recovered his breath, looked at a slip of paper in his
hand, and then mysteriously glanced at Mr. Priestley,

who had been biting his lips and affecting to look
unconcerned ever since Mr. Bowler had been on
his legs. And Mr. Priestley rose, with some emotion, and with sundry wavings of his hands, to propose the health of a gentleman whose name he was
sure would be received with cordiality, even by
those who did not agree with him in religious
opinions. Bentley felt an unpleasant sensation in
the palms of his hands and feet, and began playing
with the tea-spoon in the saucer.

"He," Mr. Priestley, "had always found Mr.
Bentley, his respected friend," (several of the poorer
classes, whom Bentley had often assisted, here
joined with the chairman in endeavouring to raise a
loud applause, but it did not succeed,) "he had
always found his respected friend, and he might
say, he hoped without offence, his brother minister,
most anxious to cooperate with him in all matters
affecting the common welfare of their flocks. He,
Mr. Priestley, had his own opinion, and probably
many who heard him had theirs, of the expediency
of a state religion. But, as the laws of the land
had decreed that one religious denomination should
have the ascendancy over the rest, he trusted all
would obey those laws so long as they continued to
exist." Bentley felt uncomfortable.

"If, indeed," continued the speaker, "all churchmen were like Mr. Bentley, Christians would, indeed, be at peace. Nothing could exceed the
liberality, the Christian liberality, of his sentiments;
worthy a religion of which the first principle was
peace on earth and goodwill to men;" and he concluded with proposing Mr. Bentley's health.

"How kind!" said an old woman to her next
neighbour.—"Just as it should be," exclaimed a
stout, honest-looking tradesman; "I like to see
good feeling among the gown! Live and let live,

is my motto; and persecute no man for his opinions!" Bentley rose to return thanks; the kind-hearted, zealous, pious Bentley, who wanted nothing but instruction to understand and avoid the false position in which he felt himself placed, and who really was struggling (day and night) beyond his strength to spread what he deemed true religion among the thousands of Hawkstone, just as the Irish constable threatened with his solitary arm to surround the mob. That he said but little, and that little with an embarrassed air, and in a voice too low to be heard, might naturally be expected. And he sat down vexed with himself, and to the evident disappointment of some few and the triumph of many, with only a few encouraging "hear, hear," to cover his retreat.

"Quite a break down," whispered Mr. Mason, the Quaker, to Mr. Bryant, who was the great orator of the place, and had been assiduously writing notes on a scrap of paper for some time past; "quite a break down."

And certainly, through some cause or another, the Church does break down generally, when it attempts these rhetorical harangues. Popular eloquence is not its forte, and never has been, for what reasons we leave our readers to inquire; but Charles Bevan, if he had been asked, would have said, that man, in delivering a message from his Maker, has only to deliver it, and not to trouble himself with the results; to deliver it plainly, intelligibly, effectively, so that no excuse may remain for inattention, and that all the rest is in the hand of Heaven; and, therefore, popular preaching, and popular speaking, and appeals to the passions, and all the trickery of platform discussion and proprietary chapels, are out of place in members of a Church, and only do harm. Certainly, Bentley felt as if he wished such were the case, and he might not be called on again to make speeches at the Temperance Society.

Not so Mr. Bryant. Another mysterious look was exchanged from the chairman, and the great orator of Hawkstone arose, and with a deep and portentous voice he poured forth, as the newspapers described it, "a flood of eloquence, which held his audience in rapt attention," and "electrified them with lightning bursts of feeling" for more than half an hour. In fact, the chief amusement of the meeting had depended on Mr. Bryant, and of this he was well aware, for the day had been fixed purposely for his convenience in attending. His exordium was like Mr. Bowler's, but more pathetically bespeaking indulgence for his defects and diffidence. From this he proceeded to describe (and his eyes opened and flashed as he advanced, and his arms began to move) "the grand and solemn scene which he then saw before him; so many intellectual beings congregated together under the wide vault of heaven (applause), without distinction of sect or party (applause again), to emancipate themselves and the whole earth from the great crime of drunkenness (reiterated cheers)." Mr. Bryant, in looking over his speech in the morning, had doubted about "the whole earth," but it told wonderfully well; and the inhabitants of Hawkstone felt each like an Atlas with a whole universe resting on his shoulders. He proceeded, says the newspaper from whom we borrow, to depicture in the most gratifying terms "the moral and intellectual condition of his hearers, free, enlightened, religious, liberal, without bigotry, without vice. It was a sight to rejoice the heart of Englishmen" (cheers again, though some of the older members refrained, as not liking to applaud themselves). From this he digressed to give a graphic sketch of the drunkard "rolling in the

gutter, which made the blood of his audience thrill
with horror," and he pointed out the absolute importance of binding even children from their youth
by a solemn vow to abstain from all spirituous
liquors. "Impossible," he said, "to begin too
early;" and Mr. Armstrong, the Baptist minister,
nodded a most hearty assent. He then enlarged
on the value and necessity of associating ourselves
in every good cause; enumerated the hundred affiliated societies which had sprung from the central
one in London; trusted that they should always act
unanimously, and keep up a close and affectionate
correspondence with the body from which they had
derived the first blessing of a temperance committee. Without union, the very object of the
society must be lost. Without the society, there
could be no temperance. He would intreat them
to stick heartily together, and mark any one who
ungratefully or insidiously should sow the seeds of
— (Mr. Bryant here paused for a moment, for the
word "dissension" had risen to his lips; but, for
some reason or another, he did not like it, and
luckily had time to change it)—" should sow the
seeds of disunion among them."—Loud cries of
" We will, we will!" And here the newspaper reporter observes that some allusion was intended
to a feeling of discontent which had spread among
many of the members in regard to the conduct of
the committee, and which Mr. Bryant was most
anxious to prevent from breaking out into open
schism. And he therefore proceeded to point out
the solemn duty of not quarrelling with persons in
authority, especially for minor points, lest the very
object of the whole society should be defeated by
such jealousies and animosities.

Having dwelt for some time on this delicate
topic, he passed, to use the language of the news-

paper, " with singular felicity" to the " picturesque
and romantic ruins within which they were that
day assembled." " He trusted, indeed he felt assured," (and here he gazed round with a scrutinising
eye,) " it was impossible, indeed, that any papist
should have intruded into their truly protestant
assembly."— "No, no," cried the party.—"He gladly
accepted their answer. And yet if the Pope himself had been present, drinking tea with them, he,
Mr. Bryant, would have boldly stood his ground,
and dared him to defend his bloody and atrocious
system." As this was uttered with the greatest
vehemence, and Mr. Bryant's clenched fist descended
on the table at its close with more than an ordinary
thump, it was followed by a round of applause.
And certainly he was right in supposing that few
true Roman Catholics would have made their appearance in such a heterogeneous congregation.
And then the speaker burst forth into the most imposing portion of his harangue. " He compared
the deeds of darkness which had formerly been perpetrated within these walls," (how and when, he
would have been puzzled to say, for the simple
reason that he had never heard,) " and the innocent,
the sublime recreation of drinking tea under their
ruins, with tea-tables spread in the chapel, and
kettles boiling where the altar had stood. He spoke
of the enormities of monasteries, of vows by which
men bound themselves without any authority from
the Bible ; of absurd abstinences and fastings from
good things which God had created to be enjoyed
in moderation; of silly idle mummeries, and men
and women dressed up to distinguish themselves
from their fellow-creatures."— (And here, in the
ardour of his gesticulation, he nearly knocked off
from the breast of his next neighbour an immense
blue rosette, with which all the members had de-

corated themselves, and especially the gentlemen
stewards, the bearers of white wands.) He showed,
and with the greatest truth, how a number of men
or women congregated together without the superintendence of their spiritual superiors, and, following only their own will and fancy, must fall into
mischief, as monks and nuns had done: and from
thence he traced the corruptions introduced by them
into the pure Gospel of Christ, with which every
one had mixed their own notions and mere human
speculations, instead of adhering simply to the truth
as it was taught by God. Nothing could be more
successful than his demonstration, and admirably
was it received; for Mr. Bryant was a clever man,
and not an ineloquent man, and a religious man,
and had studied parts of the Romish system with
no little insight into its faults, whatever he might
have learnt of its virtues. One point, indeed, he
omitted: he had intended to speak of the absurd
religious processions and pilgrimages in which Roman Catholics indulge, with music, and singing, and
other vain solemnities ; but the chairman, as it was
getting late, was obliged to remind him that they
had not yet sung the hymn, and that the band was
becoming impatient.

The hymn therefore was sung, all standing ; and,
as it was one of Watts's, which Mr. Priestley had
previously eviscerated of all peculiar doctrines, it
gratified all parties, and offended none. And the
members were just about to rise from the tables,
when a fresh arrival was announced which caused
considerable sensation. Several of the stewards
jumped up to receive the stranger ; several others
looked round for a seat. The bottom of the table
fell wholly into commotion, what with curiosity,
and what with a wish to do honour to the new
comer. Mr. Bryant himself and Mr. Priestley ad-

vanced hastily to the outer gate of the priory, and
proceeded to introduce into the chapel, and to present first to Mr. Bowler the chairman, and then to
the gentlemen of the committee, — whom, gentle
reader, whom do you suppose? Was it the tall
dark stranger, who had left the chapel just before
the society came into it? No! it was a young, thin,
pert-looking, beardless man; not ungentlemanly in
his dress or manner, had it not been for a contemptuous turn about the nose and lips, and a cold
sneering expression of the eye. But the contempt
and the sneer were now meant to be subdued into
the most urbane and courteous demeanour; and the
cordiality with which he shook hands with Mr.
Bryant, and the ease of his deportment to the chairman, and the perfect confidence and self-command
with which he surveyed the long tea-tables, and
then turned up his glass to look at the mullions of
the windows, completely won the hearts of the tea
party.

"A very fine young man!" whispered Mrs.
Hutchings, the butcher's wife, to Miss Spence, who
sat by her side; "a very fine young man, indeed!
and, they say, so clever. I even heard he has
written a book."

"Indeed!" said Miss Spence. "I hope he will
make a speech."

And, to the great delight of Miss Spence, she observed a little bustle and whispering at the top of
the table, and a short confabulation between Mr.
Priestley and the chairman, which was followed by
Mr. Priestley rising from his seat, amid a clatter of
spoons, to call attention, and craving the chairman's
permission to propose a toast. He prefaced it by
some pertinent observations about "unexpected
honour," "duty of hospitality," "distinguished talents," "illustrious representative," and closed with

announcing the health of Mr. Marmaduke Brook. The cheering was not very enthusiastic, for few persons knew any thing of Mr. Brook, except that he had offered himself as a candidate for the borough of Hawkstone at the next election, and on the Radical interest. But Mr. Marmaduke received it, such as it was, with considerable nonchalance, and stood with his glass to his eye, and beating his boot with his whip, until it had subsided. He then advanced at once to the table, and, bowing round to the chairman, commenced his speech.

He thanked them cordially "from the bottom of his heart." (Where Mr. Brook's heart was, it would have puzzled a moral anatomist to discover; but, then, persons who are poor must always talk most of their riches.) "They had conferred on him an honour, such as he had never received before—such as he should carry engraved on his heart" (heart again!) "to the last day of his life. Stranger as he was, coming among them thus unexpectedly, by the merest accident, as he was taking his ride"—(Mr. Bryant bit his lips to prevent a smile, for the whole plan had been concerted that morning at Mrs. Maddox's cabinet council, and all had agreed that no better opportunity could occur of presenting the Radical member to his hoped-for constituents than the Temperance tea-drinking among the ruins of the Priory)—"how gratifying, how inspiriting, it must be to him to be welcomed by such a distinguished, and enlightened, and splendid assemblage with such hospitality, such urbanity, such"——(Here, unhappily, Mr. Brook had forgotten the last word of his triplet, and was compelled to cover the blank with a cough, which the hearers, who seldom heard such triplets, drowned in loud applause.) "He saw among them, and he rejoiced to see, some of those learned, and pious, and liberal-minded men,

G

whom, since his coming into Hawkstone, it had
been his good fortune to meet, and to obtain from
them their promise of support in his approaching
canvass." (Cheers from the little group of dissenting
ministers, Mr. Bentley remaining silent; and one
or two faint cries of " Brook for ever!" from the
bottom of the table, but as they were not taken up,
the perpetrators of them slunk back in their seats
as if abashed.) " Such men were an honour to their
country, and he did from his heart" (heart again!)
" rejoice to see them sitting here side by side, sinking all speculative differences, abjuring all empty
dogmas, confining themselves to the great truths of
benevolence and charity (hear! hear!), and pledging
themselves and those around them to the grand, the
magnificent maxim, that religion was a thing between man and his God; and that every man had a
right to worship his Maker according to the dictates
of his conscience. Am I right," continued the
speaker, elevating his voice, " am I right, my enlightened countrymen, in declaring that you, like
myself, are pledged to this heaven-descended truth?"
(Two-syllabled epithets have always great effect on
a popular ear, and accordingly the remainder of the
sentence was lost in an uproar of applause, and
cries of " Yes! yes!" in which nothing more could
be heard from Mr. Brook, but something about
" nailing colours to a mast.") " The days of bigotry,"
he proceeded, amidst cries of " hush! hush!" from
the most influential of his supporters, " the days of
bigotry are gone. No more should a tyrannical
despot trample on the birthright of man. The very
spot in which we are assembled, this roofless pile,
these yawning ruins, these——" (here again a cough
in the defect of a third synonyme) "speak to us with
a voice which should penetrate into every heart,
that superstition and persecution are at an end.

(Cheers.) The moment the light of reason had arisen, like a sun above the horizon, carrying in its orb brightness, and brilliancy, and splendour, and illumination, and lustre, and light," (at this climax the uproar became immense,) " it had burst with a lightning torrent on these dens of superstition, had torn open their inmost cells," (intense, thrilling interest, and deep silence,) " had shattered these fabrics of superstition, had overturned these abodes of bigotry, had crushed those bloody altars, had"——
Here the speaker became choked either with emotion or with having nothing more to say, and the audience, though rather disappointed of the end of the sentence, announced their sympathy by loud rappings. And as no one knew that these were only figurative expressions, by which Mr. Marmaduke Brook intended to say that Henry VIII. had driven out a number of poor old religious men to starve in the roads, had pulled down their houses, turned their chapel into a cow-house, and put their money into his own pocket, the sensation caused by such a gorgeous description was perfectly unparalleled. Happy it was that no old monk made his appearance at that moment, for in their horror of persecution for religious opinions they would infallibly have torn him to pieces.

Mr. Marmaduke having now recovered his speech, proceeded to inform his hearers that on such an occasion he should not think it proper to touch upon politics ; and accordingly he proceeded to give them an outline of his political opinions. He professed himself a thorough reformer — a reformer of all abuses, but without violence, without revolution. " He trusted to the good sense, to the prudence of Englishmen, to work an entire change in the present corrupt system of government, without moving an arm—by changing the laws," he said, "not by dis-

obeying them. So long as the laws exist they ought
to be obeyed; but every nerve should be strained
to procure a change, as soon as possible, by consti-
tutional means — by moral force — by passive resistance ; — petitions, meetings, agitation — all were
laudable — all were necessary — to regenerate the
mass of society : only abstain from violence. He
pointed out the enormous revenue now enjoyed by an
hereditary monarch and an hereditary peerage, and
contrasted them with the starving condition of the
manufacturing population — the very population on
which " (and here the factory men were loud in
approbation) "the whole wealth and welfare of the
community depended. They were the sinews of the
country ; they were its only hope — enlightened,
cultivated, intelligent ! How comes it," said the
energetic speaker, " that this important class is degraded into the melancholy condition of pauperism
and demoralisation in which we now behold it ?"
(Here Mr. Bryant, who three days before had administered to the Mechanics' Institution an abridg-
ment of Watts' Logic in the form of a lecture, could
not help coughing. Something irritated his throat;
and the cough had the effect of diverting attention
from the little paralogism with which the speaker,
without perceiving it till too late, had brought himself
too closely into contact.) " He would say a few words
upon the corn laws. (Cheers.) It was the corn
laws, it was dear bread, which had worked this frightful effect." (Here some one jogged his arm, and on
casting his eye on a bit of paper slipped before him,
he read " Bowler — a landlord," and upon this with
great adroitness he changed his tone.) " He was
not for destroying the agriculturist. No ! he was
for giving him his due ; securing him a fair remuneration. But until something was done to enable
the manufacturer, now ruined by competition with

foreigners, to carry on that competition more fully,
—to give higher wages to his workmen"—— Here
a coarse vulgar voice from the bottom cried out,
" They'll never give us higher wages than they can
help ! " and Mr. Marmaduke, turning to the quarter
from which the voice issued, asked urbanely, " What
did his excellent friend suggest ? He entirely
agreed with him. He went with him fully in his
observation ; but he might be permitted to say (*i. e.*
as Mr. Smith, the proprietor of the factories, was
not present),—he might be permitted to say, that
the workmen had in their own hands the power of
increasing their wages : they might use all lawful
combination—lawful combination, he repeated, to
obtain their demand. They might assemble and
go before their masters, and exhibit a moral force,
which would extort the admiration of the world
(loud applause), and at the same time raise their
wages." " Allow me to detain you for one minute
with a few facts " (and the speaker searched in a
copious pocket-book for some papers and memoranda), " only a few statistical facts, showing how
you, gentlemen, would be benefited, and the agriculturists as much, by destroying the present taxes on
your bread. Facts are the only argument."

And then, with a great display of cool calculation
and accuracy, he proceeded to read them from a
paper a long list of figures and prices :—Wheat per
bushel, so much ; duty, so much ; wages, so much ;
cotton, so much ; brandy, so much ; which astounded
the hearers by the business-like learning it displayed, and enveloped the whole subject in a mist
of multiplication and subtraction.—"A sound man!"
whispered Mr. Bryant. — " No theorist," said Mr.
Priestley. — " A good practical man of business —
understands figures," subjoined one of Mr. Lomax's
clerks ; and the effect was very favourable.

"But I have detained you, gentlemen, too long"——("No! no!" from the whole body.) "I should have said 'ladies and gentlemen,'" continued the speaker, as if recollecting himself, and dexterously resolving to relieve the dry statistics by an allusion to the bright eyes and matchless beauty with which he was surrounded. "How could I forget," he continued, with a self-reproachful tone, "those brilliant forms, the fairest portion of creation, who are foremost in all good causes, and whom I rejoice to see, on this most interesting occasion, enjoying this innocent delicious beverage," and he took up a tea cup.—"What's beverage?" asked deaf Mrs. Lloyd of her clever son from the National School. "Something to drink, to be sure!" said the pert boy, who had been spelling the word that morning, and he looked sneeringly at his mother.—"What a fine thing it is to go to school!" thought Mrs. Lloyd, and she eyed her boy with admiration; till her attention was called back to Mr. Marmaduke Brook, and, with her hand turned up to her ear, she succeeded in catching the most prominent portions of his succeeding sentence,—"eyes raining bright influence"—"heaven-beaming innocence"—"fairy forms"—"flowers of creation," and sundry other appropriate phrases which Mr. Brook had by him at all times, kneaded up in a ready-made sentence, and used on all occasions, when it fell to his lot to propose the health of the ladies. Magical was the effect produced by it on the ladies of the Temperance Society, who had never heard it before. They blushed, they simpered, they looked down, and the sensation took a palpable form on the same evening, by a resolution of the chief personages to raise a subscription of sixpence a-head, and purchase a large silk banner of the palest blue, with "Reform and Liberty" worked on it by their own fair hands, to be presented to Mr. Brook himself at the ensuing election.

"And now," proceeded Mr. Brook, "I will add but one word more: but it is on a subject of the most overwhelming importance. I am, gentlemen, a decided advocate for the Ballot. (Uproarious applause.) I am an advocate, gentlemen, for ensuring to every Englishman the right of voting according to his conscience. (Hear! hear!) But how you can vote according to your conscience, if your vote is to be known, I cannot discover! What can be more atrocious, more tyrannical, than for a landlord to say to his tenant, or a master to his workman, 'You know little of politics, vote as I wish—abandon your liberty of thinking'? What can be more derogatory to the dignity of a free and reasoning being, amidst the light of the nineteenth century, than to be told that he is incapable of judging on the affairs of government,—that he cannot be trusted with the management of his country—that some tyrant of a landlord"——Here again a friendly jog reminded Mr. Brook of the agriculturist chairman: but as Mr. Brook turned round ready to pay a flaming compliment to Mr. Bowler, as the only intelligent benevolent landlord whom he had ever met with, that gentleman, he saw, was fast asleep; and, indeed, his being awake would have mattered little, since he had long since abandoned all trouble about politics, and made a point of giving his vote to the first man who asked him.

The sight, however, of Mr. Brook's slumber reminded the speaker that his speech should draw to a close; and so to a close he drew it, with the usual protestations of ineffaceable gratitude for the honour they had done him,—with the most profound deference on all points whatever to their wishes and opinions, as the guide of his life,—and, if he might be allowed to propose a toast, with "the health of those pious and excellent gentlemen to whom their spiritual welfare was committed, for whom he entertained the highest respect, and trusted they would always exert their influence in spreading knowledge, and order, and peace, and charity throughout the whole of this favoured land."

And here, amidst enthusiastic cheers, Mr. Marmaduke bowed to the assembly, and shook hands with the chairman, who had woke up just in time, and was rubbing his eyes, and with Mr. Bryant, and Mr. Priestley, and the Baptist minister, and the Independent minister, and, escorted by them, amidst the wavings of handkerchiefs and hats, and cries of " Brook for ever!" he left the ruins.

Two horses were at the gate : himself and young Mr. Thomas Maddox, who had not appeared before, lest suspicions of a designed visit should be roused, mounted together.   Hands were again shaken, and hats taken off; and as soon as they had turned the corner, Mr. Marmaduke Brook burst into a loud laugh, in which Mr. Thomas Maddox most humbly and deferentially joined; not a little proud to think that he had been seen on horseback in company with a would-be member of parliament.

CHAP. VII.

IN the mean time Bentley had slipped away, soon after Mr. Marmaduke Brook's appearance, and was walking home alone through the park, uncomfortable and dissatisfied with himself. He had heard things which he did not like, though why, he could scarcely explain, and had done things which he felt to be wrong, though no one was likely to reproach him with them. And yet what could be better than his motives? There was a population under his care ignorant and turbulent, and amongst whom habits of intoxication, encouraged by the prevalence of distress and by the gambling spirit of manufacturing employment, were rapidly spreading. One after another pothouse after pothouse in the streets of Hawkstone had been converted into splendid buildings with pillars, and carvings, and illuminated interiors, and pawnbrokers' shops opposite, to supply means for the pale, haggard beings who all day long dropped in to spend their last pence in purchasing a temporary forgetfulness from hunger and misery. And without some efforts made to check this fountain of evil there was no hope for Hawkstone. Why not take advantage of an engine which had done so much good in America, and was converting even Ireland, by hundreds at a time, to sobriety and decency? What was the harm of men binding themselves by an open resolution to do that which was evidently right, and binding themselves all together without regard to religious distinctions in a matter where religious opinions clearly could not alter the

duty? Bentley was perplexed for the solution,
and yet could not make up his mind that Temperance Societies were the good thing which he
had once fondly believed. It did not occur to him,
and no wonder, since no one had taught him, that
by God himself, long prior to the nineteenth century
there had been founded a Temperance Society,
with its initiatory vow, its appointed officers, its
festive meetings, its solemn sanctions; moreover
with an especial promise of aid and blessing from
Heaven; and that Bentley himself had been created
an officer to govern this old society, and not to
supersede and destroy it by any new association of
his own, or of human invention: it never occurred
to Bentley that such a society was the Church.
Of the Church as an associated organised body
politic he had entirely lost sight; just as if a subject living in the British empire, perhaps a magistrate charged with the administration of its laws,
were to forget some day by any strange halluci-
nation that he had already a Sovereign, and a Parliament, and statute laws, and tribunals of justice
binding him to execute his office, and were then to
frame or fall under some new invented constitution
and governor set up by a popular enthusiast, — continuing all the time to sit on the bench and administer justice in the name of the old establishment.
Strange contradictions and painful perplexities
would assuredly arise in such a conflict of relations:
but not more strange or more painful than those to
which Bentley had been exposed, when as a minister
of the Church he had attempted to fulfil an end of
the Church by means not appointed by the Church,
and in conjunction with men who were in open rebellion against it.

And why was Bentley not alive to such simple
truths? Because, as we said before, no one had

taught him. He had been brought up as a boy under parents of lax principles, who never spoke to him of religion: from them he had been transplanted to a school, where, with the exception of a dull sermon on the Sunday,—a sermon on morality only,—and a chapter in the Greek Testament on Monday, in which nothing was thought of but the syntax, religion again was as if it did not exist; and all vice was allowed to flourish, without effort to correct it, if it only had cunning to escape the eye of a master who did not wish to see. From school he went to Cambridge. And here the first germs of his religious feelings began to develop themselves. He was thrown (by accident) among a set of clever, cool-headed, profligate young men, who formed themselves into a sort of club, of which the motto, if the spirit had been expressed, would have been a dilemma between Atheism and Pantheism. He was caught by their sparkling vivacity, overawed by their sarcastic pretensions, involved with them in a rivalry of mere intellectual power, in which he was encouraged by the hope of obtaining a fellowship, for which nothing but intellectual power was required. And the very studies of the place, engaging him almost solely in mathematical speculations, fostered in him a dry, critical, cold-hearted, sceptical tone of mind, which was prevented from hardening into avowed infidelity solely by the natural warmth of an affectionate disposition, and the blessing of Providence. The very circumstances of a place of education, in which, as at that time was the case unhappily in both universities, the externals of religion had degenerated into empty forms, and yet were still strictly maintained as instruments of College discipline, necessarily engendered doubt as to the sincerity of its professors, and the reality of its system. He saw the chapel service enforced strictly on the

pupils, and neglected by the tutors — attendance on
it selected as a fit punishment for trivial offences,
and a refusal to receive the Holy Communion visited
as a sufficient penalty by the most trifling fine.   He
found himself within the walls of the chapel kneeling
side by side with an avowed Socinian, a professed
Jew, and an hereditary Roman Catholic.   And
yet the authorities of the College, without hoping
or attempting a conversion, were satisfied with
exacting from them all an external act of worship,
which to any sincere believer, either in Socinianism,
or Judaism, or Popery, must have been revolting
and impious.   He attended lectures on divinity,
but instead of the positive truth of the Gospel, they
turned on grammatical disquisitions, or evidences of
Christianity — evidences, which, if belief had been
strong in the Church, would scarcely have been
deemed necessary to be taught.   Of ecclesiastical
history, of religion either as embodied in a social
system, or as a vital habit of the heart, he heard
nothing.   Church livings and Church patronage
were the only forms under which the Church appeared: and its political connexion with a mere Tory
party, who upheld it as an instrument of government, rendered it peculiarly obnoxious to the contempt of a liberal Whig; and by liberal Whigs he
was surrounded.   At this stage in the formation of
his character, when he had already done much of
which, at a later date, he bitterly repented, and was
on the eve of doing worse, it pleased Providence to
throw in his way one of those many biographies,
with which a peculiar school of Divinity has endeavoured to supply the place of the Acta Sanctorum,
or Lives of the Saints, of Romanism.   It was taken
up first in mere idleness: but it happened, or
rather it was ordained, that it should rouse a train
of serious reflection; and Bentley became an altered

man. A new world seemed opened to him, — a
world of feeling and passion, to which the dry, cold
associations of his past life gave new zest. The
book which first touched his heart was read again
and again with avidity. Others were procured of
the same stamp. Hymns, sermons, devotional exercises, preachers, doctrines, all formed on the same
model, were at Cambridge within reach, until he
had worked himself into a fever of religious excitement, in which remorse and triumph, despair and
confidence, love and fear, alternated in strange confusion, and his imagination was filled with a wild
phantasmagoria, obscuring all the plain duties and
sober realities of life. By degrees this passed away.
But still excitement of feeling was the predominant
element in his religion. He entered into holy orders
with a fervent zeal to redeem, if possible, his past
life by an entire devotion to his duty. But of this
duty itself he had never formed a clear and definite
notion. And notwithstanding his horror of Popery
as a religion of forms superseding the vital doctrines
of the Gospel by the craft of a priesthood, he fell at
the very first outset of his ministry into precisely
the same error which led to the corruptions of
Popery — that of making the object of his ministry
to be the salvation of men, instead of the plain,
straightforward, uncompromising enunciation of the
message committed to his charge. His first thought
was man, as if the glory of God depended on man's
obedience. And thus he laboured for his flock with
an energy exhausting his own strength and often
defeating its purpose. Night and day, morning and
evening, Bentley's thoughts and actions were engaged in devising and executing plans for winning
souls to God. Sermons, — lectures, — visits, — ex-
hortations, — some new association, — a prayer meeting, — attractive music in the church, allurements

for charity,—besides innumerable parochial designs for ameliorating the condition of the poor, in penny clubs, and blanket clubs, and benefit clubs—and then the schools, week-days and Sundays,—the gaol,—the workhouse,—all these suggested themselves and pressed on him with an anxiety which allowed him no moment of respite for quiet contemplation or scarcely for prayer. Measuring the rectitude of his exertions by their success, and seeing them constantly fail, he was constantly miserable. Every new scheme was seized as gladly as if no schemes had been already provided by the Church whose minister he was. A character of bustle, and vacillation, and excitement, pervaded all his undertakings. His best efforts to do good were generally out of place. He was constantly exhorting—constantly debating; bringing religion before men at all times, seasonable or unseasonable, with no rule to guide him but his own conscience; and his conscience could never be at rest.

His very phraseology acquired an affected, technical character which destroyed its force. It was violent without warmth, and strained without power. And singular to say, as he began, so he proceeded; and with all his dread of Popery, which he never ceased to denounce in the strongest and often in improper language, he gradually adopted all the worst principles of Popery, and brought them into action. Like Popery, he endeavoured to bring men to religion by appeals to the fancy, the feelings, the reason, instead of plainly and simply setting before them the truths of God, and leaving them in the hands of God to work their fruit. Like Popery, he learned to look with contempt on the Catholic constitution of the Church, and, if not to despise bishops, at least to depreciate their authority. Like Popery, he formed his own standard of opinion, and fixed his own centre of obedience, instead of submitting to the standard and the centre fixed by God in the Catholic Church. Like Popery, he had his saints and his fathers, recent indeed, and selected by himself, and canonised by himself on account of their agreement with his own opinions, to whom he deferred implicitly as individual men, while he stigmatised as criminal any reverence for the Fathers of Primitive Christianity. Like Popery, he shut up the Bible from the comprehension of the people. The book, indeed, he distributed abundantly, but as he threw each reader on his own powers of interpretation, and cut off from them the sound comments and typical illustrations of Christian antiquity, he might as well have given it to them in the Arabic text; for what uneducated man could find out the one true doctrine in the variety of possible interpretations, and who could take an interest in a work, which he could not understand without assistance, and in which assistance was denied him? Like Popery, he encouraged the growth of a multitude of voluntary self-organised bodies, emancipated from episcopal control, and which were intended to perform the various functions of the Church, but by a different machinery; just as if a man to whom nature had given legs should insist upon walking upon stilts. Monastic, indeed, they were not: Bentley would have shuddered at the word. But perhaps they had all the evils of monasticism without any of the good, as we may see hereafter. Like Popery again, Bentley preached loudly the doctrine of justification by faith, and practically inculcated justification by works; for he threw men on their own internal emotions, tested their goodness by their feelings, which after all are only works of another kind from alms, fastings, and mortification of the body, but without the advantage of pro-

ducing like them external good. They produced
no good at all. Like Popery, Bentley indulged in
forms, and laid on them the greatest stress—forms
of speech, forms of intonation of voice, forms of
society, abstinence from certain amusements, associations with certain persons, the reading of certain books. Unhappily they were forms of his own
creation, or adopted from his party; not the forms
of the Catholic Church. Like Popery, at the Council of Trent, Bentley tampered with the Catholic
apostolical creed—added to it—omitted from it—
fixed his own limits as to what was essential and what
non-essential—and denounced an anathema on all
who did not subscribe to his peculiar views. Like
Popery, Bentley tampered with the sacraments. If
monasticism introduced a second baptism, a second
vow of obedience, a second commencement of a new
life, which invalidated the former, Bentley had his
notions of conversion, which went precisely to the
same point. If Popery, in order to satisfy a curious
reason, explained the mystery of the Holy Communion by the irreverent theory of transubstantia-
tion, Bentley had his theory likewise, constructed
for the same purpose, but equally destroying the
nature of a sacrament, by denying the inward grace
of it, as Popery denied the outward sign. Bentley
had also his confessional: not a private confidential
chair, in which he might guide the consciences of
his flock, but open confessionals, where he encouraged every one in the presence of every one
to recount their spiritual experiences and throw
open to the common gaze that sanctuary of the
heart which God has so carefully hidden beneath
the veil of diffidence and shame. And this confessional he endeavoured to extend, by putting up
a box in his church to receive communications from
his flock, without the pain or difficulty of personal

intercourse. Unhappily, this plan he was obliged to abandon, for just as monks and friars are charged with leading away silly women, so Bentley found his box filled with communications from ladies, who, as any one might naturally expect who knew his real goodness of heart, his talents, and his piety, looked on him with something more than the reverence due to their pastor.

In short, not to multiply instances, or to enter into the abstruser points of resemblance, Bentley had by degrees become a Papist in every thing but in name, and, what was more important, without the power which enabled Popery to wield so long the spiritual destinies of the world. He had no association to fall back upon; no organized system; no arm of terror; no mysterious foreign authority to speak to his flock from behind a veil; no antiquity; no pretension to learning; no deep knowledge of human nature; no secular force; no wealth: and the consequence which was necessary followed, — his flock melted away under his eye. A few he retained almost against their will, for they did not coincide with his notions. Others attached themselves to him enthusiastically for a time, and then dropped off, as soon as Mr. Bryant had appeared in a new chapel, and with new eloquence. The poor he could not hold; for all that he told them they required, they found in a more palatable and intelligible shape in the dissenting chapel. And for the better classes he had nothing to animate activity, to regulate feeling, to enforce self-denial, to satisfy a doubting reason, to answer that craving which, in an age of scepticism and dissension, yearns for some permanent authority, some bond of union, to quiet the distraction of the mind. He never placed before them *law—stern, inflexible, external law—a law over reason as well as over will—a law of God,*

H

definite and immutable, intrusted to the custody of an incorporated society, and through the hands of that society to be held up before the eyes and grafted on the heart of man. And without such a law, what becomes of man's intellect, or his passions, or his activity, or his happiness? He spoke to them of reason, of conscience, of feeling, of utility; but when his hearers asked themselves whose reason, whose conscience, whose feeling, whose sense of utility, was to be their guide, each man found it was his own: and those who were satisfied with their own gladly followed his premises to their legitimate conclusion of self-indulgence in all things; and those who were not, looked about them weariedly and anxiously for some ark of rest, —and an ark of rest, of false and treacherous rest, they were about to have.

As Bentley seated himself on the point where the stranger had turned aside in the morning to replace the broken bench, and gazed down sadly and bodingly on the town in the valley beneath, he fixed his eyes on some white glittering pinnacles just rising unfinished above the smoke, and recognised the great object of his alarm, the new Roman Catholic chapel, for which Lord Morden, the Whig minister, had given the ground, and the Earl of Claremont had subscribed a very large sum; the rest being supplied from some mysterious fund, of which no one could give an account, but which, from the splendour of the building, and the number of others of the same kind which were rising throughout the country, appeared almost inexhaustible.

The thoughts which passed through Bentley's mind, as he gazed on this hateful object, were most bitter. His ministry had failed; and he had sought for the credentials of his ministry, not in a formal appointment from the appointed rulers of the

Church, but in the success of his labours. He had found the town effete, indeed, and paralysed by the long incapacity of its old rector to attend to their spiritual wants; with little but a formal religion, and those forms dwindled into shadows. He had thought to revive the spirit of religion without them, —to make men hearty zealous Christians, so as to need no support from mere external ordinances, —just as if, when a sick man has fainted, and the circulation stopped in his limbs, we should proceed to restore the circulation, and at the same time to cut off the limbs. And now all had failed; and the church, lying as it did, on his first coming, in a state of suspended animation, had been apparently killed, and prevented from coming to life again by his zeal and energy, which had cut off the channels through which the life-stream was to flow.

Bentley did not see all this; but he did see that something was wrong; and he sighed most heavily. And as he looked down on the dull red mass of vapour that hung over the town, through which the setting sun was now shooting its diverging rays, other thoughts than of his spiritual duties rose in his mind. There were, indeed, thousands of souls in that large place, for which, in some shape, he, and he alone, was responsible; and he felt bitterly that the account he must render of them was full of evil. But there were also thousands of bodies, thousands of living beings, of whom all but a small proportion were in poverty and misery; —mothers, with the hearts of mothers, who were hanging over starving children; fathers, with arms of strength, and hearts almost desperate with disappointment and suffering. There were hundreds and hundreds of children who were toiling day and night without hope, without relief, like drudges in a mill, forced from their beds in the cold grey mornings before

they had slept out their melancholy weariness, sent
back to their beds again to think with fear of the
coming day; many worn with midnight toil, snatching their hasty meal of dry bread or cold potatoes,
apart from their parents, under the eye of a stern
task-master, and in the midst of grinding wheels
and tainted air,—oh! how unlike that beautiful, that
merciful nature, on which Bentley himself was
gazing,—the hills—the woods—the green meadows
—the sparkling waters—the bright blue sky—the
glorious sun,—all which God has made for man, but
especially for man in his childhood, as the nursery
in which he might be reared under fair sights, and
gentle sounds, and softest colours, and a liberty of
innocence, to see his Maker around and above him
at every step, in every thrill of pleasure, though
shrouded under a mystery of grandeur and of
beauty.

And they were left to themselves. Some hand,
Bentley knew not how, had severed those unhappy
beings from the ranks above them. He did, indeed,
visit, and visit daily, their miserable abodes, and
came back choked with tears, to sit down to his
solitary meal, which he could scarcely provide for
himself, and which was often sent away untasted to
relieve some famishing family. But what could
one hand, a hand of poverty like their own, or one
voice, or one mind, do with such a mass of ignorance
and distress? When he stood among them, and
spoke of religion, they gazed on him with a stupid
indifference, as if asking what right an individual,
young and solitary like him, could have to command
their minds. If he gave them relief, it was snatched
without gratitude; for there was nothing about him
to fear, and therefore little to excite love. In vain
he exhorted the few unoccupied persons, principally
ladies, who could undertake the task, to visit and

assist in relieving. They did assist him as they could; but they had neither authority, nor power, often not judgment sufficient, to turn those visits to account, in forming habits of obedience, or religion, or even prudence. The population was a body without a head, — a mass of fermenting passions, sufferings, high stimulated desires, half-instructed reason, — with no power above them to control, to guide, to be the object of affection, to sympathize with them, or to awe them. And not long since they had been admitted to the right of voting for members of parliament — to a share in the supreme government of the country. And as Bentley recalled these things, and gazed on the sun sinking behind a hill, and thought of a declining empire, he started up suddenly from his seat — for he had lost his watch.

CHAP. VIII.

UNHAPPILY for the unity of our story, our three principal personages at this moment have diverged, each in different directions, without knowing or caring at all for each other's movements. And the reader, who must hold in his hands the several clues to their proceedings without confusing them, will, we fear, be not a little puzzled. The stranger has left the ruins, and wandered into the park; Bentley, while sitting on the bench, and ruminating on the state of his parish, has just discovered the loss of his watch; and Miss Mabel has been occupied the whole afternoon, and we must now return to her. She left Mrs. Bevan's a little ashamed, a little perplexed, and, perhaps, a little angry, with the lecture which she had received. But her official duties were all before her, and her spirits rose with the calls upon her exertions. The accounts, accordingly, of one society were settled, and the plan for the other arranged; and the meeting for the Irish attended; and Mabel had the satisfaction every where of finding herself employed as secretary, and consulted as oracle—for persons are always glad to find those who will take trouble off their hands, and never hesitate to consult those whom they are not obliged to follow. And, the work of the morning despatched, and an invitation being accepted to eat a family dinner at Mr. Morgan's at five o'clock, Mabel resolved to employ her afternoon in a visit of charity. She would go and see poor Mrs. Connell, and the burnt boy.

It was with some difficulty that she made her
way under a dirty archway, and over a heap of
rubbish, through the narrow, stifling, and offensive
alley in which the poor family had taken refuge.
Some tattered linen was hanging to dry across it ;
heaps of dung and offal lay before the doors ; and a few
pale miserable faces peered out of the broken case-
ments, as Mabel's black silk cloak, carefully wrapped
round her, was seen threading the low passage.
Every one prepared at once their tale of sorrow or
complaint.   One had been neglected in the
distribution of blankets ; another's child had been
whipped at the National School, and would not be
sent any more unless the committee would scold the
master ; a third had found fault with the soup ;
a fourth was meditating how to extract from
Mabel an order on the Benevolent Society for wine
for her sick child, then lying in a high fever ; and
a fifth, a masculine, red-armed Amazon, had taken
those arms from the washing-tub before her, and,
hastily wiping them, came forward, with no pacific
voice, to expostulate with and denounce poor Mabel
for having said something to Mr. Bentley in dis-
praise of her drunken husband. One face only, a
fair, soft, delicate face, still bearing traces of great
beauty, but worn with care. and sorrow, shrunk
back, as if trembling and ashamed, the moment
Mabel appeared, and hastily withdrew up the stairs
of one of the most miserable of the hovels. Mabel
herself had caught her eye, and started, for it was
poor Margaret, who had been her pride and delight
at the National School, whom she had petted and
brought forward on every occasion, employing her
as scribe and monitor, and in a variety of other
trustworthy offices, even dressing her in her own
cast-off clothes, and turning, in fact, the poor girl's
head, until, to Mabel's horror, a change was per-

ceived in her character and appearance: her quickness became levity; her eye, naturally lively and open, now shrunk from meeting Mabel's; and it soon became too evident that Margaret was lost. Mabel, indeed, did not abandon her: exertions were made by Mr. Bentley, and other influential persons, especially by Mr. Brown, who employed George Wheeler in his service; and it was some satisfaction to Mabel to think that all that could be done was done, and that George, who had caused her ruin, was compelled to marry her.

Whatever strictness Mabel was inclined to enforce in melancholy cases of this kind, she could not forget that something was to blame in herself; and the moment she caught sight of Margaret's humbled, penitent, anxious face of patient suffering, she resolved to do what she had not done before, and to visit her again. And she was rather pleased to find, when asking for Mrs. Connell, to hear that she and her husband and children had been offered a shelter by Margaret herself, and were now living under the same miserable roof. Making her way past a little knot of dirty ragged children, who were playing with a crab-shell, and, young as they were, intermixed their play with oaths and words which Mabel could not hear without shuddering, she ascended the ruinous staircase; and her authoritative knock at the door was answered by the bustling appearance of Mrs. Connell, her black ragged hair straggling from her torn cap, and many symptoms indicating that she had not passed a day of that total abstinence recommended by the Temperance Society.

The room, however, was neater than Mabel had usually found to be the case in similar alleys. The broken panes were partially covered with paper. There were one or two chairs with their full complement of legs; a little range of crockery orna-

mented one wall; a common print of a Scripture
subject, which Mabel recognised as one of her own
gifts to poor Margaret when at school, was pinned
over the fire-place; and two large geraniums in
the window gave something of an air of refreshment
and comfort. It was with some little difficulty that
Mabel made her way past the loquacious Mrs.
Connell, full of her own distresses, and tales of
complaint against her drunken husband, to the
heap of straw covered with an old brown coat,
which lay in the corner, and on which the boy who
had been burnt in the fire was now stretched. He
was asleep, and, just as Mabel came to the bed-side,
a ray of light struggled through the dim casement,
and fell on his face. It was exquisitely beautiful;
the forehead open, the lips half closed and full of
intelligence and sweetness, the hair clustered thick
in natural ringlets, the ear delicately small, the
nose finely formed; and, though childhood even
amongst the poorest is still full of beauty, Mabel
was struck at something of a higher character in
the form before her. She stood looking on him for
some minutes, with that delight and composure, not
unmixed with melancholy thoughtfulness, with
which a sleeping child, helpless, unconscious, peaceful, pure, and yet surrounded with so many dangers,
is regarded by a feeling mind. And she did not
turn away till the boy, disturbed by some noise,
threw out his arms, opened his eyes, and, uttering
an oath, and throwing from him a Bible which
Margaret had placed by his side, once more composed himself to sleep. Mabel shuddered again,
and would have remonstrated with his mother on
permitting him to grow up in such habits, but she
had left the room; and, on turning round to look
for her, she observed Margaret herself, who had
endeavoured to escape observation by withdrawing

behind a screen, on which a new-washed shirt was hanging to dry, and was affecting to busy herself with preparing something in a pipkin over the scanty fire.

As Mabel approached her, she turned round, and, almost sinking with shame, could not venture to lift up her eyes; and, at the few kind but sad words with which Mabel addressed her, she covered her face with her hands, and, sinking in a chair, burst into tears. With this sight all Mabel's severity vanished; she spoke to her once more as she had used to do'; and as the sound of her voice recalled past days and happier times, poor Margaret's agony of weeping increased, and it was with some difficulty that Mabel composed her sufficiently to proceed in some inquiries respecting her husband. At the word "husband" all Margaret's distress was again aroused.

"Where was he?"

"He had gone to find work at the quarries in the forest."

"How was he going on?"

Margaret was silent.

"Was he kind to her?"

She faintly answered "Yes." But Mrs. Connell, who had entered the room again, looked as if she were very much disposed to say "No."

"Where was her infant?"

And here Margaret once more burst into a passion of tears. "George had taken it with him to a relation's."

"Why?"

"To get it taken care of."

"But why not leave it with its mother?"

"We were starving," said Margaret, "and he said it would be better off."

"Was he fond of the child?"

Margaret was silent, and Mrs. Connell could refrain no longer, and said, " No,"—that he was " a brute."

Margaret sprung from her chair, and put her hand before the woman's mouth. But it was too late; and, with all the feelings of an Irish mother, in whom no hardship and no distress can eradicate the love of her children, even of her foster-children, Mrs. Connell proceeded to enlarge on George's bad conduct both to his wife and his child; but to the child especially — he seemed to hate it. Mabel listened with great pain. She thought how often love which ends in crime turns into hatred, and how little hope there is of permanent peace and comfort in an union which remorse and shame must embitter, and how hard it is to restore what has once been broken by sin. But while Mrs. Connell, unchecked by the imploring eyes of Margaret, who yet could not deny her statements, was proceeding in the full flow of her eloquent indignation, another step, harsh and heavy, was heard ascending the creaking staircase, and a short rude knock at the door was followed, without waiting for an answer, by the entrance of another person.

" Is your husband here ? " said a rude, stern voice to Mrs. Connell, which, as Mabel's dress appeared from behind the screen, was softened down into something of bland hypocritical gentleness; " is your husband here, my good woman ? " And, on looking up, Mabel saw a middle-aged stout man, with a hard iron face, rough whiskers, and bushy hair, a patch upon the mouth, the eyes small, and twinkling with deep lurking cunning, yet capable of concealing their expression, and his dress that of a butcher. But there was something about his whole appearance singular and almost unnatural, — a certain contrast between his dress and his

manner, which was felt rather than understood, and
an evident desire to make observations upon others,
without being able to face others himself. Mabel
was struck equally by his change of tone and
manner when he perceived who she was. He made
way for her as she went up to the place where the
poor boy lay, and his bow was that of a person
capable of moving in a higher situation. And it
appeared that he now thought it necessary to show
some sympathy for the poor woman.

"How is he to-day?" he asked of Mrs. Connell;
"is he better?"

And, as he came up to the bed-side, the boy
opened his eyes, and a greeting took place between
them as of an old and a young associate, familiar
with each other, and of whom the elder had initiated
the younger into much that was evil: and the look
with which he gazed upon the boy did not escape
Mabel. It passed over his countenance for a
moment, lighting it up with a strange expression of
exultation, and hate, and treachery, which made
Mabel feel uncomfortable in his presence. But it
was soon over; and he turned to repeat his question,
"Where was Connell?"

Mrs. Connell herself seemed to stand before him
in awe and fear. She faltered out, "that he was at
the public-house."

"As usual," muttered the man. "As usual.
And why do you let him go there?"

"How can I prevent it?" said the poor woman;
"he takes all he can, and leaves me to get on as I
can; and it is his only comfort. He does not sleep at
night, and can't get work in the day; and no one
cares for us; and, to tell the truth, Mr. Pearce," she
said, gaining courage from despair, "it's bad days
with us, and it were better we were back in our
own country. Would to God we had never left it!"

"Pshaw! pshaw!" was the reply, and he was about to leave the room, when Margaret, trembling and faltering, came up to him, and asked if he had seen her husband.

"Where is George, Mr. Pearce?"

The man started and coloured, but only for an instant. "Up in the quarries, I suppose. How should I know?" he said; "am I to be answerable for all the stray husbands in the place?"

"But he told me," said Margaret, "that he was going to see you—that you were to get him employment."

"Did he?" answered the man; "then he told a lie, and you were a fool for believing him."

"And you have not seen him, then?"

"How should I have seen him, I tell you again!"

"And my baby," once more she faltered out,— "you have not seen it?"

The man uttered a coarse expression of impatience, and, as Margaret burst into tears, he retreated hastily out of the room.

It was some little time before any one spoke after this scene. At last Mabel broke the silence by some observations on the sick boy, who lay with his fine face buried in a rough dirty heap of clothes, and apparently sulky and impatient at being made the subject of remark. It was in vain that Mabel addressed to him some of the usual commonplaces on the duty of bearing pain patiently; on its being a warning; on the necessity of profiting by it; on the opportunity which he now enjoyed of reading the Bible and saying his prayers. He either said nothing, or muttered some indistinct sounds, which told more of sulkiness than gratitude: and Mabel, as she withdrew, could not help lamenting to Mrs. Connell how little he seemed to have profited by sickness, and entreated her to remember the awful

responsibility of rearing up her children in the way
they should go, and of the misery of seeing a son
turn out ill.   There was a strange passive indifference in Mrs. Connell's face as Mabel uttered the
word "son," and a look of intelligence in poor Margaret's eye, which, however, did not intend to tell
any tale.   But Mabel observed them not; and, after
leaving a trifle from the funds of a District Visiting
Society, and promising to call again, she withdrew.

CHAP. IX.

As she turned the corner by the back gate of the
little public-house called the Bricklayer's Arms,
she once more caught sight of the strange man
whom she had just met. But the repugnance which
she had felt at his presence made her turn away her
eyes. And she did not notice that, after looking
up and down the street, to observe if any one saw
him, and whistling at the same time with an affectation of indifference, he slipped quietly into the
yard.

And we must follow him.

A nod of familiar recognition to a dirty, slipshod
abigail, who performed the domestic offices of the
public-house, and another to her equally dirty mistress, showed that he was no stranger in the place; and
he entered without hesitation a little back room communicating with the tap, where, round a deal table
covered with mugs of beer and tobacco-pipes, sat
six or seven ill-looking ruffianly fellows, with rough
caps on their heads, and dresses such as are worn
by navigators, excavators, and persons employed on
railroads. His entrance caused a movement among
them. One or two took off their caps; others shuf-
fled with their feet, as if prepared to rise; and all
seemed awkward at first, as in the presence of a
superior. But he nodded to them with a mixture
of condescension and familiarity ; and they were
soon placed at their ease again by his taking up a
dirty newspaper stained with beer, from which one
of them had been reading, and asking what news.
Before an answer could be given he had exchanged

a sign with one of them who sat at the head of the table, and seemed to possess some command over the rest, and to be better drest. And after a few words whispered between them, the other left the room.

"And so, sir, we are to have an election after all," said one of the remaining party.

"And what good will an election do you?" said a shrewd, cynical-looking man at the bottom of the table, who appeared to have had a somewhat better education than the rest.

"What good will parliament or any thing do us," rejoined another, "until we get the charter?"

"And what good will the charter do you?" said the cynic.

"Why, give us what we want, and put all things straight. Is it not a crying shame that with your representative government, as you call it, here are we, the thousands, ay, the millions, without any voice at all, or any one to represent us, or care for us, or give us any thing but a jail for a poor-house, and Botany Bay for a country residence? If we are to have representatives, let them be real ones — men who will do as we tell them, and only speak what we choose to hear."

"Fine governors we should make!" said the cynic.

"And pray why not?" was the reply. "Do not we know as much of government as the king's ministers themselves? cannot we find out what the people like, and do it just as well as they can, and better too? We'd soon make short work of it. Down with your civil list! down with your pensions! down with your corn-laws — and your landlords, grinding the poor to death that they may put their high rents into their pockets! Down with your poor-bastiles! down with your kings!"——

" And dukes, and princes, and marquises, and lords, and all the crew of them !" said another.

" Here's a health to them all, Mr. Pearce !" and he turned his glass upside down, and looked up significantly in the face of the last comer.

" And your taxes," rejoined Pearce himself, " and your tithes, and your church-rates, and your parliament clergy, your archbishops with 50,000*l.* a-year, and your bishops with 20,000*l.*, and your parsons, who, having plundered the Catholics, would now willingly burn and hang them, and send over an army to Ireland to extirpate what they call the bloody papists — do you say ' down ' with these, too ?"

" Ay, ay, down with them all !" rose at once in a chorus from the whole table ; " down with them all —the sooner the better."

" And how will you down with them ?" asked Pearce, winking, and looking at them with a cold sarcastic smile on his lips ; " what is the use of your talking when men should be acting ?"

" And we are going to act, are we not ?" was the reply.

" Going !" said Pearce ; " cowards are always going to act. What have you done to prepare yourselves when the time comes ?"

" Something," said one of the youngest ; and he threw a heavy stick upon the table, which Pearce took up and examined, feeling one end of it, and drawing out a short pointed weapon which fixed into it.

" Sharp —pretty sharp," he muttered, as he closed it up.

" Sharp enough," said its owner.

" And do you intend to use this ?" said Pearce.

" Use it ?" cried five or six voices at once, and the whole party opened their eyes as if in astonishment

I

at the question coming from such a quarter —
" Use it ? Why, what have you sent Blacker to us
for, if we are not to use them ?"

" *I* send Blacker to you !" said Pearce. " *I* wish
you to use them! Who ever heard me say any
thing of the kind ? I recommend you all to claim
your rights as Englishmen; and if they attempt to
put you down by force, why, rather than have your
necks straightened on the gallows, it might be as
well to try something else. But my advice is, obey
the law. Alter the law if you can, but do not break
it; it only does harm. Show yourselves in a strong
attitude; let your enemies and your persecutors see
that you can defend yourselves. Moral force is
invincible. This is what I recommend, and always
shall. So Blacker will tell you: he is a fine fellow,
and you cannot have a better leader."

There was a curious mixture of blank surprise
and disappointment in the faces of all assembled, as
Pearce uttered these words and turned whistling to
the window.

" But I thought, Mr. Pearce," said one of them,
at length taking courage, " I thought Blacker had
orders from you ?"

" Orders from me !" fiercely cried Pearce as he
turned round sharply on the speaker. " Orders
from me, Blacker ! " — as the man who seemed the
leader of the gang re-entered the room — " Blacker !
have you told these men that I have given you
orders — that I have any thing to do with this ?"
and he took up the dagger stick.

" I ? " said Blacker, stammering. " No, sir, never.
No one ever heard me say any thing of the kind. I
told them you were a friend to the people, and
wished them to have their rights, and were no
monopolist or aristocrat : that is all. If any one
says more than this, it is quite a mistake."

" Quite a mistake, quite a mistake," hastily repeated Pearce. "Moral influence is what I recommend—peaceable pressure from without—force of
opinion—imposing attitude;—show your strength
—but do not violate the laws, do not violate the
laws!"

He then whispered a word to Blacker—received
a short answer, and, with a hurried good morning,
he left the room.

" Now that is what I call courage!" said the
cynic; and others seemed inclined to say the same.

But Blacker took his seat at the head of the
table, and, making a sign for silence, soon drew
their attention to other things. There were signs
and countersigns exchanged, mysterious communications respecting Lodges and Brethren, and work
to be done. Several produced weapons like the
one exhibited before; and the aspect of fierce determination, with which they gradually regarded
each other and their leader, brightened with satisfaction when Blacker pulled out a handful of sovereigns and proceeded to divide them.

" And now, Captain Blacker," said the cynic, as
he pocketed his money, "you are a great man, and
a clever man among us poor ignorant fellows, who
cannot read or write; but may such a stupid fellow
as I am take the liberty of asking where all this
comes from?"

" Come from?" replied Blacker, with a laugh.
" Who minds where his money comes from, when
he finds it snug in his own pocket? Do not trouble
yourself about that."

" Why, I do not trouble myself much about any
thing," said the cynic, chinking the money in his
hand; "it is all the same to me, if I get my pot of
beer and my warm fire-side, how the world goes

with other people. But that fellow Pearce, they
say he has plenty of these," and he held up a sovereign to the light; "and you seem to be pretty good
friends with him. Eh, captain?"

Blacker laughed again, but with a look which
checked further inquiry, and contented himself
with saying that the business was over and he must
go. "One thing," he added, "you may be sure of,
my lads. There are people cleverer and greater
than I or Mr. Pearce, or any one in this place, who
will be very glad to see you have your rights, and
won't mind assisting you if you help yourselves.
Only remember your business: mind your oath,
keep your counsel, do not get drunk, stand by your
brethren, and obey your captain. Is not this it?"

"Yes, yes,—we will, we will,"—and Blacker left
them.

As he passed by a little room at the other end of
the passage, the door was ajar, and he was beckoned
into it by Pearce, who was standing to watch for
him. The door was shut after him; and Pearce,
drawing himself up to his full height, and planting
himself with an air of determined and commanding
authority within a few feet of him, sternly demanded what he meant by letting those fellows
suppose there was any communication between
them. Blacker, a man clever and self-possessed,
but evidently under the control of Pearce, and
awed by him as by a master, hesitated and coloured, and began to excuse himself and deny it.

"None of your excuses or denials," said Pearce;
"you know who I am, and you know that I know
every thing. Never tell *me* a lie!" and he fastened
on him a look of penetrating and contemptuous significance which Blacker could not face.

"You have not told them any thing," said Pearce,

after a pause. "I know that well enough. But
you have allowed them to suspect, and with us that
is as bad. Remember your oath, sir; and remember
that if I have but two eyes in my head, I have a
hundred in my pocket, and hands too, — hands," he
muttered in a low but audible whisper, "which will
do any thing I bid them, and which never spare a
traitor."

The word "traitor" restored Blacker to his self-
possession. He came forward, protested against
deserving such a charge, acknowledged that he
might have been careless, promised that he would
take care to remove any impression of the kind;
and Pearce, receiving his excuses, shook hands with
him at last, and apparently restored him to favour.
"And now go," he added, "and send that brute
Connell to me directly. Stop," he cried, as Blacker
was leaving the room; "I have one more thing to
say. Come back, and shut the door. Have you
seen *him* to-day?"

"He was at the inn this morning at eleven
o'clock, I know," said Blacker; "and afterwards
he went to Atkinson's, for I watched him there;
and canny Charles was to watch him afterwards.
George the hostler told me they thought he was
going away in a day or two."

"Did they know who he was?" asked Pearce.

"No," replied Blacker.

"And you did not give them a hint?"

"Not I. I merely stood about in the yard when
they were talking about him, and so found out what
he was doing."

"Has he seen Connell yet, and the boy?"

"Yes, yesterday morning. Connell told me he
came to Wheeler's wife, saw the boy, and seemed
struck with him. Connell said it was quite strange
to see him. The boy behaved ill, and swore, upon

I 3

which Connell had a sermon given him, and something was said about his being sent to school."

"Very good, very good," muttered Pearce; "this will do. Has he been to the Priory yet?"

"Not yet, I am sure," said Blacker, "for I have had my eye on him ever since you ordered me, and he cannot have gone anywhere without my knowing it."

"Let me know," said Pearce, "when he does go; "for it cannot be long first. And so the old Lord is come back? You will have an eye there too, Blacker, and an eye on my Lady."

"I saw her go up to the Priory about an hour ago," said Blacker, "in a little low phaeton, with a servant on horseback."

"To the Priory?" muttered Pearce. "Humph! And where is *he* now?"

"Canny Charles will tell me this evening," said Blacker.

"Find out if he is gone to the Priory too," said Pearce, "and let me know at once. I shall be at my lodgings all the evening. And now, good day."

But, once more, Blacker was called back before the door had closed, and Pearce, shutting it carefully after him, and looking round the room as if afraid lest the walls had ears, came up to him, and laying his hand on his shoulder, and looking fixedly in his face, said to him in a low voice, "Are you sure of Wheeler?"

"As sure as I am of myself," was the answer.

"Humph!" muttered Pearce. And once more looking Blacker in the face, as if he would penetrate into the very bottom of his thoughts,— "He knows things," said Pearce, in the same low distinct voice, "he knows things which he should not know, and he has threatened to disclose them."

" Has he ?" asked Blacker, as if alarmed.

" It is against our laws," said Pearce—and he paused. " And our laws must be obeyed," he continued.

For a moment Blacker seemed to shudder and recoil from Pearce's touch; but Pearce, with the same fixed, searching, significant gaze, retained his hold of him.

" Our laws must be obeyed," he repeated, " and to the letter, or all is lost. Blacker, my fine fellow, there must be no flinching."

" I never thought of flinching," said Blacker sulkily, and yet seemingly nerving himself to hear the rest.

" I never thought you did," said Pearce; " I know you too well." And with an encouraging clap on the shoulder, and a relaxation of his countenance, he let go his hold. Blacker seemed to recover and take breath, as if from a species of fascination.

" Keep watch on him," said Pearce—" and that is all."

There was something significant in Blacker's eyes, as he looked up and repeated " That is all?"

" Yes, all—that is all : " and then, as if correcting himself, " for the present, that is."

" Very well," said Blacker.

" Good bye. And now send Connell."

It was some time before Connell arrived, and in the meanwhile Pearce paced backwards and forwards along the sanded floor of the little room, with his arms folded, and resting every now and then, as if in intense thought, with his forehead on the mantel-piece. Once his dark, gloomy, but energetic eye caught a gaudy-coloured print like a valentine over the fireplace. It represented three hearts transfixed with arrows, with the words " Mary, Jesus,

and Joseph" over them, and a devotional inscription
at the bottom, containing an invocation to all three.
He crossed himself at the sight, muttered over
some form of words, which might have been an
Ave Maria, and then relapsed into thoughtfulness,
from which he was disturbed by a low knock at the
door.

"There are no letters, sir, to-day," said a little
girl who opened it with fear and trembling. "But
here is a parcel come by the coach. Three and
sixpence, sir, to pay, from Preston."

Pearce took the parcel, and eagerly tore it open.
Some papers containing lists of names and printed
tracts, apparently for circulation, he put into his
pocket, and then sat down to open a letter in cypher,
which it cost him some trouble to translate.

"The cypher changed again," he muttered. "Why,
they are more cautious than ever. Has there been
any treachery, I wonder?" and he proceeded to read:
"'You will have no more letters by the post yet, for
the post-office people have noticed the foreign letters.
Government has got wind of something. F. C. will
forward those from Lyons in a parcel by coach to
the Hen and Chickens.' Humph! more caution.
'You have committed yourself to Wheeler. He is
not one of us, and never will be, and has his own
views and plans, and you will never be able to make
use of him as you propose. He has even threatened,
unless we do what he wishes. He is too sharp and
too wicked for you. If you cannot get the papers
from him quietly, we must not mind ———' (here
was a blank). 'He might ruin us all.'

"Fools!" said Pearce impatiently. "Fools, to
think I needed to be told this! 'You will send us
word regularly of V.'s movements. He has sold
his Yorkshire property,—we learned this by X. Z.,
and has made up his mind to live at the P. You

will let us know how long he remains at H., and
whether he goes to the castle and sees L. E. She
is quite firm; and at present so is he, and there
seems to be no chance of any change. But they
have not met since they parted at Florence, and we
have resolved on waiting patiently a little longer,
and making another trial.' "

As Pearce came to these last words he laid down
the letter with a cool smile, which implied no little
contempt of the writer, and no inclination to enter
into his views. "Another trial!" he muttered.
" Have they not had trials enough already? Do
they think to bring him round now, with his obstinacy and what he calls his conscience, when he
has once got out of their net? They might have
done it once, when he was younger and knew nothing ; but he has fallen into other hands now, and
they are no match for him. No!" and he looked up
triumphantly ; " those two will never be one now ;
and, what is more, they never shall be. Never!
never! I have sworn it by my hatred and my
vengeance — sworn it on my knees, if my hand and
the power it wields can prevent it. Never, never!"
and it would have given a study for the picture of
a fiend to have watched his face as he uttered these
words. But the paroxysm of passion was momentary. He smothered it over, assumed the same
cold iron cast of countenance, and proceeded to de-
cypher the letter. " ' If all fails, and he will not
come over, we must try something else. He must
not be allowed to remain at H., where he will do
us great harm. He makes no secret of his intentions, and will work against us in every possible
way. But you will take no steps to attack him till
you hear from us. If he can be brought over by
fair means, well and good ; if not, we must be rid of
him in some other way.'

"Rid of him in some other way!" repeated Pearce. "Rid of him in some other way! Yes, there are many other ways of getting rid of him. Men have been driven from their homes by disgust, by disappointment, by threats, by abuse, by calumny, by fear. There is no difficulty in this. But this would not be vengeance — not my vengeance. To make him drink of his own cup — to stab him with his own dagger — to have him here with my foot upon his neck, and tell him it was I who did it!" He stood fixed in the very posture which he would have assumed had his deadly enemy been lying under his feet; and his eye lighted up with fierce exultation. The letter, however, was not finished; and with the air of a man who could shake off all personal feeling and apply himself at once to business, he reverted to it. "'You will beware of the Abbé; he is still at the old Lord's: but he is, you know, a mere Protestant at heart, and you must not trust him. We shall soon have him removed, and you may communicate freely with the person who comes in his stead. Of course you will do what can be done for the Liberals at the election. Make use of Wheeler's set if you can safely. But again remember that he has his own plans, and must not be trusted, and, unless he gives up the papers, all may be lost. Write to us every other day if you have any thing to communicate, and send your letters under cover to X. Z.'"

Pearce had scarcely time to read the end of the letter, when he heard another knock at the door, and, with a heavy lumbering tread, his face inflamed with habits of intoxication, his eyes bloodshot, and an expression of haggardness and fear in his lip and mouth, Connell came in.

"Drinking again, sirrah!" said Pearce to him, in the same cold, stern voice which he had assumed towards Blacker. "Drinking again!"

Connell, like every other person who came into contact with this singular personage, seemed to quail under his eye, and stammered out some excuse.

"I will have no excuses," said Pearce. "You have been at the public-house all this morning, and all yesterday afternoon."

Connell attempted to deny it.

"How dare you," said Pearce, in his low, distinct voice, which seemed to thrill through and fascinate his hearer; "how dare you tell a lie to me, who know every thing that you say and do? You went at four o'clock yesterday afternoon to the Swan tap; you there met Roberts and Jackson; you sat drinking with them till six; you then went down by the Brewhouse lane; you spoke to a person by the way, and you told him, half-drunk as you were, that you would meet him at the Ruins to-night, and help him. You know whom I mean. And now, when I know every word you utter, and every thing you do, how dare you tell me a lie?"

The poor wretch, as if aghast at the presence of a supernatural being, listened without a word of reply, and showed by his silence the accuracy of Pearce's statement.

"I tell you again," said Pearce, "that I have eyes in every place, and tongues to tell me every thing. Never lie to me, for it is of no use. And now, sirrah, give me a true account of all that passed when the gentleman who saved the boy came to see him. Tell me every thing, at your peril!"

Connell, faltering and frightened, endeavoured, but very imperfectly, to give a clear narrative, and Pearce listened patiently without interrupting it. He knew human nature too well to attempt to hasten him. It appeared by Connell's story that the stranger had made inquiries the day after the fire, and had found out Margaret's lodging, with the view of giving the poor people some relief; that on seeing the boy he seemed struck, as Connell expressed it, all of a heap; had stood gazing on him, as he lay on the straw, with a look of painful surprise, as if struggling to retrace past circumstances, and bring to light some dim and indistinct vision. He had lifted the cluster of brown hair from the boy's forehead; spoken to him with a voice softened and sad, as if with an interest deeper than that of ordinary benevolence; had returned more than once to look on him, and had groaned heavily as a ray of light fell more full on his face. It was not till the boy spoke, and spoke, as he had done to Mabel, in language which revolted the ear, that the stranger turned away, as if in disgust and disappointment; and rebuked both Connell and his wife for permitting one so young to be brought up in such profaneness and vice. Even then he called Connell aside, and interrogated him closely on his family, the number of his children, the age of the boy, where he was born, and other questions of the kind.

"To all which," said Pearce, at this point of the story, "you answered properly?"

"Yes, sir," said Connell.

"And boldly?" asked Pearce.

"Yes, sir, as you told me."

"Did he seem to have any doubt, or suspect any thing?"

"Nothing," answered Connell.

"You are sure, nothing?"

"Quite sure," said Connell.

"And then," said Pearce, "he offered to send him to school, did he not?"

"He did," said Connell. "And I told him I must think of it."

"Very good," said Pearce. "You will let me know when you see him again. And you will give

no answer of any kind till I have told you what to
do. And now, man, tell me what Wheeler gives
you for helping him at the Ruins to-night?"

Once more Connell seemed aghast at the secret
knowledge which Pearce possessed of all his movements. "Five shillings, and beer," he stammered
out.

"And you are to carry away what you have got
there to the quarries to-night? How many of these
things have you got there?" And he pulled out of
his pocket a pikehead weapon of the same kind as
that which had been produced by one of the gang
in the other room.

"I do not know," said Connell.

"How many carts are there to be?"

"Two," said Connell.

"And pray how came Wheeler to trust you, a
drunken sot as you are, with this piece of work?
Why, for five shillings and a pot of beer you would
betray your own father!"

"I won't betray him," said Connell. "Why
should I? What should I get by it?"

There was a pause, during which Pearce collected his countenance into the same piercing, sted-
fast look with which he had awed Blacker, and,
coming up close to the ruffian, he said, in the same
low distinct voice, "But Wheeler could betray you!"

Connell started, as if shot. The blood forsook
his cheeks, and he turned to Pearce with a look of the
most abject, supplicating terror. Without appearing to notice it, Pearce continued looking stedfastly
on him, and again uttered the same words, "But
Wheeler could betray you!"

"Who told him?" exclaimed Connell. "Who
told him? I never confessed to any one but the
priest. No one upon earth knows it but the priest,
and you."

And in the same low distinct tone of voice Pearce whispered, " Wheeler knows it, and can give you up at any time. And this is why he has employed you for a work which, if you chose to peach, would cost him his own neck."

The poor criminal sunk down in a chair, and trembled from head to foot. Pearce allowed him a few minutes to recover; but he had no intention of relieving him from his fear. He pulled a newspaper out of his pocket, and, casting his eye over a file of notices and advertisements, proceeded to read one which described Connell's person exactly, and offered a large reward of more than 500*l.* to any one who would give information which might lead to his apprehension.

" Wheeler," said Pearce again, " has seen this, and he is a needy man, and a cunning man ; and no one here has seen it, but himself and me. You are in his power, and for that reason he ventures to trust you. But he has been to the police, and, I suspect, about this."

Connell's hat had fallen on the floor, his arms had dropt, as if lifeless, by his side, and the sweat broke out in large drops upon his forehead ; while Pearce, so far from comforting or encouraging him, proceeded to read the advertisement again, comparing every point of the description with Connell's appearance, and going over them slowly and steadily, as if wholly insensible to, or even taking pleasure in, the agony of his victim. At last Connell could bear it no longer, and he fell down on his knees, and, wringing his hands, intreated Pearce to save him.

" You can save me, you know you can !" he cried ; " you can do any thing, — you promised you would, — you saved me once before, when you brought me from Ireland !"

" I can save you, I know," said Pearce, " if only

we can stop Wheeler's mouth. He's a troublesome and a dangerous fellow, and 500*l.* would soon tempt him. He has seen the paper, and he knows you did it, and can give information all about it, which would hang you up in a minute; and, as I tell you, I have seen him talking with the policeman. Nobody else has seen it, and there are no placards here, nor likely to be, or I can stop them; so you are quite safe, except from him."

" How did Wheeler find it out ?" asked Connell, falteringly.

" I am sure I do not know," said Pearce, " but he told me all about it; told me where you hid the gun after the shot was fired ; and how, when the old man struggled, you knocked him back with the butt-end ; and where you threw away the frieze coat; and about the marks on your waistcoat ;" — and, with his eyes fixed steadily on the convulsed countenance of Connell, he proceeded slowly : " He knew every word the old man said; how he begged for mercy, and prayed you might not go to hell for it ; and spoke to you of the tithes he had forgiven you, and the potatoes he used to send you through the famine."

Connell put his hands before his face, and groaned with anguish. " Oh, Mr. Pearce!" he cried, " if you had not put it into my head, I should never have done it! He never did me any harm, except putting me out of that bit of potato ground."

" I put it into your head, man!" said Pearce; " how could I put it into your head ? I told you, if a parson kept you out of your rights, you might give him a little fright, that was all, — and then you went and shot him !"

" You told me," said Connell, " that he was a parson, and all parsons ought to be got rid of; and you said he was an enemy of our religion, and

cursed by the blessed Pope, and a devil; and that
there was no harm in getting rid of devils; and
then you said there would be no difficulty, and I
might make a clean breast of it at confession, and
do a little penance, and all would be right, and I
should get the ground, and no one be the wiser;
and this was the way to make ould Ireland free. I
remember every word, as well as if it were yesterday; and the devil put it all into my heart. Would
to God I had been murdered myself rather than
have done it!"

"Pooh! pooh!" said Pearce, "what is all this
fuss about? It is not the first parson who has been
punished in Ireland for keeping what does not
belong to him, and it won't be the last; and you are
no worse than others. The only thing to think
about is how we shall stop Wheeler's mouth — that
dangerous, treacherous fellow; I would not trust
my own life in his hands for a mint of money.
"Eh?" he added, and looked aside at Connell, as if
hoping that a thought might suggest itself to him,
without requiring to be expressed. "Eh?" he repeated, "how are we to stop his mouth?"—and, as
if leaving the question to work its way, he went to
the window, and whistled.

Connell once more buried his face in his hands,
and continued silent.

"At what o'clock," said Pearce, after a pause,
and turning sharply round, "are you to be at the
Ruins to-night?"

"Ten o'clock," said Connell.

"Any moon?" said Pearce.

"I do not know," answered Connell, doggedly.

"Any one to be with you?" asked Pearce.

"No," said Connell, in the same dogged way.

Pearce went again to the window, and began
again to whistle. "He's a vile heretic, that

Wheeler," he continued, " and one that will do us mischief;" and, as he uttered the words, a careful observer might have detected a little faltering in the voice, as if arising from a momentary swelling in the throat; but he stifled it with a short cough, and the cough broke the stupor in which Connell seemed sunk.

" I thought," he said, " he was a friend of your's, Mr. Pearce?"

" No friend of mine," said Pearce: " I tried to bring him round, and make him useful, but he would not do for us. Blacker is the man I like — a sound, honest, trustworthy fellow. Wheeler has got too much of the devil in him; and he knows a great deal more than is quite convenient, more especially for your neck, Connell,—eh, man? A rope and a gallows, and no priest to anoint you; no pleasant prospect, eh?"

" But Wheeler won't peach," said Connell; " why should he give me up? Why, I could give him up, for all that."

" Ay, ay, so you could; but pray what would you gain by that? How would it save your own neck from paying forfeit for the parson's bullet, by putting Wheeler into gaol for his tricks with those arms? And, after all, he would only be tried, and perhaps acquitted; or the lawyers would let there be some flaw in the parchment; or else there would come down a warrant from the Secretary of State, and he would only be sent to Botany Bay, and get a good place there, or be returned to his family. Why, they could easily get up a petition for him, and find plenty of members of parliament to threaten ministers if they did not let him go; and ministers do not like to provoke people now-a-days. But it would be very different with you, my man. They may not mind much in Ireland; but you are in

England now, and English people have not much
sympathy with shooting at landlords and parsons,
though they are Protestants, and do like to let their
own land as they choose. I suspect, man, your
chance would be small."

Connell once more let his hands drop as in
despair. And Pearce continued standing at the
window, and affected to watch the drops of rain
which were chasing each other down the glass.

" Are you sure," he said, once more, " there will
be no one but you two to-night ?"

" Not till the carts come," said Connell, " and
they are not to be there till ten o'clock."

" Humph !" muttered Pearce. " He's a slight,
weakly fellow, that Wheeler ; I could twist him
round my thumb."

" Not when he has his pistols with him," said
Connell.

" Does he always carry pistols ?" said Pearce.

" Always, on such nights," answered Connell,
sharply ; and there was another pause.

" That's a deep well in the Priory court," said
Pearce, " by the great yew tree; how many feet
water are there in it ?"

" Twenty," muttered Connell, " or thereabouts ;"
and they were silent again.

" There was a man," continued Pearce, " in
Hawkstone, some years back, who fell into a well,
and was never heard of again for thirty years, when
they found his skeleton in cleaning it out."

Connell was silent ; but something had come
across his mind, and he started up, and, confronting
Pearce, who endeavoured to avoid his eyes, said,
with a voice in which bitterness of suffering was
mingled with anger, and scorn, and defiance, " Mr.
Pearce," he said, " are you the foul fiend himself,
or only his head clerk ? Blood enough already, for

your head and mine! Blood enough already!" And he left the room.

Pearce stood for some minutes motionless, half-alarmed, half-surprised, and chilled with that shame and remorse, which even the most hardened and most guilty cannot shake off, when rebuked by inferiors guilty like themselves. But his was not a mind to give way to such feelings. He whistled, as if to turn the current of his thoughts; and once more began pacing the room. He uttered nothing; but his thoughts were dark and deep, and showed themselves in the workings of his stern and malignant features. They were thoughts of a vast and deep-laid conspiracy, in which the fate of kingdoms was involved, and in which, though a subordinate, he was an active and accomplished agent. They reverted to the days of his youth, when he had been taken up by one of its most penetrating leaders, and tutored in all the mysterious craft of intrigue—an intrigue of which religion was the pretext, and ambition the mainspring, and which was carried on by a machinery at once so gigantic in its extent, so secret in its operations, so united in its combination, so steady and undeviating in its aim, and so adapted in all its parts to the passions and wants of human nature, that to a human eye nothing could resist it, or save even thrones and kingdoms from falling under the rod of a religious tyranny. He thought of the lessons which he had there received; of acquiring power, and exercising it remorselessly and fearlessly, with one sole view to the aggrandisement of his society; of the modes by which the minds of men might be laid open, and be made slaves to those who were privy to their weaknesses and crimes; of the grand rule of all worldly ambition, "divide et impera," set friend against friend, power

against power, and you become master of both.
He took from his pocket the papers which had
reached him in the packet, and contemplated with
exultation the account there given of the progress
of their influence, and the increase of their revenues ; while the governments and countries over
which they were stretching their arms in secret
sat still in unsuspecting confidence, unconscious of
the mischief which was working in their very
vitals.   To be engaged in the management of such
a secret and gigantic plot was in itself full of interest and excitement to a mind like his.   It gave
him, palled as he was at an early age with a licentious life, something still to stimulate his enterprise
and feed his imagination.   It exercised all the
powers of a penetrating and calculating intellect :
it gave him a personal importance which atoned
for the degrading sense of dependence and inferiority, to which his low birth had exposed him
in early life ; and the bitterness of which, to his
haughty spirit, had been aggravated by the contemptuous repulses which he had encountered in
his effort to obtain a footing in higher classes of
society : and if it held out a prospect of revenge
upon the classes who had thus despised him, it
touched him also in a tenderer point; without
which, perhaps, he would never have thrown himself, with his whole heart and soul, into the position
which he then occupied—a position of great risk,
requiring the utmost delicacy of management —
bringing him into contact with agents whom it was
impossible to employ without risking treachery on
their part, and whom he could only hope to control by playing them one against the other, and
fearlessly resolving to sacrifice any of them the
moment they became dangerous.   Pearce had his
private ends and personal ambition ; and his am-

bition was a longing for revenge. It burned in his breast with a deep, steady, resolved hatred, which never allowed a thought of pity to come before it and its victim ; and which, if ever conscience intruded for a moment, threw itself at once into the form of justice—of a deserved and equitable requital for a deadly injury ; and assumed even the appearance of piety, because the same blow which laid the being whom he hated at his feet laid prostrate also the enemy of his faith, and the determined and dangerous antagonist of the religious body to which he was solemnly pledged, and in whose prosperity he was told that the interests of Christendom were involved.

But the thoughts could not continue for ever. There was work, active work, to be done. A few minutes later, a respectable clerical-looking person, with his face closely shaven, a dark head of hair, and a pair of green spectacles which completely covered his eyes, issued from a little garden gate, which communicated with a back street of Hawkstone ; and, after threading one or two narrow lanes without any houses in them, he opened another similar door by a private key, and soon found himself in the little study of the Rev. Patrick O'Leary, the bland, liberal, and accomplished Roman priest, who had recently settled in Hawkstone to superintend the erection of what the people persisted in calling a new Catholic Chapel.

CHAP. X.

WITH Bentley's narrow income, and the numberless
calls upon it, the loss of his watch, which he valued
also as a legacy from an old aunt, was a very serious consideration : and he resolved to retrace
his steps to the ruins in the hope of recovering it.
It never occurred to him, that as the obligation of
the Temperance Society only bound men to abstain
from one sin, and this on the ground of its inconvenience, a member of the society might feel no
difficulty about a distinct sin, particularly where
tempting from its convenience. And he did not
recollect, that, just as he was entering the archway into the ruins, there had been a little crowd
and crushing of some bystanders, in the midst of
which it was not impossible that his watch had
either been stolen or forced from his pocket. He
walked, therefore, as fast as he was able, back
through the park. But the sun had already set.
The sound of the returning band, as it entered the
High Street of Hawkstone, reached him from a
distance, and told him that he would find the ruins
deserted. Twilight was coming on, and, if Bentley
had honestly confessed, he would have acknowledged that he preferred a visit to the Priory in
broad daylight. As the thought came across him,
he laughed at his own folly, and walked towards it
so much the faster. And yet notions, and fancies,
and idle tales, which were current about the place,
would occur to him. For there was a gloom and
an evil destiny which seemed to hang over the spot,

and the family to which it belonged; and many
were the stories which tradition preserved, some
old and some more recent, which, mixed up with
popular superstitions, almost seemed to imply that a
curse from Heaven lay upon them. In the vault
underneath the Oratory there lay, not the remains,
but the place where the remains should have lain, of
Sir Roger de Hawkstone, the bold profligate cour-
tier of Henry VIII., by whose arm the monarch
had expelled the monks, plundered their possessions,
including the most sacred ornaments of the chapel
and the altar, and made over the whole property
around to his avaricious minion. And the remains
of Sir Roger de Hawkstone never reached their
place of rest in holy ground. He was seized suddenly with his death pangs in the midst of a mad
drunken revel, in the hall of his new house, the hall
which, after the example of the Protector Somerset,
he had built out of the fragments of the consecrated
cloister, and, like most of the nobility of that day, had
hung with tapestry, and adorned its sideboards with
chalices and plate, which he had plundered from the
chapel itself. He died, and the room where they
laid him in state caught fire with the torches: and
before the flames were got under, the whole wing
of the house was a mass of ruins; and only one
blackened mutilated limb could be discerned and
extricated to give it the mockery of a Christian
burial. By that lay his two wives; one who had
died by poison, administered, it was always believed,
by her own husband; the other, in giving birth to
a still-born child. By them lay three children, all
childless, two daughters and one son, — the son
snatched away in his boyhood; the eldest daughter
killed with a broken heart; the youngest, the proud
haughty Lady Eleanor, childless also, and brought
to her grave with hands stained with blood and a

tainted fame.   Then followed another branch of the
family, of whom but one, the good Sir James, had
escaped the hereditary curse.   His successor was
murdered by a mob close by the tall ash tree, which
shot up by the Priory's chimney.   His son, Sir Hildebrand, had left behind him a name of vice, and
debauchery, and superstition, with which mothers
in the neighbourhood would frighten unruly children,
and threaten them with the "wicked Sir Hildebrand."   Then came a son, who was driven from
his estate by a dishonest law-suit, and the property
passed into a line, which had gradually encumbered
it with debt, harassed the tenants, parted with some
of its finest portions ; involved itself in election
squabbles, and profligate extravagances, until, followed by the hatred of all around him, the last
owner, General Villiers, had taken refuge on the
Continent, where he died, and his only son laid
him, not in the grave of his fathers, but in the
Strangers' Cemetery at Rome.   But, before that,
another name had been added to the melancholy
catalogue — a name never pronounced by any of the
older peasantry without an affectionate and reverent
sorrow — the good Lady Esther.   She was the wife
of General Villiers, and daughter of John Earl of
Claremont, whose estates adjoined the Priory.   And
like her father she was a Roman Catholic, but a
Catholic more than a Romanist ; scarcely tainted
with the sins of Popery, and a character such as
might be formed, and, we may trust, has often been
formed, in the school of Fenelon, Pascal, and Bor-
romeo.   Even she had not escaped the general inheritance of evil : compelled by her father, against
her will, to marry General Villiers, she had found
him cunning, narrow-minded, jealous, and re-
vengeful.   One son was born to them, whom she
was permitted to bring up for a few years, and

whom, as far as childhood can be formed, she had
formed to be the image of her own character. About
that time the embarrassments of the General thick-
ened on him: his temper became soured, his conduct tyrannical; losing all sense of religion himself,
the deep earnest piety of his wife provoked from
him only contempt and persecution. And, without
listening to her earnest and tearful prayers, he took
her child, now grown to be a boy, from her care,
carried him abroad, and left her to linger out one
year and three months in patient solitary suffering,
and then to be borne amidst the tears and blessings
of the poor to her last earthly resting-place in the
Priory of Hawkstone.

And even beyond Lady Esther the curse seemed
to continue. At the death of General Villiers, the
title to the large estates of Hawkstone had been disputed. His son remained abroad for years, under
circumstances which no one understood; and even
now, when his title had been acknowledged, and his
fortune increased by a considerable bequest from an
uncle, it was reported in Hawkstone that Ernest
Villiers had become himself embarrassed; that his
estates in Yorkshire were to be sold; that he was
about to turn Papist, if he had not become one
already; and, as the only mode of escaping from
his difficulties, he was to marry his cousin, Lady
Eleanor,—not a very probable combination: but the
sale of the Yorkshire estates had been announced
that very day in the papers, and Bentley, as he approached the ruins, sighed to think of the futility
and mutability of all earthly grandeur.

Before he descended the brow of the valley, the
twilight had deepened so much that he found it
difficult to search for his watch along the path which
he was retracing. The stars were coming out one
by one; the horizon in the west was fading into

the dark sky, and a pale crescent moon just faintly peered over the stag-headed skeleton of a great oak, round which the Hawkstone brook was rippling, and which was known familiarly among the cottagers by the name of Prior Silkstede's Oak ; for this also had its tale, and a tale of sorrow. It was named from a village legend of the last prior, a weak but not vicious man, who had been harassed and persecuted by Cromwell until, in an evil hour, he consented to surrender the Priory to the king, rather than risk the miserable fate of the monks of the Charter House of London, five of whom had already died under the hardships of their usage ; five were brought, by the severity of their imprisonment, to the brink of death, and many others had been executed. But no sooner was the surrender made, than the most bitter remorse had seized him. When the visitors came to carry off the vestments and plate, he had stood on the steps of the altar, and solemnly denounced the sacrilege, repeating the curse imprecated by the founder of the Priory upon all who should disturb his gifts. When forced to desist by one of the commissioners, he had gone to the foot of the old oak, and, there gathering round him the peasantry assembled on the spot, had warned them, with a bitter confession of his own infirmity, against partaking in the evil thing, and bringing down upon their heads the wrath of God. He had then left them, and wandered, no one knew whither, till one morning he was found lying on his face, cold and stiffened, with his hands clasped, as in prayer, under the old oak tree, turned to the already-demolished Priory, as if he had come to die at least within sight of its walls. And none of the villagers liked to pass at night near the Silkstede oak. Many were the fearful appearances which were recorded to have been seen there ; and latterly they had singularly multiplied. When the keepers made their morning rounds, the trampled grass and broken bushes betrayed that persons had been there in the night; it was generally supposed poachers. Voices had been heard, and even figures seen, about the ruins by late market people. And even Mr. Morgan had laughingly told Bentley, that, on his riding over the night before to Hurst, he also had passed near them, and seen a light moving about within the chapel. Bentley was not sorry to find that it was becoming too dark to search for his watch, and that his wisest plan would be to cross the valley at once, and make his way into the high road. He was not superstitious, but he was not a scoffing sceptic, and therefore he was not ashamed to feel a certain awe, and even credulity, in all that related to the mystery of a world of spirits. To effect his purpose it was necessary to follow the path by the oak, and then strike off along the Priory wall, passing under the great east window of the chapel, and so gaining the little rude bridge which crossed the brook below it. But as he approached the oak he could not help starting at the sight of a figure beneath it. It was a female, seemingly of the lower orders, sitting with her head buried in her hands, and motionless, as if in deep distress. She no sooner heard the sound of footsteps than she sprang up, with a faint cry, and was hastening to meet Bentley, until, as she came near, she turned back suddenly, as if she had mistaken the person, and diverged into the thicket, where he lost sight of her. Bentley stopped to see if she would appear again, or wanted any thing, but to no purpose; and he passed on, wondering what could have brought a poor woman, at so late an hour, to such a place. But his wonder was not to cease: as he turned the corner of the north wall, and was making his way, with some difficulty, over the frag-

ments of the building and broken ground, on which
the dormitories had stood, not without fear of falling
into some of the choked-up vaults and arches with
which the ground was full, his eye turned to one of
the lancet windows, rich with thick painted glass,
and still perfect, in the little oratory adjoining the
chapel. Was it his fancy, or the reflection of the
moon? But a faint glimmering, which struggled
through one of the panes, fixed him to the spot. It
grew in a few moments clearer and clearer; and
Bentley could not doubt that there was a light
within. He would have gone at once to see who
was there, but he remembered the rusty chains and
padlocks with which he had seen, a few hours before, that the iron grate was fastened; and he was
too well aware how many turbulent and evil-dis-
posed persons there were in the neighbourhood of
Hawkstone to expose himself to any collision with
such visitors in such a spot. He stopped, therefore,
holding his breath, and, it must be confessed, with a
beating heart. But the light remained stationary,
and, seemingly, was the reflection of a lantern, not
immediately in the oratory, but in some adjoining
passage. His next impulse was to move gently to
the window, and look in, but it was at too great a
height from the ground; and his prudence then
suggested that it would be quite sufficient to mention the next morning to Mr. Atkinson what he had
seen, and to pursue the inquiry by daylight. But
just as he had reached the east end of the chapel,
he was again startled by a clashing and fall of something like arms; and a rough voice just above him,
seemingly from the hollow of the wall, uttered a
dreadful oath, to which another voice muttered out
a grumbling, sulky answer. Bentley drew himself
close to the wall, and buried himself in a huge mass
of elder and ivy, driving from it a flight of sparrows

which had nestled there for the night. In another
minute he heard two persons jump down on the
pavement, and the light from the lantern streamed
up. Some words passed between them, which
Bentley could not understand, about "number nine"
and "fourth lodge;" and then one of them he heard
departing, with a promise to return in about half an
hour, while the other proposed to remain. Could
Bentley have seen into the chapel, he would have
recognised in the former the coarse, ruffianly Irish
vagrant, whose boy had been saved on the night of
the fire. The other he might also have recognised,
though with difficulty. He was younger, respectably dressed, with a quick, clever eye, but with features marked with passion and intemperance, and
quivering at times with a lurking fear and suspicion of detection, as if he was in possession of some
fearful secret, and was loaded with the consciousness of a deadly crime : and Bentley would scarcely
have remembered in him the sharp intelligent lad
at the National School, always foremost to answer
questions and gain prizes, who, having left the
school thoroughly tutored in reading and writing,
and thoroughly untutored in any thing else, had
soon plunged into a reckless career of vice, and had
become one of the most notorious profligates of
Hawkstone — a Socialist. He had covered up his
lantern, and was pacing backwards and forwards at
the east end of the chapel, whistling at intervals,
while Bentley, drawn up close to the other side of
the wall, and unable to move without making a
noise in the bough of ivy, was deliberating, with no
very comfortable feelings, what he should do. But
before he could make up his mind, the same brutal
voice which he had heard before called out, "Who
goes there ?" and at the same time the lantern was
flashed out upon the building. Taken by surprise,

Bentley was on the point of answering, when a timid plaintive voice from the bottom of the building uttered faintly, "It's only I, George."

"Who's I?" said the brutal ruffian.

"It's Margaret," answered the female.

"And what do you want here with your whining and pining, and spying out what you have no business to spy? How came you here?"

"Connell told me I should find you here," said Margaret, with her voice faltering.

"And what do you want to find me for?"

"I want"—— said poor Margaret, and she ran up to him, and put her pale, wan, anxious face into his hands; "O George! I am starving: I have no friends, not one upon earth, and you have left me; and I am alone, and perishing, and I want!—O George, George! give me back my child!"

And she fell down, and clasping his knees looked up to him longingly and earnestly with her eyes streaming with tears, and her long hair cast back from a countenance where delicacy and beauty were still struggling with care and sorrow.

"Fool! what brings you here?" was the only reply which the ruffian vouchsafed, as he shook her from him. "Go back quietly, and here's something to keep you from starving," and he flung her a piece of money.

But she heeded it not. "No, not money; I want no money; I want yourself, George; I want you to love me—to love me as you did when you married me!"

"Married you?" cried the wretch with a hoarse laugh; "married you!—what's marriage?"

"Yes, married me!" said Margaret, with a firmer and prouder voice. "I am your own lawful wedded wife. No one has a right to separate us; you cannot leave me. Did you not take me to your chapel? Were we not married regularly, truly joined to-

gether for ever ? Would to God we had gone to
the church as my father and mother did before me !
It could not have been so then."

" Why not?" asked the man insultingly. " What
have your priests to do with marriage? What are
their accursed contrivances, except to fasten persons, neck to neck, like galley-slaves, instead of allowing them their freedom ? No, my good girl,
we are wiser now. Go back quietly ; find out another husband; I give you full leave, and shall
never complain. Much better do this than whine
and whimper in this way."

"Never, never !" cried the horror-struck, indignant Margaret. "O George ! you did not say this
when you knew me first. You swore to me you
would never desert me. You used to kiss me, and
love me, and call me your treasure, and hang over
me, O how fondly! Do you remember when our
child was born?"

" Dolt ! idiot !" exclaimed the irritated man.
" Hold your tongue, and begone!"

" May God help me ! God have mercy upon me !"
faltered the poor woman as she sunk upon her knees.

" Ay, ay, that's the right thing," cried the man
with a horrible sneer; "go to your priests and your
prayers, they'll comfort you ; nothing can be better
for you women."

" Nor for men either," she roused herself to say.
" George, George ! the time will come when you will
die, and then you will think on me; and you will
know that there is a God in heaven who avenges the
poor ; ay, in another world ! "

" Ha! ha!" was the answer, as he burst into a
loud laugh, which made the walls of the chapel
ring, and Bentley's blood run cold.

" Yes," pursued Margaret, " there is a hell, and
you will know it, sooner or later !"

" And so this is what you get from your priests?"
said the man. " What right have they to tell me
what is to become of me? They know nothing better
than I do! Don't they tell each man to judge for himself? and why am I not as good a judge as they are?
Why, they do not believe what they teach themselves.
Here have been five or six of them here this evening,
keeping me from my work, all of them the best
friends in the world, smothering each other with
kindness, and to-morrow they will get up in their
pulpits, and swear each that the other is a liar.
No, woman, it's all a sham from beginning to end, —
a lie to cheat and frighten us, and we are beginning
to know it. We'll have no more priests!"

Margaret shuddered with horror. " Oh George!
where have you been since you left me, that you
have learned to speak in this way? What horrible
company have you been keeping?"

"The company I chanced to meet," said the man.
" And I have learned what I have learned, and
am what I am, and could not be otherwise; so do
not be afraid, Margaret," and he seemed softened
by her deep compassion for him. " Do not be
afraid, Margaret; we cannot help our opinions, you
know. We do not form them ourselves, and no
one has a right to punish or blame them. Why,
even your priests tell you this, and your precious
Whig ministers, all of them together; do not they,
my good girl?"

And he attempted to put his hand on her shoulder,
but she shrunk back as from a touch of contamination.

" And so, George," she asked with a deep groan,
" you are become an atheist?"

" An atheist!" said the man with an effort to
laugh. "An atheist! no, not an atheist. We are
religionists, rational religionists, all of us. We do

just what your priests do, and tell us to do. And
we take their Bibles and read them ourselves, and
if we do not like or understand what we read, why
we know it is false. We use our reason, as they
recommend us, and think for ourselves. And as
for atheism — no, Margaret, so long as there is
good brandy in the world, and good beef, and pudding, and a good fire, and a snug house and plenty
of money, why a man can't be an atheist. He can
worship these, you know, just as your gentlemen,
and your manufacturers, and your Chancellors of
the Exchequer are worshipping their good things.
What care they for any thing, if they have but
plenty of money?—and a good filled purse," he cried,
rattling some sovereigns in his pocket, "is as good
a thing to worship as any other. No, Margaret,
never call me an atheist! It's a mere calumny —
a bugbear."

"And you are rich, then?" faltered Margaret,
looking up at him with a famished poverty-stricken
face.

"Yes, it is better times now with me," said the
wretch, "than when we used to be starving together without a fire, and scarcely clothes to cover
us. And here's something for yourself. Take
this," and he endeavoured to put two or three sovereigns into her hands, but she let them fall without
notice.

"And what are you doing?" she asked.

"Doing?" said the man; "doing a great deal
that one of these days you'll hear of. You should
have been here five hours ago, up in the wall as I
was, and heard that young jackanapes who wants
to be member of parliament tell us what we ought
to do. We are going to recover our rights, my
girl; and we'll have a little gentle agitation, a

little moral influence, a little quiet pressure. Ah, ah!" he cried, and threw open his coat, so that the light fell on a couple of brace of pistols. "A little moral influence! ha, ha! moral influence of starving mechanics, with guns on their shoulders and pikes in their pockets. Hark!" He stopped. "Is that ten o'clock?" and the distant chime of the Hawkstone bells just faintly reached Bentley's ear. "Stop here, Margaret," he said to the poor woman, who was trembling with alarm, "and you shall see what you shall see, and know pretty well what I've been doing, — only," and here he uttered a horrible blasphemous oath, "if one word of what you have seen this night ever pass your lips"——— and he looked at her and put his hand on his pistols, "as sure as you are a living woman!"———

"Does no one know you are here?" said Margaret, faintly.

"Not a soul but that Irish brute Connell, who dares not peach."

"I fancied," said Margaret, "as I was waiting for you, that I saw another person coming. I fancied it was the parson."

"The parson!" exclaimed the man. "How I should like to catch the parson at ten o'clock at night in the Priory ruins, prying into my secrets! — if I would not slit his throat from ear to ear with as much coolness as he would mend his own pen!"

Bentley heard it, and at that moment the cold air irritated his throat, and he was on the point of coughing.

"Hold the lantern, girl, and do not be frightened!" and, giving her the lantern, he lighted a match and went down to another part of the ruins. And the next minute the poor girl heard a rushing, wavering, roaring sound, and a rocket with a prodigious train of fire rose up into the air, throwing a glare of light on the masses of walls and the grim grotesque faces with which the traceries were studded.

"Did you see that, Margaret?" said the fellow as he returned; "is not that a good blaze? Do you think we do not know how to manage our fire? and won't we make a firework of every house and farm in the country, unless they do as we choose? What's the use of science, and lectures, and Mechanics' Institutes, if they cannot teach us a little useful chemistry? Come here, girl," and with a hoarse diabolical laugh he pulled her into the antechapel.

"Now, look out there to the north, over the pillar, two minutes more :" and he began to whistle, and, before the two minutes had expired, the poor terrified Margaret saw in the distant sky another rocket shoot up, which broke and fell in a shower of sparks, but at the distance of several miles.

"Do you see that?" said the man; "is not that a clever mode of talking secrets with one's fingers at six miles distance? Now then, look there, through the window, out by the hills, where the quarries are. There it goes!" he cried.

And another rocket shot up in that direction.

"Once more come along, you poor fool!" and he dragged her reluctantly to the outside of the chapel, round to the east end, and within a few feet of the bushes in which Bentley was hidden. "Look out for the forest, there ought to be two there to-night. Ay, I thought they were awake;—fine fellows those pitmen! capital coals they work, and capital hammers they have." And as two rockets rose up side by side, over the dark outline of the mountainous district which formed the mining part of Hawkstone Forest, the man seized Margaret by the arm, and almost crushed it with his violence. "And now you see what I have been doing; and if you dare breathe a word of this!"—— and once more he threw open his coat. "If I have a tongue that can talk in this way, I have eyes that can see through stone walls, and ears in every house in the parish; and sooner than we'd be baulked of our rights, there's not a man of us who would hesitate to put you quietly out of the way, in the twinkling of an eye."

"You would not murder me?" cried the almost fainting Margaret; "you would not bear to have me murdered?"

"Murder you!" said the villain. "What do you use your cant words for? Murder means to do something wrong, and the bloody Whigs would hang one up for it. No, I would not murder you; but I tell you what I would do,—I would very quietly, and impelled by necessity,"—(and the fellow laughed at his own ethics,) "and purely under the influence of circumstances, my good girl, because I could not help it, you know, and for the good of the community at large, for the general utility,—ha! ha!—to promote our happiness and comfort, (and what business have we with any thing else, as your parsons and your philosophers — ha! ha! — have been telling you for ages?) — why, Margaret (and he lowered his voice to a deep hoarse pitch, and put a pistol to her ear), "I would blow out your brains this instant."

"Spare me, spare me!" cried Margaret, sinking down on the ground.

"Spare you?" said the man, "to be sure I will; you have not peached yet, and do not intend to peach: and now get you gone, for I have some more work to do, and cannot stand here chattering. What are you stopping for?" he cried, with an oath, as the poor woman, who had risen up almost stupified, lingered and seemed summoning up courage to approach him again. "What do you want more?"

And once more she ran to him, fell at his feet, and clasped his knees. " O George, George! forgive me! spare me! don't kill me, don't be angry, only tell me, and I will go away quietly, quite quietly. You promised you would — O George, George! where is my baby?"

The wretch uttered a horrible imprecation, and almost stamped upon her. "What have you to do with your baby, you fool? What have any of us to do with babies, when we are starving and dying piece-meal? — men enough in the world already, without having more to breed a famine!" (Margaret's blood ran cold.) "Away with you!"

"No!" she cried, gaining courage with despair; "I will not away, I will not leave you! you promised I should know where it was. My own child, my beautiful baby! you took it away, and you shall give it me again. Would to God that I had died before I slept that night! We were starving, we were dying; but so long as that baby was on my breast, I could bear any thing. And now"—— and a flood of tears followed at the thought of her own misery and desolation. "Tell me," she continued, "tell me only one thing, — is it safe? is it well? does it seem to know you? are they taking care of it? You promised they would take care of it. You swore to me it should want for nothing; that it should be quite happy."

"Ay! ay!" said the man, with something like a groan, "quite happy! It wants for nothing, woman, take my word for it, and never will."

"My God, my God!" cried the miserable woman, as she caught the gloomy expression of his eye, and a bitter smile about his lip, "it is not — no, George, you would not deceive me! you would not kill me! you do not mean"—— and she stopped, choked with her dreadful anticipation.

" Go along, Margaret. Go along, and ask no questions. What's the use of asking questions? It's all right."

" All right — and my baby is well? Thank God! God Almighty be praised! O bless you, bless you! dear, dearest George! — quite well — you are sure, quite well?" And her voice faltered as she caught again the gloomy expression of his eye, though she thought it seemed moistened for the moment.

" Ay, go away — go away! all's right — all's right," said the man.

" No! no!" said Margaret, for she knew his notions of right, and that every thing expedient was right, and she trembled at his repetition of the phrase; for, hardened as he was, he rather wished to avoid a lie. " Do not say all's right. Tell me with your own lips my baby is well, quite well."

" Nonsense!" said the man; " why then, quite well." But the words choked him, and he tried to slur them over.

" And I may see it?" exclaimed Margaret. " I may see it? When may I go? I am barefoot — look, George, since you left me I have not had shoes to my feet: but miles, oh! millions of miles, would I walk to have one sight of my darling baby — one kiss! When may I go? to-night?"

" Yes, to-night, fool!" cried the wretch, exasperated and infuriated with her perseverance.

" And at once?" exclaimed Margaret; " and with you?"

" Yes, woman!" he cried, as he became furious; " at once, and with me!" and he seized her by the arm with a horrible execration, and dashed her on the ground a few yards off, close by the buttress of the chapel. " There! there!"

And Margaret saw fresh mould and turf, which had been disturbed, and the horrible truth flashed upon her. She raised herself up on her knees, and gazed on him like a furious tigress; and before he could recover himself, she had sprung and fastened round his neck. "Monster! murderer! Murder! murder! help! help! He has murdered my child! Help! help!" and her cries rang through the walls of the ruin, and startled the screech-owls in the wood. "Murder! murder! help! help! take him! seize him! he has murdered my child!"

"Silence, woman! silence!" muttered the man, as he vainly endeavoured to release his neck from her iron grasp. "Silence!"

But Margaret's shrieks and cries for help did not cease; and, without speaking, he contrived to disengage one hand and seize his pistol. But the next moment he was pulled upon his knees, and the pistol went off. There was a man wrestling with him in the bushes, wrestling desperately and franticly; and as they rolled together on the ground, the villain saw that it was a young figure, of little strength, and unarmed. It was Bentley. "A priest, by all that's holy!" he muttered; and throwing away the pistol, the only one which had been loaded, he coolly prepared himself for the struggle, with the certainty that he must be the master. "Not very wise to be here at this time of night," said the wretch as he succeeded in turning Bentley under him, and getting his knee upon his chest. "Not very wise to be prying into other people's secrets at this time of night!" and Bentley, sickening with the pressure, began to relax his hold of the ruffian's neck. With one hand pinning him down, with the other the man began to fumble in his coat, and a dreadful oath showed that he had a difficulty in finding what he sought. Bentley took the opportunity of springing up once more and making a last desperate effort; but his strength

was nearly exhausted. " Down! down!" cried the
villain. " Lie still!" and he dashed him to the
ground : and as Bentley's eyes turned up, he saw
something in the murderer's hand which glittered
in the moonlight : his eyes closed, and, having just
time to utter a prayer, in the next minute he was
senseless.

CHAP. XI.

IT is now time to return to the spot on the side of the hill, where, in the afternoon, the stranger had stopped and looked back, to catch the music of the Temperance Society, as it issued from the outskirts of the wood. As he saw the banners and the people, a dark shade came over his countenance, and with a gesture of impatience he turned away to pursue his solitary walk. One only expression escaped him as he stood a little farther on with arms folded, as if in deep and painful thought; but our readers may like to hear it, for it was uttered from the bottom of his heart. "O Rome! Rome! thou curse of the earth! what crimes thou hast to answer for!" and he then passed on.

But, buried in thought, he scarcely heeded even the magnificent scenery through which his path took him. He followed it once more to the top of the park, and then struck off down a steep declivity, the sides of which were furrowed into three deep ravines formed by the descending waters. The little streams themselves fell over masses of rock, here spreading into dark pools, and there eating unseen into the overhanging banks: and above them the sides rose steeply, covered with old oak trunks, and thorns, and fern, from which the deer were startled and bounded off as the stranger approached. At one point the eye could pass down over all this depth of wood, and range over a plain beyond it, then lighted up with the bright evening shadows. To the west lay the forest of Hawkstone, stretching in a long black ridge, and terminated at one extremity by three conical mountain heights folding one behind the other, between which the sun was preparing to sink, and was then melting down their hard clear outline into a flood of the palest gold. Still nearer lay Claremont Castle, with its ruined keep and broken tower, hanging over the Hawkstone brook, which there widened into a stream, and wound snakelike through the meadows. Lord Claremont's modern house was not visible; it was hidden by a projecting grove of oaks: and at one time the stranger, who had before scrupulously avoided looking in that direction, seemed to make up his mind to face the sight, and tried to discover it; but in vain. At the bottom of the ravine, just where it opened and the stream made its way into the lower park, he rested against a gate near an ivy-covered, old brick building used by the keepers in killing the deer, and gazed on two gigantic firs whose tall red stems, all scarred and peeled, bore up their mass of dark green foliage from the bottom, nearly to a level with the top of the bank. Beneath them, but planted so as to form a group, was a fine stone pine carefully enclosed; and the ground round its roots seemed to have been recently stirred, as if by some hand anxious for its growth; and as the stranger looked upon the pine, his thoughts wandered off to a still brighter clime, and to hours when he sat amongst the gardens of Florence with another person at his side (and he gave an audible groan at the recollection), gazing on the tall wild outline of the same trees as they jagged the blue horizon of an Italian sky.

" Lady Esther's trees, sir," said a respectable old peasant, coming up and taking off his hat to the stranger, and exhibiting one of those fine, placid, sensible old faces for which the peasantry of England were once famed, and which even now may occasionally be seen on the Sunday in the open pews of a village church, looking up attentively to the preacher, and catching and applying every word. " My barometers," as Charles Bevan used to call them, when I wish to know if my sermon is understood.—" Poor Lady Esther's trees."

The stranger turned, took off his hat also, and looked mournfully on the intruder, who also seemed struck with something, without exactly knowing what.

" Sir Robert Haswell, the great painter," continued the peasant, " used to say those were the finest trees in the county; and he never came to the Priory, but my lady and he used to come up here; and I have seen them stand half an hour together close by this gate looking at them."

The stranger only answered, " Yes, my good man, they are very fine trees." " And what," he asked with a faint smile, " is that young tree?"

" That, sir," said the old man—" that's Master Ernest's pine—planted when he was born: and please God he may come to see how it is grown. Not a day passes but I look after it. But oh ! sir ; it is a sad thing for the owner of this fine place to be in foreign parts, and all this going to ruin ; and the people caring nothing for any body, and knowing nothing of the landlord, except when they pay their rents. It is not good, sir, nor right; and things cannot be well when we are all left in this way to ourselves without our betters to take care of us."

" Certainly not," said the stranger, " but we will hope your master may come to live among you."

" Oh, sir, I hope he may ; but there is bad news

at the house, they say. People talk of his having turned papist, and being in debt, and selling all his property, so soon after he has got it again. But then, it is not my business to talk of master's affairs. And I beg your pardon, sir."

"How long has he been absent?" asked the stranger.

"Ever since Lady Esther's death, sir. I have not set eyes on him these twenty years. The old General took him away before, but he came back then for a few days, and ever since that he has been with him in foreign parts, except when he was at college. And things have all gone wrong since the General's death, and now, just as we thought things were coming right, why, they say he's a ruined man."

"I hope not," said the stranger half smiling. "We must not believe all we hear."

"Oh, sir, if he would only come back and settle among us, and take an interest in us, and teach us what to do! Now, sir, things are all at sixes and sevens, and the bad people at Hawkstone are riding over the country; and the miners out there," and he pointed to the forest, "are getting arms, and having torchlight meetings. And the farmers won't pay their tithes, and the church is tumbling down, because the parish won't make a rate, and the poor care nothing for any body, for their wages are ground down almost to nothing, and nobody comes to see them. And if they want justice, they must go to Mr. Smith the cotton man, whom they have made a magistrate of, because he votes for the radicals, instead of having it from their own landlord. In short, sir, I wish it were the old times again, when landlords, and tenants, and labourers all hung together; and we had none of those ugly factories corrupting the men and women, and no fine talk

about reform, which for my part I believe is all
nonsense. If people want reforming, they had
better reform themselves, and that is the only way
of reforming."

"I think so too," said the stranger. "This is
the way to the house, is it not? Good afternoon."
And the old man pointed out the path, looked after
him with a sort of wonder, and could not help muttering to himself, "how very like!" A short turn
of the path soon brought the stranger in view of
the house. It was one of those "old and reverent
piles," which no one has so well described as
Wordsworth, with deep bay windows, and wrought
gables, porches, and mullioned arches, high twisted
chimneys, and pinnacles wreathed with ivy, and all
the rich quaint carving of the Elizabethan age. At
one corner stood a fragment of an older building, in
the shape of a square massive tower, called Sir
Bevor's tower, which rose up from the terrace, and
recalled by its dark solid masonry the days when
the lords of Hawkstone had been knights in armour,
and Sir Bevor himself, whose figure lay cross-legged
in the cathedral of ——, had led a body of its yeomen
to the Holy Wars. Although an incongruity in
architecture, the tower formed a feature of no little
interest. Not so with a line of building of modern
Italian taste, raised on the site of the wing, which
had been burnt down on Sir Roger's death. It
connected itself with the stable-yard, and was intended for offices. But there was a disproportion
and gaudiness about it which shocked the eye; and
the stranger evidently regarded it with considerable
disgust. And yet, on the whole, few English mansions were more striking than Hawkstone. Its
green terraces sloped up the hill behind, and were
connected with the house by balustrades and vases.
In front, beneath a rough overhanging bank, lay a

small sheet of water, reflecting in that calm sunny afternoon every line of the building, its oriels glittering with the sinking sun, and the rich foliage which bent over it from the back. And at the corner of the tower lay a small square platform studded with parterres and vases in the old French taste, and commanded by a range of windows in the south front, to one of which, a richly wrought Gothic oriel with a small lancet adjoining, the stranger looked up, and gazed at it evidently with considerable emotion.

As he approached the house, he did not observe that there were marks of carriage-wheels on the broad gravel before the door, and that the great gates which opened into the stable-yard were open. The old housekeeper, who had been in the house ever since Lady Esther's time, and indeed had been her favourite maid, was very ill. And a young grand-daughter, to whom the stranger gave a note from Mr. Atkinson, the steward, led him timidly through the great hall hung round with pieces of armour and stags' heads, and through the ante-room and dining-room, with its oriel window and huge cumbered chimney-piece, and the retiring-room, which more modern taste had enlivened with gilded cornices and fretwork, now faded and dull. And there were pictures of mailed knights, and stiff ladies in ruffs and farthingales; and venerable old gentlemen in wigs and brocaded coats; and a few good busts; and in the library, a long, oak-wainscoted apartment, opening into various recesses, and dark with painted glass, there was a large collection of books, on which the stranger looked with evident satisfaction. The little girl could not, indeed, understand his movements. He seemed to open the doors as if he knew the house thoroughly. Before one or two pictures he stopped with earnest interest. The others he passed by carelessly; and she endeavoured in vain to repeat some of the lore connected with them, which she had learned from her grandmother.

"Would he like to see the curiosities? the fine embroidered velvet pall, which had been brought from the Priory when it was pulled down, and which Sir Hildebrand, the sallow dissipated-looking man whose portrait, in the costume of Charles II.'s time, hung on the north side of the dining-room, had turned into a coverlet for his bed?" The stranger declined.

"Should she show him the great gilt cup, which was also brought from the same place, and which Sir Roger had in his hand, and was drinking out of it, at the very time when he was taken with the convulsions of which he died." The stranger shook his head; he would go upstairs into the gallery, and look at the pictures there, and his little guide need not follow him. He would prefer looking at them by himself. And half-doubting, notwithstanding Mr. Atkinson's guarantee, if she might trust him there without her, and looking back wistfully, as he ascended the grand staircase, she took her bunch of keys, and proceeded to reclose the doors of the rooms through which they had passed. At the top of the staircase a pair of folding doors, with pillars and richly carved capitals, opened into the long gallery, ceiled with stucco-work, and lined with portraits, and furnished with old cabinets and curious encoignures, and high-backed ebony chairs and marble tables, all of which the stranger passed unnoticed. His eye was fixed on a door at the end of it, which he seemed rather surprised to find ajar. He opened it gently, very gently, almost as if he was afraid of disturbing some one within. It was a large lofty room, hung with tapestry, containing a

heavy-carved bed, heavy-carved wardrobes and
cabinets, old worked chairs, and a toilette laid out
with a rich silver apparatus for a lady's use ; and
over the fireplace was a full-length portrait of a
lady also. It was the bedroom of Lady Esther.
And as she looked down from the picture on the
cold melancholy apartment, herself all radiant with
youth, and beauty, and the brilliancy of her bridal
attire, the contrast seemed too painful to the
stranger. He turned to a smaller portrait, only
half finished, in which the same high noble countenance, but marked with lines of care and sorrow,
was bending over a young child, and watching him
with tears in her eyes, as he lay sleeping, not on her
bosom, but in the arms of a nurse ; and the tears
came into the eyes of the stranger likewise — tears
which fell faster as he stood by the side of the bed.
For the last time he had been in that room it was
darkened, and hung round with funeral lights ; and
he had been brought there, awe-struck and wondering, to cast a last look on a gorgeous coffin ; and
the time before that the room was also darkened,
but, instead of the trappings of sorrow, there only
lay upon that bed, covered decently with white, a
pale, cold, unmoving figure, resting as it were from
a great agony, and every line of sorrow softened
into peace ; and the stranger well remembered his
being lifted up upon the bed and giving a kiss ! —
how chill and awful ! — to that marble forehead. And
the day before that, he had been also brought into the
same room by the old housekeeper, now lying ill ;
and how well he recollected that hour. Years
had passed away, but as he now stood by the bed-
side, the whole scene came back upon him with
a vivid distinctness, which almost appalled him.
There was the pale faint form of Lady Esther, supported by pillows, turning round longingly to the

door where he was expected to enter, and waving to
have the curtains undrawn that the light might fall
once more upon the face of her beautiful boy; and
he had been wrapt in her embrace for minutes
without either of them uttering a word, and he himself hearing nothing but the beating of her heart,
and feeling a stream of tears falling on his face.
And then she moved him from her, and turned him
to the light, gazing on him with a look of sorrow
and affection which he had never forgotten. And
once more he was buried in her arms, and he heard
prayer on prayer, faintly, yet all distinctly, poured
over his head with the energy of a dying saint.
She had made a sign, also, to her maid, to bring her
something from a casket on the dressing-table; and
whispering to him softly, "They will not prohibit
this, they will not take this from you," she put
round his neck with her own thin transparent hands
a chain of her own hair, from which hung a plain
little cross of gold; and the cross she put gently into
his own hands, pressed them together, and looked
up to heaven, and once more kissing his forehead
with a long fervent kiss of blessing, she motioned
to the servant that she could bear to part with him,
and as she sunk back upon the pillow, he was taken
out of the room.

Nor were these all the recollections of that chamber. No! almost ashamed of himself for their intrusion, he thought of days still earlier, and of very
different occupations, when, as a child, he used to
play by his mother's side in that same room, and
make her show him the treasures of those silver
boxes, and tell him stories; when he would sit at
her feet, (there was the stool before him, just as it
used to be, at the foot of the great ebony chair,)
playing with his puzzle, or learning his lesson, or
looking over picture-books; not alone, but with a

companion of his own age, or, as he always used to
call her, his little wife, his cousin Eleanor. He
dared not trust himself longer, but moved, with his
arms crossed, to another door, which opened, seemingly, into a little sitting-room belonging to the
suite.   The curtains were closed, and it was nearly
dark, but a door beyond was open, and a stream of
rich light from the narrow lancet window fell beyond
it into a small Gothic oratory, which had been fitted
up for the use of Lady Esther.   There was the
richly wrought niche over the altar, containing a
crucifix of the purest ivory ; the canopied fan-like
roof, the silver lamp, the illuminated Missal, the
small gold candelabra, the footstool where Lady
Esther used to kneel, all exactly as he remembered
it when, as a child, he had been allowed occasionally
to look into this sacred recess, where, several times a
day, Lady Esther used to retire in the midst of even
her most busy avocations, and where, since General
Villiers had gone away to the Continent and taken
her son with him, she spent the greater part of her
time in prayer.

But the stranger saw none of these. For before
the altar, her back towards him, and her head upturned as in a posture of the deepest devotion, there
was a female figure kneeling, who did not hear his
approach, and yet whose thoughts at that moment
were full of him, were praying for him. It was
Lady Eleanor. He could not doubt it. It was her
tall, graceful form ; the exquisite shape of her head,
the slender neck. Even the dress he recognised ;
the same which she had worn when they parted,
three months before, at Florence. What a meeting !
He stood for a minute fixed to the spot, not astonished
to see her, for he knew she was in the country, but
amazed that their first meeting should be in such a
place, so consecrated to the recollection of them

both. Gathering all his resolution to bear the meeting as he ought, he recollected himself sufficiently to endeavour to withdraw from intruding or disturbing her at such a moment. But the noise he made in moving roused her attention. As she turned round, she caught his figure retreating through the outer door, and, before she knew what she was doing, his name had escaped from her lips. In a moment he was at her side, on his knees before her, covering her hands with kisses ; and she, slightly endeavouring to withdraw them, was looking as if a load had been taken from her heart, and a long-hoped-for, long-delayed joy, a joy too great for utterance, had suddenly arrived. But it lasted only for a minute. His eye caught the crucifix over the altar, and he shuddered ; and dropping her hands and rising up before her, with an altered tone, which made the blood forsake her cheek, and leave on it a fixed look of disappointment and despair, he faltered out, " Forgive me ! forgive me, Lady Eleanor —I have no right—I am not master of myself. I am much to blame—I was not prepared to meet you. Forgive me for the intrusion. I did not know you were here."

" They told me," said she, faintly, " that you were in Yorkshire. I came here to see poor Collins, who is very ill, and wished to see me before she became worse."

" You have been," he said, " at Claremont, then, some days."

" Yes, my father came down on Saturday."

And there was a dead pause.

" And you will stay here, then, for the autumn ?"

" Yes," she replied ; " perhaps all the winter."

They were silent again ; but Ernest was recovering himself.

" We shall meet, then ; we must meet often," he

said, with a firm but painful effort. And a slight gleam of hope came across her mind. " We shall see each other very often, as in old times."

" Yes," was her faint answer, and all hope had vanished, "as in old times."

" As friends ? "

" Yes, as friends."

" Not as common friends ? " said Ernest.

" No," she replied, for she also was gaining strength ; " as very dear friends."

" As brother and sister ? "

" Yes," was her answer, and her eyes filled with tears ; " as brother and sister."

And once more he took her hand, and pressed it reverentially to his lips. But the effort was too much for her, and she sunk down in a seat, and cried violently.

He stood by her in silence, waiting for her feelings to find vent, and his own tears falling fast with hers. By degrees her emotion subsided, and she looked up, and stretched out her hand to him, which he took in both his own. " This is sad weakness, Ernest, sad weakness," she said ; " but you will not think I wish it otherwise. Act according to your duty, as I would act by mine. Do not think me wicked enough to wish that you should tamper with your conscience. I mean,"—she corrected herself (for she knew how the word conscience is abused) —" with your faith, with your religion. Better for us both to be miserable, separate, than to be joined without God's blessing."

" Not miserable, dear Eleanor, not wholly miserable," said Ernest ; " you will have your comfort, and God will give me mine. We cannot be miserable, you know" (and he vainly attempted to smile), " when we are doing His will."

" May God forgive me the words!" she said, and she lifted up her hands. " No, Ernest, we will not be miserable. We can love each other, even now, as brother and sister."

" And we can pray for each other," said Ernest.

" Morning, and evening, and every hour," she exclaimed fervently. " O Ernest! if you knew ——" but here her voice failed. " Let us come out," she resumed soon, " out into the open air. This room is stifling."

And he gave her his arm, and, by a winding staircase at the corner of the tower, they made their way out on the terrace.

It was a still delicious hour. The birds were carolling in the trees, the waters glittering in the sunshine, the swans on the lake oaring their way in little fleets, the deer lying under the oaks with no footstep to disturb them. One solitary fleecy vapour was sailing gently across the setting sun. The flowers looked up, as they passed, as if delighted to waft their fragrance to them. The very air breathed like balm upon their heated foreheads, and Ernest, much as he loved at all times to dwell with nature, felt that he never before had known the power of its soft gentle music in lulling a troubled heart, where the heart was right with God. The turret clock struck four as they came out upon the terrace. It was five before they left it. Now that all hope was over, Eleanor, quieted and resigned, could almost talk to him as she used to talk ; could begin to feel to him as she used to feel before she had ever thought of him except as a playmate and a brother. He asked for the good Abbé St. Maur, who was still at Claremont with the Earl. He spoke of foreign scenes, where they had travelled together. He even ventured to tell her much of what had passed since they parted at Florence, while still there was a lingering thought that he might yet be converted into the Romish communion, and thus claim Eleanor's hand on the only terms on which Eleanor, with all her love for him, would listen to his affection. And then he entered on his plans; told her why he had remained in Hawkstone privately, partly in his dread of meeting her until all his arrangements were settled, but chiefly that he might compare by himself the real circumstances of his two estates, and decide which he should part with, that he might reside entirely on the other.

"You know," he told her, and Eleanor looked up to him with a pride which she no longer attempted to disguise, "that I hold the possession of land a most solemn and responsible trust. A landlord is the king of the soil, and as a king, he cannot have a divided empire without doing injustice to one portion of it or the other. I have, therefore, resolved to sell my estates in Yorkshire. They are quiet, comparatively happy, compared with these; here, every thing is turbulent, and full of evil, I fear of serious danger. And I have chosen to station myself here, and by God's help, I hope to try what can be done in one little spot, at least, to save us from the iniquities, and follies, and approaching curses, of this unhappy land—done," he said, (and once more a pang went to Eleanor's heart, but he was resolved that, cost what it may, his decision should be definitively known,) "done as a Protestant may do it—as a devoted son of the English branch of the Holy Catholic Apostolical Church may hope to do, and may pray for God's blessings on his labours."

"May you have them, Ernest," was her only reply. "And you shall have my prayers, and you will give me yours?"

He said nothing, but pressing her hand led her to the carriage, which had just drawn up, and the meeting was over.

CHAP. XII.

THE carriage rolled away; turned down the sycamore avenue out of sight; and then it was, that
Ernest felt the struggle which he had been making. The excitement was gone: the delight of
seeing her, of walking by her, witnessing the purity
and elevation of her thoughts, feeling that she
loved him, though she could never be his—the
consciousness that he was sacrificing himself to
what he believed his duty—all seemed to vanish
with her, and a cold dreary blank fell upon his
heart. The very sun itself, and the bright landscape which had soothed him so before, now became
melancholy and inanimate. The whole of life
seemed stretched before him as a long, dreary, te-
dious waste. And more than once his resolutions
failed; more than once an evil tempter whispered to him, that forms of faith were not essential
to religion; that charity was the essence of piety;
that opinions are not controllable, and, therefore,
are not to be censured; that marriage is a civil
ceremony, convenient and conducive to the tranquillity and morality of states, but that no solemn
spiritual union is implied in it, which should prevent
it from joining as one body those of different communions in spirit, or rather, a living member of the
Church and one who was cut off from its fountain
of life by heathenism, or heresy, or schism. Happily
he had been well taught, and he repelled the suggestions manfully.

And now we must ask forgiveness for a long, a very long parenthesis, to interpret much that has passed, and all that is to come.

Some outline of Ernest's history the reader must have gathered already. He was the only child of Lady Esther: as such, and as heir to the large Villiers' property, he was reared up from his infancy in habits of command, which, but for the watchful care and discipline of his mother, would have moulded him into a little tyrant. He had within him the proud haughty spirit of all the Villierses. Around him he saw nothing but obsequiousness to his wishes, and a stiff ceremonious mode of life, not relaxed, but rather increased by the strict adherence of Lady Esther to the principles of the Roman Catholic Church. So long as he continued as a child under her care, his imperious disposition was kept down by her rigid but affectionate superintendence. But when the General, soured in temper by pecuniary embarrassments, and incapable of sympathising with her devotional habits, insisted on executing the miserable condition proposed at their ill-assorted union, of bringing up the boys in the religion of the father, and the girls under the wing of the mother, Ernest was taken from her, and placed first under a well-intentioned but injudicious tutor, who endeavoured to eradicate any seeds of Popery which might have been implanted by his mother's influence, and to form him to habits of religion by violent appeals to his feelings, and by continual theological controversy, which his mind was not capable of bearing; for few persons seem to understand, in the education of children, that the religious frame of mind, not the religious knowledge, is the effect to be sought for—that a child's religion consists not in quoting texts of Scripture, or in making long prayers, but in reverencing, loving, and obeying the parents and teachers whom God has placed over them; in worshipping God through them and in them; and seeing Him dimly and faintly beyond them as a mystery, and only as a mystery, which gradually clears up into open day as obedience to His earthly representatives prepares the heart and soul for obeying Himself. Young as Ernest was, his feelings were chilled rather than warmed by these efforts to excite them. And with a sagacity common to children, he soon detected the latent weakness and even insincerity, which must exist, wherever there is an habitual forced effort to excite religious feeling by outward professions of it. He was, in fact, even as a child, disgusted with religion; and, if at any times he thought of it with pleasure, it was in the recollection of his mother — of the little simple hymns which he had learned at her knee, of her own unaffected devotions, of the prayers rather than the preaching which formed her religious exercises both by herself and with him, and especially of that tone of unhesitating, unsuspecting authority with which she always spoke, and which, he knew not how, seemed wanting in his tutor's admonitions.

From his tutor's he was sent to Eton. And at Eton, as he rose to the top of the school, his talents developed themselves gradually, and with them the imperiousness of his temper, which made him stand aloof from the rest of his companions, and confine himself to the society of one friend who was of a similar disposition to himself; and which soon brought him the reputation of a haughty and overbearing boy. And yet Ernest was not overbearing in the common sense of the word. To weaker boys he was kind and gentle; to the generality careless; to his superiors really haughty. His companions disliked him, and the masters could not understand him. And there was only one occasion, a rebellion, on which he came forward prominently, and by a bold, independent act, which set all the school at defiance, prevented considerable mischief. But for the most part he lived alone; his walks were solitary, his reading generally at night, when others were gone to bed. He seldom joined in games; and when he did, it seemed to be as if in scorn of himself, though no one excelled him in any sport which he chose to undertake.

From Eton he came to Oxford. And still the same reserved and exclusive mood made him regarded with fear by inferior men, and with dislike by nearly all. The one or two friends, indeed, who were admitted to his rooms, spoke of him with enthusiasm. But when thrown into general society there was a sarcastic expression about his lips, a thoughtful irony in his language, and a gloominess on his brow, which repelled every approach. Gloominess, we said, for Ernest was far from happy. He had nothing to fill his mind. Ordinary follies and dissipations he had none, for he had too much pride. Against worse excesses he was saved by the daily and almost hourly recollection of his mother, whose picture hung over his fire-place, and who seemed, to his fancy, to embody the perfection of pure, delicate, dignified, and commanding woman. He made no effort to obtain any distinction; left competitors whom he might easily have vanquished to carry off prizes without rivalship, chalked out a line of reading for himself, and attended to his lectures only sufficiently to avoid censure. He always took his place in the class-room on one seat, rather out of sight, which no one else ventured to appropriate; and when a tutor spoke to him, he answered with a reserve which, without the slightest disrespect, discouraged all attempts to gain his confi-

dence. And in the mean time his imagination was
running wild in an endeavour to find some realisa-
tion for dreams of ambition, and knowledge, and
goodness, without which life seemed to him a waste.
Around him all was mean and petty — meaner and
pettier the more it was compared with the marks of
giants' heads and giants' intellects stamped upon those
remains of past generations, beneath the shade of
which he was living. He saw statesmen succeeding to
the helm of the greatest empire formed by man, and
yet bowing to each gust of popular clamour, dreading
to assert a truth or hazard a principle; hiding in
false shame or falser fear the grandeur of their own
destination, and breaking and frittering up a glorious
system in vain attempts to purchase (from a mob)
security for the superstructure by surrendering instalments of the foundation. Still nearer he beheld in his own university a congeries of grand in-
corporations armed with wealth, talent, influence,
and dignity, capable of commanding the education
of the country, of beating, as it were, almost as the
heart and pulse of the British empire, and of spreading its arms to grasp on every side the command of
all its moral movements; and yet no grand scheme
of improvement—no organised resistance to the mis-
chiefs which were gathering on the country—scarcely
a recognition or sense of the awful responsibilities
laid by Providence on the rulers of such a body,
seemed to break the dulness and repose, in which
the constituted authorities of Oxford clung to the
narrow lines of existing associations and habits.
" What," thought Villiers to himself, " what would
Oxford have been made at such a crisis in the hands
of Popery!" Nor, when he turned to his book-
shelves, filled as they were at each return of the
season with the newest publications, and searched
through on each fresh arrival to discover some sa-

tisfaction to his longing after energy and power,
did he find what he required. Novels, reviews,
magazines, trumpery histories, autobiographies,
Scotch metaphysics, and, still worse, Scotch œcono-
mics, met him till he turned from them with loathing. Once he caught with delight at one of Carlyle's
publications ; and plunged into a course of German
studies, till here, also, he discovered the same hollowness, and vanity, and coldness, though masked
under a more pretending mysticism. And his final
refuge lay in the old and great writers of Greece,
whose empire over the human mind he seemed to
share, as he was enabled to stand by their side and
to appreciate the justice of their conquests. From
Philosophy (the step was necessary), he came upon
Theology. And the controversy of the day, which
brought before him as the one prominent object,
the Image of the Church, seized at once upon his
mind, and opened to his fancy all that he had so
long been dreaming of. Here, then, was the power
for which his heart was yearning, and for which all
Nature seemed to cry aloud, — a power divine,
though upon earth, bearing in its hands the keys of
Truth, opening and closing at will the fountain
springs of good and evil, swaying the hearts of
men, and overruling the oscillations of their reason,
and capable of binding into one the straggling elements of society, till all affections should be absorbed in one object, and every movement subdued
to one law. It was a grand conception for a grand
mind ; and from the moment that Villiers realised it,
he became an altered being. A load seemed to have
been taken from his breast ; the world wore a
brighter aspect ; life had an object, and reasoning a
foundation in truth. He could now venture to do
what before he had often feared to do — to think and
to inquire into the destinies of man and the Provi-

dence of God. And it was in this frame of mind, before he had time or opportunity to study the reali- sation of his idea in the history of the Church, and to penetrate deeply into the differences of the va- rious communities of Christians, that he was sum- moned to join his father at Rome.

CHAP. XIII.

It was a warm and brilliant evening, about a month
after his arrival there, that he stood on the steps
which lead up to the Palace of the Senators : but
not alone. With him, but a little retired behind
him, and watching him with deep earnestness, stood
a pale, calm, silent figure, in the garb of a Roman
ecclesiastic. His thin lips were compressed in
thought : his eyes, deep set, and filled with a singular lustre, were fixed on every movement of
Villiers : his hands were not merely crossed on his
breast, but clasped and folded, it seemed in prayer :
and over all his face, on which high intellectual
power and purity was stamped, there was spread a
chastened yet ardent humility, strongly contrasted
with the bold and commanding contemplativeness
of his companion's eye. One seemed bowed down
by a weight above him, beneath which he nevertheless moved with power and willingness, not
without enjoyment : the other stood as lord and
monarch of all around him, free and bold to move
in any direction, to search into any mysteries, to
mould every thing according to his will.

"And this, then," said Villiers after a long silence, "this is the Capitol—the Capitol of Ro-
mulus and Numa, of Scipio and Marius, of Cicero
and Augustus. And here, then, was the throne of
the world !"

And as he turned to look upon the paltry modern
edifices by which it is disfigured, a slight tinge of
sarcasm fell from his look upon his companion.

" And there," said his companion, stretching out his arm toward the dome of St. Peter's, " there *is* the Capitol—the Capitol of Rome and of all Christians ! "

" And where," asked Villiers, "are its triumphs?"

" Not," said his companion, and his eyes turned up to Heaven,—" not where our heathen triumphs have now passed for ever. Those which are gone are passed into heaven, and those which are upon earth are before you. Look," he said, and pointed to a long procession of pilgrims (it was a year.of jubilee) which was winding its way between the colonnades of St. Peter's.

As Villiers turned to look at his companion, his eye met from him a steady, piercing, but sad and anxious gaze; and even his own proud spirit quailed before him. Neither of them spoke for some minutes; and the silence seemed scarcely broken by the deep and almost internal, thrilling, low voice with which the ecclesiastic asked him when he intended to leave Rome. Villiers felt that a fascination was upon him—how, or from whence, he scarcely knew—and he tried to break it by answering coldly, " In a week." But the effort was vain.

" And you will go from hence," said his companion, still in the same charmed voice, " to Athens ?"

" Yes," said Villiers; and he affected to answer as if he did not feel the spell. " I must tread the ground where Plato taught; where Socrates died; where Æschylus dreamed; and where the people that have subdued the minds of ages are now lying in the dust. Athens has been before me, as the first place of my pilgrimage, ever since I read the Phædo."

" You have visited, then," continued the ecclesiastic, "the tombs of the Holy Apostles. You have studied all the wonders of that art, and the history of that wisdom, with which this place has enlightened the earth. Have you descended into the Catacombs?"

Villiers felt all that was meant, and simply answered "Yes."

"And from Athens," continued his companion in the same low unearthly voice, "you will go to Delphi, the oracle of the heathen world, to Egypt, to the Pyramids."

"I hope to do so," answered Villiers.

"To stand," continued his companion, "on the summit of mighty structures, on which the storms of ages have beaten, and beaten in vain; and to bring before your eye at one glance the mystery of time absorbed in eternity—of change coeval with immortality?"

"Such have been my thoughts," said Villiers.

"And such are mine," replied his companion. "But I need not quit this spot. Are we not at this moment at the Oracle of the Christian World —at the Pyramids of human empire—one and the same empire, whether its throne be placed on one side of the Tiber or the other?"

Villiers made no answer, but the thought struck deep; and his companion knew it, and refrained from disturbing it for some minutes.

"You are young," he continued at last: "who would have expected thoughts so deep from one so young? Have you ever thought that, as time may be swallowed up in eternity, and yet both co-exist together, so extension may be swallowed up, and space all but annihilated, and yet exist? You have railroads in England,"— and a faint contemptuous smile played on his cold lips: "are you not proud of them, as triumphs over the greatest of fetters cast on man's soul by God, the fetters of space?"

"They are grand proofs," replied Villiers, "of the power and dignity of man."

"Yes," replied his companion; "to see beyond the vision of the eyes, to hear beyond the hearing of the ears, to stretch out our arms over the world, removing mountains and bridging oceans without moving from our place,—is not this ubiquity, and is not ubiquity an attribute of Deity? And so far as science and machinery enable man to realise this problem, so far they bring him nearer to the perfection of his nature. It is, indeed, a wonder. Look," he said, and he took from his pocket a packet of letters: "one post this morning has brought me letters from every quarter of the globe." And with calmness free from all ostentation he showed Villiers the post-marks on nearly twenty.

"Your correspondence is extensive," said Villiers. "Must you reply to them all?"

"They must be replied to," said his companion (and Villiers observed that he did not say "*I* must reply"), "to-day."

"I observed one," said Villiers, "from England; from a place well known to me—from Hawkstone. May I ask if you know any one there?"

The ecclesiastic slightly coloured, and, simply saying that his letter was accidentally put into the post there, he proposed that they should descend the steps of the Capitol and pass on to the Campo Vaccino.

The conversation of that hour sunk deep into the mind of the ambitious, thoughtful, imaginative Villiers. The next day and the next found him again with his friend, who had been introduced to him, soon after his arrival, as a countryman of his own belonging to the English College; and had con-

N

trived, without any appearance of intrusion, and as sought for rather than as seeking him, to become his daily companion. Without any seeming design, sometimes in the pursuit of amusement, sometimes in a plan of study, sometimes by accidental coincidences, Villiers found himself through the means of Macarthy brought into contact with all that could most engage the affections and stimulate the imagination in the papal city. All its ancient lore was even more familiar to Macarthy than to himself. When Villiers entered with avidity on an examination of its ruins, Macarthy seemed to have made them for years his favourite study. He carried him to unexplored recesses, illustrated half obliterated inscriptions, brought forth from an inexhaustible memory quotation on quotation ; and whenever Villiers was at a loss for a point of history, if Macarthy omitted for the time to supply the information, he was sure the next day to revert accidentally to it, and to show that he was master of that subject. Villiers did not know that the paleness of his cheek and thinness of his frame were due partially to the midnight studies with which he prepared himself to be in all points the assistant, and at the same time the master of his companion. The versatility and multiplicity of his talents (still without officiousness, or bustle, or ostentation, for Macarthy was discharging what he conceived a duty to his Superiors, not thinking of himself,) engaged even more the admiration of Villiers. If Villiers expressed an admiration for Dante, in a few days Macarthy would lead round the conversation to him, and pour forth stanza after stanza of his most exquisite poetry. If he proposed to devote a day to the sculptures of the Vatican, the morning slipped past unheeded, as Macarthy illustrated their history with anecdotes and theories of art. At one time

Villiers expressed an inclination to play billiards, and to his surprise, when after some days' delay Macarthy allowed him to find a table, and after some reluctance was induced himself to play, Villiers was beaten by him. One law Macarthy seemed to have laid down to himself. He never entered on any subject, nor took part in any pursuit, in which he was not Villiers' superior. Villiers was young; and the society of Rome at that time was gay and brilliant. Without any departure from propriety or clerical gravity, Macarthy did not hesitate to share it with him, and whatever attention was paid to the handsome, and noble, and wealthy Englishman, Macarthy was not long in any company without drawing the chief interest round himself, and bringing Villiers to stand beside him, the spectator and admirer of his power. But Villiers one day spoke with enthusiasm of the austerities of a monastic life; and by some seemingly natural and accidental circumstance, he was led to call on Macarthy late on a cold wintry night, and found him without a fire, with a single candle to light his studies, his solitary meal evidently untasted, and the door of his bedroom open, through which Villiers could not avoid seeing a rude hair shirt, not displayed, but apparently lying casually, ready to be put on. And let us do Macarthy justice. In all that he did, however calculated to raise himself in the eyes of Villiers, there was neither affectation nor selfishness. He was placed by those to whom he had sworn obedience, and whom he regarded in the place of his Heavenly Master, to play a part, to accomplish a work, and that work the fascination of Villiers: and as the whole powers of his mind were thrown into his duty, the affections of his heart became involved likewise. And Villiers could not have found in the world one who more dearly loved him, or would have sacrificed for him more readily all that he valued, excepting only the one absorbing interest of his Society and his Church. He could not witness Macarthy's private devotions; but they were never uttered without prayers, and often tears, for him—prayers that he might one day be brought home to the bosom of what Macarthy deemed the true Church, and that Macarthy himself might be the instrument of his salvation. One night, when they were making an expedition in the Abruzzi, and were compelled to occupy the same room, Villiers was startled to hear his name repeated again and again in the disturbed dreams of his companion, in tones of affectionate anxiety, and mixed with entreaties for blessings on him, which went to Villiers's heart. At another time, as they were crossing a winter torrent in the mountains, Villiers's foot had slipped from a wet rock, and he was plunged headlong in the stream, incapable, from the fury of the waters, of exerting his powers of swimming. In a moment Macarthy was by his side, and by their joint efforts he reached the bank. From that day the charm was completed; and it began to work.

"How are you advancing?" was the question put soon after to Macarthy by the superior of his Order. "Why did you not bring him here last night, to see the washing of the feet of the pilgrims?"

Macarthy sighed, and answered, "that he had every hope of bringing Villiers over in time, but that his was not a mind to be dealt with rudely." And while he uttered these words, something of pain and shame flushed across his face, as if, even in the conversion of a soul, trickery and artifice were unworthy either of man or of the Gospel. And, indeed, nothing but Macarthy's real and deep belief

in the rectitude of his own views, which gave
warmth and sincerity even to his most elaborate
manœuvres, could have prevented Villiers from de-
tecting and revolting against his ingenious artifices.

At one time, Macarthy would take him to an hospital, where, among the sick and dying, instead of
unfeeling hirelings taken from the lowest orders, he
saw young and delicate women habited in a religious dress, and ministering with tenderness and
devotion to the poorest sufferers. And as they
came out, penetrated with the spectacle, Macarthy
would ask, as if inquiringly, whether there was any
thing of the kind in London, or, as he would correct
himself, among the Protestant sects.

Another morning, the newspapers had brought
word that some treaty of commerce had opened a
port in China to European settlers. And scarcely
a day elapsed before Macarthy called on Villiers, to
tell him that he might now have an opportunity of
witnessing the consecration of a bishop, which was
to take place immediately. " We are sending out
a bishop and seven missionaries to China," he said,
quietly.

" So soon?" asked Villiers.

" And are we to leave the poor heathen a day,"
asked Macarthy, gravely, " without preaching to
them the Gospel ?"

" And how can you manage this ?" asked Villiers. " In England, it would take years even to
propose such a plan, much more to complete it."

" We have our colleges," answered Macarthy,
" and devoted men always ready to go in bodies
wherever they are sent. We are not under the
crown."

And Villiers was silent, but he treasured up the
fact. Oftentimes Macarthy would speak to him of
his mother, as of one with whose character he was

N 3

familiar; and as the tears came into Villiers's eyes
at the recollection of her sainted life and sainted
death-bed, Macarthy would turn aside ; and not in
affectation or hypocrisy, but in deep unfeigned pain,
would silently breathe a prayer, that the son might
yet be restored to the communion of the mother ;
and Villiers understood his thoughts.

"Perhaps," said Macarthy to him one evening,
"you had better not come to-morrow, as usual, to
hear the music in our chapel. There is a com-
memoration of the dead ; and one name you would
hear mentioned in our prayers, which might affect
you painfully. Lady Eleanor was a benefactress to
our Order. And I fear," he continued, "you could
not join with us in praying for her now."

It was almost the only bitter word which Macarthy had ever used, but it went to Villiers's
heart.

At another time, when Macarthy perceived that
his friend was suffering under depression of spirits,
and with the acuteness habitual to his Order had
discerned that there was something on his mind —
some remorse which required to be calmed — Macarthy led him through a church by a confessional,
where a penitent was kneeling. Something induced him to stop to look at a piece of sculpture,
and to decipher a long inscription ; and, as he
glanced round to observe Villiers, he saw that the
shaft had struck him. They left the church, neither
of them speaking : not a word passed till they found
themselves in the open Campagna, beneath the solitary sky ; and, as Macarthy sat down to rest himself
on the fragment of an old ruin, Villiers, with a
deep groan, knelt down before him ; and, hiding his
face in his lap, entreated him to hear his confession.
A by-stander might have observed a look of joy
and exultation in Macarthy's lustrous eye pass into

tenderness and sorrow, almost into a tear, as he bowed his head down upon Villiers, and prayed God to bless him; but he knew too well the art of fascination.

"No," he replied, to Villiers. "I understand you; I know your wants; I mourn for you; but I cannot give you relief. Your faith, if so it may be called, repudiates that holy sacrament, cuts you off from that blessing to penitent sinners, and you must bear the burden; I cannot relieve you. If you need confession, and can conscientiously receive absolution, you should have recourse to your own clergy. There is Mr. De Courcy, who preaches at your chapel." And he named a young, gay, fashionable clergyman, who nominally under the pretext of his health, but in reality to indulge his amusements, affected to take the spiritual charge of the English residents at Rome, by reading prayers to them on a Sunday, and rehearsing a sermon of Blair's.

No physician watching the crisis of a deadly disorder ever studied so deeply each shade of symptom; touched so delicately on every spring which could work a favourable change, gave himself up so completely to the perplexities of a varying and complicated disease, as Macarthy, preserving all the time a profound silence on any point of controversy, watched over Villiers. Villiers had launched one day with enthusiasm into the vision of an empire placed in the hands of one great mind, unshackled by the fetters of a popular government, and devoted with honesty and self-devotion to the good of mankind. The same afternoon, Macarthy stopped in their walk at the gate of one of the colleges in Rome; and, after some little delay, they were led into a small cell. The stone floor simply matted over, the single wooden chair, the simple deal table

covered with papers and books, the image of the
Virgin under a niche, with a lamp burning before
it, and the fireless hearth, even in the midst of
winter, were familiar to Villiers; and he felt no
surprise. But he was not prepared for the noble and
almost awful figure of the occupant of that humble
apartment; for the command with which he raised
himself from his seat, and bestowing no look on
Macarthy, who stood trembling in his presence,
pointed to a map of the earth before him, and with
his eyes fixed upon Villiers — " Beware," he said,
" young man; remember that it is nothing to gain
the whole world, and to lose your own soul."   He
then waved his head for them to withdraw; and
Villiers learned from his still awed companion, that
he had seen the general of the Jesuits.

There were many Germans at Rome; and Villiers, who did not understand the German language,
endeavoured to converse with them in Latin.

" Oh!" sighed Macarthy, " if but one language
could be spread over the whole world, to unite us
all together in our devotions as in our converse,
would it not be a blessing?   Would it not almost
repeal the curse of Babel ?"

They spent morning after morning before the
works of art, with which every palace in Rome is
filled ; and while other curious visitants passed
rapidly through the galleries, some chatting idly on
common matters, others scanning, with absurd pretensions to criticism, the grandest works of the
great masters of painting and sculpture, and others
lounging lazily on sofas to gaze, through opera-
glasses, on the sufferings of saints, and admire the
anatomy of the muscles in the form of a crucified
Redeemer, Macarthy would draw Villiers apart,
and fix him before some figure of the Blessed Virgin ; tell him how in its softness and its dignity it

was a type of the Church; and, as he watched the
picture, drawing into itself, by degrees, the thoughts
and affections of his companion, Macarthy asked
himself how any system of religion could rule the
heart of man which did not appeal to his imagination through his senses. With great care and
judgment he withdrew Villiers from the popular
spectacles of religious ceremonies, and from every
thing which could suggest to him the too painful
system of artifice and deception with which Popery
amuses and controls its followers. He showed him
no relics; led him through no tawdry churches;
carefully prevented his reading any popular books
of devotion; spoke soberly and sadly on some im-
postures, which at the time were claiming to be
miracles; and only on one occasion had committed
a mistake, when Villiers had remarked with some
severity on the exhibition of a dirty doll hung
round with beads, and crowned with paper flowers,
before which a crowd of market-women were paying their devotions. He had made a faint apology
for it—the usual apology of Popery—*Populus
vult decipi, et decipiatur.* But the indignant and
astonished look with which Villiers turned round to
see if he were speaking seriously,—his demand to
know whether God has given to the Church commission to deceive,—to do evil that good might come,
—to rule by lies,—as they startled Macarthy himself, threw him also on his guard; and though the
principle had been laid deep in his own mind by the
whole system of his religious education, he never
broached it again. But to one spectacle in particular
did Macarthy accompany his companion. It was the
ceremony of the Pope's blessing the people in the
great area before St. Peter's: and as the venerable
old man rose from his seat over the grand entrance,
and the multitude fell down before him hushed into

the profoundest silence, Macarthy felt Villiers kneeling by his side, and kneeling even after the cannon from St. Angelo had broken the trance, and the shouts and cries of the struggling crowd around them had dispelled the magic of that wondrous scene. But Macarthy did not lose the opportunity. The next day, as they parted, he left in Villiers's hand a note-book, closely and carefully written through.

"Yesterday," he said, "we both were kneeling side by side, I to receive the blessing, and you, I trust and believe, not scornfully resolved to reject it, of a poor old man. You think," he continued, "that the whole was a delusion. And, if you did not love me, you would despise me for becoming the slave of such an imposture as the papal supremacy. This is the language of Protestants. I do not like that you should despise me. I have therefore brought together in this book the testimonies of antiquity, —of Catholic antiquity," he repeated, — "to the truth of our doctrine ; and, perhaps, you would like to look at them."

The next morning Villiers received a note from him, to say that he was called away suddenly from Rome. Days passed, weeks passed, two months passed, and Macarthy did not appear or write. He had planted the seed securely, and he was too wise to stand by and disturb the process of germination. Villiers himself, with the departure of his companion, disappeared from the general society of Rome. He was intently occupied, in the mornings, in the libraries to which he could gain access, in his solitary walks involved in abstracted thoughts, and far beyond midnight his lamp was seen burning in his room, till his countrymen of the Piazza di Spagna spoke of him as a prodigy of learning, or as a recluse soon likely to be involved in the net of Popery. One only Englishman might be seen with

him at times, climbing feebly the steps of the
Piazza, for he was just recovering from a long illness. And as the passers-by saw him, with Villiers's assistance, mounting the acclivity, and observed his sunken cheek and glassy eye, they marked
him as one who would add another to the victims of
the stranger's burial-ground. He was a clergyman of
middle age, bearing no marked character upon his
features or figure, quiet, equable in temper, resigned and cheerful, as one whose past life had
neither been ruffled by great shocks of sorrow, nor
stained by memories of evil, and whose knowledge,
accurate and sound rather than universal, had been
obtained by a patient, steady, undeviating course of
study, in which he was seeking not for the display
of talent, or the satisfaction of a presumptuous curiosity, but to prove and develope truths which he had
already embraced heartily under the teaching of his
Church. In this good, simple-minded, sensible man,
a type of the character of the English Church in
general, Villiers became deeply interested. His
perfect simplicity, his freedom from effort, his abstinence from all attempts to display himself or to
influence others, the tranquillity with which he retired
unnoticed in society, and the openness, not without
thoughtfulness and discretion, with which he spoke
in private, fell upon Villiers with a degree of novelty
and freshness. It was a relief after the depth and
brilliancy which had marked the conversation of
Macarthy ; and from the profound carefulness with
which his every movement seemed to have been
regulated, as if some design and object lay beneath
each action. But there were other bonds of union
between them, and each week more and more time
was spent by them together ; and as Beattie's health
improved, before tables thickly strewed with books,
till the day which brought to Villiers a letter from

Macarthy. It was short, but ardent and affectionate. He apologised for not writing before, by the pressure of business; made no allusion to any thing which had passed between them, and only hoped that he should see Villiers as soon as he arrived in Rome; or that, if he had left Rome, Villiers would carry with him, wherever he went, the remembrance of one who dearly loved him. Villiers's brow worked painfully as he cast his eyes over the letter. He was in Beattie's room, immersed with him, as usual, in a pile of folios; and as he laid the letter down, and rested his face upon his hands, Beattie looked up quietly, and saw by the close pressure of his fingers that he was engaged in some internal struggle. At last he recovered himself, and simply saying that it was a letter from Macarthy, who would be in Rome next week, he resumed his writing.

On that day week, Macarthy arrived in Rome. If any one had imagined from his absence or his silence that he had lost sight of Villiers, he would have done him grievous injustice. His absence had been contrived for the very purpose of giving free unsuspected scope to the working of the suggestions which he had made to him. A double time had been allotted to the prayers in which he entreated a blessing upon his labours, and as he fondly deemed it, upon the head of his friend, by his restoration to the unity of the Church. His asceticism was increased; his voluntary penances made more severe. And though, too often, a chill and deadness of feeling hung upon him, as if his devotions would be unheard, at times he mistook the excitement and enthusiasm of overwrought sensibility for a divine inspiration within, and solaced himself already with the thought of embracing his friend, as his own work, and as such, adding him

as a worthy conquest to the triumphs of his idolised
Society. His heart beat as he entered the gates of
Rome. It throbbed quicker, under an outward
veil of perfect composure, as he ascended the staircase to his apartment, almost expecting that Villiers would be there to meet him. But the room
was empty, the evening past, and Villiers arrived
not. The next day came, and though Macarthy
remained within, listening to every step that approached his door, it closed in blankness and disappointment, and all his dreams seemed vanished.
And yet, in what way an honest ardent mind like
Villiers's, bent upon simple truth, and ready from
inclination to receive it, could escape from the overwhelming evidence which Macarthy believed that
he had placed before him in favour of the fundamental article of his own religious creed, it was
hard to imagine. Should he go himself and seek
Villiers? But Macarthy was too proud to seek,
where he desired to be sought, and too prudent to
risk repulsion by an officious over-zealous attempt
to attract. The third morning relieved his anxiety
in some degree. It brought him a little note,
simple, and cold, and avoiding even the usual
formal expressions of regard — to say, that if Macarthy was disengaged, Villiers would come to him
that evening; and he did come. But, from the
first moment of his appearance, Macarthy saw that
all his feelings were changed, and that something
had occurred to break the spell of his own personal
influence over him, and that Villiers was no longer
his captive. The formal apology, the hand laid
coldly in his own, and suffering motionless the
pressure of Macarthy's — a pressure which Macarthy
instantly checked — sufficiently told the tale of some
secret estrangement. Macarthy's pride came at
once to cover his disappointment, and enabled him

to meet the cold and severe look of Villiers with equal reserve and self-possession.

"I am come, Mr. Macarthy," said Villiers, and his voice faltered as he said Mr., and something of his former tenderness seemed returning, — "I am come to replace in your hands a little book, which you were good enough to trust me with before you left Rome. You intended, I am well aware, that I should study it thoroughly, and I hope, therefore, you will excuse me if I have interleaved it, and added to it suggestions and corrections of my own." And as he placed the volume in Macarthy's hand, and met Macarthy's eyes, surprised, and yet unflinchingly fixed to meet his, some misgiving arose in Villiers's mind as to the justice of his severity. Macarthy said nothing, but opened the book. He found it, indeed, interleaved, interlined, filled with MS. notes in Villiers's handwriting, and with references, which had evidently been drawn from a very deep and extensive course of reading.

"And is there," said he, "any thing in this book, Mr. Villiers, which should have worked the change which I cannot but perceive — any thing which should destroy our former regard for each other? It was drawn up with a very different intention.",

"I do believe it," replied Villiers; "I cannot have been insensible to your anxiety, a well-meant but ill-regulated anxiety, to win me over to your own form of religion. I neither complain nor condemn. It is a good and a Christian zeal, when conducted with reverence for truth; but I do lament, lament bitterly, Macarthy, that you should have endeavoured to convert me, even to what you believe to be the truth, by an imposture."

Macarthy's colour leaped into his face, and he half started from his chair, but sat down again, confronting Villiers with an open indignant look which demanded explanation.

" May I ask," said Villiers, " if this collection of authorities and testimonies to the doctrine which you desire to impress on me was compiled by yourself from the original writers?"

" It was made," said Macarthy, " as I intended to express at the time I gave it to you, from our own controversialists. I wished you to see the line of argument which they adopted, and the evidence on which they proceeded."

" And you have never verified them yourself?" said Villiers.

" I have not," replied Macarthy; " I have myself faith in my teachers, and am willing to accept their statements. It is our practice, and our first lesson, to discard doubt in the honesty and correctness of those who are placed to rule over us."

" And as a collection from your controversialists you gave it to me?" said Villiers.

" Most assuredly," replied Macarthy. " I never imagined that you would mistake it for any thing else, or myself for a man of so much learning."

Villiers's face in a moment resumed all its old cheerfulness and affection. " I have done you wrong, Macarthy, a grievous wrong; but you must forgive me;" and he stretched out his hand, which Macarthy met and took, but did not press, for he was offended as well as amazed.

" I did you a grievous wrong, dear Macarthy," continued Villiers, " and I must make a full reparation for it."

" May I ask first," said Macarthy, " for an explanation of this rather singular conduct?"

" Macarthy," said Villiers, " when I first took up your volume, I was overpowered with the accumulation of evidence which it brought to bear on your favourite dogma. I found an array of names, whose authority it was impossible to dispute; distinct enunciation of the doctrine from the earliest times, which no art could misinterpret; and quotation on quotation which, it seemed clear, no opposite testimony could overcome, or even balance. For one day you had conquered me. But I happened to return to it, and to light on a passage quoted from St. Cyprian, a striking and overwhelming testimony, as you have there extracted it, to the papal supremacy. A copy of St. Cyprian was lying, may I not say providentially, by me, and I turned to the passage in the original. What was my astonishment to find that the words on which necessarily turned the whole propriety of the application of his expressions to the See of Rome were acknowledged as a well-known interpolation even by the Romanist editor, and were carefully excluded from his text, — the very text, remember, to which your reference was given."

Macarthy's eye continued firmly facing Villiers; and he proceeded : " One discovery," he said, " of this kind induced me to examine further, — to examine laboriously and honestly, and not without assistance, but with a single desire to discover truth. And shall I tell you the result ?"

Macarthy begged him to proceed.

" I found," said Villiers, " that nearly every important passage was garbled in the same manner, and in the face of direct warnings against the corruptions, which corruptions it was impossible to doubt had been originally fastened upon the text by papal transcribers and editors. I found that other passages which were not garbled were yet wholly misapplied — that what the ancient Fathers had spoken of the whole Catholic Apostolic Church, without any restriction to the branches in communion with the Bishop of Rome, was employed as if those epithets

had been used, as you abuse them now, exclusively
to designate your own peculiar branch. I found that
spurious documents were appealed to as genuine ;
and obvious interpolations of whole sentences admitted without a hint or warning. I catalogued
the list of authorities, and affixed their dates, and to
my astonishment discovered the art with which ancients and moderns—Fathers of the Catholic Church
and doctors of the Romish schools—were mixed together, to present an overwhelming catena of testimonies, out of which but two or three were valid,
as legitimate evidence. And when I compared the
real accounts of the constitution of the Church in the
ages which we are bound to follow with your own
description of them, I could find little but direct
contradiction. Pardon me, Macarthy, if, as I read
this compilation of forgeries and deceptions, (for I
can call it little else,) and imagined you to have been
the author of it, and this for the purpose of in-
ducing me to embrace a system of religion based
upon this one foundation, I did resent it, and did
forget all that I had formerly felt for you. When
we have been deceived in one point, we suspect deceit
in all. Before this, others endeavoured to persuade
me that pious frauds were an essential part of your
system. But I never could willingly believe it.
And when once there fell from your lips that hateful maxim, *Populus vult decipi, et decipiatur,* I
persuaded myself that you were speaking in irony.
May I believe so still, and that your controversialists alone are responsible for this cheat ?"

Macarthy did not look up. A slight pang crossed
him as he felt that the maxim so hateful to Villiers
had been uttered by him, not in irony, but in sober
seriousness ; and that if the imposition, of which
he had been the unintentional aider, was gross
and enormous, it was still in perfect consistency

with the principles of that dominion over men by human arts, though for religious purposes, which his life was devoted to maintain.   But the shock to his mind was great.   He received the book, carefully locked it up, and then taking Villiers's hand, " I never intended to deceive you," he said, simply : " are we friends again ? "

And the pressure of Villiers's hand showed that his confidence was restored.

CHAP. XIV.

But in Macarthy's own mind confidence was not restored. Villiers from that hour made no attempt to resume the subject. Whatever fascination had been previously thrown round him by the apparent grandeur, unity, and splendour of the Romish system, the discovery of the hollowness and vanity of its fundamental assumption, and of the artifices with which it was supported, had dispelled the whole illusion. He now walked the streets of Rome almost with loathing, as a scene of imposition pitiable and pardonable in the deceived, but frightful and impious in the deceivers. As he examined the doctrinal errors of its system, he could detect in all of them the element of popular influence which the lust of rule required, and to which, and not to truth, it clung with such vigorous tenacity. And as he read the history of modern days, and especially of his own country since the Reformation, he could enter with heartier sympathy into the struggles, and compassionate with more indulgence the errors, of the minds by which, in one portion of the globe, popery had been resisted and exterminated, though not without loss. But theology, as yet, had been taken up by him only as a theory—as a vision for the imagination ; and when the first vision which he had formed broke up before his eyes, he was left in a state of dreary doubt and coldness, without any foundation on which to rest — any positive system, either to realise in himself, or to inculcate upon others. The thought, therefore, of bringing Mac-

arthy from error never occurred to him; and even
if it had occurred, the natural delicacy of his mind
would have shrunk from obtruding on a task to
which he was not called, and for which he possessed
little fitness. Even if he had undertaken it, what,
according to his then views, could he offer Macarthy
in exchange for the system which he would abandon,
and which, false and hollow as it was, was still a
splendid falsehood?

In the mean while Macarthy's own mind was
working upon itself. It is not true that the quarrels
of friends are the renewal of friendship. Friendship
is a delicate plant, and every rude touch, though it
does not uproot, shakes and mars it. And the suspicion and resentment once felt by Villiers, though
cast away at Macarthy's frank declaration, had left
the shade of an evil association with his name, which,
unreasonable as Villiers confessed it to be, he could
not altogether dispel. Their intercourse became
less frequent; and Macarthy himself pleaded occupation and study in excuse for it. And when they
did meet, Villiers was pained to see a marked alteration in his manner and appearance. He became
gradually reserved and silent; his mind was apparently engaged in abstracted and anxious thought;
and his eye was restless, and no longer possessed of
that singular power of penetration with which he used
to fascinate those with whom he conversed. Lines of
care began to mark his countenance. From a frank,
open apology of occupation, he seemed driven to find
excuses for avoiding a meeting with Villiers. If he
came to him, it was late in the evening; and in the
day-time he never walked with him, as before.
When Villiers called on him, he evinced impatience
and anxiety for his departure. And at last, after
having been informed several times by the porter
that Mr. Macarthy was not within, Villiers received

an embarrassed note from himself, pleading that he was peculiarly circumstanced at present, and must deny himself the pleasure of seeing him so often. Villiers, of course, acquiesced, with some surprise, and still more of offended pride. In his thoughts he charged Macarthy with foolish resentment at the refutation which had been given to his polemical theories. Alas! he little knew the misery which he had caused to him, and the fiery trial through which he was now passing. Weeks had passed without his seeing him, when, on sending once more to know if Mr. Macarthy was in Rome, an answer was given that he had left it, and would not return for some little time; and Villiers gave up all hope of seeing him, and prepared himself for his journey to Naples. He was to depart the next morning. But before he quitted the Eternal City, he gave himself up to spend one more evening among its ruins, to stand once more by moonlight on the steps of the Capitol, to listen once more, in the cool silence, to the plashing of the fountains among the colonnades of St. Peter, and to sit once more on the topmost range of the Colosseum—that image of the fortunes of Rome—that concentration of its wonderful history, and still more wondrous character.

The moonlight was streaming in masses through the dark piers of that gigantic structure. The distant hum of the corso scarcely reached his ear as he ascended to a favourite point, from which his eye could command the whole area. There was the enormous pile, reared by human art to gratify the meanest craving of an enormous ambition. There was the ground polluted with the blood of hireling gladiators, to slake that thirst for excitement, that avidity for power, which converted even the theatre of Rome into a butchery and charnel-house. There was the scene of martyrdom; and Villiers blessed

himself that the day of persecution had passed for
ever, till he remembered the Inquisition. He sat
immersed, not in thought, but in a dreamy, melancholy, trance-like stupor, under the immediate presence and eye, as it were, of an awful spirit, which
seemed to fill and haunt the ruins. And he heard
no step behind him till he was touched on the
shoulder, and a low hollow voice sounded in his ear,
" Villiers — dear Villiers ! "

He turned round, and, disguised and enveloped
in a large cloak, he saw Macarthy. As the moon
emerged from a cloud and fell upon his face, Villiers
was shocked, and startled to see its haggard cast and
ashy hue. It was the image of secret anguish ;
and every trace of coolness and resentment vanished
from Villiers's mind in compassion.

" You are ill," he said, " Macarthy ; how came
you here at this hour ? They sent word to me, only
yesterday, that you had left Rome."

" Did they ? " said Macarthy. " I knew nothing
of it ; but, thanks be to Heaven, I am here. I have
escaped them. Only you are yourself in danger.
This is no safe place," he said, looking round him,
" for any one, much less for us. These dark passages and cells have a bad reputation ; and two men
were stabbed in them last week."

Villiers knew it, but he was fearless.

" I could not leave Rome," he said, " without
once more coming here by moonlight. But you are
ill, Macarthy, dear Macarthy ; what is the matter?"

" Not ill," replied Macarthy, " not ill, only in
torment. But I have borne it. I have gone through
the worst ; and if I can but breathe another air, I
shall be well."

" And what have you suffered ? " said Villiers.

" It is a long tale," replied the other, " and I
have but a few moments. Hush ! " he continued,

" we are observed. Did you not see a figure moving round that corner ? "

Villiers looked, but all was still.

" There are two of us," he said ; " and we can have given no cause of offence to any one. Be not alarmed."

Macarthy drew breath more freely, but proceeded in a low voice, almost in a whisper—

" You," he said, and his voice faltered tenderly— " you whom I loved so dearly, whose name has been in all my prayers, the thought of whom has been the last to soothe me at night and to wake me in the morning,—you whom I have sought to make my own, until I have at times forgotten my God,— you have been my destroyer ! "

Villiers looked up with amazement.

" You have made me," Macarthy continued, with a sepulchral voice, " an Infidel. No," he continued, after a pause, and drawing himself up once more to stand as he used to stand when he would command and rivet his hearers, " not an Infidel. Thanks to my God, thanks to better thoughts and prayer, I have not lost all. Something is true within me in what we have learned and felt of Christianity : but what, or how much, or where, or how it may be found, I know not. I cling to it as to a flitting shadow, which I expect will every moment vanish also from my grasp ; and but one thing on earth am I sure of—that Popery is a lie ; and they know that I know it ; and I have been in their hands." And Villiers shuddered at the tone of mingled terror and loathing with which Macarthy uttered his last words.

" I have been in their hands, Villiers," he continued ; and he bared his arm, and Villiers saw that it was blackened and almost paralysed as by some dreadful torture.

" They found my book—your book," he said.
" They watched my reading as I followed it. They
had their confessional; they wrung from me every
thought of my heart. I had been their chosen minister, in the possession of their secrets. Judge,
Villiers, if they would spare me ! "

And he again looked trembling behind him to
catch a creaking sound, which seemed like a step
creeping stealthily along the dark vaulted passage
at his back.

" Move out," he said to Villiers, " into the open
air. It is better in the light."

" And how, then, are you here?" asked Villiers.

" I have been bound down," he said,—" solemnly
and awfully bound down; and one voice was raised
to save me, or I should not be here. But I am
escaped from them — escaped for the present,
though every movement is watched. I saw you
from the wretched place where I have taken refuge
for the time, and traced you here to wish you farewell,—to tell you that you may think of me when I
am gone. But it is at the peril of my life. As you
value it, do not come near me, nor write to me.
You are yourself in danger, and should leave Rome
without delay."

" And why not leave it with me ?" asked Villiers.

" I cannot," said Macarthy ; " I am bound hand
and foot, and dare not stir. And if I could escape,
where am I to go ? "

" To England," said Villiers, " to your own
country, with me."

" And what could I do there?" said Macarthy.

" Our church," said Villiers, " is open to you.
We do not deny your orders."

" No," said Macarthy, " you do not deny our
power to minister; but will you, can you, trust to

us to minister, at least for years, till you have tried us; and meanwhile—hark again, surely that was a footstep?"

And Villiers advanced to look into the dark passage, but all was still and silent, and only the hooting of a solitary owl broke the breathless calm that reigned around them. The unhappy man sunk down and buried his face with his hands, till Villiers once more suggested his endeavouring to reach England.

"England!" said Macarthy, "where the prisoner is freed by the very touch of the soil on which he stands! England, the refuge of the world!" And he seemed to revive at the thought.

"And our church," repeated Villiers, "is still open to you."

"Yes," muttered Macarthy, "if it be true. And if truth be found upon earth, I would fain hope that it is there, though at present all is dark around me. I can believe in nothing. I can only suspect and disbelieve;" and he heaved a deep groan. "Life and the world, and earth and heaven, are all a blank."

"Will you not examine further and inquire?" asked Villiers, tenderly.

"Inquire!" cried Macarthy, with a bitter laugh of irony. "Have I not inquired once? And what has been the end?"

And then, after a pause, he resumed, as if the possibility of so doing had dawned upon him.

"And if I could inquire, where should I be meanwhile? Outcast, degraded, despised; rejected with suspicion by those to whom he comes, and persecuted even to the death by those whom he abandons; his heart broken; his mind distracted—friendless—without books—without support or guidance—shut out even from the channels of aid from God, if such there be; starving, perhaps, and destitute of all things ; — you bid the wretch whom you have shaken from his faith and tempted to your own — you bid him inquire ! Villiers, is it not a mockery ? Do you remember," said Macarthy, after a long silence, "do you remember that miserable man" (and he alluded to a case which they had witnessed), "the apostate priest ? Do you recollect his shame and his sins, when he was driven from the shelter of his Church, and exposed naked and defenceless to the temptations of the world, which he had never known before ? Why should not my end be like his ?" And he sprang up in desperation, and stood trembling on the very verge of the precipitous wall, till Villiers seized his arm, and, entreating him to be calm, reminded him of the hour and scene when his own life had been saved by Macarthy's arm.

"Can you," he said, looking stedfastly into his distracted eye — "can you speak of poverty, and destitution, and friendlessness, while I am living ? "

Macarthy's pride, controlled and subdued as it had been by his former position, in which the grandeur of the body of which he was a member compensated for the humiliation of the individual, had now resumed its sway, and almost scornfully he withdrew his arm. "I cannot," he said, "be dependent even upon you." But, recovering himself, he continued : "One thing there is which you might do, and which I could accept without shame. You might procure me admission for a time to one of your colleges." And his eye turned up in hope as the thought struck him. "There I might be safe for a time, and at peace ; and there, with the necessary help, I might perhaps — once more —" he stopped — and then added faintly, "inquire."

Villiers did not understand him, and looked at him for an explanation.

" Our colleges?" he asked.

" Yes," said Macarthy, "you have literary colleges, where there are libraries, and religious services, and good associations, and discipline, and shelter from temptation, and learned men, and means of living with quiet and respectability at least, upon comparatively humble means. Ours are always open to receive any converts from your faith to ours: they are admitted to a shelter immediately; and in that awful crisis which must take place in the transition from one communion to the other, they are nursed, and watched, and disciplined, until they are strong enough to return once more into the world. You must have such refuges in England; and in them I might still be saved."

" Alas!" said Villiers, mournfully, "I know of none such. Colleges, indeed, we have, wealthy and numerous, but they have not been used for such a purpose; perhaps they could not be."

" Not one?" asked Macarthy again, "not one? not a single place of refuge for the miserable beings whom you are daily almost execrating for remaining in popery, and calling on them as their only salvation to come over to your Church? And do you thus cruelly endeavour to break down the roof and walls of the home in which they are sheltered, and to turn them adrift and naked upon the world without caring where they go? And when they come and sit down before your own doors, craving for some shed to cover them, you bid them wait and inquire. Oh, Villiers, can this be the Church of England — of England, the merciful and the wise?"

Villiers sighed deeply, but could make no reply.

" Then," said Macarthy, after a lengthened silence, "all is lost." He started up and listened, as a fragment of stone detached from the wall fell down in

the dark passage through which they had passed,
and both fancied they heard a suppressed cough.

"Come," said Macarthy, "let us separate.   I
have been followed and watched for days; and to
be seen with you might ruin me."

"And why?" asked Villiers.

"Because," replied Macarthy, "I know all their
designs upon you.   Beware, Villiers, how you trust
to any one.   Leave Rome immediately.   At Naples—
even in England—even in the farthest part of the
globe, remember that there is a power seated here
which has a thousand eyes and a thousand arms, and
can walk the earth invisibly, working its will at
any moment and in any place; and its eyes are
fixed on you."

Villiers understood the allusion, for he knew
that Macarthy was a Jesuit.   But why he should
himself be their object he could not imagine.

"Are you not aware," said Macarthy,—"can you
have been so long in Rome, so long with me"—(and
he groaned again), "without seeing the intense
avidity with which every Englishman of rank and
influence is brought within the range of their fascination?   Upon England their eyes are fixed as on
the one great hope of restoring their empire.   Every
concession to an insane toleration, every popular
movement, every trembling and shaking of the
boughs of the English Church, every foreign alliance or foreign commerce which threatens either the
downfal of the old English antipapal system, or the
revival of a papal influence, they watch and foster
with an art which almost defies detection, but in-
sures success.   Your name is on the list of those
from whom it hopes much.   Your mother's memory,
your last associations at Oxford, and all which they
have witnessed in you here, have marked you as
their victim.   Beware of every one.   Beware"—

But before the word was finished, there was a rush behind. Macarthy staggered and fell into the arms of Villiers; and before Villiers could disengage himself, a figure, muffled up, leaped past him into one of the deep dark passages on the other side. Villiers sprung after him, and all but grasped his neck, but with a tremendous effort the assassin shook him off, shot down the steps, and disappeared in the labyrinth. Villiers rushed back to find Macarthy bathed in blood, and stretched dead upon the ground. His arms were crossed as if his last thought had been prayer. But the dagger had reached his heart, and life had fled.

CHAP. XV.

As the spring of that year came on, the loiterer on the Chiaia at Naples might have observed, day after day, at a certain hour, an English carriage drawn up before one of the principal houses on that delicious suburb.   After delays, often very capricious, a little, thin-visaged, mean-looking old man, with a soured and fretful countenance, would be assisted into it by his valet for his morning drive.   And if the loiterer had also loitered before in the Piazza di Spagna at Rome, he might have recognised the same carriage and the same old man at the hotel, which was then occupied by General Villiers ; but the valet had been changed.   Just before the General left Rome his former courier, upon some pretence or other, expressed a wish to remain behind, and to recommend in his own place the present stout, active, useful, obsequious, and accommodating, close-shaven, though rather sinister-looking person, who, after almost lifting the fretful General into his carriage, and arranging his large silk handkerchief, his muff, his snuff-box, his cane, his newspaper, and his poodle, without a murmur at the General's angry complaints at the cold air or the hot sun, took his seat behind the carriage with the air of one who was now master of the vehicle and of all that it contained, and ordered the coachman to drive as usual towards Pausilippo.   The same loiterer might also have observed, that on one or two occasions a young man, singularly contrasted with the feeble and pinched figure of the General, tall, and nobly formed, but with a deep melancholy impressed upon his countenance, and dressed in mourning, had taken his seat on the opposite side of the carriage, but with a look of weariness and ennui. Little conversation passed between them, except some tart remarks of the old man on the dress or gesture of his companion, on his still continuing to wear mourning, or on some accidental interference with the silk handkerchief, the cane, the snuff-box, or the poodle, which seemed to constitute the only interest in the eyes of the decrepit valetudinarian. His remarks on passers-by were snarling and ill-natured. His observations, when made on the contents of the newspaper, of which he carefully perused all the advertisements, scarcely went beyond some faded reminiscence of past gaiety recalled by the columns of the Morning Post, or the price of stocks. He dozed during a great part of his ride ; and if, when he woke up, he found his companion engaged in reading, he made some angry complaint that he could find no one to talk to him ; or would ask, sneeringly, if that was one of the new popish books from England, and when the young man intended to turn monk.

With ill-disguised impatience, and sometimes with less of respect than became a son toward a father,— even a weak, fretful, irreligious, and mean-minded father, —Villiers either answered shortly or remained silent. And the drive seldom concluded without some suggestion from the General that, if he could not make a more agreeable companion, he might as well remain at home — a suggestion which Villiers would gladly have adopted, had not his father, in the cat-like spirit of a mouse-tormentor, whenever he found him engaged in some study or interesting occupation, called on him to come out and accompany him. Each day, and almost each hour, brought with it some little vexation of this kind, which fretted Villiers's temper, and disturbed even his own self-respect. In his own mind miserable and doubting, still suffering from the shock which the frightful scene in the Colosseum had given to him, with no grand object before him to occupy his life, and with the daily presence of littleness and lowness in all that he saw of man, whether in the vicious infirmity of his father, or in the habits of a Neapolitan population, he became morbidly sensitive to the annoyances to which he was subjected even in the presence of society. His father's life had been more than idle or useless; it had been vicious; and Villiers knew it. And in old age a paralysis of mind was coming on which extinguished all hope of repentance. He had been a cruel husband to the mother whom Villiers adored. And in more than the little habits of daily intercourse, in threats of casting off his son, and depriving him of his inheritance, he was a tyrannical father. One person only in the house seemed to bear with him imperturbably. It was Pearce, or Mr. Pearce, as the servants, who dreaded him as much as they disliked their master, universally called him. It was he who slept in his master's room, who arranged his gouty stool, unfolded and dried his newspaper, purchased his peculiar snuff at a peculiar shop, made his posset, and administered it at night — even fed his poodle, and shaved his beard, without extorting from the old man any very violent outbreak of anger. A spell seemed to be laid upon the General by the very presence of Pearce. There was something in his look penetrating and cunning, and yet, when he chose, commanding, which at first disgusted even Villiers himself, as it overawed his father. But Pearce to his young master was more than attentive; he was obsequious and flattering, as clever servants can be even to intelligent masters. He made himself useful in a thousand little ways, gradually superseded Villiers's own man in many trifling offices, which the cleverer eye and head of Pearce better understood. And at last he attained the grand point which he had gradually but unsuspectedly worked up to, of paying Villiers's little bills, obtaining free access to his room, and at times even copying for him a letter, or writing out some extract from a book which Villiers might wish to preserve. Villiers could not like him, but could not deny that he was a very clever, very obliging, and very useful fellow. Nor was his appreciation of his attainments diminished, when one day, having received from Pearce a transcript from a passage in Burke, in which a Latin quotation had been misprinted, he found that the error had been corrected by Pearce, who, on Villiers expressing surprise, informed him that he had been taught Latin when a boy.

And in the meanwhile what were Villiers's own occupations? He could scarcely tell himself. Stunned and horror-struck at what he had witnessed at Rome, he had delayed his departure in the hope of finding some clue to the murder of poor Macarthy, but could reach none. Strange obstacles and delays were thrown in his way by the police themselves. Once, when a cap had been found in the dark passages of the Colosseum, and a hope was raised that it might serve to trace or identify the assassin, it disappeared from his possession, and he could never find it again. Nor, indeed, was assassination so uncommon an event at Rome as to create generally the interest and suffering which it had caused in himself. He was at last advised by a judicious Italian, and advised with a degree of significance, that his search was hopeless, and that it would be necessary to abandon it; and with a sickened, loaded heart he followed his father to Naples.

Youth, by a strange elastic power, soon recovers even from the most frightful shock. But Villiers, even at Naples, did not recover. By degrees, indeed, the horrible vision, with which his dreams were at first haunted, died away. He no longer heard Macarthy's last " Beware!" ringing in his ears, or saw his ghastly haggard face gazing on him through his curtains at midnight, and almost reproaching him with his death. Though at the first moment all the tenderness of affection, which he had once felt, seemed to revive, afterwards the later train of association resumed its place. And especially as his temper and patience became embittered by the trials of his father, he found himself at times almost regarding poor Macarthy's memory with the same resentment as if he really had meditated the deception which he involuntarily practised. It is a sad and awful trial, heaviest perhaps of all to which human nature can be exposed, when a bold, noble, ardent mind is placed under a feeble, petty, contemptible government, which it cannot reform, and may not shake off. One only blessing can enable it to be borne, when the bold mind is actively engaged in some high and energetic work, which makes all other things seem little, and sanctifies and elevates the temper to be patient even as its Divine Master. But Villiers had no such work. His first dream of grandeur and of truth dispelled, and dispelled so horribly, he fell back into a state of dreary inactivity. He could take no interest in the ancient associations of Naples, and all that surrounded it, for the study reminded him of Rome and of Macarthy; and he was obliged, as the thought struck him, to close his book, shut his eyes, and take refuge in the crowded noisy streets of the luxurious city. Here he could find nothing to elevate, little to attract, but everything to effeminate and sensualize. At times he plunged into violent bodily exertion, mounting his horse, and penetrating, though with vacant eye and indolent mind, the distant scenes of the surrounding country, or taking with him some young boatmen and sailing on the bay at midnight, when his solitary dinner with his father, and the still more solitary evening, while his father was dozing in his arm-chair, had left him at liberty for the enjoyment of real solitude — the solitude of a vision-peopled nature. And these moments, when he threw his mind as it were upon a couch, and casting off all exertion of thought, all memory, and all fore-castings of the future, gave himself up to the luxurious influence of that delicious climate and glorious scenery, became at last his only enjoyment. They soothed and tranquillized him, and yet excited his imagination — acting almost like an opiate on his distracted mind, and filling him with a dreamy languor, full of luxurious sensibility, but full also of a deadly poison. His religious feelings, however crushed and chilled by what had passed, happily were not destroyed. They had been, and continued to be, his safeguard through all the worst forms of temptation to which, amidst a dissolute society, separated from all the influences of his Church, and from all examples of high rectitude in his own countrymen, he was necessarily exposed. Once, in a moment of intense weariness and self-reproach which followed a scene of contemptuous vexation from his father, and almost of recrimination on his own side, (for Villiers's sense of dutifulness was rapidly sinking,) he happened to be drawn by an acquaintance to a gambling-table, and had all but given himself up to the impulse of gaming himself; but a vision of his mother, of her prayers and injunctions, came

across him, and he left the room with precipitation.
At other times, when, as he fondly thought, a better
spirit was moving within him—a spirit of peace and
love, undisturbed by idle controversies, and resting
calmly in the great truths of religion, in which
all creeds united, — he would abandon himself, not to
the contemplation, but to the soft gentle influences
of nature, tracing a hand of love and a vision of
glory in all her works, in the bright stars, the breathless night, the eternal ocean, the soft air that fanned
his brow as he lay stretched in his boat upon the
sea, or sat listlessly on some wave-eaten promontory, listening to the lulling waters, or inhaling
fragrance from a flower. Startled as he would have
been to hear the right and only name due to such
vague and idle dreamings, he was sinking into a
species of Pantheism, but knew it not. And meanwhile, as the luxury from without was creeping on
him, the strength within was dying away. His
energy was gone, his sense of duty deadened, his
self-command and self-respect powerless against the
continued annoyances of his father's society. In
later years, when, proved and disciplined by sufferings, Villiers looked back upon the scenes of this
period, it was always with a keen and deepening
remorse — remorse which in the secrecy of his own
chamber found vent in stated days of humiliation
and penitence. He was not indeed led to any open
violent breach of filial respect, though to this he
was often tempted; but his good taste saved him
from it — it would have been ungentlemanly. But
the cold reply when his father asked him some
painful question; the dead silence to which he
abandoned himself during their meals; the reluctance
to meet half-way even the occasional overture of his
father to a more amicable communication; the irritation which betrayed itself towards any of the in-

numerable frivolities with which his father endeavoured to beguile the lingering weariness of an old
age without a hope and without a virtue; at times
even the tart and harsh reply; the neglect of any
attempt to soothe, or amuse, or elevate, his father's
mind; and the forgetfulness of prayer — of that
prayer for his correction and amendment which
might have availed, even when all human help
seemed vain, — all this came back to Villiers when
his father was gone for ever, when he had forgotten
the bitterness of feeling caused by the hourly exhibition of his father's frivolities, his whims, his
weaknesses, the offensive habits into which a self-
indulgent old age too often sinks, and the petty
wearying spirit of revenge with which he consoled
himself for the acknowledged superiority of his son.
and displayed his mean jealousies and resentments
by thwarting and almost insulting him. It came
back on him when the realities of religion had been
unveiled before him; and as he stood by his father's
grave, he asked where his spirit then was, and
whether he himself might not have done something
to rescue it while it was upon earth.

By degrees also, as his father's infirmities increased, instead of redoubling his attentions, and
devoting himself more assiduously to enliven his
sick room, Villiers was tempted to absent himself, and to enjoy his freedom by prolonging his
rides or boatings. To Pearce — the active, obsequious, ever-ready Pearce, who understood all the
old man's humours, and had now obtained a complete command over him, so that the poor decrepit
being, sinking into dotage, scarcely dared to move
without asking permission and advice from his hireling,—Villiers abandoned his father. The excuse for
retiring himself was easy and ready, though it was
not without some pang of self-reproach. His father

disliked himself, and liked Pearce. His own presence only seemed to cause irritation, or his patience was so exhausted that he required repose and relaxation. Alas! how easily we can excuse what we like.

One evening the General had been more than usually querulous and sarcastic upon the companion of his tête-à-tête dinner, until it amounted to rudeness; and Villiers's suffused face showed that he was treasuring up a store of bitter feeling. As it grew later the old man's weariness increased. One by one, Pearce endeavoured to engage him with the many childish but expensive gew-gaws, in which his frivolous mind still endeavoured to find relief from the monotony of existence. The parrot repeated its lesson, the poodle had performed its tricks; and as Villiers lifted up his eyes from some poetry which he was reading, an involuntary expression of scorn rather than of compassion rose to his lips, but was checked in time. The heat of the room became oppressive and the air offensive. Again and again Pearce was summoned to shift the valetudinarian in his deep-cushioned easy chair. His gouty stool required moving: Villiers left it to be arranged by the servant. He wished to be lifted round; and another arm was required. Villiers, when requested to assist, coldly complied, but without any expression of thankfulness from his father or of acknowledgment on his own part. He was evidently treated as a slave. Again he was required to leave his book to ring the bell, and Villiers became fretful. The poodle nearly threw him down as he returned to his seat; and Villiers pushed it aside, and almost kicked it, which drew a howl from the little ugly animal, and the howl drew a violent coarse exclamation from the impatient General. Villiers closed his book, and prepared to leave the room; but his father authoritatively called him back. Villiers coldly pleaded an engagement, and escaped. But he was overtaken at the top of the stairs by Pearce, who delivered some bitter and insulting message to him, which the artful messenger took care should assume its full force of provocation, and should sting Villiers more deeply by coming from a servant. Villiers bade the man begone, and closing the door violently behind him, issued into the street.

The hurried passionate step with which he paced the long avenues of the royal garden, into which he had entered as the first place of refuge, gave way by degrees to more quiet and composure. The evening was calm and warm; all the stars above him seemed to look down on him, as if to sooth him with eyes of peace and love. The hum of the city was dying away, and except the roll of an occasional carriage, few sounds but the plashing of the sea disturbed the stillness. As the cool air played upon his forehead, his resentment sunk by degrees into that morbid state of self-pitying, self-congratulating sensibility, in which, forgetting our own faults, we consider ourselves the victims of the faults of others, and, instead of rising up to battle with our temptations, indulge our vanity and indolence by contemplating ourselves as interesting sufferers. If Villiers could not realize his dreams of ambitious action, he could find some gratification of his visions in this placid and painless self-martyrdom. It soothed him, flattered him, enabled him to dwell dangerously on the trials to which he was exposed, and on his father's conduct, and permitted still to lurk within him all his disrespectful unfilial feelings of resentment and contempt, without calling them out so prominently as to ensure their reprobation by his conscience. He sat down by the side of the water, and as he gave himself up to the melancholy luxuriousness of indolent sensibility, and felt the charm

of nature, in calming his troubled thoughts, they fell,
as they often fell, into poetry. And he all but completed a beautiful and pathetic sonnet, in which he described his own broken spirit—weary, sick, helpless,
hopeless, the sport of idle thoughts, and chained to a
sinful world; while the spirit of Nature was invoked
and blessed as his mother, as his nurse, watching over
him, notwithstanding his follies and his faults, with
tender pity, soothing every pain, bearing every infirmity, and leading him on with a mother's hand
to a higher and nobler state of being. It was a
picture full of fascination. Villiers contemplated
it again and again. Again and again a vague wild
feeling of devotion rose up to the spirit of Nature;
he gazed with a visionary eye upon the stars above—
with a mysterious sense of infinity and power on
the ocean before him — with tenderness and sympathy even on the orange blossoms, which exhaled
odours on each side, as if they felt for his sorrows,
and delighted to minister to his relief. In the meanwhile his father was calling for him to assist him to
his bed. But Villiers had forgotten the reality in
the dream, as persons often do who write poetry.

He found some perplexity and entanglement in
arranging his last line, so as to express with sufficient vividness the intensity of his feelings; and, as
the night was becoming cold, he rose to return
home. The gates of the gardens in which he had
been lingering had been long closed, but he had
been favoured with a private key; and as he passed
along, and within the iron railings, to the gate
through which he was to obtain egress, he observed
two persons, one of whom resembled the figure of
Pearce, and the other was a young and seemingly
delicate female, in the dress of a peasant, standing
on the pavement, and engaged in deep conversation.
As Villiers opened the gate, Pearce, whom he did

not recognise, had just seized the hand of his companion, which seemed reluctantly yielded up to him,
and he had put it to his lips. But he was startled
by hearing the gate grate on its hinges ; and with a
few hasty and affectionate words the two separated.
The young girl, as she passed Villiers, dropped a
slight courtesy, as if recognising him; and as the
light of a lamp before an image of the Virgin fell
by accident (no, not by accident; for things which
in moments of indolence or sin lead us into temptation, and end in misery, are not accidents) fell by
some mysterious overruling providence full on her
features ; and Villiers beheld a tender and pensive
face of exquisite beauty, which timidly glanced up
at him as he passed. He did not turn to look, for
his mind was one of singular delicacy in all that
regarded woman. But that face, once seen, was
fixed before his eyes. The sight had given to him
a strange mysterious impulse, which seemed to touch
a hidden chord, and to awake a new spring of life
within him. He had never been sensible of any
thing like it before. He dashed his hand across his
brow, and walked hastily on, but the face was still
before him. It came that night and looked upon
him in his dreams, and his first thought on waking
fell on the same vision. The next afternoon the
carriage came to the General's door as usual; the
General himself was lifted in ; the muff, the handkerchief, the snuff-box, the cane, the poodle — all
were deposited. Pearce was at the door waiting to put
up the steps; the General was feebly and querulously
demanding where Mr. Villiers was, that he might
drive with him, and read the newspaper to him, but
no Villiers appeared ; his servant only came to say
that his master had an engagement, and could not
come. The angry General, in a passion, ordered
Pearce to lift him out again, and the carriage was

sent away; and the sick man was deprived of his drive and fresh air, almost the only thing which recruited and supported him during the day.

Half an hour afterwards, Villiers himself was floating indolently in his boat, on the blue glad waters of the Bay of Naples; and, as he lay stretched at his ease in the stern, with his Petrarch open before him, and his eyes half shaded from the sun, the boatmen rowed him gently, as if the very plashing of the oars disturbed his repose; and followed, as he bade them, the line of coast, entering into every little bay, and bending round each ruin-crested promontory, while Villiers gave himself up to his usual luxury of dreaming. But this day his dreams were not of empire; empires had lost their charm. Solitude, retirement, sympathising hearts, domestic affection, had found their way into his thoughts. Nations he could not find subjected to his will, and ready to be moulded by his hand. But one human heart — pure, gentle, delicate, and devoted, if such there were upon earth — might still be his; and he might lay one head upon his bosom to find there shelter and repose from the dangers of the world. He might nerve his arm to fight battles, or to endure toils, for the one weak and helpless being who might look up to him as her only strength. And he might find one mind docile, and susceptible, and unperverted by the cold maxims of a false refinement to hang upon his lips as the fountain of truth, and to image in every thought and action the maxims which he could teach her. Still he might be a sovereign. And as the hope flashed across him, he closed his Petrarch, laid his head back upon the stern of the boat, and, as he closed his eyes, there came again before him that fair, and pensive, and exquisitely beautiful face which had glanced up at him on the night preceding, beneath the lamp of

the Virgin. He was roused by the sound of oars
from an approaching boat, a little fisherman's boat,
apparently returning from Naples. It neared them,
rowed by a single old man, but rowed vigorously
and steadily; and in the stern of the boat, amidst
baskets of fruit, and singing to her father, as he
rowed, her hymn to the Virgin, there sat (it was a
strange coincidence, and coincidences act as spells
and charms upon the strongest mind) the same
figure, the same exquisitely beautiful face, which
he was striving to recall to his fancy. Villiers
sprang up, rubbed his eyes, watched the boat as it
passed them, and exchanged a greeting with his
boatmen. And again the beautiful face glanced up
timidly, as if expecting possibly a recognition from
Villiers. And as the little boat shot round a promontory and disappeared, Villiers ordered his own
boat to follow. It seemed a providence — and a
providence it was. But in the world are two powers
of providence; and the good is discernible from the
evil only by the holy energies with which we strive
to turn accidents into virtues.

The boatmen were gaining rapidly on the little
bark, when Villiers, as if recovering himself from a
momentary impulse, ordered them to stop. And
affecting to be busily engaged in disentangling and
examining some sea-weed, which had gathered round
the rudder (for passion is full of craft, and even
Villiers, proudly and fiercely honest as he was, could
not allow his boatmen to see what was passing in
his mind), he made them rest on their oars until
the little bark ran alongside a broken flight of steps
in the cliff. The old man moored it fast, took out
his daughter in his arms, and with her basket on
her head, and still singing, she tripped lightly up
the steps, and entered a little cottage hung with a
trellis-work of vines, which stood on the verge of

the precipice.　Villiers waited, still busily examining the sea-weed, but finding nothing that he
wanted.　And when no one appeared again at the
door of the cottage, he gave the signal for their
return to Naples; and as he returned, the boatmen
observed that he did not throw himself back to
dream with closed eyes in indolence, but sat up
with his head buried in his hands, thinking.　He
was engaged to dine that day with the ambassador,
to meet the Duke of Newburgh and Prince Castel-a-
Mare, and all the rank and brilliancy of Naples.
And Villiers sighed at the burden which awaited
him, and at the dulness, formality, and heartlessness
of high rank and fashionable life; and his fancy
wandered off to a little cottage trellissed with vines,
and a seat scooped out in the native rock, from
which he might gaze upon the blue sea and the
glorious sky, free and untrammelled, but not alone,
—with one to whom he might himself give dignity
and honour, instead of receiving it from others.
But the dream was broken by the boat touching
land, and the first sight was the obsequious Pearce,
with a face not merely of feigned but sincere consternation (for his schemes as well as his gains were
at stake), who had ran down to the beach to inform
him that his father had been seized with an attack of
paralysis.　He had been violently excited by Villiers
declining to drive with him; had indulged, Pearce
took care to inform him, in expressions which Villiers was obliged to command him to desist from
repeating, and in the midst became speechless.

Villiers soon stood by his father's bed-side, not
without remorse, yet still excusing himself.　The
physicians were present, and all agreed that by
avoiding any future excitement, and with great care
the patient might recover.　And Villiers no sooner
heard it than the load passed from his mind, and

he found his fancy again wandering off to the trellised cottage and the blue sea. One year before had any one told him that he could stand by what might seem to be the death-bed of his father, and that in that awful moment a single thought of self or self-enjoyment could intrude upon him, he would have spurned the charge with indignation : but admit self in little things, and great things will not exclude it.

The patient did recover, so far at least as to resume his usual habits; and with the usual habits came the former temper, and with the former temper came Villiers's former trial. And at first the shock and warning which he had once received operated as such warnings are designed to do. He bore with his father more patiently, if not more humbly, from the fear of bringing upon himself more future remorse, if not from filial duty and Christian affection. But the health of the poor old man seemed at last quite re-established, the memory of the sick-bed scene died away, Villiers's heart was full of other things; it was possessed by a feeling — and possessed persons are not masters of themselves.

As the spring came on, he himself became an altered man. Even his common acquaintance observed that his eye was lighter and his step firmer — that life seemed to have a charm, and time an object for him. He mixed indeed in the general society of the place far less than ever; but when he was induced to join a party, he was cheerful, and even playful, instead of reserved and abstracted. His pride and coldness seemed to be thawed by some better and happier influence. There was more of natural dignity and command in his manner, as if he was conscious of standing in relations and a position which give to men individual consequence and character. Even the Countess of Lurley stopped one day behind the screen, as she came into her

drawing-room, to observe him tête-à-tête with her
little boy, playing with him upon the carpet, and
taking the child with fondness to his arms, as it
screamed out with delight at some little frolic with
which Villiers was amusing it.

"You! exclaimed the Countess, "you, whom we
are all so afraid of, playing with my child!" What
can have happened to you?" And the lady smiled
significantly. But Villiers faced the look calmly and
steadily, and only remarked, that persons when
happy in themselves were generally fond of children; and that he was, he thanked God, very happy.
And again the lady smiled significantly; but Villiers shook his head; and he was not a person
whom even the gay and lively Countess presumed to
banter.

If the servants of the General's establishment had
been examined on the subject of their young master's
change of feeling, (and servants in general know
more than any other persons in the house, and,
though treated as unworthy of any respect, yet must
be admitted, whether we like it or no, into our
greatest secrets,) they would have brought together
a number of little facts, which they had themselves
frequently put into a conjecture in the servants'
hall, and might have constructed from it a tale.
The groom would have stated, that soon after the
General's illness Villiers had resumed his rides, but
the groom's attendance was dispensed with, and the
horse's head was always turned in one direction.
His master's daily ride, without variation, was along
the road which winds to the north, by the side of
the bay; and the groom also had remarked that the
horse, Villiers's favourite Mameluke, never bore
marks of having gone to any great distance. The
cook would have complained that now, when the old
General was ordered to dine early and in his own

room, her young master's late dinner was again and
again spoiled by waiting for him. Frequently none
was ordered, and when ordered little was tasted. He
had also asked her to write out a recipe for some
little delicacies, which she had often tasked her skill
to provide for him (for the servants all were fond of
their young master, though not a little afraid of
him), on the pretext that he knew a friend who would
perhaps like to have them. The housekeeper, the
good-natured fat Mrs. Boucher, knew nothing that
was going on out of doors, but when bruised fruits
and bad vegetables were brought into the kitchen,
she never ceased to wonder why her poor little
Pauline did not make her appearance again, with
the finest melons and newest eggs that ever came
into the Naples market. And when the name of
Pauline was mentioned, the housemaid would look
significantly and resentfully at Mr. Pearce, and
Mr. Pearce would bite his lips and leave the room.
Pearce's manner, indeed, had undergone a great alteration. He could seldom or ever obtain leave to
absent himself from the General's side. If he left
the room, the bell was rung instantly to recall him
for some trivial purpose, to pick up a book, or move a
chair, or what was more frequently the poor old man's
real wish, to amuse him with some of the Naples
gossip, which, partly forged and false, and partly
collected from various sources known only to himself,
Pearce was always able to retail, and to insinuate in
the midst a variety of little hints which it was his
object to impress upon the old man's mind. At last
his master's confidence had reached so far that he
was called on even to open and read the letters
which Pearce brought from the post. And this
advance was a great satisfaction to Pearce, for it
saved him some little trouble, and enabled him to
bring the letters direct from the post to his master,

without delaying, as he had before been used to do, in his own little room, with bolted doors, and the keyhole carefully closed, before he made his appearance with the budget. He was only surprised, just about this time, to find that no more letters arrived for his young master ; and on inquiring at the post-office, he was informed that Mr. Villiers had given orders for them to be delivered to none but himself.

It was about a month after the General's attack of paralysis that Pearce obtained leave one evening to go into the country. He was seen to take the road which runs along the north side of the bay. And it was late when he returned. As the footman opened the door for him, he was surprised to see his face distorted with passion, his eyes full of malignity, his lips almost bloody with the compression of his teeth. He went hastily into his room. When the General rang for him he pleaded illness; and was heard by Villiers's man all the night striding up and down the room, muttering incoherent exclamations of jealousy and revenge. He made his appearance the next morning, ill-disguising, notwithstanding his wonderful powers of self-concealment, the passion under which he had spent the night. And there was a fierceness and strangeness of manner in his mode of addressing Villiers, which almost amounted to insolence, and which Villiers, unconscious as he was of what was really passing within him, or of any cause of provocation given by himself, was disposed to attribute almost to incipient insanity, and desired his own man to keep an eye upon him. This manner continued for some days ; and during them Pearce was employed, as often as he could escape from the General's room, (even to whom he showed an impatience and violence of temper which the old man could not understand,) in writing long

letters, which he took to the post-office himself ;
some of them, as the clerk at the post-office observed, being addressed to a female, and the others
to persons at Rome, Lyons, and England, especially to a town called Hawkstone. Nor was he
without receiving letters in return ; and after perusing them in his own little room, some he would
carefully burn, picking up and destroying every
fragment which escaped the flames ; and others he
locked up anxiously in a little box, which he deposited in a corner of his room, under a loose plank
in the floor, over which he never forgot to draw
a huge and heavy bureau. By degrees his manner
became more calm and subdued ; a change which
he attributed, as he told the General, to some favourite medicine which the General had recommended him as an admirable specific for the headache, which he pleaded as a cause for his altered
appearance. And the General was pleased and flattered by his own success in working a cure. To
Villiers also he resumed his usual deportment, was
still more assiduous and obliging, even made him a
humble apology for his former manner, and attributed
it to indisposition, a rush of blood to the head, to
which he was subject from a child ; asked if he could
get his letters from the post as usual (which Villiers declined) ; and but for a dark malignant scowl
upon him, which he seemed to indulge, as if in-
demnifying himself for perpetual self-restraint,
whenever he looked back on Villiers passing him,
no one would have remarked in him anything but
the officiousness of a remarkably clever, bustling,
and rather fawning servant, who seemed, as he often
acknowledged was the case, to have known better
days.

CHAP. XVI.

In the meanwhile Villiers, unconscious that he had
caused suffering to a single human being, was enjoying what he had never before enjoyed in his life
— happiness. The vision which he had pictured to
himself — the vine-trellised cottage, the seat scooped
out from the living rock, the gazing on the deep blue
sea, the face, the exquisite face of innocence and
beauty, not yet indeed to lie upon his bosom, but to
look up into his eye with wonder and all but adoration — the mind simple and docile, which he
might mould like wax to take from him every stamp
of truth — the one idolized object on which he might
pour, unchecked, the whole tide of his affections, —
all this some mysterious hand had realized for him ;
and earth to him was now a heaven.

" Will he not come to-day, father ? " almost whispered the poor Pauline, as one evening the old man
and herself had stood for more than an hour on the
rock beneath the cottage watching for the approach
of Villiers's little boat, rowed now only by himself.
" Will he not come to-day ? " and she crept into her
father's arms, and he felt her hot tears stealing
down her cheek.

" My child ! " he replied, " my darling child ! even
these tears I am thankful for. Your happiness is too
great, and every pain mixed with it is like an expia-
tion for it. If you suffer as well as rejoice, your joy
may yet be lasting." And as he bent his reverend
grey head over her delicate neck, and gave her his
blessing, Pauline looked up fearfully but fondly to

ask him with her look why he should speak so sadly.

"My child," he continued, "I am old, and have seen the world, and know what lies in human nature; and though now we are living lonely on this little nook of rock, in better times I have served in armies, and walked with nobles in courts and palaces. And yet, if there rose before me all whom I have ever known of noble beings — and Providence permitted me to choose for you the noblest and the best, —I scarcely know that I could fix on one to whom I could consign you for ever with so much hope and so much joy as this young Englishman." And as he said this, he felt the poor girl's face laid closer on his bosom, as if thankful and proud of his praise. "But that such a lot," he continued, " should have fallen upon you, so young, so poor, so destitute of all help,"—he corrected himself, and reverentially taking off his cap, added, —" of all help but heaven, this is to me strange and almost fearful. And I tremble lest so great a seeming good should be only a temptation, and should end in evil." And he lifted up her face and looked gravely and steadily into her eyes yet wet with tears. "My child, he is rich, and you are poor; he is young, and I am old. When I die, and I shall soon die, will he still be to you all that I have been?" And Pauline shuddered, and once more buried her face in his bosom.

"Have you told him," he continued, "all that he ought to know?"

Pauline faltered "Yes."

"Everything?" asked the old man, searchingly.

"And again she answered "Yes. How, father, could I help it; how could I hide anything from him—from him who loves me so dearly?"

And Pauline spoke the truth. Almost one of the first questions which Villiers had put to her,

when he dared to do so, and felt that now their
whole souls should be open to each other, was the
one so natural to a devoted and therefore a jealous
heart, and yet so hard to ask and to answer: "Was
the hand now to be his own never devoted to another?" Villiers knew not how to frame it — had
hesitated — had asked it more by looks than words;
and Pauline understood it, rather by her own wish
to answer it than by his expressions. And though
her reverence for him was so great, that often,
when he led her to speak of herself, she would hide
her face, and sit beside him without the power of
doing more than answer "Yes," to his interro-
gations: now her look sprang up with confidence
and courage, and meeting his anxious and inquiring
eye without shrinking for a moment, she said to him,
that there were things which she wished to tell him,
which he had a right to know, but that she could do
it only in writing. A pang struck to Villiers's heart.
He withdrew himself coldly and proudly from her
side, and walked from the seat where they were resting to the edge of the cliff. It seemed as if the
glory of his vision was departing, and some rude
hand had swept the brightness from the blossom of
his beautiful flower. But he heard a sound as of
a sob near him. And Pauline stood a little way behind him, as not daring to approach, her face covered with her hands, and the tears streaming
through her delicate fingers.

"You are angry with me," she said, faintly (and
all his fondness returned). "You are angry with me
for not telling you at once. I will tell you now —
this moment — anything rather than that you should
be angry. I can bear anything but this;" and she
burst into a flood of tears. "I know," she continued, taking her hands from her face, "I know
what you would ask me. Never, never! O that

you could look into my heart! Never till you came."

Villiers's heart leaped with joy. And he sprang forward to catch her to his bosom; but he checked himself, for she was not yet his; and with a superstitious reverence he would not allow even his own affection to presume on her exquisite delicacy. He thanked her, and blessed her fervently.

" Stop," she said, you have not heard all; "there has been one who was kind and good to me—kinder than I deserved. And my poor father is old, and soon will be unable to work ; and he feared for me, if he should die and I should be left alone. But when I told him that I would rather die myself, he did not urge it. And the person who was kind to me once is kind to me no more. He knows that it is vain to ask for what I have given to another."

Villiers understood the tale, short and broken as it was. One impatient question came to his lips; but as he checked it, Pauline herself anticipated it.

" You must never ask me," she said, "who it was, for I could not tell it — no, not even to you; and I know you will not ask me."

And as she looked up firmly, and with unsuspecting confidence, to demand his promise, Villiers gave it readily, and kept it honourably.

" And now, my darling child," he said, "your father is calling us. Let us go to him; and I will read to you, and you shall sing to me your own dear hymn."

" And you are not angry with me now," she said, timidly. And as she caught his look of deep affection, her heart bounded within her, and she sprang off like a fawn to seek her father, and find her lute.

Two years afterwards, Villiers was lying in a miserable stifling chamber, bound hand and foot,

and his brain on fire. And in the midst of a
paroxysm of raving, in which even the stern sturdy
men who were placed to guard him could scarcely
prevent him from bursting his bands, the voice of
some poor singer in the street, led there as by a
pitying angel, commenced the same simple strain.
Villiers caught it, and strove to sit up upon his
low pallet. His eye gazed wonderingly around
him; and, as the simple music still fell on his ear,
tears began to flow; and visions, far other than those
which had nursed his phrenzy, came gently on him.
He was sitting on the seat scooped out of the living
rock, and his own Pauline beside him; and behind
them was standing the venerable old man, listening
to their solemn vows, and blessing them: and then
he was floating with them both on the smooth swelling waters at evening, just as the moonlight began
to ripple on the sea; and a fairy, gentle voice was
singing the same sweet hymn. And then they were
both tending together a sick bed in a vine-trellised
cottage, watching over the patient sufferings, soothing every pain, bearing with every infirmity of a
dying father — Pauline's father, not his own. The
scene changed, and there was a holy chapel — a
holy ceremony — a stoled priest. And then they
were both kneeling again before the same dying
bed; and the old man was lying with his arms
crossed, looking up gratefully to heaven, and blessing God that now he could depart in peace. But
the music ceased — another thought came upon Villiers; and with a shuddering groan he sprang up in
agony, and called wildly for his child; and the
keeper sternly bade him lie still, and not make a
noise.

While these delicious moments, so bright and so
soothing, even when recalled in dreams, and gone
for ever, were gliding on, where was the aged,

miserable, sinful father of the young, happy — and as his own deceitful conscience whispered — innocent young man. He was sinking daily into his dotage. As if still further to remove the obstacles which might have embarrassed or embittered the full enjoyment of the happiness to which Villiers was now abandoning himself, almost, thought Villiers again, by a good providence (as if a good providence ever administered to us pleasure, except that it may nerve us to duties), the General, instead of wishing for his son's presence, expressed more openly his aversion to him, and frequently passed whole days in his own room without seeing him. Pearce was acquiring, every hour, more influence over him — was becoming more necessary to his comfort; and from suggesting advice, and hinting opinions, he had now assumed the right of dictating to his master. And his master faintly and timidly succumbed to all that he proposed. Something in this beyond the mere art of ruling, which Pearce had so deeply studied, might have been discovered by one who knew all that passed in the long confinement of the old man's room, to which Pearce unmurmuringly devoted himself. He felt that it could not last long ; and the gradual approach of success in his grand object encouraged him to discharge the most wearying and even offensive offices, without exhibiting more impatience than was necessary to keep the old man, as he called his master, in proper order.

Pearce, like Villiers himself, knew (for things of the kind are known far wider than we imagine, when we hide our eyes and think we are not seen) that the General's life had been one of vice. But he knew nothing of particulars. And among all the various arts which he employed to obtain the knowledge of this important secret, in conformity with the leading principle and policy of

the religious school in which he had been brought
up, none had succeeded in throwing clear light
upon the subject, until one day's post, among a
number of letters, brought one written in a coarse,
vulgar hand, and marked *private*. On this occasion
Pearce did not proceed, as usual, direct to his master's room. He retired first to his own, and there,
with bolted door and the key-hole carefully closed,
he found little difficulty in mastering the secret.
He had been employed before in a foreign post-
office, and had there learned much, which he found
eminently useful to him in after-times. As he
placed the packet of letters, as usual, on the little
table by the General's easy chair, where he sat
propped up with pillows, his thin, peaked, wrinkled
features peering malignantly from a large fur cap,
and his legs wrapped carefully in blankets, Pearce
retired where he could command a view of what
passed, in a large mirror, without being supposed to
watch him. He saw the thin bony fingers, almost
like claws, of the old man stretched out to grasp
the letters, which he could scarcely hold. The spectacles were shifted, and Pearce himself was called
to wipe them. The letters once more were feebly
taken, and laid one by one aside, as the old man
scrutinised the post-mark, till he came to the one
marked private. His pale face became of an ashy
hue; his hand shook violently; and casting a cowardly side glance at his obsequious servant, to see
if he was looking, he thrust the letter under the
folds of the blanket. Pearce waited in vain to be
asked to open and read the letters as usual. He
then proposed it himself; but the unhappy old man,
in a trembling husky voice, told him he might go
and leave him, for that he wanted to sleep. His
bell rang again for Pearce, about an hour after; his
countenance had then resumed its ordinary look,

and Pearce observed nothing, but that he must
have moved from his chair himself (an exertion
which he had been incapable of making for weeks),
and that the remains of burnt paper were lying
under the grate. The look of exultation which
Pearce cast upon his prey, now completely in his
hands, was even heightened, as the old man asked
for his son, and Pearce could inform him that he had
been absent for several days, and (as he took care to
add, maliciously,) that he was seldom at home now,
since the General had become worse. No one
knew where he went to.

This was a falsehood, for this secret also Pearce
had long penetrated. It was a spot which he himself had known—respecting which he had himself
indulged dreams and visions—visions far different
from Villiers, but which never occurred to his mind
without filling him with the spirit of revenge and
jealousy almost to madness.

On that day he said nothing more. Two days
after he was summoned to read a letter from the
General's lawyer, alluding to a power reserved to
the General in some marriage settlement of leaving
his property to another branch of the family. And
Pearce took care to sigh. And when the General
fretfully asked him the meaning of his sigh, he hesitated, and at last was compelled reluctantly to lament that Mr. Villiers did not show as much respect and affection for his father as became a young
man, heir to such an estate. Another night the
General's rest was broken by a ringing of bells and
disturbance in the house, and Pearce took care to
inform him that it was caused by his son, who constantly came in late. Another time he went still
farther; and appearing with a face of astonishment
and reserve, as if possessed of some melancholy secret, which he was resolved to hint, but not to disclose,

he permitted the General to extort from him a confession that there were sad stories about Mr. Villiers,
and he feared he was going on ill. And a few words
were enough to suggest all that he wished to the old
man, whose mind with readiness suspected in others
all that he had been guilty of himself. With vice, indeed, even in his son, he could readily have borne;
he would have admitted it as a matter of course:
but when Pearce hinted at something else, at the
possibility of his son abandoning himself to an in-
fatuation, as he called it, and throwing himself
away for life in a degrading connexion, he touched
a chord in the old man's mind which lay entwined
with all his favourite schemes, and awoke his most
violent passions. Mean and paltry as his usual
habits were, since from the extravagances of a luxurious youth he had become calculating and selfish,
he had formed and cherished for years one plan
having a show of dignity—the marriage of his son
with his cousin, Lady Eleanor, and the reunion of
the old family estates of Claremont and the Priory. We all know how deeply an idea once admitted, and allowed to shoot out into fancies and
dreams, in the morbid indolence of a sick room, or
an unoccupied old age, will take possession of the
whole man. To touch this, to hint a doubt of the
possibility of realizing it, was to throw the General
into a violent outbreak of temper. This had been
one of the most embittering subjects on which he
had harped to his son, till even the natural inclination which Villiers might have felt towards the
project gave way beneath the tormenting and overbearing indelicacy in which his father dwelt upon
it. And in his heart of hearts he had resolved that
no such mercenary thoughts should ever be connected with that marriage tie, which, whenever
and to whomever it should bind him, he recognized

as most sacred and most ennobling. On the same subject Pearce himself, thoroughly master of his tactics, had at first indulged his master in assisting his fancy, and joining in his calculations. And now, as if seizing on every opportunity to exasperate the poor enfeebled man, on this he artfully touched each day, contriving to separate the two objects, and to present to the general's mind the possibility of realizing one if not the other; and if he could not effect the marriage through his son's wilfulness, at least of uniting the estates. There was one difficulty, one prejudice, as Pearce well knew, most difficult to surmount: Lady Eleanor was a Roman Catholic; and though the old man, careless of religion, could have borne to see her united with his son for the purpose of uniting the estates in the person of his own heir, he was not yet prepared to throw his own property into the hands of a Papist. His prejudices against popery were strong, and vulgar. Of its really deadly and destructive nature he knew nothing. But he disliked it—disliked it the more from the vexation which his union with Lady Esther had brought on him; and this obstacle Pearce was to remove. It was not a mere thought of his own. If we could have obtained possession of that mahogany box, buried under the loose plank, and covered with the huge bureau, in Pearce's little room, and could then have perused the letters, which, with the Roman postmark upon them, he had received from time to time, we might have obtained a deeper insight into the springs and objects of his conduct. But whatever caution and slowness he had originally shown, his success became more and more apparent each day. The poor old man was soon entirely at his disposal. A hint dexterously thrown in one day, and accompanied with one of those significant looks which Pearce could so

well assume, revealed to the terrified General
that the secret, which he thought was buried in his
own bosom now, and would be buried for ever in
his grave, was known also to another person, and
that person his servant.   In vain he endeavoured
to persuade himself that his conscience had taken
alarm too quickly—that Pearce's words meant
nothing.   Pearce understood it all, and contrived
without delay to repeat the hint, dropping also a
little circumstance, which removed all doubt.   Farther he did not go.   He never threatened, or presumed upon his possession of this knowledge ; though
the General would have purchased his silence by
any humiliation.   His attentions were redoubled ;
his manner still more obliging than ever.   And the
General became bound to him, and ready to comply
with all his suggestions, far more than any menaces
or violence could have made him.   It suited, however, Pearce's purpose cautiously to open the subject
of religion.   With a most artful and delicate hand
he contrived to touch even the seared and hardened
conscience of his victim by fear.   He himself affected
and exhibited a devotional spirit.   At times he led
the General to ask questions, which brought on
some tale of superstition, some thoughts which
awakened in the unhappy man fears of a future
state, and longings for more safety in the prospect to
which he was compelled to look forward.   Pearce
dwelt with energy and fluency on the peace and
comfort of his own mind, relieved from all the burden of past sins by the absolution of his priest, and
secure in the intercession of the Saints.   The old man
listened, and wondered at the new tone of his servant, now almost become his companion ; but the
ideas were not lost.   They came home to him more
and more when his rest began to be disturbed at
night by strange noises, which Pearce, always

ready by his bed-side, took care to interpret and comment on, till the old man shook in his bed, and the cold sweat stood on his brow. Then Pearce would drop suggestions of the peace and comfort which were ensured to all who were members of the One Church. But the old man gave no signs of change. And the noises became more frequent, and his rest more disturbed. At last he was awakened from his sleep one night by a figure standing by his bed-side. The old man started up in an agony of terror. The figure motioned him to remain still —uttered some words to him, and disappeared. And Pearce, awakened, or rather affecting to be awakened, by his cry of terror, found him senseless.

A few days after that, he had a long interview with his son, in which he violently and peremptorily insisted on Villiers immediately abandoning the connection which he had formed, and returning to England, that he might prosecute his favourite plan of a union with Lady Eleanor. Villiers steadily refused. His father menaced him with the consequences of his refusal. Villiers begged that he would act as he thought fit. His father bade him depart, and almost imprecated a curse upon him. And Villiers proudly left the room, and never again saw his father alive. Pearce had heard all that passed. As Villiers came out of the room, stung to the quick with the language which his father had used towards the being whom he cherished most upon earth, exasperated most of all by the violent effort with which he had compelled himself to leave his father in ignorance of the real nature of his connection with her, that he might not irretrievably provoke him to do that which would so deeply injure her, Pearce met him, and for a moment the fierce passion of the vindictive wretch overcame his caution ; he uttered something which made the veins in Villiers's forehead swell almost to bursting, and his eyes flashed fire.

"Villain!" he cried, "whom did you say? going to whom?" And Pearce no way intimidated by the arm that was lifted ready to crush him, with bitter and insulting sarcasm, asked of him again if he was going to his —— Before he could finish the offensive word he was levelled on the ground. "To my lawful wedded wife!" said Villiers; and, spurning the fellow from him, he rushed out of the house.

Two days afterwards the physicians ordered the General to remove to Rome. And solitary, with none but Pearce now with him, and sitting by his side, the miserable old man drove for the last time from the Chiaia, bearing upon every feature of his face the mark of terror and of death.

CHAP. XVII.

It was late one night, nearly twelve months afterwards, that a calash covered with mud, and the
horses ready to drop with exhaustion, drove rapidly
into the Piazza di Spagna. As they whirled round
the corner, the single traveller who was in it.
stretched himself out to catch a sight of a house before
him, in which, while all the other windows in the
square were dark, and the inhabitants buried in
slumber, two windows were still lighted, though
thickly curtained. As the carriage stopped at the
door, without waiting for the exhausted postilions,
who could scarcely get off their horses to put down
the steps, Villiers sprang out of it, haggard, pallid,
and in the deepest mourning. He tottered as he
entered the house, and caught sight of the face of a
servant, full of that mysterious gloominess and
forced sympathy which is worn by domestics when
death is approaching, or has already fallen upon a
family. The servant opened gently the door of the
saloon ; but Villiers made an effort to pass by, and
proceed at once to his father's bed-room. But the
servant detained him. " Persons were with him,"
he said. And when Villiers asked if there was any
hope, the man shook his head. He would have
asked if the last awful moment was close at hand ;
but there is a strange and awful feeling which it is
no superstition to observe and realise when death is
near us, a stillness and creeping of the flesh, we
know not how, which told Villiers that his father
was now lying in his last agonies. The servant left,
promising to come back the moment Villiers could

be admitted into the sick room ; and Villiers knelt
down, overpowered with awe, and in that awe almost
forgetting his own misery.   But a smothered cry of
great agony and terror from the adjoining chamber struck upon him ; and he could bear the delay
no longer.   The next moment he was in his father's
bed-room.   The curtains of the bed were open : by
the bed-side stood the nurse and Pearce ; and two
priests, habited in their vestments, were preparing to
administer the rite of extreme unction.   But it was
too late ; Villiers glanced upon the bed, and saw
that all was over.   The ghastly features, the convulsed
mouth, the eyes still staring, the hands clutched
fiercely on the bed-clothes, the hair standing on end
— Villiers saw it all, and sank again upon his knees
in intense agony ; for now, when it was too late, he
asked himself if this might not have been averted.

He was roused from a stupor by the necessity
of removing from the room.   And as he was passing
to his own apartment which he had occupied before,
Pearce came up to him, and insolently ordered the
servant to prepare a bed for him in the north room.
The servant stared at the person who presumed to
give orders in a house where Villiers himself was
now master.   But Pearce repeated the order, and
desired Villiers to make himself at home.   And
Villiers, unheeding everything, and staggering under
remorse as well as suffering, looked at him, scarcely
knowing what he said, and was persuaded by the
old housekeeper to retire and lie down, though not
in sleep.

Sleep, indeed, except in rare and feverish fits,
had not visited him for weeks.   The moment he
closed his eyes there came before him that one
vision, that pensive, delicate, exquisitely beautiful
face, which had haunted him so blissfully ever since
its first appearance.   But only once or twice did it

appear in all its beauty, radiant with joy, as when
he first called her his own, or calm in the pensive enjoyment of deepest happiness, as when he
sat by her side on that seat of rock, and taught
her lessons of goodness from his own manly, upright heart. These were the appearances which he
dreaded most; and by a secret instinct, whenever
they approached, he started from his broken slumber,
not daring to face the agony which would await him
on awaking. More frequently the vision came in a
very different guise; but Villiers could bear it better,
for there was no deceit in it, no frightful revulsion
from the dream to the reality. It came pale, and
wan, and feeble, but still beautiful; sometimes attired
as one who, sickening under a fatal disease, was
still able to be removed from her bed, and propped
up with pillows to breathe fresher air; sometimes
with a sleeping child lying in her bosom;—then
with a few sweet flowers strewed upon her forehead,
the lips motionless, the eyes closed, the head enveloped in its grave-clothes. But to-night it came
in a form more fearful. The delicate beautiful
face came, indeed, and looked upon him as before,
but it changed suddenly into the horrible and ghastly
figure which he had witnessed on his father's death-
bed. It seemed to utter on him fearful reproaches;
to imprecate a curse upon himself and on his children, with the same voice with which his father
had bade him depart, in the last words which he
had spoken to him while alive. The eyes glared
frightfully upon him; claws were stretched out to
seize him; a cry—the cry of agony which had
pierced him to the heart from his father's room—once
more rang in his ears; and shaking from head to
foot, the big drops standing on his forehead, his
heart beating with terror, and his breath gasping, he

R

struggled out of his sleep and looked wildly round
him.

A clock was ticking on the mantel-piece, and a
few flickering gleams strugged from the dying
embers on the hearth. He sat up on the bed, and,
breathing more freely, attempted, not to sleep again—
for this he dared not do—but to pray for forgiveness
for the neglect, the undutifulness, the harsh, unforgiv-
ing spirit, which, as a son, he had shown to his now
miserable father—for the self-indulgence in which
he had abandoned him to the artifices of a menial—
for the proud unbending temper with which he had
kept aloof from him ever since he had left Rome,
receiving no letters except a rare statement of his
father's health from a physician; and resolved on
making no overtures for a reconciliation, lest he
should be supposed to be actuated by mercenary
policy. At the time all this had appeared to him
innocent, even high-minded and just. Now he knew
that it was sin; and sin the beginning of all others—
the dishonouring of parents, even of parents who
are sinful themselves. And then for the first time
it struck him that the judgments of God are just.
He had forsaken his father for a device of his own
heart, and a desire of his own eyes: and the desire
of his eyes had been taken from him. The punishment had fallen just when the sin was consummated.
And he who had left his father alone in the world,
to sink into his grave in the arms of hirelings, and
with no consolation but the delusions of an anodyne
for a guilty conscience, purchased by an act of apos-
tacy, and after all snatched from him at the last,
was now himself left alone in the world, stripped
of his dreams, his hopes, his affections—like a
wreck abandoned by its crew, and tossed idly on the
waters.

One little gleam of soothing thought—soothing,

because it revealed a duty as well as an enjoyment—stole on him when he remembered that, widower as he was, he was still a parent. And as the fondness of the father awoke in him a train of softer feelings, the tears coursed each other down his cheek. He rose, threw his dressing-gown around him, and, opening his writing-case, among papers which he never left behind him, and which were carefully labelled and concealed in a secret drawer, he sought for a miniature, delicately finished, over which he hung in silence, recalling all the scenes with which it was associated,—the light step,—the look of pensive sweetness, varying with each thrill of affection into deep devotion for himself,—the delights of those hours when he had hung over her as she sang, or when she had seated herself at his feet, looking up archly but docilely to hear what he would read or teach her,—the thousand little acts of love with which she had solaced the last days of her venerable father (for she, thought Villiers, with a pang, never despised and never neglected the author of her being), — the simple look of wonder with which she had listened to his question, when he told her that perhaps poverty might be their lot; and would she still love him?—and then the lingering illness, the patient suffering, the tears for him alone, the prayers over the head of her child, the fervour with which she commended it to him, with her memory as its safeguard—all these recollections stole out one by one like stars upon an evening sky, till he seemed once more to be living in the midst of the realities—to have an object and a being still before him, whose presence would rule his life and elevate his thoughts—whom he might almost adore now, even as he adored her when living. And his heart, once touched with this emotion, passed on to a higher region, and to the only Being who is

present always, and can elevate and sanctify the
soul, and whom the heart of man may indeed adore.
He knelt down, and prayed earnestly, not only for
forgiveness of past sins, but for strength to bear
their punishment, and to atone for them, as far
as men may atone, by humility and dutiful obedience for ever after. He prayed also for a reunion
with her whom he had lost; for a blessing on his
child: and by degrees all his thoughts and affections concentred round his infant; and he felt
that it was an object which might absorb him wholly,
and be to him his happiness and life.

He was still kneeling, with his face upturned to
heaven, and the lamp which he had lighted had
flickered and died away in the socket, leaving only
the gleam from the ashes of the wood fire, when he
heard a slight noise in a distant corner of the room,
and looking up, observed a thin streak of light stealing
on the wall. At first he thought it a reflection
from the fire ; but it grew wider and stronger, and
the heavy tapestry curtain behind which it appeared visibly moved. At another time Villiers
would have advanced without a fear to examine the
cause. But all that he had suffered and witnessed—
the thought of what was lying at that moment beneath
the same roof—the recollections which had so long
haunted him—now chilled him with a superstitious
awe. He remained motionless, and hidden by the
huge chair before which he was kneeling, with his
eyes fixed on the increasing glimmer of light. An
exclamation almost escaped him as the curtain was
slowly withdrawn, and a human face peered out
from behind it. It looked round cautiously—
advanced—the whole figure appeared, and Villiers
saw that it was Pearce. His eye glanced first upon
the open writing-case and the packet of papers, as if
he would willingly have seized upon them. Then,

furtively looking round the room, he stole to the bed-side, and, gently peeping through the curtains, started back, and almost stumbled and fell, as Villiers sprang up from his kneeling posture and demanded what he wanted. An ordinary person would have required some little time to recover from such a shock ; but Pearce, in emergencies of the kind, was not an ordinary person. Prepared and composed in a minute, he answered that he had heard Villiers moving ; was afraid that he was ill; had come to see if he could be of any service. Villiers eyed him with some suspicion. But Pearce still preserved the same composure. And on Villiers assuring him that nothing was the matter, Pearce begged his pardon, and retired through the regular entrance. Villiers did not return to his bed till he had examined the passage behind the heavy tapestry curtain, and finding a secret door in the wainscot communicating with a narrow staircase, he contrived to block it up with some furniture. But it was daylight before he was able again to close his eyes.

It was late the next morning before any one would venture to approach Villiers's room. His bell had not rung. And it was only the good-natured house-keeper, Mrs. Boucher, who had courage at last to take him some breakfast without his asking for it. She found him dressed ; but so pale, so thin, so thoroughly wretched in appearance, that the poor woman, after placing the tray on the table, could not refrain from sitting down in a chair ; and, hiding her face in her apron, she burst into tears.

"Oh, sir! Oh, master Ernest!" she cried, as she sobbed violently, "if you had but been here, this would not have been — if you had but answered the letters!"

Villiers himself was leaning his face upon the mantel-piece, and the tears streaming down his cheeks

R 3

But at the mention of letters he raised himself up to ask " What letters ? "

" Ours, sir," said Mrs. Boucher, " which we, that is I and the butler, made bold to write to you, to tell you what was doing."

Villiers had never received any. " I had," he said " but one or two letters from here, and they came from Signor Villetti, the doctor ; and they all told me things were going on well, till I heard from Mr. Beattie, and then I came here immediately.

The poor housekeeper seemed amazed. " Then, sir," she said, " there has been some foul play, and that Italian doctor ought never to have been brought here. It was not we who sent for him, but that man,—I suppose we must call him Mr. Pearce now. And the General, poor man, would never hear of any one else."

And the ice once broken, the motherly, loquacious Mrs. Boucher proceeded to explain to Villiers all that had passed in his absence ; how they had been ordered suddenly to Rome, no one knew why ; but Pearce had pretended some advice from the doctors ; how, when they reached Rome, no visiters were admitted but one or two Englishmen, whom the servants had not seen before, and, by degrees, a priest from one of the colleges ; how Pearce had contrived to take the whole management of affairs upon himself, carefully excluding the servants from even seeing their master, except when they caught sight of him as Pearce assisted him down the stairs to take his usual drive ; how, more than once, Pearce had brought with him a sort of lawyer, and Mrs. Boucher, on passing the door of her master's room, as it stood ajar, had seen him with a pen in his hand, and Pearce standing by to guide it as he signed a paper ; — and then came complaints of Pearce's increased arrogance and domineering habits,

which none of the other servants could endure,—
just, Mrs. Boucher said, as if he was master of the
house. "Oh, sir!" she concluded, "I am afraid there
has been foul play, and you will find things very bad."

Villiers scarcely entered into the latter part of
the sentence, but the former struck him to the heart.
And he asked to what she alluded. Upon which
Mrs. Boucher proceeded to enumerate many little
facts. As she passed the General's door one day,
she had heard high words between Pearce and his
master; and when the General wanted to drive one
way, Pearce would order the carriage to drive another. And the old man was not allowed to see any
of his old friends; and the doctor, Signor Villetti,
would prohibit him from having things to eat and
drink which he used to be fond of. "And then,
sir," she continued, sinking her voice to a whisper,
and looking anxiously round the room, "one day,
as I was going up stairs, and Mr. Pearce had gone
out, I was standing just by his door; and what should
I see, to my wonder, but the door softly open, and
your poor father himself looked out. It was in this
very room, which Mr. Pearce had put him into.
And he made me come in. He could hardly walk;
and there he sat down in that arm-chair; and there
was nothing about him comfortable, no book or any
thing; and they had taken away his dog Fido, sir,
that you remember—a little ugly thing it was, and
always getting in the way. I remember one night
it nearly threw me down the stairs. It was the
night we got to Rome: I was coming up stairs in the
dark." And where Mrs. Boucher's reminiscences
would have carried her no one could have prophesied. But Villiers recalled her to his father. "Oh,
sir! I was going to tell you what he told me, and what
I got the butler to write off by that night's post. I
would have written myself, sir, only my handwriting

is bad. And yet I had some good schooling, and
my father was in very comfortable circumstances,
and brought me up well. I used to go to school at
the Park-gate—old Mrs. Bond's, close by the great
elm near the Priory ruins."

And once more Villiers impatiently recalled her.
Mrs. Boucher begged pardon, and at last Villiers
learned from her that the General had complained to
her of ill-treatment; had said that he was very much
afraid of Pearce; that Pearce had become a tyrant, and
he could bear it no longer. Only when Mrs. Boucher
had proposed that he should be sent away, the unhappy man turned pale, and said, "No, that could not
be." And then the good woman had ventured to
say something about Mr. Ernest, and that he ought
to be sent for. And the General had seemed sad
and downcast; and complained that every one had
deserted him—that even his son would not come
near to him. And Mrs. Boucher added, "He seemed
to speak, sir, as if he would have given a great deal to
see you. And I do think he loved you, sir, though he
was rather hasty at times. But then sons ought
to bear with their father: I am sure I did with my
poor old mother, who was bed-stricken for years."

Villiers groaned aloud, and shuddered, as he still
stood with his face covered with his hands, and resting on the mantel-piece. He lifted it after a pause,
during which Mrs. Boucher sat with her hands folded
in her black silk apron, and asked her if——he dared
not name his father; and checked himself to say,
"Had there been much suffering?"

Mrs. Boucher shook her head mournfully, and
once more proceeded. "He had been much disturbed at nights. A servant, who slept over-head,
had often been kept awake by his groaning; and
there were sometimes hard words from Pearce, as if
he were threatening instead of comforting him.

One night he had been taken very ill, and Mrs. Boucher had been summoned to assist. It was a long time before the doctor came, and Mr. Pearce, who seemed extremely impatient for his arrival, had left the room to hasten the messenger.

" And then," continued Mrs. Boucher, " as the poor old gentleman looked up, and only saw the other nurse in the room, he made signs to me to send her away, which I did; and then, though he could scarcely move, he put his hands so-together, and shook his head. It was the most piteous sight I ever saw. He was so pale and thin, and his hair quite white. And then he made signs to me to give him his keys, which I did, and he pointed out one. and making me lay my ear almost down to his lips, he whispered, ' When I am gone, give this to *him* — you know whom I mean. He has not been kind; but I won't be hard to him: let them do what they choose.' And just then Mr. Pearce came back, and was quite angry that I had been in the room alone. He took up the keys, as they lay on the bed, and I never saw them since. Hark, sir! there is some one at the door."

The knock was repeated, and Mrs. Boucher bustled up to make way for Pearce himself, and another person, seemingly a notary. It was with a face of almost savage exultation, scarcely intended to be stifled, that Pearce announced to Villiers that he was come to seal up some drawers. Villiers himself, almost forgetful as he had been of any other circumstance, in the thought of his father, was now aroused to demand by what right he entered on this office. And nothing further was needed to induce Pearce to enter at once on the real object of his intrusion; and desiring his companion to open a black portfolio, he placed before Villiers a formal document, which he requested him to read. Villiers did read it—read it with his eyes almost blinded with tears, for he saw his father's signature, shaken and abrupt, as of a person in the extremity of illness. It was formal, however, correct, without a flaw, duly signed, and witnessed. Villiers knew nothing of law, but, to all appearance, it assured him that the menace held out by his father had been fulfilled, and that he was a beggar. All that could be left away was given to the Jesuits' College at Rome, with the exception of a large legacy to Pearce. The landed property was given to Lady Eleanor, and Villiers himself not mentioned. He was a beggar; and the effect was, for the moment, stunning. That which for months he had thought of, and spoken of as possible, was realized; but reality is a very different thing from imagination— and he found it so.

It required, however, but little time for him to recover himself sufficiently to return the document, and to request that he might be left alone, and not subjected to intrusion upon questions of business at such a moment; and Pearce retired, taking care, as he looked him in the face, to lift up a mass of hair from his own forehead, and to exhibit a scar, which had been there ever since the evening when Villiers had last left his father's house at Naples.

It was a dreary and fearful interval which ensued between that hour and the day when his father's remains were deposited in the grave, according to the rites of the Romish church. One person only was admitted to him—Beattie, who was still at Rome, in recovered health, and to whose judgment Villiers willingly committed the task of making the necessary inquiries into the validity of the will. There were moments of stupor, of amazement, such as falls upon the mind when some great shock has changed the whole face of the world around us.

Then came attempts to realize the present and the future; then some object before him brought back all the past: and, for the moment, the present seemed a dream, till the reality once more flashed upon him. At times came a conflict between his conscience and his suffering. Angry thoughts would rise; the recollection of past ill-treatment; efforts to excuse himself; then recollections of his own joys, and his own sorrows; then he was once more sitting on the rocky seat, or under the shade of the vine-trellissed cottage, till he started up to find himself in his dark, dreary chamber. Once, only, the vision returned to him again, and again bringing something like peace — the vision of his motherless child; and the thought that there was still a centre, round which his affections might gather — a being for whom he might toil, though in poverty and pain — who might look up to him, and love him, and cling to him, and cherish him when he was old and in sickness. But here a pang shot across him; for what hope could he have of meriting that filial duty towards himself, which he had himself denied to his own parent. Every thing ended in remorse; and even remorse was sweet, for it was real, and true: it bore on it no delusion. And as he bowed himself to the ground, and prayed, Villiers began to feel what religion is; he felt it in its first beginning — sorrow and shame.

He left his room but once. It was after every one in the house had gone to bed; and even the nurses, who were sitting in the chamber of the dead, were appalled when they marked the agony in his countenance, as he opened the door and motioned them to withdraw. They listened at the outside, and heard him draw the bolt and prostrate himself on the ground, and then all was silent; only at times a suppressed groan reached them: but they dared not enter. And the cold grey dawn struggled in through the curtained windows before he opened the door and returned to his own room. But from that night Villiers was an altered man. Even Beattie was surprised to see the calmness and self-control, the almost childlike gentleness with which he did and suffered all that was necessary in the distressing scenes through which he was obliged to pass. He made only one request—that Pearce might be prevented from coming near him. Every thing else, which, in a former day, would have galled and stung him to the quick, he now submitted to patiently and meekly, as under punishment—a punishment which he recognised as just. He requested only a single alteration in the arrangement of the funeral; but it was intended to express more respect and honour for the dead. And during the last melancholy ceremonial, except the strong and almost convulsive grasp with which he kept his hand within his bosom, clasped on that which Beattie knew to be a little golden cross, Beattie himself would have observed little in his manner but quiet resignation and sorrow. Villiers, even in his youth, was no friend to scenes and exhibitions of emotion.

The second evening after all was over he was sitting alone in Beattie's room, reading—reading, because he was expecting every moment that Beattie would return and bring him information of the circumstances relating to the will. Not indeed that this had ever formed a prominent feature in the bitter thoughts which forced themselves on him; but when at times an almost Quixotic feeling of contempt for wealth, and insensibility to his worldly position, had obtruded themselves, the thought of his child came across him—of his duty to others—and of the necessity for ascertaining and enforcing right wherever it seemed to have been violated. And he admitted with Beattie the obligation of obtaining sufficient information as to the validity of the document. As Beattie's step was heard coming up the stairs, a slight pulsation of the heart revealed to Villiers that his composure was not entire indifference ; but it ceased the moment he caught sight of his friend's face, and saw in it that the case was hopeless. Nothing, Beattie explained to him, could be more correct or formal than the will. He had indeed made inquiries of the servants ; and from them had ascertained much which Mrs. Boucher had stated to Villiers himself, and which awakened no little suspicion of unfair influence having been employed to obtain the present distribution of the property. Hesitatingly and carefully watching the effect of the suggestion on Villiers's countenance, Beattie added that litigation might be possible ; but Villiers shook his head reluctantly. And Beattie then added that he had suggested the possibility of this to the parties now interested in the will, and had not hesitated to express an opinion that it might be overturned ; but he had been met by a threat—a threat of disclosures most painfully affecting the poor General's character ; and Villiers impatiently stopped him, exclaiming, "Never ! never ! "

He sat down without delay to write two letters,— one to Lord Claremont, to inform him that he had no intention of endeavouring to disturb the will, and making one request which he knew would be granted, that he might be allowed to possess the picture of his mother which hung in her bed-chamber at the Priory. The other letter was to his uncle in Yorkshire, an old, penurious, singular character, who possessed, however, some parliamentary interest, and being himself unmarried, had often shown symptoms of attachment to his nephew, even to the extent of contemplating him as the heir of his property. Villiers asked of him nothing but to obtain some situation or commission in the army, which might enable him to support himself. And the letters sealed, he took leave of Beattie for the night, promising to see him the next day before he left Rome for Naples, to make the necessary arrangements for placing his child in some fit and eligible care.

CHAP. XVIII.

IT was not, perhaps, till his arrival in his own room at the hotel, that Villiers for the first time in his life felt what poverty was. He was to part with his servant. And as his servant took his wages, and a donation far beyond what he might have expected, Villiers was pleased with the honest hearty way in which the man thanked him, as having always been a kind and good master. He had tasted scarcely any thing that day, and his spirit having returned with the removal of suspense and the necessity of exertion, he would have asked for something to eat, but the thought came to him of his child, and of the necessity of depriving himself of comforts for the sake of that dear being, and he checked the order which he had been on the point of giving. His servant insisted on remaining to pack his trunks; and Villiers, who had been nurtured in habits which made him peculiarly sensitive to the distinctions of rank, and to the refinements of life, once more felt the reality of his altered position when he gave orders that his portmanteau should be carried to the place from which the vehicle of a courier, with whom he had engaged a place, was to start the next morning. He was young, and still amenable to false shame; and as, accidentally, he met an English acquaintance just as he was mounting the vehicle, and noticed the curiosity and hauteur with which his friend's glass was levelled at him, and the cold bow (his circumstances being known) with which his own distant recognition was returned, a momentary chill, followed by indignation, came over him at the thought of the heartless world with which he was now to grapple; but it was momentary only. Once more he remembered that he had been sinful, and was under punishment, and his equanimity returned.

Side by side with his humbler companion, on whom but a short time before Villiers would have looked, not indeed with contempt, but with something of wonder and curiosity as a being of a different species (for Villiers had been nurtured in some of the worst habits of an exclusive English aristocracy), now he exchanged the little courtesies of fellow-travellers, and, notwithstanding the oppression on his spirits, endeavoured to ask him questions, and even to take an interest in the willingness with which the honest and sensible man opened to him his ideas and history, till he came to explain that he had engaged in a life which he did not like, and had sacrificed much that he enjoyed, even postponing a marriage with a young person to whom he was engaged, and all to enable him to support an aged father, who had lost everything by imprudence. But as he came to this part of his tale he observed that Villiers had buried himself in his cloak, and was sitting with his eyes closed and his brows knit, as if in great pain; and with a tact not uncommon even to uncultivated minds which are familiar with the world, he contrived to stop, and, as the vehicle was mounting a hill, to jump down and walk by the side, leaving his companion to his thoughts; and those thoughts were, as if at every step an eye were opening and a tongue were planted in every mouth, to witness and proclaim one crying sin to a remorseful heart. Just as the vehicle reached the top of the road which crosses the Monte Albano, and Gui-

seppe, the courier, was about to jump into it again,
a light calash drove rapidly round the corner behind them, and nearly grazing the wheels of the
other carriage, galloped on, as if in great anxiety
to reach the next stage before them. Villiers himself had scarcely noticed it, he was so plunged in
thought. But Guiseppe made some remark on the
speed with which the horses were going, and also
on the sinister looks of a single traveller who had
ensconced himself in the corner, and, as he passed
Villiers's vehicle, had thrown a large red handkerchief over his face, which Guiseppe had only been
enabled to see by observing it peering from the
glass behind, as if unwilling to be recognised, and
yet anxious to observe.

"I never knew," he muttered to himself, as he
once more seated himself by Villiers's side, "I never
knew any good connected with such quick travelling; there is always some mischief before or behind." But Villiers made no reply. And the rest
of the journey was spent in silence. Guiseppe understood that his companion was in distress and
sorrow; and respectfully forbore to intrude on him,
except by little attentions which Villiers noticed
with kindness, and which left upon his mind the
valuable lesson for after-life — that no class is so
humble in which courtesy and benevolence, and
even delicacy of feeling, do not exist. It did much
to re-awaken a sympathy between himself and his
inferior fellow-creatures. Meanwhile, as he receded
from Rome, the sufferings of the past week began
to soften and die away under the influence of the
open air, the beautiful scenery, and the rapid motion. His thoughts wandered forwards; and though
he dreaded the bitter recollections which awaited
him at Naples, the thought of his child, whom he
was going to rejoin, and from henceforth intended

to devote himself to rear, gained on him every hour.
It was the star still left in the horror of thick darkness which had fallen on him — the spark from which
a fuller light might hereafter be kindled — the
centre round which alone upon earth his memories
and his hopes might gather, and find happiness and
duty still. He thought of it as lying in its dear
mother's arms, as he had first beheld it; as learning
to stretch out its little arms to him, even though
unable to speak; as laughing brightly at his approach;
as playing with the hair of his head, and crying
to be taken by him and tossed; as reviving many a
little trace of that face, pensive and exquisitely beautiful, which had first entranced him; and as about to
become an image — of himself, Villiers would have
said, had he dared to conclude the sentence : but
then came the consciousness of his sin, of his own
undutifulness and cruelty (he would have used no
lighter word); and he could only breathe a prayer
that his child might not be the image of himself.

It was with such a thought in his heart that the
vehicle drove into the dirty narrow street of Fondi.
He had passed it more than once before, and was
well acquainted with the formalities attending pass-
ports. It was therefore with some surprise that he
found Guiseppe detained in the police-office for a
considerable time, and with still greater that he
saw him come out accompanied by one of the officers, who informed Villiers that there was an informality in his papers, and that it was impossible
for him to proceed till they had been examined further. There was a singular hesitation and strangeness in the man's manner; and when Villiers begged
to know the nature of the informality, he could only
reply, vaguely and impatiently, that there was suspicion, irregularity, and that there must be some
delay.

" How long ? " inquired Villiers.

" Perhaps three days," was the answer.

At another time, Villiers's indignation would have vented itself abruptly, and not very wisely. But his temper had been schooled, as well as other defects in his character; and after endeavouring to remonstrate calmly, and to explain, but to no purpose, he took leave of Guiseppe, and removing his portmanteau, submitted to be shown to a miserable little albergo, there to content himself with remaining until the difficulty could be removed.

On looking round the wretched room, which was all the accommodation supplied him, he was himself surprised to find how little such external appearances affect us when the mind is occupied with either deep sorrow or deep joy; especially how estranged it becomes even from the thought of them, when there is a consciousness within of having acted wrong — of being under punishment. Punishment in a palace is a mockery; and to feel that he was suffering a punishment, — to resolve on bearing it manfully, and patiently, and gratefully, and to look up to the hand which inflicted it with the prayer, that such a spirit might be perfected within him, was becoming every hour more and more the temper of his mind.

In the evening he strolled out to relieve his thoughts, painfully depressed and overwrought by several hours spent among papers, and arrangements which were full of bitterness for the future as well as for the past, and with only one bright thought of consolation — the thought of his child. As he returned into the narrow dirty street of the little town, close by the Dogana, a crowd was collected round a door. A few faces seemingly more adventurous than the rest were prying into a hovel; but the most part with countenances indicative of alarm and conster-

nation, mixed with that curiosity and fascination of
terror which is so common in uneducated minds,
were standing aloof, and spreading the news of
some disaster to every passer-by. On Villiers
inquiring the cause, he found that the first case
of a fever, which had been for some time anticipated, had just broken out, and one of the persons
employed in the Dogana had been its victim. The
poor fellow was alarmingly ill. But no one dared
to approach him. And it was only on Villiers
going into the miserable place, where he lay, and
summoning the terrified by-standers to assist him
in moving the sufferer, and in providing him with
some comforts, that they ventured to risk the infection. It was some relief to his mind to be
engaged actively in a work of charity. The tending
by a sick bed brought back to him the memory of
two other sick beds, both of them associated with
remorse. In this case there could be none. And
as the only old woman who could be found to remain with the sufferer as nurse was timid and
inexperienced, Villiers himself sat up with the sick
man during the night. The poor woman, who
was a Roman Catholic, and had, therefore, been
brought up in pious horror of heretics, among whom
she had been taught to class the members of the
English Church, was surprised to see him spend
no little part of the time on his knees. She had
been told that Protestants never knelt in prayer
— that they never prayed at all; and her amazement was great. The morning came, and the patient was better. His gratitude was intense to
Villiers; and in expressing it, he added to him a
warning, which surprised him, but to which he
paid little attention. He told him that his detention had been brought about apparently by a traveller, who had preceded him by a few hours, and

who had had some secret conference with the chief
of the office, and he hinted to him the necessity of
being cautious, if he had any secret enemy, or was
conscious of offences against the government. Villiers smiled, and thanked the poor fellow for his
advice; but did not think it worth while to make
further inquiries of him respecting a suggestion so
obviously unfounded. Nor, indeed, could the man
have given him any further information than the
vague notion which he had gathered from some
incidental remarks of his superior. He was, indeed,
too ill to be communicative, and though better,
when Villiers the next day took leave of him, on
receiving his passport, and with it apologies for the
delay, nothing more passed between them.

It was a bright and joyous afternoon, as Villiers
once more re-entered Naples. The sun was dancing
on the blue waters of the bay. The fringe of glittering suburbs, which stretched round its magnificent
curve, flashed on the eye like marble. Vesuvius
towered in the distance, curling up a thin wreath
of smoke upon the golden sky. The road was full
of gay-dressed peasants, with their brilliant many-
coloured costumes and antique ornaments of gold
and pearls. The lazzaroni, capped and buttoned,
were lying about, basking their swarthy muscular
limbs among the painted stalls of water-melons
and summer fruits. The Chiaia was swarming with
equipages, and gay boats were skimming about the
bay. The whole spectacle was luxury and enjoyment. But to Villiers, over it all, there hung a
black, motionless, fearful veil like a pall. He sat
back in the humble conveyance with his eyes closed,
his brow knit, his lips compressed in anguish, and
a weight pressing upon his chest, which compelled
him every now and then, to the alarm of his fellow-
travellers, to heave a deep groan, and stretch his head

out of the window, as if gasping for breath. He
had answered so gently to their first inquiries, if he
was ill, and yet with such firmness, that they at
last permitted him to remain unnoticed. The vehicle stopped on the Chiaia; and Villiers, muffling
himself up, called to him, from among a group of
fishermen, an old familiar face, which recognised
him at once. He bade the man see his portmanteau
removed; and having sunk down in a little boat,
which was drawn up on the beach, they were soon
launched upon the bay. The honest fisherman saw,
and partly understood, the cause of his evident
anguish; and though he remained silent, a by-
stander might have seen him dash away something
from his eyes as he looked upon Villiers, and observed the tears streaming down through the hands,
in which his face was buried. He held his arm for
Villiers to rest on, as he rose to step from the boat,
at the little moorings, close by the steps in the cliff,
under the trellissed cottage, and the seat of rock;
and Villiers caught at it, for he was ready to
fall. But as his foot touched the ground, a better
thought seemed to nerve him, and he sprang up
the narrow path, impatient till he could see all that
now remained to him of joy and hope upon earth,
and could clasp his child to his bosom. He faltered
for one moment as he passed the seat in the rock;
but the next he was at the door of the cottage. It
was closed. He rapped, that Marie, the nurse, who
had the care of the child, might hear him; but Marie
was evidently out. He looked in at the window,
but could see no one. The cradle was there, but
it was empty. Once more he rapped, but to no
effect; and while waiting in expectation of an
answer, he observed that the flower-bed in the
front had been trampled on, seemingly by men's
feet. He was startled by a little cry of surprise

and dismay from a young girl, whom he recognised as the daughter of a neighbouring peasant, and who endeavoured to run away when she saw him. But he compelled her to come to him; and on inquiring for Marie, the nurse, he could at first obtain no answer. Evidently there was something to conceal. At last the girl stammered out that Marie was at their own house. And Villiers hurried to it. A scream of dismay from the poor woman was the first greeting. The few incoherent words which he could extract from her were sufficient to inform him that his last hope was gone. Two nights before, a false alarm of fire had been given at the door of Marie's cottage. Startled from her sleep, she rushed out with the child in her arms: two men, who had given the alarm, met her at the door, offered to hold the child while she ran back to secure her little property; and while she was hastily collecting what was most necessary to save, they had disappeared. A small boat had been seen moored at the bottom of the steps, which was never seen again. Every spot had been searched, and all the neighbouring cottages — every inquiry made — but the child was lost.

It was past twelve on the following night, when a man and his wife, who had been employed at times in the establishment of General Villiers while he was at Naples, and who still lived in the house to take care of it while untenanted and unfurnished, were coming home from a rustic fête. As they came within the light of a lamp which hung before an image of the Virgin — the same lamp which had first revealed to Villiers that face which he never forgot— they saw a figure leaning against the wall, the hat slouched over the face, and the legs bent as if unable to support themselves. It was evidently a person ill. He moaned as they approached; and

suffered them to raise his hat, and to reveal a face
ghastly with suffering of body and of mind, but
which they still were able to recognise as their
young master's. He scarcely replied to their astonished inquiries ; and, on their asking if they could
take him home, he sank down, muttering faintly
that he had no home. A passer-by aided them in
raising him, and carrying him to the house ; and,
on the arrival of a physician, they learnt that he
was in a high fever — partly the result of infection,
from his watching over the sick man at Fondi, but
aggravated greatly by agony of mind, and the
violent exertion with which he had exhausted himself in endeavouring to trace his child.

We need not dwell upon the days and weeks
which followed — on the wanderings of mind upon
past scenes — the incoherent ravings — the violence
with which it became necessary to coerce him — the
wretchedness of every thing around him, in a large
deserted house, with none but its two poor inmates
to soothe and nurse him ; and then the dreadful
dawning of returning reason, only to reveal to him
again the misery of his lot. Providentially, with
the passing of the crisis there came some relief
to him in the person of his friend Beattie, who had
traced him out, and followed him from Rome. He
watched by him at night ; held his forehead when
splitting with pain ; administered his medicines ;
read to him, prayed with him and for him ; led his
thoughts quietly and gently to see the dispensations
of an overruling goodness in their true light ;
opened to him future prospects of usefulness and
duty ; and, by his simple and unaffected piety,
wrought upon the mind of his friend even more
than Macarthy had wrought with all his brilliancy
and force of genius.

It was one evening, after Villiers, leaning on

Beattie's arm, had returned from his first attempt
to venture into the open air, that he asked Beattie
if he might now be allowed to look at some letters
which had arrived for him, and which his physician
had prohibited him from reading before. He felt
stronger, and able to bear it; and Beattie gave them
to him. One was from Lady Eleanor. She did not
say that she was compelled to write herself, because
Lord Claremont had sternly refused to do so: but
with high-minded, yet feminine dignity, she expressed her full conviction that the disposal of
General Villiers's property had been influenced by
the wrong suggestions of others; and her earnest
desire that, if possible, the will might be set aside,
and the estates revert to Villiers, instead of coming
to herself. Villiers smiled as he pointed out the
paragraph to Beattie. But the first lines which he
wrote, when able to take a pen in his hand, were to
express, not only his admiration and gratitude for
his cousin's noble disinterestedness, but the impossibility of his permitting any change to take place
in arrangements, in which he felt it his duty patiently
to acquiesce. Another letter was from his uncle,
dated from England, and informing him that he had
obtained a commission for him in the army, as the
only thing which he could procure. Another was
from the Horse Guards, ordering him to join the
regiment, to which he had been appointed, in Canada,
without delay. And the fourth was from Pearce,
with some insolent inquiry about a matter of business, which Villiers read patiently, and replied to
briefly without a single expression of indignation at
the insult.

The letters read, he raised his eyes, and looking
steadfastly upon Beattie, told him that he was now
ready and able to bear his answer to one more inquiry. Every search had been made; the assist-

ance of the police had been obtained; communications had been made in every direction. Had any trace whatever been discovered of the child?

Beattie shook his head mournfully: and Villiers, clasping his hands, and closing his eyes for a few minutes, during which his lips were moving in silent prayer, endeavoured to compose himself to entire submission. As he opened his eyes again, he found Beattie was kneeling by his side, looking on him with the deepest affection and commiseration, and prepared to pray with him, as the best mode of soothing and comforting him. And by an hour afterwards Villiers was able to turn his attention to matters which required immediate arrangement, and to prepare composedly and steadily to enter on the new line of life to which he seemed to be called.

CHAP. XIX.

TWELVE years passed away; and we may pass from the sick bed of Villiers to the saloon of the English ambassador at Florence. It was brilliantly illuminated for a state dinner on a Friday. The tables glittered with plate. Wax lights in alabaster vases threw a soft moonlight radiance on gorgeous pictures, and marble statues, and jewelled guests. The cool plash of fountains, amidst pillared porticoes and perfumed flowers, mixed lullingly with soft strains of music. And the exquisite taste of the noble ambassador, who was a notorious profligate, threw round the scene an air of refinement and fastidiousness, which almost oppressed enjoyment. The gorgeously-dressed domestics moved in silence on the velvet carpets. Even the creaking of a door or the derangement of a dish seemed to inflict pain on the sensitiveness of the voluptuous host. Every one spoke in a low voice, as if a sound beyond a whisper was an infringement on the solemnity of the festival; when the countenance of the illustrious ambassador was seen to assume a haughty gloom, as he observed a very ill-disguised yawn distorting the countenance of one of his youngest guests in the regimentals of a distinguished corps. Captain O'Brien really was extremely tired. He had enjoyed, or rather suffered some little experience of state dinners, when aide-de-camp to his uncle, a late Lord Lieutenant of Ireland. But with all his habits of society and good breeding the young vivacious Irishman was not proof against the som-

nolent influence of the ambassador's grandeur. He
endeavoured to rouse himself by obtaining the attention of a very lovely and elegant woman who sat
next him, and whose conversation had been hitherto
engrossed by an elderly white-headed gentleman on
the other side of her. He observed that she refused
every dish presented to her; and the second time
that O'Brien offered her some preparation of meat,
she asked for vegetables only. O'Brien trusted she
was not ill; and with perfect unaffectedness she replied that she did not eat meat on fast-days. O'Brien
for a moment opened his dark animated eyes with
some degree of incompetency to understand her.

"I thought I had the pleasure," he said, "of addressing an English lady, or, though we are aliens
in Ireland, may I not say a countrywoman?"

The lady smiled, and only replied that he was not
mistaken; but that English ladies might be Catholics.

O'Brien coloured, and apologised.

"We are commanded by our Church," she continued, "to practise these little self-denials; and I
have often thought it might be very beneficial if
other religious communities enjoined them likewise.
But English Protestants, I believe, have entirely
discarded them."

O'Brien knew little either of Roman Catholics
or of English Protestants, in matters of theology.

"One person," he replied, "I knew, who was a
Protestant, and who always fasted on Friday. I
knew it well, for it was connected with matters of
deep interest to myself. By the by," he said, forgetting the solemn quiescence which reigned around
him, and speaking across the table to an old military
officer covered with orders, "how delighted I am to

hear that Villiers has come into possession of his property again. I saw it in the papers this morning."

The ambassador's face assumed a deeper gloom than before. The old General shily answered "Yes," and coughed, as if to intimate that the subject might as well be dropped. But the warm-hearted young Irishman had fallen on a subject very near his heart.

"Have you heard the circumstances?" he continued. "The property was left away by his father to his cousin, and his cousin has given it back to him; and there was some statement of a paper being found in a cabinet. But one thing is certain, that Lady Eleanor has behaved most nob——"

But before he could finish the word, the ambassador, near whom he was sitting, in a very cold and formal voice of condemnation, begged to introduce him to Lady Eleanor Howard, who was sitting by his side. O'Brien's fine features were once more suffused with a very becoming flush. But Lady Eleanor soon relieved him from his momentary embarrassment.

"Mr. Villiers, I presume," she said, "is a friend of yours."

"A very dear friend," said O'Brien.

"You must not then think too well of his cousin," said Lady Eleanor. "I am sorry to say she has had no opportunity of acting nobly; and the newspapers, those miscalled sources of information, have, in this case, as in most others, been egregiously wrong."

O'Brien bowed, and was prepared to make some lively compliment. But Lady Eleanor, with quietness and simplicity, continued: —

"As Mr. Villiers's friend, you will be happy to hear that he is in Florence."

O'Brien almost clapped his hands; but a look from the ambassador froze him into quietude.

"He arrived this morning," said Lady Eleanor, "and will, I hope, meet us here this evening."

"And may I ask," said O'Brien, "if the statement respecting the recovery of the estate is true?"

"It is true," was the reply, "in its principal facts. But the recovery is simply owing to the law. General Villiers, it was only recently discovered, had no power to alienate the English estates. He had overlooked a codicil in his grandfather's will; and to me it has been a great satisfaction that they should still be retained in the original line."

"And there was no paper, then," asked O'Brien, "found in an old chest? The whole story sounded so like a romance, that I distrusted it from the first."

"There was a paper found by Mr. Beattie, an intimate friend of Mr. Villiers, but found some years back, which implied that the General's will had been made under undue influence; and this probably would have had the effect of overturning the will itself, if it had been brought into litigation. But you are Mr. Villiers's friend, and you will not be surprised to hear that he refused to take advantage of it. There were circumstances connected with it, which would have involved further discussion of matters, which it was more honourable to the memory of those who are gone to preserve in privacy."

"How like him!" exclaimed O'Brien. "Lady Eleanor must pardon me if I intrude such questions; but Villiers is the best and dearest friend I have in the world. And they laugh at me for raving whenever he is mentioned."

Lady Eleanor was interested in her companion's enthusiasm.

"Is it possible," he continued, lowering his voice,

"to tell you a very long story without drawing the attention of this whole solemn meeting?"

"If you are repeating what is good of him," replied Lady Eleanor, "you need not be alarmed. I fear, generally speaking, it is only scandal which attracts attention."

"And may I begin at the beginning?" asked O'Brien, laughingly.

Lady Eleanor prepared to listen, and O'Brien, relieved from his ennui, delighted at having obtained the attention of his fair neighbour, and still more at being indulged with the full expression of his admiration and affection for his friend, proceeded, with all the natural eloquence, energy, and vivacity of a well-educated Irish gentleman, to recount his story : —

"We were quartered," he said, "in Canada some years since, when Villiers first joined the regiment. At that time, and in our own regiment, duelling was a prevailing fashion. Scarcely any one was allowed to join us without being compelled to engage in this, which now I will call detestable, practice of murder. But then I thought differently. When Villiers first came out he was just recovering from illness, and evidently in great distress of mind. At that time I did not know the cause; but he was allowed for some weeks to remain much to himself. And young and thoughtless as we were, we felt it right to give him some indulgence. But you must be aware how little young men of high spirits, and thinking only of amusement, can bear with melancholy and gloom in others. Villiers was always gentlemanly, kind, and considerate, but he was reserved and depressed; and there was a superiority of mind and manner about him which we construed as haughtiness. A month or two passed, and we became impatient of his continued retirement. In particular, we observed that he never joined the mess on a Fri-

day; and as this was a convenient day for parties, his
absence became marked. I need not say how soon,
where offence is sought, offence may be taken. And
I, as one of the youngest and most hot-brained
— I will add a stronger word, as one of the most
unprincipled of the party — boasted that I would
compel him to attend the mess or insult him. It
was not difficult to find an opportunity. Lady
Eleanor will have no wish to hear details, of which
I shall always be ashamed. But I did, (and O'Brien
lowered his voice, and with the colour mounting to
his face, hung down his head as he proceeded,) I did
at the mess-table make observations which he could
not avoid overhearing, and which led to a gentle
expostulation on his part, to some insulting reply on
mine ; and at last, when he rose to leave the room,
to language for which, in the ordinary code of
society, no reparation could be given but bloodshed.

" I was sitting in my room late that night, having
made all necessary preparations in case I should fall,
and wondering that I had not yet received any communication to fix the meeting for the morrow, when
I heard a rap at the door, and drawing myself up to
receive, as I expected, Villiers's friend, to my extreme astonishment I saw Villiers himself. He was
perfectly calm and self-possessed; and there was a
gentleness and dignity in his manner which gave to
him such a superiority over me, that I could only
escape from it by rudeness. 'I am come,' he said, 'Mr.
O'Brien' (for I was then only a lieutenant), 'to express
to you my forgiveness for your having insulted me
to-day as you have done : I am willing to believe
that the act escaped you in a moment of thoughtlessness. But I am come also to express to you with
my own lips that no such act, whether proceeding
from thoughtlessness or deliberation, will induce
me, I trust, to comply with that false code of ho-

nour which thinks it possible to wipe out disgrace only by committing either suicide or murder. When you have been visited as I have been, you will feel, I cannot doubt, that there is another code, far higher and far more awful in its chastisements than that of human society, and to which we are all amenable. By this code I am not only bound to abstain from seeking your life in revenge for an injury offered to me, but I am bound to give you my free and hearty forgiveness, which I now tender you; and to seek the first opportunity, in some legitimate way, of evincing that this forgiveness is not one of words only, and that my present act is not the act of a coward. Until that opportunity is presented I must be content to remain under the stigma which your act has thrown on me. I perceive,' he continued, as he observed me about to indulge in some expression of irritation and contempt, ' I perceive that it will be useless to prolong this explanation.' And before I could give vent to my violence he had withdrawn.

" 'Coward! hypocrite! fool!' were the first words which came to my lips. They were repeated by the greater part of the mess, when the story became known. Villiers himself was of course shunned and sent to Coventry; and the commanding officer was only prevented from showing similar feeling by his private connection with Villiers's family. In the mean time Villiers retired from our society, without seeming to shun it. I thought his manner was that of a man struggling against a violent temptation, and suffering under bitter mortification. But he was calm and patient in his exterior, and refused to notice the little acts of insolence and contempt with which the youngest among us now ventured to molest him. He bore with it for at least six weeks. At the end of that time my corps was ordered on an expedition. Our business was to occupy New-town height, which commanded the river at Toronto, and the rebels were in great force underneath it. I shall not easily forget the march we had, in the dead of night, through the woods, and a morass in which we sank up to our knees, expecting every moment that the enemy would fall upon us. It was the most perilous expedition of the whole war. Here was the height—there the river—here we passed through the forest." And O'Brien, once embarked in his military manœuvres, endeavoured to assist Lady Eleanor's comprehension by ranging bonbons and comfitures on the table, much, if we may venture the pun, to the discomfiture of the refined ambassador, and not a little to Lady Eleanor's disappointment, whose thoughts were far less engaged with the military tactics than with the anecdote of Villiers.

"Just as we were on the point," continued O'Brien, "of debouching from the forest (debouching, you should know, means issuing out, and is a military phrase,)—just here, by this green bonbon, you see, the alarm was given, and in an instant we found ourselves surrounded. I had advanced before the rest, and was cut off from behind. Four of the rebels fell on me. I received a wound across my sword-hand—here it is" (and he held up his hand), "which completely disabled me ; and I was on the point of being cut down between them, when one of my assailants was cloven across the head with a sabre-blow. An officer threw himself before me, bidding me make my retreat, and he would cover it. A second assailant was stretched by him on the ground. But before any of our own men, whom he had rallied, could come to our assistance, I received another blow, under which I fell to the ground, stunned and senseless. When I recovered my consciousness, I was lying on a bed of leaves in a deep thicket, the light of morning just dawning, and only one person with me, who was employed in bandaging my wounds,—and that person was Villiers. I was perishing with thirst. He had procured some water in a hollow stone, and some biscuit, which I afterwards found was all that he had for himself. And when, with a mixed sensation of resentment, indignation, and shame, I interrogated him as to the reason of his presence, he charged me to be silent, for that we were still near the enemy's outposts, and that we must wait till night before we could venture to move."

" What had brought him on the expedition ?"

" I found subsequently that he had learned, after we had left our quarters, that we should probably be surprised ; had obtained permission from the commanding officer to follow with a few men ; had come to my personal rescue : and when the rest had been compelled to retire, he had thrown himself, with me, into the wood, had dismissed those who carried me, and had remained himself watching by me till a reinforcement could be sent, and I could be removed. And, now, will Lady Eleanor excuse a stranger, if he has taken up her time with a tale of such a man ?"

" And you both escaped ?" asked Lady Eleanor.

" We lay covered all that day, not daring to stir ; and in the evening a movement was made by our troops, which compelled the rebels to decamp, and we escaped to head-quarters."

" And from that day," continued Lady Eleanor, " I presume, you date your friendship with Mr. Villiers ?"

" No," replied O'Brien, " not from that day. It was too noble, too oppressive kindness. What with shame, and what with gratitude, I could not feel to

him as a friend. I wished to apologise to him pub-
licly, but he would not hear of it. Of course, he
was received among us again ; and every one spoke
of him as a fine, noble-hearted fellow. But those
who have injured seldom forgive ; and I could
scarcely forgive him, even for saving my life by an
act of heroism which made me so immeasurably his
inferior. And he knew this ; and never sought to
do me any more kindnesses till I was taken seriously
ill : and then, when all my other noisy companions
deserted me, or only came to pay a hurried visit,
and excuse themselves for not staying above a few
minutes, I was left alone, terribly depressed, and
would have given worlds for any society. He never
came . near me, however, till one day the nurse
begged him to come, and said she knew I should
like it, — and I did like it. If he had been my own
brother, he could not have been more kind, more
affectionate. As soon as he found that I took pleasure in seeing him, he had his bed moved into the
next room, and was with me constantly. And from
that time he has been my friend. Such a friend,"
he continued, looking on Lady Eleanor with his
large full eye suffused for a moment, " as ——
But I must not weary you with my enthusiasm."

Lady Eleanor was not wearied ; she was any
thing but wearied : but there was one question which
she longed to ask, but scarcely dared.

" My little observation respecting fasting," she
said, " has brought from you a very interesting
anecdote. Mr. Villiers was then a Protestant ? "

" Oh, yes," said O'Brien ; " he never was any thing
else. But he used to do a number of things which
I am afraid are not very common among Protestants.
I know he associated very much with an American
bishop, near whom we were stationed ; and I suspect
what he saw in America very much confirmed him

in many of his opinions. I have private reasons for knowing that he regularly set apart a tenth of his income, and it was very small, for charitable and religious purposes; and he often urged me to do the same. He used regularly to stay at church."

And the young officer, in using the ordinary expression applied to the most solemn act of Christian devotion, little thought of the censure it implied upon the great mass of Christian congregations who do not stay, but go away.

"I have known him," continued O'Brien, "ride twenty miles for the purpose on a Saturday, and return on the Monday. He had regular hours when he used to disappear; and even in the middle of the day I am convinced that he was in the habit of praying. I was young and thoughtless," continued O'Brien, "and have been worse than thoughtless; but I have learnt from him lessons which will be a blessing to me to the end of my life."

"His Excellency will drink wine with you, sir," interrupted the plumed chasseur of the noble host, whose indignation at his young guest's vivacity was considerably mollified when he observed the attention paid by Lady Eleanor, whom his fastidious taste recognised as a model of refinement, to O'Brien's animated conversation. The interruption, however, did not prevent O'Brien from returning to his favourite theme.

"I fear," he said, "that with all his goodness he is, and has been, very unhappy. I rarely saw him smile."

"Perhaps," said Lady Eleanor, "his unhappiness may have been the cause of his goodness?"

"It was not goodness," replied O'Brien, "if I might trust his own account, which caused his unhappiness. He never recovered the loss of his child and wife."

"Wife!" repeated Lady Eleanor, thrown off her guard, and her eye lighting up as if a weight had been removed from her mind. O'Brien looked surprised.

"Perhaps," he said, "I am betraying confidence. But I know what falsehoods are often circulated. He certainly was married in Italy to a young person, whose portrait in a moment of great distress he once showed me. She must have been exquisitely beautiful. Poor thing! she died of a decline within a short time after her marriage, and the child was lost in some extraordinary way."

He was silent, and Lady Eleanor would have willingly induced him to continue, but knew not how, without betraying the deep interest which she felt in the tale.

"She was the daughter," added O'Brien, "of an officer in the Spanish army, of high rank, but who had been driven from his country through political disturbances in which he had become involved."

"I had heard something of this," replied Lady Eleanor; "but I had fancied she was of low birth."

"No, certainly not," answered O'Brien. "They were reduced to great poverty, and the father supported himself by his own hands; but there was certainly good blood."

Once more there was a pause.

"He seems," said O'Brien, "to have doted on his child, though it was so young. I shall never forget a scene I witnessed, and which led to his telling me these facts; for otherwise he was very reserved, and rarely spoke of himself or his own affairs, even to his most intimate friends."

Lady Eleanor begged him to proceed.

"There was a young soldier," he continued, "in the regiment, who was very ill-conducted and dissipated; and after a number of reprimands and slighter punishments, it became necessary to have him flogged. Villiers happened to be the officer who was ordered to superintend the execution of the sentence — never a very pleasant task ; but though most gentle in himself, he was remarkably firm when it was necessary to punish. I have seen him do things, without moving a muscle, which our greatest disciplinarians would have shrunk from. In this case something led him to have a communication with the poor culprit before the flogging commenced. He heard his story, — who he was, — how he had been brought into his present state. It appeared that he had been kidnapped from his parents when young, and had been thrown into every kind of temptation, and ruined by bad company. I shall never forget Villiers's face as he came upon the ground after the interview. It was pale as ashes. His lips were nearly bitten through. But he took his position, — gave the signal, — never shrunk, till after the tenth lash, when the poor fellow uttered a hideous cry, and Villiers dropped to the ground. He was taken up senseless ; and I never saw such agony as he evinced when he recovered. It was this which brought me to know the circumstances which had occurred to him before he joined the regiment. What made him feel most acutely the loss of his child was the sense that he himself had been undutiful to his own father."

Lady Eleanor sighed deeply.

" But I am distressing you," said O'Brien, " by these melancholy reminiscences. And here is the signal for breaking up our solemn festivities — for a more solemn dinner I never saw."

———

" Who is that distinguished-looking man ?" asked the Duchess of San Lorenzo, as she reconnoitred with her glass the brilliant groups which began to

fill the ambassador's saloons on the breaking up of
the dinner party.

" Do you mean," asked a lively conceited little
abbé, who had attached himself to her side — " do
you mean that tall mustachioed Russian bear, who
is leaning against the pillar ? "

" No, — the one on the other side by the window."

" Oh, that slim youth with the long flowing hair
and the collar turned down to expose his Byron
neck !   That is the young English lord who writes
the verses for the fashionable albums."

" How can you suppose I mean him ? " pettishly
replied the duchess.   " Who would apply such an
epithet as distinguished to him ? "

" Is it the robust figure who is taking snuff out
of a gold snuff-box, with a hand covered with gold
rings, and brushing off the dust from his gold brocaded waistcoat ? "

" How can you ask such a question ?   Do you
see Lady Eleanor Villiers ? "

" If your Grace were not in the room," replied
the little abbé, " I should say how can I possibly
see any one else when she is here ? "

" Well, look to the right of her, — not the young
officer ; that is Captain O'Brien ; but the person in
black — rather dark — without any thing very
marked about him, — so simple and quiet, and yet
with such an eye.   See, the ambassador is coming
up to him.   He must be some one of consequence,
for I never knew our punctilious host throw away
such urbanity and condescension on ordinary mortals.   See, Lord Claremont is introducing him.   I
declare the ambassador is shaking hands with him ;
and old General Fitzwilliam is moving towards
him.   Do find him out, and bring him to me."

And the little abbé fidgetted away to execute the

duchess's orders, full of the gratitude which he should excite in the interesting stranger, by introducing him to the great leader of the fashionable world of Florence, whose fiat, notwithstanding her frivolity and levity, stamped consequence on any one whom she condescended to notice. As he approached Lady Eleanor, Villiers and O'Brien were conversing with her, — O'Brien with his usual animation, and Villiers even cheerfully. He even laughed at some story which the young Irishman was relating; and Lady Eleanor looked pleased to see him shake off his gravity. The little abbé found no difficulty in insinuating himself into the group, requesting an introduction, and offering his assistance in exploring the classical scenes of Florence; all which courtesies Villiers received gently, but with a little distance of manner which might easily have been mistaken for hauteur. But the abbé could not be repelled. He proposed an introduction to the duchess; but Villiers bowed coldly, almost sternly; and expressing to Lady Eleanor his hope that he had sufficiently done his duty in paying his respects to the ambassador, he shook O'Brien by the hand, and retired, unobserved, from the gay throng.

CHAP. XX.

WHEN Villiers came to Florence, it was for a week
only, in order to conclude some necessary business
with Lord Claremont connected with the restoration
of his property.   But the week passed, and matters
were still unsettled : the month came, and he was
still there.   It became necessary to fix the period
of his return to England, and he found himself still
postponing his departure ; each day becoming more
loth to leave the place.   Why ? he never thought
of asking himself.   But day slided into day unobservedly : at last some private business rendered it
necessary for Lord Claremont and Lady Eleanor to
go for a short time to Venice.   Villiers, by Lady
Eleanor's request to her father, was not asked to
join them.   It was proposed that he should remain
at Florence till their return ; and the good Abbé
St. Maur, the French Roman Catholic priest who
resided in the family, proposed to remain with him.
Villiers found, to his surprise, that he would gladly
have accompanied his uncle to Venice ; he found
also, to his no less surprise, that with the departure
of his cousin the whole charm of Florence disappeared ; and that the house, which before was so
full to him of animation and enjoyment that he
could not bring himself to quit it, had become a
dreary vacuity.   He was not indeed without thoughts
and occupations which filled his mind ; but even
these had lost their absorbing interest, until, in one
of the blank moments of chilliness which fall on us
when a vacant chair reminds us of an absent being,
a light flashed across him ; and the good Abbé ob-

served that, after a silent breakfast, Villiers walked
for more than an hour up and down the same walk
in the garden, his eye occasionally glancing up to a
particular window, and his pace hurrying after each
glance. The Abbé was an attentive observer ; but
he never intruded upon confidence: and except that
he looked into Villiers's face with more of kind and
affectionate interest than usual, as Villiers brought
him his stick and covered his silver hair with his
hat, previous to their going out for their usual
walk, there was nothing to betray what was passing
in the mind of the benevolent and simple-minded
ecclesiastic. Perhaps, however, something of this
might be gathered from a letter which he sat up
that night to write, and which we can insert at
length, because, by our usual faculty of ubiquity,
we were present at the post-office at Rome when a
stout, sinister-looking person, no other than Mr.
Pearce himself, came there to ask for letters for the
Rev. Mr. O'Dogherty, then an inmate in the Jesuits'
College ; and by the same faculty we followed Mr.
Pearce into a small house, previous to his returning
to the College, and by means of a process familiar
to himself, were there able to read the letter with
him before it was resealed and taken to its original
destination. It ran thus : —

 " My dear O'Dogherty,
 " I received your last letter with some surprise,
and reply to it with much pain. But, as a Christian
minister, I cannot hesitate to speak what I feel. I
never can take a part in any intrigue or plot, however desirable the object may seem. I do not think
that plotting and intriguing can ever be serviceable
to the Church of Christ, or to the cause of His truth.
And, devotedly as I am attached to our holy Church,
I have lamented most deeply that others have so

frequently endeavoured to assist and support it by
what I must consider artifices unworthy of such an
object. Surely we have suffered enough already for
such conduct. I can well understand that the person of whom you speak should be an object of interest to all those who are concerned in restoring
England to the unity of the faith. I have seen
enough of him here to be assured that, wherever he
is placed, he must exercise a powerful influence.
His high-mindedness, his integrity, his firmness,
his conscientious strictness, his ardent enthusiasm,
and his command of property and rank, would render
him a most important convert ; and I should rejoice,
like yourself, to see him received into the bosom of
our holy Church. More than this, it is my duty, at
proper times, and in an open honest manner, to set
before him the truth, and to lead him, as I may
have opportunities, to embrace it. But this is very
different from becoming a spy upon his actions,
communicating his thoughts to others, or undertaking any secret manœuvres to accomplish such a
desirable result. I deeply grieve that you should
have known me so ill as to make to me such a proposition ; for however cautiously your letter is
worded, I cannot read it in any other sense. And
I will frankly declare, that no zeal for your order,
or vow of obedience to your superiors, or prospect
of benefit to the Church, can justify your engaging
in such schemes. I must distrust, and deplore, and
deprecate, any organisation, or religious association,
which proceeds upon such principles. It is founded
in falsehood and deceit, and must end in heresy and
schism. You will call me a Protestant ; but my
heart is Catholic as your own. I would even charge
you to abstain from these intrigues, by the hope
which I have that they are not required ; and that,
if all things are left to the hand of Providence, He

will bring out the end which we all should desire.
His mind is at this moment any thing but settled.
He has been shocked in America by the full development of what is commonly called Protestantism.
He abhors that licence of self-will and of private
judgment which casts off all deference to authority,
all belief in the testimony of the Church, and in the
social principle by which the Church, as a body politic, exists. And he is too acute not to see that it
must lead to every kind of dissension and heresy;
and, with the banishment of truth, must banish
order, and goodness, and religion from the world.
All this he thoroughly understands, and requires no
one to teach him. Much of it, I suspect, he derives
from early impressions; much from his own generous nature: and he speaks often to me of an
American bishop (so called), who appears to have
exercised considerable influence over his mind, and
to have taken pains to point out to him the working
of these principles of mischief in that unhappy
country. I have also reason to believe that he has
friends in England, a Mr. Beattie in particular,
whom he consults on these points, and who is very
much tinctured with the new notions that are springing up in the English Church. I mention these
things that, if your views with respect to him are
simply to extricate him from error, your mind may
be in some degree relieved. It would be idle, however, to disguise that he is at present a strict con-
formist to the English communion, and carries out
its rules with far more scrupulousness than I have
ever observed in any of his countrymen. He is,
indeed, so conscientious, that I cannot imagine his
becoming a member of any society, least of all of a
religious society, without endeavouring fully to act
up to its spirit and its rules. At the same time, I
cannot but perceive that he has once entertained a

strong predilection for our holy Church; and though
some degree of repugnance to it succeeded in consequence of circumstances which occurred to him some
years back, (circumstances, let me remind you,
which had their origin in the artifices and intrigues
then employed to win him over,) since he has been
in Florence, and especially since he has seen the
conduct of Lady E., I have reason to think that his
feelings are very much mitigated. He often speaks
to me of the possibility of such a reform in the
Church as would restore the unity of Christendom.
Unity appears to be his chief thought. He dreads
the anarchical spirit which is rising up against the
truth; mourns over the impotency of secular governments to arrest the torrent of change; longs to
see once more the Church of his own country re-
asserting her spiritual power, and gathering the
people under her wing. And this, he thinks, cannot
be achieved until its arm is strengthened, and its
spirit renewed, by the restoration of peace and concord to the whole Church of Christ. So much I
am at liberty to tell you without violating confidence. Nor, indeed, am I possessed of his confidence further than that he seems to take pleasure in
conversing with me on such subjects. You hint at
other things — at the influence which Lady E. may
have upon his mind, and the probability of this
winning him over, even if every thing else failed.
Once more let me warn you not to engage in such
speculations, or in any manœuvres to effect such an
object. If such a union as you contemplate should
be ordained by Providence, I can imagine few more
likely to be blessed, as I have never seen persons
apparently more suited to each other, more pure,
more high-minded, more able to appreciate, and
support, and improve each other's character, and to
give a wonderful strength and support to the cause

of our Church in England. But let us leave such
designs to Providence : let us leave to Him also
to accomplish the great end we have in view — the
conversion of England. I pray for it as you pray.
But I cannot bring myself to view the Church of
England as you do, or to confound it with that heterogeneous and fearful mass of heresy and dissent
which has overrun that unhappy country. It has,
indeed, severed itself from the see of Rome ; but so,
also, our own Church in France has denied much
that you, on your side of the Alps, consider essential
to a right faith in this article. The English Church
has preserved the creeds, the four first councils,
her apostolic succession, (all this, strongly as you
would deny it, I cannot, in common honesty, refuse to allow,) her respect for primitive antiquity,
though individually it may have been neglected,
the Holy Scriptures, and a sound principle of interpreting them by the aid of the teaching of the
Church. I know how strongly you repudiate such
concessions ; but as I differ from you in many other
points, so I lament, and can only anticipate evil from
a refusal to acknowledge in others palpable good.
It is not honest ; it is not Christian. And sadly as
the individual teachers and members of the English
Church have neglected or misunderstood her teaching, sadly as her rulers may have failed to enforce
her discipline and to uphold her authority, I can no
more charge the sins of individuals upon the communion itself than I can reject our own Church, because, as we all confess, its rulers from time to
time have so deeply sinned. If this spirit of concession and of charity prevailed among us — if our
own Church would acknowledge that the English
Church was a true branch of Christ's Catholic Body,
and would seek to restore communion with it by
correcting what is amiss in itself, and by abstaining

from troubling the peace of others, I cannot but
believe that the English Church also would rejoice
to see the wounds of Christendom healed, and would
not hesitate to remove any thing in her own practice
which might reasonably offend a sister or a mother
church.   But so long as we violently condemn what
we are not called on to judge, and cut off from salvation those whom the early Church would not
have excluded, and confound those who at most are
erring in inferior matters with gross heretics and
deliberate offenders against Christ's laws, and send
out emissaries to trouble the peace of Christian
communities, — so long, I must think, that we are
sinning against God, and though a zealous and affectionate son of our Holy Church, I cannot 'expect
that a blessing will be vouchsafed upon her labours.
I know to what I should expose myself if these
my opinions became generally known. But I am
now old, and life has no longer any thing to tempt
me. I have thought deeply and honestly on these
things; and when I am called on, I shall not hesitate to declare my conviction. I pray, as you pray,
for the restoration of England to the unity of the
Church; but I pray also that we may discharge our
duty in preparing for this great work by cutting off
our own offences. England indeed is important,
and you are right in directing towards her your chief
thoughts. Her wealth, her intelligence, her weight
in the councils of Europe, her science, her command of the seas, her vast empire, her commerce
and her colonies, which would give Christianity
access to every part of the world, her language,
which is spread over the whole continent, her gigantic resources of every kind, her very position on
the globe, point her out as the strong arm of Christ's
Church — as the great sanctuary of Christ's truth.
With England doing its duty for the cause of the
Gospel, what triumphs might we not expect for

that Gospel even to the end of the world? In all this we heartily agree. But beware lest your zeal for Rome make you the preacher of another gospel than that which Christ and his Apostles preached. Seek not to make England a handmaid of the Pope rather than a handmaid of Christ. Think not of a spiritual empire over the minds and bodies of men, but of proclaiming to them truth, and truth only. And then you will not be tempted to engage in those plots and conspiracies (I cannot call them by a milder name) in which none take refuge but those who have objects at heart which they cannot trust to God's providence to accomplish, or who have not faith in his power. You know that I have always remonstrated against any such means of effecting Christian objects. They have brought upon us already hatred, shame, persecution, contempt, and punishment — punishment most deserved, though most severe. They have arrayed against us not only kings and princes, but people and priests. They have made the very name that you bear a by-word for falsehood and cunning. And the principle on which they were adopted at the first has led to other acts and other doctrines, which have roused even bishops and fathers of our Church to protest against your system as against the Antichrist, which is to come. Forgive me this freedom. But as an old and beloved friend — as one with whom I have borne much, and whom I cannot believe to be yet entangled irremediably in the meshes of a most dangerous policy,—I warn you, and pray for you, that you may yet be preserved in the simplicity and innocency of Christian charity. My letter of course you will destroy. And my secret, so far as my opinions may be a secret, is, I know, safe in your hands.

"From your affectionate brother in the Lord,

"PIERRE ST. MAUR."

The effect of this letter upon the person to whom
it was addressed, it is unnecessary at present to explain.   One thing also may be observed, that it was
not destroyed.   The admissions in it were too important to permit their being lost.   And the simple
unsuspicious St. Maur little thought, that in making
such a communication to a bosom friend he was
betraying himself to a whole community.   In the
meanwhile the absence of Lord Claremont and
Lady Eleanor threw him every day more into the
company and confidence of Villiers, whose respect
for his office, for his age, for his singular simplicity and piety, and for the absence of all bigotry
and bitterness from the strictness of his religious
opinions, was increased as he became more acquainted with the trials through which he had
passed.   By degrees each opened his mind more
freely to the other.   And St. Maur felt no scruple
in suggesting to Villiers all the considerations which
rendered the union of the Church under the Roman Pontiff an object of such paramount interest
and importance.   He pointed out the impotency of
any national church to resist the aggressions of the
civil power.   He showed the necessity of its allying
itself with that civil power, if left without any other
arm to strengthen its authority.   He recounted the
temptations of Erastianism, and the corruptions and
laxity of discipline which such secularity involved.
He dwelt much on the same grand view of Christian unity which Macarthy had before with picturesque effect, and all the eloquence of enthusiasm exhibited to Villiers at Rome.   He asked
how doubts could be resolved without some one
authoritative expositor of divine truth — how dissensions and schissms could be prevented where
doubts were permitted — how the picture of the
Church, as delineated in the Jewish polity, could

be developed except by establishing within it some visible centre of unity, with one Great High Priest and one glorious Temple. All the ordinary processes by which the Scriptures have been pressed into the service of Romish controversialists were familiar to him; and he adopted them with a simplicity of faith and sincerity of conviction which gave, at times, even to vague inferences and metaphorical analogies, the force of argument. Villiers listened. And when he brought forward the result of his own inquiries on primitive antiquity, and with a noble indignation protested against the forgeries and falsehoods by which the papal supremacy had been maintained on this ground, the honest, unreserved St. Maur threw him off his guard at once, by conceding the point, by allowing the doctrine to be a mere modern development, but a development of expediency.

"Development!" repeated Villiers to himself; "Development!" and he dropped the abbé's arm as they were walking in the gardens of the Palais Pitti; and while the old man rested himself against a vase, Villiers was thoughtfully pacing the terrace before the grand fountain, which shot up a column of water high into the air, and then spread it out and developed it in a fan-like canopy and dome of silver.

CHAP. XXI.

" Development!" again repeated Villiers, " Development!" as he stood the next morning watching
a young orange-tree which was shooting out its
tender leaves from a newly-planted stem, when a
servant came to announce to him that a gentleman,
with letters of introduction from England, was in
the saloon.   Villiers's thoughts were still upon the
subject of development, when he found himself
facing a young man with an easy rather than a gentlemanly address, and a disagreeable sneer upon a
cold sceptical countenance, which made Villiers,
who was sensitively alive to such physiognomies,
throw into his manner all the coldness and reserve
which was consistent with his usual politeness.   The
gentleman had brought an introduction to Lord
Claremont from an under secretary of state, with
whom he had become acquainted by writing a political pamphlet in defence of the Irish education
system.   And he introduced himself by a name
which Villiers had never heard before, but with
which our readers are already acquainted, Mr. Marmaduke Brook.

Mr. Marmaduke Brook was what is commonly
called a man of the world.   He had raised himself
from a comparatively obscure rank to a certain position by the address with which, both at school
and at college, and in after-life, he had insinuated
himself into the acquaintance of persons of rank,
and attached himself to them.   As is usually the
case, his liberal and democratical theories were per-

fectly compatible with a profound and fulsome reverence for rank in itself, and a great degree of soreness and discontent at the reflection that he did not possess it. But, clever and acute as he was, he soon learned that intimacy and influence with the fashionable and aristocratic world, which constituted the great object of his earthly ambition, was not to be attained by mere servility. He affected, therefore, considerable independence; never condescended to flattery, except where he saw that this was the only bait which he could offer; and assumed a tone of equality, and even of superiority, which threw ordinary companions off their guard, and in which, however surprised at first, they soon learned to acquiesce. The same policy he proposed to follow with Villiers; but for once in his life he found himself completely baffled by the simplicity, but coldness, of Villiers's manners. His talent, however, and a certain power of accommodating himself to the tastes and habits of any society, enabled him by degrees to force himself even upon Villiers, whose acquaintance he soon found it was important for him to obtain. And notwithstanding the repugnance, amounting to antipathy, with which Villiers regarded his selfish and worldly character, and his avowed principles of liberalism, both in religion and in politics, it frequently happened that Mr. Brook was permitted to intrude his company upon the abbé and himself after the introduction of the first day had been attained.

It was on one of these occasions that the abbé and Villiers were standing in the gallery of Florence, watching a young artist who was copying, on a large scale, the celebrated " St. John." The ardent intelligent features of the boy—for he was scarcely more —had struck Villiers; and he had been led, as he usually was led by such a spectacle, to inquire into

his history, with something more than common
curiosity, as if some secret hope, which nevertheless
he knew to be vain, was still to be fulfilled by the
inquiry—as if he were about to find something which
he had long lost. But the boy's story was still unfinished, when the abbé came up and stood with
him, watching the young painter's progress.

"And you are copying this picture at large," said
Villiers, "for an altar-piece?"

"Yes, sir."

"And it is to be four times the size of the original?"

The young artist assented.

Villiers paused a little. "Suppose," he continued,
taking the abbé's arm—"suppose that in effecting
this enlarged copy—this development, you were to
insert a feature, or a colour, or a portraiture of your
own, what would your employer say to you?"

"I suppose, sir, he would not buy my picture."

"And suppose," added Villiers, "that in copying
the face you left the eyes of the same size as the
original, while you made the nose of the magnified
proportion, what would you produce?"

The boy laughed, and answered that it would be
a monster.

"You would not call it," said Villiers, "a development, but a destruction of the original?"

"Certainly not."

"So that there are two laws," said Villiers,
"which you observe in your process of development,—first, to insert nothing of your own; and
secondly, to develope the whole together, not omitting
any part?"

The abbé smiled, for he knew what was passing
in Villiers's mind.

"And will not these laws," Villiers continued,
turning to the abbé, — "will not these laws apply to

the office of the Church in developing the doctrine and the discipline of the Gospel? Must she not beware of introducing anything of her own in the pure simple word of Revelation? And when she does expand and illustrate its general doctrines, must she not take care to embrace them all, to omit none, to bestow equal attention, and develope in equal proportions all alike, lest she make not a copy, but a monster?"

The abbé assented.

" How far your Church," continued Villiers, " has observed the first rule, might be a separate question. But consider only the second. You say that in the fourth and later centuries the doctrine of the unity of the Church was developed into the papal supremacy. Were there not other doctrines which should have been developed also, and which you have suffered to remain in less than their original proportion— the doctrine of the authority of the whole college of the Apostles, of their Apostolical privileges separately, of the Episcopal power, of the independence of the civil state, of the authority of Scripture? Were not these essentially parts of the system of primitive Christianity; and have you not so neglected these, while you expounded the doctrine of the visible unity of the Church, that they have been overlaid, as it were, and suppressed under the partial exaggeration of a single counterbalancing feature?"

Before the abbé could satisfy himself with an answer, Mr. Brook, who had seen and joined the little group, ventured, in defiance of Villiers's very cold recognition, to take a part in the conversation. " You are speaking, I find, of the new doctrine, which is causing such a sensation in England. It is singular to see how you high churchmen are coming round by degrees to the truth."

Villiers opened his eyes widely, and looked at him.

" Mr. Brook must excuse me for begging that he will not apply to me any title but that of churchman. I know nothing either of high or low ; and it is the use of such party words which has already done incalculable injury to the cause of truth and peace."

Brook quailed under the eye of Villiers, but soon recovered himself. " And yet you must allow," he said, " that there are parties in the Church, and that those who have adopted what are called High Church views are also putting forward their doctrine of development."

" We must allow," said Villiers, " that a few individuals who have hitherto maintained principles in accordance with the great body of the Church are now running into extravagances, and endeavouring to propagate error. But we must be very cautious whom we confound with them."

" I confess," continued Mr. Brook, " that I am rejoiced to see any approach at last to liberality and freedom of view. Why is religion, any more than any other art or science, to be excluded from those improvements and expansions, which the progress of knowledge and civilization must produce ? We know how experience increases knowledge, how prejudices are removed, and errors corrected, by the advance of time. You speak of antiquity ; but we, as Bacon truly says, are the real ancients. Surely there is no reason why dogmas of theology may not be amended and corrected as well as theories of any other philosophy ?"

" But one reason," said the abbé, gravely, — " that religion, the Christian religion, is a revelation, and that philosophical theories are discoveries : one comes from God, the other from man ; one is given to us perfect at once, the other is imperfect, and perfected only by degrees."

"Ah!" said Brook; "but then you take for granted the fact that your theological dogmas—for instance, your Athanasian Creed —are revelations."

Villiers coloured indignantly.

"Mr. Brook will feel," he said, "that, in speaking to a clergyman, and even to a lay member of the Church, who heartily believes what he promised to believe at his baptism, it is at least becoming to speak with respect of the faith which they profess. Whether there are not higher motives for reverence, whether the bare possibility of such doctrines having come from Heaven may not be sufficient to alarm us against treating them with sneers and sarcasm, I will leave it Mr. Brook's own good taste to judge."

Brook had not been accustomed to hear levity on such subjects rebuked, and he was rather surprised. But his courage was not daunted.

"I can assure you," he replied, "that I had no intention of giving offence ; far from it. But may I venture to ask the abbé how he proves the fact of the revelation of this or that doctrine ?"

"Assuredly," said the abbé; "by the testimony of the Church."

"Testimony to what, my dear abbé?" asked Villiers.

"To the particular doctrine," replied the abbé, "which is called in question—testimony that it has been handed down from the Apostles; and their supernatural commission, of course, is attested by their miracles."

"That it has been handed down!" asked Villiers. "Then this would imply that it has been transmitted unchanged. You must identify it, must you not, throughout?"

"Certainly," said the abbé.

"And is it easy," asked Villiers, "to identify it without preserving it unchanged? If a messenger comes to me from a friend with a letter, stating that he is to bring me a young infant, and, when I ask for the infant, he produces me a full-grown man"——

"You mean the development of the infant," interrupted Brook, laughing. But there was something in the illustration which had suggested itself that seemed to have pained Villiers, and he was silent. The abbé was evidently perplexed, but recovered himself.

"Surely," he said, "if you were in India, or some still more remote country, and a considerable time had elapsed between the writing of the letter and the arrival of the messenger, you would not be surprised to find that the child had grown? You would not doubt its identity because it was no longer a mere infant?"

"No," said Villiers; "because in the child itself there is a principle of growth; and its alteration is so necessary that it must be implied in the original message."

"And is it not so," asked the abbé, "with divine truth? Has not that also within it a principle of growth? Was not the seed sown by our Lord upon earth, and left by Him expressly to be developed, after his Ascension, by the Holy Spirit in the mind of His Church?"

"Of His Apostles, assuredly," said Villiers. "But the question at issue is, whether any, since the Apostles, have been entrusted with the same power of developing it?"

"What do you understand by development?" asked the abbé. "What is precisely the process of it? and then, perhaps, we may obtain more insight into the truth."

"I mean by development," said Villiers, "the application of a general rule, or a general principle, to the particular cases which fall under it. Thus the Fourth Commandment, and indeed all the other Commandments, are given to us in the form of specific enactments, which virtually, and by natural implication, contain in them, like the Trojan horse, a whole host of legitimate inferences and precepts of conduct. The duty of observing the Sabbath involves the duty of obeying all other positive commands of God; and the duty of obeying positive commands in general applies to every instance which occurs of the kind. So the doctrine of the divinity of our Blessed Lord involves a multitude of other doctrines;—as, that he is most humbly to be adored; his atonement—that he is to be blessed and loved by us; his humanity—that he is to receive from us all such regards and expressions of affection as are due to a perfect human being, partaker of the same nature with ourselves. So, also, when two or more doctrines are put together, from these new relations and combinations will flow out new deductions and conclusions, just as all the theorems in Euclid are drawn out of the first axioms, problems, and definitions, by means of arranging them in various groups and forms; just as chemical elements produce an infinite diversity of effects, according as they are thrown into different mixtures and proportions. Saltpetre and charcoal, separately, are harmless: combined, they explode in fire."

"You are right," said the abbé. "And is not the whole process of Christian instruction, and of Christian obedience, such a process of development? Has Almighty God given to us any more than the first general principles of conduct to guide our moral life, and the first general truths of the Divine nature to embrace in our intellect, leaving it to our conscience and our understanding to draw them out and apply them to our practice?"

Villiers assented.

"You teach a child his creed," continued the abbé. "Is he to learn nothing more? You impress on him the Ten Commandments. Will they alone suffice without some process of development?"

Villiers shook his head.

"Where, then, do you condemn us," asked the abbé, "if we think, that in the polity of the Church, as in many portions of its teaching, something, nay much, may have been left, at the first preaching of the Gospel, to be expounded and drawn out in succeeding generations?"

"Precisely so, precisely!" interrupted Mr. Brook. "I am delighted to hear you. This is precisely what we contend for. You think with us, that there is no necessity to adhere blindly and bigotedly to old formularies of dogmatic teaching—that new light may from time to time stream in upon the truth,—that we, in fact, in the nineteenth century may be much more capable, after longer experience, and with our increased civilization, of distinguishing between truth and error than our ancestors 1800 years since. This is the very principle which our great dissenting divines, and, indeed, all our best modern philosophers, are anxious to establish, and which what are called the orthodox churchmen are so peremptory in condemning."

The abbé seemed startled at such zealous approbation and support from a person whose principles were fully as obnoxious to himself as they were to Villiers. "You forget," he said to Mr. Brook, "one very essential difference; it may be necessary that doctrines should be developed. But it is not the same whether they are developed by an individual, or by the Church. You would leave them to the tender mercies of private judgment; each man thinking and inferring, and applying for himself. With us, this privilege is reserved to a proper ecclesiastical authority."

" You object, then," said Mr. Brook, " to our theory, because it places the determination of truth in the hands of an individual ?"

" Certainly," said the abbé.

" Because," continued Brook, " you think an individual is not competent to decide, and that he requires correction, assistance, external rule ?"

" Certainly."

" And in whom, in the view of a great portion of your Church, does this power reside? Is it not in the Pope ? "

" Certainly," said the abbé; " such is the doctrine of many."

" And in the Pope, as an individual independent of councils ? "

" Not with us," said the abbé; " not with the Gallican Church, but with Jesuits and ultramontanes."

" And you repudiate their view ?" asked Villiers.

" Assuredly."

" And why ?"

" Because I can find no promise made to justify such an infallibility."

" Have you not," asked Villiers, " promises as distinct, and language as decisive, in the opinion of many, as you have for the papal supremacy generally?"

" We adhere," said the abbé, " to the practice and principles of many past generations, in the Church, in conceding to the Pope great power and authority, though it may be difficult to limit it precisely."

" But you profess," continued Villiers, " to regard the whole body of the Church assembled in her councils as the authorised expositor and developer

of divine truth — not the individual Pope. The
Pope is, with you, only an important member — a
voice in the Church? "

" Certainly."

" And you condemn and excommunicate us,"
continued Villiers, "not because we reject the authority of the Pope, but because we reject the authority of what you conceive to be general councils,
and therefore, legitimate representatives of the
whole church? "

The abbé was unwilling to make the concession, but could not refuse. He made some observations respecting the importance of recognising
the papal authority as an element in the tribunal of
the Church, but was compelled to acknowledge that
it was difficult, or almost impossible, to define accurately its extent, or to say when disobedience
became a crime.

" And yet," concluded Villiers, " you do not
hesitate to excommunicate us, and to cut us off
from salvation, because, in our own judgment of
the doctrines and practice of the Primitive Catholic Church, and according to the practice of our
own immediate ancestors, we have not allowed to
the Pope such an extent of prerogative, in a matter,
by your own confession, never accurately defined, as
he himself would claim. You have done the same,
have you not? You do not, in the Gallican Church,
allow to him what is claimed by him in Italy. What
right have you to modify or circumscribe his prerogatives, which we have not in England? And
if we have committed a deadly sin, are you not
guilty likewise? And yet you join in excommu-
nicating us. Is this Christian? "

" We are justified," said the abbé, " by the general
voice of the church, which you have rejected."

" I know not," said Villiers, " where you will

find such rejection. It has been our professed and recorded desire to adhere to the general voice of the Church. But the voice which we recognise is that of the old Church of the Apostles, and of the first centuries, not that of modern days. And it was not because the Council of Trent developed Christian truth, but because it altered and corrupted it, that we discard its decrees."

"You agree, then," said the abbé, "that Christian truth must be developed, and developed by the Church?"

"Assuredly."

"We have driven away Mr. Brook," remarked the abbé, as that personage retired to join another group at the other end of the gallery. "Tell me now, for we can speak more at ease, what are your real objections to our theory of development."

"First," replied Villiers, "as I before said, that, in professing to develope, you change and alter. Secondly, that you claim for those to whom you assign the task of development an authority and weight as a representative of the whole Church, when in reality they form but a part of it. Thirdly, that not content with requiring to their teaching such amount of moral respect as is fairly proportioned to the goodness and wisdom of human teachers, you impose their dogmas as infallible decrees, and made the reception of them essential to salvation. Fourthly, that in so doing you transgress the express commands and warnings of the early Church, which drew a broad and distinct division between that portion of the Christian faith which was to be imposed on and received by all as essential to salvation, and that which, however true in itself, or correctly deduced from fundamental credenda, was not itself established as fundamental by God. Fifthly, that you transgress by the same act not

only the commands of God, but the whole analogy
of the Church. When we would rear an oak, we
know that we must plant an acorn; and that acorn
is itself the oak in a certain stage of development.
But if we buried a young tree as we bury the acorn,
would it live? And when we would rear up in the
mind of man the full expansion of Christian truth,
we must plant in it first the general principles, the
filaments of all truth, organised and concentred as in
a seed or germ; for instance, as we find them in the
Creed; but not expanded in a more developed system.
In this manner we do not load the mind with more
than it can bear; we do not exact from it more
implicit faith than is necessary; — above all, we do
not require its assent to the correctness of the logical faculty in man as exercised upon divine truth,
in which attempt it must, by its nature, be liable to
err, and has no guarantee against error from a
divine promise. We require truth only in historical testimony — that such and such doctrines have
been received from God. We leave the logical
faculty scope to exercise itself subsequently, and
the various ramifications and details of doctrine to
shoot out and grow, according as they are required,
under the care of a teacher and the labours of the
pupil conjointly. But you, my dear abbé," continued Villiers, as he hastened to close the conversation on observing the return of Mr. Brook —
" you, that is, your Church, would plant in every
mind at once the full-grown tree; and if the mind
is incapable of receiving it, if it hesitates to place
as much confidence in the reasoning of man as in
the word of God, you cut it off from salvation.
And thus you compel the mind either to an unlimited credulity, or an unlimited scepticism. And
Romanists, in proportion as they enter zealously
and heartily into the spirit of their system, and are

not saved from it by some happy inconsistency, which perpetually embroils and perplexes them as in the Gallican Church, must become either infidels or fanatics."

"And yet," said the abbé, "if authority has been given to the Church thus to develope, and thus to impose its development on its members——"

"If!" replied Villiers. "But in that *if*, how much is included! You cannot show me any such authority in the Scriptures conceded, to say the least, to any but the whole Church as the full representative of the Apostolical body; and your Church is but a part. The Romish see, and those who have acceded to it, form but a portion of the Christian body, are representatives but of one Apostle. You cannot produce any such practice from the Primitive Church! for I deny that the Nicene Creed was a development—it was a statement. It was no more a development of doctrine than Magna Charta in its own language was a development of the English constitution. It was a declaratory law — declaratory of facts and doctrines already in existence. And the reasonings of the Council of Nice did not tend to draw out new positions from the Scriptures, but to justify old. And if by the inspiration of the Holy Spirit they were authorised to decide at all on such an essential point as the amount of credence requisite for salvation, they were authorised also to decide that that amount should not be exceeded. With the anathemas—the most solemn anathemas—of the Church which you profess to follow protesting against you, how can you appeal to it? Did not the half of Christendom separate from you on this very ground, that you tampered with the creeds? Either you are condemned by the voice of the ancient Church, or, in despising its condemnation, you own yourself to be a new

Church; and with a new Church comes a new doctrine; and with a new doctrine where remains the
faith once 'for all delivered to the saints?' 'the traditions which we are bound to hold fast?' 'the
Gospel, one and unchanged, which cannot be
preached other than as it was preached by the
Apostle, though preached by an angel from Heaven.'
It is because your doctrine of development destroys
the very fact of revelation—that it overthrows the
very foundations of truth and faith, that therefore
it is so fearful. And yet upon it your doctrine of
the supremacy is founded, and all your departures
from the faith and practice of the primitive Christianity—departures, as they appear to us—are attempted to be justified. Your worship of saints,
your adoration of images, your terrors of purgatory,
the licentiousness of your indulgences, the frightful
blasphemy of your language to the blessed Virgin—
every thing which compelled the Reformation, and
with the Reformation brought on the frightful excesses to which sectarianism and infidelity have
proceeded in these later times."

"You are still discussing, I find," said Mr. Brook,
as he resumed his position by the side of Villiers
with a mixture of freedom and servility. "I must
take my stand with the abbé. We find in England
that there are no greater friends to liberty of conscience and general toleration than the Catholics."

"Roman Catholics, I must beg to call them,"
said Villiers; "unless, indeed, such a name implies
a self-contradiction."

"Oh!" replied Brook, "I have no objection to
any name. What is there in a name? Words are
but signs; and one of the strange absurdities of
the present day is the contest for names."

"You do not think it an absurdity, do you?"
said Villiers, turning to the abbé. "You would

not allow me to call you any thing but a Catholic,
without remonstrance, I am sure?"

"Certainly not," said the abbé; "for Catholic is
the title of the Church given to it in the Creed; and
if I am not Catholic, I am not a member of it."

"And if not a member of the Church," continued
Villiers, "you are not, we shall both allow, an heir
of salvation? At least, you have no promise or
assurance of it?"

"Assuredly," said the abbé; while Mr. Brook
listened with a sarcastic expression of contempt.

"You are one, then," said he, "of the new Oxford
school—the P——"

"Sir," interrupted Villiers, "I am afraid you
are proceeding to apply to me an expression which I
never permit to be used to me. For the same reason
that I objected to your use of the word Catholic, I must
protest against any one applying to me another word
which, besides that it calumniates a good man as
being the leader of a party in the Church, condemns
all who accept it as being followers of an individual
teacher, instead of being followers of Him whom
only we may recognise as our Master. It is virtually to unchristianize them; at the least it repre-
sents them as schismatics. You will oblige me by
never employing it when you are choosing to describe any religious opinions which you may suppose
me to hold. I beg to wish you good morning."

"You have been rather severe on Mr. Brook,"
said the abbé, as he took Villiers's arm to assist
himself down the stairs.

"I did not mean to be severe," said Villiers;
"I have no right to be severe on any one. There
is too much here" (and he put his hand to his
heart) "to humble and shame me, for me to undertake the office of a censor. And yet I am naturally
hasty; and they used to call me haughty. But it

certainly is a trial to me to meet such men; and
the present day abounds with them. I can bear
enthusiasm of any kind, for it must contain good,
and only requires to be rightly tempered and directed ; but the cold, sneering, unfeeling, flippant
sophistry which has crept into the spirit of the day,
and which men call liberalism, is—— However, we
gain nothing by speaking of it."

"I fear you have offended him," said the abbé.

"It is very possible," answered Villiers; "but I
must risk his offence rather than permit him to
indulge in that tendency to give nicknames, which
has done more harm to the Church, by forcing men
into parties almost in despite of themselves, even
than heresy itself. It is the fomenter of all
schism."

"But I thought," said the abbé, "that you and
all other Protestants cared little for schism. Surely
your Church is overrun with it; and what have you
done to prevent it?"

"My dear abbé," said Villiers, "why will you,
an educated, well-informed, and conscientious Christian, suffer yourself to think and feel of the English
Church as the Romish communion, whether in
ignorance or design, teaches the most violent of
her members to speak; misunderstanding or mis-
representing our principles, and confounding us
with those sectarians who have gone out from
among us, but are not of us ? We, by the voice of
our Church, are as deeply interested in the cause of
unity—are as solemnly pledged to maintain it—as
you are. If we differ in the mode of preserving it
—if we think that the creation of a visible centre
of unity in the person of one supreme bishop is
neither consonant to the divine form of Church
polity, nor conducive to the end desired—if we
would rather adhere to the old apostolical system

of the first centuries, than adopt your new developed theories—and if, owing to your violent attacks upon us and to our own weakness and individual faults, we have been unable to retain within our fold a large number of our sheep, as you yourselves have been unable to retain the branches of the reformed communions—this is no proof that we repudiate or despise unity, but that we have been unwilling to preserve it by a wrong principle, and unable to preserve it by the right."

"And you will not, then, accede," said the abbé, "to the theory of development?"

" " "I think it," said Villiers, "the most insidious, the most fatal, the most fertile in mischief, of all those rationalistic principles on which Romanism has built up its system. Grant this doctrine, and you grant a power to subvert the faith, to destroy truth, to erect a spiritual despotism of superstition and tyranny, which must end in a spiritual anarchy. You grant, I think, the very principle for which all heretics, and schismatics, and infidels are clamouring; and upon it must be charged those odious excesses and crimes which have disfigured the Christain Church since the Romish supremacy was established, both in those who have upheld and in those who have resisted it."

"And yet," said the abbé, "you allow the necessity of some development?"

"Assuredly," said Villiers, as they reached the house, and stopped under the gateway. "Assuredly. If I were to sum up my own view of it, it would be that development itself is an operation contemplated by God himself" (and Villiers removed his hat as he mentioned the holy name) "in his whole scheme of Christian instruction — but development confined properly to the Church, limited by laws which will prevent it from either

x 3

adding, or taking away, or altering, from becoming, in fact, any thing but development—when carried on by individuals, subject to the watchful control of the Church ; and when enunciated by the Church, to be enunciated without any such sanction or enforcement as would alter the terms of communion prescribed by the Apostles, or narrow the gates of Heaven, or enlarge the articles of the Christian faith, which by them were selected as fundamental, and enforced as essential to salvation.   The Epistles are in this way a development of those forms of doctrine which were taught to candidates for baptism before the Scriptures were completed.   They were written by Apostles, of whose inspiration there is no doubt. And yet even they were not enforced upon Christians as terms of salvation.   The catechumen was pledged to the Creed, not to the Scriptures.   And can a privilege not claimed by Apostles be claimed by a single bishop, or by any of their successors? Let the Romish Church develope her system of belief as we have developed ours in our Articles.   Let her, if she chooses, impose her development upon her own clergy and teachers.   She may reason rightly or wrongly, and be responsible before the Almighty for her error.   But she will not be guilty of the sin with which she is now charged, of fixing arbitrary conditions of salvation for which she has no sanction but her own voice, and so cutting herself off from Christendom by cutting Christendom off from herself.   Remove your excommunication, and you restore peace and unity to the Church."

The abbé sighed deeply.   "I fear," he said, "that these are dreams which can never be realised."

"Let us pray," said Villiers, "that they may be realised—realised without compromise of truth. And to earnest prayer who can deny that even this

great boon may be granted by Him who is the
'Author of peace and the lover of concord?' But
how, I often wonder, how can you offer to Him
your prayers for such a blessing, when your acts
are the daily cause of discord and confusion?"

"In what way?" asked the abbé.

"In this way," answered Villiers. "You begin
with forming an unauthorised theory of Church
unity. To justify this, you are obliged to recur to
your theory of development: to sanction that, you
must claim infallibility; and infallibility being presumed, you cannot escape from intolerance: and
thus you place yourselves in hostility to all around
you who are not of you; and you introduce enmity,
and with enmity persecution, wherever your faith
prevails. For, be assured, it is not possible for
Christians to be deeply and sincerely religious, and
yet to live in love and charity—perfect love and
undisturbed charity—with those whom they believe to be in the wilful commission of deadly sin,
and abandoning their own salvation. How can
subjects exercise a true loyalty to a monarch whom
they regard as a heretic, and therefore, perhaps, as
worse than an infidel? How can provinces live together happily and affectionately, as parts of one
and the same empire, when they are distracted by
the claims of a foreign allegiance, involving the
peril of their souls? How can parents and children,
wives and husbands——" But here Villiers
stopped. A memory of the past came to his mind,
and a thought for the future; and, hastily closing
the conversation, he returned to his room.

CHAP. XXII.

IT often happens that an accidental conversation does more than weeks of reflection to bring out, and arrange, and fix principles which shape our conduct through life. And so it was with Villiers. General, vague, and desultory opinions, strong, indeed, and permanent, but not consecutively combined, on the subject of Romanism, had possessed him for several years. The subject had occupied his attention, painfully and anxiously, of late. It had mixed itself with many floating day-dreams. He felt that it was intimately connected with his future plans and welfare. But he was remarkable for seizing on the clue of an argument, and following it out rapidly, and tracing the connection between its several stages. And his discussion with the abbé had led him to a somewhat connected view of different features in the system of Romanism, which, separately, he had always regarded with great aversion. The doctrine of development had presented itself to him as a speculative question. But excommunication, intolerance, the bitterness of sorrow, if not of hatred, which the Romish theory fosters in its children towards all who differ from them, and the consequent impossibility of forming any social union where Romanism is an element amidst contending systems — this now pressed upon him with tenfold force. The remainder of the day after the conversation with the abbé he passed in his own room. It was over the apartments occupied by the abbé, whose own mind was anxiously engaged in watching every turn of the young Englishman's opinions and feelings; and who knew not whether to augur well or ill for the object nearest to his heart, as he heard Villiers pacing backwards and forwards with an agitated step; now stopping, as if to think; now throwing open his window, as if to calm the turbulence of his feelings by gazing out on the bright sky, and cypress terraces of the garden of the palazzo. More than once the abbé caught the sound of a suppressed groan, as he threw himself on his knees and remained in prayer, — praying that he might be enlightened in the truth; praying as fervently that he might be guided now in the path of duty, and be enabled to withstand the strong temptation to which he felt that he was exposed every day that he remained in a spot where Lady Eleanor was present. He sent his apologies to the abbé for not joining him at dinner; and when the abbé ventured to seek him in his own room in the evening, he met Villiers's servant carrying the letters just arrived from the post, and preparing his master's travelling apparatus.

" Are you leaving us at once, so soon?" exclaimed the abbé, — " packing up!"

But Villiers did not hear him. He was hastily opening a letter in Lady Eleanor's handwriting. He read it; and turning to the abbé, said, "I was going away to-morrow morning; I have lingered here too long, and ought to be in England. But this letter must detain me. My uncle is ill. They are bringing him here at once, and expect to arrive to-morrow. Of course I cannot leave him. But," he continued with a deep sigh, "I must remain here no longer than is absolutely necessary."

The abbé understood him, and did not press for any explanation.

When Lord Claremont's travelling-carriage drove
into the court-yard the next day, Villiers was on
the steps to receive him. He assisted Lady Eleanor
out with outward calmness ; only she observed that
his hand shook as it took hers, and was withdrawn
in a moment. And her own mind was as much
alive as his to every little sign which might indicate
what passed within. Lord Claremont was assisted
to his room. His medical attendants were soon with
him. But when Villiers waited to see them after
their consultation, he was shocked to hear that
the illness was of a more serious nature than had
been apprehended, and might probably terminate
in paralysis. He was to be watched carefully. The
uncle had done little to win the affections or command the gratitude of the nephew. He was a cold,
dull, formal, uncharactered man, who seemed incapable of being touched by anything but the claims
of the Whig party to his vote in parliament, and
the influence of his daughter, to whom he occasionally showed signs of attachment far beyond
what could be expected from his selfish, phlegmatic
nature. But Villiers had been taught a lesson. He
spent the night on a sofa in his uncle's room, without permitting any one but the servants to know it.
And he was comforting himself while dressing the
next morning in his own dressing-room with the fal-
lacious hope that the patient was better, when he
was alarmed by the hasty ringing of bells, and the
hurry of footsteps along the passages. Before he
could ring to inquire, his own man knocked hastily
at the door, and entreated him to make haste,—Lord
Claremont was in a fit — was dying. Villiers was
in a moment by his bed-side. The poor old man
lay insensible, and one side of his face was distorted by a seizure of paralysis. Lady Eleanor, her
hands clasped round him, was chafing his temples,

and though evidently in fearful agony of mind, did not permit it to render her incapable of giving the requisite orders. Villiers took his place at her side, assisting her in all that she did, or hastening the arrival of the physicians. Half an hour elapsed before they came. Lord Claremont showed no signs of recovery, and Lady Eleanor's firmness was evidently giving way. She neither wept nor spoke, except to ask for something seemingly required by the patient. But Villiers saw, by the working of her lips, that the suppression of feeling could not last much longer. The physicians came, and at their request he led her from the room.

This is not a love-story; and we have no wish to involve our readers in the details of love-scenes. Both Villiers and Lady Eleanor possessed strong minds — strong both in the energy of their emotions, and in the control which they exercised over them.

But the strength must have been superhuman which could have preserved the secret of their hearts wholly unrevealed from each other at such a moment. Every word of encouragement and consolation on the part of Villiers, however anxiously guarded by him, conveyed volumes to Lady Eleanor's mind. And even the violence which she put herself on her own feelings, and the embarrassment with which she listened to him, and the tremulousness of her voice when she begged him to return to her father's room and obtain a report from the physicians, was sufficient to ensure Villiers that happiness was within his reach; that he needed only to ask for it and obtain it; but — and with the *but*, instead of joy, there came intense misery. He had made no declaration. She had uttered nothing like confession. But both knew what the other felt; and both knew also that there was a gulf between them which neither could pass. The first thought of each upon separating was a fear lest a betrayal had taken place—a betrayal which, unaccompanied by any farther declaration, might compromise the happiness of the other. The second was a resolution to make the explanation instantly, if it could be done. The good abbé was at hand ; and he was the first person to whom, as to her confessor, Lady Eleanor committed the secret of her affections, entreating him to take some opportunity without delay of assuring Villiers of her unalterable resolution never to engage in marriage with one whose religion was different from her own. The abbé lost no time. The next day Lord Claremont was better, and the abbé insisted on Villiers leaving the sick room, and coming out for fresh air.

Villiers — distracted, absent, almost vacillating, and recovering from his vacillation only to be filled with remorse at his weakness — suffered the good old man to take his arm. They strolled into the great square ; and the abbé led him up into the gallery, as to the place most likely to occupy and amuse him. He brought him into the tribune, and soon commenced a conversation with the young boy whom Villiers had seen there on his last visit, and who had excited his interest by his skill in copying the "St. John." The abbé led him on to tell his story. Villiers became gradually interested in it. It was a tale not unlike that of his own parents, though in humbler circumstances. There had been a marriage between a Romanist and a Protestant — then had followed the usual estrangement of affection, which ended in bitterness and persecution, as soon as religion, which at first was a mere name both with the husband and the wife, became a passion and a duty. There had been the same separation of children — the son following the faith of the father, the daughter that of the mother. Then came the sickness of the Protestant father, his death-bed, and the poor boy's account of his mother's agony of mind; and the torture and persecution to which his father was exposed by her relatives, even in his last moments, to induce him to change his faith, did more than any arguments could have done to steel Villiers in his resolution. The father died; the child had received his last injunctions to remain steadfast in his faith. The mother, dotingly fond of him, and bent on saving him from a state, as she conceived, of utter ruin to his soul, strained every nerve to win him over to her communion. Her efforts were seconded by all the arts and influences which could be exerted by the priests with whom she was surrounded, but in vain. The boy had doted on his father; his father's last words, last look, the solemnity and fearfulness of his last hours, had all impressed themselves indelibly on his mind. He was proof against reasoning, against prayers, even against his mother's tears; until exasperated and in despair, and resolved, at the suggestion of a priest, to make one final trial of severity, she drove him from her door, and almost threatened to lay her curse upon him. But it was all in vain. He left her (this had happened in Ireland), and took refuge with the clergyman of the parish, who had supported him through all his trials. By him the talent which he possessed for painting had been discovered; and he had been introduced to the notice of a nobleman, who had enabled him to come abroad to study. The tale was short, simply, but affectingly told.' And as Villiers turned away in thought, the abbé made a general remark on the evil and misery of mixed marriages; which led him to speak of his own particular opinions — of his own private recommendations to those over whom he possessed

influence — of the satisfaction which he had in
knowing that those in whom he was most deeply
interested — one especially, who was his own chosen
charge (and Villiers understood the allusion),
participated fully in his views, and was unalterably
resolved to act on them. The good abbé sighed
with affectionate compassion, as he made the communication ; and there mixed with the compassion
a pang of disappointment at the breaking up of his
most darling hope ; but his conscience reproved him.
And Villiers, thanking him, and giving him to understand that he comprehended his meaning, assured
him also of his own unchangeable determination to
act upon the same principle, and of his desire that
it should be known.

It had struck twelve the same night ; the light
was still burning in Villiers's room, and his servant
was hurrying backwards and forwards with preparations for packing, when the abbé, to whom a
letter had just been delivered, knocked gently at
the door, and begged five minutes' conversation.

It was the good old man's last opportunity, his
last effort. Wholly as he had composed himself
more than once to face the disappointment of his
dearest hopes, and to leave Villiers to himself, as
the moment of Villiers's final departure approached,
he had received another command from a quarter
which he was bound to respect, and resolved to
make one more attempt, to speak openly and fully,
and urge what still remained to be urged, that the
young Englishman might be won over to the Church
of Rome, and (what the abbé would scarcely dare
to confess to be equally the object of his prayers)
might be united with Lady Eleanor.

It was no surprise to Villiers to see the abbé.
Where minds are severally engaged in the same
thoughts they fall together into the same acts. He

placed the abbé in an easy chair, sat by his side, took his hand, and with affectionate respect entreated him to speak without reserve, if he had any thing to communicate. And the grey light of dawn began to steal in through the half-closed curtains before that communication was closed. Villiers, on his leaving the room, threw himself on the bed, agitated, exhausted, alarmed, uncertain, full of vacillation once more; and at every wavering thought came in the vision of Lady Eleanor. He had gone through the other trials of his faith; had exposed the historical fallacies of Popery; had witnessed and shuddered at the moral perversions which followed upon its theory; had sifted the rationalising speculations on which its claims to empire were founded : one point remained untouched, and to this the abbé had addressed himself. Villiers closed his eyes; and in a feverish distracted dream he fancied himself standing in a venerable cathedral; the service of the Church of England fell on his ears. He was kneeling, praying, when the building shook from its base; the pillars tottered; the roof cleft open till the stars were seen through the crevices; great masses of mortared stone, fragments of arches, bosses, columns, tombstones, hurled themselves around him; a black chasm yawned beneath the altar and swallowed it up; the worhippers and priests fled with cries of terror : and as there gathered round him in their place a host of frightful demon visages screaming in triumph, Villiers saw through a distant aisle a figure — a female figure — beautiful, pure, innocent, and holy—the figure by whose side he had watched over his uncle's bed — beckoning him to escape, and to escape with her. It was the weakness, the distraction, the coldness, the irreverence, the approaching ruin of the English Church, which the abbé had been urging on his

thoughts. A ray of light fell on his eyes, and he
awoke up to the sense of his trial. Alas! how
many bitternesses, how many weaknesses, how
many pangs of remorse and fear crowd often into
that moment of awaking! Till he had raised himself from his pillow, partially dressed himself, knelt
down, read, meditated as usual, even in spite of
wandering thoughts and distracted affections, Villiers thought of postponing his departure, of remaining; of considering all that the abbé had urged,
quietly and impartially with him. He would not
see Lady Eleanor, he said to himself, more than
was absolutely necessary. He could command his
feelings. He need not suffer her to know what
passed in his own mind; and it was cruel to desert
her in the moment of her trial. He was bound to
remain with his uncle; and to refuse to listen to
the truth was obstinacy. He was bound to give to
the objections of opponents a fair and candid consideration. His hand was on the bell to counter-
mand his carriage, but his eye fell on the open
Prayer-book on his table — on the words "Lead us
not into temptation;" and when his servant came,
his first word was to hasten the horses. He went
to his uncle's bed-side, who was still asleep, and
much recovered. He sent Lady Eleanor's maid to
ask if she had any commands for England; but
Lady Eleanor only sent a kind verbal message in
reply. The carriage drove into the court-yard;
and when the abbé pressed his hand, while he yet
lingered on the steps, and asked him if he would
think on what he had heard last night, Villiers,
with a deep sigh, replied, "I go to think; go to
inquire. — God bless you; and bring us both to the
truth. Drive on." And the postilions whirled the
carriage through the gate on its road to England.

As it turned the corner of the street Villiers's eye caught that of a man dressed — it almost seemed disguised — as a Jew, who stood with a young shabby boy in his hand, apparently watching the carriage. It was an eye whose expression he knew. Even in the boy there was something which touched him, he knew not why. He looked back as the carriage drove on; but the man had disappeared. Villiers did not know that he had been lurking round the house the whole morning, or that he had been ever since Villiers's arrival in daily communication with the Italian porter, or that, as he followed the carriage with his eyes, his teeth firmly set, his face scowling with malignity, he had been secretly imprecating curses on him, curses on the abbé, curses on all that belonged to him. He did not recognise him as Mr. Pearce.

CHAP. XXIII.

THE great bell of Christ Church had long ceased
to toll; the streets of Oxford were silent and deserted; and all but a few lights were extinguished
in the dark quadrangle of ———— College, when
the sleepy porter was summoned to answer a hasty
knocking at the gate. It was opened to a tall gentlemanly figure, apparently just arrived from a long
journey, and still in his travelling cloak and cap.
He asked for Mr. Beattie's room.

"No. 12., one pair of stairs to the left," answered
the obsequious porter, who suspected a stranger of
rank, and proceeded to show him to the narrow
archway and stone stairs which led to Beattie's
room. The stranger tapped, heard the usual words
"Come in;" and as he stood before Beattie himself,
who rose from his large reading-desk, and shaded
his eyes from the candle to receive his visiter, it
was some seconds before they mutually exchanged
recognitions.

"My dear Villiers!"

"My dear Beattie!"

"Where did you come from?"

"Before I answer your questions," said Villiers,
"will you give me some tea?"

Beattie's tea-things, untouched, stood on a side-
table, and his kettle was simmering on the hearth.
And Villiers was soon installed in a large leather
reading-chair, from which Beattie was obliged to
remove its usual occupants, a heap of folios: and

the solitary reading-lamp having been exchanged
for brighter lights, the simple-minded Beattie placed
his stool by Villiers's side, and asked for an account
of his movements. Villiers repeated to him every
thing. When he told him of the recovery of his
fortune, Beattie made no remark, offered no congratulations, only looked on him with more of
melancholy, affectionate interest, as if such an event
only exposed him to more perils and heavier responsibilities. When he spoke of his feelings towards Lady Eleanor, Beattie seemed alarmed, but
was relieved by the frank and firm tone in which
Villiers declared his resolution never to unite himself (he was compelled in a low voice to say "again")
with one who was not united in the same church
communion with himself. But when at last Villiers
entered on the subject of his conversation with the
abbé, on his doubts, his anxieties, his misgivings,
Beattie covered his face with his hands and sighed
deeply.

" You saved me once," said Villiers; " you gave
me peace and satisfaction once : can you give it me
now ? —— Peace and satisfaction ! " he repeated, as
if correcting himself: "alas! whatever befalls me,
that must be for others."

Beattie did not move. He sat immersed in painful and anxious thought, sinking, it seemed, as he
drooped his head, under a sense of fearful responsibility. Villiers also was silent. At last Beattie
roused himself as the clock of St. Mary's struck
twelve.

" You must leave me now," he said to Villiers,
"for our hours, you know, do not permit late visiters. You will breakfast with me to-morrow, will
you not ? "

Villiers readily assented ; and at the great gate,
to which Beattie went with him to rouse the sleepy

porter, they parted with a warm but silent pressure
of the hand.

When Beattie's servant came to his room the
next morning he observed that his candle was
nearly burnt out. He must have sat up very late,
contrary to his usual practice. His Prayer-book
lay open on the table, and the pages were still wet
with tears. Several closely-written sheets of paper
were lying on his desk, as if he had been striving
to collect and arrange his thoughts. And as the
servant knocked at the door of the little closet
which served for his bedroom, he found him already
drest and at his devotions.

Punctually as the chapel bell commenced he
was taking his usual solitary walk under the avenue
of horse-chestnuts in the garden, when he was
joined by Villiers.

" You must take me with you into chapel," he
said. " Shall I be considered an intruder ? "

" Ten years since," said Beattie, " perhaps you
would have been ; but let us be thankful it is not
so now. Ten years since, even in this place, even
while we were retaining as a form the daily service,
and employing it as a roll-call for our students, or
even as a punishment, and secretly willing to abolish,
or at least to shorten it,—even when it was thought
unnecessary for any fellows to attend it, except a
single tutor,—even then, I remember, there were
some few, a very few, who understood and who
valued this old form. But now this feeling is
general. We seldom have strangers—our friends,
I mean—staying with us without their attending
our services ; and you will find that the movement
has spread in various directions through the country.
The daily service is no uncommon thing at this
day, even in our village churches."

" And this is owing," remarked Villiers, " to the
Tracts for the Times ? "

"It is owing," said Beattie, "to the good Spirit of God."

"Employing," returned Villiers, "as subordinate agents, those who first originated the movement in this place?"

"I never like," replied Beattie, "to dwell much on subordinate agency or secondary causes, either in the Church or in Nature. In either case it tends to veil from us, or to withdraw us from, the one great Cause. If we regard ourselves in this light, it engenders either conceit or timidity; and if others, it gathers us round them as heads and leaders of party."

"And yet," said Villiers, "you will not deny that the Church of England owes to those men who originated the Church movement here a great debt of gratitude?"

"Assuredly," replied Beattie; "I honour them myself most highly. But you must not forget that other causes and agencies were in operation at the same time, without which their efforts would have failed. They found a field well prepared by others for the seed which they proposed to sow. The extravagancies of an opposite system, the rash violence of the enemies of the Church, the spirit of docility and reverence which characterises our institutions in this place, were all in their favour; but the main arm of their strength was the Church itself. If they had come forward in any other character than as her servants, promulgating her avowed doctrines, sheltering themselves under her authority, ranging themselves by the side of her great teachers and masters in days gone by, and promising reverently to submit themselves to her guidance and control, be assured they would have been signally discomfited. We have no toleration here for founders of new sects and theories. And, so far as the great body of the clergy is affected by our principles, they would have resented indignantly the attempt to influence them to join a party; they would have demanded a censure by Convocation sooner than adopt the principles which they have adopted, unless they had been convinced that they came to them with the sanction of the Church. I think you will see this soon. You will find that if the movement changes its ground, as it is now threatening to do, and becomes an individual speculation, it will be reprobated and condemned at once. You have not found, have you, that as the English clergy have been roused to think more deeply, and reason more acutely, they have become generally less attached to their Church?"

"I think not," replied Villiers.

"No," said Beattie, earnestly; "she may well be proud of this; that she holds us in a willing submission to herself, using no threats, employing no violence—permitting and encouraging us to examine her declarations freely, and ruling over us, not as a tyrant, but as a parent. There are some men," he continued, "young men, very young men, who are clamouring for a sterner, stricter rule; for a more imperious, sweeping dogmatism; for a more uncompromising exclusiveness. And this they would call strength and power. But the strength and power of the Church should be like to that which is exhibited in the analogy of His works who is the head of the Church; and we see nowhere there such marks of overwhelming despotism. The Almighty sets before us, in this life, good and evil, blessings and cursings, truth and falsehood, but permits us to choose, and judge, and walk in seeming liberty; and his Church, to be his minister, must do the same. Too great strictness and strength in the Church is a sign that there is something wrong in her constitution or her temperament. There must be something out of order, some derangement of forces. But the chapel bell is down. In your time, do you remember, every one was allowed to straggle in till the Psalms were nearly over. This, also, you will find changed in many colleges."

As they returned from the chapel, Villiers could not help remarking on the improvement which he observed in the devotional appearance of the young men. Beattie corroborated it.

" And do you find," said Villiers, as they sat at the breakfast-table, " that this improvement extends to practical self-denial? Ten years since, if we had been breakfasting together, as now, on a Friday, we should not have confined our meal to dry bread; now, neither of us feel any difficulty in doing this openly. Is this also becoming common with the young men?"

" Not common yet," said Beattie. " But I have observed many things tending to it which are encouraging. Ten years since I remember a professor of divinity remarking to me that there were more dinner parties among the senior members in Oxford during Lent than at any other season. Now I have known many instances of young men giving their large parties early in the term, that they may not fall during Lent."

" And this is voluntary?" asked Villiers.

" Perfectly so," replied Beattie.

" And done in recognition of the authority of the Church?"

" Probably," said Beattie; " for it is done by those who are not in any way influenced, either by party or enthusiasm, scarcely by consistent religion, and who, therefore, can be governed only by a sense of authority." Beattie's servant here en-

tered the room with a box, which had just arrived
by the mail.

"I know what this is," he said; "and you shall
see it opened at once."

Villiers's interest was roused, and his admiration
still more, when Beattie carefully unfolded from its
wrappings of silver-paper an exquisitely-wrought
chalice of silver-gilt, enamelled with Scripture subjects, and inlaid with gems.

"It is intended," said Beattie, "for our college
chapel."

"And from whom does it come?" asked Villiers.

"This," replied Beattie, "I am not at liberty to
publish.   We have fallen latterly into a practice of
giving what we give anonymously, and avoiding
subscription lists.   Ten years since this would have
been sent in the form of a punchbowl, or a coffee-pot,
or a silver corner-dish."

Villiers was silent, but thoughtful. At last he said
—"And what is your own opinion of this revival in
the English Church?"

"I look on it," said Beattie, "as the Athenians
must have looked on the young shoot of olive, which
sprang up out of the trunk in the citadel, when it
had been cut down with axes and burnt with fire.
It shows not only that life is not extinct, but that
if not extinct after such a trial, humanly speaking,
there is nothing which can extinguish it.   It is one
of the chief things which rouses my impatience,
when I hear the Church of England lightly spoken
of as weak and perishing."

"And yet other Churches," said Villiers, "have
had their revivals also."

"Surely;" replied Beattie, "the foundation of
every new monastic order in the Romish Church
was intended as a revival. But observe the difference. In other instances the spirit has shot up in

some form of novelty ; it has emanated from some individual — has generated a party. Instead of adhering to existing laws and institutions, it has delighted to invent new ; it has cast off all restraint, and fed itself with enthusiasm and fanaticism. Such a revival indicates the weakness rather than the strength of the body in which it takes place. But the revival which we have witnessed in our own time has been, strictly speaking, a revival of the spirit of the Church, within the Church, under the control of the Church, encouraged by the ministers of the Church, throwing itself back upon the laws and the teaching of the Church, and placing itself from the first under external control and guidance. It is a natural, not an artificial revival. It has not been produced by stimulants, and therefore it is as much an evidence of the internal strength and vigour of the Church as the recovery without medicine of a man at the point of death is a proof of the strength of his constitution."

"And yet," said Villiers, "the Church of England ten years since was at the point of death."

"So," replied Beattie, "it seemed to us. Threatened by the people, treacherously protected and corrupted by the state, robbed of her revenues, mutilated in her bishoprics, disorganised and enfeebled in those collegiate bodies which ought to form her greatest strength, her authority neither asserted by herself nor recognised by others, her testimony set aside and supplanted by an empty rationalism, her education emptied of every thing which could give it life and power, her churches deserted, her children running off without a warning voice into every kind of dissent, and the population swelling like a running tide around her, and menacing to swallow her up, like those fabled springs destined to overflow and drown the mortals who forget to keep them under cover and confined within their proper bounds — such was the condition of the Church. Who would have dared at that time to prophesy that it should, within ten years, simply by the assertion of its own principles, be more deeply rooted than ever in the affections of its children, more feared than ever by its enemies, more able than ever to take its stand as the guardian of this empire, and to spread out its arm to the most distant continents as the converter of the heathen? Yet surely this is now true."

" And yet," said Villiers, " there must have been some malformation, some secret mischief, which had reduced her to her previous state. Without some radical defect no church could so have fallen."

" My dear Villiers," said Beattie, after a pause, and placing his hands on his friend's shoulders, " will you endeavour to remain for five minutes in this position, standing upright without moving a single muscle?"

Villiers stopped (for they were now walking on the terrace in the college gardens) and endeavoured to do so, but found it impossible.

" Or," continued Beattie, " will you try and walk up to that plane-tree yonder in one straight line without a single divergence?"

Villiers shook his head.

" No," said Beattie, " it would be impossible; for the law of progression, as in human minds, and in individuals as in societies, is a law of continual oscillation. We bend from side to side, wavering at every step; if weak, falling wholly, not to rise again; if strong, recovering ourselves by some great effort, and advancing at each fresh struggle with more directness, but never upon this earth without a tendency to vary from the central line. Do not therefore measure the weakness of societies by their oscillations, or even by their falls (for they are human, and cannot escape them), but by their recoveries — recoveries through their own internal strength, when to common eyes they seemed wholly lost. Look round on all the churches in the world, on all civil societies which history presents, and search if you can find an instance of any human polity recovering itself from oscillations so fearful as those by which the English Church has been shaken at times from her centre. Think what a tremendous shock to all opinions and all institutions was given by the stroke which severed her from the tyranny of Rome. And yet, though she bent for a time beyond her equilibrium, she righted, and recovered in her doctrine both the principle of authority and the talisman of an hereditary Catholicism, without which she would long since have been fractured to atoms, like the Protestant communions in Germany. She was saved here by the arm of the civil power, which grasped her (roughly indeed and tyrannically) when she had shaken off her hold upon the Papacy ; but yet rescued her from falling wholly into that worst anarchy, the government of self-will. That arm itself was then fractured; and the Church fell to the ground, and to human eyes was utterly destroyed. And yet suffering, and persecution, and martyrdom, only purified and strengthened it ; and it came out of the convulsions of the rebellion stronger than before — the monarchy supported by the Church, and the Church supported by the monarchy. The Revolution came ; and the monarchy was split from top to bottom. It stood indeed, and a superficial view might not detect the flaw. But the principle of popular election, however disguised and disclaimed, was admitted into the constitution. And since then the Church has been placed to contend against it, breaking out as it has done in a thousand different forms. She has contended with it under the most difficult circumstances; her hands tied, her movements restricted, her principles corrupted, her resources curtailed, her operations betrayed by the necessity of recognising a nominal monarchy, which, in reality, was a democracy. If the monarchy had wholly disappeared, her course would have been plain and her opposition unfettered. But she has fought like a woman defending her house and husband against robbers; her husband himself being all the time one of their accomplices, and endeavouring to silence and corrupt her. We measure strength," continued Beattie, " not by mere exertion, but by exertion against resistance, and under disadvantages. Think in this point of view on the very existence of the Church of England at this day as all but a miracle."

" And yet," said Villiers, " is not the existence of the Church of Rome a still greater miracle ?"

" Have you overlooked," said Beattie, " the fact that the Church of England all this time has been contending not only with secular powers and popular licentiousness, but with the strength of the Church of Rome, put out to crush her as its most dangerous opponent; disguising itself under every variety of form, and ransacking all its resources ? Are you not aware how much of the popular movements against the Church of England has been fomented by Rome? how earnestly Rome has bent herself to destroy us? and still we are not yet lost. Every fresh degree of power which you think you recognise in the Church of Rome is another attestation to the strength of the Church of England, which, single-handed, has resisted and survived such aggressions."

" And yet," said Villiers, " think of the enormous power—of the wonderful organisation of the Church of Rome. Where are we to find this in the Church of England? Look at her monastic orders, at her discipline, at her influence on the people, on kings, on learning, on education, on all that gives power to rulers. Surely the Church of England, by her side, is as an emaciated sick man or a mutilated cripple."

"Emaciated she is," said Beattie; "mutilated she has been. She is weak, and will long continue so —weak as Samson before his hair grew again— as Achilles robbed of his arms — as the Giant blinded for the moment. But if even in her weakness she has fought with the strong arm of popery, and not been yet destroyed, what will she do in her strength?"

"And yet," replied Villiers, "surely there is in popery a principle of power and of permanence which no other polity can realise. Think of the concentration of its forces round one centre; of its unity of action; of its emancipation from all secular control; of its sternness, its exclusiveness, its uncompromising demand of subjection, its unflinching singleness of aim, the enthusiasm which it contrives to awaken, both in the ambitious and the devout; of its command over the imagination, of the elasticity of its practice coupled with the immobility of its theories. Remember how amidst all her errors, and worse than errors, she preserves axioms of truth, and misleads her followers chiefly in questions of fact, which they are unable to examine. Observe how she bends to her purpose every passion of human nature; how she unites the most licentious indulgence with the most intolerant asceticism. Weigh well the power that lies even in the extravagance of her claims to empire over both mind and body; and when you reflect on the willingness of weak man to fall down and become the slave of any one who professes power to govern, and willingness to save, and a divine commission to justify his acts and fulfil his promises, will you venture to indulge hopes that any such power can ever be developed in any other Christian communion, much less in the Church of England, which from the very nature of its constitution is distracted between double principles, and encumbered and enfeebled by its own professions of moderation."

" Villiers, dear Villiers," said Beattie, " have you not shifted your ground? You have spoken of the strength of Rome, most truly. But when you ask if such a strength can ever be developed in the Church of England, tell me, would you wish that it should be developed? When I speak of strength in the Church, I speak of such a strength as a Christian may pray for, and a church delight in. I do not ask for a sick man that he may recover his muscular force by becoming a maniac, though a maniac be stronger than a giant. And when you ask whether the Church of England could ever become in herself as powerful as the Church of Rome, I answer, God forbid! for I know not how such an object could be accomplished without her constructing a system equally false, equally sinful, equally unchristian. Be assured that truth, that goodness, that reason, that Christianity, must in this world appear weak and wavering, compared with bold, unscrupulous, unbalanced vice. It must recognise a whole circle of duties, and this must beget occasional doubt and timidity. It must be humble, and therefore want self-confidence. It must cling earnestly to truth; and truth, in this world of darkness, lies beneath a veil, and can neither be comprehended by our own eyes, nor exhibited to others, except mixed up with seeming inconsistencies, which destroy its fascination, and perplex and repel those who are easily attracted by the seeming simplicity of falsehood. It owes allegiance to an external law, which

law is often difficult to consult, and still more difficult to understand in its precise application. Hence
it must be slow and submissive. It is passionless,
and will seem to want energy. It is disinterested, and
therefore without the stimulus of selfishness. It is as
a stranger in the world, and the world will not cling
to it. It has faith, and therefore despises and throws
aside the instruments of human power. It has no
object but obedience upon earth ; and the voice of a
martyr at the stake will sound to human ears far
fainter than that of a conqueror on a field of battle.
And yet, Villiers, strength, real strength, may be
found, even in this form, far greater than in the
shape of an uncompromising, universal, infallible,
spiritual empire, which has no foundation for its
power but ambition and intrigue. Look up," continued Beattie, " at that beautiful spire," and he
pointed to the spire of St. Mary's, which rose above
them into the clear blue sky from the midst of its
forest of pinnacles. "If you saw two men, one
hurling himself down headlong from the summit
of that spire, and another balancing himself on
the point, in which would you recognise more
strength ?"

" Certainly," said Villiers, " I should see no proof
of strength in the act of falling."

" No," replied Beattie, " nor in the indulgence of
a single passion, nor in the headlong pursuit of a
single object, nor in the carrying out of a single
principle, nor in the exercise of rule when all op-
posing forces are subjected to us, nor in a claim to
universal dominion, nor in a dream of infallible authority, nor in the threat of tyrannical punishment
upon all who disobey our will, nor in any excess or
extravagance, whether of reason or of affection, in
which the mind is possessed and carried away by an
idea, instead of possessing and subjecting it to the

control of strict external laws. Even so it is with
the Church of Rome. Its very unity is the proof of
its weakness. It has no doubts; it admits no opposition; it sets itself no bounds; it is without scruple,
without hesitation, without difficulty; it can adapt
itself to all circumstances, carry out its one un-
varied purpose by any means, resolve any perplexities, fathom any problem, indulge any inclination,
enrol in its body any variety of character; and
therefore, with the physical strength of a giant it
has the moral weakness of a child: and moral
strength and moral weakness are the objects to
which we must look in the constitution of a church.
But a church which, while it asserts its own independence and authority, can submit itself to the
authority of another power as equally ordained of
God, which can break loose from a tyranny without
falling into a democracy, which can demand obedience to authority while it exercises and encourages
free thought, which can decide on necessary questions without intruding on things unnecessary, which
can hold fast an unwavering faith while it disclaims
any right to dogmatise presumptuously, which can feel
and act upon the sense of error and wrong in others,
and yet shrink from harshly judging and condemning them, which can reverence antiquity and yet
admit of improvement, which can so embrace and set
forth counterbalancing truths, that while equally
supported by authority they are difficult to reconcile
by reason, and which will open its arms to receive
her children, not upon terms of her own invention,
but upon the terms prescribed to her by another, —
such a church, I conceive, in the very doubts which
she acknowledges, even in the seeming inconsistencies which she encounters, even in the difficulties
which she prepares for herself in her apparent hesi-
tations, and scruples, and vacillations, exhibits an

internal self-command, a power of vision, and a power of action, which, even in this world, is worthy of all admiration, and in another must triumph ultimately over all persecution. It has pleased Almighty God to place the Church of England upon the pinnacle of his temple, where he placed his Catholic Church of old; and so long as she is there supported, though with a bruised foot, and trembling hand, and fearful eye, so long I recognise in her a power which cometh from above, and which none but God can supply to his own chosen and favoured servants."

" And yet," repeated Villiers (after they had stood some minutes by the side of the plane-tree, from which a large arm had been recently severed) — " and yet the Church of England is weak; we cannot deny it."

" Yes," replied Beattie, " weak in her organisation; not weak in her principles, or her formularies, or her theory. In these, for all practical purposes, she possesses greater elements of power and durability even than the Church of Rome. Look, for instance, at the very fact which is too often fixed on as a blemish, and as a source of imbecility. One of her first fundamental principles is obedience in all temporal matters to the civil power. While she asserts her own independence and supremacy in spiritual things, she admits the same independence, and supremacy, and divine right, in the State. Logically, the position is a paradox: superficially viewed, it threatens to enslave her. And yet what is the truth? If you would plant any institution or polity firmly upon the ground, you must place it upon two foundations. It must have two feet to rest on, that when one gives way, or slips, as in this world it always will do, the other may recover it. Rest all upon a single power, embark all on a solitary plank, and when that fails all is lost. Thus in the English Church, allied as she is, or associated, or, rather, combined and amalgamated, with the State, when the State becomes weak, or corrupt, or fails in its duty, the Church is ready to support and correct it. And when the Church is exposed to mischief, then the State is ready to interfere. We may not be able to measure precisely the right degree to which these interferences should be carried. Certainly in all such exigencies there will be occasional excesses. But through these successive oscillations the right line may still be preserved; and the history of the English Church, the history of its extension, of its prosperity, of its durability, is to be traced through a series of actions and counteractions between the State and itself, and so will continue until some rash and foolish hand severs the two; and both spiritual and temporal power, left to themselves, will fall without an arm to save them."

" I understand you so far," said Villiers. " But if this double power, this binary construction of influences, is essential to the preservation of a polity, how is it that the Church of Rome has maintained her position with her perfect unity and simplicity of system?"

Beattie paused, as if in surprise. " And have you, then," he asked, " been so blinded by the professions of Rome as not to see that she also has acted upon the binary principle, and by it has consolidated her power, and maintains her existence? What would Rome have been if she had not employed the civil arm in the first period of her history? How did she prosecute her aggressions except by the aid of a power which derived its forces from a source different from her own? It was not the bishops of Rome who conquered the empire of popery, but the bishops of Rome allied with kings and emperors, who, even while they acted as the ministers of a church, claimed to themselves supremacy in the state. Rome indeed boasted, and demanded, and pretended to rights and authority far beyond the Church of England, or the Catholic Church of old; but whenever she practically succeeded in her objects, it was by an alliance with some civil power, upon terms as near as possible the same as those which we recognise in England. And when the State became weak and impotent, or rebellious, and unwilling to do her bidding, to what other machinery do you attribute the power of Rome?"

"Undoubtedly," replied Villiers, "to her monastic bodies."

"Yes," continued Beattie, "to her monastic bodies, beginning from the first societies of recluses and penitents to the last grand and fearful conspiracy of Jesuitism. And what are they but a civil power—an organisation, framed as it was by Rome independent of the regular government of the Church —having a power of its own, and a power founded on temporal privileges and possessions—on wealth, character, landed property, talent, combination, every thing secular? No, Villiers, do not dream of a state of things in which a spiritual power can exist detached from a temporal power in some shape or other, or a temporal power detached from a spiritual. Keep them combined, yet distinct: subject them one to the other, mutually and reciprocally : be not afraid of the logical paradox, but try the construction practically, and you will find it the only source of strength and permanence."

"Alas!" said Villiers, "where is it to be found now in the English Church? Has not the State all but cast it off? Will she not soon be compelled to stand before the world with only her spiritual blessings, and spiritual menaces to overawe her rebellious

z 2

children ? And when she is thus left solitary, upon your own principle and prophecy, what is to be her fate but ruin ?"

Beattie made no reply; but he took Villiers's arm and led him out of the gardens into the quadrangle, and up a flight of narrow stone steps, which landed them on the leads of one of the highest towers in Oxford.

" Look round you," said Beattie.

And Villiers did look, and gazed with admiration on that glorious maze of spire, and pinnacle, and turret, and dark cloistered courts, in which lay green lawns and trim gardens embedded like jewels, every stone calling up some recollection of the past, and even the abodes of common life tinged by them with a sacred gloom.

" Have you ever thought," said Beattie at last, " to what arm, to what power the Church of England has been indebted, under Providence, for its revival, for its existence at this day ?"

" I have," said Villiers; " it was to this place; to this university. It was Oxford which first stemmed the torrent of revolution, and recalled England to her senses."

" No," replied Beattie, " it was not Oxford — not the university only, but the colleges of the university, which, if the Church has been saved, saved her at that crisis. The university is a creature of the crown, and can be destroyed by the crown. He that makes can unmake also. But these colleges were not creatures of the crown. They are independent bodies, holding their property and their influence by the same laws on which the peasant and the noble hold their cottage and their castle. And it was because the State could not touch these colleges, that the colleges, and through them the university, were enabled to resist the tyranny and

folly into which democracy would have driven the
State, and turned its aggressions against the Church.
But for these colleges all would have been lost."

"And how," asked Villiers, "do you connect this
with our past conversation?"

"Dear Villiers!" replied Beattie, gravely, "when
foolish, thoughtless young men in our own Church,
or enemies of that Church from without, speak contemptuously of weakness in the English Church,
and how it is to be removed, and of its desertion
by the State, and of the want of organisation to
enforce her claims, or of any temporal power to
enable her to regain her hold over the affection and
obedience of a revolted population, think of what
you see here, and it will give the answer. These
are the piles and buttresses by which we may support her even now; these are the bulwarks and
towers which no human force will be able to overthrow; these are the hands (only let them be multiplied and stretched out wherever the work of the
Church is to be done) with which that work is to
be accomplished. Close up your hand," he continued; and, compressing all but Villiers's little
finger, he said, "Now try with that little finger to
force this iron bolt into its staple."

Villiers tried, but in vain.

"Grasp it," said Beattie, "with your whole hand,
with a college of fingers." And the bolt shot into
its place.

CHAP. XXIV.

DAY after day passed, and Villiers found himself still lingering at Oxford, sharing Beattie's simple breakfast, accompanying him in his evening walks by the side of the river, dining with him in the hall, and kneeling beside him in the chapel. He saw few persons beyond the ordinary society of the common room, for Villiers was not fond either of exhibiting, or being exhibited, or seeing others exhibited. He had little curiosity to see men who were talked of in the world, merely that he might observe their countenances, or watch for some peculiarity of manner or expression, or be enabled to say that he knew Mr.——, and Dr.——, and Mr. ——; his knowledge being confined to the formal generalities of a morning visit. And he cherished a painful impression that where the thoughts of men are laid open to the world in their writings, it is as well not to seek for more close intimacy, lest valuable illusions should be destroyed, and inconsistencies of conduct be discovered. It may be, that Villiers was too proud and independent either to lead or be led. In the mean time he made his observations. He remarked in the habits of the place a return to more simple living : conversation was more deeply imbued with a reverential and religious tone. As he passed through the dark quadrangle at night, he heard less frequently than in his own days—far less frequently—the sound of noise and revelry. The general deportment of the older members struck him as far more spiritualised and

elevated; and that of the young as more chastened
and subdued. There was much indeed to please
him in the whole tone of the society into which he
was thrown, and in which he was received at once
with a frankness and courtesy, which, while it
recognised his own rank, asserted also a rank and
independence of their own for those who paid it.
And yet, thought Villiers, these men, in this age of
wealth and adoration of wealth, in which every
man's consequence is measured by his money, possess perhaps only an annual pittance, scarcely sufficient for the ordinary comforts of life. Villiers
did not remember, that though individually poor,
collectively they were rich, and that while their
own poverty secured them from conceit, their corporate wealth gave to them a consciousness of
position and self-consequence which secured them
from humiliating dependence. Villiers was surprised to see the general similarity of opinion which
prevailed among them, combined with independence
of thought. He watched with pleasure the little
interchanges of courtesy which prevented the familiarity of friends from sliding into too great a
liberty. He saw the power which united action
gave them, both in the work of education and in
the furtherance of any object necessary for the good
of the Church. Especially he was struck with the
voluntary deference and respect paid to the head of
the society in which he was living; and with the
absence of all pretension, or selfishness, or conceit,
even in those whose talents and position claimed
for them the greatest authority. He was even
amazed at the liberality, the profusion, with which
demands of charity were answered from men who
had nothing to depend on but their little annual
stipends. When he remarked these things to
Beattie, and asked to what cause he could attribute

it, Beattie's reply was still the same, "to the collegiate principle." Place men in colleges, he would say, place those colleges under a good system, and let that system be subjected to a proper superintendence from the bishops of the Church, and you will form men like these every where.

"And yet," he continued, with a sigh, "even here all is not right. There is much still to be done to bring us to a perfect state, many good practices to be recalled, many forgotten statutes to be enforced; and the stream which was flowing so steadily and so rapidly in this direction of improvement has met a check, which will throw it back for years. You observed," he said, "a specimen of the mischief at work yesterday after dinner."

"Do you allude," asked Villiers, "to that forward conceited person who spoke so fluently and so petulantly in the common room, on the subject of Popery and the Church?"

"That," replied Beattie, "is one of the leaders, if such a boy can be called a leader, in the new movement. He has written much which has startled and alarmed us."

"But he has only just taken his degree," said Villiers, with astonishment.

"Not long since," replied Beattie: "but in this day, when every one can publish what he likes, and as he likes, and when he likes, and publish anonymously, it is in the power of mere boys to circulate doctrines and rouse fears, the mischief of which cannot be cured by the oldest and the wisest."

"And when he was speaking so contemptuously of the Church, and so boldly in excuse for the corruptions of Rome, was he speaking," asked Villiers, "merely sentiments of his own, or such as others would share with him?"

" Sentiments, I hope," replied Beattie, "which only a few — a very few — would respond to ; but still which may be traced even here. But you have been abroad, and are not well read in the theological publications of the day. And yet," he continued, " I fancied, when you first came to me the other evening, that you had fallen in with them, and had been yourself tainted with this new poison."

Beattie covered his face with his hands as he had done before, and once more seemed lost in painful and anxious thought.

" And what then," asked Villiers, gently, " is this new theory at which you are so much alarmed? Surely such a person as that young man in your common room cannot be an object of anxiety. Surely ——, ——, ——, and others like them, who originated the movement in the Church, cannot have abandoned it to such hands, and cannot be unable to control it ? "

Beattie sighed deeply. " I will not reply to your last question," he said, "because I could not speak without seeming to condemn ; and to condemn is not my place. We are responsible for all our deeds, for our silence as well as for our utterance, not to individual brethren, but to the Church and to its Head."

" And what then," continued Villiers, drawing his chair nearer to his friend — " what is this new theory, or heresy, or what may it be called, which so alarms you ? "

" Alarm," replied Beattie, " is not perhaps the proper word. We have no right to be alarmed at any thing which befalls the Church, in which all that happens must ultimately work together for its good. Call it rather vexation ; for so much of these extravagancies proceeds from a silly love of notoriety, that I am afraid to dignify it with too much attention."

"And what is the nature of the extravagance?" asked Villiers. But before his companion could reply, a step was heard at the door, a submissive knock was given, and on Beattie's giving the usual permission to enter, a stout, thick-built, swarthy man, with sunken and cunning eyes, and his features covered with a thick beard and enormous whiskers, put his head in, as if afraid to venture without reconnoitring his ground. Villiers turned to see his entrance, and as the man's eye fell upon him he hastily retired, muttering an apology, and saying that he would return when the gentleman was disengaged. And though Beattie called after him to enter, he hurried hastily down the stairs.

"Who is that man?" asked Villiers. "Have I not seen his face before?"

"He is a stranger to me," said Beattie; "some foreigner, I suppose, with a petition. But I was about to tell you something of our new heresies here. Villiers resumed his attention, and Beattie proceeded.

"I need not tell you, Villiers, how natural it is, when power is used against us unjustly and tyrannically, to rise against it in resentment, and not content with throwing it back within due bounds, to annihilate it altogether. None of us should be surprised that the aggressions of the State upon the Church within these few years should have produced a tendency in the Church to reciprocate an aggression upon the State. Perhaps the seat and beginning of this mischief may be traced to a dream of spiritual empire and ambition, fostered by the just claims which the Church has revived to her spiritual independence and authority, but exaggerated far beyond the sanction either of history or

reason, and exaggerated by the natural provoca-
tions caused by the alternate imbecility and violence
of our civil government. There is a struggle to
place the Church once more in a position of power.
It is felt, felt most truly, that there can be no peace
for the country, no safety for truth, no right encouragement for goodness, no strength in the government, until the spiritual authority of the Church
is once more recognised. To re-establish it, it is
not necessary to subvert the authority of the State;
but young, rash men, once possessed with an idea,
are carried away by it. They would make the
Church the only power, and subject the State to
her. To do this they must divest the State of its
own sacred character and divine institution; and
they hesitate less at this profanation, because the
powers that be are now wielded by the populace;
and thus their very hatred for democracy leads them
to adopt the worst theory of democracy, and, like the
Jesuits, they become at once political radicals and
spiritual despots."

Villiers recalled his conversation with Macarthy,
but remained silent.

" When," continued Beattie, " they look round for
means to realise this dream of ecclesiastical empire,
they see that in each single nation the civil power
must be stronger than the Church. The only hope
for the Church in such a struggle must be in a close
union with other foreign Churches. Hence the
vision of a so-called Catholic Church, not distributed
into various branches connected at one root, harmo-
nising in essential articles of faith, communicating in
all works of love, but gathered round one visible
local centre, and formed into a monarchy upon
earth."

" It is a vision," said Villiers, " very natural, very
romantic; far more easily understood, and seem-

ingly far more capable of realising the ends of the Church, than the true doctrine of a Catholic body, ramifying from one root, and each branch retaining its individual existence together with its corporate unity."

"And it fails," said Beattie, " only in a few points — that it has no sanction in the primitive constitution of the Church, and on examination is discovered to be as unsound in theory as it has been proved to be mischievous in practice."

"It may be so," sighed Villiers.

"But the dream," continued Beattie, "has been once realised — realised in the papacy ; and hence their eyes are turned to Rome with a strange mixture of envy and wonder."

"And this accounts," said Villiers, " for the soft and gentle terms in which they speak of Rome; for their unwillingness to believe ill, or to hear ill, of her."

"Yes," said Beattie ; " while they do not hesitate to exhaust ridicule and reproach upon the follies of what they think the opposite extreme (though it is in reality the same), while they anathematise every thing like private judgment, self-will, disobedience, want of faith, irreverence to antiquity, they know so little of the real history and nature of popery, and are so completely blinded by its pretensions, that they would throw a veil over all the enormities into which popery has fallen by precisely the same vices, and seem totally ignorant that the whole of popery (so far as it is a development of the doctrine of a universal spiritual monarchy) is only a pre-development of the spirit of dissent — just as the tyrannies of Greece were identical with their democracies."

"Something of this tendency," said Villiers, " was

observable, was it not, in the very earliest writings of the Oxford school?"

"Something," answered Beattie. "But it seemed excused by the violent, thoughtless abuse which Puritanism had heaped even upon the Catholic parts of the Romish system, and therefore upon our own Church. It was necessary to defend what was true in popery. And we tolerated it more readily from the excess of our aversion to liberalism, which was then triumphant, and because the apology for the good parts of popery was coupled with the most un-flinching denunciations and warnings against the evil."

"And this," said Villiers, "has now been changed?"

"It has," said Beattie. "Followers have learned to speak softly and gently of every thing in that system, and leaders have uttered no warning against it."

"And yet," asked Villiers, "however fair and specious the papal supremacy may be in theory, how is it that men who are acquainted with the history of the Primitive Church, and who appeal to its authority, can reconcile themselves to such a palpable usurpation and novelty?"

"In the first place," said Beattie, "they are young men, and not learned men. Their knowledge of ecclesiastical history is limited, for the most part, to modern compilations; and those compilations they have chosen to seek in writers of the Romish communion. As for any deep and accurate know-ledge of ecclesiastical antiquity, or the writings of the Fathers, it would be absurd to expect it from men only a few years emancipated from their boyish studies, and most of them more disposed to talk and write than to read and think."

"And yet," said Villiers, "they must have some knowledge of history; they cannot be so utterly

and absurdly ignorant as not to know that the
Romish supremacy is a novelty, and is allowed to
be such even by their own controversialists."

" They have two theories," replied Beattie ; " one
derived from one Romish authority, and the other
from another.   One is the right of development ;
the other, that even usurpation may be justified by
prescription.   They have fallen thus, in the former,
into the worst doctrine of the liberalism of the day, in
opposition to which the movement commenced ; and
in the latter they not only show themselves ignorant
of the fact that in the English Church the papal
usurpations can claim no prescription, because they
were constantly protested against, but they also
put forward a maxim utterly destructive of the very
foundations of the Church, and of all positive institutions of God."

Villiers sighed.   " But," he continued, after a
pause, " if these men hold this theory, they must
consider separation from Rome not only as inexpe-
dient, but as criminal.   They must not only condemn
the Reformation and the Reformers, but they must
be anxious to restore the English Church to the
Romish communion without delay."

" Such, I believe," said Beattie, " is the case.
Remember, I am not speaking of any individuals.
I will not be led into imputing motives, or censur-
ing conduct, in others ; much less do I mean to say
that such notions are general : but in some I do
believe they prevail."

" And they must believe," added Villiers, " that
the English Church, on being severed from Rome,
forfeited many great privileges — perhaps even her
sacramental power.   Can it be otherwise ? "

" I," said Beattie, " could not find any way out of
this dilemma, which would not also justify every
kind of dissent.   But others may.   At least, I trust

they have some honest solution of the problem, otherwise I cannot understand that they should be able to remain, as they do, in the Church of England."

" Surely," said Villiers, " you do not mean to say that any man, seriously and firmly embracing such a theory, can remain in the Church ? How can they believe reunion with Rome to be necessary for the validity of the Sacraments, and therefore for salvation ? how, even, can they desire it on the ground of expediency, without striving to accomplish it ? and how can they strive to accomplish it while remaining within the bosom of our own Church ? "

" You might have added," said Beattie, " necessary for the validity of their own orders."

" Their own orders ! " exclaimed Villiers, springing up, — " their own orders ! Do you mean that any English clergyman, any honest man holding such opinions, can continue to exercise his functions ? "

Beattie sighed deeply.

" Seriously," resumed Villiers, " would you have me believe that there are men, clergymen in the English Church, who not only profess such doctrines, but, professing them, think it possible to retain their commission in that Church, and secretly to use their influence for bringing it over to popery ? "

" You ask me questions," said Beattie, " which I would rather not answer; but I know that it is not impossible for clergymen in the Church to hold these opinions, and to remain exercising their functions in it, upon the ground that subscription to the articles of that Church is not incompatible with a recognition of the decrees of the Council of Trent."

Villiers sat for some time silent, as if struck with amazement.

" Beattie," he said, at last, " what would our

courts of law say to an officer in the Queen's service, who, when a French army was invading this
country, should not only, as a theory, think subjection to France desirable, but should also conceive
it his duty to further that object by every means in
his power, especially by the influence which his
commission gave him with the soldiers of his regiment?"

"That he was a traitor," said Beattie.

"And what," continued Beattie, "if instead of
going over at once to the enemy, he remained under
his colours, only secretly and fraudulently throwing
out insinuations, and projecting plans, and carrying
on correspondences, and assimilating his practices
to those of the enemy, and endeavouring to discontent his soldiers with their position by repeated
sarcasms upon England and panegyrics upon France,
and lamentations over the struggle by which the
freedom of England was to be maintained? What
if he defended himself with alleging that he could
not act as an individual, that he waited till the
whole army should throw down their arms, and that
in the mean time he felt himself at liberty to prepare and stimulate them gently so to do? What if
he satisfied his conscience by pleading that the good
of England was his only object, though he fancied
that good to lie in enslavement to the power of
France?"

"I should say," exclaimed Villiers, interrupting
him —but he checked himself. "No, Beattie," he
said after a pause, "let us not judge others, lest we
be judged ourselves. Let us leave such men, and
such consciences, to the judgment of One who sees
the heart, and to whom they are responsible. I
dare not judge any one."

"Neither," said Beattie, "will I. But it is my
lecture-hour, and we must separate."

CHAP. XXV.

THEY did not meet again till the bell was ringing for the hall dinner. There was but a small party ; and as they assembled round the great Gothic fire-place, while the servants were carrying the dinner to the high table, Villiers was introduced to a foreigner, a French abbé, who had been invited by the same young man whose forward and rash language had attracted his observation on a previous day. The abbé was evidently a man of education, quick and acute in his remarks, and keenly bent upon observing every thing that passed. His manner affected a politeness which bordered upon fulsomeness ; and he showed particular anxiety to become acquainted with Beattie, and to draw him into conversation. He threw out many innuendos and covert suggestions, which might have led to the subject which generally occupied attention, namely, the state of the Church in England ; but Beattie quietly permitted them to drop, and turned the conversation to questions of general literature. The abbé was not to be repulsed. He ventured, at last, to make comments on the characters and writings of some of the most conspicuous among the leaders of the Oxford movement ; and, with a want of tact not unfrequently found in a manœuvring mind, he even boldly questioned Beattie on his own opinions. This took place in the Common Room ; but Beattie made some excuse for going to the other side of the fire-place, and rang the bell for coffee, while the abbé, a little discomfited, threw himself upon Villiers with similar curiosity, but was once more defeated by Beattie returning to Villiers; and pleading business with him, he took him to his own room.

"You seemed very reluctant to gratify the abbé," said Villiers, as they ascended the stairs.

"Very reluctant?" answered Beattie. "I am not satisfied with his appearance; and I do not like the admission amongst us of foreigners of the Romish communion, who come without introduction and without object, as far as they profess, but who, I cannot but suspect, are acting as spies upon all that passes among us at this critical moment. I am not fond of meeting them myself, still less of introducing them to our general society, where we speak often unguardedly, as round our own firesides; while, in reality, we are in a public room, and open to the observation of strangers. In addition to this, I entertain a most serious objection to associating on terms of familiarity with Romanists. They believe us heretics; we believe them in this country to be at least schismatics. In general society we must lay aside the appearance of such a belief, and act hypocritically; and the hypocrisy often ends, with us, at least, in the opinion that our differences are of no moment."

"And would you act in this exclusive manner to all who differ from you in religion?" said Villiers.

"To all," answered Beattie, "who are not themselves members, and who do not allow myself to be a member, of the Catholic Church. I know no other bond of union in society to which we can trust but the bond of the Church. And I am sure that to confine ourselves within the limits and combinations which she has formed for us is a far safer and a far better security for peace and concord than to endeavour to throw down or overlook these party-

walls; and frame a new heterogeneous body upon
no principle but that of arbitrary fusion, and the
negation of all positive truth. But in the case of
Romanists," he continued, " the inducements to this
caution are, with me, far stronger than with any
other sectarians. I have studied the history of
Popery, and cannot but regard it in the light of an
aggressive intriguing conspiracy, aiming at universal empire — an empire professedly spiritual, but
essentially secular. I speak, remember, of the
popery of Rome ; not of the catholic elements of
truth and goodness, which it contrived to preserve
in its system. I know that at this moment, as often
before, the agents of Rome are exerting their utmost
efforts to embarrass the English Church ; that they
have emissaries in every part of the empire ; that
their operations are not confined to doctrinal discussions, but are deeply mixed up with political
movements, even with insurrectionary disturbances,
in England as well as in Ireland. Such has been
their conduct at all times ; but the present is a
favourable moment, and they are turning it to their
purpose with more than common enterprise and
assiduity. There are a few persons among us — the
persons of whom we spoke this morning — who laugh
at all such suspicions, and seem to take delight in
playing with firebrands, and walking about blindfold
on the edge of a precipice. Whether they are right
or wrong, time will show. In the mean time, I
avoid, as much as possible, the society of foreign
popish priests. We cannot meet for controversy ;
and I can hold no other voluntary correspondence
with the avowed enemies of my Church but controversy. Where, indeed, a person of a different communion comes and asks for a serious discussion upon
any difficulties which may occur to him, the case is
different. For instance, that Jewish-looking man,

who came to my rooms the other morning. I like
neither his looks nor his manner; but I have not
hesitated to see him more than once."

"And who is he?" asked Villiers. "I caught
but one glimpse of him, and fancied I had seen him
before."

"He tells me," said Beattie, "that he is a Polish
Jew; that he was at Rome (perhaps you may have
seen him there); and that a Father Matthias, of the
English college, converted him to Romanism. He
became, however, dissatisfied with what he heard
and saw of their system, particularly with their adoration of images, and came to England. And here,
he says, he has met with such a number of sects
among Protestants, and has been so harassed by
the doubts and difficulties which they have raised
against each other, that he is even thinking of returning either to Judaism or Popery, if he cannot
be satisfied with the doctrines of our own Church."

Villiers shook his head. "Not a very promising
state of mind," he said.

"I fear not," replied Beattie. "Indeed, few states
could be more unpromising. And there is something in his look so full of cunning, and, at times,
even of malignity, that I should refuse to have any
thing to say to him, except that I do not like to
omit any opportunity of possibly doing good. He
seems remarkably anxious to hear my opinions on
Popery, and is at times very abusive against it himself, with the view, I am inclined to think, of trying
if I am willing to defend it."

"Has he asked for money?" said Villiers.

"No," answered Beattie. "Had he done this, I
should be inclined to suspect at once that he belonged to a class of swindlers who not unfrequently
obtain access to us here under pretence of religious
difficulties or persecutions, and seldom fail to prey

upon our unsuspicious benevolence. But he describes himself as provided with means of his own."

Villiers shook his head again. "I confess," he said, "that, were I you, I should be even more on my guard against such a man than against an avowed foreign ecclesiastic. When I was in America I became acquainted with a person who, from circumstances, had been thrown very much behind the scenes with the emissaries of Rome. He mentioned to me several instances where most serious evil had resulted from their intrigues."

Beattie sat musing for some little time. "I scarcely needed," he said, "this caution. But many similar facts are known to me, and, I assure you, I am on my guard. And now let us turn to a more agreeable subject. While I am making tea, will you find out that noble passage of Burke, in his 'French Revolution,' where he speaks of the destruction of the monasteries, and of the value of the principles of incorporation in the Church, and in society generally?"

"Can it be so late?" said Villiers, while they were still discussing the use and abuse of collegiate bodies in the Church. "Is that twelve?"

And the deep-toned clock of St. Mary's, followed by strokes from many another spire and tower, compelled them to separate for the night. Beattie followed him down the stone stairs, which were already dark, the lamps having burnt out. The street was empty. But as Villiers passed down to the Angel Inn, where he was staying, close at the corner of the street which leads into the dark Radcliffe Square, between St. Mary's and All Souls' College, two men were standing, with their backs to him, engaged in deep conversation, but sheltered, under the shadow of the wall, from the light of the moon. They were speaking earnestly in French,

and Villiers fancied that he heard his own name
mentioned ; and as he turned to look at them as he
passed, he was surprised to see the Jew in company
with the French ecclesiastic whom he had met that
day at dinner.

" I tell you I am sure. He is as great a heretic
as ever ; and so they are both," was all that Villiers
caught as he moved on. It was too little to justify
him in stopping to demand an explanation ; but he
resolved to prosecute some inquiries in the morning.
He went into the coffee-room to write a letter,
which the sleepy waiter promised to commit carefully to the driver of the mail, which passed through
to Hawkstone at two o'clock in the morning ; and
as he was going up stairs to his room, the chamber-
maid met him, with apologies for having shifted him
to another apartment, — one, she said, more airy and
convenient ; the other had been wanted as part of
a suite for a family. Villiers made no remonstrance.
His new room was preferable to the other. His
servant had moved all his dressing apparatus, as if
no change had been effected. And after trying the
lock of a door, which seemed to lead into an adjoining
room, and finding it fastened on the other side, he
sat down, trimmed his candle, and opened his desk
to examine some papers. His eye fell on a packet
sealed with black, and carefully secured. It contained documents, which he never parted with, full
to him of bitter recollections, and which yet he never
looked on without some gleam of hope that they
might one day restore to him his child. He opened
it, and the tears fell thick upon the papers. The
certificate of his unhappy marriage, memoranda of
all the facts relating to the loss of his boy, as minute
an account as could be obtained of every point which
might lead to his recognition, and which had been
drawn up, by Beattie's care, at Naples, while Vil-

liers himself was lying in his illness; some family papers of his wife's, relating to her own birth and connections; and the miniature of his wife herself, in all her beauty. — Villiers once more, for the thousandth time, perused and reperused these precious memorials, until a heavy step passing his door, and entering the adjoining room, roused him from a sort of stupor, and he prepared to lie down. Once, as he was undressing, he fancied he heard a slight grating sound, as if some one was trying the handle or the lock of the door, but it did not return, and, resting his head on his pillow, he was soon asleep.

He rose soon (for it was Sunday morning), that he might attend the early Communion with Beattie. It was one of the last days which he proposed to pass in Oxford, and, except the hours of Divine service, he spent the greater part of it with Beattie. It was a time of deep and solemn reflection to him ; and softened and elevated by the feelings which Oxford, more than any other place, breathes upon a Sabbath rest, he spoke unreservedly to his friend of the future as well as the past; of his repentance; his submission to the will of God ; his recognition of the hand of Providence in the judgment with which he had been afflicted; of his earnest desire to devote the remainder of his life to the service of God and the Church; of his resolution to divert his thoughts from the great temptation which he felt would interrupt that purpose if he once involved himself in a union even with the most admirable of women, severed from him by her religious faith. Beattie listened to him, as they paced backwards and forwards on the broad smooth level lawn of St. John's garden, silently, but not without emotion.

" I shall look to you, dear Beattie," he said, " for much assistance, for advice, for suggestions."

But Beattie shook his head. He was not fond

of giving advice; and he had no great confidence in his own suggestions. It was one of his first maxims to undertake no responsibility to which he did not seem obviously called by the hand of Providence.

"Place yourself," he replied, more than once, "under the guidance of your bishop; he is the proper person to direct you. At any rate you will have done your duty ; and whatever be the result, you will have no cause for self-reproach."

"But you will come and see me ?"

"Indeed I will."

"And you will not refuse to tell me if I am wrong in any thing I undertake ?"

Once more Beattie shook his head and smiled ; but it was a smile of affectionate confidence, that there would be few occasions for such admonitions.

"And now of my more private matters;" said Villiers, "I must trouble you once more. You will, I am sure, look over again the papers which you drew up for me at Naples; I must have accurate copies of them taken and placed in the hands of a friend — of more than one friend ; for I tremble at times lest I should lose them, and then all hope would be lost of recovering what at times I still believe God in his great mercy will restore to me. I will bring them to you to-morrow ; and in your hands, for the time, I know they will be safe."

Beattie readily promised. Even he himself, though neither sanguine nor romantic, and notwithstanding the impenetrable mystery which hung over the loss of Villiers's child, and had baffled every research, — even Beattie, as he looked proudly and fondly on the noble and almost sacred character of his friend, did not despair that blessings were still in store for him. He wished once more to examine the documents, and consult upon them a legal friend who had enjoyed considerable experience in the detection of similar cases.

Villiers's arrangements were all made to leave Oxford for Hawkstone the following day. Once more the midnight bell tolled out from the towers and steeples before he could bring himself to separate from Beattie, and before Beattie had half concluded all that he was endeavouring to explain of the proper organisation of the Church, and of the necessity for restoring it at this time to meet its tremendous responsibilities, by the restoration of the collegiate principle, cleared from the errors of monasticism. Once more they roused the sleepy porter at the gate, who, notwithstanding the nightly disturbance of his doze, stood obsequiously with hat in hand to open the wicket for Mr. Beattie's friend.

" I will bring you the papers to-morrow," were Villiers's last words.

To-morrow came. Villiers rose to go to chapel and to breakfast with his friend for the last time. He went to his desk to obtain the papers. Every thing lay as usual — the lock uninjured, money to a considerable amount untouched, some rings, private papers, confidential letters, all safe; nothing was missing : but when he looked for the packet sealed with black, it was gone.

We have no wish to exhibit characters created for respect under the influence of mere feeling. Villiers was not indeed a hero of romance, with whom every emotion is a hurricane of passion. He possessed a wonderful control over himself, and for mere passion entertained a profound contempt. He therefore neither tore his hair nor wrung his hands; but his consternation was great. He searched through all the drawers — ransacked every corner — endeavoured to recall every clue by which he

might remember where the papers were mislaid.
He had seen them only two nights before. The
notion of robbery was laid aside when he examined
the desk and found every thing untouched. His
room, moreover, had been kept locked during his
absence, and he had the key in his pocket. Unwilling to make a charge so vague, which might
unjustly expose the whole household to suspicion,
he sent privately for the master of the hotel.
But no light could be thrown on the loss. Only
one person, when interrogated, seemed to entertain
a suspicion. A foreign gentleman, a Jew, who
had been staying in the house, happened to meet
Villiers's servant at the door of his master's room,
while he was removing his things to his new apartment. He had come into the room to ask some
frivolous question, and had looked about him : and
on inquiry of the chamber-maid, it was found that
he had complained to her soon afterwards that his
own room was noisy, and had asked to be moved into
the one which adjoined Villiers's, and communicated
with it by an inner door. It was found also that he
had left Oxford that morning by the earliest conveyance, and gone to London. Slight as the clue
was, it recalled to Villiers's mind the sound which
he had heard in the keyhole the night when he was
last examining the papers, — the mention of his
own name in the street, — all that he had heard
from Beattie, — the strange look, which nevertheless
seemed to be not new to him : and writing a hasty
note to Beattie, he proceeded without delay to
London, in the vain hope of tracing the stranger.
It is needless to say that all his efforts were
vain : baffled and wearied, he was obliged to resign
himself to his loss. And now that all hopes of
recovering his child were gone, he consoled himself by planning how he should devote more com-

pletely himself, and all that he possessed, to the
service of his Maker. He had no longer any object
in either sparing or accumulating. Unselfish in all
his thoughts, he never had contemplated his possessions, enlarged as they were by his uncle's death,
as a means of personal aggrandisement. But so
long as there remained a possibility of discovering
his child, so long he felt the obligation of guarding
and preserving for him all that he might have a
right to claim. That obligation was now all but
destroyed: recovery seemed hopeless. And after
remaining in London for some weeks to make the
necessary arrangements with his lawyers, Villiers,
with a heavy and weary heart, came down to
Hawkstone on the very night of the fire : and to
that place we must now, after this long retrospection,
carry back our readers.

CHAP. XXVI.

WE trust that our readers will be able to pass from the grave and sobering thoughts of the preceding chapters to a more insignificant scene, and yet one not unconnected with them, and will now take their stand with us by the side of poor Mrs. Crump's arm-chair, and look out of her bow-window into the High Street of Hawkstone.

Although Mrs. Crump's afternoon had closed angrily and gloomily, her prospects brightened up when the next day arrived ; for about twelve o'clock brought an event in her monotonous life, no less than the arrival of a strange gentleman at the side-door of Messrs. Silkem's residence, and evidently a visiter to Miss Mabel Brook herself. None but persons in Mrs. Crump's position can fairly appreciate the envy with which at that moment she would have regarded persons possessing, like ourselves, the privilege of following this visiter into the house, and of hearing every word that passed. There is in fact a remarkable faculty possessed by authors — that of ubiquity, by which they see every thing, and hear every thing, and can give a most accurate report of all that passes in the most secret and confidential communication : and as these pages may perhaps meet Mrs. Crump's eye, we shall not hesitate on the present occasion to take advantage of our privilege, and give her full information. The gentleman then in question, as Mrs. Crump herself perceived, was rather of that age which is most appropriately described " as the same age with every body else;" that is, he was neither young nor old; but he was portly, of a military aspect, with whiskers, and even an abridgement of mustachoes; and he was enveloped, though the day was by no means cold, in a blue military cloak, with a profusion of silk cords and tassels depending from his neck, round which there also hung a massive watch-guard and chain, which to Mrs. Crump's admiring eye were composed of solid gold. He inquired respectfully of Mabel's little Abigail, if this was the residence of the celebrated Miss Brook; upon which the little Abigail, frightened out of her wits at the sight of so formidable a stranger, hesitatingly replied, "No—Miss Brook's name was not Celebrated, but Mabel."

"Miss Mabel Brook! It is the same personage," said the stranger. "Pray present to her my card, and say that I beg the honour of an interview."

The card was of the most polished character, bearing on it in full blazonry the title of Major O'Keefe, Honorary Secretary to the Royal and National Grand African Colonisation and Timbuctoo Civilisation Society, No. 94. Suffolk Street. Before Mabel had had time to inquire of her little maid the appearance of the stranger, or to recover from the trepidation naturally produced by the approach of such a titled personage, he had himself followed up the stairs, and even made his appearance within the door of Mabel's sanctuary. With his hat gracefully waving in one hand, and the other pressed respectfully to his breast, he bowed repeatedly; and then approaching Mabel, he begged to know if he had the honour of addressing that well-known ornament of society, that example of genuine benevolence and enlightened liberality, whose name had reached far beyond the narrow sphere to which her beneficent exertions were un-

happily limited?   " Was it Miss Mabel Brook
whom he then had the pleasure of beholding?"

To this overpowering exordium it was impossible
for Mabel's modesty to do more than colour and
look confused, and say, "Oh! oh!" and beg that
he would take a chair; which, throwing aside his
blue envelopment, and studiously displaying, not
only his massive chain, but two equally massive
rings upon his fingers, as he passed them negli-
gently through his copious hair, he proceeded to
do.

" Madam," he commenced, " I will make no apology for thus intruding on hours dedicated to the
sweetest labours of an enlightened charity ; but I
have been deputed to wait on you by the committee
of that noble and illustrious society, to further
whose object I have devoted, I might say sacrificed,
myself — the Royal and National Grand African
Colonisation and Timbuctoo Civilisation Society,
No. 94. Suffolk Street.   You must be aware,
madam, of the deep interest which benevolent individuals have recently taken in the fate of Africa.
Wilberforce, Macaulay, Stephens, Smith, Hopkins,
Johnson, Thompson — hundreds of the most illustrious characters of the day—feeling the blot which
that unhappy country now makes on the face of
the globe, have resolved to wipe out this dark stain
from the age.   They propose to rouse the country,
madam ; they will sound the tocsin throughout
the length and breadth of the land ; they will summon together the great, the noble, the learned,
the pious, — all that dignifies human nature and
society, — Prince Albert, Madam, himself, and the
Bishop of —— ; and from the platform of Exeter
Hall there will go forth a voice which will be
heard in the inmost depths of the spice-breathing
forests of Africa, and by the swarthy natives of the

farthest south, saying to them, 'Be free! be civilised! be happy!' Madam——" But here, as he
was obliged to pause in order to take breath, Mabel
also took the opportunity to express her deep sympathy with the society, of whose formation she
had been made duly acquainted through the public
press; and also to hint at the admiration which the
stranger's glowing language and energetic delivery
had already excited in her mind.

"But, madam," he resumed, "I must not longer
deprive myself of the pleasure of offering to you
the tribute to your numerous virtues, which the
committee of our illustrious society have desired
to pay you. They have begged your acceptance,
madam, of this diploma, which I here present you,
and entreat that you will allow your name to be
enrolled among the Honorary Vice-Presidents of
the Ladies Affiliated Association, for the furtherance
of our benevolent object."

And with these words, from a pocket which
apparently contained a number of documents of the
same shape and size, the stranger produced a huge
sheet of printed paper, blazoned and adorned with
a variety of allegorical figures, and containing a
long and dignified list of visitors, presidents, patrons,
vice-patrons, honorary governors, that is, governors
who were not allowed to govern, subscribers, and
supporters; resolutions moved by Lord A., and
seconded by the Bishop of B.; and at the bottom,
in a copious and most tortuous hieroglyphic, the
signature of Augustus Philadelphus Wilberforce
O'Keefe, honorary Secretary and Treasurer. But
that which most surprised, and, it must be confessed, most delighted Mabel, was a letter addressed
to herself by the body of the committee, expressing
their admiration of her character, their desire to
show their sense of the benefit which, in such va-

rious capacities, she had rendered to the cause of true benevolence, and the unanimous applause with which she had therefore been elected to a seat at the board of honorary vice-presidents of the Ladies', &c. &c. &c. The honorary secretary and treasurer was not insensible to the favourable effect produced on the honorary vice-president.

"Madam," he proceeded, "will you now permit me to explain to you, succinctly but precisely, the object of our most important undertaking, in which we fervently trust you will both sympathise and co-operate with us?"

Mabel bowed, and placed herself in a listening posture, not forgetting, however, that too ready an acceptance, even of such an honour, might compromise her own dignity, and therefore throwing into her countenance a cast of critical and judicial severity, to temper the blandness of her general demeanour.

"Our object, madam," said the secretary, (and he drew his chair closely and confidentially to her side), "is to pour the light of civilisation and liberty over the vast regions of Africa—a fourth part, madam, of the habitable globe."

Mabel bowed assent.

"We feel, madam, that nothing can reclaim those miserable nations from their present degraded position, or put a stop to the horrors of slavery——"

Mabel gave a shudder.

"Yes, madam, the horrors of slavery! What Englishman, what female—what tender, delicate, affectionate heart—a heart, madam, like your own, does not glow at the name of liberty? How can we release these miserable regions from their state of darkness and thraldom, except by pouring in upon them the light of civilisation? It is our wish, madam, to establish relations with all the tribes in the interior of Africa. We propose to develope their resources, to modify their institutions, to carry out the principles of an enlightened utility."

Mabel looked all attention.

"To do this, madam, we have obtained from a most eminent French traveller accurate statistics of the population, commerce, manufactures, literature, and religion of those vast regions ; and we find, on authentic calculation, that by turning the labour of the people into manufactures and agriculture, more wealth would be created than by selling them as slaves."

Mabel bowed.

"Once, madam, impress this great truth on the mind of the sovereigns of those districts, and by the inevitable operation of the great law of our nature, prudential self-love, the slave-trade will be abandoned, manufactures and commerce will be introduced into the dark regions of Timbuctoo, and will bring with them all the blessings of life which they have diffused upon our own favoured shores."

Mabel here did not bow assent, for the word manufactures reminded her that she had just come from the dying bed of a poor stunted factory child, whose arms had been crushed in the machinery, and whom his mother, with ten starving children, was vainly endeavouring to support upon cold potatoes and water — the father spending his wages in the intervals of work at the public-house.

"Madam," continued the secretary, "nothing but knowledge can work this miraculous change. 'Knowledge,' madam, as the great Bacon says — 'Knowledge is power.' And one of the first debts due by our civilised continent to our unhappy brethren of Africa is to give them knowledge."

"You intend, I suppose, sir," inquired Mabel, "to establish schools among the blacks?"

" Certainly, madam, certainly — schools of all kinds. One of our first thoughts, madam. I may mention to you privately, madam, and confidentially, that a most distinguished person has already placed at the disposal of the society a sum of 1000*l.* to found a professorship of political economy in the great capital of Africa. The Rev. Dr. Mason, that celebrated writer and divine, has also been pleased to place at our disposal all the unsold copies of his lectures on that science (and I assure you they amount to a large number of volumes), for the purpose of circulating them among the negroes."

" How interesting!" said Mabel. " And pray, sir, do the negroes understand English?"

" No, madam, not yet, not exactly: but Dr. Jones, who understands the languages of all the savage tribes both in Africa and in Europe, and has published some beautiful translations from their literature and poetry, has undertaken, for a mere trifle, not above three or four hundred pounds, to render them into the vernacular tongue, the Ashantee dialect — a man, madam, that, of prodigious power! wonderful memory! extraordinary fancy! His opinion is, that the chapter on rent and wages will tell wonderfully in opening the eyes of the natives to the true theory of wealth. He has some notion of publishing a little volume himself, of translations from an Ashantee poem, one of them a splendid epic — wild, madam, and irregular, wanting in the unities, but sweetly touching — spirit-stirring — the peripateia especially!"

" I should like much to see it," said Mabel; " there is something so interesting and affecting in the wild life of the native African."

" Certainly, madam, certainly," said the secretary; nothing can be more so. It is to be published by subscription. Would you allow me to put your name on the list?"

Mabel, however, was prudent and economical even in her enthusiasm, and was obliged to decline; pleading the many calls on her purse.

"We shall hope, madam," continued the secretary, "to print it at Timbuctoo. Our expedition takes out a printing-press, — one of our first objects. We shall have a newspaper, madam, weekly at first, but we do not doubt of its circulation soon reaching to a considerable extent, and then we propose to publish it daily; the *African Sun* it is to be called — allegorical, you see, emblematic of intellectual light. It will contain all the European news — our parliamentary reports, which will give the poor blinded natives an interest in a free government — the rise of stocks — authentic accounts of prices — the state of shipping — quotations of foreign articles in the British markets, — every thing, in fact, which can enlighten the mind as to the true principles of wealth, and enable them to comprehend and labour to attain themselves the blessings of civilisation."

"How delightful!" said Mabel.

"Yes, madam; and a country, that, of prodigious resources! fine inland river, that, the Niger! gold-dust, ivory, elephants, monkeys, lions, alligators, snakes, crocodiles. The Niger itself, madam, contains more crocodiles than any river in Europe."

"Does it, indeed?" asked Mabel. "And are they good to eat?"

"Not exactly, madam, not precisely; though Capt. Biffen — the great traveller, who has spent months in the interior shooting, and has given the world that delightful and interesting account of his sport — bagged twenty elephants, fifteen buffaloes, and ten boa-constrictors in one day, besides a tiger and baboon — he says, indeed, that the green fat just below the last joint of the off fore-paw is exquisitely delicious, and would rival turtle — beat it, indeed, out of the market; but our thoughts have rather been turned to science. We long to introduce into our own beloved country the same blessings of knowledge which we would diffuse in Africa ; and what branch of knowledge more interesting, more valuable, more refreshing and expanding to the mind — carrying it, madam, up to the great Cause of all things, and filling it with wonder and admiration — than the study of Nature, and Nature's works!"

Mabel smiled, and assented.

" And yet, madam, think, even in this favoured land, and among our own enlightened peasantry, and even our artisans, how few know the difference between an alligator and a crocodile!"

" Very few," said Mabel, a little alarmed lest any question on the subject should arise which might betray her own ignorance of this important point.

"Oh! madam, we look forward to the day when not only in the Regent's Park, but in every town in England, there may be a zoological collection — live birds and beasts of all kinds. We have entered already into a contract with the proprietors of the Surrey Gardens to supply them every three months with two live crocodiles. They seldom live longer than three months in this climate — cold, madam, and damp, compared with the genial atmosphere of their own delightful land ! They will become a branch of trade — open a new line of profitable speculation. We calculate that the prime cost of one, all expenses and duties paid, will be scarcely more than what any private gentleman of moderate fortune might easily afford, if he wished to keep one himself."

" Indeed!" said Mabel.

" Then, madam, think of our own trade ; what a market for our own commodities ; how delightful to introduce among the blinded hordes of those benighted regions our own enjoyments — brandy, rum, gunpowder, fire-arms. We have already contracted for 500 stand of muskets with a great manufacturer at Birmingham, warranted, madam, not to burst till the third time of firing. Opium, again ——"

" Opium ! " inquired Mabel, rather alarmed. " I should not have thought it desirable to encourage a taste for opium among the negroes."

" Oh ! madam, not for the world, not for the world ; it is not with a view to encourage any pernicious habit ; not that, madam ; but commerce, you see, must be free, free as air. Fetter its wings, and, ike the imprisoned eagle, it pines and dies ! "

Mabel was enchanted with the metaphor, but could not help reverting to the objectionable character of an opium trade.

" You see, madam," said the secretary, and he drew his chair still closer, and subdued his voice into a persuasive and didactic tone, " you see, madam, the state and prospects of this country are so alarming in consequence of our commercial speculations, that it becomes absolutely necessary for us to look round on all sides, and to provide means for developing them farther. Capital, madam, must be employed, otherwise how could we pay our National Debt ? Our shipping must be kept up, or what is to become of our duties? In fact, madam, our whole existence depends on our manufactures and commerce ; and opium, madam, is one great branch ; two millions of money annually are invested in it. What would the Chancellor of the Exchequer say if this branch of his revenue was cut off ? No, madam, it is not for us to interfere with or fetter the natural expansion of trade ; it will take its own

course, and work out its own end, and nothing but
mischief can follow from attempts to overrule it.
The nineteenth century has long since exploded the
old absurd theories of restrictions upon commerce.
But then, madam, do not suppose we are insensible
to our moral influence. It is by showing to the
poor natives our superiority in all points of knowledge, by compelling them to look up to us for the
supply of their wants, that we intend to acquire a
control over them, and lead them on in the glorious
path of civilisation. We take out a steam-engine,
madam, which is to work the gold mines : gold
mines, we know, there are in abundance; labour
cheap and plentiful ; and the negroes will work
almost for nothing if kept properly in order. Why,
in our own factories children work twelve hours a
day for 6d. ; and it will be hard if the negroes in
their own country cannot be induced to do the same.
Stimulate their wants, madam, enlarge their capacity for enjoyment, open to them new views of advantages, and you will find that even the negroes
will become as industrious, and as civilised, and as
happy, as our own artisans."

Mabel, however, said nothing, for again the word
" factory " had raised up a painful vision before her
eyes ; and she turned the subject by pointing to an
engraving on the diploma, which represented a
splendid range of buildings, with a quay, and shipping in the distance ; and on the foreground, a lady
of most amiable deportment, with a helmet on her
head and a spear in her hand, sitting in what to
ordinary mortals must be an uncomfortable position, on the tire of a wheel, and stretching out her
hands to a group of negroes, not attired with perfect
decorum, or rather, not attired at all (for modern
art seems to have dispensed with the superfluity of
dress). The above-mentioned negroes were also em-

ployed in carrying some huge bales, carefully corded, and marked Messrs. Baldwin and Co., Merchants, Timbuctoo. Above was a splendid irradiation of light pouring down from amidst a mass of dispersing clouds.

"This print, I suppose," said Mabel, "is emblematical?"

"Yes, madam," said the secretary, "partly so — a little device of my own" (and he smiled with conscious dignity); "but partly real. It is the architect's design for the new town of Albert-Ville, on the banks of the Niger."

"Indeed!" said Mabel. "It is very beautiful."

"Exquisite, madam; one of the most charming and complete things which Mr. Plasmer has produced! Great genius that, madam! very great genius! You see, here is the Crescent; Victoria Crescent it is to be called, in honour of her most gracious Majesty. Here, in the centre, is the hotel, a most spacious and convenient house, containing baths, billiard-room, ball-room, theatre adjoining, admirably ventilated kitchens, tap-room, and separate spirit-shop at the back for the accommodation of the natives; a noble range of houses and warehouses on the banks of the river: the whole to communicate with a railway direct from Timbuctoo."

"Indeed!" said Mabel. "It is a magnificent idea!"

"Magnificent, indeed," said the secretary; who seemed as if by this time he had exhausted his eloquence, and wished to draw the conversation to a practical closing point. But Mabel's thoughts had before this turned to one other consideration.

"And I presume, sir," she said, pointing to a central tower, round which the buildings were picturesquely grouped, "I presume this is to be the church?"

"No, madam, not exactly, not precisely; it is

B B 4

the tower of the observatory. We are to have an
observatory. You are aware how anxious the world
of science has long been to establish a chain of
observatories over the whole earth. They have built
one at Botany Bay. The grand celebrated Association for Science, where all the philosophers assembled last year, particularly begged that one of our
first things should be to build an observatory, and
teach the negroes the use of the telescope. How delightful it will be to see the swarthy Abyssinian villagers, with eyes upturned to heaven, scanning the
wonders of the starry world, or calculating the
transit of Venus! How elevating to their minds! how
enrapturing the prospect! We may owe even the
discovery of a new nebula, or the just outline of one
of the mountains of the moon, to one of those poor
creatures who are now rambling in their native
forests, believing, in their miserable ignorance, that
the stars are sparks of fire, and the moon only
three feet round. Sad, indeed, to reflect, that never
till now have we endeavoured to give them juster
and more ennobling views! And how delightful
the thought, that at length the clouds of darkness
may be unrolled from their eyes!"

"And where is your church to be?" pursued
Mabel.

"Oh! why—why—oh!" and the secretary hemmed
and coughed. "Why, madam, you see"—and he
coughed again—"we have been desirous to rally
under one grand banner of enlightened benevolence
all the great and good minds of the present day; and
to do this without risking those sad discordances and
disputes on antiquated dogmas which must intervene,
whenever, in these days, the subject of religion is
mixed up with more practical pursuits. We have
therefore thought it better (and the government
quite approve of our principle) to leave religion an

open question. But there will be a church, madam. Do not be alarmed; there is to be a church."

"I am glad to hear it," said Mabel. "And I suppose you will have clergymen and missionaries?"

"Oh! certainly, madam, certainly. We have thrown open the whole field to competition. Any clergymen of any denomination will be invited to accompany the expedition. And we rather think of allowing to a certain number a free passage, provided they bring proper recommendations from their respective congregations. Something, indeed, was suggested by the government about providing them all land in the colony according to the number of their flocks : but we really dread mixing up the clergy with any secular or temporal pursuits; it removes them from their purely spiritual duties and character ; and therefore the committee have resolved not to hold out such temptations. Besides which, it would be inconvenient, as the land is of some value, and may be wanted for commercial purposes."

" And have you had many applications or offers from clergymen?" asked Mabel.

" Oh dear, yes! certainly; three Baptists, two Presbyterians, four Wesleyans, and six Rational Religionists have sent in their testimonials; besides one Unitarian clergyman, who intends to open a business in the ivory and spirit line."

" Indeed! " said Mabel. " But is not the ivory and spirit line rather a temporal and secular occupation for a clergyman?"

" Why, rather so, madam, rather, perhaps; but then, you see, the gentleman must live in some way. He cannot preach and starve. If he is not paid for his services, he must support himself. "

" Very true," said Mabel. " But where is the church to be built—our own church, I mean?"

" Why, madam, this has been rather a difficult

question for the committee. They have not liked
to pledge themselves exactly to any one religious
denomination, as I before said. They feel that it
would be presumptuous in them to decide on those
deep theological discussions which are now agitating
the religious world. They will have no objection
to any clergyman of the establishment building his
own church, but they feel it would be a departure
from their fundamental principle to allow it to
appear prominently in the plans of their own architect."

Mabel looked rather puzzled.

" Sir James Perceval," continued the major, " did
indeed propose at the board, that a church should
be built at the expense of the Association, but it
would not do. Such a clamour was raised, and all the
various denominations came at the next meeting and
protested; and there was a violent altercation, as
there must be when you bring together into one place
or under one roof a number of persons who differ
on a subject on which they all feel warmly. Sir
James was obliged to withdraw his motion. But
he is a Conservative, madam, as you know, and does
not like the idea of not doing something for the
Church; and as his party is tolerably strong, they
have proposed, by way of preserving peace, what
will certainly be carried. One of the largest store-
rooms in the settlement is to be set apart every Sunday, and different hours appointed by the governor
for the several services of the various denominations;
so that they will all meet amicably under the same
roof, and no undue preference be given. And thus
the natives will have the opportunity of hearing the
truth set before them in all its various forms, without any attempt on our part to prejudice their minds;
the Association undertaking the cleaning out of the
room."

Mable looked disappointed. But before she could say more, there was a double knock at the door below, and the secretary, seemingly most ready to seize the excuse, rose to depart. Once more he waved his hat most gracefully, apologised for the long time during which he had trespassed on Mabel's attention, and trusted that his explanations had been satisfactory — hoped that she would as soon as possible co-operate with the central committee, by forming an Affiliated Ladies' Association in Hawkstone, and collecting an annual fund — and begged to know whether she would wish her own subscription to be annual, or, as most of the other honorary vice-presidents had preferred, would make her contribution immediately in a donation of five pounds, which he could receive at once, and which would exempt her from any further trouble. Happily for Mabel, she had presence of mind to request time for consideration, and the more so, as, in her own heart, Africa, with all its interesting features, was balanced by a recent proposal which had been made to her that very morning through the Rev. Mr. Armstrong and the Rev. Mr. Howell, the Baptist and Independent ministers of Hawkstone, to aid them in an important work nearer home — no less than the sending out a deputation from the clergy of the Protestant communions of England to convert the Pope. The eyes of Protestantism, and particularly of Protestantism in Hawkstone, by the rapid rise of a new Popish chapel among them, had been opened more than ever to the enormities of popery, and to the fearful strides which it was making in England. And it was thought that a grand effort should be made to stay the evil at the fountain head, by endeavouring to act at once on the conscience and understanding of the Papal court; for which pur-

pose a deputation of the most eloquent dissenting
ministers had offered their services to go to Rome,
provided their travelling expenses were paid, and
their families maintained by their congregations
during their absence.   And it was thought that the
presence of so many distinguished lights of the dissenting interest, differing in all other points of religion, yet all agreeing in their abhorrence of
popery, might have a salutary and awakening effect
on the mind of the Pope himself.   At any rate, as
Mr. Howell said, it would be a satisfaction to deliver
their consciences, and to preach the Gospel once to
the people in the very bosom of Antichrist.

All these thoughts and reminiscences passed rapidly through Mable's mind—a mind capacious
enough to grasp both projects at once, and active
enough to organise committees, and collect subscriptions, for both, if her finances had permitted her.
Gratitude indeed—gratitude for the honour which
she had received so unexpectedly and so wholly
without solicitation—began to preponderate, when
the door opened, and her little Grey School girl,
once more half frightened out of her wits, announced,
as she held it ajar, that there were two more gentlemen down stairs, who wanted to see Miss Brook:
one was Mr. Bevan, and the other, she did not
know who.   Mabel hastily arranged some papers of
school accounts which she was looking over, and
omitting to put out of sight the blazoned diploma,
which lay open in all its grandeur on the table, she
prepared, with a dignified look of business, to receive
her new visiters.   Only, it must be confessed, she
wished the stranger, whoever he was, had come
without Mr. Bevan ; for Mr. Bevan, she thought,
was always laughing at her, and would always intrude his own strange Oxford notions ; and, to say

the truth, she was a little afraid of him. She had, however, no time to ruminate, for steps were heard coming up the stairs, and presently Charles Bevan entered the room, and with an apology for the intrusion, he begged permission to introduce to her a gentleman, a friend of his, who was staying in Hawkstone — Mr. Ernest Villiers.

CHAP. XXVII.

It is not from any wish to tantalise the reader needlessly that we must revert, at this point, to another personage, in whose fate, it is hoped, they have not lost their interest during so many intervening chapters. Ernest's visit to Miss Brook was connected with the disappearance of Bentley. He had been directed to Bentley's by Mr. Atkinson, in order to procure some information on a subject of great interest to him. Bentley was not at home, and his housekeeper was beginning to feel uneasy, especially as he had been seen walking back late in the evening to the Priory ruins. In default of Bentley, Ernest resolved to apply to Charles Bevan, whom he had slightly known at college; and Bevan brought him, for information, to Miss Brook.

But while all this was passing, what had become of Bentley himself? We left him at the moment when he sank senseless under the knife of the ruffian. As his consciousness gradually returned to him, he awoke to the sense of a rough jolting motion, apparently through some unfrequented road, for the boughs of trees crashed as they moved along. There was a sound of hoarse brawling water close to him, like a torrent; and as he faintly opened his eyes, he saw above him the moon streaming brightly through a dense mass of foliage. As he became alive to a sense of his situation, he tried to rise from the bottom of the cart in which he was lying, and look round to discover into whose hands he had fallen, and where they were carrying him. But on applying his hand to his chest, he found his clothes saturated with wet blood. Some rough hand had indeed attempted to bandage up the wound; but, faint with the loss of blood, he sank back, and had scarcely strength to relieve the uneasy position in which he lay, with nothing but an old sack to break the jolting of the cart over the ruts, and a quantity of hard poles for his support, which by the glittering of the moon on their points he perceived to be pikes. One heavy tramp he could hear close at his side, as of a man attending to the horse. And as he once more endeavoured to rise up, and thought of appealing to him for assistance, a rough voice close at his ear muttered to him " to lie still, and keep his eyes shut." The voice was hoarse and hollow, but there was something of kindness in it, which gave Bentley a feeling of hope. It was also Irish, with a strong brogue; and Bentley fancied it was familiar to him. Presently the cart stopped, and two other voices, as of persons who had just overtaken it, were heard speaking together in an under tone, as if afraid of being overheard. Half fainting and half bewildered, Bentley was unable to collect his thoughts, to know what course he should take. But as he opened his eyes once more, the light fell upon a rough face, begrimed with black, looking steadfastly upon him.

" He is alive!" the fellow cried, with an oath, " as sure as my name's Jack."

" Is he? " said another voice. " And what in the world are we to do with him?"

" Why did not Wheeler put him down the well at once?" said the first; " he would have laid snug enough there for ever, and no one the wiser. Who is it, Connell? "

" It's the parson," returned the same voice which had before told Bentley to lie still, and which he now recognised, as having heard it often when visiting poor Margaret and the boy after the fire. " It's the parson! "

" These parsons," rejoined the first speaker, " are always getting into scrapes, meddling with other people's business. Why can't they let folks alone, to do as they like? What is it to them what we choose to do? But them that meddles burns their fingers."

" Hark!" muttered the other, " there's some one coming."

" It's only the water," was the reply.

" And if we do meet any one, what a mess we are in," said the first, " with a murdered man in the cart, and all these confounded pikes too. I say, Jack, let's throw him over at once."

And Bentley could perceive, by the steep ascent of the road, and the brawling of the torrent at some distance below, that they were probably passing along a steep precipitous bank overhanging the river. His head began to swim, and he was on the point of making another effort to rise and cry for help, when Connel's low mutter was heard again, close at his ear, " Lie still, lie still; they shan't touch you!"

" And you're the fool that begged him off, Connell," said the first speaker, " to get hung yourself for your pains!"

" It's I that did it," answered Connell; " and I'd do it a hundred times. Didn't he give me to eat when I was starving, and my wife too? Didn't he offer sums of money to any one who would save my poor boy out of the fire? Didn't he come and visit us afterwards often and often, and always a kind word in his mouth, and something to help us in his hand? I've done bad enough jobs in my day to them as was my enemies, but I do not desert them that's kind to me: and I do not intend to desert Parson Bentley; and, what's more, none of you shall touch a hair of his head."

" Why, he isn't one of your own craft, after all,"
said the first speaker, with a sneering laugh. " He's
one of your heretics, isn't he ?"

" May be," said Connell, " and more the pity ;
but he has been kind to me and mine, for all that."

" Better get rid of him at once," said the second
voice. " Dead men tell no tales !"

·Connell said nothing, but laid a whip vigorously
across the horse, which made him move on rapidly.

" Why, you ar'n't the man, surely," said the same
voice, " to mind putting a dangerous fellow out of
the way. You've done such a thing before now."

Connell groaned, and laid on another lash of his
whip.

" Why," pursued the voice, " they tell me, in Ireland, you folks no more mind popping at gentlefolks
from behind a hedge, or knocking at a man's brains
with a flint stone in a stocking, to find if they are
at home or not, than we mind shooting at a cock
sparrow. Eh ?"

Bentley heard another deep groan.

" Why, you know," continued the speaker, " if
your priest there, or whoever you call him, were to
bid you knock out the parson's brains, here, this
moment, you'd do it at once."

" Ay, but he wouldn't," muttered Connell.

" Ay, but if he did, would you do it ?"

" But he wouldn't," said Connell.

" But if he did ?" pursued the speaker.

" He wouldn't," repeated Connell, doggedly ; and
no other answer could be extracted from him.

" And what in the world do you intend to do
with the parson ?" said the first speaker.

Connell made no reply.

" I tell you what, Jack," said the other. There's
no use our meddling with this job any more ; let's
stick to the other cart, and go round by Birking

Lane, down the copse. If Paddy will put his head
into the noose, let him."

"And what shall we say to Wheeler?" said the
other.

"Let Wheeler shift for himself," was the reply.
" He's a rogue and a rascal; 3s. 6d., and a quart of
beer for this work : and he gets all the penny subscriptions from the club and pockets them, and no
one knows any thing about them. He does not care
a fig for any one of us but himself, with all his fine
talk about liberty and rights.—Hark! again, here's
some one on horseback, sure enough." And the two
men fell back and joined the other cart, which was
coming slowly up the hill behind, at no great distance.

Bentley, on hearing the approach of a horse, was
inclined once more to call out and obtain assistance;
but again Connell's rough hollow voice bade him
lie still and say nothing, " all was right;" and he
thought it better to comply.

"Good night, sir, good night." "Why, rather late,
isn't it?" was all that passed between Connell and
the stranger on horseback. He turned back, however, for a minute, repeated some kind of password
in a foreign language, and asked if the other cart
was coming. Connell said, ' Yes,' and the stranger
once more bade him good night, in a tone implying
a superior education and habits of society, and rode
off. Bentley was now left alone with Connell; and
he was hoping to obtain from him some information
as to his destination; but Connell, without speaking,
jumped up on the cart, and seizing the reins, urged
on the horse over the rough road, till Bentley,
in an agony of pain, was obliged to raise himself
up and entreat him to stop.

"Better not, better not," said Connell.

But on Bentley's entreating him to go quietly,
for he was very ill, he jumped down, and getting

into the cart, endeavoured to arrange the pikes in such a manner as to make a less uneasy bed. As he did this, there was a strange gentleness and softness about his voice and manner which surprised Bentley, little used to the contrasts of the Irish character. He lifted him up almost like a child, fastened the bandage more tightly about the wound, and taking off his own coat, folded it up, and put it as a pillow under the head of the sufferer, and then covered him with a sack.

" Don't be afraid, sir, don't be afraid; I'm your friend; I don't forget you; I'll stand by you; only we must get on." And once more he jumped on the front of the cart, and urged on the horse to a trot. Bentley closed his eyes, and endeavoured to compose his thoughts into prayer ; but his head swam, his senses became confused with pain and weakness, and he lay gazing up in the sky with a bewildered sensation of something frightful in which he was involved, without any distinct perception of what passed, except that a large ball of light lay close to his eyes, and a number of sparks were dancing about before them, and burning him. Once or twice he groaned ; and Connell, checking the horse, turned to ask what was the matter, and tried to arrange the pillow more comfortably for him. How long he lay in this state he could not tell ; but the road from the deep copse-wood, which clothed the steep banks of the torrent, now emerged suddenly upon a wide heath, without a tree of any kind. Huge sweeping hills, destitute of all cultivation, spread far before them ; but apparently they were approaching human habitations, for the road became tolerably smooth, and several groups of men passed by, and exchanged with Connell the same good night, and the same mysterious foreign password, which the gentleman on horseback had used before. Bentley's eyes, however, were now closed in a sort of stupor, from which he was roused by the cart stopping, and by his feeling Connell's arms placed gently under him to lift him up.

"Now, sir, get up—I'll take you out. Don't be afraid—only for your life do all you are told, and don't fear, otherwise your life is not worth a straw. —I'll be with you."

And Bentley, on looking up, found that the cart had stopped in a little yard surrounded by low sheds and buildings, apparently workshops; for large bars of iron were lying about, and heaps of coal, and tools used in mining and excavating. The gate by which they had entered had been carefully closed and barred by Connell; and once more begging Bentley not to be frightened, he raised him up softly, and, lifting him out of the cart, half led and half carried him into a little outhouse, where he arranged some straw, and, laying him down, covered him once more with some sacks. Bentley was by this time in a burning thirst, and he entreated some water, on which Connell disappeared, but returned soon with a cupful of liquid, which he declared would do him good, but which, on tasting, Bentley found to be whisky; and he was obliged, once more, to ask for water. Connell tossed off the whisky himself, and soon brought him a broken jug, out of which Bentley drank with avidity.

"Now, sir, lie still here, and I'll be back presently."

Recovered by the water, Bentley felt his senses becoming clearer, and he could look round and observe by the moonlight the objects around him; and what was still more comforting, he could compose his thoughts to prayer, and prepare himself for the worst which might await him. Where he was, he knew not; but there was a lurid glare in the sky

above him, and a rushing grinding sound as of
wheels and machinery not far off, which led him to
suppose that he might have been taken up into
Hawkstone Forest, among the coal and iron pits;
and it was a thought by no means calculated to
allay his alarm. He knew that for several months
there had been rumours of insurrectionary movements among the workmen employed in this district; that it was the refuge of the worst outcasts of
society gathered together within the last three or
four years by the opening of the mines, and left
without any superintendence or control; that it was
the boast of Hawkstone Forest that no policemen
dared come near them; and that as the enormous
profits of Sir Matthew Blake, the proprietor, increased, he was employing every day a larger
body of labourers, and accumulating a mass of vice
and sedition, which threatened soon to break over
and deluge the country with some serious mischief.

He lay for more than an hour ruminating on
these thoughts, and resigning himself into the hands
of Providence. He would have risen to look round
him more carefully, and to discover any means of
escape, but his wound had become exquisitely painful, and escape in his present state was hopeless.
Just as a clock, apparently in a workman's cabin
near, struck two, a light as from a lantern appeared
in one corner of the shed where he was lying, and
from a door in the partition five or six men issued
out, and came up to the place where he was lying.

" And so this is he?" said one.

" Yes," said a voice, which Bentley recognised as
Connell's; and at the same time Connell came up
to him, and taking hold of his hand, pressed it hard,
as if to remind him of his former injunctions, and
to reassure him.

" Why, 'tis a bad wound," said another, stooping
down, and examining the bandages, which were

full of blood. "That Wheeler's a dangerous chap;
he'd as soon stick a man as look at him."

"Well, parson," said a third, who seemed to be
the head, "we've heard you're a kindish man, and
never grudge your help to the poor, and that's
more than some of your cloth can say; and, may
be, though we are resolved to have our rights,
we've no wish to injure them that do not grind and
starve the people. Now, I tell you what, you've
been fool enough to go spying and prying into
other people's secrets, and have got a knife into you
for your pains : do you think that will be a lesson
to you never to talk of such secrets again?"

Bentley tried to speak, and to remove the notion
that he had any wish either to discover or divulge
their secrets; but the man put his hand upon his
mouth, and bade him be quiet.

"There's one here," he said, "you must thank if
you hav'n't your mouth stopped more effectually;
but he's told us all about you. Are you willing to
take the oath?"

Bentley asked "What oath?"

"Why, our oath—never to tell to any living soul,
be he magistrate, or police, or what not, or friend
or foe, any thing you have heard or seen of us."

Bentley replied that he was at their mercy—
that he had done them no harm, and never intended to do them harm—that it was by mere
accident he was at the Priory—and he was willing
to do any thing, not unworthy of a clergyman, to
save his life.

There was a laugh and jest from several of the
party as he came to the words "unworthy of a
clergyman," but their leader silenced them.

"You'll take the oath, then?"

"I will," said Bentley, "if it is not an oath to
do any thing wrong."

"You promise, then?"

Bentley faintly answered "Yes." Something in his conscience whispered that to take an oath of such a nature, even under such circumstances, was an act of doubtful propriety, to say the least; but he had not been brought up in a very strict school of casuistry; his virtues and his religion had both been matters more of feeling than of deep reasoning. And bewildered, and alarmed, and worn out with pain, he consented to do all that was required.

"Take him up, then," said the leader. And while two men raised him in their arms, he found Connell gently lifting up his head, and once more whispering in his ear — "not to be frightened, and do all that he was bid." It was with some difficulty that they bore him through the narrow door in the partition, and which was concealed by a projection of the wall, and difficult to discover. But the passage widened afterwards, and led down by a flight of wooden steps, rotten and broken, which seemed ready to fall under their weight.

"Take him softly, mind his head, put your hand under his shoulder," cried Connell, as they lifted him down the last step; and the leader, from a huge ring of rusty keys, proceeded to open the padlock of a low door in the wall.

"Now then, is all ready?" he asked.

And once more turning to Bentley, he reminded him of his promise to take the oath, and that his life depended on it. "If you don't," said he, "why it's only left for us to take care of ourselves; and you may judge," he said, "whether we can't easily give you a quietus, which won't require any oath or any swearing whatever. And if you break the oath —"

"He won't," said Connell, "he won't break it —

I'll pledge my life for him — I know he's a man of
his word — my life for his we're safe with him."

"He'd better not," said the leader. "There was
but one man ever broke that oath, and he was a
Scotchman, and turned informer; and I'll tell the
parson what became of him."

And he stooped down, and whispered in Bentley's
ear a few words, which made his blood run cold
with horror. "And now is all ready?"

"Do not be afraid, do not be afraid," muttered
Connell in Bentley's ear, as he raised him to stand on
his feet. "There's no danger, only take the oath."

But Bentley was afraid — and well he might be.
He stood on the verge of a dark pit or well, down
which hung an iron chain; above, by the light of
one or two tallow candles, he saw nothing but the
roof of a sort of cave hewn out of the solid rock,
and dripping with water. The men had nearly
stripped themselves naked, and were turning a
windlass, by which Bentley saw a low shallow
wooden tub rising to the top of the well. It no
sooner reached the surface than the captain of the
gang bade them put over Bentley a rough blackened
smock-frock; and himself getting into the tub, Bentley was placed in it likewise, and, supported in the
arms of the other, he felt the chain rapidly lower;
the glimmering light of the candles became fainter,
the aperture of the well began to contract; and as the
light above fell with a dimmer lustre on the rough
damp rockwork, out of which the shaft was exca-
vated, the dense pitchy mass of darkness in which
they were sitting themselves seemed to rise rapidly
above them.

"I have money," said Bentley to his companion;
"what will you take to set me free?" as he vainly
thought of propitiating him.

"Money have you?" said the man; "then you'd
better give it to me."

"Here," said Bentley, as he put a quantity of silver into his hand. The man looked on it scornfully, and put it into his pocket.

"Where are we going?" asked Bentley.

"You'll soon see," said his companion. "There, mind your head."

And as the bucket swung against the side of the shaft, he with some difficulty saved Bentley from the concussion.

"Catch hold of the chain. Have you strength to hold on yourself?"

"No," said Bentley, faintly, for he was becoming giddy.

"There now—here we are," said the man; and the bucket touched the ground with a shock which nearly threw him out. In a minute Bentley found himself seized by two men, naked to the waist, and begrimed with filth; a third bore two rough-shaped torches, and with the captain of the gang following, Bentley was carried along a steep, plashy, descending passage, hewn out of the rock. The air was stifling. The glare of the torches fell fearfully on the low ponderous roof, which seemed ready to crush them as they advanced, and before them was a black depth of darkness, into which it was impossible for the eye to penetrate.

"Stop," said the captain, when they had advanced as much as a hundred yards in this way. "You must wait here. Put him down."

And resting Bentley with his back against the rock, they disappeared. Left alone in utter darkness, in the bowels of the earth, and in the hands evidently of designing and desperate men, he felt his whole soul sink with alarm. He continued, however, to pray fervently; and with every prayer his strength increased, and his presence of mind returned. As a light appeared in the direction in which they had come, he almost began to hope that

it was the same party returning; but it was only
Connell. Once more he brought Bentley a cup of
whisky, and entreated him to drink it; and rather
than disappoint him, Bentley placed it to his lips,
but could not swallow it.

"You'll take the oath," said Connell; "mind
you take the oath. There's nothing in it; only not
to tell, that's all. If you don't, you're a dead man.
I promised you should take it; or do you suppose
Wheeler would have let you off? Why, they had
you at the side of the well in the ruins, and were
just about to heave you in when I came back; and
I had a regular tussle with them. But I do not
forget, sir, what you've done for me, — and I with
no friend in the world, and a miserable wretch that
might as well be put an end to myself. You'll pray
for me when I'm gone, sir? you'll pray for my
soul, won't you?"

And as the light fell on Connell's haggard countenance there was an expression in it of terror and
suffering, which made Bentley, even in his own
alarming position, almost forget himself in compassion for his poor companion. He had no time, however, to say any thing, for the captain and the
others returned, once more lifted him in their arms,
and carried him along by a continuation of the
same low winding excavation in the rock. On
turning a sharp projecting point, Bentley perceived
a wider opening; the roof was higher, and supported
by two masses of rock, which had been left to form
natural pillars; another flat mass in the middle
served as a sort of table, and against the side were
fastened three torches, the red glare from which
fell on those men who stood round it, the lower
part of their faces covered with black crape, and
one of whom seemed to start when he saw Bentley.
On the table was a Bible, a skull, a glass containing
a red liquor, a drawn sword, a brace of pistols, a

dagger, and two pikes such as those which Bentley had seen in the cart. It was not indeed at first that he perceived all this, for the sight so sickened him that he would have sunk back and fainted, had not Connell, who was at his side, once more put the spirits to his mouth and forced him to swallow some.

"We'd better make haste," said the man who had seemed to recognise Bentley; "there's no time for speechifying; and he must get his wound drest. Make him kneel down."

And placing him on his knees, and supporting him, they put the Bible into his hand, and proceeded to administer the oath. It was a strange, awful rhapsody — strange, in that it mixed up religion and rebellion, bloodshed and justice, appeals to the Divine Being, with pledges of crime to man, — but binding the swearer, never on earth, or sea, in winter or summer, in trouble or wealth, to friend or foe, living or dying, to reveal the secrets, or do harm or hurt to any member of the society by whom that oath was administered to him. Bentley shuddered with terror as he heard the curses imprecated on him who should violate it : and when at the close he heard the most holy names appealed to to give sanction to it, (for even a society of rebels and murderers find they cannot govern without the aid of some appeal to another world, cannot rule without professing their belief in a religion,) he was about to make a solemn protest and remonstrance against such an awful mockery, but Connell pressed his hand, and fear once more predominated over the voice of his conscience. He could not say "Amen" as it was uttered in a deep voice by all the persons present, but he kissed the Bible as it was placed to his lips, and was about to rise, with a deep sense of degradation and remorse, when he was forced down once more on his knees, and each

person taking up one of the weapons off the rock
which served for the table, and holding them close
at his breast, he was ordered to repeat after them,
" May these pikes pierce my heart, and this blood
be on my head, if I break this oath which I have
taken ! "   At the close they put the glass to his
mouth, but Bentley shuddered with horror as the
smell betrayed its loathsome contents, and with
unutterable disgust he threw it from him, and the
glass fell to the ground.

" He refuses it ! " said the leader. " Away with
him ! "

" He tasted it, he did taste it," cried Connell ;
" look upon his lips : " and with dexterity he contrived to smear upon them some of the blood which
had fallen on his own hand. " He's a safe man !
I know he's safe ! Take my life for his. I know
he's safe ! " And with all the eloquence of an Irishman the poor fellow began again enumerating all
Bentley's kindnesses and charities, and urging his
claims to mercy. " But he's gone," he cried, " he's
clean gone ; " as he turned and found that Bentley
had fainted away.

" Carry him off," said the leader ; " we'll hold
you responsible for him."

" Yes," said Connell ; and with the help of one
of his companions he bore him away.

END OF THE FIRST VOLUME.

Printed by A. Spottiswoode,
New-Street-Square.

HAWKSTONE.

VOL. II.

LONDON:
Printed by A. SPOTTISWOODE,
New-Street-Square.

HAWKSTONE:

A TALE OF AND FOR ENGLAND

IN 184—.

IN TWO VOLUMES.

VOL. II

LONDON:
JOHN MURRAY, ALBEMARLE STREET.
1845.

HAWKSTONE.

CHAPTER I.

THE sun was streaming in through the lattice, when Bentley awoke to a full consciousness of what had passed in that frightful night. As he threw his eyes round the little low whitewashed room in which he lay, he could recognise nothing as familiar to him; but it was clean and decent. The pallet on which he was stretched was furnished with a white curtain; a deal table at the side contained a bottle and glass, and some linen, which seemed intended to be used in dressing his wound; and his clothes had been carefully folded and arranged on an old worsted-worked chair at the foot of the bed. There were also on the walls some coarse coloured prints representing saints, and one of the Blessed Virgin with the Infant Saviour in her arms; and a roughly-carved crucifix of bone was placed over the chimney; and lying on the bed, turned down so as to mark the place, was a volume, which Bentley took up, and found it to be a book of Roman Catholic devotion — " the Hours of the Blessed Virgin." Before he could look into it farther he heard the footsteps of two persons coming softly up the stairs; and one of them gently opening

the door, they both came in. One was a man —
young, but his countenance marked already with
strong lines, and his dress that of one of the superior
miners. As Bentley looked on him he almost fancied that he recognised his face; and the same
kind of impression seemed to be made on the man
himself, for he started slightly on seeing Bentley,
and took care to place himself with his back to the
light, that his countenance might be less noticed.
The other person was a female. She was dressed
in a habit of coarse black stuff, only relieved by a
square fold of linen of the purest white round her
neck, and a white bandage above her forehead to
confine a black veil of the same stuff with her dress,
which veil hung down and concealed her hair, and
all but a portion of her face. She had a rosary of
large black beads round her neck, with a crucifix
of ebony depending from it; and the singular purity
and serenity of her features, accompanied by a look
of abstraction, grave and solemnised, yet full of
mildness, gave to a face by no means young or
beautiful an expression which riveted the attention of Bentley more than any thing he had ever
seen.

"How are you this morning?" asked the young
man. And he proceeded, with a hand evidently
skilled in surgery, to unfasten the bandages of
Bentley's wound, and prepared to dress it anew.
Bentley thanked him for his trouble, and would
fain have asked where he was, and who were the
parties before him; but the first attempt he made
to question his attendant was replied to by a surly
admonition to remain quiet: and the burning of
his hand and blackness of his parched lips were
enough to justify the warning against any excitement. With a tread evidently accustomed to a
sick room, and moving noiselessly about, without

officiousness, the Sister of Charity (for the female
was one of those admirable women) aided the man
in his operations; and when they were concluded,
and the Sister had smoothed the pillow, and placed
some toast-and-water by the bed-side, they both
withdrew, leaving Bentley to fall once more into a
disturbed slumber. When he awoke he was apparently still alone, but his curtain had been closed,
and stretching out his hand to put it aside, he saw
the same female as before; but she was kneeling
with her back towards him, and with her eyes upturned to the image of the Virgin, she was repeating to herself her devotions, with a depth and
fervency of feeling which Bentley dared not intrude
on. He let the curtain silently fall again, that he
might not interrupt her. When they were finished
she rose up and quietly approached the bed to see if
he was still asleep. Bentley could not but thank
her earnestly for her care of him; but his gratitude
was mixed with a strange feeling of suspicion and
dislike at being thus brought into contact with a
Roman Catholic, of whom he entertained all the
vague and irrational alarm which has been diffused
among Protestants by the coarse indiscriminate
abuse of every thing that is found in their system.
It was irrational, because indiscriminating; because
it made no separation between the Catholicism and
the Popery of the system, and thus gave as many
triumphs to Popery as it gave to it opportunities
of evading just condemnations, by exposing the
fallacies of unjust. At one moment there flashed
across him a suspicion that the whole was a pre-
meditated scheme. He thought of the new chapel
rising at Hawkstone,—of the zeal with which he
himself had preached against Popery,—of the importance which would be attached (for Bentley, like
most other adversaries and advocates, rated his own

services rather high, and like most other popular preachers, sank at times into a little vanity) to the removal of so dangerous a foe as himself to the corruptions and abominations of Popery. But to reconcile such a thought with the mere accident which took him back to the ruins, and with the mode in which Connell, Roman Catholic as he was, had acted, was impossible. It was in vain that he endeavoured to draw from the Sister an explanation of his situation. She denied, and apparently with truth and sincerity, all knowledge of what had passed, and showed no desire to hear any thing. And again recommending him to repose, she left the room.

About an hour afterwards she returned with some food for him; and when Bentley, invigorated by it, requested her to procure a Bible for him, she seemed more disposed to enter into conversation. A Bible, indeed, was not to be procured, except an old copy of the Vulgate; but she brought him some books of her own devotions, and among them Thomas à Kempis's " Imitation of Christ;" and as she placed them on the table, she could not help saying, " But, perhaps, you will not like these; they belong to us."

Bentley raised himself up to look at them, and laid them down in despair, while something like an expression of disgust and indignation passed over his countenance. " And you have no Bible?" he asked.

" Yes," she replied, " here is one; but it is in Latin."

" And you cannot read this?" he asked.

" No," said the Sister; " but we have portions read in the chapel; and we have the 'Lives of the Saints,' and our 'Hours,' and many other devotional works."

Bentley sighed deeply.

"And you are one, then, of those," she replied, "who believe that every thing Catholic is corrupt?"

Bentley made no objection to her use of the term Catholic, for he was little aware of the danger of allowing it to be thus abused by restricting its application to Romanism.

"I do, indeed," he said, "lament bitterly over the sad delusions in which you are lying; and I would do much to win you from them."

"We think," she answered, "that you rather are labouring under delusions, and preaching corruptions. You have broken off from the great body of the Church, beyond which there can be no salvation; and you have invented new rites, and new doctrines of your own; and your lives exhibit no high picture of what a Christian's should be. And instead of being united in the bond of peace, you are broken up into factions and dissensions; and the State, on which you leaned for support, is now found to be a broken reed, and is ready to pierce your hand."

Bentley was surprised to hear the mode in which the Sister addressed him. He did not know that controversial questions made a considerable part of the education of Roman Catholics, whether male or female, who are destined by their Church for positions of trust; and that the corporate character of the monastic societies in which that Church abounds gives to their members generally a dignity and self-confidence in the importance of their own position, as well as a sense of honourable dependence and obedience, which unite the two great elements of what is called good manners, and invests even persons raised from the lower classes with a superior character and address. He roused himself, however, to remonstrate with her on what he considered some of the grosest abominations of Popery. But her answer to all he said was steady and quiet. It was the Church who taught her; she did not like in such matters to depend on her own judgment: she believed what the Apostles believed, and what the Fathers taught; and would not willingly be wise in her own eyes, or trust to her own understanding.

It was in vain that Bentley referred her to the Bible. The Bible, she said, was to be read under the teaching of the Church; it might easily be wrested to the destruction of rash and ignorant men, who would listen to no guidance: and she could not put upon it, by her own judgment, weak and fallible as it was, any meaning contrary to the received declarations of the Holy Catholic Church. Into all this discussion the Sister entered temperately, and yet earnestly, and with a power of expression and reasoning which excited Bentley's surprise. Still more surprised was he to find that all his own observations were powerless against her. He spoke strongly, as he felt deeply; and used expressions which, however just as a description of the form which Popery assumes in the lowest and most ignorant of its followers, were neither true nor respectful in regard to the person whom he was addressing. For this is the great secret of Popery, and the mystery of its strength, that under the same forms and outward comprehension it contains several distinct applications of itself, and becomes all things to all men, without any open compromise of opinion. The answer of the Sister was still the same. She asked Bentley on what authority he rested his own belief, and he answered, on the Bible.

She replied, " On your own interpretation of the Bible, is it not?"

And when Bentley, though earnest at first in asserting the one clear, self-evident sense of the

Bible, was compelled to acknowledge that different interpretations might be and were given and defended, and that each person must take and must defend his own upon his own responsibility, she preferred, she said, the opinion of the Church to the opinion of any individual.

And when Bentley, abandoning his first ground, threw himself on the authority of the Reformers, she answered, that she preferred the testimony of a Church which traced itself to the Apostles, and had continued firm for eighteen hundred years, to one only two hundred years old, and which had its origin in individuals like Henry VIII., Luther, and Calvin. Bentley spoke of the virtues and holiness of the Reformers; but the Sister replied by the lives of the many self-denying holy men who have lived in the Romish Church. She asked if Protestants could boast of more, or even of as many? She contrasted the comforts and indulgences of many a Protestant clergyman, his domestic blessings and modern refinements, with the discipline and asceticism of a monastic life. And though Bentley poured forth all his eloquence against such corruptions from Gospel truth, he could not deny that, in itself, a life of self-denying religion was higher than one of mere innocent enjoyment.

"And you are yourself a nun?" he said; for, added to other defects which incapacitated him from entering successfully into the controversy with Popery, he knew little of its interior regulations.

"I am a Sister of Charity," she replied.

"And your occupation is ——"

"To attend the sick, chiefly," she replied, "in this place. But we have also a school, and we visit the poor, and give our priest information which he requires in the management of his flock."

"I cannot but wonder," said Bentley, "that you

have been allowed to establish yourself here. Is
there not a law against it?"

The countenance of the Sister underwent a
change; and, almost with indignation, she exclaimed, "And do you forbid others to do what you
neglect to do yourselves? Have you not allowed in
this place, as in so many others, a miserable population to spring up, whom you make the slaves and
the tools of your own covetousness? Are not your
manufacturers and your mining proprietors accumulating thousands every year by the sweat and the
blood of the poor? Do they not draw them from
places where they may be within reach of religion,
and herd them together here without a church, or a
minister, or the Sacrament, or the Bible, leaving
them in the midst of a land which calls itself Christian in a state worse than heathens—worse, because without the knowledge of their God, or the
means of approaching Him, you have given them the
knowledge of the world, and of the devil? And when
we would come among them, and devote ourselves
to their care, you repel us with jealousy and abuse."

Bentley was silent.

"Will you think," she continued, "how many
horrible accidents necessarily happen in this district? Scarcely a day occurs without some loss of
life or limb by explosions, or falls, or entanglement
with machinery, without speaking of the fearful
disorders to which labours like these are subject.
Has Sir Matthew Blake, or any other proprietor who
thrives in luxury upon these risks and sufferings—
has he laid by any portion of his vast wealth to
found even an hospital for those who lose their
strength, or their limbs, or their life, in pampering
his insatiable covetousness? And if we have been
sent here to undertake this work of mercy, are we to
be treated with scorn and contempt?"

Bentley was still silent, for many most painful thoughts were crowding on him.

"But you are weary, I see," she said, gently, as he sunk back on his pillow; "and you must not talk any more. I was wrong in allowing it. But you are a Protestant; and whenever you hear our religion abused, will you remember that you were once nursed by Catholic Sisters of Charity?"

Bentley replied, with fervour, that he should never forget it. And as she left the room he lay back, with less anxiety, to think over the prospect before him. He would, indeed, willingly have made use of some of the devotional works which the Sister had brought him; but in the midst of the most elevated piety he was startled and terrified at the language in which the Blessed Virgin was appealed to, and made the centre of the worshipper's hopes and affections, almost to the exclusion of the Almighty. And as this frightful instance of the Mariolatry of the Romish Church was brought back palpably to his mind, he felt the favourable impressions die away which had been made by the Sister of Charity. Why or how it was that he was unable to cope with her in argument he could not see; but he felt that his cause was right, and yet he knew not how to defend it—knew not, in one word, that the principles of the Sister were, for the most part, true, but that her facts were false; and that nothing but a knowledge of facts could show the inconsistency between the professions of Popery and its real conduct—between its pretended antiquity and real novelty—and so enable the Church to defeat it by its own arguments. In the midst of these reflections he once more sank into a sleep, and woke to find the Sister again sitting by the side of his bed, and another female in the same dress, but older and more matronly, looking on him with her.

"He is young, and seems good and amiable," said the elder Sister. "How sad that he should be lost in heresy, and cut off from the Church!"

The younger sighed; but Bentley awoke just then, and they told him that it was necessary to look at the dressing of the wound. As Bentley prepared himself for the operation, the same man came into the room whom he had seen at first, and catching his full face in the light, Bentley could not refrain from calling him by his name. "What," Cookesley?" he cried— "How are you here?"

But Cookesley stood behind the Sisters, and with his finger to his lips motioned him to be silent. The Sisters seemed surprised at the recognition, but Cookesley himself made some remark on Bentley's having mistaken him, and, busy with their work of benevolence, they seldom indulged in idle curiosity. The dressing finished, however, the man proposed remaining a little to make some medical inquiries of Bentley, and the Sisters withdrew. He waited for a short time with his finger to his mouth, until they had gone down stairs; and then coming up to the bed-side, he suffered Bentley to put out his hand, which he took kindly as that of an old acquaintance.

"Cookesley," said Bentley, "is it possible this can be you?"

"And I may say the same to you, may I not?" answered the other. "Is it possible this can be you?" And he affected to smile, but it was with an expression of shame and sorrow, which he could ill conceal.

"And what are you doing here in this dress?" asked Bentley. "Have you left London? I thought you were walking the hospitals there? When we met last you were just going there."

Cookesley affected again to laugh, and said, "Oh,

that's all over ; but you see, happily for you, I have
not forgotten the art."

" And your father and mother," said Bentley, " do
they know you are here ? "

" Oh, yes, yes, all's right," muttered Cookesley.

But Bentley saw by the working of his countenance that all was not right ; and as the recollection
of days came over him when they had been schoolfellows together and companions, living in the same
town, and associating in all their amusements, he
could not help feeling alarmed at his present appearance under such circumstances.

" Are you in business here ?" said Bentley.

" Yes, yes, in business; but you must not ask
questions."

And the hard dirty hands and coarseness of dress
refuted Bentley's suggestion.

Cookesley, however, would not allow him to say
more, but proceeded cautiously to the door, called
to some one at the bottom of the stairs, ordered
them to make no noise, and not to come up stairs ;
that the sick person was going to sleep, and he
would watch him for half an hour. And then returning and bolting the door softly, he came and
stood before the bed.

" Bentley," he said, with a low voice, " can you
keep up your nerves ? are you frightened ?"

" I am in the hands of Providence," said Bentley ;
" and though I know that I must be in danger, I
can resign myself to Him."

A slight sneer passed over Cookesley's face at the
mention of Providence.

" Providence has not taken much care of you
just now," he said, " except that you have met with
me ; and I can't forget old days."

" Providence will take care of me," said Bentley,
firmly ; " I have no fear."

" You have taken the oath ?" said Cookesley.

" I have," said Bentley.

" And do you mean to keep it ?"

" Most assuredly !"

" Your life depends on it," said Cookesley.

" And are you then," asked Bentley, " mixed up in all these criminal proceedings and plots, whatever they are ?"

" And so you did not recognise me," said Cookesley ; " but of course you could not. You didn't like the taste of our wine, ah !"

" Horrible !" exclaimed Bentley, shuddering at the recollection. " And you to partake in such a frightful act of mockery ! "

" It may be mockery, or mummery, or any thing you please to call it," said the other ; " but what are your crowns, and sceptres, and bishops' wigs, and judges' red gowns, but mockery and mummery? And it does very well to hold our fellows together. They believe it all ; and we wiser ones——"

" O Cookesley, Cookesley !" cried Bentley, " are you then one of the leaders of these abandoned men ?"

" I am one of those who can serve you in the scrape you have got into. How you managed to get into such a mess I can't tell ; but they do say you grave people do sometimes commit little indiscretions, like sillier folks ! Eh ! Bentley."

And in Cookesley's face there was an expression of ironical intelligence which made Bentley feel uncomfortable.

" What brought you to the ruins at that time of night, Master Bentley, eh !" and he laughed significantly.

" Mere accident," said Bentley ; " I had lost my watch."

" Mere accident, pure accident !" replied Cookesley, with the same significant, intelligent laugh. "All these things are mere accident. And so, when that fellow Wheeler was going to shoot his wife, you, like a gallant hero, preferred getting stabbed yourself."

And again he laughed. All this to Bentley's mind was unintelligible; and he was proceeding to explain the facts, but Cookesley, looking at a heavy silver watch which he pulled out of his coarse workmen's trousers, told him they had no time for joking now. "You must do something for me at once, or I cannot help you."

"I will do nothing," said Bentley, "unless you will tell me something of yourself, where you have been, and what you are doing. I cannot commit myself farther in perfect blindness as to the hands into which I have fallen."

"Would you hear my history?" said Cookesley, "It is short enough.

"I went to London, as you know; I carried there much the same kind of education that young boys get at school and at home. I walked the hospitals, cut up bodies and cut off limbs, till I cared no more for the living than I did for the dead. We had a good merry party together—Charles Brown and Harry Morson, and all that set. My father complained that I spent all his money; my mother, that I lost my religion. You know, Bentley, as a boy, I always hated canting and preaching; and my mother did nothing else, and my father used to laugh at her. We spent our mornings in tossing about dead men's flesh in the dissecting room, and our afternoons in dressing wounds and plastering fractures; and at night there was the play, and the Shades, and the little rattlers, and a thousand other little nameless amusements. And then came the constable; and then more applications for money:

and there were other persons I had to support besides myself; for I, too, have done foolish things." And once more he threw into his countenance, evidently agitated as it was by the tale he was telling, another glance of ironical intelligence. "And all this went on till one day — but never mind," he said, abruptly, "why look back to what can't be helped. You were more fortunate than I was. You were sent to college, and I suppose there you did learn to be grave and serious. And I never had any one to take care of me. Turned adrift in London — all of us together, all young, no homes to go to, and all kinds of misery to witness — why it turns one's stomach and hardens one's heart. And that's the best I can say for myself and for hundreds of others. How can they expect us to come to any thing else?" And Bentley gazed on the altered, vitiated, and melancholy countenance of one whom he had known as a boy full of spirit and promise, and he saw Cookesley's eyes moisten for a moment; but the unhappy man soon cast away the feeling.

"Bentley," he said, with a low voice, "it matters little what becomes of me. A few months may make me a great man, or see my head spinning on the gallows. And what matters it? '*Mors æterna quies*,' as you know we used to learn at school, and as our old master, Dr. Ellison, always repeated when he showed us how the brain thought, and the nerves felt, and the stomach lived of itself—'*Mors æterna quies!*' And perhaps my time is come; and I've had enough of life. 'Tis but a poor thing after all."

And Bentley would have followed up the subject, and spoken to him in a different tone, but Cookesley once more checked him.

"We have no time now for talking of these matters. You are in a bad plight, I honestly tell

you; and though I can be of use to you, and will be
for old remembrance sake" (and he pressed his hand
kindly), "you must do as I bid you. Are you
strong enough to write?"

"Quite," said Bentley, for he felt much better.

"Here then," said Cookesley, "take this pen,
(I'll hold the paper,) and write to your old housekeeper that you will be home in two or three days;
that you are staying with a friend, and have sprained
your ankle, that's all."

Once more Bentley felt a little scruple at putting
his signature to a false statement, even under his
present circumstances. But once more the warning
of Cookesley that he was in danger triumphed over
his conscience, and he wrote the letter.

"We must keep the thing quiet," said Cookesley. "If they get frightened about your disappearance, and begin making a search, all is over
with you; it would be as bad for you as for Wheeler,
or for us. Hush it all up; and in a few days I
think we can manage to send you back quietly. One
thing I can tell you is, that you have had a most
narrow escape already: nothing but the earnestness
of that Irish fellow Connell, and the way in which he
told our people what you had done for him, and how
much you did for the poor, would have saved you.
We've too great a stake just now to trust ourselves
in the mercy of any one. And we've hands with
us which are ready enough for any job, and would
as soon put a foe out of the way in a dark night by
the side of a coal-pit, as soldiers would in open day
on a field of battle. And after all, where's the difference?"

"Cookesley," said Bentley, "I entreat you not to
talk in so frightful a manner."

"Pooh! pooh!" muttered Cookesley. "'*Mors
æterna quies! Mors æterna quies!*' What does it

signify to either of us? And now let me give you
another warning. Speak to no one; know no one;
and do not attempt to move. I'll do my best for
you. And now I must go and send your nurse to
you! Eh! Bentley!—rather a different nurse from
what we have in our hospitals. I've sometimes
thought," he continued, becoming grave, and his
voice slightly faltering—" I've sometimes thought,
that if I had had such persons about me at St.
George's, and had fallen into good hands like
you, and had been taken care of, with a home in
London, a college, and persons to advise me and set
me a good example—I've sometimes thought I
should have been a different kind of person. Eh?
Well, ' *Mors æterna quies! Mors æterna quies!*'
Mind what I tell you, and keep quiet. Good-by."

CHAP. II.

It was about the same hour that Cookesley left
Bentley on his bed, when Charles Bevan and Villiers, to the extreme interest and jealousy of Mrs.
Crump, who was still at her bow-window, and to
the equal surprise and curiosity of the Miss Morgans, who were assuaging their noonday appetite
by a couple of cheesecakes at Machem's the pastry-
cook's, arrived, and knocked at Mabel's green entrance
door. At the announcement of Villiers's name it was
impossible for Mabel, with all her dignity, to prevent
a slight suffusion of gratified pride and expectation
from mixing with her surprise at a visit so unexpected from such an interesting and important personage. She had already in her own mind (having
heard early in the morning of the removal of his incognito) settled that he was to accept the office of president of the Ladies' Missionary Society, to become
patron of the National Schools, to revive a dropped
subscription of the old General of five pounds five
shillings annually to the Benevolent Society, to
undertake to support Lady Sudborne in holding a
stall at the next bazaar, and to place himself in confidential communication with her, Miss Mabel, on all
the important questions of the Hawkstone charitable and religious associations. She had almost
pledged herself to lay before him at the first opportunity the papers of the Rome Missionary and Papal
Conversion Plan. But Mabel was a person prudent
in her zeal, and resolved for the present to withhold any communication on this subject until she

had discovered whether, what she sadly feared, Villiers was an Oxford man. "An Oxford man" was Mabel's expression; for Mr. Bevan had long since warned her against the vulgar use of the other epithet applied to the opinions which all men who support the Church are supposed to hold.

Her agreeable feelings were not at all diminished by the frank, kind, and, at the same time, the respectful way in which Villiers apologised for his intrusion; for Charles Bevan had already explained to him Mabel's character. And whatever opinion Villiers might entertain of the soundness of her views, or of the expediency of her mode of carrying them into effect, he could not but esteem and be disposed to like her.

" Never," he said to Bevan as they came to the door, " never ridicule individuals who are endeavouring zealously and honestly to do good, though in a wrong way, until they have been shown, and refused to follow, the right way. This way our Church of late years has failed to point out; and I admire the earnestness and the motives of those who, without her aid, are striving to do good, far more than I condemn their mistakes, or excuse that inactivity on our part, which is the real cause of all the mischief. Teach them the right way, and where there is honesty and zeal we shall have all their exertions with us."

Bevan agreed, but he felt also that there was a little rebuke contained in the words; for he was himself inclined, though not ill naturedly, to laugh at individuals as well as at opinions which he did not approve of, and to amuse himself with Mabel's inconsistencies rather more than was quite agreeable to that lady's feelings. Villiers, older in mind, and sobered down by trials, never laughed at any one.

"I am come," said Villiers, after the usual introduction, "to request some information from you, as the person most acquainted with the subject, respecting the state of the schools in Hawkstone. I want to place a poor boy at one; and both Mr. Atkinson and my friend Bevan assure me that I cannot apply for advice to any one so well as to Miss Brook." Mabel inclined her head with dignity, and begged they would be seated.

"I believe I may venture to guess," she said, "at the object of your bounty"— for she had heard as much from Mrs. Connell; and however well bred, she could scarcely resist the temptation of bestowing her eulogistic patronage on so distinguished a person.

"Mr. Villiers must be aware of the admiration which we have all felt for the heroism with which he rescued the poor boy from his frightful danger."

Villiers smiled; and acknowledged that he was desirous of putting Connell's boy into some good school. He had found him sadly neglected, apparently accustomed to very bad company, as might indeed be imagined. "But there is something about him," he said, "which has singularly interested me—an extraordinary likeness. And it will be sad if the hand of Providence has saved him from an early death, only to make him criminal and miserable in after-life."

Mabel gravely assented; and with a little conscious importance she proceeded to turn over papers, and tickets, and little piles of bills, and an assortment of flannels and ginghams which had just arrived for the choice of the Dorcas Society.

"My list of schools," she said, "is rather long. There is of course the National School, and the Grey School, and the Bluecoat School, and Mr. Elton's Academy for young gentlemen, and Mr. Dawson's Seminary, and the Establishment at the top of the High Street, and Mr. Polewell's Commercial Gymnasium. But I wished particularly to find out a paper (I dare say you have seen it in the shopwindows) — but it was for to-morrow — a grand public examination of the boys at the New National Athenæum and Polytechnic Lyceum — quite a new thing for Hawkstone. The plan has been tried in London, and succeeded admirably. Government have assisted us here; and Dr. Bray, the celebrated Dr. Bray, the secretary to the parent institution in London, has come down. And Mrs. Maddox takes great interest in it. Indeed it seems as if it would quite work a revolution in our system of education — so easy, and yet so comprehensive."

"Pray," said Bevan, "my dear Miss Brook, do not trouble yourself on my account, for I know the paper by heart. It has been before my eyes every day during the last week. There was a syllabus of the subjects of examination in it, was there not?"

"Oh dear, yes," said Miss Brook. "But you are laughing, as you always are," she continued, as she looked up, and caught a smile on Bevan's lips.

Villiers also smiled, but it was a grave smile, with no tinge of sarcasm.

"Why will you charge me with laughing," said Bevan, "when I am by far the gravest person in Hawkstone? Besides, I can show you that I am serious. Did not the summary of the last examination run in this way:—Analysis of physical sciences — causes, properties, affinities, attractions, energies; *Fire* — ignition, combustion, flame, caloric; *Water* — decomposition, fluidity, solidity ; electricity, magnetism, atmospheric gases, space, motion; new theory as explanatory of— horizontal, ascending, descending, reflected, pedulous, rolling, diagonal, rotary and planetary motion ; recapitulation of moral principles, concluding with rhetoric, ethics, geology, pneumatics, astronomy, metaphysics, moral cosmogony, politics, botany, chemistry, history, ancient and modern, poetry, manufactures, agriculture, mnemonics, horsemanship, dancing, arithmetic, geometry, cookery, the art of swimming, painting, sculpture, anatomy, music, ontology, and deontology?"

"Stop, stop!" cried Mabel; "all the latter part is your own invention."

"My own invention!" said Bevan. "You know that every one of thèse was contained in the paper, though they might not all have come together in one clause."

"But you are laughing at it," insisted Mabel.

"Mr. Villiers," said Bevan, "saw the paper himself; and we both read it together."

"I hope Mr. Villiers will not suffer himself to be corrupted by your sad new notions," said Mabel, partly in sober sadness, and partly in curious inquiry as to the state of Villiers's principles.

Villiers only bowed, and smiled again.

"I ought not," he said, "to trespass on your time, which I know is so fully occupied; but my friend Bevan told me that you could give me information generally on the state of the schools and education in Hawkstone. Connected as I am with it, and hoping soon to be a resident in the neighbourhood, and to take an interest in its welfare, I am naturally desirous to ascertain the state of its population and its principal wants."

Mabel was delighted; it was the very thing which she had anticipated — evidently an overture to her accepting the office of head almoner, and prime minister of charities to Villiers himself. And once more commencing an ineffectual search among papers, and linen, and work-baskets, (for Mabel had a work-basket, though she had no time to use it,)

c 3

she was obliged at last to abandon the task, and resuming an erect and important secretarial posture, with pen and ink before her—" Mr. Villiers," she said, " would probably like that I should begin at the beginning. He" (with a stress upon the word) " will, I am sure, be rejoiced to know that we have established an infant school lately, and have seventy children in it already."

" What a frightfully large family !" said Bevan; " and all orphans too !"

" Orphans !" said Mabel ; " no, not orphans. I think Betsy Hatchett is the only one that has lost her mother. Oh, yes! there is Jane Jobson ; but I do not recollect any other. How could you think they were orphans?"

" I thought," said Bevan, " you and Miss Atkins, the schoolmistress, had undertaken the care and education of them ?"

" And so we have," said Mabel; " but that does not make them orphans. Their parents are alive for all that."

" Did you buy them ?" asked Bevan, gravely.

" Buy them ! What can you mean ?"

" I mean, did their parents sell them to you? How did you come into possession of them ?"

" Possession of them !" said Mabel. " How I wish, Mr. Villiers, you would teach Mr. Bevan not to be so sarcastic !"

" I am not sarcastic," said Bevan ; " I am speaking seriously. Suppose some morning a policeman were to come into my room, and find me busy in teaching tricks to your little dog there" (for Mabel did indulge in the luxury of a pug dog), " and encouraging it to come to me at all hours, and to follow me, and not you, when I called it—taking care of it, in fact, and educating it in an infant dog's school ; and when he looked at the collar round the

neck, suppose he found it marked, not with my
name, but Miss Mabel Brook's, with a charge to return it to the owner if lost;—do you not think he
might fairly ask me how I came into possession of
the little animal, and whether I had bought it?"

"Little animal!" said Mabel. "It's such a
beauty; only look at its tail! Is it not a beauty,
Mr. Villiers?" And Villiers was obliged to stoop
down and pat the little monster; but he did not say
it was a beauty, for he never said what he did not
think.

"I hope the poor little thing will never fall into
your hands," said Mabel, taking it up, and fond-
ling it.

"And why not?" said Bevan.

"Because you would not know how to take care
of it, in the first place; then, you would never love
it as I do; and, I am sure, it would never love
you."

"Not if I taught it tricks," said Bevan, "and
made it stand upon its hind legs, and put out its
paw, and perhaps spell a word or two with letters
on the ground? You know there have been reading pigs; and why not a reading dog? I can't tell
you how many tricks I know which I could teach it
—to jump up when bidden, and to wag its tail, and
toss up a bit of biscuit from its nose and catch it in
its mouth, and to ring the bell. In short, it might
learn any thing, and become quite an accomplished
dog, highly educated and enlightened, even for
these days."

"I do not think," said Mabel, "that teaching a
dog tricks is the way to make him love you. It is
feeding it, nursing it, having it with you, taking it
out on your walks, keeping it constantly with you
in your room, talking to it, as I talk to my little
pet. Don't I talk to you?" she said, stooping down

almost to kiss the dog. "When it looks up to you every day for its food and comfort, and knows no one's voice but yours, it will love you, and not before. I cannot tell you how my poor pet whines and moans when I am away from it, and how it bounds about and frisks when I return."

"But do let me try the experiment," said Bevan; "do let your dog come to me every day, and let me teach it some tricks."

"No, indeed!" said Mabel; "for if it did not love you, it would not obey you, or learn any thing from you, unless, indeed, you had recourse to a whip, which I could not bear; and if it did love you, why it would not love me. And I think it ought to love me, for I saved its life. There were some idle boys going to drown it, and I bought it of them, when quite a puppy, for a shilling; and therefore, as I gave it its life, I think I have a claim that it should love me; and it does love me very much." And the dog put out its tongue to lick her hand.

"I must confess," said Villiers, "that Miss Brook's theory of affection seems as sound as it is deep. It would scarcely be fair, perhaps, to ask if the fathers and mothers of the seventy infants entertain the same opinions?"

"I am afraid the fathers and mothers," said Mabel, not exactly understanding the drift of the question, but feeling that some mischief was contained in it, "I fear the fathers and mothers have no theory of affection, or of any thing. They are a most sad, ignorant, profligate set, who bring up their children to nothing but vice and idleness. These sad manufactories, Mr. Villiers, they have quite ruined Hawkstone. High wages to-day, and none to-morrow; and the children, as soon as they can earn a penny, sent to the factories, and the mothers the same; never at home by their own fire-

sides : so that if we did not step in, and take the
care of the poor little children, I know not what
would become of them. Not less than three infants
have been burnt to death here, in their cradles,
within the last eighteen months. And as soon as
they begin to run about, they are allowed to play in
the streets, where they hear and see all kinds of
horrible things. Surely," she turned to Bevan,
" you would not wish such a state of things to continue, though you do ridicule our infant school ?"

" I must protest," said Bevan, " against such an
insinuation, even from a lady's lips. I do not
ridicule infant schools, and I do not wish such a
state of things to continue. But whether infant
schools are exactly the best means of remedying it,
I may, perhaps, doubt."

" But what can you do ?" said Mabel.

" Why, having objected," said Bevan, " to your
plans, I think I am bound to produce my own ; and
I will therefore propound to you my theory—an
Oxford theory, Miss Brook."

" Oh, no, no," cried Mabel ; " I will hear nothing
of your Oxford notions. I know what they will be ;
something about Popery, I am sure." And she
looked inquiringly at Villiers, to see what impression was made on him by the word Oxford. But
Villiers only smiled in his own quiet way, with a
tinge of sadness in it.

" Shall I tell you a story, then ?" said Bevan.

" Oh ! by all means," said Mabel, " provided it is
not about some Popish saint."

" No," said Bevan ; " my story is about a
doctor. There was, once upon a time, a doctor,
who lived ——"

" In the west of England, of course," interrupted
Villiers, laughingly ; " all heroes of tales, in this
day, live in the west of England !"

"Yes," said Bevan, "in the west of England; and he was called in one day to see a poor man who had a mortification in his chest, and was evidently dying. And in the same village there lived a lady, one of the most benevolent of her sex, charitable beyond her means, president of five societies, secretary to five others, patroness and superintendent of the infant school; and I rather think," he added, glancing at the splendid diploma which lay open on the table, "that she was an honorary vice-president of the Grand Royal and National African ——"

"Mr. Bevan, Mr. Bevan!" cried Mabel, half laughing and half offended, "I must not be caricatured in this way. You know you are joking at me."

"Pray," said Bevan, "allow me to finish my story. In the same village, then, with this doctor lived this lady, who, among her other charitable avocations, had taken much interest in the distressing state of the poor sick man; and one morning, about twelve o'clock, she called on the doctor, and was shown into his private room. 'Dr. Morris,' she said, 'I have called to speak of the state of poor Jackson. What is to become of him?' 'Madam,' said the doctor, 'I fear there is little hope; the disease is approaching the vitals: and unless we could expel it from thence, I see no chance of his recovery.' 'Well,' said the lady, 'I quite agree with you. But still something must be done. We cannot allow the poor man to go on in this way, without some effort to save him; and the nurse and I have just thought of two plans by which, at any rate, some good will be effected. You say the limbs and extremities are not affected yet.' 'No, madam,' replied Dr. Morris. 'Don't you think, then,' said the lady, 'it might be as well to save them, at least?' Dr. Morris seemed puzzled by the question.

'Don't you think,' continued the lady, 'you could cut off the arms and legs—amputate them, you know—and so they would be saved, at any rate; the disease could not get to them.' Dr. Morris rose silently, and rung his bell. 'Or else,' said the lady, 'the other plan nurse and I thought of was, without amputation, to apply a tourniquet to the limbs, so that the blood from the body might not flow into them, or only a very little now and then; and so it would not matter what became of the vitals, and the arms and legs would be kept quite sound, and we could employ them as we liked for any useful purposes of society.' By this time the doctor's bell was answered, and, with his assistant, approaching the lady, he begged her to keep herself quiet, persuaded her, under pretence of refreshment, to swallow a composing draught, and immediately sent for her friends, that she might be taken home under their care, and not be allowed to escape again."

"Not very complimentary, I must confess," said Mabel, with an offended air. "But I do not see what this has to do with our infant school."

"Will Miss Brook," said Villiers, "allow me, whom she will not suspect of sarcasm, to interpret the allegory? I suppose Mr. Bevan thinks, and I confess I think with him, that parents and young children — very young children especially, and such as are admitted into infant schools—are as members of one body, drawing their life and support, and bound all to hang together from one common centre. Nature has so formed them, and we must deal with them accordingly. He meant, I imagine, to suggest, that either to save such children from the infection of corrupt parents by separating them wholly, or to attempt to save them from infection while they still continued in communication with the vitals, was a futile attempt. I do not agree with him that the propounders of such a scheme should be committed to the care of their friends; but I confess I do think the scheme itself is rather visionary."

"But," said Mabel, "we do not separate them wholly from their parents. They go home every night; and are at home on the Sundays, and several hours in the day."

"And there," said Bevan, "if their homes are such as you represent, they must learn either from your example to despise their parents, or from their parents' example to despise you. And which do you think is more likely?"

"Yes," said Mabel; "but then we stand to them in the place of parents. I teach them to look up to me as their mother; and indeed I am sure they have the greatest affection and respect towards me, for they always courtesy when they meet me in the streets; and one of them, quite a little one, worked me the other day such a nice pincushion; indeed, I have had several. It is quite a pleasure to receive such little presents. I only gave 6d. to the first, who worked a sampler for me; and no less than six girls have commenced doing the same thing. It shows their affection;—and so young, too!"

"Seventy children!" muttered Bevan, "seventy children! The last Shah of Persia had only sixty-four!" And he put his fingers to his lips, as if calculating a sum. "Pray," he said, "how is it that the mothers are obliged to send their children so young to school?"

"Because," answered Mabel, rather fretfully, "because they have so much to do. Many of them have large families, others have their work in the, factories; and it is impossible for one person to attend to all these things. You know you must

have an eye on children perpetually, or they get
into such mischief."

" Have any of the mothers in Hawkstone," asked
Bevan, " as many as seventy children ?"

" How can you talk such nonsense ?" said Mabel,
becoming angry. " Poor things !" she continued,
more placably, for she could not help laughing at
Bevan's smile ! " What would become either of
parents or of children with such a family ?"

" And what then is to become of you, Miss
Brook, and of your seventy children ? I have been
shuddering at the thought of your fate ever since
you avowed your condition."

" How you persist," said Mabel, reproachfully,
" in taking every thing I say so literally. I do not
mean," she said— and what she was about to say no
one can tell, for she stopped short, and coloured,
and laughed— " I mean, of course, that persons
who undertake to educate children are their parents
metaphorically ; not exactly parents, you know, but
in a figure."

" That is," said Bevan, " finding the parents
unable to educate their children, you undertake to
educate them instead."

" Exactly," said Mabel.

" And the parents give them up to you ?"

" Yes."

" Wholly, or only in part ?"

" Of course, only in part."

" And pray, what part is that ?"

" Why, to teach them their lessons, and keep
them in order, and all that," said Mabel.

" And you propose to teach them every thing
that is good, and make them obedient, and dutiful,
and religious, and every thing they ought to be.
Is it not so ?"

" Certainly," said Mabel, " we wish to make them good children."

" And pray, have the parents to teach them any thing else ?"

" Why, yes — no — yes," said Mabel, hesitatingly. " No, I do not know that they have."

" And pray, do you find this an easy task ? How do you set about it ?" said Bevan. " For I assure you I have had some experience in education, and find it by no means easy to make persons good, parti- cularly children. You whip them, of course ?"

" I hope not," said Mabel, indignantly. " I trust all punishment of that kind is discarded with us. It is not fear that can make children good."

" Nor, I conclude," said Bevan, " do you find that learning their letters, or repeating their col- lects, or singing together ' the cat purs — the cock crows — the dog barks — the pig grunts,' or jump- ing about like little Merry Andrews, clapping their hands, and pretending to be in play, till they yawn with sleepiness — you do not find, I suppose, that this assists much in forming them to virtue ?"

" Of course not," said Mabel, angrily. " We make them good by their love and affection to us; we wish them to respect us, and be grateful to us, and do every thing we bid them, for our sake."

" For your sake, and Miss Atkins ?" asked Bevan, half afraid lest he should offend her too much by his playful interrogatories.

" Not exactly ours only," said Mabel, " but for the sake of the subscribers generally, and all the ladies who have helped to establish the school."

" And whom they see," said Bevan, " once a month ! Is once a month time enough for children to learn to love persons ?" he asked.

" Why will you continue to take my words so literally ?" said Mabel. " I only meant to say that

we endeavour to make the children do right by
enforcing their duty to us, and exciting their affection and gratitude to us."

"And I know no means but affection and gratitude," said Villiers, kindly, coming to her support,
"which can be efficacious, humanely speaking, in
education. Miss Brook will find me on her side."

And Mabel was soothed and pleased with his
approbation.

"Suppose, then," continued Bevan (and Mabel
affected to stop her ears, saying, she would not
listen to any more of his suppositions — they were all
equally bad); but Bevan persevered — "suppose,
my dear Miss Brook, some fine morning, these
seventy children were to come to your door, telling
you that they had learned to love you very much,
and to respect you, and, as is naturally the case
with the affections of all young people, that they
now cared little for any one else; and did not like
their parents, who treated them harshly, and were
bad people, nor their homes, which were not half
as clean and airy as the school-room; and that you
had told them you would be a mother to them; and
that they loved you much better than their real
mother, and would do any thing you bade them —
pray, should you not be taken a little by surprise?"

"Indeed I should," said Mabel; "and my first
orders would be, to go back to their parents, and to
honour their father and their mother; and to remember that I was only their teacher, and not to
be regarded by them in the place of a real parent."

"Only a metaphorical one," said Bevan, laughing.

"I do not like sarcasm," said Mabel, gravely.

"Will you let me tell you the sequel, then, of
the story of the doctor," asked Bevan.

"No, indeed, I do not wish to hear any more."

" But I must, indeed," continued Bevan ; " Mr.
Villiers told it me himself."

" Oh, Mr. Villiers!" cried Mabel, " I did hope to
have had your support; but I am afraid you are
corrupted also with these sad Oxford notions."

Villiers only smiled, and shook his head.

" I must tell you the sequel," said Bevan. " The
day afterwards, the same lady (for she had made
her escape by a side door) called again on the
doctor, and informed him that she had taken into
consideration the difficulty of preserving the limbs
from corruption, in case they were amputated ;
and that she had a remedy which would remove
this objection. She had spoken to another man,
who had consented to have the limbs, when cut off,
fastened on to his own body. ' And you know,' said
the lady, ' that they may be fastened on quite
tightly—sown on, in fact; and if they cannot be
kept alive without being attached to some body or
other, why this will do ; and so they will still have
a body to supply them with nutriment and life, and
to direct their movements.' It will be as good as
their original body, metaphorically, you know,"
said Bevan, archly.

Mabel was silent, and almost inclined to be
seriously indignant. " I am no philosopher, you
are aware, Mr. Bevan," she said ; " but I only know
that the infant schools have been established by
some of the most religious and good men who ever
lived ; and I do think we should exert ourselves to
save these poor infants from being led astray and
ruined by the example of their parents."

" I am sure," said Villiers, as a pacificator, " that
Mr. Bevan will join with you most cordially in this
opinion ; and so we must all."

" Most cordially," said Bevan ; and he stretched
out his hand across the table in token of an ami-

cable capitulation,—" most cordially; only," he continued, as he took Mabel's hand, which was very reluctantly given him, and lay passively in his own — " only, I must tell you one more story."

Villiers could not help laughing at his pertinacity.

" There was once on a time," said Bevan.

" Indeed, indeed," cried Mabel, " I cannot stop to hear any more stories; I have heard quite enough : but Mr. Villiers will excuse me, I am sure. I am obliged to attend a meeting of the Dispensary Committee at one o'clock; and, instead of giving him any information respecting the schools, we have wasted all the time in hearing Mr. Bevan's sarcasms."

" Stop, I entreat you!" said Bevan, " one moment; you must stop, only one more. There was once upon a time a gentleman, and he lived ——"

" In the west of England?" asked Villiers again.

" No, not in the west of England, this time," answered Bevan, " but at Bagdad; and this gentleman was very fond of young animals of all kinds; and one day they brought him a young lion (it is true, indeed—perfectly true), which they had found in the reeds on the banks of the Tigris; it was not much larger than a cat — quite an infant, Miss Brook. The gentleman took compassion on the poor little creature, and was particularly desirous to rear it up in good sound principles — very different principles, indeed, from those of its father and mother, who were wandering about the desert sheep-stealing and horse-stealing, and exceedingly fond of raw flesh. He thought the best way to accomplish this would be to place himself to it in the place of a parent — not a real parent, you know, only a metaphorical one. And as he had no mamma lioness to give it suck, he constructed a large

VOL. II.   D

leathern bag, with which he endeavoured to supply
the little monster with food after its natural fashion.
The gentleman, as I said before, was particularly
anxious to extinguish its taste for animal food, and
hoped that by proper tenderness and management,
especially by teaching it to stand upright on its
hind legs, and to pick out the letters of the alphabet,
this horrible taste would be extirpated, and that it
would learn to live on milk and vegetables. It
was, indeed, allowed every night, and once or twice
in the day, to be in company with another grown-
up lion and lioness, who were kept in a cage, and
fed with raw meat, which the young one, at those
times, was allowed to partake of : but this the gentleman did not mind. His reliance was placed on
the leathern bag, and the letters of the alphabet.
And the young lion grew, and the old gentleman
continued to pet it and feed it with his own hand,
and the leathern bag ; and when the Pasha, who
knew more of lions than the gentleman, warned
him that it was not so easy a thing to wean them
to live upon potatoes and turnips, the gentleman
still replied that his lion could tell the letters of the
alphabet, and would, therefore, soon lose its taste
for blood. And at last the lion became as large as
a young donkey, and could tell every single letter
correctly, and the gentleman was quite proud of his
success ; when, one morning, it was found in its
master's room, amusing itself with the remnants of
its master's skull !"

" How horrible !" cried Mabel. " What can you
mean by such stories ?"

" I mean," said Bevan to Villiers, as they went
down stairs after taking their leave, and promising
to call for more information again — " I mean that
we in this country are endeavouring to nurse an
infant monster in the shape of the children of those

classes, which we have permitted to grow up in vice, and ignorance, and poverty, and who are now beginning to alarm us with their menaces and strength; and that if we have nothing better to crush the instinct which it derives from its parents, 'ἔθος τὸ πρὸς τοκέων'—you remember the passage in Æschylus—than our leathern bag and our letters of the alphabet — Woe to us when the child grows up!"

Villiers was silent; for it was a thought not new to him, but full of fear and sorrow.

"And yet you must not," he said, "indulge your humour too much with Miss Brook; you will give her offence and pain her. And she is far too amiable a person to treat with disrespect."

"Disrespect?" said Bevan, "I would not offend her for the world! But she is under the influence of the absurdities of the day. And ought we not to be reminded that infants have been placed by Providence in the hands of their parents, and belong to them as their property? That except by parents, or persons fulfilling all the duties and occupying the position of parents, they cannot be properly educated; because the education of infants can only be conducted through love and veneration; and their love and veneration, if directed to any one but their parents, is misplaced, and will only lead to a dislocation of the first elements of society—domestic attachment?"

"It is true," said Villiers.

"And will our education," continued Bevan, "be placed on a proper footing until we give up our usurped authority over the infants of the poor, restore them to the hands of their parents, stand by them ourselves only to aid and assist the parents in the work of education, and turn our attention rather to improve the parent than the child, rather to make the vitals of society sound, and the spring of life pure, than to save the limbs while the vitals are mortifying, and to filter the waters of the stream while the cattle are every hour polluting the fountain-head above?"

Villiers sighed. "I fear," he said, "we have rather trespassed on Miss Brook to-day. And certainly the course of conversation led us away from our object. Will you call with me again to-morrow?"

"With pleasure; and afterwards shall we go to see that quack exhibition, the Academy, or Lyceum, or whatever other fine name it bears? You observe how classical and Athenian every thing is becoming, at the very time while the same parties, who thus nickname their modern absurdities, repudiate the notion of encouraging Latin or Greek, and talk of nothing but modern science and utility."

"I am not very fond," said Villiers, "of appearing as a spectator at exhibitions the principle of which I disapprove of. But wishing, as I do, to see as much as possible of the state of things in Hawkstone, I will depart from my general rule. And now are you disposed for a walk? And you shall tell me what is the condition of the place in your own mind. Which way shall we proceed?"

"I have one favourite walk," said Bevan — "towards the Priory ruins, if you have no objection. And I wish to see a poor person on the road."

"None," said Villiers. And the two friends (for the morning conversation, in exhibiting a similarity of principle and object, had done more than renew an old acquaintance) commenced their walk to the ruins.

CHAP. III.

"AND all this is yours?" said Bevan to Villiers, as they stood together on the same brow where Villiers had rested before on his former visit to the Priory.

Villiers made no reply, for he seemed immersed in thought.

"It is a lovely prospect!" continued Bevan, not noticing his companion's abstraction. "Look how beautifully the light is falling on that gable with the ivy drooping down from the broken tracery. See, it is stealing round that pillar, and throwing it out from the shadow. Oh! is not that exquisite?" And he quite clapped his hands (for Bevan was an enthusiastic admirer of Nature) as a cloud passed away, and a gorgeous light fell on the mass of foliage and old gnarled trunks of oaks, which started out of the red sandstone rock on the bank behind the ruins. "And the rush of that water!" he exclaimed; "can any thing be more soothing and delicious? But you do not enjoy it!"

"I should enjoy it more," replied Villiers, "if it belonged to any one but myself. Neither of us indeed would perhaps regard the ruins of a religious house as the most agreeable object for enjoyment, however picturesque they may be. But men's minds do not seem to contemplate things now in such points of view. A ruin is a ruin, whatever its original destination; and break it up into picturesque groupings, tint it well with lichens, hang it with ivy, and place it in a good framework of wood and valley, and the eye once satisfied, no one seems to care for any thing else. I confess I cannot do this. And I do not enjoy the sight of those ruins, for the very reason that they are my own."

"And yet property," said Bevan, "has its charms and its uses, if properly employed."

"It has," said Villiers; "and yet the burthen of it is heavy. When you reminded me that all this was mine, I thought of a Being who said the same of this, and of all the kingdoms of the world,—'All this is mine, and I give them to whomsoever I will.' I have sometimes wished that Providence had placed me where you are placed, in the quiet independence of a college life."

"Our college life," said Bevan, "has many charms. It relieves us from all the troubles and anxieties of an establishment, gives us a home without many of the discomforts connected with a family, and secures us a degree of respectability, independent of fortune, which is useful to ourselves, and also, I think, to society, in these days, when money is every thing."

Villiers looked disappointed, and scanned Bevan inquiringly; and one who knew the workings of his countenance might have observed a slight, very slight curl of the upper lip. "I thought," he said, "that Oxford men sometimes gave other reasons for their attachment to Oxford?"

"What more would you want?" asked Bevan, sedately. "Ease, comfort, independence, respectability, usefulness to society,—where could you have learnt that any thing more was necessary? Surely not from this age?"

Villiers, plain, straightforward, never speaking except exactly as he felt and thought, and never indulging even in the most moderated irony, still seemed perplexed. And Bevan perceived and understood his thoughts.

" You wish me," he said, " to speak of other
blessings which we enjoy at Oxford. Do not suppose that I am insensible to them ; but they are
things rather to be known and felt, and acted on,
than talked of."

" Yes," said Villiers ; " your daily service, the
society of good men, your time for study, your
noble associations, the freedom from temptation,
the space you occupy in the country, as fulfilling
its noblest duties, your defence of the Church, and
of all that the Church values,—these are the things
which I was thinking of. Oxford has long seemed
to me the Thermopylæ of the age. And when the
barbarous host pours down upon us with their gold,
and tumult, and jargon, and parade, it is there that
the few must take their stand who dare to resist
the invader. Whether they will be overwhelmed
or not, is in the hands of Providence."

" And yet," said Bevan, " Oxford is not all that
it should be. It has improved, has been raised from
the lamentable state in which it lay not long since,
but it has many defects. The very enjoyment of
its life tends to make us indolent and selfish, and
unable to bear with the little frettings and rough-
nesses of life. It makes us dreamers also, inclined
to indulge in theories of what should be, rather
than to grapple manfully with evils as they are.
We have too few duties. Except those who are
immediately engaged in tuition, and the care of the
neighbouring parishes (and they are comparatively
few), we have no appointed work, except to study ;
and study by itself, without active duties and occupations to form a solid foundation for it in the
mind, is perhaps an unhealthy employment. The
consequence is, that so few Fellows of Colleges
reside at Oxford ; and even those who would wish
to enforce their residence scarcely venture to do so."

" And why ?" asked Villiers.

" They dread," said Bevan, "bringing a large
number of persons to live constantly together, who,
having nothing to do but to read, will probably
become troublesome, restless, and even quarrel-
some."

" But why not," said Villiers, " engage them all
in tuition,—allot to them each some portion of the
management of the students ? "

" We cannot," said Bevan, " without diminishing
the emoluments of our tutorships ; and, these diminished, we should not find superior men to devote
themselves to the drudgery of tuition. Besides
which, I doubt if we have discipline sufficient, and
habits of obedience, to hold together a body of
Fellows, each in his allotted place. Our societies
are kept together in much harmony and good will,
because few are in residence at a time ; and among
those it is effected by a gentlemanly spirit of mutual
accommodation, and by the general habits of society, rather than by strict discipline. This is one
of the things lost in our day, and perhaps it can
never be recovered."

" Perhaps not," replied Villiers.

" Indeed it would be hard," continued Bevan,
"to find men who would devote themselves, as the
work of their whole life, to the task of education in
a college, with only the trifling remuneration which
could be offered them under your plan. Few men
now think of dying in a college. Perhaps, as I said
before, the life itself is enervating, and disqualifies
us for our task, if continued too long ? "

" And therefore," said Villiers, smiling, " you no
sooner obtain a fellowship than you look out for a
living, and resolve to marry ? "

" We look out, I believe," replied Bevan, "for a
position where we may have regular and active

duties to discharge, particularly as clergymen. I
have heard many Fellows, as soon as they were
ordained, express themselves strongly, and I do
believe honestly, as if they felt that a residence in
Oxford, enjoyable as it is, was incompatible with
their ordination vow."

"And yet they are needed there, surely," said
Villiers, "to provide learning for the Church, and
to defend it by their writings: even to hold up a
high standard of principle and theory, as well as of
conduct, which is so soon lost in the bustle of the
world."

"Yes," said Bevan, "if any one would come forward and appoint us our tasks, and make us feel
that we are following this as our proper vocation,
fixed by Providence. But we have not been accustomed to look at our institutions in this point of
view. And after all, until we have all our active
duties and employments, as well as our opportunities
for study, I fear the attempt would fail."

"And so, as soon as you can leave Oxford, you
all marry?" repeated Villiers. And there was something in his tone of voice as if he was sounding the
depth of his companion's mind.

"We marry," said Bevan, "for what else can we
do? You would not wish a clergyman to place
himself in a parish alone, without any one to relieve the solitude of his fireside when he comes
home from his painful, and wearying, and thankless
ministrations? As a single man he commands no
station in society; he cannot attend to many things
which only a lady can properly superintend. He
must be embarrassed, to say the least, with his domestic arrangements. But there are also numberless parochial employments in which he cannot well
take the lead, but his wife may. In the present state
of society a wife is, at least, as indispensable to a

parochial clergyman as it is to a member of any other profession, who is never recognised as fixed respectably in life, or even usefully, till he is married."

"And with the marriage," said Villiers, still probing the real opinions of his companion, " with the marriage comes the establishment, and with the establishment the house and the furniture, and the hundred knicknacks of our modern refinement, and the footboy in livery, and the pony-chaise, and the respectable table, and the spare room for occasional visiters ; perhaps the piano and the harp, for you are gentlemen yourselves, and those you marry have themselves been brought up to these comforts; and the position which you occupy in the parish, or the town, requires that you should live respectably, and respectability, in modern eyes, is determined by the —— "

" Horse and gig, you would say," interrupted Bevan.

" No," said Villiers, for he was fastidiously alive to vulgarities, and could never enter into the wit of slang, " by these comforts and refinements."

" It is too true," assented Bevan.

" And then," continued Villiers, " when the school-house is to be built, and the church enlarged, and the organ fitted up, and the schoolmaster paid, and the poor relieved, without being sent to the workhouse, and the out-lying districts to be provided with additional curates and chapels, the clergyman is drained of his own means by his own necessities, and must look to bazaars and penny-subscriptions, and all the precarious mockeries of modern charity, to provide for the wants of his church ; and, after all, provide for them ineffectually."

" Remember one thing," said Bevan. " If your

present system involves a large expenditure by clergymen on their own families, it provides also the funds from private sources ; for so long as the parochial clergy retain their present respectability (let us use the word as the world uses it), so long the situation will be filled by respectable men ; that is, by men who have private property of their own, and increase it by the little fortunes of the persons whom they marry. But lower them down to a style of living and position in society which, however good, and simple, and primitive in itself, would be wholly unintelligible, and without claims to respect in modern eyes, and our clergy would soon be filled only from the lowest classes."

" I am not sure," said Villiers, " whether the funds brought into the Church in the way you suggest are at all equivalent to the increased expenditure of the clergy, entailed on them by their present mode of life ; and perhaps a different mode of life might provide for them other resources which are now closed up ; and private bounties to the Church might flow more liberally, as they did of old, when men saw that their gifts were not expended in private, but in public works. But you mistake me if you suppose I would sweep away our parochial system, as it now stands, further than that I would willingly see our clergy, within proper limits, and gradually, setting the example of more simplicity in their habits of living ; and from them it would penetrate into other classes of society. But I do think that on our Church system, as constituted at present, something else might be grafted to supply its present defects. We do require collegiate bodies, and without them our Church will be scarcely able to retain her position."

" Monasteries," said Bevan, archly.

" No, not monasteries," replied Villiers ; " far from it!"

" And why not monasteries ?" asked Bevan, looking up into Villiers's face with an expression of
curiosity and interest ; " why not monasteries?"

" It would be more fit," answered Villiers, " for
me to ask you, the learned man of Hawkstone, the
history of monasteries, than for you to ask me.
But I have read that history carefully ; and I trust
the days of monasteries will not be revived in England."

" And yet," said Bevan, " think what monasteries
have effected in their generation. How they opened
a refuge for the scattered atoms of society, the men
without homes or families, and who, without homes
or families, could become only useless, if not mischievous — how they preserved in the world the
form, at least, of a higher tone of piety and self-
denial — how they exhibited, to common eyes, religion and the Church in a tangible shape, visible
and powerful, and clothed with all the outward
ornaments so necessary to give it weight, and even
to make it intelligible to minds that can comprehend nothing but sense."

" I have thought of all this," said Villiers.

" Again," continued Bevan, " remember how
they stood between the Church and the crown at
the time when the ecclesiastical power without this
support, must have been crushed by the secular
arm — how again they stood between the crown
and the barons, and aided the former in amalga-
mating the civil elements of society, and in forming
oligarchies into monarchies : think again how they
stood once more between the barons and the people,
and threw up their great corporations strong in
property and talent, to protect the people from the
tyranny of their masters — to set an example of
kindness and good management — to introduce arts
and refinement, and a refinement not like our own,

divested of religion, but turning all the energies of the fancy to embody and illustrate, and enforce the doctrines of truth."

" I know it all," repeated Villiers, gravely.

" And to our monasteries," continued Bevan, "we owed our libraries, our churches, our cathedrals, our architecture, painting, sculpture, agriculture, music, — even our ecclesiastical endowments and our parochial system, — how much of all that sweetens as well as ennobles life!"

" With some qualifications," said Villiers, "I admit it."

" And," continued Bevan, sarcastically, "when our monasteries were swept away, came our poor laws."

" Yes," said Villiers, with a strong expression of indignation.

" And for our monasteries," added Bevan, "we have now —— "

" Yes," cried Villiers, impetuously, "we have our factories and our poor-houses, where, night and day,

' Men wake as monks of old, but not for prayer —
Men quail with famine's pangs, but not for God —
Men crush their limbs with toil, but all for gold —
Men live and die in shame, but not for sin.'

O England! England!" And Villiers drew his hat over his brow and walked on hurriedly.

Bevan followed him in silence, and they both sat down together on the trunk of a huge oak, which had been uprooted in a late storm, and lay along the side of the declivity.

" And yet," said Bevan, gently, "with all this before you, you would not restore our monasteries?"

" No," said Villiers, "I would not. From the first they seem to me to have been formed upon false principles, and to have been the strongholds of Popery ; and of Popery, if I venture to speak at all, it can be only with abhorrence."

Bevan was struck and surprised. He might have expected some expression of sorrow and re-probation for the corruptions of Popery ; but he was little used to language of this kind from any one except persons very different from Villiers. And the warmth with which Villiers spoke when roused contrasted strongly with the usual reserve and quietness of his manner. But Villiers, sobered as he had been by trials, was still a man of quick and almost passionate feeling ; and without feeling, who can move or rule the world?

" I abhor," he said, standing up with his arms folded on his breast, and looking stedfastly on Bevan — " I abhor a system which, professing a zeal for religion, aims mainly at dominion — which destroys the constitution of the Church, and with the constitution, its safeguard for the transmission of truth, in order to raise up a tyranny where God has appointed equality — which pretends to antiquity and authority, while it forges and falsifies the docu-ments on which those pretensions are rested — which, abandoning its simple duty of witnessing to the truth revealed to it, thinks only of governing men — which, to govern men, consents to employ trickeries and falsehoods, and mummeries — which would hold them in ignorance and bondage, lest enlightenment in the laity should infringe on the exclusive usurpation of the clergy — which would sever all the ties of society, separating children from their parents, and husbands from their wives, and subjects from their kings, and kings from their subjects, and rather create a chaos than want a field fitly prepared for spreading its own dominion. I abhor," he continued, "that which you abhor, its frightful popular idolatries — the audacity with which it has tampered with the most solemn positive institutions of God — the wretched, compromising, expediency-rationalism with which it has made itself all things to all men, that it may win, not souls, but bodies — the laxity of its morals set side by side with the severity of its discipline — the grasping, meddling, covetous, ay, sanguinary spirit with which it has stretched its arm over the whole world, introducing schism, and heresy, and rebellion, and murder, as the means of propagating religion, that is, of establishing its own power. And when I speak of such things," said Villiers, " I speak strongly ; and we ought to speak strongly."

" And yet," said Bevan, calmly, " placed by the side of dissent, Popery has its fair side. Even compared with our own Church it has much to admire and imitate."

" Not Popery," said Villiers ; " not Popery. Popery is the spirit of rule, of ambition, of self-will, of rationalism, of dissent itself; and as such, it has nothing fair. To serve its ambition, it has made use of religion, and preserved much that is noble and good, because it knows that without nobleness and goodness no rule can long be permanent. And it is this Catholicism, not Popery, which we admire."

" It is sad," said Bevan, " that in our own Church we have not something of this spirit of rule, some of that worldly prudence which would restore our discipline and our power."

" God forbid !" exclaimed Villiers. " God forbid !" He was thinking solemnly on a solemn subject, or the expression would not have escaped him. " Better any weakness in the Church, than a scheming, manœuvring, grasping spirit to get possession of men's minds, and then of their bodies,

and then of their wealth, for one lust will follow
on the other. Our Church has indeed its faults, but
they are faults of individuals, not of the system.
Popery sins rather in its system, and its virtues
are exceptions, and individual."

"Are you not too harsh in your judgment?" said
Bevan.

"And violent, you think," said Villiers. "Every
one, now, who feels strongly, or speaks strongly, is
thought violent. And, perhaps," he continued,
calmly, and smiling at his own earnestness, "moderation is always best; but I have seen popery,
and know its workings, which those who speak of
it with quietness have rarely done."

"And you, then," said Bevan, "are not one of
those who would rebuild these ruins? You ought
rather to look on them complacently. Does it not
delight you," he said, as they entered under the
gateway of the outer court, "to see this old corbel
tottering to its fall, and the rents in that stone
roof?"

Villiers did not answer; for he was examining
the structure with a curious eye, pacing and re-
pacing the gateway to measure its length, and
searching in a heap of rubbish overgrown with
nettles for part of the carved groining which had
fallen down.

"Observe," he said, as they entered the inner
court, "how well they arranged their buildings.
The chapel, or rather church, occupying the most
prominent place, vast, elevated, and ornamented, as
the centre and object of the whole cluster of buildings. Then the refectory, which stood where that
large oriel window is hanging—just there. You see
the low stone pillars of a crypt under it, which, in
fact, formed the kitchen and the cellars; and all the
buildings round — dormitories, offices, and all, were

left low, and almost insignificant. That which belonged to God was first and foremost, that which belonged to man in society was next, that which belonged to the individual was last and lowest. And now our houses are palaces, and our churches are barns."

" Our club-houses, at least," said Bevan, laughingly, " are an exception. They represent man in society, and are splendid enough to represent him as he should be in that capacity."

" Yes," said Villiers, "but it is a society of selfishness ; merely an aggregation of individuals, with no bond to hold them together but their own self-indulgence."

They stood now within the roofless chapel; and Villiers uncovered his head, and Bevan likewise. " Hark !" said Bevan, " what noise was that ?"

" I heard nothing but the brook rushing," said Villiers.

" Yes! there again," said Bevan; " surely there was a noise up there. And he pointed to an old narrow archway, high up in the wall, against the east end of the chapel, and close above the iron grated door which led into the Villiers's vault. Villiers's thoughts were full of other things.

" It is too early in the day for ghosts," said Bevan ; but Villiers, he perceived, had no relish for any thing approaching to a jest. And as he stood gazing on the iron grating, and then as if recovering himself, proceeded once more to pace the chapel in its length and breadth,•as if to take its measurements, Bevan passed out into the cloisters, and was examining the remains of the wall which had enclosed the Prior's garden. Villiers had just completed his survey, and was proceeding to clear away some nettles which had sprung up, and nearly hid an old knight templar's cross-legged figure, when Bevan appeared again at the arch of the

cloister, and beckoned him to come that way; his
hand was held up to motion to him not to make a
noise, and Villiers walked towards him. " Look,"
said Bevan, with a low voice, as he turned the angle
of the buttress, " look up in that corner, by that
mass of ivy, under the window; who can that be?"

" It is a woman," said Villiers.

" And what can she be doing?" said Bevan.

*   *   *   *   *   *

The church clock in Hawkstone had struck one
on the night after Bentley had paid his calamitous
visit to the Priory ruins. From a starry moonlight
sky it had become overcast with clouds, and a heavy
steady rain was pouring down; while gusts of wind
shook the far-scattered gas-lamps, and seemed ready
to extinguish them. The streets were entirely deserted; and, except the pattering of the rain, no
sound had disturbed the sleepers in the High Street,
except, about an hour before, a horse's sharp trot,
coming in from the road to the forest. On the
horse was mounted a respectably-dressed person,
muffled up in a rough cloak, who, after taking his
horse to a stable belonging to the Mason's Arms,
and from thence passing by a private way into the
little green door of the garden belonging to the
Romish priest at Hawkstone, finally retired for the
night to his lodgings at the post-office. A solitary
policeman (for, with manufactures and minings,
there had arrived at Hawkstone, also, the necessity
of a police) stood at the corner of the street, with
his iron-bound hat and glazed cape gleaming in the
gas-light. He also, like Bevan in the ruins, was
struck by hearing a noise; but it was a noise very
different from that of a clashing of iron; it was one
low deep moan, as of a person exhausted and yet
in agony; and then all was still again. The man
stopped and listened, fancying it the wind; and
then to satisfy himself he continued his patrol round

the corner of King Street, till he came within three
or four doors from the post-office. But here he
stopped; for, crouched up on the step of a door, and
exposed to all the pelting of the rain, was a female
figure. His first impression was to order her to go
home. What business had she there at that time
of night? But the poor creature made no reply,
and only continued to rock herself backwards and
forwards, clasping at the same time to her breast
what appeared to be an infant wrapped up in her
mother's shawl.

"Go home, go home," said the policeman; "what
are you doing here?"

And the poor thing opened her eyes, and catching sight of him, sprang up and fell down at his
knees. "Don't strike me again — don't strike me
again — do not murder me, George," she cried; and
then she lowered her voice to a whisper. "I won't
tell — indeed, I won't."

"What's the matter?" said the rough policeman;
"what's the meaning of this, woman? who's going
to murder you?"

"I won't tell, indeed," she continued; "it's all
safe, only don't strike me:" and she clasped his
knees, convulsively. "Any thing but that."

"Any thing but what? Get up, my good woman,"
said the policeman, "get up." And he raised her
up, made her relinquish her hold, and placed her on
the step of the door. As the light from the lamp
fell on the face of the policeman, she passed her thin
wan hands over her eyes, and throwing back her
hair from her young and beautiful face, she gazed
wildly, as if to ascertain where she was. But all
seemed to be a dream.

"Don't be frightened," said the kind-hearted, but
blunt man. "I'm not going to do you any harm.
I won't murder you."

She looked on him wistfully, and then, after a pause, she said, "Why not? I never did any thing for you. I never gave up all for you. Hah!" she cried, as she seemed to catch sight of and recognise his policeman's dress. And closing her lips firmly, as if resolved not to speak, she once more clasped her bundle to her breast, and seemed rocking her baby to sleep.

"What in the world is the matter with her?" said a second policeman, who had now come up.

"I suspect she's out of her senses," said the other. "Look at her clothes, all torn into shreds. She has evidently been through the woods; and her feet— there—one of her shoes is gone, and the other is all covered with blood."

"There's blood here, too," said the other; and he pointed out some large spots on the poor creature's tattered gown, together with some bits of mud, which had apparently been thrown at her.

"How came this?" said the second man, pointing to the mud, and trying to rouse her from her stupor by jogging her arm.

"They flung dirt at me," she said; "the boys flung at me. They called me bad names. But I am not bad—not now," she repeated, faintly. "I was once, but *he* tempted me." And she groaned deeply.

"What's the matter with you?" said the first man; "where are you hurt?"

She remained silent, and bit her lips.

"Where's your pain?" said the second, in a kinder voice, and trying to encourage her. She pressed her hand to her temple, where there were the marks of a contusion.

"Here," she said, "here—he struck me here. There's a great weight here, like lead. Please, sir, to take it off. I'm very ill."

"Are you cold?" said the policeman.

And she shook her head mournfully.

"Are you hungry?"

And again she shook her head.

"Arn't your feet sore?"

And she looked down to her feet, which were covered with blood, but once more shook her head.

"What can we do with her?" said the first policeman to the second. "I suppose we must take her to the station."

But before they could consult further, she sprang up, with a shriek which rang through the deserted street, and chilled their very blood. "Fire! fire! it's on fire. He's set it on fire. Oh, my brain!" And with both her hands clasped on the back of her head, she gave another piercing and horrible cry.

"What in the world is that? What's the matter? Oh, dear me, policeman, what can be the matter?" cried a voice out of a window, which had just opened a few doors below. It was Mrs. Jones, at the post-office.

"Only a poor woman," said the policeman, "not quite right in her mind."

"Oh, drive her away — pray, pray drive her away; do not let her stay here, for the world. What business has she here?"

"Do not be afraid," said the policeman; and as Mrs. Jones put up her window, he muttered a curse upon her for a hard-hearted fool. But another window opened, and another voice, that of a man, from the same house, demanded authoritatively, what was the meaning of such a noise in the streets at that time of night. It was Mr. Peters, or Pearce, or by what other *alias* he chose to pass. The same answer was given. And with something of an oath at the woman for disturbing his slumbers, Mr. Pearce told them to take her to the station; and, closing his own window, retired again to rest. Alas! how little do people within the houses of a town think at night of those who are without!

"Wouldn't you like to go home, my good woman?" said the policeman.

"No, no," she murmured weakly, for, as if exhausted with pain, she had sunk once more on the step. "Not home, not home! He'll strike me again; and it would kill me. Oh, to be struck by him!"

"Who's him? Who struck you?" asked the second policeman, pertinaciously endeavouring to extract the facts, but ignorant of the mode of doing it, and becoming impatient. But once more she seemed to catch sight of his policeman's dress, and her lips were sealed. "He did not do it," she said, doggedly. "It's false. He never meant it. 'Twas all play. I know he did not mean it. Am not I his wife? Am not I his Margaret, that he used to love so—that gave up all for him. Yes—all, all!" And she groaned again bitterly. "He couldn't do it. Go away, go away," and she pushed the policeman from her. "Let me get up," she continued, as the man endeavoured to take hold of her, and lead her away. "Let me get up. I'm wanted." And she folded her dress about her, as if preparing to depart quietly. "My baby wants me. I have not given it its supper. I must go home."

"Why, what's this?" asked the policeman, trying to uncover the shawl which she had enveloped in her arms; "I thought this was your baby?"

The poor woman looked at him, as he withdrew fold after fold, but it was with a vacant stare. The shawl contained nothing but some straw, which she had apparently taken from a barn, and made up to hold in her arms like an infant.

"What's this?" asked the policeman, as he un-

covered it. And Margaret, letting her eyes wander
idly from the bundle to the man, suffered it to fall
from her arms with an expression of utter desolation.

"I'm not well," she said. "I don't think I'm
quite right here," and she laid her forehead on her
hands. "Things seem to go round with me. You
won't hurt me, will you? I'm a poor woman."

"Hurt you!" said the policeman; "no, to be
sure not. You had better come with us, and we'll
put you into shelter. Here, take hold of my arm."

But once again she sprang up. "Hush!" she
said, "it's crying for me; and I waiting here. It's
cold. It wants me. Yes," she repeated, with a low
voice, and shuddering all over, "it's cold — very cold
where they laid it, and dark and lonesome. And
the rain beats upon it. And I not there to keep it
warm. Let me go, let me go," she screamed.
"There's its cry again — my baby's cry!" And
bursting, with all the strength of a maniac, from the
hand of the policeman, she rushed along the street,
turned down some alleys, which she appeared to
thread familiarly, and was lost in the darkness of
the night. What passed in the remainder of the
night no one knew. A cottager indeed, about two
miles off, had been awakened, about four o'clock, by
three frightful shrieks under his window; but he
was too terrified and superstitious to rise and inquire what it meant. The under-keeper at the
Priory also, in going his rounds early in the morning, had found a bonnet torn and dirtied, and under
the bushes, in the same place, marks as if a person
had lain there recently. And it was early in the
afternoon when Villiers and Bevan reached the
ruins.

"It is a poor woman," said Villiers, as he stood at
the angle of the great north transept, looking at her.

" But observe," said Bevan, " she has no bonnet; her hair is all torn, her gown in tatters, and her feet without shoes, and swollen, and lacerated!"

She was, in fact, kneeling down on the wet grass, on a spot where the turf seemed recently to have been raised and replaced. And with part of the blade of a rusty knife, which she had picked up, she was digging out the earth with all her strength. Villiers and Bevan approached quietly without being perceived.

" I'm coming," she said, " I'm coming, my own darling — wait a moment, I'm coming. Don't cry, for it kills me! He did not mean to hurt you. I know he did not. His own baby!"

And she continued to scrabble up the mould with both her hands. " I'm coming, darling, darling! he shan't hurt you. Ah! ah!" And throwing down the knife, and stopping both her ears with her hands — " It's that scream!" she shrieked, — " its last scream!" And she sank shuddering to the ground, and lay as dead, with only a slight convulsive twitching of one hand, showing that she was still alive.

" Poor thing!" said Bevan, " what can we do with her?"

" We must take her to a cottage," said Villiers, " and then make inquiry for her friends. She can scarcely be a native of this place."

But Margaret heard their voices, and, turning up her delicate face, beautiful, even disfigured as it was, she was recognised by Bevan, who had, like Bentley and Villiers himself, seen her when they went to see Connell and the boy after the fire.

" What can be the meaning of this?" said Bevan, " It's poor Margaret Wheeler!"

" Margaret! Margaret!" she repeated, faintly. " Yes, he used to call me his own Margaret; but that was when he loved me. Who are you? what do you want?" and she turned fiercely towards Bevan and Villiers. "What right have you here, spying out secrets? There are no secrets. He will kill you too. Go away, go away, I tell you. He has nothing to do with it. I did it. It was I—not he!"

"Did what?" asked Villiers, gently. But Margaret was again resting on her knees, with her face buried in her hands, and apparently hearing nothing.

"There is evidently something mysterious in this," said Bevan. "I wonder if we could find any trace of information. There is something here." And gently lifting her pocket without disturbing her, he took out of it a gold watch. "What can be the meaning of this?" said Bevan.—"Why this is Bentley's watch; here is his crest; I know it by the old-fashioned chasing; it belonged to his aunt. He showed it me the other day as a curiosity."

"Singular!" said Villiers. "Take care of it. But let us first attend to this poor creature." And with a quiet soothing voice, he endeavoured to persuade her to get up and come with them.

"Oh! gentlemen," she said, "you are very kind, very good, if you would but help me. You see it's cold and wet; and I am its mother. There's no one else to take care of it. And they have smothered it; and I cannot get this off." And once more she began to scrabble up the mould. "Make haste! make haste! or it will die. It's crying for me!" she said; and she laid down her ear to the ground. "I'm coming, I'm coming, darling! Make haste!" And, with all her strength, and straining every nerve, she tried to remove the turf. "Help me, help me!" she cried; "help me, help me! I'm coming, darling—coming, coming!" And her voice became fainter and fainter, and her movements more convulsive; and repeating the same words again and again, till they died on her lips, she sank down lifeless.

As the persons whom Bevan went to fetch were removing her to the keeper's cottage, which was the nearest place of shelter, Villiers looked back at the ruins from a little distance, and observed a man, who had emerged from the chapel, go hurriedly to the spot where Margaret had been found, and after hastily endeavouring to efface the marks which she had made, he looked round as if afraid to have been seen, and leaping across the brook, he struck off into the copse, and disappeared among the bushes.

" There is something in this which requires to be examined into," said Bevan.

" Yes; and we will do it to-morrow, but quietly," was Villiers's reply. " Never make a bustle; say nothing, and we shall unravel the mystery."

" I will go back," said Bevan, " and look at the spot, and then go into Hawkstone and see Mr. Bentley, while you wait till Mr. Morgan comes out."

" He stopped at the keeper's cottage as he returned, and called Villiers out. He had found, on closer examination, that the ground had been trampled on as in a struggle. In one place was the mark of a man's knee on the wet clay, and the grass had been stained with something. Bevan almost feared to say what he thought it was. But the most alarming thing was a fragment of a white cravat, with the mark of a bloody thumb on it, and the initials T. B. in the corner. Bevan was horror-struck as a thought flashed across his mind.

" I must go immediately," he said, " into Hawkstone."

" Instantly!" said Villiers. And as Bevan, hurried and agitated, reached Bentley's door and found Mrs. Alsop almost in tears with her anxiety about her

master, a little urchin brought a note to the door
from Bentley.

"Thank God, thank God!" exclaimed Bevan.

It was Bentley's note, written under Cookesley's
direction.

"And where did you bring this from, boy?"

"From Cuxteth Heath."

"And who gave it you, — Mr. Bentley?"

"No, sir."

"Who was it?"

The boy hesitated to tell; and Bevan was obliged
to threaten him.

"It was a man in a drab jacket."

"A workman?"

"Yes."

"Does Mr. Bentley ever go there, Mrs. Alsop?"

"Not that I know of, sir."

"Has he any friends in that direction?"

"I never heard, sir."

"Why did you hesitate, boy, to tell us about it?"

"The man gave me a sixpence, and told me not
to say anything."

"This is Mr. Bentley's watch, is it not, Mrs.
Alsop?"

"Yes, sir," said Mrs. Alsop; "to be sure it is.
Where did you find it?"

But Bevan, anxious and perplexed, thought it
best not to inform her.

"This is certainly Mr. Bentley's handwriting,"
he observed. "Here are the crossings of his t's,
and his y at the end of his signature. But it seems
cramped and awkward: how the letters straggle;
and the lines are not straight. Here, boy, come
with me." And he returned to Villiers, at the
keeper's lodge, taking the poor trembling urchin
with him for further examination. And the result
of the examination was, that both gentlemen sent

for their horses, and, late as it was, and near sunset, accompanied by the keeper and one of his men, they set forward to Cuxteth Heath.

"It's a bad place, sir, that heath!" said the keeper, a thick-set, sturdy English yeoman. "It's the place where Jack Roberts was robbed last week. The men in the forest are a terrible set. But I've brought my rifle, sir; and I see you've got a good stick, sir; and here's another for you, Mr. Bevan." And the party set out.

CHAP. IV.

THE sun had set for some time behind the huge grey granite range of mountains which bound the wild district known by the name of Hawkstone Forest. The shadows of the evening were deepening; and the glare of the furnaces and iron-works blazed out more luridly upon the blackened disfigured hosts of workmen who were standing about in the steep narrow street of Howlas, the village, or almost town, of low wretched houses which had sprung up recently, since the opening of the works by Sir Matthew Blake. The men themselves, instead of going home after their work, or laughing and talking openly in the street, were gathered together in little knots. One or two of them had dirty newspapers in their hands, from which they were reading out portions to groups of others. Even the women, slatternly and hollow-eyed, seemed to take a deeper interest than ordinary in what was passing; and, with their babies in their arms, forced their way into the little knots of political disputants, and added their angry voices to the arguments which exasperated their husbands against the existing state of things.

" Bread risen two-pence a gallon !" sighed Jenny Ball, a poor wan-looking creature with two young children hanging about her. " And I've nothing to give them. And John gone away to find work !"

" Work !" responded Mrs. Jubb, a red-armed and red-faced virago. " Where's he to get work ? Arn't

three more furnaces to be blown out to-morrow?
And what's to become of us then?"

" Let's go to Sir Matthew at once," proposed the
more decent and pacific Mrs. Smith, who seemed to
have more confidence in the tender mercies of a
money-making age than a longer experience would
have justified.

" Go to Sir Matthew!" cried Mrs. Jubb. " What
good would Sir Matthew do you, or ten thousand
the like of him?"

" Isn't it by us," asked Mary Adams, " that he
makes his money? And there he is, a hundred miles
off, as rich as a Jew."

" John," said the first speaker, " did go to the
house. He told me it was such a fine place—
all beautiful gardens, and trees, and fine servants;
and just as he came up to the door, Madam Blake
and her children were all going out in a fine gilt
carriage. But the servants swore at him, and would
not let him come up. And then he met Sir Matthew,
riding by himself in the park, and spoke to him, and
told him who he was (poor fellow! he hadn't
touched a bit of bread that day), and Sir Matthew
fell into a passion, and told him to get about his
business. ' He left all that,' he said ' to the agent.'"

" And the agent deserves to be shot!" cried the
virago.

" And he'll have his deserts soon," muttered a black-
looking ruffian, with a quantity of hair about his
face.

" Ah!" murmured Jenny to herself, " it was the
agent drove us here. We never thought of leaving
our cottage while my lord lived on his estate; and
we had our garden, and kept a pig and a cow; and
every thing went well with us, till my lord went
away. And then Farmer Speed wanted to pull down
the cottage, and declared the garden took John from

his work. And the agent did not mind so long as he got the rent; and so we were turned out on the world."

"And came up to the hills to get work!" cried the virago, with a bitter laugh. "Work for three months, and then starving!"

"If we had but saved a little," said Mrs. Smith, more quietly, "it would be something."

"And how's a poor man to save?" asked Mrs. Jubb. "Don't they grind down his wages to the lowest they can?"

"I remember," said Jenny, "when we had our cottage, my lady and the young ladies used to come and see us very often; and every Monday morning either Miss Mary or the clergyman came, and we gave them sixpence to put by for us; and when we were ill, or wanted some money to buy a cow, or the like, there was always something to look to."

"I should like to see Madam Blake, or her fine daughters, doing anything of the kind," cried the virago. "Why they'd be afraid of coming near us, for fear of blacking their fine gowns."

"They live so far off," interposed Mrs. Smith, in a mediatorial tone.

"Aye," rejoined Mrs. Jubb; "they don't like to come here, up in the hills, where they get all their money from. It does not do among fine ladies and gentlemen to be a coal-merchant, or an iron-man."

"Madam Blake did come up here once," said poor Jenny; "I recollect, just about the time of the election; and she rode up in a fine carriage, with some fine ladies with her. But she didn't speak to any of us, and held her handkerchief to her nose all the time, as if she was afraid of catching the plague."

"Aye," continued the virago, "I remember, too. And when my girl Susan, with the young ones, got close to Miss Julia, madam's daughter, and was looking at her fine dress, what did Miss Julia do but told her to get away, a nasty dirty thing, or she'd spoil her gown!"

" Well! they'll all get their dues very shortly," muttered the same ruffian as before. " That's one comfort."

But further remarks from him were checked by a burst of uproar from a large body collected round an orator at the corner of the street. " Down with them! down with them! down with the rascally Tories!"

" That's right!" thundered the speaker, as soon as the clamour had subsided. " Down with the Tories! They are the men that suck your blood, and grind your life out. What care they for the people's groans, or the cries of your starving children, so long as they can fatten in luxury, and keep you all chained like slaves?"

" Down with them! down with them!" was again clamoured forth from a hundred voices. " Down with the bloody tyrants!"

" Sir Matthew ain't a Tory," cried a voice from the mob. " No!" continued the speaker, " he's worse; he's one of your brutal, cheating, palavering Whigs, that are always promising the people to do something for them, when they are out of place themselves, and when they get in they are worse than the Tories, ten times over. No, my friends, the Charter! the Charter! Nothing will do you any good but that. Hurrah for the Charter!"

And caps, and hats, and voices, and hands, all simultaneously went up into the air.

" What do they mean by the Charter?" asked Jenny of Mrs. Jubb.

" I'm sure I don't know," was the reply; " but it's something, my man tells me, is to raise the

wages, and give us bread for two-pence a gallon,
and beer for nothing."

" And tea and sugar?" asked Mrs. Smith, who
was remarkably fond of that beverage.

" Oh !" said Mrs. Jubb, "tea and sugar is to be
supplied by the parish."

" And there are to be no poor-laws?" asked Mrs.
Smith.

" No poor-laws, no poor-laws!" caught up the
mob. " Down with the poor-laws!"

" And no parsons!" said another voice.

" And no gentlemen!" cried a third. "Down
with the parsons! down with the gentlemen!" Down
with the parsons! was the universal cry.

" And your bishops!" exclaimed another man,
with a huge head of red hair, and in the dress of a
butcher, with something sinister about his eyes, and
a singular demeanour, as if with great powers of disguising himself he was still not perfectly at home
in his dress.

" Yes, your bishops!" continued the orator. "I'll
just read you here a paper, telling you how much
they grind out from the sweat of the poor. Here's
the Archbishop of Canterbury 100,000*l.* a-year;
the Archbishop of York 90,000*l.*; the Bishop of
Winchester 80,000*l.*; the Bishop of Durham 50,000*l.*
— and all for doing nothing."

" No bishops, no bishops! No parsons! Down
with the parsons!" re-echoed the mob; and it may
well be supposed the substantives were not allowed
to stand alone, but were supported by various very
expressive and not laudatory epithets, which, as we
are not writing for a class of readers who might
wish to be initiated in them, we do not feel it necessary to repeat.

" And yet," whispered poor Jenny Blake to the
woman standing next her, " I've known a good

parson. When we had our cottage and our garden," (and the thought of it seemed to bring water
into her wasted eyes,) " our parson Harris (and he
was a real gentleman, and the son of a Lord) used
to come and see us regularly; and he'd sit down in
our cottage, for I always kept it clean; and we had
some nice crockery, and two geraniums, and flowers
in the garden, and all comfortable. And he'd talk
to us quite friendly like. And when John got the
fever, and nobody else would come near us, Parson
Harris came just as much as ever; and used to
send us wine, and read prayers to him every day."

" Prayers !" cried the virago; " what's the use of
prayers and such stuff? All cant and humbug — a
vile methodistical canting crew!" And poor Jenny
was silenced. But she thought of Parson Harris,
and of the Bible he had given her, and of the advice by which she had profited, and of the quiet
Sunday's walking with John to the village church
through the green cheerful meadows, and of the
change which took place in him after his illness,
in which the parson had contrived to make him
think seriously of many things which he had before
neglected. And she remembered how thankful she
had been, and happy, though she could not exactly
say why, when, in obedience to the parson's injunctions, they had both come together to partake of the
Holy Communion; and had felt more love and confidence in each other than ever before, because
they had now some foundation for it in the promise of God to bless them. But at Howlas there
were no parsons and no church. And though the
Methodists had run up a small red-brick conventicle,
with pointed windows and shutters, in which Mr.
Ebenezer Starling, the shoemaker of Hawkstone,
used to preach every Sunday evening, religion was
a word with which the inhabitants of the Howlas

coal and iron works felt that they had nothing to
do. Sir Matthew Blake was the only power on
which they felt dependence. And as religion had
no obvious tendency to lay open new veins of coal,
or to raise the market for iron, or to cheapen the
wages of workmen, Sir Matthew felt that it was a
subject with which he had no right to interfere.
His object was income! and with income he was
perfectly content. We must not, however, do him
injustice. He had lately subscribed twenty pounds
to build a chapel-of-ease at Howlas, on the earnest
remonstrances of the bishop, and representations
made by his agent of the alarming state of the
workmen, and of the need of some moral control
over them. And it should also be said in his favour,
that he had done this even at a time when the
income from his iron-works had dwindled from
15,000*l.* to 12,000*l.* a-year ; and the late cold spring
had so raised the price of early forced strawberries,
that Lady Blake, at her last London party, had
been obliged to give two guineas a pottle for them.
Sir Matthew had observed this item in his monthly
accounts just before he signed his cheque for the
church, which otherwise he had intended to have
made thirty pounds. But, as he properly said, justice to himself and to his family was the first thing
to be considered. And with such enormous drains
upon his income, and the necessity of keeping up
his station in society (Sir Matthew had himself
in his youth wielded a pickaxe in the mines which
were then his own), it was, he said, imperative on
him,'—he felt himself, in fact, conscientiously bound,
to be prudent and economical.

By degrees, the hearers and talkers in the dirty
blackened streets of Howlas dropped off to their respective habitations, — some to a cold comfortless
hearth, round which a knot of ragged children quar-

relled over their scanty meal of potatoes and salt;
others to endure the scolding of their more thrifty
but ill-tempered wives; and others to drive out the
thoughts both of past and future, by prolonging
their beer-house orgies, with a few reckless comrades, till midnight — but all fevered and fretted
with a sense of misery and want, from which they
saw no relief in peaceableness or order; all throwing
the burden of their distress, not on their own im-
providence or vice, or on the avarice of their employer, but on their rulers and the laws; all busily
engaged in dreaming of a coming hour, when their
own physical powers would work their relief, and
the grand revolution would arrive, in which all men
would have their rights — or, to interpret the phrase
according to its real meaning in their ears, when
every one would have every thing. As the last
knot of talkers broke up, with the breaking down of
an old tub, from which a fluent frothy chartist orator
had been addressing them, two of the party disengaged themselves from the rest, and passed down
a dark back lane, till they reached the open road.
Blacker was one; and the other, a stout close-
shaven, iron-faced person, whom, notwithstanding
the substitution of a brown for a red head of hair,
and rough corduroy trowsers, and smock frock, for
the butcher's blue apron, might have been recognised
by the cunning of his eyes as Mr. Pearce.

" And now," said he to his companion, " tell me
the whole story."

And Blacker, with that mixture of freedom and
deference which conceited men exhibit to those
whom they regard as connected with persons superior in rank, and yet wish to ape and imitate in the hope of obtaining the same advantage
for themselves, proceeded to recount some of the
facts which have been lately placed before the

reader, — the sum of them being, according to his version of the story, that Wheeler had found his wife and the parson Bentley at the Priory ruins at ten o'clock at night, when he was removing the arms — that a scuffle took place — Wheeler had stabbed Bentley in the side — then alarmed at the consequences of a discovery, which might not only have risked his own life but have involved the detection of the whole plot in which he was engaged, he had proposed, with the two men who came down from the forest with the cart to take away the arms, that the wounded man should be thrown into the priory well; but just as they were dragging the body to it, Connell returned, and having, for some reason or other, some influence with Wheeler, he had begged Bentley off, on condition that he should be brought to take an oath of secresy, and be put under strict guard for some days, till he could be taken back to his home, if his wound proved slight ; and thus the whole story might be kept quiet. The fear that any inquiry after Bentley might lead to the discovery of the plans, which were expected to be ripe for action in a few days, was the principal consideration which induced the reckless brutal Wheeler to consent to the reprieve of his victim.

Pearce listened to this tale with his brow knit in thought, and his little twinkling eyes almost retiring farther into his head, as if that they might pierce deeper into all its consequences and applications. He did not interrupt Blacker with a single remark — suffered him to proceed in his own half-familiar and half-consequential tone — permitted him even to lay his hand on his shoulder, to assume something of an admonitory style, and to recommend him to say nothing to Wheeler; until Blacker, presuming on his silence, proceeded to address him —

"Now, my good fellow, I would advise you to go back to Hawkstone, and we will —— " But at this point Pearce quietly removed the hand from its familiar posture, and begged his presuming companion to attend to his own business. " I have not chosen and recommended you to my friends, Mr. Blacker, for the purpose of giving us advice, but of executing our orders. *We* are perfectly aware of the course which is to be pursued. And you will do well to remember this . . . Have the goodness to tell me, sir, where they have taken the clergyman to?"

Even Blacker himself, accustomed to see Pearce in different situations as well as in different attires, was thrown back, and taken by surprise at the decided authoritative tone in which he now spoke. But Pearce knew his man — a vain, weak, ambitious person, educated (for, in the present day, who is not educated?), who could write, and read, and cipher (for he had been educated at a National School), and made use of his accomplishments to write speeches for meetings of mechanics and Chartists, and to read not only as many Sunday newspapers as he could obtain, but even a higher class of publications on politics, religion, and all the other interests of life, which a certain class of writers are now endeavouring to lower to the comprehension, and submit to the judgment, of the people, — meaning by the people the majority of the nation, as told by the head. Blacker's ambition was that of a little, bustling mind, fond of obtaining importance by being admitted to secrets, trusted with a little power, and permitted to associate with persons above him. He was just the character which the system of Romanism would have seized on and turned into a pliant instrument in the hands of religion. And though there were points in his character which made him dangerous, because those who are fond of hearing are inclined also to be fond of talking, he possessed a certain degree of influence with the lower classes of workmen and his general companions, and was free from many of those faults, such as drunkenness, which rendered it impossible for Pearce to trust others. Having the key to his mind, Pearce knew how to rule it; and by alternate confidence and mystery, by maintaining his own superiority, and at the same time flattering his tool with occasional panegyrics, and prospects of advancement to a still higher share in the great work before them — and especially by allowing him to have glimpses of the important part which Pearce himself was playing, and of his confidential communication with other great personages — he found it easier, as well as safer, to employ Blacker for his purposes than Wheeler, whose thorough selfishness and profligacy placed him beyond all control. Wheeler, also, he had incautiously admitted to some part of his confidence before his character became thoroughly bad; he had even trusted him with some important papers, which Wheeler was to transmit to another party. But, with as much cunning as Pearce himself, he had pretended to lose them, and still retained them in his own possession, with the secret resolution of not giving them up, in proportion as he found that Pearce began to distrust him, and was employing Blacker to perform many important services which had before been committed to himself. Among these was the distribution of sundry sums of money, of which Pearce appeared to have considerable command, though he managed it with economy and prudence in the prosecution of his plans. In fact, Wheeler had formed views and objects of his own, which Pearce would willingly

have made subservient to his own, could he have
made Wheeler a pliant and submissive instrument.
And when this became impracticable, the next thing
was to remove him.

But, for the present, we must leave the con-
federates, and return to Villiers.

CHAP. V.

VILLIERS himself was an active and indefatigable
walker; but Bevan's slight frame, and evident inability to endure much exertion, suggested to the
keeper the necessity of waiting for their horses at a
farm-house occupied by one of Villiers's principal
tenants. The boy, a shrewd cunning little imp, was
then placed before the keeper, and they rode on.
The road ran in the same direction with that along
which Bentley had been carried. It rose up from
the rich valley in which the ruins of the Priory lay,
and mounted along the side of a deep ravine, at the
bottom of which a torrent, sparkling at intervals
through a hanging mass of oak and hazel thicket,
was dashing over a bed of limestone rock, and
hollowing its passage through a labyrinth of little
caverns and crags. As it ascended, the view opened
over a wider expanse of high table-land, thinly cultivated, but dotted over with miserable cabins. At
intervals the brown moor was broken by heaps of
coal and slag, and the blackened sheds and tall
chimneys belonging to the steam-engines, which
drew the water from the pits; and, above all, rose
the gaunt jagged outline of the mountain ridge,
which was known as Hawkstone Forest. Villiers,
who had known the district as a boy, when permitted to accompany the keeper in a shooting expedition, before its solitude had been disturbed by
the discovery of its mineral treasures, was pained at
the change which had taken place.

" And yet," he said to Bevan, " these are the
elements of wealth ; Nature intended them to be
employed in the service of man.   They foster industry, stimulate arts, contribute to the comforts of
life.   Alas! that all this should be purchased at the
expense of so many higher and holier interests —
that the treasures of a nation should be supplied by
converting its populace into demons !"

And as Villiers uttered these words, he pointed
out to his companion a gang of blackened, de-
bauched, ferocious ruffians, who were just returning
from the pit's mouth with some carts.   The keeper,
a shrewd, sensible, English yeoman, happened to
overhear him.   He fancied, also, that he perceived
some sign of recognition between the boy and the
people in the road ; and, riding up to the side of his
master, and touching his hat, he ventured to suggest that they should ride on, as the evening was
closing round them.

" It is a dangerous thing, sir," he said, " to make
more show, or say more than is necessary in these
places.   This is no regular road ; and they may be
after inquiring where we are going.   I know these
people here well ; and if your honour will trust me,
I think I can manage to find what we want : but we
had better press on." Villiers readily complied with
his suggestion.   But just at that moment, and as
they were preparing to cross the head of the ravine,
which was there covered thicker than before with an
underwood of hazel along its precipitous sides, the
drivers of the carts seemed to have received some
signal, or else clumsily to become careless of their
driving, and drew across the road so as to startle
the horses, and throw the whole party into confusion.   As the keeper remonstrated, and was occupied in getting clear of the obstruction, the boy
managed to slide off from the horse, plunged into the

thicket, and before any of them could recover their surprise he had let himself down by branch and rock to the bottom of the hollow, and was making his escape through it without the possibility of pursuing him. The keeper and Villiers both leaped from their horses to follow him, but it was too late; and, as they turned to vent their indignation against the carts, which had caused the obstruction and escape, they observed a sort of significant laugh and chuckle between two of the most ruffianlike pitmen, who seemed to be captains of the gang. But the carts moved out of the way; the men touched their hats as they passed, not without a look of triumph as at the success of some little manœuvre; and the keeper, a cool thoughtful Englishman, having calculated the advantages of expressing his indignation, and perhaps his suspicion, thought it better to take no notice, and move on.

"There is some mischief here," said Villiers to him, as they rode on. "You understand this district better than I do. What is the best course to pursue? Had we not better go at once to a magistrate?"

"Magistrate! sir," exclaimed the keeper; "there's no magistrate can do us any good in such a place as this. Why, the whole ground, sir, under our feet is tunnelled and hollowed out; and half the people are under the earth, while the other half are above it. And a pretty set it is,—the very scum of all the worst places in England, which has taken refuge here; and not a soul to take care of them, or keep them right. Heathens, sir,—worse than heathens! and miserable, too. It's a hard life they lead—women and children, all of them in darkness and filth, and cold. I have heard some of the poor children tell of what they have gone through; and it makes one's blood run cold." Villiers at any other time would have encouraged the sturdy yeoman in his communications, for he knew that much was to be learned from them. But his increasing anxiety in regard to Bentley, and his conviction that some mischief had happened to him, would not allow him to think of anything else. He reproached himself with not having endeavoured to pursue and recover the boy; but the keeper soon satisfied him that the attempt would have been hopeless. The side of the ravine was at that spot nearly perpendicular; and none but a boy, unencumbered and accustomed to expert climbing, could have found his way to the bottom; and even there it would have been impossible to prevent his escape among the hollows of the rocks. " In addition to which," continued the yeoman, " we must have left our horses here ; not among friends, sir; I did not like the looks of that gang. And I suspect they knew more of the boy than it was convenient to confess."

" And what, then, are we to do?" asked Villiers.

" I think, sir," said the keeper, " if your honour will trust to me, I can find out something about the matter. I know something of this pit-folk ; and one of them, if I can find him out, owes me a return for a kindness which I once did him. He is rather a superior kind of man, better educated than the rest; and if your honour will keep quiet, and say nothing, he may be able to help us."

They had now reached the middle of the flat moor, in which the great iron works of the forest were situated ; and hastening on as the evening closed in them, they came at a turn of the road upon a point, where they looked down on the wilderness of blackened cabins which had grown up round them. Tall chimneys vomiting clouds of smoke, which blighted and encrusted the whole side of the mountains; vast sheds roofed in with iron

plates, and seemingly in ruins; gigantic wheels
turning and groaning; and levers of steam-engines
heaving as if wearily, but eternally, up and down;
the whole surrounded with rows of squalid little
cottages, without garden or fence, or creeper, or
any thing to suggest comfort or give enjoyment;
and at their dunghill-piled doors and fractured windows groups of filthy men and haggard women,
some drunken and others quarrelling and blas-
pheming, — such was the picture which presented
itself. Villiers looked round, but in vain, for a
spire or tower — any thing indicating a church;
but there was none. Two shabby meeting-houses
he passed; but when he thought of the work necessary to be achieved, and remembered what he had
seen in America, he had little faith in the power of
meeting-houses to promote either the peace or the
morality of the empire. It was with a heavy heart
that both Bevan and himself followed the guidance
of the keeper to a little inn, neater than any other
building, and dignified with the name of the Blake
Arms Commercial Hotel; and consigning the horses
to the ostler, they waited in a decent parlour the
return of the keeper, who went to search for his
acquaintance. Two hours passed heavily without
his appearing. Both Bevan and Villiers were too
anxious to converse; and even the mountain air
had failed to give them an appetite for the meal
which the waiting-maid served up to them. At
last a knock was heard at the door, and the keeper
made his appearance. He was evidently dismayed;
and Bevan, whose courage was not quite of so high
a pitch as Villiers's, began to think with regret on
the chances which had led him into such an expedition. The keeper explained, however, that he
had contrived to find his acquaintance — that he had
sounded him with respect to Bentley — and was

satisfied that the pitman knew more than he was
willing to disclose.

"In fact, sir, from what he said, I cannot help
fearing that things are as bad as we thought. I
tried him, sir, by threats, but that would not do;
for he would not say a word. Then I went to promises, and offered him money; but this would not
do. At last, sir, I thought it best to mention your
name; and then he told me that he had been obliged
to me for some kindnesses, and that if a gentleman
wished to speak with him, he would not mind seeing
him. But he was a gentleman himself once, though
now he is only a pitman, and would not regard so
much what he said to you. So, sir, if you like to
come along with me to the Horton works, I will
contrive to get you a chat with him: but I think,
sir, you had better come alone; only, please sir, I
hope you will take care and not commit yourself,
for these are dangerous folk to deal with."

Villiers promised to be cautious; and, under the
guidance of his keeper, he proceeded to the Horton
works. It was now pitch dark. The streets, if
streets they might be called, were only dimly and
partially lighted by a stray candle or two from an
occasional shop or public-house, and by a lurid
glare which spread over the horizon above the roof-
tops. Many more persons were straggling along
them than they had met earlier in the evening; and
shouts of vulgar revelry and singing were heard
from the beer-shops, which occurred at every step.

"Don't mind, sir," said the keeper, as Villiers
seemed to hesitate at the corner of a filthy alley,
"don't mind, sir; Cookesley is a man I think you
may trust. He has told me often that he was born
to better things."

And it was indeed Cookesley, the same whom we
have met already at Bentley's bed-side, who had

become acquainted with the keeper in some shooting excursion, and with whom Villiers was now to
communicate.   Villiers smiled at the thought of his
servant suspecting him of fear; and made his way
as quickly as he could through the mud and filth of
the nearest approach to the Horton works.   If he
had had no other object in view, he would have
been repaid by the sight which met him at the
entrance — a sight by daylight only dreary and offensive, but in the night-time even sublime.   He was
groping his way in the dark, and had stumbled and
nearly fallen in crossing one of the tram-roads, with
which the whole ground was cut up ; and, in recovering himself, he had been all but run over by
a line of coal-waggons, which were moving along
the path ; when, on looking up, he saw a vast range
of cavern-like arches yawning before him, and
within each, in a deep recess, a furnace, vomiting
forth a blast of flame too bright for the eye to rest
on.   Above him, ranges of chimneys, which broke
the long line of ragged roof, were themselves throwing up a roaring blaze, and flaming out like towers
and steeples amidst the ruins of a sacked town,
abandoned to general conflagration.   All around,
the very earth seemed to breathe forth fire ; here
playing in lambent blue flames, and there throwing
out great volumes of ruddy smoke, amidst vast
mounds and piles, which, by daylight, were ashes
and refuse, coals and slag, but by night wore the
aspect, among the flames, of ruined ramparts and
battlements, and walls of buildings recently devoted
to destruction.   The buildings themselves, mostly
of cast iron, presented vast arches and framework,
which, seen with the glare of furnaces behind them,
showed like enormous cloisters, of which the interior
was partly consumed and partly still on fire.   The
noise of wheels, the rushing of the flames, the hiss-

ing of water, the beating and throbbing of gigantic engines on each side, the cranking of chains, and the deep hoarse blasts of the furnaces, sounded in Villiers's ears more awful than any thing he had ever heard even in the battle-field. Nor was the irresistible suggestion of an earthly Pandæmonium anyway counteracted by the form of human beings grim with intemperance and exhaustion, and pale as spectres in the glare of the fires, who moved about in silence; here tossing about enormous bars of white hot iron, as if they were so many sticks; here seizing and passing them from side to side that they might be pressed under ponderous rollers, which tossed off from them, as the bars appeared and reappeared beneath their jaws, a shower of flakes of fire and molten metal. In one place half-naked workmen were feeding the piles of fuel, into which the blasts poured their torrent of flame; and in another, with unwieldy crowbars they were breaking open the furnaces themselves, and pouring out the liquid lava of metal to run in streams of dazzling brilliancy into a labyrinth of currents. Villiers stood amazed; the noise was too deafening to hear or to speak. And the keeper, who was more familiar with the place, took him by the arm and led him round to a shed in the back part of the buildings, where a dark figure was standing against the wall, and spoke to the keeper on their approach with a manner and language far superior to what might have been expected from his dirty fustian jacket, and hands and face begrimed with filth.

Few persons possessed in a greater degree than Villiers that tact and knowledge of the world which enables us at once to see the accessible points of human character, and to meet them upon that footing on which they most wish to be treated. His pride was that of station, and had nothing in it

either personal or selfish ; and he knew that among
the poorest of men, reduced by fortune from their
original position as gentlemen—that even where the
degradation has been caused by vice—still there are
few things to which the mind clings with so much
fondness as the name and old associations of a gentleman. It was as much from delicacy of feeling,
from essential good nature, from the confidence
which his own honour induced him to place in
others, as from policy and manœuvre, that he resolved to throw himself at once upon the feelings
which it was possible the unhappy man before him
might still retain from his former situation ; and
therefore dismissing the keeper, he took Cookesley's
hand, led him into the shed, where a dim rushlight
was burning on a plank, and making him sit down
on the only seat there was, he proceeded to tell him
openly his name and his object. A short-sighted
manœuvrer would have endeavoured to hide both,
and would have thought it prudence. Villiers hated
mystery, and had no fear, that he should practice
concealment ; and his course was the wisest.
Cookesley knew both before. But the openness and
manliness of the communication, the confidence
which it reposed, and the little marks of respect
which Villiers showed when he alluded to his knowledge of Cookesley's former condition, won instantly
on all the unhappy man's better feelings. Something of his own self-respect returned on finding
himself treated with respect by a man like Villiers.

" I think, sir," he said, " we had better put out
this light, for I should not like to be seen holding
communication with you here. They would suspect
something ; and we are rather a lawless set. Stay,
sir, you can come round with me to see the works.
Gentlemen often do that at night, and then I can
answer you any questions which it is safe for me

to do without our being noticed. You have put
confidence in me, sir. I am sure I may put confidence in you."

He then proceeded to tell him so much of Bentley's
story as he had heard himself: that he had been
found late at the Priory ruins by Wheeler, and
Wheeler's wife with him; that there had been a
scuffle, and Bentley had been stabbed; and that he
would have been thrown into the well but for the
interposition of an Irishman, whom he had been
kind to; and that he was brought up into the forest
to be sworn to secrecy, and kept there till he could
return without compromising any one. "He is
here, sir; and I happen to be a friend of his—an old
schoolfellow, though I am now in this plight; and
I will do every thing I can for him."

Villiers was thoroughly shocked; shocked at the
suggestion which Cookesley took care to give of the
cause of the scuffle; shocked at the narrowness of
the escape; shocked at Bentley's present situation.
"Was the wound dangerous?" he asked.

"No, sir; I was myself, as you have heard, bred
for a doctor, and have taken care of it. But he
must be kept quiet."

"And can I see him?" asked Villiers.

Cookesley not only shook his head, but answered,
peremptorily, "No! It would be as much as his
life is worth, and yours also, sir, for you to do any
thing of the kind. They would make away with
him at once, if they suspected that the business was
discovered."

"But, my good friend," replied Villiers, "a
magistrate's warrant would surely enable me to find
him, and take him home?"

Cookesley put his hand on Villiers's shoulder, and
whispered to him to be silent—that they were overheard. And he proceeded to show Villiers some

machinery, and busy him in some information respecting the process of casting. But two men followed them, and came close to Villiers to scrutinise
him with a look of suspicion, as soon as he could do
so without exciting observation. Cookesley led him
away.

"I'll walk home with you, sir, myself. It is an
ugly path to find, and pitch dark; and, to tell
the truth, I do not like the looks of those men who
overheard you just now. This is not a place, or a
time, to talk of magistrates and warrants."

He seemed to breathe more freely as they reached
the road which led into the town. But even then
Villiers perceived that he looked frequently behind
him, and avoided opening his lips on the subject of
Bentley till they reached the inn-door, and Villiers
asked him to come in and sit down. He came in,
closed the door of the room carefully, and, taking
his seat at the table, he said, " Sir, I have done you
a kindness, and done it at my own risk; for, of
course, if you were resolved on going to a magistrate, you might soon lay hands upon me, and so
could others too. But I trust to your honour as a
gentleman, that you will not let my name be known
in this affair, in which I have no concern except as
wishing well to Mr. Bentley, and able, perhaps, to
be of service to him, if all things go quietly. But
I tell you fairly, that I can give you no more information; and I would earnestly advise you not to
seek for it. If you will take my recommendation,
gentlemen, who know something more of this place
than you can, you will keep yourselves within doors
this evening: let no one know who you are, or
what you want, and get off as early to-morrow
morning as you can. And if you want never to see
Mr. Bentley again, and to send him down to the
bottom of a pit-hole with a dozen holes in his body,

I, who know the hands into which he has fallen, would advise you to go to a magistrate, and come up here to search for him with a body of policemen. If you would have him safe, you must hush up the matter, and not let a soul know it. Good evening, gentlemen."

There was a mystery, and a seriousness, and, at the same time, an obvious reasonableness in his words, which shook Villiers's resolution to make no delay in obtaining a magistrate's assistance. He stopped Cookesley, as he was taking up his hat, and questioned him once more on the motives which rendered it so great an object with Bentley's assailant to retain him a prisoner. His promise of secrecy had been given; and if the story of the origin of the scuffle was true, he was himself deeply interested in maintaining it. Why not allow him, at once, to return to his friends? Cookesley would not remain to listen; but shaking his head, and saying that he could answer no more questions, contented himself with once more repeating his warning to them to say nothing, and then Bentley might be saved. "But be assured," he said, "that the first move which a magistrate takes to find him, his life is not worth a farthing. Good evening, gentlemen; good evening, keeper: you are an honest man, and I hope you are not playing me the rogue in leading me into this trap."

Villiers assured him that no advantage should be taken of his information to involve him in any inconvenience: and as he went out of the room with him, he unobservedly slipped some money into his hand, which Cookesley, not without a slight effort of resistance, was easily induced to pocket.

So long as he had before him the fine generous countenance of Villiers, his frank and sincere manner, and his voice full of truth, Cookesley, fas-

cinated by the mere influence of his high-minded
character, felt no fear at the breach of confidence to
which he had committed himself. He had, indeed,
betrayed nothing beyond what was necessary to
preserve the life of Bentley, for whom he was really
interested. His warning had been salutary and
wise. He knew that any open attempt to search
for him, or to release him (for he was, in fact, a
prisoner, strictly watched, although his comforts
had been kindly provided for by himself and the
grateful Connell, with the aid of the good Sisters of
Charity) would be futile, and only lead to some desperate mode of baffling all further inquiry. But he
knew, also, that among the banditti with whom he
was enrolled, and in whose insurrectionary movements he was deeply involved, an informer of any
kind would be soon detected, and unscrupulously
visited with summary vengeance. He had, indeed,
been wisely silent on the principal reasons which
rendered Wheeler and his gang so anxious to keep
Bentley in their hands. They believed, from his
presence at the ruins, that he must be acquainted
with the secret of their arms and plots, and that
any inquiry which might be instituted into the
attack on him would lead to the discovery of
Wheeler's crime, and, through him, to a knowledge
of the preparations and plans which they were forming for an outbreak of violence—blind violence
and futile outbreak, but to which they were encouraged by the secret promises and negotiations of
Pearce. And Pearce himself had a political object
to answer by producing a popular commotion at
that crisis, and alarming a timid ministry unfavour-
able to the projects by which Romanism was paving
its way to gradual exaltation. The brute passion
of the mob, and their love of plunder, was a sufficient stimulus to render them, in his dexterous

hands, a pliant body, which he could wield at pleasure through his subordinate agents, without compromising himself personally by taking the lead. His quick eye, his ready suspicious intuition, the impenetrable secrecy which he threw round his own movements, the art with which he played instrument against instrument, his obvious interest and influence with some higher power, the facility with which he extracted and combined information from his various spies, and the command which his powerful intellect enabled him to exercise over uneducated and vulgar minds, — all this, coupled with his power of disguising himself, and accommodating himself to any character which he chose to assume, rendered him an object of mingled fear and admiration. Each man felt that he was at his mercy; and it was Pearce's chief object that they should be strongly impressed with such a feeling : and his one great rule of policy was, to obtain over them severally an entire command, by possessing himself of some secret which would make them dependant on him for their safety.

All this Cookesley, far superior to his miserable comrades in education and mind, however debased by profligacy, thoroughly knew. He had struggled more than any other against Pearce's assumption and pretensions, but in vain ; and having no support in his own conscience, or confidence in the wretches with whom he was thrown, he finally succumbed to him, as under a species of fascination. What, therefore, was his alarm when, as he came out of the inn-door, and had proceeded a few paces down the street, he heard a step follow him, and found a hand seize him by the arm.

" You must come with me, Mr. Cookesley," said the deep voice, which he immediately recognised to be Pearce's. " I have something to say to you."

Cookesley actually shook under the grasp of Pearce; but he endeavoured to assume a tone of indifference, and followed him into the Black Lion, a little public-house opposite to the inn.

"Bring a light!" cried Pearce. "Leave the room! Shut the door! Why do you stand there?"

And the little waiting-girl, to whom his orders were fiercely addressed, ran away as fast as she could from such a ferocious guest.

"Cookesley," said Pearce, coming up closely to his panic-struck companion, "you are a traitor!"

Cookesley staggered back, and sinking down in a chair, affected to ask him, with surprise, what he meant?

"I mean," continued Pearce, fixing on him that steadfast searching look for which he was so remarkable—"I mean that you have betrayed Wheeler and his set to that person at the inn there, Mr. Villiers. And you know what traitors deserve, and what in this place they are sure to meet with."

Cookesley endeavoured to stammer out an explanation.

"No words," said Pearce, in the same unbroken tone, "no explanation. You think, like some others, that you can act without my seeing you. You did not suppose that I was by, when that fellow the keeper came to you, or when you were putting out the candle in the shed, and showing Villiers the works—ah!—or when you talked of magistrates and warrants. Be advised," he continued. "When you would do a thing which I am not to see, or speak a word which I am not to hear, get upon the topmost stone of Hawkstone Forest, or out at sea, out of sight of land, and even then beware lest the birds and the fish should prove tell-tales. And now you have been closeted with them over

G 4

there, and you have told them where that poor wretch Bentley is to be found. How much money had you for this job?"

To the former part of the sentence Cookesley was preparing to answer, boldly and firmly, that he had given no information whatever; but the latter rather disconcerted him.

"I must know all," said Pearce. "How much money did he give you?"

And Cookesley pulled out three sovereigns from his pocket. He was preparing to offer Pearce a share, in the hope that it would mollify him, but Pearce thrust his hand aside in disdain. "So you think I am to be bribed like yourself, Mr. Cookesley; and you a gentleman born!"

"Gentleman!" sighed Cookesley, "gentleman! I'm no gentleman!"—for with his courage and self-confidence sank all his other better feelings, and he seemed to think that the only escape from degradation was to bury himself at once in its lowest depths.

"Do you suppose I want money?" said Pearce. "I that can have the command of hundreds—aye, thousands?" And he pulled a pocket-book from his coat filled with bank-notes?"

"And what then do you want, sir?" asked Cookesley. "I have told nothing but that Mr. Bentley is here, and that the best thing is for his friends to remain quiet, and say nothing."

"And Villiers, then," said Pearce, almost gnashing his teeth with hatred as he used the word, "knows nothing of the place where Bentley is lying?"

"Nothing," said Cookesley. "I would not tell him."

"Nor about the arms?" continued Pearce.

"Not a syllable," said Cookesley, thinking that

he had mitigated his case. But Pearce would allow nothing of the kind.

" Fool ! that you were," he said, " to stop short in your treachery — to think that you could tell so much safely, and to be afraid to tell all. Do you suppose," he said, " that Wheeler and his crew will let you off, because, while only half a villain, you have been wholly a fool ?"

" Villain !" cried Cookesley, starting up in fury, and recovering his energy. " How dare you call me villain ?"

Pearce stood unmoved, and only smiled.

" Sit down, sit down, Cookesley. Do not make a fool of yourself with me. You know there is no great harm in speaking truth; and what are we all but —— ? Would you call us honest men yourself?" And he clapped him on the back, with a laugh, and something of a kindly manner. Cookesley answered, sulkily, " No !"

" Well, then, shake hands. I only meant to frighten you. Nobody knows any thing of the matter but myself. And I'll tell you honestly, I have a greater regard for you than for any of them put together. I like a man of education. None of your half-sot, half-brute, that could do nothing but break heads and get drunk. Your secret, Cookesley, is safe with me. Only take especial care that that Wheeler does not hear it. He is as dangerous a fellow as I know; and I would not give a farthing for your head, if he knew you had betrayed him."

" I have not betrayed him!" said Cookesley, passionately.

" Hush ! hush ! do not speak so loud," said Pearce. " It will be just the same with him, whether you have or not, if he knows you have been with Villiers. But you are in my care, and I am your friend. So shake hands."

Cookesley, somewhat relieved, and afraid to exasperate him, gave him his hand.

"Now will you have something to drink?" asked Pearce.

Cookesley nodded his head; and some brandy-and-water being brought in, Pearce asked for a piece of paper, and writing a few lines on it in a false hand, he folded it up, put it in his pocket, and once more shaking Cookesley by the hand, and telling him not to be afraid, Pearce left the room.

Any one who observed him would have been struck by the paleness of his countenance, as he threw off the restraint which he had imposed on himself in the presence of Cookesley. His lips quivered—his eyes glared horribly—his heart beat; and he strode along the street as if a demon were pursuing him. Then he stopped short and faltered —then hurried on—then returned upon his steps. Once or twice he took the paper from his pocket, and seemed on the point of tearing it to pieces; but the passion under which he was labouring recovered its sway, and replacing it, he pushed on across some fields which lay amidst the broken ground that surrounded the pits, until he found himself at the gate of a stone building adjoining one of the most remote works in the place. A low tap caused the door to be opened, and Pearce found Blacker, the same man whom he had parted with on the road, sitting in a low vaulted room by the side of a cheerful fire, smoking, and with a glass of punch before him.

"Is all right?" asked Pearce.

"Yes."

"Are the women up stairs?"

"No," answered Blacker. "I have sent them home for the night."

"Is the fellow asleep?"

" Yes : they dressed his wound, and he has been asleep for the last hour. I've got rid of Burke and all of them, and now the ground is quite clear." Pearce leaned upon the chimney-piece, with his arms folded, for some minutes, in a gloomy reverie. Once more he took the paper from his pocket, and prepared to tear it, and throw it into the fire; but he caught Blacker's eyes looking on him with surprise, and something like contempt ; and starting from his silence, he thrust the paper into Blacker's hand, and bade him go with it to the Blake Arms. " Give it to Villiers, and bring him here."

" And do you think he'll come ? "

" Try," said Pearce. " You know what to say."

The door closed upon Blacker; and Pearce flung himself into a chair, threw his legs on the table, and began whistling. But his voice shook. He tried to think of any thing — every thing — but where he was, and what he was doing. He rose, thrust his hands into his pockets, and with an air of unconcern walked about to look at the party-coloured prints of the Prodigal Son, and other Scripture subjects which hung on the walls, till he came to one which represented the Day of Judgment, and the miserable man quailed at it, and hurried away to stir the fire. As a knock at the door was heard, he actually sprang from his chair with terror; but it was only Blacker returned. Pearce gasped for breath as he saw him.

" You have been quick," he said. " Will he come ? "

" I have not been down," said Blacher. " I came back to say a word to you. Why you seem all aghast." And he gazed with surprise at Pearce's face, livid with contending emotions.

" I say, Mr. Pearce, you do not mean any thing bad, do you, in having Mr. Villiers up here ? "

"Any thing bad!" faltered Pearce. "What do you mean?"

"I mean," said Blacker, "that if you have any other job to do than what you told me of, I am not your man. Why you seem as if you were going to —— "

His words were interrupted by a faint voice from an upper room, asking for some toast-and-water. It was Bentley, whose kind nurse had left him, and who, waking in a fever of thirst, and hearing voices below, endeavoured to make them sensible of his want. But he trembled as he heard the hoarse voices which growled in the room beneath, and still more when Pearce called out to him to be still, with the addition of a ferocious curse on him for disturbing them.

"Remember," said Blacker, whose courage and command over Pearce rose with the perception that Pearce himself was losing his presence of mind under some evil influence — "remember, you told me that you only wanted to get Bentley out of Wheeler's hands, without seeming to take a part in it yourself. There is no harm in that; — and if you wish to get a hold over Wheeler and recover your papers, and think that Mr. Bentley can help you — and if there is a gentleman here who will probably be glad to carry him off, why neither is there any harm in that. But, man! that is not a thing to make a captain of your spirit tremble, and jump, and quaver, and look like a ghost about it. If you were going to commit —— "

"Hush! hush!" said Pearce, hastily, putting his hand to Blacker's mouth to prevent his giving utterance to the horrible word. "That is all! I want nothing more! That's all, I assure you! Only that fellow Cookesley has put me into a flurry with his treachery. That's all, I assure you!" And he seemed relieved by hearing from his own lips his intention to do nothing more.

" Shall I go, then ? " asked Blacker.

Pearce hesitated. " Yes ! — No ! — Yes ! "

" Well, what do you mean ? " said Blacker, surprised. " Go or not ? Why, you do not know your own mind to-night. I never saw you in such a way before. What are we to do if you fall into such tantarums as this, when the day comes for action ? "

He had struck the key, and the resolution was formed.

" Go ! " said Pearce, peremptorily. And Blacker, as if anxious to avoid farther doubt, left the building.

" After all," said Pearce to himself, " I need not do more than I said. There is no harm in that ; and that will be so much gain." And composing his conscience with the thought that he had not yet resolved on any thing worse, he once more sat down before the fire, and emptying (a rare thing with him) the glass of punch which Blacker had left, he gazed upon the coals, and endeavoured to occupy himself in finding out rivers and landscapes, trees and rocks — any thing which had not life, any thing which could not recall his thoughts to himself, in the burning embers.

CHAP. VI.

In the meantime Villiers and Bevan were deliberating on the proper steps for them to take.
The situation of Bentley was obviously most precarious, and might be rendered fatal by any rash
movement on the part of his friends. Under the
most favourable circumstances his character was at
stake if the story of Cookesley was true; and when
they recalled the scene which they had witnessed
at the ruins, the frenzy of poor Margaret, and the
watch which had been found in her pocket, they
scarcely dared to open their lips on the subject.
The keeper earnestly advised them to take Cookesley's advice, to return home, and wait quietly, while
he would, by means of Cookesley, keep a watch on
all that passed, and endeavour to procure Bentley's
safe return without notice or observation.

" A little money, sir," he said, "judiciously employed, will do much — much more than a whole
body of police and fifty magistrates." Bevan was
much inclined to side with him. But Villiers hesitated. It was a compromise of principle with him
to seek by manœuvre what ought to be attainable
by law. He could not bear the thought of quitting
the forest from fear of having violence offered to
them; and he resolved to remain there privately,
while Bevan returned, and to seek some opportunity
of obtaining farther communication with Cookesley,
and through him with Bentley. His mind had just
been made up, when the waiter came in with a
shabby note, which had been brought for Mr. Vil-

liers by a person who was waiting on the outside.
Villiers was surprised, but remembering that
Cookesley knew his name, he was less astonished
to find that the note came from him. It was to say
that he had found an opportunity of letting Villiers
see Mr. Bentley, if he would come alone with the
bearer, who was a trustworthy person. And again
enjoining his secrecy, and committing himself to
Villiers's honour, the writer had added, in a postscript, that one of the three sovereigns which Villiers had given him was a bad one; but he did not
wish to make any allusion to this, satisfied that a
gentleman would make it worth his while to run
such a risk for him.

This last allusion Pearce had artfully introduced;
and it had the full effect of satisfying Villiers that
the note came from the same party, who had already
exhibited so much better feeling than could have
been expected from his situation.

"Show the man in," said Villiers.

But the waiter returned, and said that the bearer
would like to speak with Mr. Villiers alone. Villiers
went into another room. Blacker told his tale
with apparent openness. He had been sent by
Cookesley—could show the way to the house where
Bentley was lying; but beyond that he knew
nothing.

"And will you go?" said Bevan to him on his
return to the room. "Will you trust yourself in
such a place as this to a man of whom you know
nothing, and upon such an expedition?"

The keeper ventured to remonstrate also, but with
no effect.

"Let us go with you at least," they said.

"No," replied Villiers; "the stipulation is, that
I come alone! and if I am to do any good, it must
be by venturing everything."

"You will take my pistols, sir?" said the keeper.

Villiers at first hesitated. "I know," he said, "that there is risk; but I must trust wholly to another arm than my own. No precaution of this kind can save me if it is His pleasure that I should fall into mischief. With Him I am safe unarmed; and to Him I shall commit myself."

Bevan, however, urged upon him the duty of providing human means of defence as well as of relying upon Providence; and he consented to take the arms. He went up stairs for a few minutes, remained humbly upon his knees in prayer, and returned, calm and composed, to accompany Blacker, charging upon his companions to remain where they were, and not to follow him.

The clouds which had obscured the early part of the night had now swept away, and the stars threw a faint light on the path which his guide took. It crossed the principal thoroughfares of the straggling town, till it fell into a tram-road between two walls, one of which Blacker cleared with a spring, and requesting Villiers to follow him, he led the way across some fields. Villiers hesitated for a moment as he looked round on the solitude of the spot, so favourable to any treachery or violence. But Blacker assured him there was no fear; and the forward, conceited young man, proud of an opportunity of making acquaintance with a gentleman, fell into the conversation which Villiers opened with a view of ascertaining the character of his companion. He found him talkative, vain, and pert, and evidently full of his own importance, to which he more than once alluded with an air of mystery, especially when Villiers endeavoured to obtain from him some information on the subject of Bentley. He threw out hints that it might not be difficult for Mr. Bentley to get away if he had any friend to help him; that he himself could show any person the way if he had a mind. All that would be wanted would be a little money. And Villiers felt persuaded that he should find no difficulty in obtaining his guide's assistance if he found Bentley capable of being moved. He talked to the young man in a kind and considerate manner; suggested that his present situation was not one fitted for a person who had evidently received a good education; hinted at his own means of being serviceable to him: and before they had reached the cottage, Blacker was congratulating himself that in serving the ends of Pearce he was at the same time providing for himself a friend of so much importance as Villiers, and whom he could now lay under a lasting obligation. He was not indeed without his misgivings as to Pearce's intentions. But he knew nothing of Pearce's feelings towards the person whom he was conducting. And accounting to himself for the strange disturbance and paroxysm of feeling under which Pearce had laboured by the anxiety which had been caused by the discovery of Cookesley's communication with Villiers, he reached the door of the cottage where Bentley lay.

Everything was silent around it. A light was dimly burning in each of two windows, both of them curtained and closed, one on the ground-floor, and the other in the room above it. But no one could be seen. And only one person was near, hidden behind a projection of the wall within a shed, which allowed him to observe what passed at the door through an aperture in some planks. Blacker bade Villiers remain, without speaking or moving, under cover of a heap of rubbish. He unlatched the door cautiously, but the room was empty, the fire burning clear, and the candle flickering in the socket. He then ascended the stairs, looked into all the rooms,

and having satisfied himself that there was no one in
the cottage, even under the beds or in the closets, he
brought Villiers carefully within the door, and led
him up the creaking stairs to Bentley's room, charging him not to say under whose guidance he had
come there.

No eye but one had witnessed the expression
of Pearce's demoniacal countenance, when, after
waiting, breathless and palpitating with suspense
for the return of Blacker, he saw him through the
aperture of the door approach, and Villiers with
him. He sprang up with a ferocious triumph,
but checked himself, lest he should make a noise.
" Fool ! dolt ! idiot, that he is ! " he muttered to
himself, " to be caught by such a feather ! He is
mine ! I have him in my power. Now what is to
be done with him ? " And he threw himself back
against the wall with the look of a gambler, whose
whole soul had been concentrated in one throw of
the dice, and to whom it had been successful.
Whatever misgivings, or relentings, or balancings
he had admitted before, between the desire of obtaining a thorough command over Wheeler through
the means of Bentley, and the thirst for revenging
himself on Villiers, all had now vanished. The
sight of the man whom he hated with such a bitter
hatred — hated as one who had been injured, and
still more as one who had injured beyond the
possibility of reparation, drove from him all com-
punctious visitings. He remembered (for even in
his paroxysms of passion he could still calculate)
that he had committed himself to Blacker farther
than was safe ; and filled himself with the very
spirit of intrigue, and conscious how little any one
could place confidence in himself, he trembled at
the thought of permitting any one to possess a
secret which might place him in the power of

another. His mind was made up; and scarcely had Villiers and Blacker mounted the stairs, when Pearce emerged from his hiding-place. He paused to listen; but everything was silent. Once he faltered and relented; but the sound of some person's footsteps coming down the stairs drove the doubt from his mind : and the first thing which Blacker heard, on his entering the lower room, was the double-locking of the door from without, and instantly afterwards the barring of the shutters.

" Mr. P——" but he checked himself before he uttered the word. "Is that you? is that you? Let me out."

But there was no answer. He rushed to the back door, which opened into a little court, but that also was locked and fastened: he shook it, but the door was firmly closed. Once more he went round to the front door, and endeavoured to open it, or to induce Pearce, if there, to undo it; but both his efforts were unsuccessful. He tried the window, but it was small; and in a place very subject to robbery iron stancheons had been firmly fixed across it, which defied all egress as well as ingress.

" Is this a joke?" he said to himself. But a little reflection on the nature of the game which Pearce with himself was playing, and on the thoroughly reckless character of the gang with whom he was surrounded and identified, prohibited him from indulging such a thought. He once more shook the door, tried to batter open its pannels, called upon Pearce, but all in vain. He sat down and rubbed his eyes and his forehead, from which a sweat was breaking in a cold dew. Then he remembered Pearce's unusual agitation. He recalled to mind how willing he had been to sacrifice Wheeler the moment he found him dangerous. A moment's reflection convinced him that as little scruple would

be shown in sacrificing himself; and, resuming his
quick thought and energy with the emergency, he
hastened instantly into Bentley's room.

It is a hard and a false thing to suppose that any
persons, however degraded in society or lost in
principle, are lost utterly: good feelings are not so
easily eradicated. And Blacker, notwithstanding
his alarm for himself, had the thoughtfulness to call
Villiers out of the room, and explain to him the
danger of their position, so as not to alarm Bentley.

"There is no time to be lost, sir," he said. "I
cannot venture to stay here myself; and I would
recommend you to follow my example. It cannot
be for any good that any one should wish to catch
us in such a trap as this."

"I do not leave this place," said Villiers, "without Mr. Bentley; and you must do as you like."

"But Mr. Bentley, sir, cannot be moved; he is
too weak. And if he could, how is he to get out?
Perhaps I or you might be able to drop out of the
upper window; but he could never do it."

"And what do you apprehend?" asked Villiers.
"Surely, in a country like England, we need not
fear any outrage of the kind you seem to suspect?"

"Sir," said Blacker, hastily, "it is too late to
argue. But I see you know nothing of the state of
this part of the country; and it is all over with me,
whether I speak or not. But we are on the eve of
a break-out; and Mr. Bentley knows all about it;
and if he got away home every thing would come
out: and rather than that he, or any friend of his,
should give warning, there are men here who would
not scruple at any thing. It is a miracle that he
was not put out of the way at the first, only that he
was always good and kind to the poor, and poor
himself; and we have no war except with the
rich."

"Outbreak!" said Villiers, alarmed. "Do you mean an insurrection?"

"Yes, sir, I mean a regular insurrection, or whatever you please to call it. And now, sir, will you think of moving, before they come and find us here?"

"I do not leave this place," repeated Villiers, "without Mr. Bentley."

"Then, sir, you cannot leave it at all, that's clear; and I must be off. Do not think, sir, that I meant you any harm by bringing you into this scrape. If you will follow me, I think I can get out; but if not, you must take your chance—and a bad chance it is."

Villiers was now alive to the full danger of their situation. He was satisfied, from Blacker's manner, that he was not a party to any evil design upon him, and was himself in peril. "Stop a moment," he said, "while I return to Mr. Bentley."

In a few words he suggested to Bentley the possibility of escape, if he could summon strength and courage. "Could he dress?"

And Bentley, half bewildered and terrified, rose from the bed and endeavoured to put on his clothes, like one awakened from a dream. He was scarcely conscious of his wound, or of the weakness which had followed it. Villiers found his clothes for him lying on a chair; only one thing was missing, but this the most important—his shoes. Blacker, who had by this time come into the room to say that he could wait no longer, was surprised to find Bentley all but prepared to depart. "But how," he exclaimed, "are we to get him out of the window?"

"Look for the shoes down stairs," said Villiers.

And as Blacker crept down, and found them lying under a dresser, he heard footsteps also and voices close at the door.

"It's too late," he whispered, "too late — they are come ; better stay still, and make the best of it. I'll stand your friend — I'll tell the truth — I'll say that ——." He was going to mention Pearce's name, but the consciousness of his complete powerlessness to resist the artifices and designs of such a man, for whatever purpose contrived, struck him dumb. "Hush!" he said; "they are at the door." And he endeavoured to peep behind the curtain without being seen, and to ascertain how many there were.

"If there are only two or three, sir, why we may be a match for them."

His suggestion was right. Pearce, with whom it was a paramount maxim of policy to do no evil himself which he could procure to be done by others, and to keep himself concealed like a spider at the bottom of his web, while he threw his nets around him to entangle his victims, as if by their own agency, the moment he had fastened the door, had retired to a little distance, and from thence had despatched a boy, whom he accidentally met, with such a message to the leader of the gang as he knew would bring them to the spot. But only three had come, and had come unprovided with weapons. Pearce himself would have made a fourth; but it would by no means have suited his purpose to take any part except that of a seeming by-stander in the issue, whatever it might be. The party were ignorant of the real state of the case; but were surprised and alarmed to find the door bolted and barred, and no answer returned to their knockings. And while deliberating what they should do, Pearce stole from his concealment, tapped one of them on the shoulder, unseen by the others, and withdrawing him to a little distance, said a few words to him, and then hastily retired. But they

were amply sufficient. And while two of the ruffians remained quietly watching the door, the other
went off for a reinforcement. None of them said
any thing but a muttered oath, but their eyes exchanged looks of the most determined and savage
ferocity; and they shook hands and exchanged
signs, as if to pledge and assure each other of their
determination to hesitate at nothing.

In the meanwhile Villiers had listened, but all
was silent; and thinking it possible that the former
might have been a false alarm, he once more resolved to attempt their escape. Bentley was dressed,
and resting upon the bed. Blacker stood at the
door striving to catch every sound; but hearing
nothing, he concluded also himself that the party
had retired for some purpose, and that they might
still have time. "Follow me," he said. And he
led them into a little low garret, which occupied a
small gable at the back of the building. With a
strong hand he tore away the decayed lattice; and
showing Villiers a low shed which lay about eight
feet underneath, asked him if he could drop upon
that, and support himself on the sloping roof while
he assisted Bentley to do the same. Villiers, full
of strength and activity, and, as a soldier, accustomed to exertion of all kinds, hesitated not a
moment. He dropped on the tiles without disturbing more than one, but this rattled and fell
to the ground; and a low growl, as of a mastiff dog
uneasy in his sleep, was heard just beneath them.
Bentley himself, now thoroughly master of his senses,
slided, by the aid of Blacker, through the window,
and was received safely in Villiers's arms; Blacker
himself followed. And creeping along the ridge of
the roof, he showed Villiers a waterbutt, by which,
with care and dexterity, it might be easy to descend.
In this, in fact, there was but little difficulty.

" We shall then," whispered Blacker, " be in a
little back yard, between the court and the works ;
and there is a gate which we can easily force, and
then reach the open fields, where we can make play
for it." Silently and steadily Villiers dropped from
the shed to the waterbutt; but as he grasped it, the
rotten supports on which it rested tottered, and
nearly gave way. At this moment a noise was
heard at the door of the building. Before Villiers
could warn Bentley to descend with caution, he had
hurried down, slipped on the edge of the butt, and
the whole, with a tremendous crash, tumbled over to
the ground, throwing Bentley upon his face, and
deluging Villiers with the water. Neither had recovered themselves, when an immense mastiff, which
was kennelled underneath, sprang to the full length
of his chain with a tremendous barking. He leaped,
and tossed, and rolled over, when caught by his
collar, as, maddened with rage, he flew first at one
and then at the other. His kennel lay close to the
gate, which offered the only egress from the little
court into which they had fallen ; and Blacker, who
still hung upon the ledge of the roof, gave himself
up for lost. Villiers, however, heard the tramp of
feet coming up the lane, and bade him jump down
without delay. " We must shoot the dog : I have
pistols with me." But just as he was taking one
out, the animal threw all his strength into one desperate plunge, his chain broke, and before Villiers
could seize his pistol, the brute had fastened on his
chest, and was dragging him to the ground. Villiers felt its teeth in his flesh ; but he remained
quite cool.

" Open the gate," he said to Blacker, " and do
you and Mr. Bentley get out while I manage the dog.
Do not mind me." And while he was still grappling

with the mastiff, he had the satisfaction to see the
gate open. But it opened from the wrong side.

"Well done, growler! Hollo! here they are!"
were the unwelcome words which came from the
ruffian who had opened it. "Well done, growler!
hold him fast!" But at this instant Villiers mastered his pistol, and fired. The shot grazed the
head of the mastiff, but no more; and Villiers, finding that it still retained its hold, threw down the
pistol, grasped the neck of the animal with both
his hands, and nearly choking it, compelled it to
loose its hold. He hurled it down violently on
the ground, close at the feet of the ruffian who had
just appeared; and the animal, on recovering itself, sprang furiously upon the man's face, as the
first object that offered, and in a moment pulled
him down, roaring for help, and vainly endeavouring to pacify the animal, whose fangs were buried
in his cheek. Not an instant was to be lost;
Blacker seized Villiers by one hand, and Bentley
by the other, and dragging them up the steep side
of a heap of slag, so that their figures might not be
seen against the sky, he hurried them into a deep
hole on the other side, and down a rugged path into
a narrow lane.

"Now, run for our lives! straight on," he said.

"Can you run?" said Villiers to Bentley.

"Yes, yes; make haste," replied Bentley; but he
was evidently sinking.

"Give him this," said Blacker; and he pulled a
flask of brandy out of his pocket, and made him
take a considerable quantity. "Come on now."
And Villiers, seizing Bentley by the arm, and almost
lifting him along the ground, followed Blacker
down the lane.

"If we get round that corner," said Blacker, as

they paused for an instant to take breath, " we are
safe." At this moment they heard steps behind
them.

" Go on," said Villiers, " yourself, with this
gentleman. I have my pistols, and will bar the
way against any of them : hurry on ! " And fixing
himself in a favourable position against the wall, he
calmly awaited the pursuers. They came up, running as in chase, two of them, and armed ; each, as
far as their figures could be seen in the dark, of a
stout athletic frame. The first thought of Villiers
was to fire at once. He closed his eyes, uttered a
short prayer, and was preparing to take aim, when
he paused to reflect that the life of a fellow-creature
was not to be destroyed until the last emergency;
and that it was better to trust to the protection of
Providence than to an arm of flesh. " I will not
fire," he said, " till compelled." But he had scarcely
made the resolution when a third man sprang upon
him from the other side of the wall; and he found
himself disarmed and powerless, in the hands of
— three policemen.

CHAP. VII.

Two hours after that Villiers was standing by the side of Bentley's bed, at the Blake Arms, watching his disturbed sleep, and ready to supply him, for the last time, with any thing he might want before he himself retired to rest. His own breast, which had been savagely lacerated by the dog, had been dressed by a surgeon, but was still exquisitely painful. Bevan, who had been suffering during Villiers's absence tortures of anxiety, but who had not ventured to disobey his injunction to abstain from following him, had also gladly laid down, with a mind relieved, and a body wearied with his previous agitation. The keeper was placed in a double-bedded room with Blacker, who had declared himself a lost man if he ever returned to the pits again; and whom Villiers had made as happy as his anxious position admitted by a promise of providing for him. The clock ticked gently on the stairs, and all the inmates of the house lay buried in sleep, without the slightest apprehension of any danger — all but one. To the keeper's infinite disgust and annoyance, Blacker tossed and rolled from side to side, and finding himself unable to rest, would fain have prevented the keeper also from sleeping by a variety of questions, which, however, met no answer but a heavy snore. Several times he rose from his bed, and opened the window, stretching out his head to catch any sound which might come upon the wind. "How I wish," he exclaimed, at last, "that morning were here! Is not that the dawn?" But at that moment the clock struck two, and, with a beating heart, Blacker returned to his pillow.

Villiers himself was not wholly comfortable. He also stopped on the stairs, to listen if he could hear any noise in the distance; and did not forget to lay his loaded pistols on his dressing-table. He had easily satisfied the policemen that there was no necessity to apprehend him, as running away after committing some offence, which they had at first suspected; and he had ordered them to overtake Blacker and Bentley, which was easily done just as Bentley was fainting, and Blacker could no longer support him. Together they carried him to the inn; but the conversation which Villiers then had with the superintendent was by no means satisfactory. Clever, active, acute, and sensible, the superintendent was perfectly aware that mischief was working round him. His means, however, of detection or repression were very limited. He did not hesitate to inform Villiers that he had privately written to obtain a small military force, which might assist him on any emergency. But the whole district was so remote, its population had been gathered together so suddenly, there was such a total absence of any resident gentlemen to organise or direct resistance to a popular disturbance, and the mass of vice, intemperance, and ferocity was so fearful, that he expressed no little uneasiness, if any explosion should occur. "One thing," he said, "he was assured of, that some other agency was employed in preparing for it besides what might be expected in a population of the kind. Communications in a foreign language had been traced; men of education were frequently seen in intercourse with the workmen. There was no scarcity of money; and he remarked, also, that great efforts were making to introduce some Romish establishments in the place. A chapel had been built, and a nunnery. But this, perhaps," he continued, " was not surprising, when the people had been so entirely abandoned by the Church. Papists were not to blame for endeavouring to give them some notions of religion. Better to be papists than heathens !"

And Villiers sighed, as he assented. He pressed the superintendent to take some refreshment, but the officer was evidently anxious, and wished to depart. He asked a second time for Villiers's statement of what had passed, and what he had heard ; and noted it down upon paper. As he left the room, Villiers observed that his eye was making observations on the size of the hall, the position of the staircase, the direction of the doors.

" You have been a soldier, I suppose ?" said Villiers.

" Yes, sir ; in the Second Dragoons."

" I have been in the army, also," said Villiers ; and he was a little surprised at the man's answer, " Thank God ! sir. Then, perhaps, you may be of use to us. If you are going to bed, sir, I think I should advise you to lock the doors of these rooms." He himself tried the handle of another, which led into the back yard.

" This is not a bad place," he said, smiling, " for a defence, if ever we should come to that. However, I must not stop. I wish you a good night, sir. If I should hear any thing, you won't be surprised at my returning."

" Certainly not," said Villiers ; and they shook hands, and parted. Villiers called after him, to ask him one question.

" Do you think," he said, " it would be advisable for us to leave this place immediately, and not to wait till the morning ?"

The officer paused to think. But a little reflection convinced them both that Bentley could not be moved without imminent danger; and there was no conveyance in which he could be placed comfortably. There was also the risk of exposure in a dark night along roads where it was probable that watches would be placed. And re-assured by the officer's expression of a hope that there was nothing to apprehend that night, Villiers retired to his room. A Bible lay upon his dressing-table; and his mind became calmed as he gave up his usual time to read the evening lessons, and knelt more than his usual time to return thanks for the hand which had been stretched out to protect him in the danger from which he had just escaped. He thought, also, of the position which he should henceforth occupy as a magistrate and a landlord, — of his duties, and difficulties, and perils, surrounded as he should be by such a population. The plans which he had long been forming were now to be put in execution; and as the evils with which he would have to contend were brought more closely under his eye, their magnitude appalled him; and the powerlessness of any single arm to encounter them tempted him at one moment to think of abandoning them altogether, but, at the next, they induced him to take refuge from all anxieties in the simple resolution to do his duty in his own province, and to the utmost of his means, without vainly attempting to calculate consequences, which must depend on a higher power. It was this principle which gave to all his movements such quietness and composure, even amidst the utmost activity. It quieted and composed him now; and though he hesitated for a moment, he resolved at last to undress, and endeavour to obtain some sleep, instead of lying down, as he had first contemplated, in his

clothes, that he might be ready for any emergency.
But he had scarcely taken off his coat, when the
door-bell of the inn rang violently.

At this point it may be well to return, for a
moment, to the chief agent in all this plot. As soon
as he had insinuated, rather than explained, to one
of the party who first came up to the door that
there was a necessity for a reinforcement, and for
coming provided with the best arms they could
find, he slunk back to his concealment in a shed
which fronted the house. He was triumphant; all
his plans had been successful; all his instruments
had proved docile, and pliant to his hand. His
machinery had played smoothly, stroke upon stroke,
without an embarrassment or a flaw. As a' mere
game, as a trial of skill, an exercise of power, the
achievement was full of satisfaction. But the mystery and secrecy in which he hugged himself, while
he saw his tools risking their lives, and all at his
disposal, without being able to involve him in their
own peril, thrilled him to the quick. His face
almost assumed a cast of dignity from the consciousness of the power which he possessed. His
eyes lighted up as he reflected that, whatever was
the result, the game must turn to his own advantage.
It was one of the deepest, and at the same time the
most difficult and perilous parts of the policy in
which he had been initiated, so to combine the
threads of his stratagems that if one should fail he
might easily grasp the others. Singleness of aim
was foreign to all his operations. With the religious
and political plots in which he was involved he had
mixed up his own private intrigues and revenge;
and he never lost sight of either. To embarrass an
obnoxious ministry, to further the cause of his religion, or, as it should rather be said, of his fraternity, to revenge himself on Villiers, to recover a

command over some of those necessary tools, who
were beginning to waver in their dependance — all
were in his mind parts of one great scheme, twisted
together like cords in a single rope. But the predominant thought at this moment was revenge. It
was very sweet. He had found his courage waver,
and his conscience begin to rouse itself, beneath the
cold, dark, dreary solitude in which he had been
waiting. And he had drank — he who in his ordinary habits refrained from all indulgence of the
kind, lest he should be led to forget, and commit
himself. He was now fortified. And if in any
wandering of thought his mind fell upon ideas
which made him falter, he lashed himself into the
full tide of passion again by calling up images of
past days, of a foreign clime, of hopes which had
been blighted, of enjoyments which had been
snatched from him, and of insult offered him, by
the man whom he had now within his grasp. And
when such thoughts failed to restore the uncom-
punctious triumph in which he would fain revel,
there was an anodyne ready at hand. He himself
was doing nothing. If blows were struck, or violence offered, he was not the guilty actor. It would
be the deed of others; and his conscience (such was
the morality in which he had been educated) would
remain clear. And after all, it was for the good of
the Church. He was obeying his spiritual superior.
He could obtain absolution. If any one had asked
him what precisely he expected to be the issue of
the rencounter which he had contrived, he would
have found it difficult to answer; for he had never
dared to face fully the probability which, fearful as
it was, lay lurking at the bottom of his thoughts.
He knew that the hounds whom he had let loose
upon their prey were strong, quick-scented, ferocious, and not to be daunted by any fear of blood.

He believed that their prey itself was driven into a corner—all but chained to a stake. He knew, also, that if any accident (for accident he continued to call it) should remove Villiers from the world, he had the means in his power of securing wealth and power beyond his most sanguine wishes, provided only he could recover from Wheeler, in whose hands he believed it to exist, a single packet of mysterious and important documents. This was one vision which opened to him. On the other hand was the chance, nay, certainty, of involving Wheeler himself in some fresh difficulty and crime, which would place him more completely at his disposal. But there was also a third. He had received that morning orders to hasten, by every means in his power, the outbreak which had long been preparing in that part of England. Its ultimate success was hopeless; its object idle, so far as the apparent agents and movers were concerned. But for these no care was entertained by parties behind the curtain, who employed them, as puppets, for their own ulterior and more extensive designs. An insurrectionary movement was required just then in that quarter to aid a political negotiation, in which the emissaries of Rome, or rather of his fraternity, were engaged; and it was to be procured at any sacrifice. Pearce knew well how soon a fray may be turned, when minds are heated and materials well laid, into a rebellion; and he felt as a man who had set fire to a train, and was now waiting in safety for its explosion. With these imaginations he solaced himself while watching the approach of Wheeler's additional party, his face laid close to the little window of the shed in which he had ensconced himself. The delay was shorter than he had expected. They came in quite sufficient strength to master any resistance. He saw blud-

geons in their hands : he had little doubt that more
formidable weapons were concealed about them.
His breath heaved quicker as they proceeded to un-
bar the door. At that instant the barking of the
dog broke upon him, and he listened on tiptoe, with
his face pressed close on the window, and his blood
almost ceasing to flow. There was a stir at the
door of the house, and figures appeared coming
back, as if in search of something, and dispersing
themselves in different directions. The pistol-shot
was fired, and he heard a shout. His knees tottered,
his breath went, all his blood seemed to rush at once
to his heart and smother him. The end—was it
come? For one moment his conscience awoke in
all its force, and flew at him like a tiger ; and if
any one could have seen his face, they would have
read in it the agony of a damned soul. He staggered into the air, leaned against the door-post,
while the cold wind sweeping across his head, from
which his hat had fallen, revived him, and changed
the current of his thoughts ; and in that position he
saw the party issue from the house ; and as one of
them hastened past, he managed, as if unconcernedly, to ascertain from him that the prisoners
had escaped.

" All ?" asked Pearce.

" Yes, all." His first thought was to thank the
fortune which had saved him from the gratification
of his wishes. But the demon-spirit rushed back to
his heart, and he felt that everything was a blank.
As another of the pursuers ran past the door-way
in which he was standing, he felt as if he would
willingly have joined in the chase. But even when
scarcely master of his reason, he was retained me-
chanically by the habitual reserve which he had
practised in abstaining from any direct participation
in the plots which he was weaving. At one time

he thought of retiring, and leaving it to the next day to ascertain results, and discover in what way they might be turned to his advantage. He had forgotten, in the thought of Villiers, that Blacker was with him, had fled with him,—had therefore betrayed himself, or could betray him, not only to Villiers but to Wheeler. Even *his* mind, under strong emotion, had been unable to retain all the complication of his manœuvres; but, like a chess-player who, at the moment when the game seems decided, discovers a move which had been over-looked—or, rather, as a gambler stripped of every thing, and roused from his stupor of despair by finding another piece of gold thrust into his hand to recommence his play,—he no sooner recollected Blacker than he started up, and recovering all the powers of his mind, plunged once more into his calculations of intrigue, and paced slowly, with his arms folded, before the door of the little shed. Just as his course was taken (and it was taken with a rapidity and determination worthy a better cause), on turning upon his heel to strike down a dark passage, he was confronted suddenly by Wheeler, breathless, and infuriated with disappointment and alarm.

"Is this any work of yours, Mr. Pearce?" exclaimed the ruffian, with an oath. "You are a man of many names and many ways. I say, sir, have you had any hand in this? I tell you, you shall answer for it with your life. There's not a man shall come here stealing and sneaking about, and like a cowardly rascal putting other people's fingers in the fire, while he is afraid to show his face himself, be he who he may. I'll not stand it, sir! We'll none of us stand it! Hollo! Jack, here seize this fellow!"

And one of his companions came up, and together

they collared Pearce, and dragged him down the gateway. Pearce's blood ran cold within him. Wheeler was furious, was armed, was half intoxicated. His nervous muscular grasp had seized Pearce by the throat, so that he could neither move nor speak. He knew that Wheeler hated and feared him—had imposed upon him—had obtained possession of documents on which all his own prospects depended,—that he was acknowledged by all the gangs of ruffians implicated in the approaching outbreak as their head and captain,—that he was full of jealousy and resentment at the endeavour which Pearce had made to supplant him by Blacker,—that he was desperate at the danger in which he was involved by the escape of Bentley, —and had long since discarded every shadow of scruple at the commission of any crime. Wheeler's clutch griped him like the claw of a tiger, and every moment he expected to be struck down. He stood perfectly motionless; and Wheeler, finding no resistance, bade his companion go and tell Roberts to find out that brute Connell, and bring him by the neck to the " Black Lion," and then come back. He could manage Pearce in the meantime. And slightly slackening his hold, so that Pearce recovered the power of speaking, he presented a pistol to his head, and bade him not stir for his life. It was not necessary to give such a caution. Pearce, with his thorough knowledge of human nature, was perfectly aware that his only course was to avoid motion, look, or word, which could keep up the excitement under which Wheeler was labouring. Sand, he often had said to himself—soft, yielding, shifting sand, is the only effectual barrier against the waves of an Atlantic. By a strong effort he threw his mind into a totally different train of thought, as if all that had happened, and especially all that he had done himself, had never been; and by this means he both recovered his coolness and was able the better to assume the appearance of surprise and innocence. But his first anxiety was to ascertain whether Wheeler's attack and accusation was a mere ebullition of drunken passion and jealousy, or was founded on any discovery of his own communication with Blacker.

"Mr. Wheeler," he said, calmly (he used this formality in addressing him, knowing that with an exasperated mind it is necessary to preserve a distance, and that too near an approach or affectation of friendship only increases the irritation), "Mr. Wheeler, you have just been grievously injured, and like other men you fall into a passion with the first person you meet, even though he is a friend. But I know what has happened, and can easily forgive you. Tell me, is there any chance of catching them?"

"None," growled Wheeler; and Pearce knew that he had gained his first move. He had induced his enemy to answer him a direct question by putting one which only required a monosyllable for reply. It was the first step to a regular parley; and this once obtained, Pearce knew that he could manage all the rest.

"How many were there?" asked Pearce.

"Three," said Wheeler, sulkily; and his hand relaxed its grasp on Pearce's collar.

".Which way did they go?" asked Pearce. But the question was injudicious. It roused Wheeler's passion by compelling him to declare his ignorance, and to speak at length; and he answered fiercely, with an oath, "How should I know? I believe if there's a man in this place knows, it's yourself." And Pearce felt the grasp of his hand tighten, and the muzzle of the pistol approach nearer to his

forehead; but he was assured that Blacker had not
been taken, and his course was now clear.

"Wheeler," he said, with coolness, "why all this
violence? What right have you to suspect me of
doing this mischief, when you know that I was the
person who sent word to bring you here? I happened to be here. I saw two men enter. I barred
the door behind them, and sent off at once to you;
and in return for this, here you are threatening to
shoot me. Put down your pistol, man, and be calm."

It was his first step to re-assume the tone of
command which he had always asserted over
Wheeler as over others; and to his great satisfaction
he found the charm was not lost. The pistol was
lowered, and Pearce began to breathe more freely.
At this moment footsteps were heard in the lane,
and Wheeler moved as if to look out. A man of
less tact than Pearce would have made an effort to
escape. Instead of this he laid his hand softly on
Wheeler's arm, and whispered, — "Stay here, don't
move; it may be a policeman:" and once more Wheeler
obeyed the suggestion. It showed an absence of
fear, and anticipated his own intention; and Pearce
knew that to obtain submission generally, we must
begin by requiring what there is no objection to
grant. It brought Wheeler's mind also, though
only in a trifling act, into accordance with Pearce;
and thus it was a step towards a renewal of sympathy. All this had been taught to Pearce by the
men under whose skilful direction he had been
brought up, and still more by his own practical
experience of human nature. He was once more
playing a game — a game of intrigue, — fishing, as he
profanely expressed it, for men, or rather getting a
savage animal whose claw was on his throat into his
net, not by hounds and spears, but by smooth
words and a gentle hand.

"Draw back," he again whispered. "Let us

stand in the shade—closer to me—here," and
Wheeler found himself drawing to the side of the
man whom a few minutes before he was prepared
to shoot dead upon the spot. Here was association
and communion.

" Are they passed?" whispered Pearce.

" Yes," replied Wheeler, in a whisper; and this
secret communication into which the ruffian was
drawn, almost without being aware of it, completed
Pearce's charm. The pistol was dropt, the grasp on
his collar removed, and now all that remained for
Pearce was to bend once more to his will, and use
as his tool the man whom he knew would not have
scrupled to be his murderer.

" Wheeler," he said, " it is not safe for us to be
here. Job Stuart's house was broken open last
night; and there are three policemen watching round
in this direction. Let us walk quietly away. Do
not hurry—take hold of my arm."

Wheeler hesitated; and looked at him suspiciously,
and once more put his hand into his pocket to seize
his pistol.

" None of your tricks, Mr. Pearce ; I know you
well. Leave go my arm."

It was now Pearce's time to affect anger and
resentment. He thrust Wheeler's arm from him
with just sufficient violence to indicate passion in
himself without provoking it in his companion.
" Go your way, man," he said, — " go your way.
What is to become of all your great plans and bold
undertakings if the leader of them can't distinguish
between his friends and his foes? How do you
think you'll ever be able to keep your men together,
or do your job, if you give way to these foolish
jealousies and suspicions. What is it to me whether
you walk with me or not? I am going to the
Black Lion. Do you choose to come?"

And Pearce walked on while Wheeler followed sulkily, yet unable to quarrel with the proposal, since it was the very place to which he was going himself, and where his comrades were assembled. In all this Pearce had shown the judgment not to think of removing Wheeler's suspicions by any argument or evidence. He knew that minds heated and bewildered cannot follow reason, and do not require it. Like huge rocking stones, they will vibrate beneath a touch, when the strongest levers are unable to dislodge them. He walked on steadily at his usual pace, not sorry that Wheeler should follow, since he knew that even such a trifling circumstance as this had an influence upon the mind in infecting it with a feeling of inferiority. At the same time he took care that no occasion should be given to rouse Wheeler's still floating suspicion, that he intended to make off and escape, in which case Pearce was sufficiently assured that a bullet might probably follow him. He therefore took care to look back once or twice, and ask, " Well, are you coming ?" At a corner of the streets where it was necessary to turn, he stopped and whistled unconcernedly, and at another he stooped down to tie his shoe, until all thought of his running away was removed from Wheeler's mind. But he was scarcely prepared for Pearce's next step. When he himself came up with him at the " Black Lion," Pearce entered at once into the long room — a sort of clubroom, furnished with deal tables, and pipes for smoking, and spitting dishes, and a gorgeous apparatus of a state-chair, hung with coarse, tawdry red and orange, and curiously surmounted with various devices. The whitewashed walls were garnished with mottoes and sundry symbols of Justice, Temperance, Fortitude, and other Christian virtues, for whose encouragement it was generally supposed that the

F. Lodge, like all the other Lodges of the Hawkstone
Odd and Even Brotherhood, had been established,
and in which its members especially delighted. It
was, in fact, one of the religious orders of the nineteenth century, springing from the same love of
exclusiveness and sociality, bound by vows, useful
in an economical view, giving importance to the
poor, and the dignity of office to the mean. One
element was omitted — the Church. In the room
were assembled a number of pitmen in their better
clothes, workmen from the founderies, and a few
better-dressed persons who seemed strangers; and
the president's chair being empty, they had formed
groups and were severally discussing questions of
politics with looks and allusions of no very peaceable
significance. It was one — one, it may be hoped,
among the few low associations of the kind, which
had been converted into a political club, and from
that into an organised society for sedition. And all
the persons present were privy to the designs which
were in progress, and were bound by oaths like
that which had been administered to Bentley in the
mine, not only to secrecy but to co-operation. As
Pearce appeared at the door he was hailed with
loud applause. However careful the veil which he
had thrown over his personal objects, and the separation which he had maintained between himself
and the actual operations of the gang, his influence
and importance were generally known; and the very
mystery in which he shrouded himself heightened
his consequence, while all doubt of his trust-
worthiness was removed by the command which he
exercised over the leaders. He walked therefore
into the room with a firm and even haughty step,
and every one giving way as he advanced, he took
his stand at the top, by the seat which was destined
for the presiding genius of these treasonable orgies.

Wheeler followed, but with a confused and bewildered air, and would have stepped into the seat of
authority as the president, but Pearce put his arm
before him to prevent him, and arresting him just
as he was on the step, he turned to the assemblage,
and with a rapping on the table called their attention to what he wished to address to them.
Wheeler paused with the rest — to listen. He was
more than surprised, he was astounded by hearing
Pearce in a fluent, off-handed speech explain to the
gentlemen present the fact of the escape of Bentley,
which few were yet acquainted with, and the
manner in which he had himself been treated by
Wheeler. He then quietly appealed to two men
present, of whom one had received the message
which Pearce himself had forwarded, to apprise the
gang that Villiers and Blacker had entered the
house ; the other had received from him the communication respecting the necessity of a reinforcement to the party. It had been no slight part
of Pearce's plan to provide himself with these wit-
nesses from the first, in case his treachery should
be discovered; and the manœuvre succeeded. Wheeler
stood confounded, half angry, half ashamed, yet
still unable to cast away all suspicion, so thoroughly
was he convinced of the depth and artfulness of all
Pearce's proceedings. He looked round to see
what impression had been made, and was satisfied,
that although there was a reluctance and fear to
express any feeling against himself, they regarded
his conduct as unjustifiable, and Pearce's character
as cleared. Pearce himself, with an eye quick as
lightning, perceived the state of their minds, and
how far he might count on their support.

" Now, gentlemen," he said, after a pause, " I
think you'll forgive me if I objected to this gentleman taking the chair of this honourable society, of

which friendship and good fellowship are the motto, until he had ——"

"Made an apology," interrupted some voice. "'Pology, 'pology," were faintly uttered by some of the more moderate of the audience at the farther end of the room, who sat enveloped in a cloud of tobacco smoke. But the demand was not taken up by that general acclamation which might have been expected. The men stood in awe of Wheeler as well as of Pearce, and dared not irritate either. In a moment Pearce caught his line.

"No," he said; "gentlemen, I want no apology. This gentleman is your captain; and he was and is still my friend. But I do want him, before he ascends that chair, to tell me before you that he no longer suspects me of wishing to injure him, or of being a traitor to your noble cause."

"Hear, hear, hear! hurrah! that's noble — that's just like a gentleman!" exclaimed the whole room, relieved from the dilemma to which they had been reduced.

"Shake hands, shake hands!" and Pearce stretching out his own hand, which Wheeler was obliged to take, though not without a shrug of the shoulder and a look of bitter suspicion, he lifted him into the chair, and stood by him with much the same attitude (to compare little things and great) with which the protector of a kingdom might stand by the throne of an infant sovereign, whom he was permitting to exercise the regal function.

These are little details; but human nature is the same in courts and cottages. And the skill and ingenuity practised by Pearce in a pot-house he had learnt from men who at the same time were practising the very same principles in influencing the rulers of nations — rulers in palaces, as, by the constitution of England, the members of the F. Lodge have become its rulers in cabins.

"And now, gentlemen," resumed Pearce, after a little pause, during which Wheeler was recovering his self-importance, "I beg your pardon for intruding upon you; and as I know you must have some weighty things to think of, now your excellent captain, and indeed all of you, have been brought into this jeopardy, I think I had better withdraw."

His words were cautiously weighed that they might sound as a question, whether it would be better or not that he should leave them. And he paused for an answer.

"No, stay, stay; we shall want your advice," was the general outcry; and Pearce did not wait to have it repeated.

"Well, gentlemen," he said, "since you wish me to be a looker-on, you know that, though I have business of my own which prevents me from taking any part in your proceedings, my heart is with you, and always will be; and I certainly am very much concerned that this vile treachery should have exposed the life of your excellent captain, and indeed, I may say, the lives of all of you, as it has. But I should think the best thing would be to find out at once who is the traitor. Do not you think so, captain?" and he appealed, with an aside, to Wheeler, who, he saw, was becoming impatient with his interference, and uneasy to resume his own authority as the first personage in the room. "Its not my business," he continued aloud, "to advise, when it would be done so much better by your own president. But there is a person here, I think, who could give him some information."

And as a cat would torment a mouse, Pearce, with his eye looking significantly at Cookesley, who

quailed under it, and turned as pale as ashes, asked
him to tell the captain what he knew about the
matter. Cookesley's heart sank within him, his
lips quivered, his eyes cowered, as he raised his
head from his arms with which he had been resting
on the table, and with a supplicating look at Pearce
he endeavoured to commence some stammering accounts. It was not the mere .sport of inflicting
torture, though this raised a smile and a sneer on
Pearce's hard features, but the policy of exercising
power, which induced him to drag Cookesley forward. But he intended nothing more than to terrify
the unhappy man; and having shown what mischief
he could do, to excite his greater gratitude and dependance, by leaving him at last in safety. It was
at once his delight and policy at times to seize one of
his unhappy dependants, and hold him, as it were,
over a precipice, threatening to drop him. He saw,
however, from Cookesley's alarm, that it would not
be safe to trifle with it, lest his unhappy victim
should betray himself. He interrupted him, therefore, before a second word was out of his mouth.

" I think," he said, " you told me that you saw
Mr. Villiers, was it not, come into Howlas, riding
with a groom, or something of the kind?"

" Yes," said Cookesley, hesitating.

" And that, afterwards, he came down to the Horton works, and asked you to show him over them.
Was not that right ?"

" Yes," faltered Cookesley, trembling for the next
question, but still hoping much from seeing that
Pearce was himself making up a story. " And then
you thought it right to let me know what he had said
to you; that he had been making inquiries about
a gentleman who had met with an accident, and
sounded you to know if you had heard anything

about it; and said something of a magistrate and a warrant?"

" Ay, ay," cried two of the black begrimed furnace-men from the other end of the room. " We heard him say that, didn't we?" And they appealed to each other. " We thought there was something in the wind."

" And so did you, Mr. Cookesley, did you not, when you thought it your duty to tell me as soon as you could?" said Pearce.

Cookesley, half exulting like a reprieved criminal, half afraid, half unwilling to tell a direct lie, and bewildered with the tricks of Pearce, like a fly who felt himself entangled in a spider's web, which yet it was too dark to see, only ventured to assent by nodding his head.

Pearce looked round, as much as to ask if any doubt could be entertained of the author of the mischief. He then engaged Wheeler, who almost growled as he turned his head to listen to him, in a whispering conversation. At the close of which, as if revealing the result of a confidential deliberation, he said, aloud, " Your excellent captain and I know this Mr. Villiers well; and you could not have a more dangerous man to deal with—could we?" And he turned to Wheeler, who sulkily assented.

" Now then," Pearce suggested aside to Wheeler, " find out who is absent."

Wheeler, scarcely recovered from his intoxication and his passion — alarmed at the personal consequences of Bentley's escape — cowed and disordered by the mistake which he had made with respect to Pearce, was to be recovered and brought up to the proper pitch of energy necessary for the object which Pearce had in view. And the proper mode of recovering him was to engage him in some of the routine duties of his office. He accordingly began to call over the names ; and, in doing it, to resume his usual feeling of importance and determination.

"Smith."

"He's sick," answered a voice.

"Corbet."

"He's gone down to Hawkstone to see his brother."

"Connell. Where's Connell? Has any one brought Connell with him?" exclaimed Wheeler, furiously, as if sure of his treachery.

"Connell, sir, I know is away at Barton Mills," said two or three voices. "He went away at six this morning." And Wheeler looked as a bear from whom its prey had just been torn. Four more names were called, and an excuse given for each. Blacker's came next.

"Blacker. Mr. Blacker."

"Ha!" exclaimed Pearce, loud enough to be heard by all the room. "Ha, Mr. Blacker! is not he here?" he repeated; and he put his finger to his lips, as if in thought. "Has any one seen Mr. Blacker?"

There was no answer.

"I saw him with you," said a pitman, who knew little of Pearce, and was therefore little daunted by his presence. "It was about three hours ago."

"With me?" exclaimed Pearce. And his first thought was to crush the speaker by one of his most ferocious looks, and compel him to retract his words. But the stout steady look with which the huge giant confronted him compelled him to alter his course.

"Yes," he said, "about three hours back, was it not, at the corner of Wych Lane?"

"Yes," said the man.

"I thought at the time," said Pearce, "when he left me, that there was something suspicious about him. He seemed hurried, and said he had a job to do ; and when he went away, he went down towards the inn."

" I saw him go into the inn myself," said a stout active lad about sixteen, " and come out again with a gentleman."

" Ha !" exclaimed both Pearce and Wheeler, as in concert. And the former again laid his head by the side of the president's ; and, as the prospect of discovery opened on them, Wheeler's conference assumed a more cordial and confidential tone.

" Yes, yes," he said to Pearce. " You see, gentlemen," he continued, speaking aloud, and to the great satisfaction of Pearce, assuming the tone of energy which was natural to him, " Blacker is a man that we have for some time had our eye upon ; he is quick enough, and cunning, and conceited, and is always talking of being with gentlemen, and becoming a gentleman himself. I know that he has done as much as he could to injure me."

" And you will bear me out," subjoined Pearce, " that he has not scrupled to tell you many falsehoods of me, in order to make us enemies. I have had him with me often, to see if I could make any thing of him, but I have never liked the man ; he's a notorious liar for one thing, and would never hesitate to bring a charge against any one, true or false. He's just the man who, if he were caught in the fact, would swear that he was set on to it by the captain himself—or perhaps," he added, laughing, " by me. What think you, captain ?"

Wheeler gave his assent, but not without a little shrug of the shoulders. " Send after Blacker, and find him out," cried Wheeler. But just at this instant (as if some secret power, according to Pearce's views, was aiding his plans) a man came in, breathless, to say, that he had just obtained information

from another, who had seen three policemen and a
gentleman with Blacker himself carrying Bentley
into the inn, and that they were all there together.
There was a dead silence.

" At the inn?" whispered Pearce to Wheeler.
" Do they stay all night?"

" Do they stay all night?" repeated Wheeler,
aloud, to the informant.

" Yes, sir, I heard it from the ostler myself.
There's no chay, and the doctor has been up, and
the gentleman has been hurt, and the sick person
cannot be moved."

" Did you hear the gentleman's name?"

" Yes, they said it was young Mr. Villiers; they'd
heard it from the keeper there, down in the park,
who is come with them."

The discovery was complete; the whole assembly
seemed thunderstruck. Pipes were laid down; half-
tasted pots of beer were removed from the lips;
eyes were turned on each other; and, to the great
delight of Pearce, Wheeler jumped up from his seat
with a violent imprecation, and swore that he would
have his revenge.

" You are sure," said Pearce again, aloud, to the
last informant, " that they stay all night? Is
Blacker at the inn?"

" Yes, sir."

There was a pause.

" What o'clock is it?" said Pearce to his next
neighbour.

" Only just twelve," was the answer. Wheeler
himself seemed perplexed. But his spirit was up;
and Pearce thought it better to make no direct
effort to guide him.

" I never heard," said Pearce to his neighbour,
" a more rascally thing. It's a sad thing to think
of," he continued, lowering his voice; but I would

not give five farthings for the neck of my good friend Wheeler, or the success of any of your plans, now this has broken out. You could not have a man against you who would do you more deadly mischief than young Villiers. I know him well. He is almost the only man I should ever be afraid of, except, perhaps, your own captain, when his nerve is up."

Wheeler heard every word, as it was intended that he should do.

" How many of you are there?" continued Pearce, as if carelessly.

" Four or five hundred," was the answer.

" Four or five hundred!" exclaimed Wheeler, fiercely: " there are four or five thousand — yes, double and treble the number — who are with us — good men and strong. Why, this moment, in this town, there are five hundred who would follow me the moment I gave the word, are there not?"

And " Yes, yes, follow you, captain, anywhere," was the shout in reply.

Pearce stretched across, and whispered to Wheeler, " Did they say, follow you to the inn?"

" Yes," exclaimed Wheeler, fiercely and aloud. " To the inn, or anywhere, wouldn't you, my boys?"

The words were no sooner uttered than " The inn, the inn!" rose up on all sides. The word was dropped, the idea suggested, and Pearce, preserving his countenance in its usual impassive coldness, secretly hugged himself in triumph.

" My boys!" said the captain, as if in doubt.

But Pearce, who was standing by him, began soliloquising aloud. " He is quite right; just like himself. Strike while the iron's hot. What a fine body of fellows! and what a man to head them! There's plenty of time!" And he took out his watch to look at it. He knew that many minds —

most minds, in moments of indecision, may be
fixed in any resolution by taking it for granted
that the resolution is made already, — minds that
never like to retreat, or to be suspected of retreating, from any step on which they have once decided. Wheeler was one of this class.

"You'll form," said Pearce, " in three bodies, I
suppose, and attack them at once. Will you fire
any rockets, to let the people in Blackmore know
what you are doing ?"

Wheeler pushed him aside. "You are a very
clever man, Mr. Pearce; but I suspect we know
better how to manage these things than you do.
We have gentlemen who have served in the army
themselves. Leave us, if you please, to manage
our own concerns."

Pearce received the repulse with the same satisfaction with which the hand experiences the
recoil of a spring, which it is testing to see if it
will break. He thought, however, that a little
irritation was no bad mode of confirming his instrument in his resolution, and putting him wholly
on his mettle by affecting a little distrust.

"Would it not be as well," he whispered again,
while Wheeler was busy in giving some orders to
one of the men (he chose the moment on purpose)
— "would it not be as well to send round to the
works and get the men together ?"

Wheeler uttered a tremendous oath.

"Confound your interference, sir; am I not doing
the very thing? I wish you would stick to your
own business. I conclude we shall see nothing of
you to-night." And he looked round on Pearce
with ineffable scorn.

Pearce was perfectly satisfied. The men had
jumped up from their seats, and the whole room was
in confusion. Wheeler had called to him three of

the stoutest and most intelligent of the party, and
was engaged in giving them directions. His whole
energy was aroused, and he spoke and acted with a
spirit and judgment worthy of a better cause, and
worthy of the National School, in which his intellect
had been so sharpened and prepared.   And just as
he rose up in his chair to make a short but violent
speech to his comrades, Pearce quietly took his
hat, and slipped out of the room.   At the door he
beckoned a rough bloated miner to him, and telling
him that having disturbed their meeting, he was
bound to leave something to make them merry, he
put into their hands enough money to produce in
the whole party the degree of intoxication, and
therefore of recklessness and violence, necessary
for the accomplishment of their work, and then he
retired into the street, as the demagogues of the
nineteenth century usually do retire, when fighting
is about to commence.

Only one thing remained. He had fired the
train, which he was assured would terminate in the
required explosion. But with that explosion it was
probable that he should be compelled to remove
from the district. Wheeler himself might be destroyed or driven away, and with him the chance be
lost of recovering the mysterious papers. How often
did he reproach himself for having once permitted
him to see them.   Upon no other part of his proceedings could he fix the imputation of being what,
with the French diplomatist, he considered worse
than a crime—a blunder; and yet, he thought to
himself, it was necessary to explain to him about
the boy. I could never have gained command over
him without showing him some confidence; and if
he has played me false, why (he chuckled as he
muttered) it is only what I have done to him ! He
despaired of recovering the documents by any influence of persuasion ; he had tried this in every

shape: but Wheeler, though not aware of all the value attached to them, saw by Pearce's frequent recurrence to the subject that they were of great moment. Himself quick, intelligent, and aspiring, he growled impatiently under the superiority which Pearce assumed over him. Before he would consent to entrust him with any of his own secrets, he had insisted on being admitted into some of his partner's; and Pearce had been compelled to show him something which might explain the nature of his own proceedings, and account for the mystery attending them, and for his refusal to take an active part in the more general conspiracy. But instead of removing distrust, the knowledge thus obtained had only increased it. Wheeler saw the real nature of Pearce's character, and kept his eye fixed on all his movements, as upon a snarling dog, which might at any hour turn on him and rend him; and nothing but the money with which Pearce supplied him could have preserved the continuance of their connection. He had taken advantage of a careless moment in which Pearce, not then sufficiently aware of his cunning, had left the papers in his possession, to secrete them, and pretend that they were lost. At one time he had even thought of making use of them himself; but they were comparatively valueless without further information, which none but Pearce possessed; and he was too deeply involved in the turbulent conspiracy of the district, and too deeply in the power of Pearce, to venture on such a step. All that he could do was to retain them in his own hands, as a sort of hostage or balance-weight, to preserve the equilibrium of their mutual suspicion. And the more effectually to prevent Pearce from recovering them, he had shifted his lodgings; and when it was necessary to meet, they had met at another public-house.

In this critical moment Pearce was resolved to make one more attempt. He contrived without difficulty to find out Wheeler's lodgings; easily obtained admittance to his room, on leaving the Black Lion, on pretence of wishing to see him; looked round on the closets and places in the miserable garret, for it was nothing more, in which the treasure might be concealed; and fixed his eyes especially on a deal box, closely locked and corded, in which all Wheeler's little property was contained, with many other papers of no little importance, besides the packet in question. He would have been tempted not to lose the opportunity, but to search at once; but while his eyes were furtively seeking for some means of opening the box, he heard voices in the street, and had only just time to hurry down stairs, and to meet Wheeler himself, and, as they were styled, three of his officers with him. Wheeler looked at him with surprise and suspicion, but was too full of other things to attend to him.

"They told me," said Pearce, "that I should find you at Blacker's lodgings. Is not this Blacker's lodgings?"

"No!" exclaimed Wheeler, with an oath.

"I wanted to remind you," said Pearce, "that a troop of dragoons came yesterday to Hakewell Barracks; so you had better make haste."

"Fool!" exclaimed Wheeler, "to think we do not know that!"

And Pearce, having lulled all his suspicions, once more went his way. He proceeded first to his own room, where he provided himself with certain cunning instruments, by which he was able to open any lock without detection; and then he waited patiently at his window, listening to catch any sound which might break the stillness of the night.

CHAP. VIII.

WE may now return to the inn-door, which Villiers, startled by the ringing, had hastened down to open. His anticipation of its cause was too well founded. The superintendent of police, with two of his men, met him in the passage; and a few words were sufficient to apprise him that the pitmen were mustering their forces, and that an attack might be apprehended on the inn. Villiers's first thought was the possibility of transferring Bentley to some place of safety. "Was there any mode of quitting the town?" But the policemen negatived it at once. Scouts had been posted on all the roads, and round the inn; and retreat was hopeless without discovery.

"No, sir," said the superintendent; "if the attack is made we must meet it here."

Villiers asked the number of the assailants.

Brown, the superintendent, shook his head. He had learned that the workmen in nearly all the works were gathering. They were a sturdy, desperate, and ferocious class, long banded together in a general conspiracy, and well armed, if not with fire-arms, at least with weapons still more formidable for close combat — the weapons of their own labour; and, what was still more alarming, there were among them men who had served in the army, and were well acquainted with the best mode of planning an attack.

"And how much time have we," said Villiers, "to prepare for receiving them?"

"I do not think," said Brown, "that we have more than half an hour. The men from the Binley and Powham works cannot join them in less than that. And it is late ; and they have had to wake them up."

"Half an hour," said Villiers, "well employed, will do much. Call up every one in the house. Stop — not there!" he cried to the man who was hurrying to the first door on the stairs ; "not there ; that's Mr. Bentley's room. Do not disturb him till the last moment. How many men are there with you, Mr. Brown ? "

"We have but eight, sir. One of them I have sent up to Mr. Jackson's, to see if he can muster any assistance among the better sort of people, — the shopkeepers, and so on. But they are a cowardly set ; and I have no great reliance upon them, even if we could swear them in as constables. They think of nothing but making money ; and making money is not the best school for learning to fight for any thing, even for their lives."

"Are there any military anywhere in the neighbourhood ?" asked Villiers.

"Thank goodness, sir ! " was the answer, " a troop of dragoons arrived yesterday at Hakewell Barracks ; but that is ten miles off. One of my men is despatched for them ; but he will have to cross the mountain ; and the road is bad, even if he manages to get there."

"Let us have no ifs, Mr. Brown," said Villiers. "When we have to fight in a good cause, we must feel sure that all things will turn out well. There must be no doubting. How long, then, shall we have to hold out ? "

"Allow three hours," said Brown.

"Allow four," said Villiers, "that we may not be

disappointed. Always give time, and prepare for the worst at once. And now for our defence."

By this time the terrified inmates of the house had been roused from their sleep; and, half-dressed, — some shoeless — some with their nightcaps on — some staggering under the dizziness of fresh-broken dreams — and all open mouthed with fright and wonder,—were assembled in the bar and the passage. There was the landlord, a stout, hearty Englishman, and his wife, with one maid, and the ostler, and boots: both of whom appeared to Villiers's searching eye as men who would stand by him, and who could be trusted. No stranger was in the house but a bagman, or, as he would rather be entitled, a commercial gentleman, who came trembling down the stairs, with one hand holding up the lower part of his attire, and with the other dragging after him a heavy portmanteau. In a very few words Villiers explained to them the facts of the case; and insisted that the women should be immediately conveyed to a place of safety, and that any others who liked it should retire also.

"We must have none with us," he said aside to Brown, "but those who are with us in heart, and will stand by us."

The landlord was the first who answered. He was the son of an old tenant on the Villiers estate, had served in the yeomanry himself, and still retained his yeomanry equipments. "As sure, sir," he exclaimed, "as my name is Bonsor, I do not leave this house while you and the sick gentleman are in it! I've heard of Mr. Bentley many a time. He always did what he could for the poor; and I'll stand by him to the last; and by you, sir, for Lady Esther's sake."

Mrs. Bonsor listened to her husband, and then declared her intention of remaining also. She had full confidence in her husband's martial qualities, and especially in his yeomanry accoutrements : she would not be driven out of her house by any set of ragamuffins. Besides, there was all the tea and the sugar, and the larder ; and the rum and shrub in the bar ; and the teaspoons and silver teapot ; above all, there was the great china bowl—the very pride and treasure of her life, — all of which were committed to her keeping ; and, with a spirit worthy of an Englishwoman, she seated herself in her great chair, and declared that nothing should make her afraid. The poor maid trembled like an aspen leaf ; but the landlady bade her take courage ; and she also announced her wish to remain with her mistress. The two men-servants seized the poker and the shovel, and vowed that they would stand by the Blake Arms to the last drop of their blood. They would not see a gentleman murdered, or their master's property injured ; and they did not care a straw for all the pitmen in the forest.

Villiers thanked them all in a manner which made them more than ever firm in their resolution to stand by him. He promised that their services should not be lost sight of; and encouraged them by explaining that he was himself an officer in the army, and had fought in sieges and battles before. But in the midst of his little address he was nearly pushed forward by some one creeping behind him, and striving to reach the door. It was the terrified bagman.

" I'll thank you, gentlemen, if you please, to let me out. I'm only a lodger, you know ;" and he affected a laugh, which fear converted into a hiccup. " I think it better to go to the Swan. Good night, gentlemen ; I hope you won't be hurt. Here, Boots, will you take up my portmanteau to the Swan ; take care, there's money in it." The Boots opened the door, threw his portmanteau after him into the street, and bade him get off for a cowardly sneak — an injunction which the shivering wretch, half dressed as he was, willingly proceeded to comply with, without giving way to any resentment at the imputation so unceremoniously thrown upon his heroism.

"Money, sir, again," said Brown to Villiers. "Money — a money-making people will never fight for any thing; their soul is always in their pocket."

It was, however, no time for philosophising — an occupation of which Mr. Brown, in his vocation, was extremely fond. Villiers, who, while he was in the army, had devoted himself with zeal to his profession, and studied it thoroughly, cast his eyes round the little garrison which he was now to maintain; and with that quick sagacity which indolent men call genius, and wise men know to be the fruit of patient study and a well-disciplined mind, he fixed on the whole plan of defence. The house was a double one, thrown back from the street, and connected with the two rows of houses on each side by a wall which formed a little recess, enclosing three sides of an open gravelled space.

"Get some pickaxes," Villiers cried to the ostler and the boots; "knock some holes in these walls for our muskets; we can command and sweep the whole front of the house from these: and here we must take our first stand. Mrs. Bonsor, will you have the goodness, with your maid, to bring down as many feather-beds and mattresses as you can, and place them against the windows in these two front parlours; and then pile up all the loose chairs and tables and drawers, any thing you can lay hands on in the passage here, as well as in the rooms. We are tolerably safe behind, are we not?"

Brown consulted with the landlord, and found
that the stable-yard at the back was surrounded
pretty nearly on all sides by stables, coach-houses,
and other out-buildings, except the gate, which led
into the garden, and through the garden into the
fields. But this was perfectly exposed.

"It may be," said Bonsor, "that they may not
come round, or think of this. We must trust this
to Providence."

"No," said Villiers; "we will trust to Providence
all that is beyond our own resources, but we have
no authority for trusting any thing to it which we
can do ourselves. Keeper, when they come up,
station yourself in that loft—it commands all the
garden, and shoot the first man whom you see
coming in that direction."

"Hollo!" cried the landlord at this moment;
"my boys! I had forgotten you." And two stout
hearty boys, about fourteen and fifteen, who had
been overlooked in the general rousing, now joined
the party, half in wonder, and still more in delight,
at the prospect, as they called it, of some fun. Villiers was not sorry for the reinforcement.

"Of course, they will not leave you," he said to
the father.

"I should like to see them," said Bonsor. "English boys! and be afraid of a set of thieves and
ragamuffins!"

"Boys," cried Villiers, "here is your work. Do
you see that heap of paving-stones? Carry as many
as you can up to the upper rooms. Quick! and do
not get in the way of your mother. Mr. Brown,
your other men should be here by this time; you
say they have plenty of ammunition."

"We have ten muskets, sir," was the answer;
"besides some sabres, which belonged to the militia;

and, luckily, the cartridges, which were intended for the soldiers, I wrote for, came on Thursday."

Why, sir," said Bonsor, " there's a little barrel of gunpowder in my cellar, which Mr. Jackson asked me to take care of for him for a few days, and that will stand us in some stead."

By this time the other policemen had arrived, and brought with them the necessary resources.

" You have your own yeomanry arms, Mr. Bonsor," said Villiers.

" Yes, sir."

" Bevan — you, I know, will not like to take a musket; but you can be of great use to me if you do not mind danger ; you can be my aid-de-camp, and carry my messages."

And Bevan gladly consented to take a post which would employ him usefully, without compelling him to shed blood.

During the whole of this Villiers preserved the utmost cheerfulness. He laughed, joked, patted one man on the shoulder, showed another the proper way to knock out the loop-holes in the wall, came to Mrs. Bonsor's assistance as she was stumbling under a heavy mattress, which was to be placed against the hall-door ; and, in particular, he won her heart by carrying with his own hands the great china bowl from the exposure of the bar into the cellar.

" We must have this filled with punch," he said, laughingly, to the good lady, " when we have sent these fellows back to their pits, and must all drink your good health in it. I do not know what garrisons would do without ladies to help them."

And the comfortable landlady, pleased with the compliment from such a nice gentleman, continued to bustle about with redoubled activity.

" My poor girl, what is the matter with you ?"

he asked Mary, the housemaid, who, having finished
her task, was beginning to reflect on the approaching danger, with the tears coming into her eyes.
" Why, you have never been in a siege before, as I
have ; it will be a feather in your cap as long as you
live.   See, you have not piled up these things properly ; just help me to move that table — now toss
up those cane chairs lightly one upon the other, so
that if any one attempts to climb over them he may
tumble head foremost into them.   Remember, the
next time you are besieged, that light things of that
kind are far better to blockade a passage than heavy
tables."

" Oh ! sir, I hope I shall never be sieged again !"
was the poor girl's reply.   And she would have
burst into an hysteric sobbing, but Villiers, without
pretending to notice it, sent her off with his compliments to her mistress, to beg that she would provide immediately the best supper she possibly could
in the bar.   " I saw an excellent round of beef
there," he said ; " and you had better put hot water
on the fire.   And Mr. Bonsor, you will produce us,
I hope, the very best bottles that you have in your
cellar.   We may want them," he said aside to Brown,
" full as much as the little barrel of something else
which it fortunately contains.   Charles X. lost his
throne by forgetting that his troops could not fight
without eating ; and I believe that the greatest man
in this day, when a popular tumult is expected in
London, always commences operations by victualling
the billets of the soldiers.   And now," he turned to
Bevan, " will you go up to Bentley — I fear he must
have been wakened by this noise — and break things
to him as well as you can ?   One thing more, Mr.
Brown, remains ; we must blockade the lower windows and doors of the house toward the stables ; and
I think we can do this with the flys and the dung-

cart, and that old broken-down coach, which are in
the yard. Let us turn them up, and leave only a
passage for us to retire into the house, in case we
are driven from our outposts." He looked at his
watch. "We have no time, my men, to spare."

And, all setting their shoulders to the work, the
barricade was soon completed.

"And now," said Villiers, as he went from room
to room with the superintendent, examining the
preparations, "I think we have done all that we
could."

"And the rest?" said the superintendent.

"The rest," interrupted Villiers, "is in the hands
of the Almighty; and to him we must commit it.
But we must give the men their supper; and, above
all, take care that they do not become intoxicated."

"The women are the worst part of the thing,"
said Brown.

"I am not sure," replied Villiers. "Occupy them,
make them take a part in what we have to do,
prevent them from sitting down and working themselves into hysterics, and women may form a most
valuable part of a garrison. I do not think, in the
present state of England, that Englishwomen must
be exempt from facing such perils as these."

"Very true, indeed, sir," replied the superintendent; and he added the reflection as an acquisition
to his philosophical lucubrations, to be produced on
the first opportunity. He would, indeed, have followed it up by some additional morality of his own,
but Mary came to say that the supper was ready;
and all the little garrison being summoned together,
they sat down to a table garnished with all the delicacies of Mrs. Bonsor's larder, the richly inlaid
round of beef occupying the centre, and the extremities groaning under a brown-powdered uncut
ham and a cold pie, on which the recreant bagman

had only commenced an assault for his supper, promising, with a hearty relish, to resume his attack in the morning.

"I must quarrel with you," my good Mrs. Bonsor, said Villiers to his landlady, who, busy and cheered with the duties of her vocation, had almost forgotten why they were assembled. "But you do not treat us to any silver spoons. I hope you have not put away your plate, as if there was any chance of it's falling into the enemy's hands. With such a gallant little army, and such a defender as Mr. Bonsor there, I hope it has never crossed your mind that they will ever penetrate into your bar."

And Mrs. Bonsor, looking with matronly pride at her husband, who had arrayed himself in his yeomanry dress and grasped his yeomanry sword, declared that she had no fear whatever — only she had indeed put the spoons into a drawer, from which she proceeded to restore them.

"I hope," said Villiers, "you have plenty of hot water. I have known a house gallantly defended with boiling kettles."

"Bless you, sir," said the landlady, we are brewing this very night, and there's a supply of hot stuff enough for a regiment."

"Well, then," replied Villiers, "we must trust this to you, and Mary, and the boys. Have you taken up all your paving-stones, my lads?"

And the boys laughed, and promised to take a good aim from the upper windows.

Cold, reserved, haughty as Villiers was thought by those who only saw him in very general society, and proud as he certainly was by nature, in the present circumstances he threw it off entirely. He was animated, lively, if not affable — for that implies condescension, but just sufficiently familiar with the whole party, down to the ostler himself, to please, assure, encourage, and confirm them in their resolution to stand by him to the last, as the finest and nicest gentleman they ever saw. A common danger levels all distinctions but that of mind. He was moreover really pleased at the genuine manliness and courage with which they had promised to support him. He respected them, and was grateful to them, and even then occupied himself in planning how he should reward them if—— But with the "if" came also the thought of the frightful danger in which they were involved. And as the party was now beginning to be cheerful and merry, and almost to doubt if the whole was not a false alarm, he left Mr. Brown recounting stories of brave defences made by small bodies against large numbers, and, beckoning to Bevan, he went with him to Bentley's room. He stopped on the staircase to ask one question.

"You have seen Bentley," he said, "and prepared him."

"Yes."

"Had you any opportunity—did you allude—could you satisfy yourself on that dreadful point? Was there any truth in that man's frightful tale, or is it a calumny?"

"A calumny—it is wholly false," replied Bevan. "I spoke to him openly: he told me enough to satisfy my mind completely, though he is bound to say no more. I will answer for his innocence."

"Thank Heaven!" repeated Villiers, fervently. "Now I can fight for him with comfort."

He entered the room, and Bentley endeavoured to raise himself from his pillow, but fell back, and could only take his hand and press it to his lips. "You have saved my life," he said, faintly, "thus far; and the Almighty will enable you now to save it wholly, if it is His good pleasure. Would that I could help you ; but I am powerless."

"Not powerless," said Villiers. "Our time must be occupied with other things. But you can pray for us."

"Yes," said Bentley, faintly, "I have done so. I will do so. It is wonderful how calm and resigned I feel. I have no fear."

"Nor have I," said Bevan; "but it will be a comfort to have prayed together." And with Villiers kneeling at his side, Bevan took his Prayer-book from his pocket.

"Read the Confession," whispered Villiers, "and the Absolution. This may be our last hour."

"Are you ill?" said Bevan to him, in alarm, as he came to the end of the Confession; for Villiers was kneeling unsupported, but nearly drooping to the ground — his arms folded across his bosom — his face buried in his hands — his whole attitude that of a man sinking beneath an intolerable load.

"No, no, go on."

And as Bevan closed the Absolution, Villiers had once more raised himself. His voice joined calmly, almost joyfully, in the Lord's Prayer. His lips moved with every petition which Bevan read from the Psalms, as most suited to their fearful situation; for Villiers never rose in the morning without committing a psalm, or a portion of it, to heart as he was dressing.

"Read," he whispered to Bevan, "the Thanksgiving, for we have much as yet to be thankful for. Read the prayer for all conditions of men, for we must pray for those who are with us, who may be called, like ourselves, before our Maker, suddenly."

But there was no time to do more. A sound, hollow, deep and swelling, like the muttering which precedes an earthquake, struck upon their ears. It was the tramp of feet, measured, firm, numberless, as of a host. Bevan calmly gave them the blessing, and they both rose from their knees. Bentley stretched out his hand once more, and uttered a fervent prayer for them.

"They are coming," he said; God bless you. Go to your posts, and do not think of me,—only save yourselves."

They were indeed coming. Villiers had scarcely time to return to the room where his little garrison was assembled, to address to them a few words reminding them of their duty to their Sovereign, and encouraging them by the prospect of assistance, and still more by the rectitude of their cause, and the never-failing protection of Providence, when the assailants, in three regular columns, issued, without uttering a word, from the three streets which opened in front of the inn, and drew themselves up in a thick mass. As Villiers looked out from a bow window in which he had stationed himself, he had expected to see a mob—a promiscuous, irregular, undisciplined multitude, whom it would be easy to baffle and defeat by the exercise of a little prudence and firmness. But he was startled to see the order with which they marched, halted at the word of command, and drew themselves up almost in a military line. He was not aware how long the movement now made had been ripening under very expert instructors, and how much education had done to infuse discipline and order even into a seditious movement, by inculcating a due regard to an enlightened self-interest and intelligence. They had no sooner reached the ground than the silence which they had observed during their approach was broken by a tremendous shout, which fairly overthrew poor Mrs. Bonsor as she was removing her tea-spoons again to a place of se-

curity, and extorted a shriek from poor Mary,
which went to Villiers's heart.

"My dear Bevan," he said, "go to those poor
women, and comfort them. Make them do something. Tell them to get linen, to scrape lint, to boil
water, to do any thing ; only do not let them remain
unoccupied. I can stand any mob, but I cannot
stand a woman's shriek."

In the meanwhile, from the dark ferocious mass
of heads now ranged in front of the inn, came forward a single person, who seemed to act as their
leader. It was, in fact, Wheeler himself; and calling loudly for the landlord by name, he summoned
him to give up to them the party whom he was
harbouring in his house. Bonsor, with the honest
indignation of an Englishman, would willingly have
faced them, and bade them do their worst, but Villiers held him back.

"No, my good friend," he said ; "I am the person who have brought you into this jeopardy, and it
is fair that I should meet it."

Accordingly he threw up the sash, and, standing
before them, unshrinkingly declared that he himself
was one of the persons whom they were seeking,
and warned them, in the Sovereign's name, to withdraw. "Misguided as you are," he said, "you are
come here to add crime to crime. You have endeavoured to secrete and confine a person who never
injured you, and never intended to injure you; and
because he has exercised the right of an Englishman
to escape, you now come to violate the laws, and to
risk the lives of yourselves and others. I warn you
to retire in time. At present, whatever offences
have been committed, neither your names nor your
persons are known. That gentleman whom you
have so unworthily treated knows nothing of your
secrets, and has no intention of betraying them.

He has bound himself by a solemn promise not to do so; and in pursuance of that promise he has concealed, even from me, the circumstances which placed him in your hands. He is a man, as you ought to know, whose life is spent in providing for the wants of the poor in your own neighbourhood; and this is the return which he meets from Englishmen!"

"Tell them," said Brown, who was standing by his elbow, "that we are armed, and will shoot the first man who approaches."

"No, not yet," replied Villiers. "Do not speak of force till all other words have failed. It is the last thing of which a mob should be reminded."

And, in fact, the quietness, firmness, and coolness of his manner, the fluency and feeling with which he addressed them, and especially his declaration that their secrets were as yet undivulged, produced an obvious effect. A wavering and hesitation was observable among the mass of heads; and even Wheeler himself retired to consult with his lieutenants.

"And who are you?" exclaimed a voice from the crowd.

"I am Mr. Villiers," replied Villiers. "Your own neighbour, who hopes to spend many years in your neighbourhood, and to do you all the good in my power; but who am shocked and astonished, on my return to England, to find that Englishmen can so far forget themselves as to be guilty of such outrages as these. But it is a satisfaction to remain ignorant of the real authors of them. And such a scene as this I trust never to witness again."

He proceeded in the same kind but firm manner to address them at much greater length. It was one of his first objects to gain time; and he knew how easily an English, or indeed any, mob are led and influenced by a good speaker. Nor was he disappointed. They listened to him with less and less unwillingness. " He's a bold chap,"—" Isn't he a fine speaker ?"—" Well, I will say, he's a man of mettle," —" I don't think he's so bad, after all," were remarks which he caught at intervals; and it is not impossible but that his eloquence might have been successful, had not a figure, who had hitherto kept entirely in the back-ground, hidden under the houses, now crept up, and mixed with the outlying stragglers, who were unable to hear what was said.

" Hoot him," said the figure to a boy. " Hiss him. Why don't you hoot and hiss ?"

" Hoot him," yelled out the boy. " Hoot him, hoot him," joined his neighbours. And the clamour once commenced, in a few moments the contagion seized the whole body, and a din and roar arose which drowned all that Villiers would have uttered. He saw that the ground was cut from under his feet. He made signs, but in vain, though he continued to stand firm and unmoved, waiting for an opportunity of obtaining another hearing. Even a mob cannot hoot for ever; and though the favourable feeling was extinguished for the time by the physical excitement which had been raised against him, he might once more have gained an audience, but the same figure in the back-ground, who had looked at his watch, and seemed impatient of delay, once more crept into the crowd.

" Why do you not have a fling at him ?" he said to the same boy whom he had addressed before. " Here's a stone."

And Villiers the next instant heard the pane of glass above his head shiver into atoms. It was like the single big drop which brings down the whole torrent of the thunder-storm. No sooner was the sound heard than there rose from the dense mass of heads a yell twice as fearful as before. "Down with him! down with him!" was the cry; and a volley of stones followed which shattered every window in the front of the house. Villiers saw that all was over. He had been struck on the head with a flint, and his face was bleeding.

"Shall we fire?" asked one of the men, impatiently.

"No, no," said Villiers, "remember my orders. Let us wait for some more deadly manifestation before we take life. Are all your men at their post, Mr. Brown?"

"Yes, sir."

"Wait, then, till I have spoken to the mob once more."

And, taking advantage of a momentary lull, Villiers admonished them again, in the Sovereign's name, to withdraw. "I warn you now," he said, "that we are well armed — thoroughly prepared to shoot the first man that proposes to enter the house; and I call Heaven to witness, that if you still persist in this outrage your blood is on your own head."

Before he could finish the sentence, a pistol was fired from the crowd—no one ever knew by whom, and a ball whizzed past Villiers, and grazed his ear.

"Now, then," he said to Brown, "all of you to your posts!" He drew his head within the window, closed down the sash, and begged Bevan to put up the mattresses against it again, so as to leave a space from which, with his own pistols, he could command the entrance. It was the only window in the house where this was possible. "Now go to the side walls. Charge the men to keep their fire, as I have ordered, and on no account to fire promiscuously, where they may hurt women or children. Ask Mrs. Bonsor to come to me: it will initiate her in her duties to put a little lint on this hurt, which is a mere trifle." It was done chiefly to relieve her mind by giving her some occupation; and the poor woman was roused from the stupor of terror into which she had fallen, and began to bustle about, with Mary, for lint and rags, pleased with the thought of being useful, and relieved from much of her apprehension for the future by finding that the first wound was of so little moment. Meanwhile, the firing of the pistol was the signal for the first attack. Twelve huge savage foundrymen, each wielding an enormous crowbar, with which they break open their furnaces, detached themselves from the front of the mob, and advanced to the door. Two blows were levelled on it, but failed to demolish it; but as the third man was poising his bar, and levelling it against the lock, eight tongues of flame leaped out of the side walls, amidst a volume of smoke and the discharge of musketry. The smoke cleared off. Six of the ringleaders were lying dead upon the ground; two others had been wounded: and, amidst a yell, partly of terror and surprise, and partly of fury, the whole mass of assailants had recoiled, and left the space in front of the inn quite clear.

CHAP. IX.

" I WILL make one more effort," said Villiers,
gazing from the window on the sad sight beneath
him. " They have obeyed me well — have singled
out the ringleaders, and marked them. It may be,
Heaven will still touch their hearts, and we may be
spared more of this frightful bloodshed." He threw
up the window again, and endeavoured to make
himself heard. But the moment he appeared the
uproar became terrific : several shots were fired at
him, amidst a volley of stones; and Bevan dragged
him back into the room.

" It is hopeless," he said. " When blood has once
been shed, a mob becomes a monster of ferocity.
The battle must be fought out. Bear me witness
that I have done all in my power to spare life."

He had no time, however, to say more. The
assailants had consulted together, and, gathering
themselves in a dense column, they rushed, with a
hideous cry, up to the front of the house. Once
more the fire from the flanking walls opened upon
them, and every shot told : Villiers himself, from
his post at the window, fixed upon the most conspicuous of the assailants, and his aim rarely missed.
From the attics the boys hurled down their paving-
stones upon a mass of heads on which every missile
did execution. The women themselves, kindled
with the excitement, now joined in the defence ;
and, arming themselves with kettles of boiling
water, and pails of scalding liquor from the brew-
house, poured them upon the eyes and faces of the

pitmen, till they shrieked with agony. Body after body fell, and was trampled on by the advancing column, who, untouched as yet by the fire of the musketry, were not aware of the danger of approaching till they were close to the house, and there, excluded from retreat, aimed their ineffectual blows at the doors and windows, and then sank, and were trodden down in a mass of carnage. Pressed and jammed together, they were unable to use their arms, or receive orders. In vain Wheeler and others in command endeavoured to make the advancing body recede, that there might be scope for a more regular attack. Every thing was confusion and uproar; howlings of the wounded and dying; shriekings and horrible imprecations, as the torrents of boiling stuff were poured suddenly on their upturned faces; blasphemous outcries, which none but demons would have uttered; and, rising above all, threats of the most horrible vengeance against Villiers and all around him. At last their efforts succeeded. The pannels of the door were smashed to atoms; the windows — the shutters — framework, — all were demolished. A breach, it seemed, was made into the house; but, to the disappointment of the attackers, both the passage and the rooms had been so filled with mattresses, drawers, and chests, and light chairs, piled up to the ceiling, over which it was impossible to climb, that they were as far removed from their object as at first. Wheeler himself, furious when he found himself thus baffled, at last succeeded in forcing his men back from an unavailing attempt, in which life after life was sacrificed without their being able to 'touch the defenders of the little fortress. Once more the mass recoiled; the space before the house was cleared; and as Villiers looked down upon it again, now piled with corpses and heaps of mutilated and

wounded bodies groaning with pain, the clock struck
four. Two hours were past of the four on which
he had calculated to hold out. There was a pause
— a silence as awful as the dead, breathless calm
between the bursts of a hurricane. And Villiers
sank into a chair, and burst into a flood of tears.

Bevan stood by him, with mingled compassion
and admiration, but left the feeling to find vent,
without attempting to check it.

"Leave me," said Villiers, "for two minutes to
myself. Go, if you are not worn out, and see that
the men have refreshments. Send Mr. Brown and
Bonsor to me ; and let me know if any one. has
been hurt."

Bevan hastened on his commission, and Villiers
fastened the door, and knelt down to calm and recover himself, and ask for guidance. He knew that
the worst was still to come. The more sanguine landlord thought otherwise. He came, in high spirits, to
congratulate and thank Villiers, as if all was achieved.
But his courage was considerably damped by hearing
the opinion of the superintendent, that another
attack would take place. "If," said he, "they had
been a mere common mob, without object or order,
they would have given it up long since. But there
is more mischief in them than I thought."

"Do you remember," said Bevan to Villiers,
"the young lion we spoke of? Bear or tiger would
be the more proper name. But this is the monster
that England has been nurturing with her manufacturing system, and instructing in her alphabet ;
and even now it is not full grown."

At this moment the keeper came in. He also
thought the battle was won. "Blacker," he said,
"had come to him, and asked to change posts
with him, as he did not like, if he could help it, to
fire upon his old friends. And he was accordingly.

stationed in the loft, to watch the garden gate.
Was it necessary for him to remain there longer?"

"Absolutely necessary," said Villiers. "You
will observe the enemy have not retreated; they
have screened themselves behind the houses, but they
are still in full force ; and if they have with them
men who know any thing of their business, their
next attempt will be upon the stable-yard, since
they cannot get into the house in the front. Do
you think it possible, Mr. Brown, for us to hold
good the side walls, if they attempt to scale them ?"

Brown thought for a minute, and shook his head.
"We must try," he said ; "but, with their number,
I doubt."

"No one has been hurt yet ?" asked Villiers.

"None."

"Have the men had their refreshment ? "

"Yes."

"How are the poor women ?"

Bevan said that he had taken them for the present into Bentley's room, and comforted them ; and
that Bentley himself was now speaking to them ;
but that they were in a sad state. Villiers then gave
his orders, and having placed Bonsor to occupy his
post at the bow-window, he prepared to place himself at the head of the little garrison in the yard.
It was now the post of danger. He had been perfectly right in his conjecture. Grady, a savage-
looking Irishman, who had been a private in the
life-guards, and flogged out of the regiment for
repeated drunkenness, was at the head of one of
the columns, and he now insisted on directing the
attack upon the side walls. "Silence those muskets," he said, "and the day is ours."

Wheeler himself saw the wisdom of the advice ;
and, though their numbers were thinned, and not
a few had stolen away in despair, it was resolved to

adopt it. Villiers was looking from the window on the heap of mangled bodies, among which two haggard miserable women, who had forced their way through the assailants, were now searching, with piercing cries, for a son and a husband whom they missed. He thought of making an effort to persuade the pitmen, at least, to remove their wounded, under a promise that they should not be fired on during the removal. But Brown interfered.

"These men," he said, "know nothing of such things. They have no trust, and no faith, and no pity; and you must leave them to themselves. Hark, sir, hark! There's no time to be lost. Do you not hear a tramp? They're coming. Hark!"

And listening, they caught distinctly the sound of a large body of men approaching.

"It's the soldiers," cried the sanguine Bonsor; "you can hear their tread.

"The soldiers," repeated Bevan, "the soldiers!" and he was hastening off, with the joyful tidings, to Bentley's room.

"Stop," cried Villiers, catching his arm. "You are not sure. Listen to that shout? Those are not cheers of defiance."

It was too true. The same dark figure which had so frequently before stolen into the outskirts of the crowd, and directed their movements unperceived, when he saw the determined resistance of the little garrison, had hastened to a hut which stood on the top of an eminence over the town. From this four rockets shot up, which were answered from Pen-deen hill, about three miles distant, on the side of which lay the great Brocas works; and the hurrah of the assailants now hailed the arrival of a strong reinforcement from that quarter. Only a few moments of suspense were given; but even those moments were as hours. Villiers alone remained calm.

"Are you all ready?" he said.   " Remember, if we cannot make good the line of wall, we retire into the house, without risk."

" Make haste," cried Brown, "they're coming."

And as they hurried down the stairs, the whole mass of assailants rushed, with horrible yells, into the little square.   Instead of attempting the house, they divided themselves, as Villiers had suspected, into two bodies; and, provided with such means as they had been able to seize, they threw themselves on each other's shoulders, and proceeded to scale both the walls at once.   Wave followed on wave. The openings made in the mass by the fire from the loop-holes were filled up, as if none had fallen. Heads, shoulders, whole bodies appeared on the summit of the wall along the whole line, — some hanging lifeless across it, as they fell under the bayonets of the besieged; others thrust forward by the advancing mass, and thrown headlong into the court; others dropping down in the intervals between the line of defenders.   The struggle was fearful.   But Villiers saw that it was hopeless; and while it was yet possible to give the signal for retreat, they mustered at the back door of the inn, and halted. One man only was missing : it was Blacker.   "He's in the loft," said Villiers, "and will be cut off;" and plunging across the yard, he dragged him down, and had all but brought him to the steps of the door, when a fresh body of men burst through the garden gate.   They fell on him with fury.   "Save me !" cried the miserable man, "save me !" as Wheeler, one of the foremost, seized and tore him from Villiers's grasp.   Villiers threw himself upon the body, and with his sabre swept a circle around him, and, placing the unhappy wretch behind him, he endeavoured to cover his retreat into the house. But it was in vain. The walls were scaled, the yard filled with ruffians, and, after a tremendous effort, Villiers found himself driven up to the steps, and was dragged by Bonsor and the keeper within the door. "Open the door," he cried to them, as they endeavoured to retain him in their arms, and to prevent him from exposing himself in vain. "Open the door. They will tear that poor wretch in pieces. Let us rescue him." But the firmness of the keeper held him fast. It was too late. Amidst the roar and outcry they heard one frightful cry, "Save me!" From the window one of the policemen saw a figure hurled down to the ground by a group of fiend-like faces, who fell on it like cannibals on their prey. And this was the last thing known of the unhappy man. When the day dawned, and the field of slaughter was examined, a limb was found, with a fragment of dress upon it, which was supposed to be his, but all the rest was indistinguishable. Villiers, absolutely sick with horror, would have sunk under it, had his attention not been called to Bevan, who, with nerves far less accustomed to such scenes, had fallen back in a chair and all but fainted. But this sight, and the necessity of exerting himself, roused Villiers anew.

"Now, my friends," he said, "we are safe. We have gained all the time we could have expected by maintaining our outposts. They cannot touch us here; and we have only to stand firm for an hour or two longer, by which time the dragoons will arrive."

"Thank God!" uttered every one present, with a deep and long inspiration.

"Why, Bevan, my good fellow, you of all men must not give way," said Villiers to him. "What shall I do without my aid-de-camp? Take some of

this," and he compelled him to swallow a glass of
wine. "Now, gentlemen, half to the front of the
house, and half to the back. Manage your fire
well. Let the boys, with their paving-stones,
employ themselves in the attics; and Bonsor, here
— if Mrs. Bonsor has any large washing-tubs, and
will fill them with water, and put some wet blankets
into them, they may be of use."

He did not tell the landlord his reason ; but he
whispered to Brown, "We have little to fear now
but one thing. Look to fire, and be ready to put
it out; but say nothing. Move that mattress closer
to the back-door—now bring that chest of drawers
against it—raise it on the table; those chairs will
fill up the passage. Are all the other lower windows
well barricaded?" and Brown having examined them
with him, they were satisfied that it would be
impossible for an entrance to be effected without
more time than must elapse before assistance would
reach them. He pointed this out to the little
party, and their stations being taken at the upper
windows, the battle once more began.

It is needless to dwell upon the madness and
ferocity with which the assailants now, like a tiger
blooded with its first prey, hurled themselves
against each front of the house. The doors and
the windows on both sides were in a few minutes
shattered to atoms and torn from their place. The
ground in front of them was piled with bodies,
which fell rapidly under the fire from the upper
windows, and still fresh waves swept up and broke
against the wall, in vain attempts to tear away the
mattresses and beds, which presented a more effectual barrier than even a wall of stone. Four
times Wheeler, who was leading on the attack in
the yard, drew back his men and paused. Four
times they fell again upon the house, hoping that

the ammunition of the little garrison would be exhausted or their courage worn out. Their own fire-arms, not many in number, had long since become useless by the failure of powder, and the stoutest hearts were beginning to think of abandoning the attempt, or, at any rate, of waiting for day-light, and for what the day might bring. They now felt that the plot which they had so long dwelt on in secret had exploded; and this was the first act. They were now committed; but if this was the beginning, what would be the end? Wheeler alone was resolved to lose no time. He had kept to himself the secret of the arrival of dragoons at Hakewell Barracks, lest it should dishearten his followers; but finding the steady and military defence which the attacked were making, he could little doubt that they had thought of sending for assistance. At any rate, news of such an outbreak travels fast, and with the morning the troops would come. He rested gloomily and savagely, like a wild beast at bay, with his back against the stable wall. Something embarrassed his feet, and he looked out to see what it was. It was a mangled, disfigured head, and he kicked it away with a frightful oath—"So much for one traitor." One of the men brought him a pot of beer to quench his thirst, but he thrust it aside, and cursed him for his pains. He was like a dog caught in a trap, and frantic with pain, whom it is not safe to approach even to set him free. The men rested on their arms and stood aloof from him; when the same dark figure, which was noticed before, once more crept forward from the gloom, and stood at his elbow.

"Captain," he said.

And Wheeler jumped round furiously at the interruption to his thoughts. "Who are you? Ha!"

and he broke into a savage laugh, in which scorn
was mingled with passion.   "You, Mr. Pearce?
Who would have thought of seeing you where
fighting is going forward? Are you sure,"—and he
lowered his voice and ground his teeth — "are you
sure this is none of your work?"

"Wheeler," said Pearce, calmly, "are you not
mad to ask such a question, when you know what I
have done for you this day? Whose fault is this
but your own? Who permitted your fellows to
bring the parson up here into the forest?"

Some recriminations only exasperate; but this
charged Wheeler with a fault which he was ready
to avow and lament, and it rather conciliated him.

"Who was it," continued Pearce, "that managed
to bring you the Brocas men just in time but
myself? And who can now, if he chooses, put you
in five minutes into the middle of that house but
myself?"

Wheeler stared at him as if asking explanation.

"I tell you, Wheeler," said Pearce, "that I can
put you, and as many men as you choose, into the
middle of that house in ten minutes,—that is, if I
choose."

Wheeler stared again; but he was so well acquainted with Pearce's wonderful skill in observing
and collecting information, and carrying on intrigues, that he believed it possible for him now
to possess some secret means of executing what he
proposed.

"And you will choose," he said, hastily, "you
will choose.   How is it?   Which is the way?"
and he snatched up the heavy iron bar which he
had been wielding, and was moving to the house.
"Stop, man, stop," rejoined Pearce. "I may choose,
and I will choose, but it must be on one condition."

" And what is that?" asked Wheeler, impetuously.

" I will tell it you fairly, Wheeler," said the other. " You know that you have in your possession papers of mine, which you have no right to keep, and which can be of no use to you, though they are to me. Give them up to me, and I pledge myself to put you in the middle of that house within one quarter of an hour, nay, in five minutes."

Wheeler uttered a violent imprecation. " They are lost," he cried. •

" No, Wheeler," answered Pearce, " they are not lost—you know they are not lost; you are not such a fool. Give me up those papers, and I will do what I promise."

" You shall do it without," said Wheeler. " Look here;" and he kicked with his foot against the ghastly head which lay before him; and even Pearce turned sick, and shuddered. " This is the way we deal with traitors; and if you refuse to show us the way into that house now, why you are a traitor, and shall be dealt with accordingly."

" Hollo, there!" and he summoned some of his men to seize Pearce. Pearce himself preserved his equanimity, as usual. " Send away your men," he said, " for you know they are of no use. You know that if my head was to be torn from my body, I would not utter a word which I did not choose; and if I were gone, what would become of your purse, ha? Stand off, my good fellows," he said to the party that approached; " do you know who I am?" and they fell back, awed by his manner and gesture.

" Wheeler," he said again, " you have now but a short time to finish your work in; in another hour or two soldiers will be here: and unless the house and all that's in it are yours by that time, you know that you are lost. No one will stand by you to be shot down like partridges. If you cannot take a poor public-house, who do you think will follow you in any other of your projects? Will you give me those papers?"

"They are lost, I tell you."

"No," replied Pearce, "they are not lost. I give you five minutes for your answer, and then I shall be off." And he took out his watch, and began to count. Wheeler remained sulkily silent. The five minutes expired; and Pearce wished him good night, and was leaving.

"Stop, come back," cried Wheeler; "if I can find them, you shall have them to-morrow."

Pearce came up to him, and looked him full in the face. "Do you think I am such a fool as to wait for to-morrow? I must have them now on this spot."

"They are not here," said Wheeler; "they are in my box."

"No," said Pearce, hastily, "they are not in your box." He spoke incautiously; and if the other had observed the vehemence and certainty with which he asserted this, he might have suspected what was actually the fact,—that Pearce, while every one else had been engaged in the affray, had contrived to return to Wheeler's room, and there, by means of his ingenious apparatus, had made himself master of all the contents of the corded deal box, among which he had not hesitated to select some documents of even more importance to their right owner than his own were to himself. He reconciled the abstraction to his conscience by the plea of necessary retaliation. The end justified the means.

Wheeler remained silent again. "And if I do give them to you," he said, at last, "how do I know that you will show us the way?"

"I will give you leave to shoot me," said Pearce.

"We may do that without your leave," said Wheeler.

"I can wait no longer," exclaimed the other. "Am I to have the papers?"

"Take them, and much good may they do you," cried Wheeler, furiously. And from a secret pocket in his rough coat he drew a packet tied with tape, and sealed with black wax, and flung it at Pearce's feet. Pearce took it up, carefully examined it, carefully deposited it in a secret pocket in his own coat, and then told Wheeler and his party to follow him.

CHAP. X.

THERE was near to, but not actually adjoining, the north gable end of the Blake Arms a long low range of buildings, which had been attached by degrees to the main fabric, and served the purpose of scullery, brew-house, wash-house, and other useful offices. Seemingly, there was an open passage between it and the house; and, externally, it presented no means of access to the interior. It had, therefore, not been marked as a point of attack; and as no window opened from the gable, it lay out of sight of the besieged. Pearce led the way to this range, and ordered them to remove a pile of old packing-boxes and hampers, which were lying loosely in one corner. "Underneath," he said, "you will find a trap-door; that door is the outer entrance to the cellars, which lie under these low buildings; from the cellars a flight of stone steps leads up into the kitchen. And I will venture to say, that no one has thought of blocking up that passage. It is scarcely ever used."

In what manner he had obtained his information it is unnecessary to explain. With his shrewdness and talent for such a discovery, this was one of the least extraordinary of his achievements. He had learned it from the men who were in the habit of carting coals into the Blake Arms, and who had often seen butts rolled down into the cellar through the inclined plane which the trap-door covered, and had themselves been admitted by the stone steps into the interior of the house.

And while this was passing on the outside, what was occurring in the interior of the house? Few things are more wonderful than the facility with which the human mind accommodates itself to any circumstances, however strange and dreadful. Satisfied that the defences were sufficient to enable them to hold out for a considerable time longer—accustomed to the fearful sights, and sounds, and work of butchery which at first had thrilled them with horror, and encouraged by the pause which had been made in the attack, and by the obvious discomfiture of the assailants, the little party had laid down their arms, and Villiers had insisted that such as were most exhausted should endeavour to take some repose, if only for a few minutes. Mrs. Bonsor and Mary were employed in carrying refreshments to them, and Villiers, with Mr. Brown, once more looked round the lower rooms, strengthening the weak parts of the barricades, and satisfying themselves that all was right. Two points he was still anxious about—the possibility of fire and the failure of ammunition. Against the former he had made the provision of the wet blankets, and for the latter he now proposed that recourse should be had to the powder, of which the landlord had spoken, in the cellar. Brown went to call Bonsor, that he might show him where it was to be found. And all three had just reached the door, which opened from the kitchen at the top of the stone steps, when they heard voices, a rush, a shout on the other side within the cellar, and, before they could recover themselves, a crash followed, the pannels of the door fell in, and they found themselves confronting ten of the most savage of the gang, armed with pick-axes, crowbars, hatchets, and pikes, and their clothes and faces smeared with filth and blood. Wheeler was at their head. Each party recoiled for a moment at the unlooked-for encounter. But it was only for a moment ; the next instant a furious conflict commenced. The steps were narrow, steep, and without any protection at the sides, and the communication between them and the vaults beyond was through a dark, narrow archway, which admitted only two persons abreast. But for this, all must have been over at once. It gave time to Villiers and his companions to stop their progress, until the rest of the little garrison could come to their assistance. Two of the assailants were hurled off the steps by a tremendous blow from the keeper. Wheeler had aimed his pike at the breast of Villiers, but the thrust was parried by the bayonet of a policeman. Brown himself nearly severed the arm of another pitman from the shoulder by a stroke of his sabre ; and the shots of the rest of the party, aimed into the dark passage, cleared it for the time. There was a moment's respite. " Block up this archway," said Villiers. " Here are tubs, boxes ; roll that hogshead to the entrance, and we are still safe." But before their purpose could be effected, the whole range of cellars behind was filled with armed men. They rushed forward like demons, some of them bearing torches, which threw a lurid glare on the horrible faces of the throng, others staving the casks and gorging themselves with their contents, — all thrusting and forcing on each other in an irresistible torrent. The foremost, who had retired within the narrow archway, were driven on by the rear, whether they would advance or not. Three of them were struck down. Four more fell under the fire of the besieged party, who had stationed themselves on the stone steps. But the crush carried every thing before it. Villiers was driven back, and thrown down just on the other side of the archway. One of the policemen was grasped, and

hurled from the steps; the others were compelled
to give way; and Bonsor, exclaiming that " all was
lost!" was hastening to make his last effort, and die
in defending his wife, when, amidst the din and
clamour of the conflict, all at once, without a moment's warning, the whole body, besieged and be-
siegers, were wrapt in a whirlwind of fire; there
was a deep, rushing, quivering shock, like an
earthquake. A burst, as of thunder, a crash, gusts
and volumes of smoke, chimneys tottering, roofs
splitting, walls opening and closing again in huge
rents from top to bottom, the ground rocking under
their feet; then came a pause; and then over their
heads the showering down of beams and stones, and
fragments of roofs and mangled limbs. All was
silent; and the clock struck five.

When Villiers opened his eyes, he looked up and
saw the grey sky just paling with the approach of
dawn, and visible through a yawning chasm which
had been broken in the crown of the vault. A
large stone was hanging over his head, and seemed
ready to fall and crush him. And stunned and
bewildered as he was, he endeavoured to move
himself, but a heavy weight was lying across him.
It was a body apparently lifeless, his face to the
ground; and, by his rough pea-jacket, it was evidently one of the assailants. Villiers drew himself
from beneath him, and raised himself to look around.
The vault was shattered; black volumes of smoke
were curling round and round within it, and issuing
from the now shapeless aperture which had formed
the narrow entrance into the cellar. The stone
steps were covered with a pile of mangled, and
scorched, and blackened bodies, among which he
recognised Brown, stretched upon the ground, but
still breathing, and the landlord apparently dead,
and half-buried under a mass of rubbish. His

thoughts wandered, like those of a dreaming man, to the scenes in which he had been engaged during the night; and at times he fancied that it was a dream, and that he would awake and find it so. But the cold air blew upon his face, and he recovered the consciousness of its reality. He made an effort to move from the spot; his hands were unhurt. A pike had penetrated through the fleshy part of his left arm, but without any serious mischief; and having been thrown behind the wall through which the archway opened, he had been secured both from the blast and the crash of the explosion. For he now remembered the barrel of powder, and was satisfied that the assailants in their fury, having begun to stave the casks, had fallen also upon this; and the torches, which had glared within the cellar, was sufficient to explain the rest. His next thought was Bentley. He made his way into the kitchen, which had been dismantled as by an earthquake. The plaster had fallen from the ceiling; the shelves had dislodged their contents; tables and chairs had been overturned; the fire had been blown from the hearth, and blazing coal still lay about the floor; and a broad rent in the side wall admitted the light through it. From this he passed into the bar, which presented a similar scene of devastation. Part of the staircase had been blown away, and he was obliged to climb up by the remaining fragments. But on reaching Bentley's room he found Bevan, with the two women and the boys, there, and in safety. They were upon their knees, too horror-struck either to speak or move. Bentley himself, who, naturally weak and nerveless, had acquired strength and fortitude by the trial to which he had been exposed, was the most composed. Bevan, whose heroism, however, had hitherto been nursed in theory, without opportunity

of testing it by practice, was completely overcome.
But the sight of Villiers, alive and unhurt, restored them partially to their presence of mind.
Poor Mrs. Bonsor's first demand was for her husband. She flung herself at Villiers's knees, implored him to take her to him, bewailed the day
that she was born, and the hour that Villiers had
entered the house; and then checking herself, even
in the midst of her agony, lest she should hurt his
feelings, she rose up, and snatching a candle, was
hastening down stairs. She had nearly fallen down
the aperture which had been caused by the explosion, but a hand at the bottom was stretched out to
save her, and she was caught in the arms of her
husband, half-scorched, and blackened, and yet
pale as a ghost, and still bewildered in his senses,
but alive. Scarcely before had Villiers seen a
sight which so relieved him. They hastened to the
stone steps, and from a mass of bodies extricated
Brown, who, like Villiers, had been thrown down
and trampled on by the rush, but had been also protected by them in their fall. One of the policemen
was also alive, and had raised himself from the
ground at their approach, and was shaking his
limbs to discover if they were still sound. The
others they were searching for, when a noise was
heard at the front of the house; and Villiers, reminding Brown that the conflict might not yet be
over, and that advantage might be taken of the confusion to effect an entrance, went to ascertain the
state of the case. He found the yard entirely deserted, but strewed with the blackened fragments
of the outbuildings, and with scorched and mangled bodies. The court in front was also clear.
The assailants had fled at the explosion in all directions. Only a few straggling faces were peering
round the corners of the adjoining buildings; and

he began to cherish the hope that the day was his
own. One more hour, and it was scarcely possible
but that the military would arrive. He sat down
at the bow-window to watch ; and the stupor and
exhaustion which follows over-excitement surprised
him with a dizziness, in which he nearly fell from
his chair. Once more the whole scene appeared
a dream. The room seemed to reel round him.
Horrible phantoms, visions of the realities which
he had witnessed, thronged round him, as in mockery and defiance. He roused himself, drew his
hand across his eyes, and once more prepared to take
his post, in case the attack should be renewed. He
summoned Brown, now sufficiently recovered to
examine the state of the defences.

"It cannot be," said Bevan, when Villiers suggested the possibility that they might still be in
danger. "It is not possible, after what has happened, that they will venture again."

Villiers cheered him with the expression of a
hope that he was right.

"But it is our business, he said, "to prepare for
the worst. All may still be lost by neglect. And
if these are the dangers and the enemies which we
are likely to encounter in this country, we must
learn perseverance as well as courage. Here is
Mr. Brown, with the true spirit of an English soldier, as ready to fight to the last, now, as he was at
the beginning."

Brown cheerfully assented. On examination,
they found that the house itself, though shattered
by the explosion, had not sustained any damage
which materially affected its security. The archway opening which had been made into the kitchen
was soon blocked up. And the little garrison,
miserably reduced in number, and thinking bitterly
of those who had been lost, once more assembled,

and Villiers insisted that they should take some refreshment again. The morning was now breaking with returning light; the consciousness and the reality of danger were disappearing. And assuming a confidence which he did not feel, Villiers cheered and comforted them, till they began to think that all danger was past.

And all danger would have been past, if the conflict had been only with a rude and undisciplined mob. But other elements were arrayed against them. And any one who in the present day should think that an outbreak of the kind is to be met as a common explosion of popular violence will be deceived, as they were deceived.

CHAP. XI.

THE body which had recoiled from the front when
the explosion took place, and those who had escaped from the yard, reassembled at some little
distance, in an open space, which served for the
market of Howlas. Dismayed, disheartened, and
ignorant of the cause of the explosion, their leaders
lost, and their passion cooled by terror, they would
have abandoned all further attempts upon the inn,
and separated, had not once more the same figure,
which has appeared so frequently, emerged from
the surrounding gloom, and insinuated himself into
the crowd. In the mass not a few were found who
had been saved, almost miraculously, from the explosion. They had been drinking in the cellars,
and many of them, though fearfully burnt, were
still in a state of intoxication. There was no difficulty in approaching, none in representing all that
had passed as a mere delusion, none in suggesting the possibility of obtaining more drink. The
Swan was at hand; there was plenty of liquor
there. Nothing was needed but to call for the landlord; and a rush, no one seemed to know how or
why, was made to the Swan. The family, already
startled from their sleep, and gazing in terror
from the windows, were compelled to open the
door. The mob (for they had now lost all appearance of an armed force) burst into the passage,
the bar, the cellar, demanding liquor. In a few
minutes the house was ransacked. Those who
were before intoxicated became now frantic, and

those who had been desirous in sober terror to
retire were now again inflamed and ready for a
fresh attack. They were ready for any thing, —
reckless and maddened with drink. Candles were
burning in the house; and one, the same boy who
has appeared before, held one in joke to the curtains of the front parlour. The jest caught, others
did the same, and before any attempts could be
made to extinguish the flames, the house was in a
blaze. "Now then, to the inn!" was the cry. "To
the inn," "to the inn!" Some one had raised the
shout from the extremity of the throng. But it
was caught up in a moment. "To the inn," "to
the inn!" And Villiers, who had heard the uproar,
and saw a glare of light rising up over the roofs of
the adjoining houses, had scarcely time to give the
alarm, and to gather his diminished garrison, when
once more the assailants plunged headlong into the
little square. They were no longer marshalled;
there was no word of command, no halt, no appearance of order. Leaping, dancing, shrieking,
howling, more of them bearing in their hands fragments of burning wood than weapons, and resem-
bling little but a horde of wild savages in some mad
and bloody revel — tossing their torches into the
air, and hurling imprecations upon all who should
resist them, mixed with obscene shouts and blasphemous curses, they rushed upon the inn. One
party advanced before the rest. In the midst of
them was a wretched man, naked all but his shirt,
whom they had dragged from his bed, at the Swan,
and at his earnest prayers had permitted him, as a
jest, to drag with him a heavy portmanteau. Round
him they danced and screamed, till the miserable
being would fain have closed his eyes and ears to
avert the sight and sounds, which seemed to him
a foretaste of his place of eternal torment. Now

they dragged him along through the mire; then
they hunted him before them; then they compelled
him to hug and embrace his precious portmanteau,
which, at last, they tore from him, burst it open,
and in one minute its contents were dispersed
among the mob, and sovereigns were rolling about
the ground. At last, as if satiated with play, a
hand was raised behind him, and he was levelled to
the ground. "Ha!" said Brown to Villiers, who
were gazing on the scene from the bow-window,
"there is our unfortunate friend; he has neither
saved his money, nor has his money saved him.
But, shall we fire?"

"Not yet," said Villiers; "the miserable wretches
are intoxicated. Blood enough has been shed already, if more can be spared: they may be incapable of doing mischief, and must be insensible to
menace." And, apparently, this was the case. They
advanced close up to the inn, dashed their weapons
against the wall, but made no effort to enter.

"Are there not some boys climbing over the
wall?" said Brown. "Look, sir, close by the wall
that has been broken down by the explosion."

"Yes," said Villiers, "there is a man helping a
boy over; look, he is giving him a torch. Let
Bonsor have an eye to the yard. I confess I
like these fiery weapons far less than the pickaxes
and pikes. Happily, they do not seem to have any
of their wits about them." And the mob indeed
had not; but there was another near them who had
—the same who was assisting over the wall the
young boy, to whom he had suggested the exploit.

"Surely," said Villiers, a short time after, "I
smell fire. There is smoke coming up the staircase. They cannot have found means to throw fire
into the house?" But he had scarcely uttered the
words, when Bonsor rushed up stairs to tell him
that the lower rooms were in flames.

"All of them?" asked Villiers.

"Three," said Brown. "They have managed to throw fire in among the bedding and chairs, and the things are too crowded for us to get at it."

It was the first moment that Villiers had felt despair. But he now sank down, and groaned aloud. Presently he sprang up, as if ashamed of his weakness.

"Can we make a sally?" he said to Brown.

Brown shook his head. "There are but five of us, and there are two women and the sick gentleman to protect, and he not able to walk. It would be certain destruction."

And at that minute the clock struck once more. "Three hours!" exclaimed Villiers. "If we could only gain a little time — half an hour more!"

But the smoke now rolled up the stairs in thicker volumes.

"Where are the wet blankets?" cried Villiers. But on examining, it was found impossible to use them. The fire had been thrown in among the loose furniture, and it was hopeless to attempt to extinguish it.

"Bonsor," said Villiers, "close fast the doors of these rooms. Help me to tear away this part of the staircase. Now throw down into the opening carpets, rugs — any thing which will close it up. You have a cistern on that floor; get at the pipe, and have water ready to keep them wet with. If we can stop the communication between the two floors, we may last out yet."

"Why, sir," said Bonsor, "I have often heard my father say that this house was built by a man who had a patent for keeping houses from being burnt. It was he who built that house in which the king and all his court drank tea in the upper room, while the under room was set on a blaze with

faggots and tar-barrels. He had something—mortar,
I think — put between all the joists of the ceilings,
so that the fire cannot get at the wood."

" Thank —" exclaimed Villiers. He was going
to finish the exclamation, but even in his deepest
emotion he hesitated to use the sacred name. He
only looked up reverently, fervently, and gratefully.
" This may help us."

And they proceeded with greater energy to accomplish what he had suggested. The staircase
was pulled away, the aperture filled up. Nothing
remained for them but to sit down and gaze upon
each other, while the devouring element beneath
them was roaring and chafing under their feet as if
impatient to obtain access to them.

" It's very odd, sir," said Bonsor, who had just
succeeded in turning the pipe of the cistern, so as
to give them a command of water, " but my father,
who was your father's tenant, sir, at Rudgely Farm,
when he built this house, always had a fancy that
it would be burnt some day or other. It's wonderful how things turn out. Who would have thought,
when he had that mortar put to the ceilings, and
this great leaden cistern built, so many years back,
that it would have stood us in this stead now ? It
looks wonderfully like a Providence."

And Villiers thought how many such Provi-
dences occur each hour, connecting the most remote
occurrences, and planned by an eye to which there
is neither past nor future in its provisions for the
dispensation of justice.

" Why," continued Bonsor, " that leaden cistern
itself, we used to laugh at him for building ; only
he would have it. And it cost him a power of
money. He had it made over the wood-house and
coal-house, and built it upon great thick walls
strong enough for a house. I shall never forget

when the bill came in for lining it with lead. But
he made the best of it, and bade us not laugh, for
one of these days we should find the use of it. I
do not know if he thought any thing of the kind of
doings we have had to-night, for at that time there
were no mines opened here. But he always had a
sort of superstition about that cistern; and so have I."

It is wonderful with what avidity minds in moments of danger seize upon omens. The leaden
cistern was something more than an omen. But
even in this light it encouraged them; and the
party renewed their exertions to keep the aperture
of the staircase closely blocked up with wet carpets.
Apparently their efforts were successful. The flames
roared underneath their feet; vast whirlwinds of
smoke gushed out of the lower windows, and swept
round them, at times almost suffocating them; but
their position was still tenable. There was no necessity to keep watch at the windows; they were protected from the attack of the assailants by the very
flames which were threatening their destruction.

"Take care, do not waste the water," said Villiers; "I think the fire is wearing itself out;" when
Brown came rushing to him in consternation. They
had forgotten the back staircase. The flight of
steps opened in a corner of the kitchen, which,
being paved with stone, was the last part which
the fire had reached. But it had penetrated there,
had crept along the dressers and ranges of shelves,
and had seized the stairs; and volumes of smoke
and flame were now bursting from the passage, on
which it opened upon the first floor. Villiers hastened to the spot. They endeavoured to tear down
the woodwork, but the fire would not allow of their
approach. Water was thrown in every way possible upon the floor; but their carpets and rugs had
all been employed on the front stairs. And as Vil-

liers was hurrying to Bentley's room, that he might
be removed to the attic, Bonsor met him, with a
face of horrible despair, to tell him that the leaden
cistern was exhausted. Villiers could only exclaim
" God's will be done! Get your wife and your
boys up stairs," he said; "there we may make another stand yet. Brown, help me to wrap Mr.
Bentley in these clothes. Can you walk ?"

" I will try."

" Make haste!"

And supported between Villiers and Bevan,
Bentley was removed into the garret. To this
there was but one staircase; and, as far as it was
possible, they contrived to block this up in the
same manner as before. And when all was done,
they assembled in one of the rooms, and gazed upon
each other's faces. Brown looked at his watch. It
was near six, and broad daylight.

" Is there not an opening in the roof ?" said
Villiers. " Go, Brown, and see if the smoke will
enable you to look out; it may command the road.
See if they are coming."

Brown left the room. He had to pass through a
dark sort of closet to reach the ladder which led to
the trap-door in the roof. As he opened the door,
by the dim light which streamed in he saw a figure
crouched up in one corner, and glaring on him
with eyes of defiance. Before he could return or
advance a pistol-ball whizzed past him; and he
threw himself upon the man. The rest heard the
shot, and were with him in an instant. The miserable man was seized, disarmed, dragged to the light,
and found to be covered with blood, and every
feature of his face disfigured. He did not utter a
word, but scowled on them like a fiend. He was evidently one of the assailants, and not of the meanest
class. He, like Bonsor and the others, had been

stunned, and had recovered, but not till the house was on fire. He had been thrown by the explosion into a dark corner of the kitchen, in which no one had observed him ; and when roused from his stupefaction by the flames, wounded as he was in his jaw, and in an agony of pain, he had managed to crawl up the back stairs. It was the only chance of escape ; and he had hidden himself in the place least likely of discovery, resolved to prolong his life as long as possible, and planted, with his last bullet, to shoot the first man who approached him.

" Villiers, Villiers !" whispered Bentley, as he raised himself feebly from the mattress on which they had laid him, "that is the man who stabbed me !"

It was Wheeler. What would have been the conduct of the others on such a discovery had they been left to themselves, it is hard to say. They threw themselves on him even now, and perhaps would have hurled him from the window ; but Bentley started up, and implored them to desist. Villiers himself rescued him. " Place him on the floor," he said. " Have you his arms ? "

" Yes."

He bade the policeman stand over and watch him.

" Shall we tie him hand and foot, sir ? "

" No," replied Villiers ; " not here—not in such an hour—not when the house is on fire. Leave him to the just judgment of the Almighty."

And for a time their attention was withdrawn from him by a crash underneath. It was the falling of the first floor. For a few minutes there was a lull in the fury of the flames, and then they burst forth with redoubled violence. The smoke began to find its way through the crevices of the planks, notwithstanding the mode in which they had been secured by the builder. The heat became intolerable; huge flakes of fire swept up into the air, and fell again upon the roof, and threatened to kindle that. It was evident that all was over.

"Open that window," said Villiers "the wind sets off from that quarter."

And Brown went to it and looked out. In doing so he roused the poor landlady from the stupefaction in which she was lying while Bevan and Bentley were praying. She had sunk down in one corner of the room; her husband had seated himself by her side, and held her in his bosom. The two boys had nestled themselves at her feet, and she had clasped both their hands in hers; and with her eyes closed, as if she dared not look on them, she was muttering to herself. Once she opened her eyes, and saw the poor servant-maid crying as if her heart would break. Poor Mary was alone, without a friend. She herself would perish with those she loved best. It was a consolation; and she beckoned to the poor girl to come and sit down beside them. They were all speechless; only the mother at times muttered a few broken words—"To die such a death! To be burnt alive, and they so young! My poor boys—my beautiful boys! To be burnt to death! Help," she cried, and rushed to the window. "Help! help, in the name of Him who died for you! Will you burn us alive—mother and children, husband and wife—who never harmed you?" But her voice was lost in the roaring of the flames. Nor was there any one to hear: the crowd had dispersed; all round the house was empty; two boys only were standing in the yard.

"They are young like you," she cried. "You have a mother. Would you like to see her burnt to death?" and she stretched herself out of the casement, till one of the boys, with fair hair and delicate features, which strangely contrasted with his poor dress, caught sight of her. "There are ladders," she cried, "there are ladders: put them up here, up by the cistern—here under the window, —for the love of God, for the love of God!"

And the fair boy, evidently horrified, endeavoured to move a ladder which lay on the ground, where it had been brought by the assailants to scale the walls; but his strength was unequal to it. Villiers came to the window. It was the poor boy whose life he himself had saved from a similar fate. The boy caught sight of him, and uttered a loud cry. "Help! help!" he said to his coarse sturdy companion, who only cursed him for a fool. And as the poor fellow was endeavouring to move the ladder, he received a slap on his face from behind, and the same figure which has so often appeared, appeared once more, and harshly bidding them both come with him, and not meddle with what did not concern them, he dragged him away. Villiers saw this; but as he looked up he saw something else. "They are coming, they are coming!" he cried; and the troop of dragoons appeared in full gallop on the brow of the hill. It was a moment of intense suffering. There was help close at hand; but it would reach them too late. The low room was already filled with a dense smoke; the heat was intolerable. There were sounds of something falling beneath them, as the ceiling was giving way, and the floor in several places seemed sinking. At Villiers's exclamation they had all fallen on their knees, all but Wheeler, who, with his face crouched as close as possible to the floor that he might escape the smoke, lay perfectly silent, but evidently in great agony; and as Bevan prayed aloud, his features settled into a horrible expression of scorn and despair. A few

minutes more must bring the troops to them; but
the delay of a minute might be fatal, and it might
be some time before they could be discerned: and
Villiers rose to go to another window, and endeavour to enlarge the opening, to give more air.
As he looked out from it he observed the leaden
cistern. It was at a considerable depth beneath him;
but he resolved to venture. The cords of the beds
were taken out, knots were tied in them, one end was
made fast round a bedstead, and in the midst of the
inexpressible anxiety of all who gathered to watch
his descent, he climbed through the window and
slided down the rope. It swung fearfully as it received the weight; but he had been accustomed in
youth to gymnastic exercises, and, setting his feet
against the wall, he contrived to land himself safely
on the brickwork edge of the cistern. But his foot
had no sooner touched it than he endeavoured to
spring up again and hold by the rope. His ancle
had touched the brick, and was blistered with the
heat, for the store of wood and coal which were
deposited in the place underneath had been set fire
to, and had acted as a furnace. He clung to the rope
with all his strength, as it swung backwards and
forwards violently over the cistern; and as his eyes
turned down they saw a sight enough to appal the
stoutest heart, for the bottom over which he was
swinging was full of melted lead. Even now his
presence of mind did not forsake him. As the
rope swung over to the edge he arrested it with his
foot, landed on the narrow brink—all but lost his
balance, and fell backwards into the cistern; but
with a desperate plunge he recovered himself, and
the next moment threw himself on the ground. He
fell upon his face, half stunned, shattered, and
bruised, but with his senses still awake. As he
rose upon his feet, he heard the dragoons galloping

into the street; and a shout from the window
over his head told him there was not a moment
to lose. In an instant he was in the front of
the house. Some dragoons had dismounted. Together they rushed into the yard, and the ladder
was raised to the window from which he had himself descended: it was the only one accessible. He
would himself have mounted, but was . conscious
that his wounded arm and bruised frame rendered
him less serviceable than others. The sergeant
therefore ascended the ladder. The women were
placed on it, and reached the ground safely. Bonsor
and Brown were preparing to lower Bentley from
the window next; but just then a part of the floor
began to give way. Bentley entreated them to save
themselves: he was prepared for his fate. He would
wait till the last. He entreated them not to think
of him; and had nearly persuaded them to let the
boys escape next, when, from the corner of the
room in which he had been crouching, Wheeler
sprang forward and thrust them aside. He leaped
upon the window like a maniac escaped from his
keeper. A prospect of saving his life once more
opened; and he threw himself upon the ladder —
his foot missed — he strove to recover himself, but
in vain. He tottered — staggered — clung to it, but
in vain; and Villiers saw him fall headlong into
the cistern. There was a cry, such as no one then
present had ever heard before, — one of such unutterable horror, that, for years afterwards, Villiers
would wake up in the middle of the night, as he
fancied he heard it in his dreams, and the cold
sweat would stand in drops upon his forehead.
Villiers sprang upon the ladder. The miserable
being had fallen upon his hands and knees in the
pool of molten lead! He saw Villiers, and shrieked
to him to save him. He called him by his name;

but it was hopeless.   He offered worlds to save
him !   " Take me out ! take me out !   It is a hell !
I will tell all—I can tell you all !   Oh ! Mr. Villiers,
help me ! I can tell you what you would give worlds
to know.   I have seen your papers — I know where
your child is.   Help me ! help me !"   And as Villiers,
struck to the heart, was almost plunging in to rescue
him, the poor wretch fell upon his face.   It was all
over.   Bentley, Brown, — all of them descended
the ladder.   They were saved — saved as by a
miracle.   They gathered round Villiers, who had
saved them ; but he had fallen against a wall, like
one petrified.   " I have seen your papers ! "   " I
know where your child is ! "   The words rung in
his ears — " I know where your child is ! "   Once
more he sprang up the ladder, in the vain thought
that all might not be lost ; but he was dragged back
by Brown and Bevan.   There was a crash — a shock
— the roof fell in — and it was all over.

" I always thought," said Bonsor to his wife the
next day, " that that leaden cistern had been built
for some purpose ! "

CHAP. XII.

WE must now pass over a space of three weeks, during which Villiers, by the strict injunctions of Mr. Morgan and Dr. Mayo, was confined to his room at the Priory. He suffered acutely from the injuries which he had received; and though he submitted patiently and calmly, the trial was most severe. His own feelings would have cast aside all thought of bodily anguish in the search for some clue to the few words which had been uttered by the miserable man Wheeler, and which in every waking hour, and even in his dreams, rang in his ears—"I know where your child is!" Even Villiers's patience and humility would scarcely have been proof against the authority which bound him to quietude at such a moment, had not Bevan and O'Brien, and, with still more judgment and sagacity, Brown the superintendent of the police, undertaken to prosecute the inquiries for him, and engaged in it with an untiring zeal and affection, which Villiers's conduct and character had rapidly won from them.

There had been little difficulty in tracing through Cookesley, who had withdrawn from the outbreak as soon as he saw the direction which it was about to take, a connection between Wheeler and the mysterious Pearce; for Wheeler, incautious and passionate, had often suffered himself to speak before his companions on subjects on which Pearce himself studiously preserved the strictest reserve. Pearce himself had been traced to Hawkstone, and

even, by Miss Brook's assistance, to poor Margaret's
lodging. But there all clue had ceased. Connell,
and his wife, and boy—all had disappeared. Margaret, who might be supposed to know something of
their visiter, was lying, in a state of insanity, in the
hospital; and O'Brien and Brown were at this time
in London, endeavouring to procure some aid from
the information of the London police. Their return
was expected this evening; and Villiers, with the
assistance of a stick, was slowly pacing up and
down the long library of the Priory, while the
shadows fell darker and darker; and at every sound
of rustling leaves or moaning wind which could
be possibly mistaken for the crushing of wheels, he
started, and his heart beat, while he listened at the
windows, — all in vain. It is a dreary hour, that
twilight before the curtains can be closed and the
lamps lighted; when nature is darkening without,
and all is cold and vacant within. And Villiers, as
he looked round upon the heavy, gloomy recesses of
the library, and then out upon the range of park,
which stretched, without sign of human habitation,
far into the wooded recesses of the hill-side, thought
within himself of solitude. He was rich, he was
master of possessions which the world might envy.
The earth lay before him with all its charms, if
they had been charms to him. The cup of life had
indeed been quaffed, and its bitterness had been
tasted—exquisite bitterness even at the brim! Still
the years of a manhood full of energy and promise
stretched out to tempt him to indulge in any dream
of ambition which rank, and genius, and power, and
influence could dare to form. And yet upon Villiers's heart there lay a dead, cold, aching void.
He was solitary. There was no one to share his
existence, to renew his being. And though Villiers knew that the solitude of a Christian was far

other than that of the worldling, the knowledge was
not yet (alas! how rarely can it be) realised, and
incorporated with consciousness. He was abandoning himself to a morbid reflection and commiseration upon his own condition, when his eye fell
upon the picture of Lady Eleanor, which now hung
over the fire-place in the library, and it operated,
as it always did, to recall him from himself to
others. He thought of that dreary solitude of the
heart in which his mother's last years had been
spent upon earth. Then his memory glanced upon
poor Macarthy, and on the loneliness which must
have fallen upon him had his life been spared, and
he himself had become an outcast from his own faith
and Church, without any shelter in the Church of
England to receive him in that fearful crisis. Then
he turned to Bentley, and took up, and tore with
indignation, a printed paper which had been sent
to him that morning, and in which Bentley's name
was mixed up with some slanderous and cruel insinuations. And he foresaw that Bentley himself
was about to be exposed to a fearful struggle, in
which he stood alone, with scarcely any but Villiers to support him.

And then his eye fell upon a portfolio of drawings which lay upon the table near him; and, as if
summoning up resolution to recall his thoughts from
morbid meditation upon solitude to immediate practical efforts to provide a consolation and relief for
it, he rang the bell, and desired the servant to make
his compliments to Mr. Plasmer, and if he had
finished his wine, to say that Villiers would be
happy to see him in the library.

Mr. Plasmer, the servant said, had dined immediately after his return from his walk into the park;
and in about five minutes the gentleman made his
appearance.

Now Mr. Plasmer was a fashionable architect and designer, and had been recommended to Villiers by a nobleman who knew his reputation, though utterly incapable of estimating his powers of art; and having arrived from London the same afternoon, he was now ushered into Villiers's presence. Villiers received him kindly; he would have received him cordially; but there was a fluency and ease about Mr. Plasmer's manner which produced the very opposite effect upon Villiers. And the architect having seated himself, without being requested, in an easy chair, he proceeded to express his admiration of the Priory, and of all that it contained.

"Only a few touches, Mr. Villiers, wanted here and there; a slight artistic finish to be given to the details; a little more rounding off of outline, and you will be complete, as I was saying to my friend Lord George the other day."

But if there was one thing which offended Villiers's fastidious taste, it was an assumption of pretended intimacy with persons of high rank; and it induced him to do what he rarely endured to do, to interrupt Mr. Plasmer in his sentence, by asking if he had walked towards the ruins?

"Indeed, yes, Mr. Villiers," replied Plasmer; "and charming they are—wondrously picturesque, and lovely. What a pity that you cannot command them from your dining-room windows here."

"I fear," answered Villiers, coldly, "that the sight of buildings in ruins, which had been dedicated to religion, would not, from choice, form any part in a landscape which I should like to command from my dining-room windows."

"Indeed! No! Ha! Mr. Villiers, certainly not," replied Mr. Plasmer, somewhat perplexed to understand Villiers's meaning.

"I was induced, sir," said Villiers, gravely, "to

request your assistance in restoring and repairing a
portion of those ruins, which I am unwilling to
permit to remain in their present state."

"Indeed! ha! certainly," said Plasmer, "they
are gone a leetle—leetle too far. The east gable
requires a leetle propping. I suppose, Mr. Villiers,
you will turf down the chapel, and plant flowers?
A lady's flower-garden, judiciously managed, will
look charming under the east window. Some of
my new designed Gothic trellis-work will be quite
delicious there."

"No," answered Villiers, with increasing coldness; "I am desirous not of turning a consecrated
building into a flower-garden, but of restoring it to
a more proper purpose."

"Ha! indeed! certainly, Mr. Villiers," replied Plasmer. "Something useful and ornamental
too — I understand. Farm-buildings? Ha! or
a conservatory? Charming things are Gothic con-
servatories, in the florid style. And yet, Mr. Villiers, farm-buildings group well in Gothic. It was
but the other day I put a superb cast-iron window,
pointed, in the florid style, into the gable of my
friend the Marquis's new stables at Matchambury
Park. We tossed up a little spire for a pigeon-
house, ran a new light battlement and pinnacles
round the pig-sties and cart-house; and you can't
think what a charming composition they made —
quite in the abbey style; and made a lovely point
from his terrace—quite natural."

"I fear you have mistaken me," said Villiers,
slowly; "it is not my intention to profane a religious building by converting it into pig-sties and
stables; and if I were building such things from
the ground, I should certainly not wish them to be
in the abbey style. My object is to restore the
chapel as a chapel."

"Ha! certainly! indeed, Mr. Villiers," said Plasmer. "Very noble! very liberal! Charming to see the number of churches which are rising every day. I have built ten myself within the last two years, 1200*l.* each—no more I assure you—cheap as dirt."

"It is not my wish," said Villiers, "to raise a building dedicated to such a purpose as a chapel with that which costs me nothing." He began to despair of Mr. Plasmer; but he still ventured to add, "I was informed that you were practically acquainted with the details of Gothic architecture, and could assist me in obtaining accurate admeasurements and mouldings from the portions which still remain."

"Indeed! ha! certainly, Mr. Villiers," said Plasmer, with a self-satisfied smile; "few men of the age, I flatter myself, are such perfect masters as myself of the delicate touches, the true taste, the fine theory of a genuine Gothic style. It was I, sir, that fitted up that gem, as Mr. Robins judiciously called it, that gem and jewel of art, Carnation Abbey, on the banks of the Thames, at Putney. My stucco, Mr. Villiers, stood wonderfully well there. When Alderman Hobson bought it—a dull man that, sir—mere city-bred, no taste, but abundance of cash"—and Mr. Plasmer, to Villiers's great annoyance, looked at him with a vulgar smile of intelligence—"he sent for me. 'Plasmer,' said he, 'you see this box'—it was a mere square house; mahogany door in the middle, four windows in front, two steps, green verandah, round sweep, laurels, flower-borders, and distant view of the Thames through the chimneys of the gas-works. Nothing, Mr. Villiers, I assure you; positively a mere nothing. However, said the alderman to me, 'Plasmer,' says he, 'my good fellow, you know next year I am to be Lord Mayor. I do not care for money. My daughters want a place; something of the antique, they tell me. I took them this summer to see Tintern, and Netley, and Fountains Abbey; they tell me something of that kind, you know. You are a clever fellow, you know, and can tell all about it. Arabella will explain to you better than I can. You may draw upon me, you know.' Well, Mr. Villiers, we set about it; and we produced, Sir —yes, out of that square four-windowed house— we produced 'the gem!' Only a few touches, Mr. Villiers. I had by me the iron frames of the Gothic windows ready made. We threw out a charming oriel in the middle—rather heavy for the wall, but we did it in wood and plaster to imitate stone,— put painted glass into the drawing-room windows— Scripture subjects, all of them, quite appropriate; bought a lot of armour, which we hung up in the hall—only ten feet square, but charmingly pretty; solemn rather—little light, dark roof, coats of arms, and stag's horns—all that kind of thing——"

But here, to Villiers's great relief, the servant interrupted Mr. Plasmer's loquacity by bringing lights and closing the window-curtains.

"And yet, sir," resumed Plasmer, before Villiers could change the subject, "this was but a mere toy. I used to smile when the alderman talked of the Abbey; but he was proud of it; and, indeed, though I say it, he had reason. It was a gem. But my great work—my Capo d'Opera, Mr. Villiers— you understand Italian—was at Lord Gormanburgh's—magnificent place that—I fitted up his dining-room there at an enormous cost. 'Plasmer,' said he, 'my good fellow' (for indeed he knew that I had a great regard for him)—'Plasmer,' said he, as we were walking one day in the picture-gallery, arm-in-arm, 'you must fit up my new dining-room.

I know your taste. It must be Gothic, pure Gothic,
every thing appropriate ; spare no expense ; draw
upon me : only, as I said, let it be all appropriate.'
Well, Mr. Villiers, we set to work — he and I together, and we produced — Ha ! I see you never
saw it. But it was something quite beyond all
description. Indeed, I may say I exhausted all my
powers upon it. It was my *chef-d'œuvre*. You
understand French, of course, Mr. Villiers ? "

Villiers bit his lip, and made a faint attempt to
incline his head in token that he was listening, but
he could scarcely succeed.

" Well, Mr. Villiers," continued the unexhausted
architect, delighted with the silence of his new
listener — " well, Mr. Villiers, I had by me a lot of
the most charming oak-carving from a church at
Antwerp—all Scripture subjects, and the stalls beautifully executed, with angels' heads, and pinnacles
and pannels—all that sort of thing, you know. Well,
we ranged them round the sides of the room, and
they looked charmingly—quite in the purest style.
Luckily, the billiard-room was next to the dining-
room ; so we knocked down the partition, made an
entrance through a charming arch, with clustered
pillars and mouldings, lighted the new room with
lancet windows, and placed the sideboard at the
end on three steps. Gormanburgh—" Here Villiers writhed a little, as unable to bear any more,
but Mr. Plasmer was insensible to the movement.
" Gormanburgh," continued Mr. Plasmer, " would
insist on having a splendid cellaret. He gave capital
wines—capital," he repeated, and smacked his lips ;
" sometimes drank a little too hard, but that was all
his friends' fault—men of the turf, you know—fond
of hard living. However, what were we to do for
the cellaret ? when, luckily, I procured a model of a
charming font, the one at Lynn, canopy crocketed, with

pinnacles and niches—all that kind of thing." Villiers writhed again, and attempted to stop Mr. Plasmer; but he was beyond the control of a sign. "As for the sideboard," he continued, "we had it modelled in stone from Edward I.'s altar-tomb in Westminster Abbey. Gormanburgh had some magnificent gold plate, church plate, which he had bought in Spain when the monasteries were plundered — chalices, patines, flagons, and that kind of thing. I recommended him to buy a couple of silver-gilt candelabra, quite appropriate; and when he gave his grand dinners, I cannot tell you how splendid it looked — all on the al—— I mean the side-board." Villiers half rose from his seat, but to no purpose.

"But the best thing after all," added Mr. Plasmer, imperturbably, "was his pictures. He had some splendid paintings, which we placed about the room, with sideboards under them— all appropriate, especially three lovely Martyrdoms, and a magnificent St. Jerome—fine colouring, delicate flesh-tints—the expression of agony wonderful. We had lamps so managed as to throw a full light upon them, so that we could see them while sitting over our wine—quite a feast of art. Gormanburgh was fond of art, à ravir. You understand French, Mr. Villiers. Well, sir," continued Plasmer, "at the other end of the room we built a gallery — three pointed arches, clustered columns, pinnacles, niches, all appropriate, and in this we placed the organ. Gormanburgh was passionately fond of music, sacred music especially, and would always have it played during dinner. The last time I dined with him we had the Stabat Mater after the first course, and the Requiem—Mozart's Requiem during the dessert: it was quite delicious, —so soothing — the whole thing—all in character— so appropriate." Villiers sat perfectly still and motionless. At last Mr. Plasmer came to a close.

"But I have reserved one triumph. It certainly was the chimney-piece. I had by me a most magnificent group of carving from the abbey of St. Jacques, in Belgium—old oak, charmingly executed, —angels, and that kind of thing, —subject, the Day of Judgment; in the middle a most splendid group of the Virgin and Child, crowned by ——"

"Stop, sir," cried Villiers, with a voice of intense horror and indignation. "Do you know of what you are speaking?"

Poor Mr. Plasmer nearly jumped from his chair. But Villiers took no notice. He rang the bell, and ordering the servant to take coffee for the architect into the drawing-room, he apologised briefly for cutting short the conversation; and Mr. Plasmer, though somewhat dismayed, and wholly unconscious of any offence which he had committed against either good taste or good feeling, bowed himself out of the room.

As the door closed, Villiers could not help exclaiming, "And this, then, is art in England in the nineteenth century. And such is the horrible profanation to which the romance of religion, without its spirit, is leading those who ought to make every work of the hand, as of the mind, minister to holiness and devotion. Art in the hands of vulgar and mercenary tools, detached from all high philosophy, from all practical piety, turned into a puppet-show, or a painted gewgaw, or made a mere toy for sale at some paltry exhibition,—art, which can dare to place the triumphs of saints and the agonies of martyrdoms as an object to luxuriate on in a banquet-room—art, which can rifle churches to furnish drawing-rooms, and mix, like another Belshazzar, the holiest vessels of the most awful mysteries with the cups to be drained in debauchery,—art, which rather than forego the decoration of a room will preserve and admire what the Scriptures denounce as an idol, and what cannot but be horrible blasphemy. Alas! thought Villiers, if we condemn as priestcraft, and superstition, and pious fraud, the employment of art by popery for the purpose of ruling minds and warming hearts to mistaken piety, what shall be said of our use of it to generate nothing but profaneness?

He sighed deeply, and then, to relieve himself, he opened the portfolio which lay before him, and in which, with his own hand, he had sketched out his proposed restoration of the ruins of the Priory. There was the chapel rising with its lofty roof, its pinnacles, and its tower in the centre of the group. Close by it was the Hall, with its oriel restored, and the porch with its flight of steps, and its tall windows, less ornamented than those of the chapel. Round it, in a little quadrangle opening to the south under a cloister, were ranged the buildings intended to be occupied by the tenants of the edifice. They were low, yet beautifully broken with buttresses, and dormers, and clustered chimneys; and Villiers, who possessed an exquisite taste for landscape gardening, had struck out a few hints upon the paper of a green sward running in between the buttresses, and sprinkled with shrubs and trees. At one side he had added a projecting mass of building, under which he had written in pencil, " School and dormitory;" and in a separate group, only connected with the main building by a low cloister, and looking out upon the south bank, was a sketch of another set of apartments, under which he had also written in pencil, "Infirmary."

He was throwing in a few additional touches with his pencil, when the servant informed him that Mr. Plasmer would be glad to see him again. And before Villiers could either decline or accept the offer, the architect reappeared. He brought in his

o 3

hand a large roll of drawings, and begged, if Villiers had time, that he would just cast his eye over them, as it might assist them in their plans for the Priory. And without giving Villiers an opportunity of resistance he spread on the table before him a long regular mason-like elevation of a building with a centre and two wings exactly alike.

" This," said Mr. Plasmer, " is my drawing for the new United Anti-religious distinction College, in the north of Ireland, — Gothic, you see, Mr. Villiers, pure Gothic. Singular what a rage there is for all that is old. The institution itself quite a novelty, but the architecture all antique. I took Westminster Abbey for my model; scale smaller, but very like, except where the old architects failed. Centre building, the principal house, dining-room twenty-eight by eighteen, two drawing-rooms, folding doors, small study, capital kitchen and offices, butler's pantry, bath-room, four best bed-rooms, — every thing complete. Here you have in the wings admirable and commodious lecture-rooms, museums, library, reading-room—wings, you observe, regular — three stories, — windows all pointed — mullions of wood—string course, corbels, bosses, and all that of my new patent stucco — stands the weather admirably, Mr. Villiers — we shall be able to take our mouldings in it at the Priory cheap as dirt."

As Mr. Plasmer paused, Villiers was compelled to make some reply, and he coldly observed that he was not fond of stucco in ecclesiastical buildings; and that every thing which might be done at the Priory he should wish to be real.

" Certainly, certainly," said Mr. Plasmer. " I made the very same remark to my friend, Sir George, when he was building his artificial ruin, — ruin, Mr. Villiers, of an abbey, at Burnham Grove, near

Bristol. Sir George, said I, you must have something real, something to interest, a tombstone or
two, or some fragments from Tintern; here they
are, quite close to you: mere brick and mortar, I
told him, was not enough for real genuine taste."

Villiers was silent, and then asked if there were
any rooms for fellows, or any chapel, in the design
of Mr. Plasmer's college.

" O, no," replied the architect; " no new colleges
in the present day have more than a Principal or
President, whatever they choose to call him. One
person at the head is quite enough to make a college,
if he has such a name. And as for the chapel, of
course that could not be—the professor of Greek
is a Unitarian, and the professor of Chemistry a
Baptist. It was never dreamed of."

" And what is the salary of the Principal ?" asked
Villiers. " With so large a house he must require a
considerable income."

" Twelve hundred a year," replied Mr. Plasmer.
" The committee have guaranteed him that. They
could not procure a first-rate scholar for less."

Villiers sighed, and begging that the architect
would excuse his wishing to be alone that evening,
he once more rang the bell, and bowed him out of
the room. Much that he had heard would have appeared exaggeration; but his eye glanced on the
newspapers on a table near him; and there he remembered the programmes of fashionable concerts,
in which the most awful subjects, the Stabat Mater,
and the Dies Iræ, were blasphemously made the
amusement of gay and laughing throngs, and, to divert the mind from their solemnity, were inter-
spersed with light airs from operas, and sung by
opera singers under the direction of prelates of the
church. He had himself seen upon the sideboards
of noblemen chalices and holy vessels, once con-

secrated for the altars of churches, and which were
now supposed to be common, because, having been
plundered by one hand, they had been purchased
from the plunderer by another. And he had been
even in London houses fitted up in the midst of
Regent Street as if they had been built in the days
of Elizabeth, and in which religious carvings, profanely but superstitiously designed for holy buildings, were now still more profanely applied without
a thought of the mysteries which they represented,
or the idolatry which they contained, to support
sideboards and decorate drawing-rooms.

Perchance, thought Villiers to himself, if art
once more in England is to be elevated and consecrated, and made the handmaid of religion and
truth, it must find some blessed shelter in some
holy place, where the minds which gave it birth
may be nursed up in prayer and meditation, shielded
from the vanities of the world, and the applauses of
a mob, and the bribery of money. It may be that
a religious home is as needful for the painter, and
the sculptor, and the architect, and the poet, as for
the philosopher and the priest.

And he rang his bell, and desiring two of his
servants to wait in the ante-room, Villiers knelt
down in prayer, and then summoning the attendants, he proceeded in their presence to fix his signature to some parchments which Mr. Atkinson
had forwarded to him that morning. They were deeds
making over to proper trustees, under the control
of the bishop of the diocese, all that part of the
Hawkstone estate which had been sacrilegiously
obtained by his ancestors from the plunder of the
Priory, that it might be employed under the direction of the bishop in establishing and maintaining a college of clergy and others in the restored
Priory, for the perpetual celebration of divine wor-

ship, the spiritual care of the parish, the education of the young, the care of the poor, the visitation and comforting of the sick, and as a refuge for the destitute and the penitent.

An iron chest stood in one corner of the room, and he affixed his seal to it and directed a label upon it. It contained the great pall, the gilded cup, the illuminated manuscript—all that he could find among the so-called curiosities of the house, which had been plundered from holy places, especially from the Priory.

Another parchment remained to be signed. It contained a surrender of all the tithes of Hawkstone, which had been in the possession of the family ever since the time of Elizabeth, to the bishop of the diocese, for the purpose of being applied in the most efficacious and fitting manner to supply the spiritual wants of the town of Hawkstone.

And when this had been done, Villiers once more knelt down and prayed and gave thanks, and rose up from his knees deprived of one fourth of his income, but lightened of a heavy burden upon his conscience and his fears.

Villiers had scarcely done this, when the noise of wheels was heard, crushing on the gravel as they advanced up the sycamore avenue. He endeavoured in vain to interpret by the sound whether they would bring to him tidings of good or of ill, of hope or of despair. He was on the point of hastening to the door in eager expectation; but, chastened and subdued with sorrow, and still more with religious resignation, he mastered his impetuosity, and though his heart beat thickly, he waited patiently for the appearance of Bevan.

And Bevan it was, accompanied with Brown and O'Brien. But they uttered no cheerful sounds as they descended from the carriage; they waited to

take off their cloaks in the hall, as having no object
in hastening to see him; their footsteps moved
slowly across the stone hall, and the moment Villiers
saw their faces, he perceived that they had made no
discovery : their search had been wholly baffled.

There was a momentary gush of tears into Villiers's eyes—a cold dead chill of disappointment—
a something of complaint; but he shook it off in
an instant, lifted up his eyes in humble prayer for
forgiveness and for patience, and then exerted himself to dispel the gloom which hung over his visiters.
He rang for refreshments, and partook of them
cheerfully with them; and cheered with the sight of
his self-command, their own hearts became lightened.
Only upon Bevan's face there remained a gloom
which could not be shaken off; and when at the
usual hour the servants had been called in and the
full evening service performed, and the rest having
retired, he was left alone with Villiers, he proceeded
to explain the reason. Villiers learnt from him
that, notwithstanding all the efforts which had been
made to prevent observation or gossip on the subject
of Bentley, all the circumstances relating to his disappearance had been made known, and were become
the subject of general conversation, but mixed up
with the same kind of exaggerations and scandalous
insinuations as had been suggested to themselves.
Nor was this confined to mere gossip. It seemed
as if some hand was busily and bitterly engaged in
giving them publicity. The most virulent attacks
had been made upon him in print, the walls were
scribbled over with his name, placards were stuck
about, the purport of which could not be mistaken,
and even the children in the streets were taught to
assemble and sing songs under his window. Bevan
had at first endeavoured to conceal this from him as
he lay confined to his bed, but he had been obliged

at last to communicate it to him, and to urge upon
him the necessity of meeting the calumny boldly
and openly. But Bentley was distracted by the
remembrance of his oath. He had bound himself
to be silent on all that had occurred that evening,
and nothing would induce him to break his oath.
In vain Bevan suggested to him that the obligation
of an oath so imposed was, to say the least, most
questionable — that the explosion had made the chief
secret public — that of those who might be affected
by his disclosures, many had perished and others
had already been seized by the hand of justice.
Bentley swerved not. He asked Bevan if he was
satisfied with his innocence; and when Bevan gave
him a full assurance of it, Bentley pressed his hand
and said that was enough: the rest must be left to
Heaven. He never could violate his oath.

But Bevan felt that his friend over-calculated his
strength, and estimated too low the nature of the
struggle which he would have to sustain. He
trembled for the consequence; and though Villiers
endeavoured to dispel his apprehensions, and declared
his own determination to support Bentley through
any trial of the kind, neither of them could disguise
from himself the difficulties and dangers which
awaited him. Bevan, however, saw that Villiers was
not yet sufficiently recovered to bear more excitement, and postponing any further consultation,
they parted for the night.

CHAP. XIII.

THE next morning Villiers was seated in the library soon after breakfast, and was examining with Bevan some of the old records of the Benedictine establishments in England, that he might select from them whatever seemed most suitable for carrying his object into effect in the restoration of a religious community at the Priory. But they were interrupted by a gig driving up to the door, and the announcement of Mr. O'Foggarty, who has before been mentioned as the Roman Catholic priest recently established at Hawkstone, and who, it was now understood, was to undertake the office of domestic chaplain to Lord Claremont during his residence at the Park, the good Abbé St. Maur being about to return to France.   Mr. O'Foggarty was not, as might be expected from his name, one of those dark, scowling, coarse, violent men who have been the appropriate growth of Maynooth, and are the curse of Ireland, as they are the bitterest enemies of England : those who distribute the offices and regulate the policy of the Church of Rome, are far too wise so to misplace their instruments.   He was bland, polished, and insinuating in his manners, liberal in his doctrine, obsequious in his attentions, and possessed of a fluency of language and of a smattering of various accomplishments, which rendered him an agreeable addition to society, and enabled him to exhibit to the few inhabitants of Hawkstone who ventured to make his acquaintance, a picture of the Romish Church, so unlike the stern, sanguinary, blackened, and mysterious character with which it was invested to their eyes by the traditions of the reign of Queen Mary and the novel of "The Monk," that their wonder was only equalled by their gratification, and their willingness to know more of a system seemingly so amiable, and so traduced.

Mr. O'Foggarty apologised to Villiers for his intrusion with the ease and courtesy of a man perfectly conversant with the world; and Bevan having retired, he proceeded to explain the nature of his business, which related to the payment of an annual sum of money, which had been left by Lady Esther for religious purposes. Even Villiers, acute as he was in the perception of character, and fastidiously alive to anything like hypocrisy or insincerity, was touched by the mode in which Mr. O'Foggarty alluded to the character and the trials of his mother.

O'Foggarty recognised the picture over the fireplace, and gazed on it silently for a few minutes. He then spoke of her charities, and of the interest which she had always taken in the religious welfare of Hawkstone, so far as she could assist the labours of her own communion.

"Mr. Villiers, I am sure," continued the speaker, "will pardon me for thus dwelling on the faith and on the zeal of one who, if human thought may judge, is now a saint in heaven. Even though he may differ from the doctrines and system in which her faith was purified, he, I am convinced, is not so illiberal as to confine the terms of salvation to his own communion." Villiers was silent. And Mr. O'Foggarty then touched on the unfinished state of the new Romish chapel, and after some general professions of liberality, to which Villiers lent a very cold and incredulous ear, the speaker thought he might venture on requesting a contribution for it from Villiers, interested as he must be in the welfare of Hawkstone, and having, indeed, on his own estate, several families who were Romanists themselves. He added, that if it were a matter of principle, perhaps he might have hesitated in making the request; but that, as Villiers was already under an engagement to pay a certain sum towards the same object, any addition to it would not involve a question of principle.

To Mr. O'Foggarty's evident chagrin, Villiers replied briefly, that to discharge a debt was one thing, and to make a voluntary donation another; that his own conscientious opinions were noway involved in paying over to the furtherance, even of a system which he condemned, that which he only held in trust for it; but that he had long since felt the solemn obligation of abstaining from giving any support, however speciously claimed, to any other religious community in England but the Catholic Church. " You must excuse me," he added, "for carefully employing these words, since upon them my allegiance to my Church is founded."

Mr. O'Foggarty endeavoured to assume a smile. "And might I ask," he said, "if, as I must suppose, you deny the same title to the Church of Rome, and confine it to the established communion of England?"

"I have no right," replied Villiers, "and no inclination to enter into a controversy at this moment on such a subject. But believing the English Church to derive its ministry from apostolical authority, its creeds and its doctrines from apostolical truths, and in all essential points (however its individual members may have sinned) to be in accordance with the ancient Catholic Church; I cannot but consider an unauthorised intrusion into her province as gratuitously schismatical; and I cannot well reconcile the notion of schism with the title of

Catholic. But you will pardon me if I decline
such a discussion, and content myself with stating,
thus briefly, the reasons why I cannot offer you
any assistance whatever in propagating a system
which, even on this ground only, I must believe to
be inconsistent with Christian charity, and destructive of divine truth."

"And yet," said Mr. O'Foggarty, "a landlord
cannot be indifferent to the spiritual interest of his
tenants and dependants; and for their sake may I
not ask for some trifling assistance to the funds
which are devoted to their benefit?"

"I trust," replied Villiers, "that I do feel interested—deeply interested—solemnly responsible
for the spiritual as well as for the temporal welfare of those whom the hand of Providence has
placed under my care. But it would little contribute to their welfare to show myself indifferent
to religious truths, to assist in rearing them in a
faith which I believe to be false, to aid in fo-
menting those schisms which must in the end destroy all religious belief in Romanists as well as
in others. It will be my duty to take care that the
truth shall be, at least, offered to them, that opportunities of hearing it, and of studying it, be
provided for them, and that they be warned of the
errors into which they have fallen. And this duty
I hope to perform."

"And am I to understand, then," said Mr. O'Foggarty, with a tone of bitterness, "that Mr. Villiers
meditates disturbing the peace and harmony of this
place by a system of proselytism, and will endeavour, by the influence of his name and property,
to withdraw his dependants from the faith of their
ancestors?"

"Rather, you should say," replied Villiers, "recall them to the faith of their ancestors; for no

one who understands what Christian truth is would
undervalue the principle of hereditary religion.
But I am unwilling to say anything which may
seem unnecessarily harsh and painful to a gentleman whom I have no reason to suppose is acting
otherwise than conscientiously in maintaining his
religious system."

"I should have hoped," said Mr. O'Foggarty,
"that, in these enlightened days, Mr. Villiers would
have been more disposed to recognise the principle
that each individual should be allowed to choose
his own religious doctrines ; and that, as the State
has no right to interfere with them, so neither has
the landlord."

"Sir," replied Villiers, "will you pardon me
for saying that I have resided long in Roman
Catholic countries, and have had many opportunities of studying the Roman Catholic system. To
me, therefore, I am sure you will not think it worth
while to address such sentiments, which cannot be
the sincere opinion of any true Roman Catholic;
which are in themselves erroneous — I might say
false ; and which are so vitally opposed to the
whole system and spirit of Romanism, that in the
mouth of a Romanist they sound to me —— "

Villiers paused, and hesitated to finish his sentence, lest he should use words too faithfully representing his own indignation at the imposition which
his visitant was attempting to practise on him.

Mr. O'Foggarty, however, was not abashed.   "I
conclude," he said, "that Mr. Villiers will not dispute the principle that laymen, however gifted and
however zealous, are not the persons to whom the
task of proselytism has been especially appointed."

"Assuredly," replied Villiers ; "but to laity, as
well as clergy, has been appointed the task of watching over the welfare of their brethren, and of pro-

moting the glory of the Almighty — if not by preaching in the congregation, yet by ministering to the wants of the preachers, and supplying to them the means of executing their duty."

" Alas ! " said Mr. O'Foggarty, " I fear that this spirit of proselytism can only engender strife, and destroy our mutual amity. To its virulence and mistaken zeal we owe nearly all the bitterness of religious life in this age."

" I should not have expected," said Villiers, " that a clergyman of the Roman Catholic Church, of which the distinctive feature, and paramount maxim is the unwearying duty of proselytism, would employ such language."

O'Foggarty slightly coloured.

" I do think," continued Villiers, " that to the spirit of proselytism, indulged by unauthorised persons — proselytism, not to the simple definite faith committed to us by heaven, but to our own superadded dogmas and opinions — proselytism, carried on in defiance of that order and discipline, which was established by the Church of the Apostles, and of primitive times, — to this I do think that we owe nearly all the miseries and dangers which beset the Catholic faith. But I mean not to give offence, when I repeat, that an agent of the Romish Church is the last person to condemn such a spirit, with which all his own ministerial functions in this land must be tainted. And I must distinguish from it most strongly the proselytism enjoined by our Lord upon all his disciples, — proselytism to the simple, unaltered, revealed faith of the Apostles, conducted by authorised ministers, and confined within those limits which apostolical practice has laid down for it."

Mr. O'Foggarty coloured still more, but did not abandon his ground.

"Mr. Villiers," he said, "must be aware (not that I would venture to suggest to him for a moment any secular or worldly considerations) that we are not without influence in Hawkstone. I confess that I had dared to contemplate with hope the prospect of congratulating Mr. Villiers on that political eminence to which his vicinity to Hawkstone, and his long family connexion with the place, justly entitle him, without alluding to personal advantages of the highest order. A dissolution of parliament is expected every day."

Villiers's indignation was roused; and by the expression of his eye, though he remained perfectly silent, his visiter saw that he had mistaken the string on which he had touched.

"Far be it from me," he added hastily, "to suppose that Mr. Villiers would for one moment permit his conscientious practice to be swayed by worldly and selfish motives. This was far from my thoughts. But I did wish candidly and honestly to indicate, without reserve, the line which not only myself but others would feel it necessary to take in the event of —— "

Villiers did not perplex him by waiting for him to finish the sentence, which he was endeavouring to round off in some ambiguous diplomatic phrase. "Mr. O'Foggarty," he said, "and every conscientious Christian will of course endeavour, in every possible way consistent with Christian duty, to give weight and extension to those opinions which he sincerely believes to be true." And Villiers gave signs that he desired the interview to close. But O'Foggarty had left one string still untouched.

"I see," he said, in a tone in which he wished to express sorrow rather than anger, "that Mr. Villiers is prepared to reject any humble aid which our influence might offer to him in promoting the welfare of this place. It is not for frail men like us to boast, and yet we cannot but exert great power over the minds of our flocks. To us are committed secrets which are hidden from every other eye." And as he uttered the words, he looked at Villiers significantly ; but Villiers heeded him not.

" To us," continued O'Foggarty, still fixing his eye upon Villiers, — "to us, mean and unworthy as we are, is entrusted in the holy Confessional the knowledge of things which no human power, no arm of strength, no dexterity of intrigue can detect, but on which the happiness and the fate of many depend. Inviolate as our secrecy is, we are yet allowed — nay, enjoined — to make our knowledge instrumental in redressing the injured, and" (here he paused, and bending his looks searchingly upon Villiers, he dropped his voice almost into a whisper) "in restoring the lost."

Villiers sprang up, but sank back again in his chair.

" Sir ! " he exclaimed, in a voice choked and broken with emotion, "I charge you, in the name of Him from whom you hope for mercy, not to trifle with a miserable man ! If you know anything, I adjure you to speak ! Have mercy upon me ! "

O'Foggarty's countenance assumed a look of surprise, as if his words had meant nothing. " I fear," he said, " I must have touched inadvertently on some secret string of sorrow, of which I was wholly unaware. I should apologise for intruding so long on Mr. Villiers's time ; " and he proceeded to draw on his gloves, and rose from his seat.

But Villiers also sprang up, and moved to the door ; and though unable to speak, he motioned to his visitant to sit down. O'Foggarty still preserved the same affected look of surprise, but took his seat, and waited, as if in astonishment, for any further communication. And Villiers soon recovered himself.

"Mr. O'Foggarty," he said, more calmly, "will excuse me, if I ask him earnestly and solemnly whether the words which he has just uttered bore any deeper meaning than a mere generality. As a minister of Him who is the fountain of mercy, he will not trifle with the misery of any human being, however opposed to his religious system."

His visiter made no effort to conceal a certain embarrassment and awkwardness of manner. "I was wishing," he said, after a pause, "to explain candidly and honestly, and without any affectation of concealment," (it is singular how the most artful minds always boast most of their candour), "the principles which must regulate the ministers of our holy Church in their dealings with those in this country who are acting to it hostilely and bitterly. Mr. Villiers himself would not expect that, trampled on as we have been, plundered, and persecuted, and maligned for years, and now only beginning to raise our heads from the dust, we should omit to employ every legitimate means to secure the approaching triumph of our holy faith. He cannot think us bound to assist the enemies of the truth."

Villiers was silent, for he was too agitated to argue; and O'Foggarty, after a pause, continued. "I will speak openly, sir, and without reserve; I will offer to you all the assistance in my power in obtaining anything which you most covet, in recovering anything which you have lost; and my means are great. I would almost venture to say my success is certain; but it must be on one condition, that we receive from Mr. Villiers such a friendly co-operation and assistance in return as may be expected from the well-known enlargement and liberality of his sentiments."

He was silent; and Villiers had sunk down in his seat and covered his face with his hands. " Do I understand you, sir ?" he said at last, " or am I interpreting your words to imply more than they really mean ?"

" Mr. Villiers," said O'Foggarty, " may place upon my words any interpretation which he thinks fit. I have said all that I am at liberty to say, and my lips are sealed beyond. Mr. Villiers may best judge whether I have spoken idly, or am likely to offer what I cannot perform. But I must not trespass on you longer." And O'Foggarty once more rose, and his eye turned to an organ which had been just placed in one of the recesses in the library.

" Mr. Villiers, I perceive," he said, " is fond of music. I am myself a slight performer. Might I be allowed to touch this instrument." And without waiting for permission, he opened it, and ran his fingers over a few keys, and then, while he fixed his eyes upon Villiers's face, he suffered the notes to sink into a soft gentle plaintive strain, at the sound of which Villiers fell back in his chair and gasped for breath : it was the Hymn to the Virgin.

" You know all, then," cried Villiers. " You can restore him to me. — Have mercy upon me!"

But O'Foggarty's face had once more assumed its look of surprise and vagueness. " I fear," he said, " that I have agitated Mr. Villiers by recalling to him painful associations. I should have been glad of some better opportunity to lay before him the cause for which I have ineffectually pleaded. Might I hope for permission to wait on you to-morrow; or may I even now return with the satisfaction of knowing that we shall experience from Mr. Villiers, not enmity, but friendship ? Shall I leave with you this list of subscriptions to our poor chapel? Lord Morden, Mr. Villiers

will observe, has given the ground; Lord Claremont
has also aided us; and Lady Eleanor, with whom I
shall soon have the honour to be associated in this
work of benevolence, and to be domesticated at the
park as his lordship's chaplain. I will leave the
paper with you, and call for it, if you allow me, to-
morrow."

He went up to Villiers, and placed the paper in his
hand; and a bystander might have seen a faint smile
of triumph derange the composure of his features.
" He is gained," he whispered to himself — " he is
ours! Once sap the principle of resistance, and he
will fall wholly into our hands." And he waited
for Villiers's reply.

But Villiers rose from his chair; he folded up
the paper without looking at it, replaced it in
O'Foggarty's hand, and requesting him to be seated
again, he stood before him, and said, with a firm
voice, —

" I wish, sir, to express to you once more, firmly
and openly, and in a manner which I trust will
preclude any further solicitation on the subject,
that I can offer no assistance whatever to your religious operations in this country. Whether the
words which you have uttered, and which have,
indeed, awakened in me painful and bitter recollections, bear in them any deeper meaning, I will
leave to your own conscience. Your system scruples not to sever the allegiance of subjects from
their sovereign, and to make your co-operation
in preserving the peace of nations and the order
of society conditional upon the extension of favour
to your cause from governments, who cannot favour
it without compromising their own religious faith.
It would, therefore, be little strange, that as you
deal between the subject and the sovereign, so you
should deal between a father and his child;" (and

Villiers's voice faltered). " Whether such conduct
be worthy of a ministry of heaven — whether it be
an evidence of truth — whether it must not confirm
those who abhor deceit and wrong in offering their
most strenuous resistance to such a system, may be
left for your own consideration. I cannot look to it
for any aid. I must trust to heaven alone. We
must part, sir, at once ; and I trust never more to
be exposed to solicitations like the present upon any
pretence whatever.

Villiers rang the bell, ordered Mr. O'Foggarty's
carriage, sternly took leave of his abashed and disconcerted visiter ; but ten minutes after, when
the servant entered the room, he was found stretched
upon the floor, insensible.

O'Foggarty knew nothing of this. The gig in
which he had been driven to the Priory was waiting
at the door, and in a short time he re-entered his
own house in the town by the same little green
garden door which has more than once been mentioned already. Adjoining to this, and within the
garden, was a small tenement, seemingly unin-
habited. And to this the priest bent his way, and
knocking gently at the door of it, was admitted by
some one from the inside into a small but not comfortless apartment. " So you are returned at last ?"
was the greeting which awaited him from a coarse,
smooth-shaven, iron-faced, sinister-looking figure,
respectably habited in black, and who, to prepare
himself for facing a visiter, had assumed a large
pair of green spectacles. " And you have fared as
I prophesied, I suppose?"

" I have not been successful, certainly," said
O'Foggarty to the inmate of the little mansion, in
whom the reader, without requiring any assistance
from us, will probably recognise Mr. Pearce.

Pearce laughed bitterly. "I told you," he said →

" I told them — I told them from the first; and yet
they will still persist in hoping to secure him. And
now I am ordered off, and you are to try your
smooth words and persuasive arts, as if they would
do any good."

" We must not judge," said the priest, blandly,
" by a single failure on the first attempt. The
aspect of things is so different from what it was,
and you yourself have been so compromised and
mixed up with this late business in the Forest, that
you must allow the necessity of withdrawing for a
time at least."

" Yes," cried Pearce, sulkily ; " I could not well
walk about the streets just yet, and shall not be
sorry to be released from this miserable prison here.
But what did he say ?"

And O'Foggarty proceeded to recount all that
had passed between himself and Villiers.

" And you touched him with the tune ?" asked
Pearce.

" Yes," replied O'Foggarty; " and he evidently
felt it."

" And he knows that you know ?"

" Evidently."

" But you did not commit yourself ? You did
not say any thing that he could take hold of ?" said
Pearce.

The other only replied by a contemptuous smile.
" You imagine, I fear, Mr. Pearce, that no one understands these matters but yourself; and yet, perhaps, there are gentle modes of proceeding more
efficacious than even murder and rebellion."

Pearce moved as if stung to the quick by the
suggestion.

" What I have done," he said, " has been done
well; no one dreamt of any other end than has happened. And we have gained all we wanted, and

shall gain more. Is not the ministry going out? Is
not parliament to be dissolved?"

"And you will add, I suppose," said O'Foggarty,
"Is not a good blow struck against the parliament
church in Hawkstone? Has your emissary, the
printer, been here to-day?"

"Yes," replied Pearce. "I have given him another
handbill; and I do not think the poor parson will
stand it much longer. They must go to his bishop,
and there must be an inquiry; and he cannot purge
himself."

"And have you sent the paragraphs to the
papers?"

"I have," said Pearce, "with capital letters and
initials, and all that. No one can mistake it. The
penny newspapers will have the whole story at full
length."

"Remember," said O'Foggarty, looking grave
and conscientious, "this is entirely an act of your
own. It is no business of mine to throw a scandal
even upon a Protestant and heretic; but if you think
it will aid the cause ——"

Pearce looked with ill-disguised contempt upon
his companion, and then he said, "You do not
mean to hint, do you, Mr. O'Foggarty, that you have
any scruple about throwing dirt where dirt will
stick, if it is our object, and the interest of our cause,
that it should stick? We were not used in former
days to be so very strait-laced and particular.
Do you affect to regret, if that poor Bentley should
be driven from his parish, and the field thrown
more open to yourself, and your own rigid sanctity
and unimpeachable virtue" (and Pearce smiled bitterly) "be favourably contrasted with his pecca-
dilloes, and a bad name light upon all that he
belongs to? Do you object to this?"

O'Foggarty affected to look indifferent, but his eyes

twinkled with the thought of the advantage which might be taken of the situation in which Bentley had become involved.

"I rather think," continued Pearce, "that it is not one of our maxims to abstain from such legitimate means of defence and annoyance."

O'Foggarty looked grave. "I cannot," he said, "interfere to prevent you from doing what you think may be beneficial to the good cause."

Pearce again smiled in scorn. "No!" he said, "the Church generally has not scrupled to make use of our assistance, even when openly she pretended to reprobate our acts. Where would Rome have been but for our arm? And how could our arm have saved her, if we had listened to the old wives' superstitions about means and ends? All means are justified by good ends; and all ends are good which benefit the one great cause. I think even the Catholic rector of Hawkstone is a little indebted to us."

"The title is rather premature, is it not?" said O'Foggarty; but he could not avoid smiling at the sound.

"Bah!" exclaimed Pearce, contemptuously, "you smooth-faced, soft-speaking gentlemen always think every thing premature. If we had trusted to such as you, should we have now our bishops in Ireland, aye, and our rectors too, and our bishops recognised in an act of parliament, in the teeth of another act which expressly forbids it? How was this done but by courage? You fancied the Conservative ministers were bold and honest. We knew them to be cowards; and that with all their fine speeches, and conditions, and precautions, when they passed the Emancipation Act, they would not dare to enforce their own penalties. They served to gull the people; and that was all Sir Robert wanted. Ask him or the Duke now to expel the unlicensed Jesuits, or prosecute a Catholic bishop for taking his own title ; and hear what he would say—though it was his own bill, and his own promise to the fools who trusted in him."

" I suppose he would say," answered the other, sarcastically, " that the times were altered — that it was necessary to legislate according to circumstances — that however solemnly he had pledged his word at the time, he had not meant to preclude himself from modifying his opinions as events occurred — that it is idle to resist the current of general opinion — that to rule a liberalized nation, rulers must themselves be liberalized—that he really could not commit himself to a general principle — and that he was an honest man and a great states- man, and had reduced the Three and a half per cents, and therefore ——"

" And therefore the people must trust him," in- terrupted Pearce. " Bah ! for a set of fools ! Why the Tories, or Conservatives as they call them, have done more for us than all the Whigs put to- gether."

" Yes," replied O'Foggarty, " the Irish education scheme, enlarged grant to Maynooth, endowments in Ireland, bishops in the Colonies, national edu- cation in England, — all tell for us. And now they talk of their new liberal colleges in Ireland, as if they had never heard of us, or knew that to found a liberal college was the first step to putting it into the hands of the Jesuits. I wonder if any one of them ever heard a syllable of our history, or knew how we managed to make our way into them."

Pearce joined in the laugh. " No," he said, " do not be afraid of being premature. Call yourself at once what you ought to be. Have your letters di- rected to you ' The Catholic Rector of Hawkstone.'

It will compel that poor old paralytic to call himself the Protestant rector; and then any one will be able to see that the Catholic must be the true, and the Protestant the false one—any one who has learnt his creed. Think what this one word has done for us—how by using words of this kind exclusively, and allowing them to no other, we have prospered already."

The other smiled assent.

" Then," continued Pearce, " build up your chapel with a tower; have a ring of bells in it. It stands well—just in the market-place. Every one will ask what it is. Make them call it a church, or, rather, the church—the Catholic church of Hawkstone; and when you speak of the other old building, call it the chapel, or, if you like, the conventicle. Keep your bells ringing from morning to night. It is not allowed by law, but who will dare to say any thing. People will ask what it means; and the answer will be that you are at prayers—three, or seven times a day—not twice in the week only, as elsewhere,"

" You are very kind in your suggestions," said O'Foggarty, rather indignantly.

" My suggestions," answered Pearce, " are very well worth attending to ; and indeed they are not mine—

> ' Sed quæ præcepit Ofellus,
> Rusticus, abnormis sapiens.'

No! abnormis sapiens is rather too strong for us; but do not mind taking advice. Was it not my advice that you should get your chapel of a good handsome style—not like the barns, and sheds, and tawdry meeting-houses, which the establishment has been raising, at 1,200*l.* a piece. People come to look ; and then they admire; and then you say that it is

the old Catholic style — the true Christian architecture; and that you alone possess it; and that the
design was given by a Catholic — if a convert, so
much the better; and that *you* (mind and lay a
stress upon *you*) do not like to build a church of
that which costs you nothing. It is astonishing how
this tells."

O'Foggarty smiled.

"Then take care," continued Pearce, "that the
persons who show it kneel down when they enter.
If you are there yourself, do not chatter and laugh,
like the Protestants, as they walk about the aisles of
their cathedrals, as if they were seeing a showplace. Keep the church open all day; people —
poor people — always kneeling about. Get up a
procession; hire twenty or thirty boys to walk
before you in surplices; get a fine cross — not a
crucifix — English people are not ripe for it. Sing
as you go through the streets. Establish a guild, a
confraternity, which will take more than a benefit-
club; and give them a fine dress: the poorer the
people are the better — the prouder they will be of
walking to church amidst admiring eyes, dressed out
in caps and vestments, and bearing tapers. Have a
distribution of loaves. Take care only to deal with
true Catholics, or likely converts. Get a bookseller; fill his windows with Catholic prints — some
really good, others gaudy and striking, for the poor.
Have tracts in abundance. Mind and attend all the
public meetings, and speak charitably, religiously,
but, above all, liberally. Sigh over the distractions
of the Church. If you can find any young men from
Oxford, get acquainted with them; lend them
books — first Fénélon and Pascal, then Bonaventure,
Liguori, and books like that. Show them your Sisters of Charity. Deal with them moderately and
quietly. Abjure all images and superstitions. Talk

of faith, and unity, and peace, and the feudal times,
and loyalty, and the middle ages—all that's romantic, you know.   They do not know anything about
it, and will swallow all that you tell them.   By-and-
by, perhaps—who knows?—you may even get up
a miracle."   But the last suggestion was stated
rather too coarsely and broadly for the more refined subtilty of O'Foggarty, and he moved as if in
disgust.

"Ah!" said Pearce, "you affect to be shocked.
But I ask you honestly—here we are, between ourselves—am I advising you anything which is not
practicable and practised?   Is not this the way in
which we have prospered hitherto?"

O'Foggarty could say nothing.

"I do think," continued Pearce, "that some have
managed things rather stupidly.   When they celebrate high mass, they have it placarded over the
town, like a bill of the play; foreign singers—Mr.
So-and-so to preside at the organ; seats three shillings, two shillings, one shilling; doors open at eleven o'clock; the Bishop of Negroland to preach.
Now Protestants sometimes do this; but I do not
think it sounds well—it is too barefaced.   And
another man, I forget his name, used to give lectures, at Clifton, on sacred music—Catholic music;
and promised, in his bills, to exhibit in the middle
of them a famous crucifix, carved I do not know by
whom, and worth thousands.   Now any one can see
through this.   I would rather take the high tone—
fasting, you know, and the hours, and the breviary,
and unity, and Sisters of Charity, and self-denial.
It will tell far more with the Oxford men; and
those are the persons to be looked to."

"Yes," said the other.   "I stayed at Oxford myself, not long since, for a few days, and was surprised to find how I was fêted, and embraced, and

questioned; and how ready they were to fly into one's arms."

"Not many?" said Pearce.

"No, not many," replied O'Foggarty,—"a little set, about half a dozen."

"And mere boys?"

"Mere boys, who had just taken their degrees."

"Learned?" asked Pearce. "Did they know any thing about us?"

"Learned!" repeated O'Foggarty. "Bah!" and they both joined in a hearty laugh. "I would get hold of a newspaper," said Pearce,—"a Whig one would do all you wanted. Since O'Connell helped them, it is astonishing how popish they are becoming. You may throw a little dirt, if you like, now and then, where it is wanted to stick. But I think more is done by praising yourselves. Get up good accounts of your festivals and processions. You have picked up ten or a dozen old men and women, who subscribe a penny a week, and you make a confraternity of them for honouring the memory of St. Bridget, or saying vespers at the altar of St. Winifred, or devoting themselves to the service and honour of the blessed martyr, Saint Any-body. Well! you fix a day for the festival, wash out the school-room, stick up some laurel-leaves in it, dress the poor people up in their finery, get together as many priests as you can, and if possible a bishop, and have service. The next day comes out a paragraph in the paper, headed in large type, 'Celebrations of the Catholic Church.—Yesterday, at the magnificent new church of St. Radulphus, the largest church which has been built since the Reformation, was celebrated the solemn Festival of the blessed and devoted martyr So-and-So. Early in the morning the inhabitants were called to their devotions by the splendid peal of bells from that mag-

nificent tower, which has been raised at a vast
expense, and may fairly be considered a model of
true Catholic architecture.   At twelve o'clock the
procession formed in the Catholic school-rooms —
put it in the plural number, it sounds grander —
under the direction of Thomas Smith, Esq., H.
Thomson, Esq., Robert Jenkins, Esq., Edward
Jones, Esq., and other influential inhabitants of the
neighbourhood.   At the head walked the beloved,
and learned, and pious pastor of the parish, the
Rev. Patrick O'Foggarty, whose devotion, charity,
and enlarged liberality, &c. &c.'   You understand
all this.   Then bring in the venerated Bishop of
Negroland, or whoever else it may be.   Always
call your bishops venerable, and learned, and holy
prelates of the Church, martyrs, and the like.
O'Connell does this, you observe.   He kneels down
before them in the dirt, and asks their blessing.   It
tells wonderfully at a distance.   When he speaks
of them, you would expect to see angels, or saints
worn away with fasting, eyes dim with watching,
lips that never speak but in words of peace and
blessing.   He talks of them and of the Irish priests,
as if they were his idols, and no one could see them
without adoring them as the very incorporation of
holiness.   O'Foggarty, were you ever at Maynooth ?"

And O'Foggarty could not resist the laugh, in
which Pearce joined.

"It tells well," continued Pearce, "notwithstanding. Certainly O'Connell is clever—he does understand it. As for the rest, you can easily manage
it. 'Service grand and imposing—devotion of the
people wonderful — many weeping, others fainting
with joy — sermon, a wonderful defence of the true
Catholic doctrine against heresy, worthy the learning, and talents, and continental fame of the vene-

rated preacher. Assemble afterwards in the school-
rooms — tastefully fitted up — elegant collation —
ladies, Protestants of rank, who took the deepest
interest — prayers for the restoration of England to
the Catholic faith — health of the Pope drank —
then the Queen, then religious liberty all over the
world, toleration, and so forth.' Enlarge on the
'reverential piety and solemnity which pervaded the
whole meeting, and which is so singularly characteristic of the true Catholic Church.'"

"Then," said O'Foggarty, with a smile, "you
would not recommend that we should do as they do
in Ireland, and hold a reform dinner in the chapel
itself, with the altar turned into a sideboard, and
the font into a wine-cooler."

"No," said Pearce; "this would not do in England. But they may do what they like in Ireland.
People here believe nothing they hear of it."

"No," replied O'Foggarty; "I heard some one
in Oxford mention this very fact in the set with
whom I was staying; and they turned up their
noses, and declared that it was false — it must be
false, — though the relater saw it with his own
eyes."

"It is a blessed thing for us," said Pearce, "that
they are so unbelieving, otherwise awkward things
would come out. They do work rather too strongly
in Ireland. They manage their election matters,
and their repeal rent, and their politics rather too
coarsely. We must contrive things with more
gentleness in England."

"We need not fear," said O'Foggarty. "From
what I saw in Oxford, if a very demon were to rise
up before them, and call himself the Pope, they
would be ready to call him an angel, and deny their
own senses, and the senses of others too."

"Because they have got a fancy, and do not choose to have it disturbed, — is that it ? "

"Yes," said O'Foggarty.

"Have any of them been abroad ? " asked Pearce.

"Not that I know of," answered O'Foggarty. "Somebody has told them — this is their general answer — or they have read about it in Fénélon or Pascal; or they cannot find what they want in their own Church; and if you ask them what they do want, they cannot tell; only it must be something exciting, fervent, enthusiastic, romantic, and picturesque — something unlike the common."

Pearce grinned a malicious smile.

"And they talk about the fathers, don't they ? " he asked.

"Not much now," said O'Foggarty. "They have got to their new doctrine of development, which does not require the fathers. One or two of them have read something, and these serve as references; and are ready to come forward and vouch for the statements, which the rest take from them; just as in the advertisement of a quack medicine, the person cured is always ready to give his name, if required."

Pearce once more laughed heartily. "A hopeful set, I must say; but, if they love us so much, why do they not come over to us ? "

"Ay," said O'Foggarty, "that is a mystery; they say they are waiting — that they cannot come without others — that they must take their religion from their fathers, and do as their conscience tells them."

Pearce once more laughed, but more loudly than before. "And will any of them come soon, do you think ? "

"I am sure I cannot say," said O'Foggarty. "They

seem to be out of their senses. If they believed the
Pope's authority, they would come over at once, for
they could not think of remaining out of the pale of
salvation ; and if they believed their own Church,
they could not acknowledge the Pope's, and thus they
would not think of coming to Rome. But some one
has told them that the oath which says that the Pope
neither has nor ought to have any jurisdiction in
this realm of England means only that he has none
as a fact, and that the 'ought' is an expletive; and
so, perhaps, they imagine that they can remain in
the English Church, and yet acknowledge the supremacy of Rome, and that the English Church says
nothing of the Romish in this, as in other points,
but what any clergyman who accepts the thirty-nine
Articles may heartily subscribe to.

O'Foggarty spoke gravely, and Pearce did not
laugh ; for even he was surprised, and felt something
like disgust.

"And after all, then," he said, "they are only the
merest Protestants, thinking and acting without any
guide or authority whatever, mere Dissenters, — in
fact, private-judgment men."

"They are blind men," answered O'Foggarty,
"following their own noses; and this they call
faith."

"You must get some converts soon," said Pearce,
"in this place. It tells wonderfully."

"There is old Mrs. Dennett," replied the other,
"who keeps the little apple-stall at the corner of
King's Street. I have talked to her a good deal.
She is an Irishwoman, and a Catholic, but married a
heretic soldier, and for years has gone to church. I
think she will come round soon. She is very poor;
and I have offered her to sweep out the chapel."

"Yes," said Pearce; "and you must get an account
of it into the papers—the Irish papers especially,

and those which are at a distance; but even close
here it does not much matter what you say, for no
one takes the trouble to read or believe a contradiction of a bold statement once put forward well.
You must head it — Conversions to the Catholic
Church.   Something of this kind :   ' The Progress
of Divine Truth has been singularly and almost
miraculously manifested in this district, under the
sacred ministrations of the Rev. P. O'Foggarty, Catholic pastor ; or, if you like it, rector of the parish.
On Sunday last a venerable lady was received into
the bosom of the Church with the usual ceremonies.
The Bishop of Eliopolis preached an admirable
sermon on this interesting occasion.   The solemn
choir service was under the direction of the talented
Mr. Simpson, assisted by a large and extensive body
of performers.   The holy building was thronged
with a fashionable and influential congregation,
among whom were many Protestants of rank, who
evinced deep sympathy and admiration.'   Then in
the London papers you may put something of this
kind, — ' We understand that a late important conversion to the Catholic Church has caused the greatest
sensation in a town not a hundred miles from Hawkstone.   The lady in question is whispered to be of
high rank and immense wealth, as well as the most
unquestionable piety and talent.   It is understood
that her return to the true faith has been caused by
her dissatisfaction with the secularity and false principles of the Protestant communion of England ; and
that she will soon be followed by a large body of
friends and dependants.'   In another paper you may
put, — ' We are authorised to state that the lady of
rank who has recently been made a convert to the
Catholic Church at Hawkstone is not Lady ——.   Her
property has also been overrated.   It by no means
equals 30,000l. a-year.   It is understood that the first

scruples were infused into her mind by reading, not
the Tracts for the Times, and other works of the
Oxford school, but some sermons of a celebrated
vicar of a certain large manufacturing town, whose
name begins with H and ends with k.'"

O'Foggarty could not help smiling. "And what
is the good of this?" he asked.

Pearce regarded him with a sneer. "You who are
to manage matters in my place," he said — "you to
ask the good of this. In the first place, does it not
give to us importance and dignity, and the appearance of success? and success will soon find followers.
Secondly, does it not encourage our friends? Thirdly,
does it not terrify the Protestants, and especially the
wild Protestants of Ireland? Fourthly, does it not
drive them into more extravagance, and more violent
abuse of all that we hold; and does not this expose
them to make false statements, and thus to ridicule
and refutation? And has any thing fed and supported us more than the follies of what they call low
church and ultra-protestantism? Fifthly, does it
not dishearten those who are still lingering half way,
and prepare them to come over? Sixthly, does it
not throw suspicion upon our worst and most dangerous enemies, if their principles are shown to be
the cause of these conversions to us?"

"But why fix on Dr. H.?" asked O'Foggarty.
"Why not on the Tracts for the Times?"

Pearce again smiled sarcastically. "Because,"
he replied, "those who put out the Tracts for the
Times are now doing us effectual service; and the less
said of them the better. We must throw suspicion
only on those who are resolved to oppose us, of
whom there is no hope, who will fight with us to the
last. Once we thought this was to be the case
with the tract writers; but now they have thrown
off the mask, if they ever wore one, and are letting

their followers run straight forward into our arms without a word to call them back, or with such a word as only encourages them to advance by showing how far they can go, and how near they may approach us, and yet not leave their own warm shelter; that is, how they may remain as Catholics, and serve the Pope, while they are members and even ministers of the English Church. If they had been ourselves they could not have managed their plans more cleverly for us, or played more adroitly into our hands. No, let us say nothing of them."

"And you would not, then," said O'Foggarty, "recommend any controversy with these?"

"No," replied Pearce, "nor yet with the others. It is not safe. Development will not go down with these last, as it will with the young ones in Oxford. They explode it at once as mere rationalism; and it is not safe to appeal to the fathers. Even W. made a mistake when he got on this ground, and was sadly shown up for his quotations and references. It damaged us terribly. If you will have controversy, let it be with some hot-headed, zealous, low churchman—that poor wretch Bentley for instance, who knows nothing of history, and professes to fight with the Bible, and the Bible only, in his hand. You are sure of driving him into absurdities; for it must end in his either declaring that every one in the world, man, woman, or child, learned or ignorant, good or bad, is able to extract from the Bible by his own eyes the one truth which it contains, and has a right to judge the Bible by his own reason, which is just what all the infidels in the world contend for; and so he will preach infidelity—and this will pave the way for us; or else he must acknowledge the need of some authority to interpret and communicate the one truth—and he knows, and his people know, of none but ours: any other they have suffered to be so long out of sight that they fancy it does not exist."

"You are profound," said O'Foggarty—"much more profound than those would imagine who have only seen you in your red shock hair and your butcher's apron."

"I have my wits about me," replied Pearce, "otherwise those who sent me here would not have trusted me. And the advice which I have offered you is the best which you can have. But it is getting late, and my things must be packed. Did you take my place in the night coach."

"Yes; I said that Mrs. Rogers would be there, at the corner of the street, five minutes before starting. And as it will be dark, you can muffle up your face for the toothache, and wrap up in this plaid cloak, and no one will see you."

"I have a pair of pattens," laughed Pearce, "and a cotton umbrella, and a black bonnet. I think I shall do — do," he continued, "better than you will. Be assured all their hopes are vain; with all your cajoleries and softness, you will do nothing here with him. You may flatter him, but he will despise you; you may make him suspected and abused for a Papist, as he will be called by all the low churchmen round about, but this will not touch him; he will remain firm as a rock, take my word for it, and will do you infinite mischief. He should be dealt with in a very different way." And Pearce, as he uttered the words, stammered and coughed; and O'Foggarty looked grave and sombre, and shrunk back from his companion's touch.

"Ay, Mr. O'Foggarty," said Pearce, after a pause; "when you read more of our books you will be less sensitive and fastidious. If a good object is to be gained, we must not falter and stick at the means. I think this is sound doctrine — our doctrine — is it not?"

But his companion remained silent. "You take the boy with you," he then asked, "from London?"

"Yes," replied Pearce. "He is safely lodged there with Connell; and I shall carry him abroad with me. Time will come round when I shall be wanted again here."

"It is cruel, is it not," said the other, "to take a boy from his father in this way?"

"Cruel!" exclaimed Pearce, "cruel!" and he ground his teeth till the foam flew out of his mouth. "They have allowed me — and if they had refused me — refused me this revenge — I would have rather——"

But he checked himself, and drawing his chair close to O'Foggarty, who shrunk back at his approach, "O'Foggarty," he said, "do you know what revenge is? Did you ever taste it, — how sweet it is, how luscious?" And he looked into O'Foggarty's eye with such a glare of demoniacal malignity that the other drew back again from his companion in fear and horror.

"Tell them," continued Pearce, "tell them that I will have my revenge. If I can have it by serving them, well and good: if not — tell them I defy them. I think," he said more calmly, "they know me too well to trifle with me. If I obey them now and quit this place for a time, it is not to abandon my revenge, but to postpone it — to make it more sweet, more pungent. But if I am in their hands, they are also in mine, and they dare not disappoint me. You will let them know this, — I wish them to understand it."

"I will tell them all which you wish to have told," said O'Foggarty, rising, and apparently de-

sirous of extricating himself from any longer conversation with so painful a companion. "I have
business at this moment, and must leave you. I
hope you will explain that I have done all in my
power to assist you and make you comfortable."

"Yes," replied Pearce, sulkily; for though bound
together by certain mysterious ties in the prosecution of one mysterious work, there was neither
cordiality nor real confidence between them; and
shaking hands coldly, they bade each other farewell.
Two hours after, at the end of the lane, the heavy
Highflyer Coach stopped to take up Mrs. Rogers,
who, wrapped up in a huge plaid cloak, and shrouded
in a black bonnet and green veil, appeared with
pattens in one hand and a cotton umbrella in
another, anxiously superintending the disposition of
a large holland-covered package on the top of the
coach, and then, without saying a word, ensconced
herself in a dark corner of the vehicle out of the
glare of the lamps.

"You have not caught him yet?" said the
coachman to a policeman who was standing by the
door.

"Who?" asked the guard, familiarly.

"Why the fellow that used to walk about in the
butcher's frock, with the red hair—the man who
had to do with the riots—Peters—Pearce—what
was his name?" The policeman shook his head,
the guard took up his horn, and, to the sound of
"Rule Britannia," the well-appointed, well-packed
coach rolled off with a cheerful rumble over Hawkstone Bridge, and out of the town, on its way to
London.

CHAP. XIV.

WE may now pass, by means of that secret key
which opens every lock, and which none but authors
possess, into the back parlour of Mr. Lomax's
counting-house. The reader will observe the front
of the mansion itself, newly decorated with stucco
mouldings and iron railings—the adjoining house
converted into the office, to accommodate the expansion of so respectable and thriving a business.
Within all is new—clerks, some pert and conse-
quential, others grave and confidential, perched up
on their lofty stools, with pens in their ears, behind
new shining mahogany desks polished with French
varnish; machines for weighing letters and sovereigns; subscription-books open on the counter;
mysterious drawers, out of which astonished eyes
see sovereigns ladled carelessly by handfuls, and
bank-notes grasped by fifties and hundreds, just
as if they were only silver-paper—the whole a
very mine of wealth. How many needy visiters
trembled, as they pushed aside the green baize
folding-doors, and faced the ministers of the sanctuary! How many with envious eyes exclaimed, as
they issued into the street,—" O, that I were a
banker!"

We pass through this outer room into another
still larger and darker, with more clerks, more
mahogany desks, more drawers full of sovereigns
and bank-notes. Beyond is a veiled glass door, and
we are ushered into the private parlour of the great
country banker himself. Mr. Lomax is there, his

bald head shining at the head of a green table; his
face not destitute of intelligence, but indented with
lines of care; his features neither coarse nor refined, neither vulgar nor gentlemanly—something
between them both,—a specimen of the middle
classes; and his eye keenly scanning each person as
he enters, as if to gauge the contents of his pocket,
and the honesty of his promises. And yet, in some
way or other, if that eye was met by another, it
failed to stand the glance, and generally took refuge
elsewhere. And Mr. Lomax was also subject to a
nervousness—a little twitching of the mouth and
hand. He had been subject to it for some time.
The arrival of the post would bring it on—the
sight of a strange face, sometimes even reading
the newspaper. But it was only a trifle—scarcely
to be named, as a drawback to his enviable and influential position in Hawkstone—as the monied
man, to whom farmer and landlord, manufacturer
and shopkeeper, were all obliged to resort in their
respective difficulties—before whom all the little
aristocracy of Hawkstone bowed down—whom even
Lord Claremont had condescended to visit, prepa-
ratory to effecting a mortgage—whose notes passed
current as those of the Bank of England—whose
wife was the lady-patroness of the town—whose
daughters the belles of its society,—whose very
name, in the eyes of the multitude, was synonymous
for credit and for wealth.

Mr. Lomax was not alone; his table was surrounded by six or seven heads, among whom, as
the newspapers word it, we distinguished the élite of
the respectable professional inhabitants of the town,
— Mr. Robertson, the late perennial mayor before
the Reform Bill passed; Mr. Atkinson, the solicitor;
Mr. Morgan, the surgeon; Captain Hancock; Mr.
Brown, the great miller. And just as we enter,

Mr. Atkinson is in the act of shaking hands with
Charles Bevan himself, whose presence seems to have
caused in the whole group considerable surprise,
but not a little satisfaction.

"I scarcely expected to see *you* here," said Mr.
Morgan.

"Why not?" asked Bevan.

"Because I thought your new Oxford notions
would not allow you to take any interest in politics."

"Really," answered Bevan, "I cannot profess to
define what you mean by Oxford notions; but for
myself, I think it one of the first duties of a clergyman to take a part in politics—not, I mean, in a
mere struggle for place and power, which is too
often called politics, but in the practical duties of a
citizen.   The state has given me a vote for a
member of parliament, and I intend to exercise it,
as I hope for the good of the country.   I scarcely
know circumstances in which the voice of the clergy
may be so needed, and may do such good, as in a
popular election."

The little party seemed rather unwilling to enter
into the abstract discussion; and Bevan therefore
took his chair, and prepared to listen while Mr. Atkinson drew up his thick ill-folded white neckcloth,
and proceeded to open the business of the meeting.

Mr. Atkinson, the gentleman in the brown ker-
seymere pantaloons and gaiters, in the black ill-
made coat and waistcoat, with the long gold watch-
chain dangling from his waistband, the grizzled
hair, the grave, sallow, thoughtful, and reserved
countenance, which, however, when called on, as
he constantly was called, to direct the politics of
Hawkstone, assumed even a degree of elevation and
warmth, and exhibited considerable tact and self-
command, and knowledge of the world,—Mr. At-

kinson, as must be known to any one who has been within a hundred miles of Hawkstone, was a first-rate country solicitor, a man of unquestionable probity, of singular influence, looked up to by all his clients with a mixture of awe and regard, one who strictly fulfilled the duties of his position, an attentive husband, a father who worked hard to provide for his ten children, a staunch supporter of the Church, a man of irreproachable character, and the most important member of the Conservative party in Hawkstone. And, by his advice, the leaders of the same Conservative party were now assembled in Mr. Lomax's back parlour, to see what could be done at the last moment (for Conservatives usually wait till the last moment) to arrest the fearful progress of events, which threatened to install Mr. Marmeduke Brook, the radical, in the chair of the member for Hawkstone, by the hands of Mrs. Maddox and a host of dissenting allies.

Their anxiety had been not a little increased by the late events in the Forest, and by the alarm which had been caused by the revelations to which it had given rise. They felt like men who were sitting on a barrel of gunpowder, knowing that a match was burning near it, but unable to discover where. "In such times," said Mr. Lomax, "it became every one who valued the peace of society, and that which is the object of society — the preservation of property and credit, to come forward boldly, and stand by the institutions of his country." And the obvious step in the power of the Conservatives of Hawkstone was to procure the return of a Conservative member for the borough on the present occasion.

It must be confessed their means were not ample, nor their cause hopeful. Hawkstone, before the Reform Bill, had been a notorious borough — noto-

rious for the silence, ease, and certainty, with which
any two gentlemen recommended to the worthy
electors, that is, to the mayor and corporation, by
the government for the time being, were sure of
conforming themselves in a wonderful way to the
sympathies and tastes of all the electors, and of obtaining their unanimous suffrages without even
asking for them personally.   It was notorious also
for the excellent turbot, and delicious venison, which
smoked on the mayor's table twice or thrice a year,
and on General Villiers's as often as he chose to
put himself to the trouble of entertaining, at the
Priory, his accommodating friends and neighbours,
and of suggesting to them that Sir William Booth,
the Secretary to the Admiralty, and the Honourable
Mr. Murphy, the new Lord of the Treasury, would
be fit and proper representatives for the borough of
Hawkstone.   It was notorious also for the singular
facility with which nephews, and cousins, and
brothers, and brothers-in-law of the corporate body
of Hawkstone obtained various official situations,
as tide-waiters, clerks, custom-house officers, and
the like.   And General Villiers's banking account
also exhibited about once in every three or four
years, synchronising with the dissolution of parliament, — a large, mysterious, but very acceptable
item, which to the steward of the General's estates
must have seemed to have dropped from the clouds.

These, as old Dr. Grant, the paralytic rector,
used mournfully to say, were the good old times —
the times of peace and order, before the torrent of
innovation had begun to menace and sweep away
the throne and the altar, and when Hawkstone lay
in blessed repose under the shade of its ancient institutions.   It must, indeed, be confessed, that,
however favourable this shade had been to the
physical growth of the members of the corporation,

and to the pecuniary growth of General Villiers's balance at his banker's, other things had also sprung up and flourished under it, which even the corporation themselves could not but regard as troublesome fungi. Nor had the altar, typified by the old grey church, or the throne, symbolised by the mayor's gilt mace, and the constable's brass-knobbed staff of office, escaped something of decay. Dr. Grant himself, who had been placed in his post of rector of the parish as the firm and trustworthy friend of the Villiers family — as the man whose opinion in all political matters, and especially in the exercise of the elective franchise, corresponded with the most undeviating punctuality with the opinions of the General — Dr. Grant continued, year after year, to preach his well-arranged cycle of compilations from Blair ; to diminish gradually the number of services, which he found himself unable to perform without a curate ; to celebrate marriages, and funerals, and baptisms with all decent regularity ; to visit the sick when he was sent for, and the school on the day of examination ; and to give away his pounds of roast beef at Christmas, and his subscriptions to all ordinary charities, with most decent regularity. But meanwhile, pew after pew, however comfortably arranged, lined with green or red, padded with cushions, curtained from observation, fell each Sunday into a state of emptiness. One after another families dropped off from their attendance, and others sprang up who never had attended ; and Dr. Grant was wonder-struck, and provoked, and exasperated, as he passed by the new streets in the suburbs, to see bricklayers, with the most irritating assiduity, engaged in raising convenient, neat-sashed, slate-roofed, galleried, gaslighted structures, and decorating them with two round pillars at the door, and a portentous inscription on the pediment, — Wesleyan Chapel — Independent Chapel — Baptist Chapel — Presbyterian Meeting-House — Quaker's Meeting — The Bible Church — Church of the Rational Religionists — New Free Church of Scotland — New Episcopal Church of England (which, when Dr. Grant came to inquire, he found meant an episcopal church which had nothing to do with bishops), — not to mention the Unitarians, Socinians, Mormonites, besides various off-shoots of Wesleyans, who still professed allegiance to the Church, and attachment to its system, only they protested against taking part in its services, or obeying its ministers.

And with these weeds, others had sprung up round the same new buildings, which disturbed the peace of old Mr. Robertson, the incapacitated perennial mayor, full as much as the new chapels discomfited Dr. Grant, the paralytic rector. A newspaper was established in Hawkstone — a newspaper, cleverly written, full of sharpness, not ill-informed, but which, to Mr. Robertson's great surprise, instead of undertaking the defence of the throne and the altar, and eulogising the ancient institutions of the town, under the motto of "Things as they are," adopted, to the infinite disgust of the corporation, a totally different course. One week came a complaint against the town-clerk's fees; another brought a remonstrance against the paving and lighting tax; then came a sneer at the head-constable; then actually an attack upon the mayor; then words were banded about of corruption, bribery, truckling, sycophancy, roguery,—all aimed at the mayor and corporation. Then followed a denunciation of church-rates; then a call to a public meeting; then petitions for reform; then large assemblages of the non-electors of Hawkstone in the great room at the Bell, with speeches, and pam-

phlets, and placards. At last three or four of the
most influential of the malcontents, including two
dissenting ministers, and Mr. Smith, the manufacturer, a recent arrival, were seen one fine morning
in a mysterious group on the outside of the Highflyer coach, hastening up to London ; and, to the
mayor and corporation's surprise and consternation,
not unmixed with anger and contempt, their names
appeared the next day in the newspapers as important delegates from the borough of Hawkstone,
who had met to consult with other oppressed individuals in other boroughs similarly situated, by
what means they might be relieved from their disgraceful thraldom, as a borough-ridden, and cor-
ruption-haunted people. These were but the mut-
terings of the storm — the first big drops of the
thunder-shower. At last the cloud burst over the
devoted heads of the mayor and corporation, and
the Reform Bill fell upon them like a thunder-
bolt.

From the dismay and prostration which this
blow had inflicted on them, the Tory party of
Hawkstone — a few and scattered minority — was
just beginning to recover ; and Mr. Atkinson was
at their head. But Tories they dared call themselves no longer. Was it conscience ? Was it
fear ? Was it that an alias was necessary to escape
from the memory of past peccadillos ? Had they
really become enlightened to the antiquated character of their former principles ? Or had they in truth
even before had no principles at all — nothing but
the name of Tory, to denote that portion of the
constituency who partook of General Villiers's annual hospitality ? Whatever was the cause, the
name of Tory was discreetly merged and sunk in
the new-coined title of Conservative. What the
precise nature of Conservatism was, no one pro-

fessed to define. When old Mr. Robertson was
charged with being a Tory, he anxiously repudiated
the accusation. When he was taxed with Liberalism, he writhed his mouth in disgust. When asked
what he was, he could only say that he was something betwixt and between — neither one nor
the other. " Medio tutissimus ibis " was his motto.
He trusted to Mr. Atkinson; and Mr. Atkinson,
though he did not think it worth while to develope
his whole sentiments or policy to his party, partly
because they would probably rebel, and partly
because he thought they had not wit to understand
him, and must consent to follow him blindfold, or
fall a victim to the enemy, cherished his theory in
secret, having borrowed it from high sources, and
confirmed it by due meditation on his practical
experience of life.

Mr. Atkinson prided himself on being an honest
man; and although so long as a dishonest system
had been firmly established under the good old days,
he had not thought it necessary either to remonstrate against or alter it, now that the corruption
had been openly denounced and overturned, he
felt that it had been wrong, and not easily defen-
sible. He therefore resolved at once, nobly and
generously, to give up what it was impossible that
he could any longer retain, and submitted, with a
smiling face and conciliating submission, to the transfer of the empire of Hawkstone from the mayor and
corporation to the ten-pound freeholders. Nor was
he content with submission. He actually professed
readiness to co-operate with the new system; and
even went beyond the authors of the change, who
had endeavoured to beguile their opponents by
declaring that it was no change at all, only an expansion of existing institutions; and himself announced that it was a change, a total alteration, a

transfer of supreme power from the king to the
people ; and that though the constitution was destroyed by it, he would henceforth willingly acquiesce in it, and proceed to carry out the new
principles to their full extent, though with due
caution and slowness. The poor ex-mayor looked
on him with alarm ; Captain Hancock, who still
remained a Tory, shrugged his shoulders ; Charles
Bevan gave him up in despair. But Mr. Smith,
the manufacturer, shook hands most amicably with
his former foe ; and the dissenting ministers even
toasted his health, and smiled significantly among
themselves, when Mr. Atkinson endeavoured to
infuse into the still-reluctant members of the corporation his own newly-developed liberality. They
accepted, not indeed very gratefully or courteously, but as instalments, the many little pieces
of patronage and privileges, which Mr. Atkinson
blandly placed at their disposal in the town, sometimes without consulting the mayor, to whom they
properly belonged. Peace was Mr. Atkinson's object. " The popular current," he said, " could not
be resisted. There was a law of fatality in boroughs
as in empires, by which they must slide by degrees
from monarchies into democracies ; and it was the
part of the wise and prudent statesman not to provoke opposition by resistance, but to accommodate
himself to the stream — happy only, if he could
prevent the ancient institutions from being pulled
down in a riot, by undertaking to remove them
himself, trowel in hand, brick by brick, and beam
by beam." In this gradual and slow removal Mr.
Atkinson was now busily engaged. Why the ancient institutions should be allowed to stand — why
it might be the wisdom and duty of a statesman
even to risk a battle in their defence, he had never
thought. They were obnoxious to public opinion ;

and public opinion was his only test of truth. And
as fame, popular fame — the fame of being an admirable town-clerk of Hawkstone, of managing its
parties adroitly so as to prevent collision, of improving its finances, and reducing its debt, — was the
darling object of the practical solicitor's ambition,
he looked only to the increase of his reputation
with the councillors of the north ward, or the majority of liberal aldermen, and rejoiced in obtaining
the reluctant and even sneering applause of the
radical newspapers, who congratulated him on his
enlightened views, or condescendingly contrasted
his enlarged policy with the dull bigotry of his
ignorant predecessors.

And yet, if Mr. Atkinson had been called a Radical, he would have repelled the charge with
indignation. He was a friend to the Church, because, as he delighted to say, its doctrines appeared
to him very true, neither fanatical nor popish, and
more calculated than any other to produce obedient
and honest citizens, who would make the nation
wealthy and prosperous by their quietness and sobriety. At the same time he would not for the
world prevent others from holding their own opinions. And other forms and doctrines might be
true as well as those of the Church. And toleration of each other's views was the fittest course for
the practical statesman to take. He therefore not
only paid his annual subscription to Dr. Grant's evening lecture, but contributed his guinea a year to the
Wesleyan school, induced one of his clients to give
a very favourable piece of ground for the erection of
a Unitarian meeting-house, and had held a plate at a
meeting in the town-hall for promoting a Baptist
mission to New Zealand, at the same time that the
bishop of that country was embarking to take possession of his diocese. He was a friend to the throne ;

but yet he was almost struck dumb, when Charles
Bevan ventured to refuse drinking the "Glorious
Revolution of 1688." And whenever King Charles I.
was mentioned, Mr. Atkinson confessed that much
good had arisen from the principle then established,
that in cases of tyranny a people might right themselves. His notion of society was, that it was a very
convenient association for the purpose of procuring
comfortable houses, decent clothes, abundant provisions. And his abhorrence of radicalism mainly
resolved itself into the pernicious influence, which
sedition, and rebellion, and agitation generally exercised on the price of stocks. In his heart, indeed,
he little approved of a very extended education of
the poor; for he found that the impertinent boys at
the Hawkstone National School paid little attention to taking off their hats to him; and Mr. Smith,
the manufacturer, complained bitterly that his educated factory men, instead of devoting themselves
to develope the resources of the country by per-
severing labour for sixteen hours a-day, were prone
to read newspapers, and congregate in debating societies. But education was a popular watchword,
and therefore Mr. Atkinson surrendered himself to
the charm, and even delivered an address to the
Mechanic's Institute, of which he was treasurer; in
which address he satisfactorily showed that nothing
could more conduce to the virtue, chastity, and honesty of the poor than teaching them the use of the
globes; that the greatest enjoyment after sixteen
hours' work was to listen to a new theory of geology; and that, indeed, man's highest happiness on
earth, and probably in heaven, must consist in being
able to anatomise an ichthyosaurus, give the right
name to the ornithorhyncus paradoxus, or discover
a new nebula under the extreme point of the last
star in Orion's belt.

But we must not detain our readers longer from the conclave in Mr. Lomax's back parlour; for after a great deal of discussion, in which all the parties spoke together at once till they were tired, and Charles Bevan, who had sat a silent spectator, was about to take up his hat and retire in despair, Mr. Atkinson, who possessed singular tact in managing a public meeting, and, that he might carry his own way last, always allowed the others to have their own way first, and to talk themselves out of breath and patience, proceeded to draw a written paper out of his pocket, and suggested that he might be allowed to read it.

"I think," he said, "gentlemen, that we are all agreed in asking Mr. Villiers to come forward on the Conservative interest." Certainly, was the general exclamation. "And that he must be asked to take an enlarged and liberal line, otherwise we shall lose the support of a great number of votes." There was a reluctant murmur of assent from a few, broken by a growled "humph!" from Captain Hancock, who sat, with his rough, honest, weather-beaten face leaning on his gold cane, in one corner.

"I have thought the best thing I could do," said Mr. Atkinson, "was to draw up a little address, which he would himself circulate to the electors, and this would explain our views better to him than any thing else. Captain Hancock again muttered "pish!" but the rest nodded assent. "Shall I read it, gentlemen?" asked Mr. Atkinson, blandly.

"By all means," said the little party. And even Charles Bevan resumed his seat, it must be confessed, not wholly to the satisfaction of the composer of the address, for Charles was rather hypercritical; and not many months before, after Mr. Atkinson had taken the greatest pains in elaborating an address to Sir Robert Peel, and had concluded

with saluting him, not only as the greatest statesman that ever lived, but as the hope of the Church,
and the " pater patriæ," Charles had poured upon
his eulogy such a storm of indignation and ridicule,
that the favourite phrase was obliged to be ex-
punged, and the panegyric confined to the two
points of establishing the new police, and reducing
the Three and a half per cents; beyond which, to
the astonishment and indignation of Mr. Atkinson,
Charles declared that no one act of the minister
would obtain from posterity, who saw the consequences of his policy, any thing but contempt and
indignation. Mr. Atkinson, however, was now
obliged to proceed, though not without having before his eyes the fear both of Captain Hancock's
blunt honest " pish!" and Charles Bevan's more
subtle sarcasm.

And he began his address accordingly. " ' To
the Loyal and Independent Electors of the Borough of Hawkstone.' " Thus far he hugged himself with the thought that no possible objection
could be raised. But he was somewhat taken by
surprise by the dreaded " humph!" from Captain
Hancock's corner. Mr. Atkinson looked up in meek
surprise and expostulation. " What possible objection," he asked, gently, " could be made to this,
the usual and ordinary form of addressing all bodies
of electors?"

" They are not loyal," growled the captain, " and
they ought not to be independent. Why do you
begin by a lie?"

" Not loyal?" exclaimed Mr. Atkinson. " The
Conservatives not loyal?"

" No," answered the captain, " there is not one
of them would die for their queen; and that is what
I call loyal. Has not your own Sir Robert Peel
told the House of Commons that it is for them, and

not for the king, to choose the king's ministers?
And do you call this loyal?"

" My good friend," interposed Mr. Atkinson,
" you should consider the signs of the times.   This
is not a day when the extreme prerogatives of the
crown can be maintained.   We must soften down
asperities — we must conciliate.   Think of the general enlightenment — of the extension of newspapers — of the ——"

But before the sentence could be concluded the
Captain had thrown himself back in his chair.   And
Charles Bevan added : " And of the National Schools
— and the mechanics' institutes — and the railways
— and the steam navigation; all of which clearly
prove that it is right that this empire should be
governed by the people, and not by their king.   Is
it not so, Mr. Atkinson?"

Mr. Atkinson bit his lips, but still endeavoured
to preserve his bland, conciliating smile.   " And I
suppose," he added, at length, " you would object to
the word 'independent.'   Your new Oxford notions,"
he added, " Mr. Bevan, are not very favourable to
liberty."

Bevan, however, made no reply, except to beg
him to proceed.   And Mr. Atkinson resumed :

" 'Invited, as I have been, by a numerous and influential body of the ——'"   But here the Captain
could not help knocking his gold-headed cane upon
the ground.   " Ay," he exclaimed, " what is the
meaning of 'influential body,' and 'independent
electors?' are they to be influenced, or independent?
Which do you mean, Mr. Atkinson?"

" I mean, of course," explained Mr. Atkinson,
" that they should give their votes freely, without
being guided by any thing which I, or you, or any
other person might say to them.   Now the Reform
Bill has been passed, my opinion is that we should

all accept it willingly, and endeavour to carry out
its principles. And one of these, surely, is that the
voters are to vote independently."

" And what, then, becomes of your influence?"
said the Captain, rather indignantly.

" Of course," said Mr. Atkinson, " I should be
very far from excluding the proper influence of
property: property is the very end and foundation
of society."

" Or of knowledge?" said Bevan.

" Certainly," replied Mr. Atkinson.

" Or of goodness?" continued Bevan.

" Surely," conceded Mr. Atkinson.

" Then," concluded Bevan, " if they are to be
under all these influences, perhaps we may as well
strike out the word ' independent ' in the heading of
the address."

" Will Mr. Lomax have the goodness to put it
to the vote."

" I move," continued the Captain, " that ' loyal '
be struck out with it ; for I hate telling the poor
ignorant people a lie. They will learn by-and-by
to think cutting their queen's throat a loyalty."

The majority, however, felt no such scruples ; and
accepting the epithets as parts of an ordinary form,
meaning nothing, they overruled both objections,
and Mr. Atkinson continued.

" ' Invited, as I have been, by a numerous and influential body of the electors of the borough of
Hawkstone to offer myself as a candidate for the
honour of representing it in parliament —— ' "

But once more the reader was interrupted by a
grumbled " humph !" and Mr. Atkinson's eyes were
lifted up to the dreaded corner.

" I do not like that ' offer myself as a candidate,'
muttered Captain Hancock. " It is we who ought
to ask him to accept it, not he who should come

and ask us to give it him.   What does he get by
it ?"

"Get by it!" exclaimed Mr. Atkinson, rather
faintly (for reminiscences came across him, which
turned the sensitive, liberalized blood, which he had
lately imbibed, into a faint blush upon his cheeks).
"Of course it is a great honour to him, and a great
advantage, and a great ——"   But he found a difficulty in finishing his sentence.

"What!" continued Captain Hancock, "to be
kept all the best part of the year in a nasty town,
swallowing night after night infamous air, and still
more infamous speeches — obliged to give up his
family and society — and to make himself sick with
committees, and divisions, and debates, — and all
for the satisfaction of being called the honourable
member for Hawkstone.   Pish !   I'll never give
my vote to a man who comes and asks me to give it
him, as if he were going to get a place or a pension
by his membership.   And as for the honour! —
why what is the honour of being the chosen of a
mob — the elect of the ten-pound freeholders — the
pet and favourite of a set of fellows, who know
nothing, and care for nothing, but getting their beer
a penny a pot cheaper, or their wages without any
labour, and who only send him to parliament to obtain this for them ?"

Once more, however, the objection fell upon the
audience without meeting any sympathy; and Mr.
Atkinson continued: "'I come forward without delay to respond to their summons.'"

"You might as well say 'answer,' instead of 'respond,'" criticised the Captain.   But the rest, who
knew little of their classics, except what they had
picked up at very third-rate schools, preferred the
Latinised word; it sounded more dignified.

"'My principles,'" continued the reader, "'are

well known to be those of the present Conservative
ministry.'"

" What principles are those ?" grumbled Captain
Hancock.

" Oh !" said Charles Bevan, " of course the principle of having no principles." And Captain Hancock nodded to him with approbation.

"'I pledge myself,'" continued Mr. Atkinson, "' to
endeavour to maintain the ancient institutions of the
country, which it is the object of a Conservative
government to preserve.'"

" Had you not better specify them?" asked Bevan ;
" the cathedral bodies, for instance ; the Irish Bishoprics ; the municipal corporations ; the spiritual
independence of the Church ; Church education ; Convocation ; the Bishopric of Bangor, with a few others?"

Mr. Atkinson looked at him impatiently, but resumed. " ' But I shall be most anxious to remove any
restraints which now exclude certain portions of the
community from sharing the full benefits of the
constitution.'"

" That is," said the Captain, " you will keep the
gates of the citadel locked and bolted, and only break
a hole in the wall for the enemy to creep in at the
side."

" Your metaphor, Captain, is rather obscure,"
observed Mr. Atkinson, as he endeavoured to parry
the objection with another smile; " but we must
hasten on. ' I desire to see the agricultural interest
preserved in its just rights ; and, at the same time,
all unnecessary burdens removed from the manufactures of the country.' I inserted this," said Mr.
Atkinson, " because I rather think Mr. Burn, at the
silk-mills, is inclined to give us his vote, if our candidate will support free trade;" and he looked round
for some marks of admiration at his sagacity. " Mr.
Bowler, and the other landlords, of course are with

us; but I think we must contrive to conciliate the
manufacturers."

"Certainly," said Charles Bevan. "And it is so
easy to do this, by making promises which no one
could ever convict you of breaking. ' Just rights!'
— 'unnecessary burdens!' Of course we must all
agree in this. Pray what are the 'just rights' of
the agriculturist, and the 'necessary burdens' of
the manufacturer?"

"Indeed, Mr. Bevan," replied Mr. Atkinson,
rather angrily, "I cannot enter into abstract discussions with you. I must deprecate the introduction
of theories and speculations into plain practical politics. I think it would be most dangerous for us
to commit ourselves to any general principles, instead of waiting for circumstances, and guiding ourselves by them."

"Like a weathercock waiting for a wind!" grumbled Captain Hancock.

"Captain Hancock, I must protest," said Mr.
Atkinson, "against such severe strictures. Will
you allow me to proceed: 'I am, from conscientious
conviction, a firm friend to the Established Church;
but I shall always be found ready to give full freedom and toleration to other forms of opinion, all of
which, if conscientiously maintained, are equally
acceptable to the Almighty, and between which we
cannot judge without assuming an infallibility impossible to man.'"

But here he was interrupted by Charles Bevan,
whose countenance had assumed a very grave expression of indignation. He took a small Bible out
of his pocket, and presenting it to Mr. Atkinson,
begged to know in what page of it he found any
principle of the kind.

"Indeed," said Mr. Atkinson, "I am no theolo-
gian, and really cannot enter into your Oxford

notions. I am very willing to support the Church, but I cannot compromise the peace of the country, and condemn others for the sake of maintaining your exclusive notions. It may be all very well for theologians; but as practical men of business, who have to engage in the affairs of the world, we really must make allowances for differences of opinions, and not involve ourselves in a war of words for the peculiar doctrines of one class in preference to another."

" That is," replied Bevan, " as practical men of business, and as politicians, you must cast away your obligations as Christians, deny your faith, defy your God, and in the very teeth of his commandments apologise for, and support, and propagate, every form of heresy and schism."

"Indeed," exclaimed Mr. Atkinson, rather alarmed by the severity of the words, "nothing can be farther from my intention. I am sure Dr. Grant will tell you that no man is more a friend to the Church than myself, or more anxious to support it. Have I not given 10l. to the new organ?"

" The Church," replied Bevan, sternly, "does not want friends but sons. It demands not support, but obedience: and it has no more dangerous enemies than those who profess to assist it, almost contemptuously pitying its weakness, instead of recognising and submitting to its authority."

" But indeed," continued Mr. Atkinson, "I have no wish to undervalue its authority. And yet, really you would not have me as a layman trouble myself about its thirty-nine Articles, or enter into all its controversies with other sects?"

" I should wish you," replied Bevan, "as a Christian, to trouble yourself with ascertaining the grounds of your faith, and learning what that Church is, of which you profess to be a member;

and then amongst other things you would learn
never to apply to it the name of sect."

" Ay !" said Mr. Atkinson ; " Catholics always
argue in the same manner."

" I presume, Mr. Atkinson," replied Bevan, " that
you mean Roman Catholics or Romanists. I beg
to assure you that they argue in a very different
manner. But this is not the place for such a discussion. May I beg you to erase from your address
all that you have said about the Church ?"

" Erase ! erase ! " exclaimed Mr. Atkinson.
" Surely you would not wish me to leave out the
passage about supporting the Church ? What will
Dr. Grant say ? "

" And what will the Dissenters say," added Mr.
Lomax, " if there is nothing in the address about
toleration and liberty of conscience? They will
charge us with being bigoted and I know not
what."

" I think I might add," replied Bevan, " what
will Mr. Villiers say, if you propose to put into his
mouth any sentiments like those which you have
inserted ?"

" But indeed," remonstrated Mr. Atkinson, " these
are not days, when we can return to those old
exploded maxims about church authority and exclusive truth. We must adopt larger views, or we
shall never be able to stem the torrent of popular
opinion."

" I suppose you mean,' subjoined Captain Hancock, gruffly, " not be able to swim down with it
quietly and comfortably, for I do not see many
signs of stemming it."

" I must insist," repeated Bevan, " on the erasure
of those words, or I must refuse my vote at once.
If I were defending my title to an estate, I should
not like to trust an advocate, who rested my title

on his own personal regard for me, and on his own
opinion that I was a fit person to possess it, instead
of exhibiting my title-deeds, and proving that it
was mine by a right independent of all his own
inclinations and opinions. And as a minister of
the Church, I cannot permit its title, as the dispenser of the one truth, and as the ambassador of
Heaven, to be perilled by resting the support of it
upon any other grounds than an external commission from above, and thus recognising in it a
power which we are not to panegyrize but to obey."

"Well," replied Mr. Atkinson, "I am sure I am
most anxious to conciliate every one. If you wish
it, and no one objects, I will cut out the sentence.
And indeed these Church matters are extremely
perplexing, and I wish we were well rid of them.
I should like, you know, to express the feelings of
Conservatives, that the Establishment must be supported; but if you are not content with this, and
require more, perhaps the best way is to omit it
altogether."

"By far the best way," replied Bevan. "The
Church will be far safer without than with such
help as you propose to give it." And Bevan looked
at his watch, and, remembering that he had an
engagement, he took up his hat and left the room.

"A very singular young man !" whispered Mr.
Lomax to his neighbour. — "Very odd opinions
those new Oxford doctrines," muttered Mr. Robertson. — "What a troublesome person to deal
with," exclaimed Mr. Atkinson, looking round more
freely, and now that Bevan was gone, caring less
for the growlings of Captain Hancock in the corner.
But Captain Hancock still further relieved his mind
by taking up his hat also, and preparing to depart.
He stopped, however, to button his great-coat, and
to disburthen his mind of a few words.

" Gentlemen," he said, " and you, Mr. Atkinson,
—you'll excuse a plain, blunt, rough man for speaking
his mind to you.   But I'll venture to tell you, that
in the way you are going on now, you will neither
get Mr. Villiers to be your member, nor find any
one worth having to help and support you. Englishmen understand trickery and shuffling.   And bad
as they may be, and worse since the Reform Bill
than they were before, they will not have anything
to say for any long time, except to honest, straightforward persons.   When you know your own minds,
and can tell your own principles, and will hold your
own course without being frightened at this, and
driven back at that, or trying to conciliate here
and compromise there, and always leaving a hole to
shuffle out at from every engagement you make,
then, perhaps, you may be able to return a member
for Hawkstone.   But I think you had better begin
by dropping your new nick-name, and returning at
once to your old Tory, who was at least an honest
man, and dared say what he thought, and do what
he knew was right.   I hate conservatism, gentlemen, and so do all sound-hearted Englishmen, as
they hate a coward and a traitor.   I beg to wish
you a good morning."

And the blunt-spoken Captain closed the door
after him, leaving the little conclave partly indignant, and partly ashamed, and even the prudent,
practical, cautious Mr. Atkinson, with all his skill
and tact, crest-fallen and alarmed, and scarcely able
to conclude the remainder of his address, which,
like the beginning, was made up of a well-adjusted
balance of promises and professions—holding out a
hook baited for each party, and which the acute
contriver congratulated himself on having happily
concealed under an enticing compound of liberalism
and conservatism ; taking care, as he boasted to his

hearers, not to commit them irrevocably to anything whatever, and leaving a door open to escape, at any pressure of circumstances, from any engagement they might make.

The reader will scarcely be interested in hearing more of their deliberations. But it may be as well to subjoin the answer, which Villiers returned to the deputation, who waited on him with a request from the party that he would come forward as a candidate for the borough, and issue in his own name, as best corresponding with the sentiments of the electors, Mr. Atkinson's well-concocted address.

" Gentlemen,

" I beg you will accept my thanks for the compliment which you have paid me. I am aware that my connection with the borough of Hawkstone would naturally give you a right to claim of me that I should undertake the duty of representing it in parliament: but, by the address which you have placed in my hands, you imply that I must enter parliament as the representative of the opinions of my constituents, and not as a senator chosen by them to deliberate, in their stead, upon the interests of the whole nation. And as such a theory, however generally adopted in the present day, is subversive of the British monarchy and constitution, I must decline to comply with it. I will also candidly confess that my principles will not allow me to adopt the tone of conciliation and comprehension, which, it would appear, is necessary to secure the votes of any large portion of the constituency. I cannot offer at once protection to the agriculturist, and a repeal of the corn laws to the manufacturer. I cannot profess adherence to the Church, and at the same time regard dissent with indifference or favour. I cannot at once promise to maintain the Irish Church, and to enlarge and give endowments and grants to its deadly enemies. I cannot uphold with one hand the British monarchy, and with the other the supremacy and irresponsibility to law of the House of Commons. In other words, I cannot profess incompatibilities and contradictions; and therefore I must beg to decline allowing my name to be proposed as a representative for the borough of Hawkstone.

   "I have the honour to be, gentlemen,

    "Your obedient, faithful servant,

     "ERNEST VILLIERS."

CHAP. XV.

It was two days after the meeting of the Conservative conclave that Mr. Lomax was sitting in the same back parlour of the banking-house—his head resting upon his hands, and his brow furrowed with deep thought. And yet, though his eye was full of anxiety, a little conscious smile of self-congratulation could not but play at times upon his cold colourless lips. Before him lay the newspaper of the day, its columns full of a most eloquent and encouraging speech of the Chancellor of the Exchequer on the flourishing state of the country. Shipping multiplied — commerce extending — customs and excise increased — public credit supported — money abundant — manufactures flourishing — interest reduced — plentiful harvest — imports decreasing — exports increasing ; — no picture of wealth and prosperity could exceed in brilliancy of colour the statistics of the newly-opened budget. It was an illuminated ledger ; and the hearts of Englishmen throbbed with exultation as they read — and not a few thought of the words of the Psalmist : " Barns full of all manner of treasure, and sheep bringing forth thousands and ten thousands in our streets." And they blessed the people that were in such a case, forgetting of whom the words are uttered — the " strange children, whose mouth speaketh vanity, and their right hand is a right hand of falsehood." — Ps. cxliv.

Among the exulting readers, not the least were the inhabitants of Hawkstone. Hawkstone had been specially mentioned in the speech as a place which had been foremost in the career of improvement. Ten years since there had not been a manufacture in the town: now, factory upon factory was rising. Ten years since it took two days to travel from it to London: now a railway was almost completed, which would bring the journey within a few hours. Whole streets were springing up in the suburbs; new capitalists speculating in its shops. It was lighted with gas, paved with granite, guarded by a new police, decorated with a theatre, enlightened by a museum. Nothing could be more prosperous or thriving.

And yet, as Mr. Lomax read the panegyric, a little bitterness mixed with his smile, and he laid down the paper upon a statement of figures, with which he had just been busied, and which he seemed unwilling to face again. He turned to another paper lying open before him; it was Villiers's answer to the requisition, which Mr. Atkinson had just left with him, after a long and confidential communication. And Mr. Lomax's face assumed the cast of Hamlet, deliberating on "To be, or not to be?" when a gentle tap was heard at the door; and Mr. Lomax started up with a vexed and timid expression of countenance, for he knew what that tap augured.

It was Mrs. Lomax. And, with an ill-disguised awkwardness and reluctance, she was come, as she often did come, even into the penetralia of the banking-house, to request a cheque.

"My dear, you are always pestering me for money!" was the greeting with which she was received. "I am a ruined man, and you know it; and yet I cannot induce you to be economical."

"My love," replied the lady, "it is impossible to keep up our establishment without money; and you have often told me that you wished us to make a proper appearance. I only want thirty pounds."

" Thirty pounds !" exclaimed Mr. Lomax, whose drawers were at that moment piled with magical bank-notes—into whose iron room, only the evening before, Mrs. Lomax had persuaded him to take her niece Martha, that she might see sovereigns tossed about in shovels. "Thirty pounds ! I tell you, my love, I have not got it; and you must do without. Let the bills stand over."

"Not got it !" replied Mrs. Lomax, with a laugh. " How can you talk such nonsense, when you have thousands in those very drawers ?" And Mrs. Lomax playfully endeavoured to open one of them; but her husband seized her arm rather roughly, and bade her sit down. "I tell you what, Maria," he said, "I cannot go on in this way any longer. I do not choose to let the world know—but you must know—that each year is involving me more and more in difficulties ; and if I were to die to-morrow, you and the children would be penniless. You must alter your way of living."

Mrs. Lomax seemed for a time dismayed by the bitterness of her husband's manner, and the evident sincerity of his words. But she consoled herself with thinking that he had often said the same thing before, and had the next day fallen readily into any proposal which she might suggest for making an alteration in the house, or giving a dinner to some of the neighbouring gentry, or providing new ball-dresses for her daughters, that they might maintain their station as the leading belles of Hawkstone. And as Mrs. Lomax was unable to reconcile the inconsistencies, she preferred adopting the explanation most agreeable to her own wishes, and satisfied herself with the conviction that her husband's complaints were only a false cry of wolf, caused by a failure in some little speculation, or perhaps by having partaken too freely of some recent hospitalities. " The stomach," she said to herself, " was out of order ; and this was enough to account for those idle fancies and depressions of spirits. A blue pill would set it all to rights." And accordingly, whenever, in their private colloquies at night, Mr. Lomax touched with anxiety upon the dreaded subject of retrenchment, Mrs. Lomax assured him that it was all bile, and had recourse to her medicine-chest as the best panacea for these financial indigestions. Now, however, Mr. Lomax's gloomy brow, and the sight of open letters before him, excited in his lady's mind some deeper misgivings. " Is any thing the matter, really ? " she said.

" Yes," he replied, fiercely, " every thing is the matter. I am a beggar, Maria, and you are a beggar, and the children are beggars !" And he put into her hand a letter which he had just received, and from which Mrs. Lomax, though little initiated in business, understood that her husband had just been a considerable loser by the very rise in the funds on which the Chancellor of the Exchequer had so warmly congratulated the country.

" Well, my dear," said Mrs. Lomax, after folding up and returning the letter, " this is a loss, certainly ; but it is only 800*l*. Surely that cannot have ruined you ! And another speculation will set it all right."

" It is not one," said Mr. Lomax, bitterly. " They have all failed, again and again ; and I tell you I am a ruined man. We must sell the carriage."

" My dear," replied the lady, " you are taking things too much to heart. You must not despair, as you are so inclined to do. Besides, the carriage is but a trifle ; and what would the world say if they saw you reducing your establishment. They would think immediately that there was something the matter; and you could not answer for the consequences."

"I do not care about consequences," said Mr. Lomax, impatiently. "You must give up the carriage and the horses, and let the girls know that they cannot go to Brighton this year. And then your servants, Maria—I tell you fairly, you must get rid of John, and you must part with your page, as you call him; and the cook's wages must be reduced. I never can support such an establishment."

"My dear," replied Mrs. Lomax, whose theory of domestic management was to soften, not to oppose, and who, in exercising her empire over her husband, had adopted the motto "imperare parendo," "of course, whatever you desire must be done. But you would not wish to do this all at once. Consider how many persons there are who would seize upon it, and spread all kinds of reports. Why you might have a run upon the bank tomorrow."

"And so much the better," exclaimed Mr. Lomax, angrily. "Better to have it all over at once than go on in this way, dreading every post, and begging and borrowing" (he stopped, and did not add 'stealing') "in every corner to save the crash from coming."

"But I thought," said Mrs. Lomax, with some dismay, "that there was not a more flourishing business than yours all over the country. Surely the public believe so; and they must be the best judges."

"Best judges!" exclaimed Mr. Lomax, bitterly. "What do they know of our losses by bad debts and failures in speculations? And now, when money is so plentiful, how are we to make any thing by

our deposits? People think that bankers are as
rich as Crœsus, because they have thousands in
their hands: but if the money is not their own,
Mrs. Lomax?"

" Not their own!" said Mrs. Lomax, soothingly.
" But it is placed in their hands to be made use of:
and surely you are at liberty to employ it as you
like, and to replace it when convenient? Why this
is the very nature of credit."

" The very nature of a system," replied the gentleman, angrily, "for leading people into debt, and
when they are in debt turning them into rogues."

" Why will you talk so wildly, my love?" said
Mrs. Lomax. " Surely you are not in debt; all our
bills are paid regularly every quarter: and as for
roguery," she added, playfully, " what would you
say if any one were to use such an epithet coupled
with your name? Who would allow him to use it?
Why your very word would pass in Hawkstone for
thousands any day."

Mr. Lomax bit his lips till the blood nearly came,
but he said nothing.

" My dearest John," continued the lady, " you are
surely taking things too much to heart. This little
loss will soon be put to rights. I cannot help thinking you ate too much of that mock-turtle yesterday.
It is this which makes you so gloomy. What will
the world say, if they see you looking so miserable
and anxious?"

And at this moment Mr. Lomax felt the necessity of attending to her suggestions, and of clearing
up his brow, for a clerk came from the outer room,
and presented several papers for him to sign. It
was the day when the half-yearly interest was due
on various small deposits, which had been entrusted
to Mr. Lomax with the same confidence as if they had
been locked up in the coffers of the Bank of England,

and for which the poor but contented owners were
both surprised and pleased to receive from him
their five per cent. with most satisfactory regularity ; though parties acquainted with the mysteries
of the money market did wonder, at times, from
what prosperous speculation the Hawkstone banker
could derive profits so much beyond the ordinary
rate of interest. And this morning our excellent
friend Mabel had sent her Grey-School girl to obtain her half-yearly thirty pounds ; and Mrs. Crump
had despatched her maid on a similar errand.
And as Mr. Lomax went into his outer room he
was faced by Miss James, with a bright red flower
in her bonnet, and a brighter smile on her face,
coming, as she said to Mr. Lomax, to the very
abode of Crœsus and Pluto (Miss James, in her
classical instructions to her little pupils, had made
a slight mistake in her mythology) to obtain the necessary resources for conglomerating (by which she
meant settling) the academical arrangements of her
establishment. Charles Bevan, also, had dropped in
with a cheque from his mother ; and he was then
chatting with Mr. Vincent, who, for certain special
reasons, was desirous of a confidential communication with Mr. Lomax on the best means of turning
to advantage a sum of two thousand pounds, which
he had accumulated as a little portion for his daughter Mary. And to all these several visitants, and
especially to Mr. Vincent, Mr. Lomax's face assumed an aspect of cheerfulness and benignity, as
if paying money was the happiness of his life, and
receiving it a matter of supreme indifference.

" What a fortunate man you are," said Mr. Vincent to him, after having agreed to deposit the
two thousand pounds in Mr. Lomax's hands for a
few months, that it might obtain a larger interest
than the funds would offer. " How comfortable

and snug you have every thing. Here am I, a poor country clergyman, obliged to scrape together from every quarter a few pounds to save my children from starving, while you are rolling in wealth, and have only to write your name to command thousands. And what an improvement you have made in your house. Have you thrown that other room into the drawing-room, as you proposed? I must just go and say how-do-ye-do to Mrs. Lomax, and admire her taste. Ah!" he concluded, shaking his head, "none but you rich bankers can indulge in such luxuries."

And Mr. Lomax affected to smile with an air of self-satisfaction; and having shaken him by the hand, he returned into his back parlour, not without hoping that his lady had taken her departure.

But Mrs. Lomax was still there. "My dear," she said, gently, "I hope you are more comfortable now. I could not help hearing what Mr. Vincent wanted with you. I am in a great hurry. Would you, if you please, give me that little cheque? Morris, the upholsterer, is waiting in doors for it."

Mr. Lomax sat down and took up his pen. "Now remember," he said, "Maria, if I give you this now, I shall expect that you do not worry me again for a long time. I really cannot go on at this rate; and if you do not retrench, things must come to a crash."

"Nonsense, my love!" replied the lady. "How can things come to a crash, while such men as Mr. Vincent come to you every day, depositing such sums in your hands without asking what becomes of it, or trusting to any thing but your word? And then there is Mr. Villiers again: has he opened his account with you yet? They say he has a mine of wealth; and is so proud that he always keeps thousands of ready money at his banker's."

"I have not seen Mr. Villiers yet," replied the banker, gloomily.

"But of course you will see him, my dear — of course you will call on him. Why do you not have the horses put to the carriage, and drive over today, and leave your card?"

Mr. Lomax was silent. He generally bowed with submission to his lady's more accurate knowledge of etiquette and society; still he could not help confessing that he had heard Mr. Villiers was a very proud and haughty man, and perhaps might not like his calling."

"Not like your calling!" exclaimed the ambitious lady, indignantly. "Surely the great banker of Hawkstone is in a position to call on any one, when he comes into the country, if it were Lord Claremont himself. If you do not pay him this attention, how can you expect that he should open his account with you? You owe it to yourself, my dear, to your station, to your family, and the girls, not to be backward in taking up a proper position in society. I do hope you will drive over this very day. Do you not keep your carriage? and cannot you give dinners in as good a style as any one in the country? I declare, since you bought those silver corner-dishes, our table is quite as respectable as Lady Sudborne's; and she does not keep a page — only a butler and a footman; besides which, she has no epergne, as we have. You certainly must call on Mr. Villiers; and then it will be quite proper to ask him to dinner."

Mrs. Lomax, once embarked in dreams of hospitable elegance and fashionable dinners, scarcely noticed that her husband was apparently engaged in arranging to fulfil one part of her proposal, and to call that afternoon at the Priory. At last he said, " I think, Maria, if you will order the carriage, I will drive over after two o'clock."

" And you will have John, of course, in his new livery," said Mrs. Lomax. " It is so much more respectable."

" Yes, my dear," said Mr. Lomax (and he sighed). " If one is at the expense of a livery, one may as well make use of it."

· " Pooh! pooh! my love," rejoined Mrs. Lomax, smilingly. " Why will you worry yourself about expenses; every thing will come right soon. And, indeed," she continued, " I cannot help thinking that Mr. Villiers living at the Priory will be a great advantage to the town. I dare say he will enter into society, and make it quite gay, particularly if he is to be the new member."

" He is not going to be the new member," said Mr. Lomax, mysteriously.

" And who is to be, then?" said his lady. " Surely you won't allow that odious Mrs. Maddox to palm her radical protegé upon the town." And if any of our readers are startled by finding such a hostile epithet applied by one member of the Dorcas Society to an affectionate sister, they must allow for some bitterness of feeling produced by the rivalry of fashionable life and political party, even among the *deæ minores* of a country town; and must reflect that it was no little provocation to Mrs. Lomax's maternal feelings that Mr. Marmaduke Brook, the clever candidate, should be domesticated at her rival's house, and should daily parade the town with the pretty Miss Susan Maddox leaning familiarly on his arm, and followed by Mrs. Maddox and the plainer elder daughter — while the mother smiled significantly and exultingly to the greetings of her numerous acquaintance.

"Mr. Villiers has refused to come forward," repeated Mr. Lomax, in a tone which implied that he should not be reluctant to have a still further secret extorted from him.

"And who is to come forward, then?" said Mrs. Lomax, catching a little smile, which her husband could not wholly suppress. "Now, you know, my dear John," she exclaimed; "you can tell me all about it. You know there is a secret. You must tell me. I am sure there is something that I should like to know."

But Mr. Lomax pursed up his lips, and affected resolute perseverance in silence.

"I must know—I will know," exclaimed the lady, looking him laughingly in the face, while he vainly endeavoured to appear unconcerned. "It is something about yourself, I am sure, John, by that smile—I know it is," she continued. "Now tell me honestly, is it not? You are to be the new member—that is it, I am sure," she exclaimed, exultingly; and she snatched up a note of Mr. Atkinson's which lay on the table. "Here is Mr. Atkinson's own hand-writing. I always said you would be a member of parliament." And she proceeded to read the note, which revealed what her wishes had anticipated, and contained a strong request to Mr. Lomax from the members of the Conservative party to allow himself to be put in nomination at the ensuing election.

"And of course you have consented," said Mrs. Lomax, triumphantly.

Mr. Lomax shook his head.

"You do not mean," said the lady, "that you have refused. You owe it to your family, Mr. Lomax, to the girls especially, not to neglect such an opportunity of giving them a position in society. It must be done, indeed. Why should not you be in

parliament as well as that wretched Quaker-man
at Broughton, who has not half as fine a business as
you have?"

"Where am I to get the money?" sighed Mr.
Lomax, despairingly.

"Money!" exclaimed the lady—"Why will you
think about money? Have you not the command
of thousands, and no one to ask you what you do
with it?"

"It is not my own," faltered Mr. Lomax, with a
groan.

"No, my love, I know that," said Mrs. Lomax,
soothingly. "It is not your own exactly, but it
is placed in your hands to do what you like with
it; and you will always have the means of replacing
it, so long as the firm flourishes, as it does now.
And I am sure I cannot see anything more likely
to make it flourish than that you should be the
member. It is so very respectable. It will give
people such confidence.

Mr. Lomax looked miserable, and sighed again.

"Indeed, my love," continued the lady, "I must
not allow you to mope and look wretched in this
way. I do hope you will sit down at once and write
an answer to Mr. Atkinson, that you will be very
happy; and then we must all exert ourselves without a moment's delay. That odious Mrs. Maddox
has been bustling about with her trolloping daughters, for I cannot tell how long, and canvassing
among the poor people. Now I am sure your influence—the influence of the bank—must be twenty
times greater. And I shall set off immediately."

"Stop, Maria, stop, my dear," cried Mr. Lomax.

But Mrs. Lomax stopped her ears instead of her
feet, and laughingly declared that she would not
listen. "He must come forward." "Think," she
continued, "what an advantage it will be for the

girls to be introduced into society as the daughters
of the member for Hawkstone. You do not know
what may come of it. I am sure the admiration
which Anne excited by her singing at Brighton last
year was astonishing; and I should never be surprised at any thing. By-the-by, they say that Mr.
Villiers is passionately fond of music. Anne must
practise some duets before he dines with us. What
day had we better fix on, Mr. Lomax? It will be
quite proper that you should give a series of dinners, as you are to be the member."

Mr. Lomax was silent.

"I suppose," the lady continued, "Mr. Villiers
will return the call immediately, and then we can
ask him for the next week : and do let us remember, Mr. Lomax, that we have a select party.
Though we do live in the town, I should not like
him to confound us with the common set of Hawkstone. If you would but have taken Rosewood
Villa when it was to be let, instead of patching up
this vulgar old house in the street, we should have
been quite respectable—as respectable as Lady Sudborne herself. However, we must make the best
of it."

Mr. Lomax still remained silent.

"One thing I must pray," continued the lady,
"that you do not ask Mr. Morgan. He may be a
very old friend of your family, and is a very good
surgeon, no doubt, and a very excellent man ; but
he is not quite the person to ask to meet Mr. Villiers, a man of rank. I will invite Lady Sudborne,
and Lady Thompson ; and if her young nephew, Sir
Joseph Scargill, in the Guards, is with her, he will
be an excellent person ; and then there is Captain
O'Brien, nephew to Lord St. Aubyn—and we met
him the other day at the races. He was evidently
much struck with Anne. And I think," she said,

" we might ask Mr. Bevan. He is not much, but
he is a fellow of a college in Oxford, and that is a
respectable thing; and he knows Mr. Villiers."

" And Mr. Atkinson," added Mr. Lomax.

" No, my love," replied the lady; " I must protest against Mr. Atkinson. No one has a greater
respect for him than I have, or more regard for his
family. But professional men are not quite the
persons to give a tone to society; and what I want
Mr. Villiers to see is, that we have a tone, and understand how to do these things. I should like him
to become quite intimate with us, and to be here
frequently; you cannot tell what may come of it.
And I understand he is extremely fastidious in his
society, and a man of the greatest fashion."

" Well, my dear," said Mr. Lomax, succumbing
partly to his lady's volubility and confirmed habits
of authority, and partly to certain calculations which
he was making in his own mind with regard to the
probable amount of Villiers's yearly balance, " I
suppose you must have your own way, as usual."

" And we must have champagne," added Mrs.
Lomax, " and every thing, in fact, in the best
style. And you must not insist on having the cloth
removed for the dessert. When we dined at Lady
Sudborne's, if you remember, last Christmas, it was
left on the table. I observed it particularly. And
even the Maddoxes have taken to the practice; it
is so fashionable: and I would not be beaten by
them in any matter of fashion for the world,—a
mere set of vulgar retired tradesmen."

Mr. Lomax sighed, and cast his eyes upon the
paper of figures which lay before him; but he said
nothing.

" And I suppose," concluded Mrs. Lomax, as she
was leaving the room, " there is no reason why
your standing for the town should be a secret. I

will only mention it to one or two persons. I do not know any thing," she added, " which will give so much strength to the bank, and so much respectability to us all. I quite long to see how Lady Thompson looks when she hears it. Sir David, after all, was only a city knight, though he did leave her thirty thousand pounds ; and, I must say, she gives herself considerable airs."

And without waiting for a reply, and leaving the Banker to the mingled pains and pleasures of his internal contemplations, Mrs. Lomax swam out of the room.

And for us it is unnecessary to follow her, except to be present one day in the following week, after the visit to the Priory had been made and returned, and the dinner invitations, carefully framed, had all been sent, and, all but Villiers's, accepted, and Mrs. Lomax's arrangements had been completed upon the most fashionable and aristocratic principles, to the indignation of Mrs. Maddox, who was duly informed of them, and to the envy of all the rest of the town. One only card remained unanswered ; but it was the card of cards : and Mrs. Lomax's heart throbbed as the servant at length brought a note to her from the Priory, and, with a countenance blank as night, she perceived that it contained an excuse. We will not weary ourselves, as Mrs. Lomax wearied herself, and her husband, and her daughters, with supposing imaginary reasons. Charles Bevan alone knew the cause. But Villiers had inquired of him respecting Mr. Lomax's position and habits of living, and then had written a civil apology. "England," he said to Bevan, " is on the point of ruin by these idle attempts at style and fashion in a class who have not the means ; and I, for one, will never encourage them. By-the-by, will you tell Mr. Morgan that I shall be detained in

the town till five o'clock to-morrow, and if he will
let me come and partake of his family dinner I
shall be very much obliged. I promised his little
boy Harry to finish my story about the hippo-
potamus to him another day; and Miss Morgan
was to practise for me that sonata of Cherubini's:
and I like the whole family much—they are so
simple and unpretending."

CHAP. XVI.

ANY of our readers who have ever had the calamity
to be mixed up with the scenes of a popular election under the blessed representative system of
Great Britain will not require to be enlightened on
the details of the Hawkstone election. There were
the usual committees, who assembled night after
night at the Bell and the Swan, and solaced themselves and their labours with the usual copious liba-
tions at the expense of the candidates. There were
the ordinary placards and addresses from Brutus,
and Cincinnatus, and Anti-Corruption, and Verax,
and the hundred other anonymous prophets, who
swarm forth, no one knows whence, on such occasions, like rats driven from their holes by a flood.
There were the libels and counter-libels; epigrams
and epithets; songs and parodies. Mr. Brook's friends
declared that Mr. Lomax was a hypocrite; Mr.
Lomax's committee insinuated that Mr. Brook, and
every one connected with him, were atheists. Both
exhausted the imagination in picturing the blessings
which, if returned to parliament, they would shower
down upon the country, and the calamities which
would follow upon the success of their antagonist.
The Odd Fellows, and the United Brothers, and
the Temperance Clubs held their nightly orgies, to
which the rival candidates respectively resorted, and
harangued the smoke-involved and porter-drinking
meetings. Each day the fever became more fierce;
and even the calmest minds, instead of looking on
the troubled ocean from the lofty post of contempt,

were drawn down into the waves, and absorbed in the tumult. Mr. Brown, the chemist, swore eternal enmity to Mr. Hopkins, the miller, because Mr. Hopkins voted for Mr. Brook, and Mr. Brown was on the committee of Mr. Lomax. Mrs. Morgan, instead of receiving a patronising nod from Mrs. Maddox, was actually cut by her in the street. Even John Hobbs, the constable, who, as an official personage, voted of course with the Conservatives, quarrelled with Peter Simpson, the brewer's dray-man, and in his zeal for the good cause received such a deadly blow upon his nose, that the mayor, who was punctilious in the appearance of his retinue, considered him disqualified for the office of attending in his blue gown and with his gilt-knobbed staff at the borough sessions. Enmity, and envy, and hatred, and malice, penetrated into every house, and scowled upon every countenance.

As the great day approached, rumours waxed thick of bribes, and threats, and cajoleries, and seductions, and defections, and treacheries, which alternately appalled each party. Watches from each committee patrolled nightly round the town, to guard the more timid voters from assault, and the more needy from corruption. The public-houses were opened — the processions marshalled — flags suspended — bands collected — and even battles fought. And such had been the extent of Mr. Atkinson's well-managed policy, and of Mr. Lomax's well-distributed money, that the Radical party began at last to tremble. And at a meeting of the committee at Mrs. Maddox's, to the great consternation of that lady, who had long since resolved to be mother-in-law to the member for Hawkstone, and to the no less dismay of Mr. Marmaduke Brook, who had resolved with equal certainty, not indeed to carry away a wife from Hawkstone, but to convert Hawkstone into a means of changing his 1500*l.* a-year commissionership of gutters into a more permanent official post of at leat 2000*l.* : it was hinted, that unless the greatest exertions were made to detach Mr. Ball at the silk-mills from the Conservative interest, Conservatism must triumph.

There was only one individual present who heard this announcement unmoved, and with a smile of nonchalance, like that of one who held in his own hands the power at any moment of preventing such a calamitous result. Mr. O'Foggarty had particularly requested that his name might be added to Mr. Brook's committee, in order that he might testify his zeal for the cause of civil and religious liberty all over the world, and might satisfactorily exhibit how cruelly the Church of Rome had been traduced by those who represented it as the restrainer of private judgment, or the enemy of Protestantism. He had been commanded to forward to Mr. Pearce daily and minute accounts of the proceedings. And Pearce had always assured him that, if it were necessary, he could ensure at any time the return of the Radical candidate; but so long as circumstances seemed favourable, and success certain, it was unnecessary for him to move. But he had sufficiently intimated to O'Foggarty the nature of the train which he had laid to satisfy that gentleman that the contest could have but one issue. The post that evening carried another letter to Mr. Pearce, which informed him of the threatening aspect of events ; and the next post brought a reply very brief but very decisive. And Mr. O'Foggarty, as he sat by his fire-side with the letters in his hand, hugged himself, as persons do, when, in secret and unseen, they await the firing of a train which is to blow up all around them, they themselves remaining in safety.

T 3

He rose early the next morning — very early, finished his breakfast sooner than usual, took his hat and stick, and made his appearance at the door of Mr. Lomax's bank five minutes after it had been opened. The head clerk (for Mr. Lomax had returned the night before with a bad headache from a saturnalia of the Odd Fellows at the Pig and Carrot, and was not yet drest) received Mr. O'Foggarty with a cheerful smile, and was proceeding to take down a large ledger to enter, as he had been in the habit of doing for some months past, the fresh subscriptions to the Catholic Chapel, as he termed it; but his countenance fell, and his blood flowed back with a sudden revulsion, when Mr. O'Foggarty, with a soft and insinuating tone, and with something of an apology, requested to receive the full amount of subscriptions which had been paid in, about 540*l.* Well trained, however, and accustomed to dissemble the pains of payment, the clerk, grasping a handful of Mr. Lomax's notes, proceeded to ask how Mr. O'Foggarty would wish to take the sum. But all his self-command was unable to conceal his surprise and dismay when that gentleman, with another bland apology, requested to have it in gold and Bank of England notes. The clerk looked up and then down, and then, with a lingering hand, unclosed a secret drawer, counted out the sovereigns and the notes, placed them in Mr. O'Foggarty's hand, and suffered him to retire without returning his polite bow, or being able in any way to recover from his stupefaction.

A few minutes afterwards Mr. Lomax entered the counting-house with the morning letters open in his hand, and not a few nervous twitches playing on his countenance. He bade the clerk take down two or three ponderous leather-bound vellum folios — ran his eye over the accounts in them — closed

the books — opened them again — then took up the
newspaper, but without being able to read it —
then looked out of the window — then started, as
the door opened, but recovered himself on finding
that it was only Mrs. Crump's Abigail, who wanted
change for a five-pound note; — and then, after
hearing the account of Mr. O'Foggarty's visit,
during which the twitches in the face became more
numerous, he retired into his back room, and there
sat down in his black leathern chair, gazing on the
fire.

And while Mr. Lomax was in this posture, Mr.
Pearce, in London, was driving about, in a hired
cab, from street to street in the City, and holding
various secret colloquies with bill-brokers and others.
He was evidently engaged in some deeply interesting negotiation. Nor were Mr. Lomax's London
bankers omitted in his round of visits. And twice
he returned to their house in Lombard Street; and
twice he was closeted with the head partner in his
sanctuary. And that gentleman, with a face of
profound and imperturbable prudence, had more
than once pored carefully over the long files of the
Hawkstone Bank account, and had closed his perusal with an ominous shake of the head. From
Lombard Street Mr. Pearce had hurried his jaded
cab to Mincing Lane; and there he had entered a
paved back court, with a black-leaved solitary poplar
in it, and ascending a flight of stairs, he had had an
interview with Messrs. Harbottle, the London correspondents of Mr. Ball, the proprietor of the
Hawkstone silk-mills. And this interview, also,
had appeared to terminate with little satisfaction to
the correspondents, who immediately, on its coming
to a close, had despatched a clerk-like letter and a
variety of stamped documents to Mr. Ball himself;
and Mr. Ball himself, with a very worn and anxious

countenance, had proceeded with them without delay
to Mr. Lomax; and Mr. Lomax ——— But we must
not anticipate.

These various negotiations and mysterious movements had taken place on the Thursday and Friday;
and on Saturday Mrs. Lomax had felt it her conscientious duty to press on Mr. Lomax the propriety, and indeed necessity, of giving a sumptuous
dinner to Mr. Bowler and several other of the neighbouring gentry; who, though they looked with no
little jealousy on the banker's elegant establishment,
were partly under pecuniary obligations to him,
and partly had no objection to a very comfortable
dinner in the town after the fatigues of the magistrates' meeting. The dinner had passed — the
champagne was pronounced excellent — the dessert
was sumptuous. Mr. Atkinson had delivered a
most eloquent harangue to Mr. Bowler, who was
fast asleep, on the increasing prosperity of Hawkstone. Mr. Warburton, who was a political economist, had enlarged on the beautiful system of credit,
on which the prosperity of the British empire was
founded, and by which every one was enabled to
bring into play, and to employ in grand speculations, every thing that he possessed, without the
necessity of allowing any part to lie dead. Many
had been the exclamations of wonder at the thriving
state of commerce — many the congratulations on
the rapid progress of the Hawkstone railway —
deep the admiration at the spirit with which Messrs.
Silkem, the linen-drapers, and Messrs. Brown, their
rivals in the trade, had expended enormous sums in
plate glass and gilded pillars to adorn the streets
of Hawkstone; some wonder, also, was expressed
that Mr. Ball, at the silk-mills, had been enabled to
invest so large a capital in buildings, particularly as
the silk trade was flat, and two other mills were

rising within half a mile, which would probably
cause a material reduction in the profits. But at
the mention of Mr. Ball's name, Mr. Lomax, who
had been silent and gloomy during dinner (worn
out, as Mr. Atkinson whispered, with the excitement of canvassing, and the responsibilities of his
approaching honours), lapsed into more serious
nervous twitches than he had experienced before;
and, hastily passing round the rich cut-glass claret
decanters, he proposed that they should adjourn to
the ladies.

To the ladies accordingly they retired. Mrs.
Lomax received them in the gay but rather gaudily-
furnished double drawing-room. She herself, ma-
jestic in a splendid turban and bird-of-Paradise
plume, was already practising the dignified manner
which became the lady of the member for Hawkstone. Her page, covered over with sugar-loaf
buttons, was dispensing coffee from a large silver
salver. Miss Anne was seated at the piano, prepared, in default of a more youthful hearer, to
perform for the somnolent Mr. Bowler the airs
which she had so studiously practised to fascinate
the ear of Villiers. Miss Lomax, less brilliant in
manner and appearance, but not less ambitious, was
enlarging to Miss Mabel Brook, who had been permitted to come in as a refresher in the evening, on
the delight with which she was looking forward to
accompanying her papa to London when the session
opened — on the probability of his taking a house
in Baker Street for them — on the prospect of admission into London society, which their acknowledged station and rank would then ensure them, —
and she even hinted at some tickets for Almack's,
which, through the mediation of Lady Sudborne,
she felt convinced that they would be able to compass. Mr. Atkinson, standing on the bright copious-

flowered rug, with his back to the fire, and his
gilded coffee-cup in one hand and his coat-tails in
the other, was congratulating Mrs. Lomax on the
prospect of the poll; and the lady was listening to
him graciously and condescendingly, but without
compromising her dignity.   The other gentlemen
were looking over some very third-rate works of art,
gorgeously bound, which were displayed on the round
rosewood table, and seemed disposed to wish themselves anywhere else ; when the street-door bell
rang violently.   Mr. Lomax quite jumped from his
chair ; and Mrs. Lomax was startled to see his colour
change.

" It is only Mr. Bowler's carriage," she observed.
" Why, my love, what is the matter ? This troublesome election has made you quite nervous."

But Mr. Lomax knew that it was not Mr. Bowler's
carriage, for no sound of wheels had accompanied
the bell.   But a heavy step was heard coming up
the stairs, and the awkward footman, whom all his
lady's care and refinement could not teach to wear
his red plush breeches elegantly, or to move without
creaking shoes, came up significantly to Mr. Lomax,
and informed him that there was a strange gentleman below, from London, who wanted to see him
immediately upon business.

" Ah !" exclaimed Mr. Atkinson, — " something,
I suppose, about Horlock's vote."

But he was surprised to see that Mr. Lomax had
turned pale, and could scarcely hold his tea-cup.
At last the servant was ordered to show the gentleman into the study, and Mr. Lomax slowly rose
from his seat, and catching hold of the chair to
support himself, he with difficulty staggered out of
the room.

" I fear, my dear madam," said Mr. Atkinson,
" that this troublesome business is too much for our

excellent friend. Nervous excitement that — over-
fatigue! but he will soon recover it, when once he
is in parliament. You will go with him, of course,
to London?"

"I rather think we shall, said Mrs. Lomax, with
dignity. I wish that my daughters should be introduced. And with their father's position and establishment, I think it will be right to show them
more of the world than they can see in this little
confined spot. After all we must confess that
Hawkstone is a vulgar place. Brighton is my
delight! Such charming society! and most fashionable too! Oscar," she called, languidly, to her page,
"remove my coffee-cup, and bring me that eau-de-
Cologne. It is wearying, Mr. Atkinson, this being
obliged to receive, as we do; but our position
renders it necessary. Pray, how do you like those
vases—are they not exquisite?"

Mr. Atkinson duly admired the gaudy expensive
ornaments which stood on the mantel-piece; and
then he pulled up his thick ill-folded white neckcloth, which was Mrs. Lomax's aversion, and walked
away to pay his compliments to Miss Anne, who,
seated at the piano in the inner drawing-room, was
congratulating herself to Mr. Warburton on the
prospect of her more frequently attending the
Opera in London. "A box," she said, "is very expensive. But I suppose in papa's new position he
will think it right to do as others do. He will owe
it to himself and his constituents to support his
position."

Mr. Warburton made no reply, but a little shrug
of contempt. And as Mr. Lomax did not return,
and Mrs. Lomax began to yawn, and the gentlemen
from the country were anxious to return home, the
party broke up.

"Well! we have had a tolerably agreeable party,"

said Mrs. Lomax to her eldest daughter, as the last
visitant closed the door. "Every thing went off
extremely well; and I do think the table looked
remarkably elegant. Mr. Bowles admired those
corner-dishes amazingly: I do not think he has
any himself."

Miss Lomax yawned, and assented.

"There is only one thing, I think," continued
Mrs. Lomax, "that we want just now, and that is
two handsome chandeliers for these rooms. We
want the gold paper well lighted up. You know
the one in Lady Sudborne's drawing-room? How
well it looks. And I think that, as the member for
the town, your papa must take care to have every
thing about him in good style. He owes it to
himself. I shall certainly make him get us some.
Do go down to the study, Mary, and see if he is
there, and ask him to come up. I will point it out
to him at once before John puts out these wax
lights."

Mary, with evident reluctance and signs of weariness, rose slowly, and proceeded to her papa's study.
She knocked, but no one answered. She opened
the door. The candles were burning down in their
sockets; a chair overturned lay upon the floor; one
of the lights flickered and went out as she approached the table, and the other burned so dimly
that she could not discern what was that black
thing lying on the ground, behind the table. Was
it her father's great-coat? She snuffed the candle
and went to pick it up, and hang it on the chair;
but before she touched it she screamed with terror,
for from the sleeve of the coat a hand projected.
"Papa," she cried, "papa, is that you? What is
the matter?" But there was no answer, and the
poor girl, screaming and shrieking, endeavoured to
lift the unhappy man from the floor.

Her mother had just arranged in her head a well-turned sentence with which she felt satisfied that she should prevail on her husband to spend at least fifty guineas in providing the splendid chandeliers, when her daughter's screams startled and terrified her. Herself, and Anne, and the servants, were the next moment in the study. " Master has fallen into a fit," said the footman.

" Send instantly for Mr. Morgan," exclaimed Mrs. Lomax, who even then did not lose her presence of mind. " Raise him up — place him in the chair. It is all this terrible election — nervous excitement, too much for him! He will soon be better. Bring some cold water and salts."

And Mrs. Lomax prepared to chafe the temples and to unfasten the cravat of her wretched husband. But just as the head had been raised up, more lights were brought into the room, and a single glance showed to all present that it was not a fit. Mr. Lomax was dead.

" What is that you have picked up in the corner?" said the footman to the page, while the rest were endeavouring to disengage the stupified, insensible wife from the corpse of her husband.

" It's a bottle," said the page.

" A bottle of what?" asked the footman. " Show it me."

" Here's something written on it," said the page. " ' Prussic Acid !' I wonder what that is!"

CHAP. XVII.

VILLIERS was mounting his horse the next day at the great porch of the Priory; alarmed by some hasty rumours, he was preparing to ride into Hawkstone to ascertain the truth of them, when Mr. Atkinson's humble one-horse four-wheeled phaeton drove into the other end of the avenue. The appearance of Mr. Atkinson himself told at once a tale of unspeakable mischief. He was haggard, bewildered, almost distracted; and it was some time before Villiers could prevail on him to enter the library and compose himself, that he might explain the state of circumstances. And when he was able to tell his tale, it was so confused, so full of dreadful anticipations for himself, so broken with exclamations of horror, that Villiers could scarcely gather what it meant.

At last he learnt the terrible event which has just been narrated. And his first thought was, that some aberration of mind, brought on by the fatigues and anxieties of the election, had fallen on the miserable victim of a vulgar ambition. But Mr. Atkinson shook his head. It was something worse — far worse. The bank had stopped that morning. The solicitor of the London bank had met Mr. Atkinson at an early hour; an examination of books had taken place; and it was found that, instead of possessing property, the Hawkstone bank had been insolvent for years; and that an enormous defalcation could already be detected, not without suspicions of fraud. Villiers made no remark, but he remembered the invitation to dinner.

"But this," continued Mr. Atkinson, "was not the worst. There had been speculations and engagements with the proprietors of the silk-mills, to enable them to commence operations. And Mr. Ball, of the silk-mills, was a bankrupt also. And so far as it could be traced, a system of accommodation bills had been contrived and carried on for many years, which would now involve even Mr. Smith at the factory and Sir Matthew Blake himself. Hawkstone, the prosperous, flourishing Hawkstone, with its new manufactories, its brilliant shops, its railroads, its coal-pits, and its iron mines, had for some time past offered a tempting field to the investments of grasping capitalists and needy speculators; and its whole existence was a fabric of credit" (accursed credit, thought Villiers, the child of avarice and mother of fraud!). "Beneath all its splendid exterior, its flourishing projects, the ground had been undermined, as it were, and honeycombed, and a single shock was sufficient to bring the whole to the ground. There was not a single shopkeeper in the town," said Mr. Atkinson, "who could calculate for one day on his own security. Each had been leaning on the support of another; filling his windows with plate glass, and lighting his counter with ormolu lamps, on credit and speculation; and a blow levelled against one would, in all human probability, prostrate them all."

"And the poor," asked Villiers, anxiously, "are they likely to suffer much? Were there many notes in circulation?"

Mr. Atkinson, who was really a kind-hearted, benevolent man, could not hear the question, overcome and unnerved as he was, without bursting into tears. His own door had been beset that morning with a crowd of terrified, desperate, ruined inhabitants — old men, who had lost their

all; decrepid women, who had now no homes to
look to but the poor-house; industrious workmen, who had saved their earnings for a coming
emergency, and their savings were all gone. And
it was with some difficulty that he had prevented
their misery and passion from bursting out into
some fierce act of vindictiveness, even against the
equally miserable survivors in the unhappy banker's
own family.

" And what of them?" asked Villiers.

" Penniless, replied Mr. Atkinson, " utterly and
entirely penniless; and chiefly their own fault —
their own extravagance! But this," he continued,
" could be borne. But there were others, innocent
of any fault but misplaced confidence, whom nothing
awaited but the workhouse. Mrs. Atkinson had been
that morning to see three persons—poor Mabel, the
aged Mrs. Crump, and Mrs. Bevan; and no words
could picture the scenes which she had witnessed."

Villiers groaned aloud. And Mr. Atkinson rose
up and went to the window to conceal the tears
which coursed one another down his cheeks.

Villiers sat down and wrote a note, and rang the
bell immediately for his groom to take it into Hawkstone to Mr. Bevan.

" And now," he said, turning to Mr. Atkinson,
who, by disburthening his mind and giving way to
his misery, had become more composed, " will you
let me speak to you candidly and openly?"

Mr. Atkinson, who seemed as if he longed to say
something, and yet could not bring himself to do so,
looked up in hope.

" I am aware," said Villiers, that in your situation you must require at certain periods large pecuniary accommodations, which were probably afforded
you by the late bank, and the withdrawal of them
under such circumstances may cause you temporary

embarrassment. I have always had reason to put the highest confidence in your honour; and it will be only a slight return for the care which you have taken of my property, if I can assist you in this emergency. But I will say, honestly and openly, that this assistance must be limited to that sum which is required by yourself personally to carry on the necessary machinery of your business; and that I can offer no encouragement whatever to that system of advances, and borrowing, and forestalling, which, whether it prevail among landed proprietors, or manufacturing and commercial speculators, is one of our greatest curses, the most sure and certain cause of the destruction with which England is now beset. I must not presume to enter into your own private arrangements; but I am sure you will understand me."

Mr. Atkinson's face lightened up, as if a cloud had passed away from his eyes. He rose and seized Villiers's hand with a warmth of gratitude, of which his cool, reserved nature seemed wholly incapable. "My wife," he cried, "my dear wife! I have ten children, and you have saved them!" and the poor man wept like a child.

But Villiers kindly but calmly begged him to resume his seat. "Your time," he said, — "every hour at such a crisis must be precious." And he sat down to his table to write a check.

"Will you name the sum, if you please?" said Villiers.

Mr. Atkinson hesitated, and looked down, as if he dared not.

"Be assured," said Villiers, "you cannot do me a greater kindness than by giving me the means of making you perfectly comfortable. In this fearful crash, and in your situation, you will require all

your composure and energy of mind. A great part
of the burden of such a calamity must fall upon
you. And if to the public distress your own private
anxieties are added, you will be unable to render the
town the services which will be required of you.
And I am well aware that your extent of business
must subject you to very heavy claims; and that
the expenses of a large family, and your own honourable moderation and liberality, cannot but confine your resources. I shall not be satisfied, indeed,
if you do not leave this place perfectly at your ease.
" Shall I say 2000*l.* ? " and Villiers named a sum
nearly a third beyond what Mr. Atkinson's most
sanguine wishes had calculated on.

Once more he sprang up, and would almost have
fallen at Villiers's knees.

" Are you sure that it is enough," said Villiers,
" perfectly sure ? "

" More, far more than I want," replied Mr. Atkinson.   " How can I ever repay you ? "

Villiers finished his check, rang the bell for Mr.
Atkinson's carriage, and was about to quit the room
on some excuse, that he might leave the happy
man to himself, but Mr. Atkinson stopped him.
" Sir," he said, " I cannot accept this without giving
you some guarantee ; my bond, at least, till I can
place in your hands other securities which I possess."

" You can do this, my dear sir," said Villiers,
" when you return home, and can deposit it with my
papers."

" And the interest," continued Mr. Atkinson.
" I cannot accept it at less than five per cent."

" My dear sir," answered Villiers, " this is not a
moment to enter into questions of political economy,
and I fear the world generally would scarcely understand me. But I have, long since, made it a

principle, in such cases as the present, not to accept interest."

" Not accept interest!" exclaimed Mr. Atkinson, opening his eyes to their fullest width, and for a moment forgetting all his miseries, and all his relief from them, in wonder at such a proposition. "Not accept interest!"

Villiers could not help smiling at the astonished and bewildered aspect, which looked up into his face.

" Not accept five per cent.!" continued Mr. Atkinson, "legal interest? I do not understand you, sir."

Villiers looked out of the window, and finding that his visiter's humble conveyance had not yet been brought to the door, he did not disdain to explain his meaning further.

" Might I ask," he said, "what profit you will yourself make upon the expenditure of this sum, applied, as it will be, to maintaining the regular machinery of your business? Will it be more than is sufficient to indemnify you for the time, anxiety, responsibility, and labour, which you must devote to its proper employment."

" Certainly not," was the reply.

" And if it were more," continued Villiers; "if in any profession or any business the profits should, for a time, exceed this limit, it is an acknowledged principle of political economy that they must soon be reduced within the limit by the natural action of competition."

Mr. Atkinson bowed.

" And if," continued Villiers, "I were to lock up this money in a chest, would it produce me any interest of itself? Can money grow?"

Mr. Atkinson shook his head.

" Its increase, therefore," said Villiers, "must

u 2

depend on the labour, industry, and talent, which are devoted to its employment, and ought to be the remuneration of them. And if I, who do not labour, receive any portion of it, I am detracting so much from the fair and equitable reward which Providence has designed for them. I am eating the bread of idleness, and you are toiling without adequate compensation. Is this equitable? Is it agreeable to that Divine law, which has commanded us to eat our bread in the sweat of our brow?"

Mr. Atkinson, in his agitated state of feeling, was unable to follow up the reasoning. He could only stare and look bewildered. And Villiers, feeling that it was useless to pursue the subject, only added, "Prior to all such reasonings, a Christian has the most distinct intimations of the will of Heaven on this subject, both from the Scriptures, and from the voice of the Church; and this is sufficient to bind his conscience. And I think you will find, on reflection, that, if the principle were generally acted on, no such fatal calamities would occur as that which has now fallen upon us. The refusal of interest would remove the temptation to give facilities for speculation. There would be no idle members of society dependant for their daily bread, not upon their own honest industry, but on the success of speculations in others. And though we might be less wealthy as a nation, we should be more honest as individuals, and more safe from misery and ruin. But I see your carriage is come to the door, and I must not detain you;" and, having shaken Mr. Atkinson's hand, he contrived, at the same time, to leave the cheque within it, went out with him to the hall-door, and saw the wondering and bewildered man, with a mixture of joy and tears, drive off to Hawkstone.

The same evening, about six o'clock, just after

Villiers had mounted his horse at Mrs. Bevan's
door, and rode off on his return to the Priory, Mrs.
Bevan, pale and agitated, and yet not without a
mixture of joy on her worn and anxious countenance, came out, leaning on Charles Bevan's arm,
both silent, both of them with their eyes filled with
tears. Charles left his mother at poor Mabel's
door; and Mrs. Bevan, admitted by the sobbing
little Grey girl, and almost unable to move herself,
ascended the narrow stairs. She tapped, and a low
half-choked voice bade her come in. But no sooner
had Mabel caught sight of her friend than she rose,
and threw herself into her arms, but without speaking; neither of them could utter a word. At last,
Mrs. Bevan disengaged herself from Mabel's almost
convulsive embrace, and placing her in a chair, she
sat down by her side, and took her hand, and held it
in her own.

Even then Mabel's thoughts were more for others
than for herself. "And you, too, are ruined," she
said, at last. "How good of you to think of me —
to come to me!"

Mrs. Bevan only pressed her hand in reply, and
looked round the room. Stunned and amazed as
Mabel had been with a blow, which at once had
plunged her into utter destitution, without a friend
who could give her assistance, or an occupation to
which she could look for support, her active conscientious mind, instead of giving way to useless
lamentations, had, after a long struggle, recovered
somewhat of its energy; and she was resolved, without delay, to face the worst, and to occupy herself
with necessary duties. It was a cold cheerless
evening, but the grate was without a fire; Mabel
knew that she had no means to pay for it. A single
rushlight burnt dimly on the table, which was
covered with account-books, and sundry heaps of

silver.   Mabel was making up the accounts of the
various little charitable funds, of which she had so
long acted as secretary and treasurer, afraid to retain
in her hands even a shilling, which was not her own,
under the menaces of the coming temptation.   The
little girl had brought her tea-things as usual, but,
except a morsel of dry bread, nothing had been
tasted; even that Mabel had grudged to herself, for
she knew not if it was her own.   The little girl
was to go home the next morning to her friends,
and Mabel (she had no money) had given her some
comfortable clothing from her own little wardrobe.
She had also asked Mr. Silkem's permission to remain one or two days longer in her rooms, until she
could look round, and find some shelter, or some
situation.   But Mr. Silkem was a Liberal, and it was
one of his first principles that every man should
take care of number one.   He had therefore sufficiently indicated to Mabel, that as she could no
longer pay for her lodgings, it would be only justice
to himself and his family that she should leave it
without any delay for another occupant.   And with
a bursting heart, and swell of indignation at his
hardheartedness, Mabel had resolved on quitting
the house the very next morning.

"And where will you go?" asked Mrs. Bevan,
tenderly.

"To the poor-house," sobbed Mabel; "I have no
other home.   I have no friends who can relieve me."

Mrs. Bevan could not refrain from weeping.
"No, my dear Mabel," she said, "you can come to
me, at least for a time."

"But you, too, are ruined," said Mabel; "you
have lost your all.   Mr. Morgan — every one is
ruined.   I cannot be a burden to you.   But it is
God's will, and I do not repine.   I can bear it — I
can work — I can wash — He will not desert me."

Mrs. Bevan could not refrain from folding her in her arms, and mingling her own tears with Mabel's. "I am, indeed, ruined," she said, "and have lost all. But Charles has still his small fellowship; and he will increase it by taking pupils. And for the present," she added, "means have been supplied us by a hand which I must not mention, until we can look round and provide some other resources. And the same hand, which has been stretched out to us, has made it a particular request that you would come and take shelter under our roof—not only you, but others: our house is large enough; and humbled, and destitute, and softened as we all shall be by this appalling stroke, we may even find comfort from being together."

Mabel looked up, as scarcely understanding her.

"I mean, dearest," said Mrs. Bevan, "that I have the means at present of receiving you; and that it is the wish of the benefactor, to whom I owe them, that they should be shared with you: you will not, therefore, be a burden to me, but rather a comfort and assistance. There are many things which we can do together, which will be good both to others and ourselves."

"Who is it?" exclaimed Mabel. "Who could have thought of me? It could not be my cousin!"

Mrs. Bevan shook her head.

"And I have no claims on any one else," sobbed Mabel. "How kind! how merciful of Providence!" And Mabel wearied herself in vain with endeavouring to guess the name of her unknown benefactor; but Mrs. Bevan checked her. "It was the wish of the same person," she said,—"his own especial request, that no notice should be taken of his aid, and no endeavour made to trace the hand which ad-

ministered it.   And he had also begged Mrs. Bevan
to put at Mabel's disposal a little purse for immediate necessities, which she was to consider as coming
from a friend, and as belonging not to man but to
God."   And Mrs. Bevan placed in her hands a
purse of twenty guineas.   For he who was thus the
dispenser of the mercies of Providence was not
satisfied with providing for absolute want, but, like
the Being whose minister he was, he had thoughtfully and minutely anticipated all the little difficulties and exigences of such an emergency, and
endeavoured to palliate them all.

"And now I must leave you," said Mrs. Bevan;
"for the same blow which has fallen upon us has
fallen on many others.   And there is one case of
misery opposite to your own door, which I have
been commissioned to relieve also."

"Ah!" said Mabel, "poor Mrs. Crump! Her
window-blinds have been down all the day; and my
little girl told me that she had had a paralytic attack about half an hour after the failure of the bank
had reached her ears.   She is ruined, too; and at
her age — poor thing! without a friend or relation
in the world — nothing but the poor-house to look
to!   I was going to her myself," continued Mabel,
"as soon as I had arranged these things, to ask if I
could sit up with her to-night; for her maid is any
thing but attentive to her, and thinks of nothing
but her wages."

"I am going," said Mrs. Bevan, "to offer her a
room in my own house for the present.   There, at
least, she will be attended to with more care and
kindness than even in her own lodging; and, together, we might contribute something to her comfort.   If we ourselves have been saved from utter
destitution, our first thought must be to save
others."

Mabel caught at the thought of being useful. And sorrowful, yet calm, and not despairing, and even with a ray of comfort in their eyes, the two friends embraced once more; and Mrs. Bevan proceeded on her errand of mercy.

No one came to the door to answer the bell, and she opened it herself. The passage was dimly lighted; and without making a noise, Mrs. Bevan proceeded up the stairs. No one was in the poor old lady's room; her wheel-chair stood in a corner, vacant. The cupboard in which she kept her sweet cake was open, and a glass was on the table, as if her maid-servant, or some one, had been emptying a decanter of wine which stood on one of the shelves. And, on moving softly to the bedroom-door, which was ajar, Mrs. Bevan saw through it the maid herself, upon her knees, before a drawer, apparently busily engaged in ransacking its contents. A low groan proceeded from the close-curtained bed, but Martha paid no attention to it, except to turn impatiently round, prepared, if it had been necessary, to repress any murmur or complaint on the part of the poor aged sufferer by a sharp reply. Solitary — destitute — friendless, with no one to watch her seemingly last moments but an unfeeling hireling, the unhappy lady was lying on her bed of suffering. Alas! how many round us are lying in the same state, because the Church has provided no shelter for them within her own bosom, and under her own ministering hands! The mistress of the house came up the stairs, but it was only to express her complaints, and wonder that Mrs. Crump had no friends to come and attend to her, and to ask how she was to be paid for her lodgings, and for some things which Mr. Morgan had ordered, now that Mrs. Crump herself had lost all her money. Mrs. Bevan had been provided with the

means of answering this question by the same hand
which had provided for the temporary necessities of
Mabel.   A nurse was sent for, Martha was dismissed, and the next day, with Mr. Morgan's permission, the poor old lady was removed to Mrs.
Bevan's house; and Mabel took her station by her
bed-side, watching over every movement, and answering every request for help, with the tenderness
of a daughter.

The next evening Charles Bevan was seated in
the library at the Priory—grave, saddened, chastened
with the blow which he had received himself, and
awe-struck with the storm of calamity, which, like
thunder from a cloudless sky, had burst upon his
native town.   Villiers had been inquiring for his
mother and her two charges.

" They are wonderfully well, considering what
has happened," replied Bevan.   " It is singular how
engagement in active duties, especially in those
which are appointed for us, soothes and quiets the
mind. When Miss Brook was asking, this morning at
breakfast, how she could recompense you for all your
kindness, my mother told her that she could not
gratify you more than by undertaking to nurse
poor Mrs. Crump.   And she has devoted herself to
it with delight."

" And will it be painful to Mrs. Bevan," asked
Villiers, " to have her house occupied by two such
inmates ? "

" My mother," replied Bevan, " has in the first
place no choice.   She has been deprived of every
thing but the little which I can supply to her; and
my fellowship is only 100l. a year; and all which I
may obtain beyond this by taking pupils is of course
precarious, and cannot amount to much.   But, without considering this, my mother is a woman of remarkable good sense, of a sincere but deep piety, of

practical habits, and active occupations; and I am
sure she would willingly devote herself to any work,
which might be really useful to others, and sanctioned by the Church."

Villiers remained silent and absorbed in thought.
At last he said, "It is a common impression, that
females cannot be brought to live together under
the same roof without jealousies and bickerings;
and that their minds are rendered frivolous and
weak by associating too much with each other. Do
you think that this is the case?"

"I think," replied Bevan, "that if females unfit
for a life of religion and charity are forced into it
against their will, if they are rigidly and unnaturally
bound down by vows, if they are excluded from moderate intercourse with others, and treated, in fact,
like mere children, as is too often the case in nun-
neries of Romanism, then their minds, instead of
being strengthened and elevated, may be deterio-
rated. But I cannot see why this should be the
case, where no such strained and artificial system
exists."

"And how many duties there are," said Villiers,
"which can only be accomplished well by females,
and by females associated together in a body. Take,
for instance, Miss Brook's infant school. None but
females can undertake the charge of very young
children, or communicate effectually with their parents, and teach their parents by degrees to aid in
the work of a sound education, instead of neutralising
it, or doing worse by their own examples. And
how can one female bear this burden. If there were
a body, while they nurtured up the young under
a cloud, as it were, of holy influences and personal
reverence, they would not run the risk of withdrawing the child's affections from its own parents,
any more than the cloud of saints and martyrs, whom

the Church teaches us to reverence, withdraws us from the one and only Being who is to be the centre of our love; while to fix our thoughts and affections upon a single saint, as the Romish system encourages us to do, necessarily tends to draw us from the immediate communion with our Lord—not to speak of the powerlessness of any single arm either to excite reverence, or to enforce obedience, or to communicate knowledge. By-the-by, what has become of that poor young woman who had the care of the infant school? I think you told me that she had also sustained a heavy loss?"

"She has lost all her savings," said Bevan. "And the school itself, I fear, will now be abandoned; for most of our charitable subscriptions, trifling as they have been, will probably be withdrawn. In the nineteenth century our first retrenchment is usually in our charities, and the second in our payment of tithes."

"And had the school no funds of its own?" asked Villiers.

"None whatever. Who would bestow permanent endowments on an individual teacher, with whose death everything may fall to the ground, or upon a self-constituted committee of subscribers, under no ecclesiastical control, who in a few years may become Unitarians or anything? The very notion of endowments without specified principles, and a fixed organisation to secure their maintenance, is an absurdity."

"Not now," replied Villiers. "Sir Robert Peel does not think so. He has now pledged the State to sanction and secure the perpetual transmission of property to any hands, and for any purpose, assuming that it is a sufficient assertion of principle to have repudiated any principle whatever. This is the ground they have taken in the Dissenters' Chapel Bill, as it

is called,—that the money was left for the propagation of no specific doctrines, by men who had no
creed, and made it a principle to have none; and
therefore it may be legitimately applied to propagate any blasphemy."

Bevan sighed. But his mind was too full of sad
thoughts nearer to himself for him to enter into
the political question.

"And I suppose the subscriptions to the County
Hospital will also fall off," said Villiers, "and the
District Visiting Society, and, in fact, nearly all the
charities? What is to become of the poor?"

Bevan sighed again. "I am not sure," he said,
"that the District Visiting Societies are the best
things that could be contrived for the poor. The
visiters are too often young and inexperienced.
Those to whom the office might be more safely entrusted are engaged in family duties; and the whole
system, perhaps, requires to be more thoroughly
permeated with a sound domestic, and Church spirit.
It is not equal to the Romish system of Sisters of
Charity."

"They live together," replied Villiers; "their
whole life is devoted to the task; they form a
religious body in the hands of the Church; and
thus they have a dignity of their own, and a proper
ecclesiastical character, which seems very much to
correspond with that of the widows in the early
Church. And from living together under rule, and
in the constant participation of the ordinances of
the Church, they acquire a tone of mind which can
scarcely be attained by individuals condemned to a
solitary life in the midst of the world. What an
admirable Sister of Charity Miss Brook would have
made, with her benevolence, her activity, and freedom from domestic ties! And how far happier and
more useful her life would have been than it has

been in furthering all the wild enthusiastic projects of a religion without a creed and without a priesthood!"

" One thing has struck me much," said Bevan, " in inquiries which I have made, and which seems to explain one obvious defect in the ministration of our Visiting Societies. I used at one time to fancy that the poor were insensible to the value and authority of an external commission. But I am convinced that it weighs with them much, and renders them far more accessible both to those who would instruct, and to those who would relieve them. And the purely voluntary character of our Visiting Societies gives an appearance of intrusiveness and presumption to their labour, against which the independence of the poorest is tempted to revolt."

" What are you founding your opinion on?" asked Villiers.

" I think it might be defended," replied Bevan, " on general principles. But the facts which principally confirmed it in my own mind were communicated to me by a clergyman who was sent by one of our bishops as a sort of missionary to the labourers on a railroad. He told me that he found them sunk in the lowest depths of ignorance and profligacy. His business was to obtain any opportunities which he could find of speaking to them, and of reading to them on the Sundays. And, among many other anecdotes, he told me that whatever abuse he encountered from them at first, or whatever reluctance they showed to listen to him, it ceased when he explained to them that he did not come of himself, but was sent by the bishop. ' Ah, sir!' they used to say, ' if you are sent by the bishop, that is quite another thing. We thought you were a methodist parson!' "

Villiers was struck with the anecdote. " And

you think, then," he said, "that if any institution like that of the Sisters of Charity was formed in the English Church, it should be regularly commissioned by the bishop of the diocese?"

"Certainly," said Bevan; "and placed under the immediate control of the clergyman of the parish. Without this they would become either futile or mischievous."

"Poor Dr. Grant," said Villiers, "would, I fear, be very much alarmed to hear of such a plan. By-the-by, how is he, since this second paralytic seizure?"

"He is very ill," replied Bevan. "Mr. Morgan told me, as I came here, that he was much alarmed for him. He, like so many others, has lost almost all that he had — all the accumulations from the profits of the living; and the shock was too great for him."

"And how should such an institution be supported?" asked Villiers, after a pause.

"Partly by a small endowment," replied Bevan, "partly by the small incomes which the members themselves would bring into the common stock, partly by voluntary offerings, and partly by little payments from the school. But I think you would find many persons, such as daughters of clergymen, widows, young females born in respectable positions in society, and left with a narrow income, who would gladly take advantage of an institution well planned, and authorised by the heads of the Church, and who would devote themselves to works of benevolence and charity as a corporate body. And still more might be found who, though they could not contribute funds, might render most valuable assistance, and be easily supported from the common stock. How many females there are around us left solitary in the world, without any home for their affections, any definite object for their labours, any community of interest or of feeling with their neighbours, any legitimate vent for zeal and energy, who, with the loss of those external appliances by which the world measures respectability, lose their own self-respect, or, in the absence of directions from the Church, throw their religious and devotional warmth into channels even of heresy and of schism! What a blessing it would be to such minds to have a home prepared for them, where the old might retire to a holy rest and preparation for the grave, nursed with a sisterly care, and devoted to meditation and prayer, and the younger might be trained in the discipline of a holy obedience and a modest activity, living under rule, and sheltered from the vanities and temptations of a life without dignity and without duty."

And as Bevan said this he looked up in Villiers's face, and observed that he was engaged deeply in thought.

At last Villiers observed, "I have often admired that little grey gabelled building which adjoins Mrs. Bevan's house. Whom does it belong to?"

"It is the remains," replied Bevan, "of an old institution, not unlike the one which we have been sketching out—a sort of *béguinage*. The old archway which led into it is still standing, and there are several windows with the stone mullions perfect, only blocked up with brick. The very chapel is remaining in a back yard; but it is now turned into a cow-house. It was destroyed at the Reformation."

"And the river runs close by it, does it not?" said Villiers, "through that meadow with the large elms in it, just under the churchyard?"

"Yes," replied Bevan. "I suppose the site was chosen from its closeness to the church, that the inmates might be able to attend the service regularly."

"And you think," said Villiers, smiling, "that Miss Brook would make a suitable inmate of such an establishment? Where can we find a head?"

And once more Bevan looked up; for there was an evident meaning in Villiers's words beyond the mere question. "I know one," he said, "who would gladly devote herself to such a work, if properly commenced, and sanctioned by the heads of the Church."

"Do you mean Mrs. Bevan?" asked Villiers.

Bevan bowed assent.

"Such an institution might prove a blessed refuge," continued Villiers, "to many of the sufferers at Hawkstone at this moment. When I think what an awful, and what a sweeping calamity has fallen upon the place, I am almost tempted to think that it must have been the scene of some dreadful sin. The lightnings do not fall, except where there is something to attract them."

"It has been the scene," replied Bevan, "for years and years, of a neglect of God—of coldness and apathy, at least, to his honour and glory. It has been haunted by heresy and schism; and heresy and schism have led to a refusal of the just means of supporting the public worship of the Church, to the withdrawal of tithes and offerings, and to the contempt of God's ministers. And where these crimes have been committed, we have the voice of the Bible itself declaring that a curse will fall. And we have added to these sins the sins of civil licentiousness, of disobedience to rulers, and of contempt of authority. And upon this we have heaped other crimes — pride, arrogance, covetousness, trampling on the poor, hardheartedness, defrauding the hireling of his wages, boasting of our strength and knowledge, and of the multitude of our riches ; thinking that no want or punishment could reach us ; vaunting our enlightenment, dishonouring our parents, tampering with divine truth, sacrificing our creed and our Church to human policy and worldly intrigue. Is not this sufficient to account for such a punishment ? Where such attraction as this exists, could the lightning do otherwise than fall ? And will it not fall soon upon the whole of England, unless it repents of the same guilt ? "

Villiers sighed deeply.

" And when," continued Bevan, " our unhappy friend Bentley, as alive as we are to these sins and these perils, had devoted himself to correct and remove them, he thought to move the mountain by his single arm ; and rather increased the evil than diminished it, by setting forth self-will and lawlessness in religion as a cure for self-will and lawlessness in all other things. He, also, has met his fate."

" And no more tidings, then, have been heard of him ? " asked Villiers, mournfully.

" None," replied Bevan. " He left his lodgings the day before yesterday, sending word to his housekeeper that he should not return. He must have gone out of the town early after daybreak, or even before. Indeed, he had been so insulted and assailed with the most coarse and virulent abuse, that I can well understand his wishing to quit it unobserved. He took leave of me the night before in the most affectionate manner, and charged me to give you what I have already brought you, his small Bible, as the only token which he could send of his gratitude and reverence toward you. And though he did not tell me what he contemplated, I could perceive that he had resolved on taking some

step of the kind, and on leaving the place for a
time, until the storm should blow over. Indeed, I
recommended him myself to go to his friends. But
he has no parents living."

"Poor man!" said Villiers; "what a cruel position to be placed in, and how hopeless! What
will be his fate?"

"To become an outcast from society," replied
Bevan, "a branded disgrace to his profession, a
beggar, perhaps, in the streets, or, at the best, to
drag on in some unknown corner of the earth, a
desolate, destitute existence — trembling at every
rumour, and shrinking from every eye, till he finds
a refuge from misery and shame only in the grave.
No shelter is open in our Church for such cases,
no homes in this country, which, when father and
mother desert us, may take us up, and rescue us
from the cruelty and mockery of the world, in the
name of the father and of the mother of us all.
Alas! poor England!"

"We must endeavour to trace him," said Villiers.
"Perhaps, even now, some refuge of the kind might
be provided for him. Let us not despair." And
Villiers took up a roll of drawings which lay before
him, and proceeded with Bevan to examine the
plans for restoring the Priory of Hawkstone.

CHAP. XVIII.

A few days afterwards Villiers knocked at the
door of an elegant modern house in one of the principal streets of London. The door was opened by
a portly butler in purple livery, attended by two
other domestics, who bore evident marks of the
hospitality of the servants' hall, and not less of the
effects and temptations of a London life upon that
class of domestics. Villiers was ushered up a broad
well-carpeted flight of steps into an elegantly-fur-
nished drawing-room. A lady with several daughters
were sitting there—one at the harp, another at the
piano, another at an embroidery frame, destined
for a gorgeous gilt ottoman which stood in the
centre of the apartment. Morning visiters were
engaged in discussing the dinner party of yesterday,
and the ball of the approaching night. Tickets
lay on the table for the Ancient Concert, and various
other places of amusement. Mixed with china
dishes and elegant bijous, were scattered the latest
parliamentary pamphlets, and a variety of religious
works, and in one corner, on a small table, lay a
manual of family devotion. One picture occupied
the wall over the fireplace, and it represented a
very pleasing, gentlemanly, well-dressed man, seated
on a sofa at an elegant writing-table, one leg thrown
carelessly over the other, and his pen balanced
gracefully in his hand, while before him lay open a
letter addressed to the Right Reverend Father in
God the Lord Bishop of F——.

The bishop himself, as the lady informed Villiers,

was at that moment engaged — indeed, every moment of his time was occupied. The old Bishop of M—— was so infirm, that his diocese had been wholly neglected, till parliament had appointed the Bishop of F—— to take charge of it; and the Bishop of F——, having already an enormous diocese of his own, containing more than a million of souls, and occupied chiefly by a manufacturing population, had vainly remonstrated against this increased burden. The post, as the lady continued to observe, brought him such a multitude of letters, that half the day was occupied in answering them. His secretary scarcely found time to take exercise; and just now the new principles and opinions reviving in the Church caused so many difficulties, and required such nice considerations and adjustments, that in the bishop's anxiety to support his conscientious clergymen, to guide the doubtful, to repress the hasty, and to satisfy all, he had involved himself in the disputes of twenty-four parishes; and at last, worn out with the insults which he had encountered from one class, and the indiscretions committed by another, he had been attacked by a serious illness, from which he was only just recovering.

The young ladies were preparing to engage Villiers's interest in a more light and agreeable discussion of the merits of a new French novel, which lay open on the table, when the portly butler opened the drawing-room door, and his lordship himself appeared. Villiers was a man of too much importance to be received as ordinary visiters, or his clergy. And to the profound, filial, and almost awful reverence, with which Villiers stood before him, as if to receive his blessing, the kind, amiable, and courteous bishop responded with a politeness and deference, which disturbed and perplexed Vil-

liers, he scarcely knew why. He apologised for
having detained Villiers so long, assured him that
he had been obliged to dismiss four curates who
were waiting in London to see him, and proceeded to the usual topics of conversation in a
morning visit. And it was only when Villiers
apologised for intruding on time so important, and
requested a private audience on business of some
moment, that his lordship conducted him to his
library. It was a large lofty room, looking out on
the smoky back court of a London house, full of
papers, reports, letters, documents, pamphlets, plans,
subscription-lists; but it contained no books. The
bishop had no time to read: he was an elegant
scholar, a sound divine; but study was now impossible. The secretary, who was writing at a side-
table, was dismissed. And every five minutes the
door-bell rang, and one after another the butler
announced, that in the next room was waiting the
Reverend Mr. Darling, to consult his lordship on
the conduct of his Unitarian churchwarden; the
churchwardens of Ringold, to complain of their
clergyman for reviving the offertory; the Reverend Mr. Montague, a deacon just ordained, and
placed alone in a cure of three thousand souls,
to request advice respecting the burial of an un-
baptized Dissenter; the archdeacon, to deliberate
with his bishop on the use of the surplice in the
pulpit; the secretary of the Christian Knowledge Society, to submit some tracts for his approval; a
deputation of dissenting ministers, to request him
to accept the patronage of a Bible Society; besides
the bishop's steward, with the accounts of a newly-
dropped fine; and the chairman of the Benevolent
Institution, to solicit him to preach a sermon in its
behalf. Still the bishop, only once looking at his
watch, resolved to devote at least a quarter of an
hour to a man of such excellence, influence, and im-

portance as Villiers. And Villiers, though he feared
that little could be done in such a space, endeavoured
to explain his plans with respect to Hawkstone,
and to obtain his lordship's approbation and support, and, what Villiers still more desired, his superintending and controlling hand. But the quarter
of an hour had elapsed before Villiers could even
approach the principal part of the communication
which he wished to make. And with real regret
the bishop heard his servant announce that the
carriage was at the door, which was to take him to
the House of Lords to a committee of privileges.
He offered Villiers a seat in it, that he might continue
the conversation; but Villiers thought it better to
wait for a more favourable opportunity. And the
hour when the bishop was engaged to the committee of privileges was the same at which Villiers
himself had been always accustomed, when in
London, to attend the afternoon service in Westminster Abbey. He congratulated himself that, as
a layman, he could enjoy a blessing, from which
even the heads of the Church were excluded by the
pressure of business. And the bishop, kindly shaking him by the hand, and wishing that he could
find in his diocese many more such laymen, and
at the same time wondering and half-doubting
whether or not Villiers himself was a safe man,
and uninfected with Oxford extravagances, requested him to communicate freely with his archdeacon, and promised that as soon as the pressure
of business was removed (when this was to happen
he could not foresee) he would give attention to
his valuable plan.

It was with a chilled and heavy heart that Villiers
took his leave of the amiable man, the elegant
scholar, the sincere Christian, the intelligent, active,
zealous ruler of his diocese, who, but for that pres-

sure of business which absorbed even the hours of devotion, and secularised even his elevated mind, might have proved an angel and apostle of the Church. But his thoughts reverted to Hawkstone, and he suffered them to become fixed on its state, its prospects, and his own duties connected with it, till he found that he had reached the abbey.

That night Villiers had a dream. He thought that he was on his way to see the good bishop, and to beseech his guidance and control, as a son would ask for counsel from a father. But instead of the streets of London, he fancied himself in an ancient, silent, and almost deserted city — loaded, as it were, with heavy, quaint, overhanging houses, mixed here and there with old carved stone portals, and sculptured gateways. There were high stone walls, grey and lichened with age; richly wrought churches, standing each in its quiet churchyard; old massive mansions with court-yards and groves around them; low modest almshouses and hospitals clustered round silent cloisters, dim with shade, but sweet with flowers; and, in the midst, embosomed in a tall grove of limes, above which the rooks were cawing and soaring like a cloud, rose the vast, solemn, gigantic towers of an ancient cathedral. He fancied that he passed down the solemn avenue of limes, with the tombstones gleaming tranquilly on each side; the low deep portals of the venerable pile were open, and Villiers reverently entered; and as he entered he thought the organ pealed forth its solemn volumes, and from one of the side-aisles appeared a train of white-robed worshippers, a choir of boys, a procession of priests, and then one bearing on high a cross, and another with a crosier, behind whom followed slowly, with eyes cast down, and hands folded on the breast, the same good bishop from whom he had parted in the morning. There was the same

lofty brow, the same benevolent eye, the same dignity
and benignity of mien. But there was something
else: Villiers felt, but could not describe it,—a shade,
a tone of spiritual life, thrown over his whole demeanour, as if his very being were tinged and
coloured with hours of prayer, of fasting, of meditation, of study, of holy peace and patient suffering,
and fruitful labour. The beautiful ritual of the
church was chaunted forth, but by the whole congregation, not by a paid choir only. And when the
blessing had been pronounced from the throne, and
the little procession was winding its way back
through the long-drawn aisles, there ranged themselves on each side the poor, the aged, the widows,
the young, the children of the schools, and not a few
of the wealthy inhabitants of the city, looking for a
repetition of the same blessing, as from their venerated father, as he passed.

Villiers thought that the good bishop saw him,
and beckoned him to follow. And when the procession had reached a massive deep-arched gateway,
the bishop dismissed all but his attendant clergy,
and taking Villiers by the hand, led him into a lofty
refectory. A table was spread, simple almost to
frugality. The bishop seated himself at the head;
and beneath him were ranged twelve clergymen in
a priestly dress, who were the hands, the ears, and
the eyes by which he swayed his diocese, and who
never left him. Strangers also and invited guests
were there, for the bishop's palace was the centre of
hospitality to the whole diocese. And the clergy,
when they visited the city, never were compelled to
frequent an inn. But there was one table filled with
poor, and other tables occupied by young students,
whom the bishop, with the assistance of his chap-
lains, was rearing up, as in a nursery for the Church.
And instead of liveried lacqueys, the little services

required were administered by a few quiet and simple
attendants, themselves in grave attire, and who
seemed to be recognised and treated rather as
brethren than as servants. A solemn grace was
chanted, a portion of Scripture read, and then with
sober cheerfulness all were welcomed to a meal, from
which every needless luxury was scrupulously excluded, and every needful comfort plentifully provided. And there was grave and even solemn talk,
chastened with benignity and courtesy. And Villiers
thought that the bishop led him on to speak of his
own plans and wishes; and when the repast was over
brought him into his own apartment, undecorated,
unluxurious, but filled with books, and furnished
for prayer. And there he listened to the young
man's petitions for aid, and his inquiries for wisdom.
And he intermixed his questions with answers, now
warning, now checking, now advising, now encouraging, and with promises of aid and counsel whenever
it should be required. And when Villiers was about
to withdraw, he thought the holy man bade him
kneel down, and, raising his hands to heaven, implored a blessing upon his head, and the comfort of
God's Holy Spirit in all his works.

But Villiers was wakened from his dream by the
rolling of a carriage, which stopped at the house
adjoining the hotel, and which house was the palace
of the Bishop of F——.   It was the bishop's agreeable daughters returning from a London party.

CHAP. XIX.

AND now once more, and for the last time, we may pass over a space of about eight years, and at the expiration of that time we may place ourselves in front of the Blake Arms Inn at Howlas, and observe how the house has been restored and enlarged, and more accommodation provided for commercial gentlemen, their gigs and their horses. Mr. Bonsor also is still there, and his bustling wife, and even Mary the maid; but her services in the commercial room have been supplanted by those of a waiter, for Howlas from a straggling wilderness of houses has swelled into an enormous town, black, dirty, filled with vice, and misery, and poverty, and surrounded by a forest of chimneys vomiting smoke, and of iron-works flaming, and grinding, and roaring, and of coal-pits absorbing in the bowels of the earth half the population each day, and disgorging them again at night, like naked demons, exhausted with labour, and ghastly with crime. Near to it also have arisen a number of vast, many-windowed fabrics, lighted up like palaces all night long, to celebrate, not the orgies of pleasure, nor the solemnities of worship, but the tortures of midnight labour. Mr. Smith is the owner of one, to which he has removed his establishment from Hawkstone; and the dammed-up mountain stream, or rather torrent, which supplied the Hawkstone river, indicates that its manufacturing importance is duly appreciated.

A horn is heard at the end of the street, and
though there are no less than three other inns, or,
as they call themselves, hotels in the place, Mr.
Bonsor's activity and Villiers's constant patronage
and support have given to the Blake Arms the
means of standing its ground, so that one of the
four omnibuses which ply to the new railway station always sets down passengers at the door. The
horn which we hear indicates an arrival of the kind;
and if we do not mind waiting a few minutes
at the door, watching the movements of some
anxious-looking policemen, who are endeavouring
to disperse a knot of sulky, ill-looking mechanics at
the corner of the street, we may be enabled to
witness the arrival. The first who descends from
the vehicle is a stout, close-shaven, sinister-looking
person, respectably dressed in black, and bearing in
his whole appearance that singular indescribable
aspect of mystery and intrigue which is too often
found connected with the looks of the worst specimens of Romish ecclesiastics. Notwithstanding
the impassive, iron-like expression of his countenance, he cannot prevent a slight quiver from
disturbing his muscles as he seems to recognise the
house; and he even asks if there is no other inn.
But Mr. Bonsor comes up to him invitingly, though
not without anxiety in his countenance; and the
stranger follows him, though reluctantly, into the
house, and asks for a private room, and into this he
is followed by a companion.

To this companion we must now request the
especial attention of the reader. He was young,
scarcely more than about nineteen years of age, but
tall, well-formed, graceful in his movements, so far
as a natural instinct and elegance has not been suppressed and destroyed by habitual association with
evil. His dress was decent, but foreign; his hair

fair and glossy, curled thick over an open forehead; his nose, his chin, the curves of his lips and of his eyebrows, were all delicately drawn by nature. A slight and premature moustache gave him the aspect of a foreigner,—of one, at least, who had been living in a foreign country. And youth would indeed have been beautiful in him, but for the coarse lines and swollen features, which, even thus early, indicated familiarity with vice. The elder of the two travellers, having carefully deposited on a table a writing-case elaborately strapped and buckled, and having bidden the younger see that their carpet-bags were safely removed from the omnibus, closed the door, examined some cupboards which were in the room, tried the lock of a door which opened into another apartment, even looked searchingly under the sofa, and then seated himself before the fire-place, and, with his feet raised upon the fender, proceeded to meditate. His thoughts apparently were not of the most agreeable nature, for his brow worked convulsively, and his lips at times even quivered; but on the return of his young companion he started up, and resumed his usual composure, though he could not suppress a glance of contempt, followed by a malignant satisfaction, when the young man rang the bell, and ordered brandy and water, which he swallowed greedily, and then with a coarse and blasphemous oath bade the waiter leave the room.

"And so you are going down to Hawkstone to-night," asked the young man, after a pause. "When shall you be back? and what am I to do in the mean time?"

"Drink yourself drunk, I suppose," answered the elder, with a sneer.

The young man only laughed, and uttered another oath.

"And what in the world are you going to do here?"
he said again, turning from the window. "What
a mystery you are making of all this! Look there,"
he cried; "what is the meaning of those policemen
and this mob coming up the street? And why are
all the windows of these shops blocked up?" And
with the impetuosity of a mind delighting in excitement, however vicious, he would have rushed
into the street, but Pearce (for he it was) seized
him and held him fast. "You must stay here," he
said; "if you were to go out, you might ruin all."

"Ruin what?" asked the young man. "Here
you are again at your mysteries! Of all mysterious
men I ever met with, you are the worst. You have
brought me all the way from Lyons without telling
me what you are about. And then you leave me
in this filthy place. I tell you what, Mr. Pearce, I
must know something more of your proceedings,
or you will not find me so compliant as I have
been."

Pearce, though a little alarmed at the bold and
resolute tone of his companion, looked on him
sternly and contemptuously, as if endeavouring to
crush his resistance at once; but the young man
met his gaze fixedly—and even Pearce was obliged
to withdraw his eye. "You may do as you like,
Master Ernest," said Pearce; "it matters little to
me. I have been your friend through life, when
every one else had deserted you. But for me you
would have starved; and it is in my power, as I
have told you again and again, to make you a great
man, and richer than you have any notion of. But
unless you choose to put yourself into my hands,
and do whatever I command, you may go back into
the streets, and beg your bread."

And Pearce was preparing to leave the room, but
the young man stopped him.

" When shall you be back, then?" he asked.

" Perhaps to-morrow," answered Pearce; " perhaps not for a week."

" And, I suppose, I am to remain here," replied the young man, sulkily.

" Yes," answered Pearce, " if you do what I bid you, and wish me to be of any use to you, you will remain here quietly till I return, or send for you."

" And what am I to do for money?" asked the other.

Pearce went to the table and opened his desk to take out some sovereigns, but as he was stooping over it, the young man threw himself upon him with a sudden spring and ferocious oath. " Mr. Pearce," he exclaimed, " I will see what there is in that desk of yours; you shall show me that packet of papers. I will not be trifled with any more."

But, active and vigorous, and determined as the youth was, Pearce was too robust and resolute to be taken by surprise; and, with a sudden effort, he shook his assailant from him, threw him to the other end of the room, locked his desk calmly, and took it under his arm.

" It will not do;" he said to the disappointed and passionate youth, " it will not do. Make up your mind to obey me, or I give you up. The papers are not in that desk, even if you had got possession of it. Do you think I am such a fool as to risk the loss of them in that way?"

The youth muttered something sullenly, but Pearce took no notice of it.

" And what am I to do here?" asked the youth. " You told me, when we came away from Lyons, that I should find plenty to do here; and that I need not enlist, if I wanted to have a more stirring life than you kept me to in France. There is no fighting going on here, is there, as there was the

last time? Is not this the very house they burned
down then?"

Pearce said nothing.

"I wonder what became of that gentleman,"
asked the youth, "whom they wanted to get at, and
tear to pieces then? I wonder if he is alive still?
I shall not forget his dragging me out of the fire,
down there in Hawkstone; and though I was but a
mere boy, I remember I would have done the same
thing for him, and have given him the ladder when
he cried out for it in this very house, out of the
garret window, only you boxed my ears, and pulled
me away."

Pearce still continued silent.

"Is there any more of that work going on,"
asked the young man, "that you have come up
here in this underhand way—writing letters, and
receiving them every day, and going about in all
sorts of strange figures? Are you going to have a
rebellion? Is there to be any fighting, Mr. Pearce,
once for all? Answer me that."

"And do you want to fight?" asked Pearce,
quietly.

"Any thing for a stirring life;" replied the young
man; "any thing rather than be moping about
doing nothing. I want to see life, instead of being
penned and cooped up as I have been."

"Perhaps," replied Pearce, "there may be more
chances of fighting here than you think for; and
more means of seeing life, and of getting on in life,
too, for a young man of spirit."

"I wish I could find them," said the youth. But
he was interrupted by Mr. Bonsor coming into the
room with a frightened countenance, and requesting
that they would remove into a back room, and allow
him to put up the shutters. "A mob," he said,
"had collected in the market-place, and was coming

up the street; and the policemen were not strong enough to disperse them, and soldiers had been sent for : and if there should be any disturbance, it might not be safe to be on the ground-floor, particularly if shots were fired, as they had been three days before, when two men had been killed."

" A mob !" exclaimed the young man, " fighting ! soldiers ! that's capital, just the thing !" And once more he would have rushed out of the room, but Pearce stopped him, without expressing the slightest surprise at the news, or making any further inquiries of Bonsor, who, nevertheless, without encouragement, except from the younger of the two travellers, proceeded to enlarge on the turbulent and alarming state of the district—an outbreak expected every day — special constables sworn in—Mr. Villiers's yeomanry ordered out—a regiment of cavalry, and three pieces of artillery sent down to Hakewell barracks — and the same state of things in other parts of England, — every thing full of terror and confusion. And there were, at the same time, pending quarrels and negotiations which threatened a war with France ; and Ireland was organised under its priests, ready to take part in any rebellious movement, or foreign invasion. The young man, Mr. Ernest, as we may call him, cast his eye upon a dirty newspaper which lay upon the table, and read out some paragraphs to the same effect ; but Pearce paid no attention to them.

" I suspect," said Ernest at last to his companion, " that you know more about these things than you are willing to tell every one."

" It may be," replied Pearce, " and it may not."

" And what kind of fellows are they," continued the young man, " who are preparing for this fun ? "

" Very fine fellows," replied Pearce.

" Do you know any of them ? " asked Ernest.

But Pearce made no reply.

At last he said, " And if you were to know any thing of them, what would you do ? "

" Join with them and fight, to be sure," replied Ernest.

" Fight for what ? " asked Pearce, curiously.

" For any thing," replied Ernest; "for fun, for the mere pleasure of fighting. What were one's arms made for — a gentleman's arms, that is ? (and you tell me I am a gentleman) — not to work upon the roads, or to sit all day at a spinning-jenny."

" You would make a fine soldier," observed Pearce, "if you had not been intended for something better. But now you must come with me; and if you do as I tell you, there is no saying what you may find yourself some fine day. Do you intend to trust to me or not ? "

" I suppose I must," answered the youth, sulkily. " But I must have some money to amuse me. I often wonder where you get all your money from, Mr. Pearce."

Pearce, however, made no answer, but put on his great-coat, and taking his writing-case under his arm, he made a sign for Ernest to accompany him. " We must go out the back way, I suppose, if there is a mob in the street." And though his companion stopped, and listened anxiously to the shouts and tumult which now reached them from the advancing mob, and would willingly have rushed into the middle of the fray, Pearce took him by the arm, and led him reluctantly into the back court-yard, and through the garden gate.

" All built up again, I see, since the fire," said his companion. " I remember every place as well as if it was yesterday. There is the very wall I climbed over, and here is the wood-house, and the cistern into which the gentleman nearly tumbled. I cannot recollect what his name was; can you?"

But Pearce hurried on without answering: and after passing through the garden, he led the way up by a bye lane, and at last stopped before a high whitewashed wall, in which was a narrow door. He knocked, and it was opened from the inside. Pearce, stepping in, said a few words in French to the person within, and then called to Ernest to enter; and though the young man hesitated for a moment, and showed signs of doubt and reluctance, Pearce, with an authoritative voice, overpowered the suspicion which came to his mind, and they both entered, and the door once more closed upon them.

The same evening, a few hours after this, there was seen standing near the ancient Priory, under Prior Silkstede's oak, and gazing curiously on the scene around him, a sturdy mendicant, habited as one who had travelled a long journey on foot, and could second his petition for alms with a moving and plausible tale of distress, whether it was the loss of all his little property by fire, or a murrain among his cattle, or a hardhearted landlord. He had a rough crab-tree stick in his hand, and a dirty, well-thumbed, and well-signed petition in his pocket. His black shaggy hair disguised much of his features; but those who had observed the twinkling, cunning, malignant, but powerful eyes of Mr. Pearce would have found little difficulty in recognising him again, even in his present habiliments. And as he gazed on the scene before him, a dark scowl gathered on his brow, and his teeth ground together in passion.

And yet the landscape in itself was not one to call up such feelings in any ordinary spectator. It was exquisitely beautiful—cheerful, and yet solemn.

In the bottom of that wooded dell, and on the brink
of the huddling brook, which fretted and foamed
along under the rough-scarped sandstone bank,
hung with huge gnarled oaks, and carpeted with
fern and moss, stood the pile, no longer in ruins, of
the ancient Priory of Hawkstone. A hand of exquisite taste and feeling had restored it to its
original state, as nearly as was consistent with the
purposes to which it was now applied. There was
the quadrangle surrounded with its low buildings,
appropriated to the chambers of its inmates ; and
every mullioned window and clustered chimney,
and jutting buttress, and sculptured corbel, bore
the impress of a master's art. On one side rose
the tower, massive, simple, and grey, and relieved
by the rich oriel which projected over the gateway,
and by a delicately-carved niche, surmounted with
a rich-wrought canopy. On the right was the hall,
lighted with tall narrow windows, and crowned
with its *louvre*. And up to it led a porch, with a
rich but low-browed arch, and flight of broad stone
steps, about which ivy and creepers were already
twining, and tinting the grey stone with the colours
of age. At one angle stood a slender turret, perforated at the top with narrow open lancets, and
from this, at the moment when the mendicant was
gazing on the pile, a silvery bell was ringing to
call the inmates of the edifice to their evening repast. To the south the quadrangle was open, and
admitted the bright warm sunshine into a cloister
green with honeysuckle and sweet briar ; and at
one end of this cloister a narrow archway opened
into the chapel, which rose high over the rest of
the buildings, with its grove of leafy pinnacles, and
its tower, gracefully proportioned, crowning the
whole as with a diadem. The mendicant gazed on
it, and again he ground his teeth in passion. But

his attention was called away by the appearance of an old but respectable peasant in a green old age, the same who had met Villiers the first day of his arrival at the Priory, under Lady Esther's pine-trees. He asked the usual questions of the beggar, who answered them plausibly and satisfactorily, and as one who had known better days; and the old peasant became communicative.

" If you want relief," he said, " you have only to go to the great gate and tell your tale, and if they are satisfied with it, you will be welcome to a meal and a lodging for the night. No poor man goes away from it without help, if he seems to deserve it. And they are not hard in examining you. Mr. Villiers is not hard either. Many a time has he told me that he would rather relieve three rogues than refuse to relieve one honest man. We call this our Hawkstone poor-house — a very different one from those you see elsewhere !"

" And is it Mr. Villiers who has built this ?" asked the mendicant.

The peasant nodded his head.

" And who lives here ?" asked the mendicant.

" There are twelve gentlemen," answered the peasant — " clergymen most of them. And there is a head — the warden they call him. Mr. Beattie is his name. And they have often other gentlemen staying with them, mostly clergymen ; but some of them Mr. Villiers's friends, lords and others, who come here to read and be quiet, generally about Lent time. And there are a number of other young gentlemen who are going to be clergymen. And there is a school; and they do a wonderful deal of good."

" And are they liked ?" asked Pearce, significantly. " They are Papists, are they not ?"

" Papists !" exclaimed the peasant; " no more

than you and I are Papists. People tried at one time to persuade us they were; but we soon found out the difference. But if you want some supper you had better make haste, for the supper-bell is down."

The mendicant hesitated. At last he summoned up courage, and composing his countenance, and preparing his tale, he ventured boldly up to the porter's lodge under the entrance-tower. One of the Fellows (Villiers had chosen the name as less likely than that of brothers to shock prejudices by unfounded associations with Monasticism) happened to be at the gate as he approached, and having listened kindly to his story, he called the porter to bring water for the beggar to wash his hands, and then conducted him himself into the hall. Its lofty, dark-raftered roof, slightly relieved by carving, and its deep-mullioned windows enlivened here and there by the escutcheons of a benefactor or a bishop, were lighted up at this moment with the last rays of the setting sun. There was a raised dais, at which were seated about twenty of the elder inmates, all dressed alike, and in gowns of a black stuff. At the head of them Pearce, even at that distance of time, recognised Beattie, and afraid of being recognised himself, notwithstanding his disguise, he gladly slunk to the end of a table in the centre of the hall, at which were seated twelve poor people like himself. It was one of the principles of Hawkstone Priory to partake of no meal without sharing it with some of their poorer neighbours.

A simple but substantial supper was served up to him, during which Pearce looked round and observed the other tables filled with scholars, attired in gowns like the companions. And even Pearce was affected with their quietness, propriety, and reverential manner. The attendants also, he observed, were habited like the rest, though in coarser gowns, and were treated more as associates in the same community than as hirelings and servants. The meal over, a simple but solemn grace in Latin was chanted from the high table, and closed with a full and swelling Amen from the whole body ; and the Warden, followed by the rest, two and two, proceeded to leave the hall. He stopped to say a few words of kindness to a poor old man, who had been seated next to the mendicant, and he made some inquiries of the mendicant himself; but with all Pearce's power of dissimulation, he could scarcely answer them coolly. And Beattie could not help remarking to a gentleman, who walked at his right hand, on the sinister expression of the beggar's countenance. The gentleman turned and looked back on him, and his eyes met those of the mendicant, which lighted up with an expression of intense hatred, as they gazed upon the countenance of Villiers. Villiers himself felt a strange indescribable sensation thrill through him, and waken, as it were, a whole train of old and strange associations, which transported him to a distant clime, and almost absorbed the consciousness of the objects before him. But he had long since schooled himself to reject from his thoughts whatever might tend to occupy him with vain regrets, and morbid imaginations. And though night after night his dreams brought back to him the image of his wife and of his child, and he never knelt in prayer without one fervent and tearful petition, that, if heaven so willed, the lost might still be restored to him, he never permitted himself to indulge day-dreams. He cast one more look, he knew not why, at the mendicant, but the mendicant had averted his head, and Villiers then followed Beattie to his own apartments.

"And now," he said, when the door had closed, and Beattie had been seated, by Villiers's own hand, in his massive abbatial chair, — "now I can communicate to you the object of my coming, before the bell rings for chapel. He is found at last. Let us be thankful."

"Who is found?" asked Beattie.

"Our poor lost friend, Bentley," answered Villiers. "But I will read you the letter which I received this morning. And we must lose no time in sending or going to him, and bringing him here. It comes from Carrington, up in the most remote part of Durham; and I have heard something of the writer, who is the clergyman of the parish."

Beattie composed himself to hear, and Villiers proceeded to read the letter: —

"SIR,

"I am sure you will excuse the liberty which I am taking in addressing you. The interest, which you have yourself shown in the unhappy person, who is the subject of my letter, will sufficiently excuse me. I am the rector of the parish of Carrington, in the north of Durham; and as such have been made acquainted with a case of the deepest distress. About eight years since, a gentleman, evidently of education and superior manners, but seemingly without means of supporting himself, came into this parish. He took a very small room in a cottage near to the church, and for some time secluded himself wholly from observation, rarely appearing out of doors till dusk, and shunning every communication even with the poor widow in whose cottage he lodged. From her I learned, after a time, that his means appeared to be exhausted. He was punctual in his attendance at Church on every occasion, but studiously placed himself out of the

sight of the congregation, in the lowest and worst
seats among the poor; and the piety, yet deep de-
jection, and shame, and remorse, which were visible in his manner, could not fail to interest me.
For some time I observed that he never attended
at the Holy Communion. At last, once or twice,
I saw him lingering and hesitating, when the rest
of the congregation was departing; and I made
another effort to see him, calling on him, and addressing him when we met, as we sometimes did
meet, in our walks; but he evinced such decided reserve and reluctance to hold any communication
with me, that I was obliged to give up the attempt,
and to wait for a more favourable opportunity. He
did, however, at last, and apparently with a great
effort, present himself at the holy table; and I shall
never forget the intense expression of awe and
misery, and yet of hope, with which he bowed his
head down to receive the sacred elements. It affected me so much that I could not refrain from
following him to his miserable home after the service was concluded; and, without wearying you
with details, it is sufficient to say, that, touched and
penetrated with holy influences, and encouraged
by the sympathy which I felt for him, he communicated to me, under a promise of inviolable secrecy, so much of his unhappy story as he felt
himself at liberty to explain. That person was the
Rev. Mr. Bentley, about eight years since the curate
of Hawkstone, and whom, by his own account, you
yourself had rescued about that time from a situation of great danger. He told me partially the
circumstances under which he had been involved in
that danger, and his history after it. You are
aware that advantage was taken, partly by public
scandal, and partly, it would seem, by the agency
of personal enemies, to calumniate his character in

the grossest manner ; and unable to refute the charges, in consequence of the insanity of the poor woman to whose defence he was sacrificed, and involved also in an appearance of mystery, owing to his rigid conscientiousness in observing his unhappy oath, you are also aware that he was unable to withstand the storm, and abandoned his post. Although his bishop expressed himself satisfied with his innocence, he was unable to protect, or even to exculpate him in the eyes of the world. His friends received him with a coldness and suspicion so galling, that he resolved to submit to any sacrifice rather than remain in dependance upon them ; and he fled here, to this remote and lonely village, not to live (for he had no means of living), but to sink in silence into the grave under the fearful curse of a blighted fame.

" After this communication my intercourse with him became frequent ; but it was admitted by him only under a solemn pledge from me that I would not betray his residence to his friends. And, though I endeavoured to impress on him that an oath illegally exacted was not binding, I found that, like many other persons brought up in his views of religion, while there was considerable laxity in some points of moral obligation, there was in others an over-scrupulous and superstitious conscientiousness, which nothing could overcome. Nor indeed, as it appeared, was it possible for him to remove wholly the suspicions which naturally attached to certain circumstances in the case.

" My own means were so small that I could only assist him by procuring for him a few pupils — the children of neighbouring farmers, whom he instructed in reading and writing ; and in this manner he earned a scanty pittance, scarcely sufficient to support him. But from the moment when he had

opened himself to me, and we were enabled to associate together more freely, a great load seemed to
be taken from his mind; and everything which I
have witnessed in him has more and more confirmed my conviction of his innocence and upright-
ness. The last seven years have been spent by him
in the patient endurance of poverty, and privations,
and solitude; and if Providence had not enabled
him to open his mind to a brother clergyman, I
think that he must long since have sunk under his
sufferings. As it is, his distresses have brought
upon him a painful and lingering disorder, which
wholly incapacitates him from any exertion whatever; and after toiling to the last moment, and
sinking under it, he has now been obliged to abandon even the little means of support which enabled
him to drag out his existence. During all this time
not a murmur has escaped him. He has permitted
me at last, and with the deepest reluctance, to make
known his situation to some relatives—surviving
parents he has none. But the replies which I have
received have been such as to preclude all hope of
assistance. Some few alms I have been enabled to
procure for him; but these have now failed: and
when I look round I can see no shelter open for
him, — no place of retirement, where, if guilty, he
might pass his few remaining days in penitence;
or, if innocent, be shielded from the calumnies of
the world, and the miseries of destitution. For our
clergy, as for our peasantry, we have provided in
this country no other refuge, in want, in sorrow,
in oppression, in solitude, and sickness, and old
age, but the poor-house and the gaol. Happily I
have prevailed on him at last to allow me to mention his circumstances to yourself; and from all
that I have heard of your character——"

But here Villiers hastily folded up the letter.

"It is not money that is wanted," said Beattie,
after a pause. "No money could purchase the
aids and consolations which he requires; and his is
not an uncommon case. Other things besides calumny will drive men from their post, strip them
of their support, plunge them in poverty, leave them,
like a wreck upon the waters, to be tossed about,
and dashed to pieces on the rocks, like worthless
and senseless fragments of society. Alas! how
true it is. For our clergy, as for our peasantry
—rather let us say, for every class of society—we
have provided in this country no other refuge
in want, in sorrow, in oppression, in solitude, and
sickness, and old age, but the poor-house and the
gaol."

"He must be brought here immediately," said
Villiers. "You can receive him at once, can you
not?"

"Of course," replied Beattie. But the deep-toned
bell of the chapel, which had been tolling for some
little time, now paused; and together the two
friends, the Founder of the college and the Warden,
proceeded to the hall.

"I have just arranged," said Beattie, "that we
should all meet here before we go into the chapel,
and return here after the service is finished. With
so many young boys under our care, we cannot
guard too carefully against their entering upon
their devotions in a hurried, unprepared frame of
mind. I do not like their coming into the chapel
immediately from their play or lessons, and still
less making their attendance at chapel a roll-call."
And Villiers, whose admiration for Beattie increased
each day as he saw him bringing all his judgment
and devotion to bear upon the formation of this new
institution, was delighted to find that all the inmates
were already assembled in the hall, each in his

place—grave, and composed, and silent; and after a short prayer against wandering thoughts and irreverent behaviour, they all proceeded to the chapel.

Whatever holy, peaceful, grateful thoughts—thoughts of deepest gratitude even in the midst of heavy afflictions—pervaded the minds of others, in the breast of one individual, during nearly the whole of that solemn service, there raged a hell. Placed with other poor at the upper end of the sacred building (Beattie had selected the place to mark in some outward form the fact that the poor are in an especial manner the children of the Church), he looked down the lofty vaulted aisle, reverently but not gorgeously lighted, and lined on each side with rows of the members of the body, both young and old, attired (for it was the evening of a festival) in white surplices. He saw Beattie take the usual seat on the right hand of the entrance, under a richly-wrought canopy of dark carved oak, and Villiers next to him. And when he observed the deep and solemn devotion of Villiers's manner during the whole of the service, his heart misgave him; and he doubted whether any machinations which he could contrive against such a man could ever be permitted to take effect. There was a full choral service, in which all the congregation joined; for church music formed an essential part of the system which Beattie had drawn up for the course of instruction: and as the full swell of the organ, blended with the clear pure chorus of voices, young and old, rose in a cloud of music into the vaulted roof, and floated along it, almost like the songs of angels, even the guilty, remorseless, vindictive spirit of the supposed mendicant lost something of its bitterness, and became more calm. The beautiful service of the Church was concluded, the organ once more pealed forth its full tide of harmony, and the worshippers once more proceeded to the hall; and there, after another short prayer for forgiveness for all the coldness, and negligence, and omissions which might have sinned against Heaven during the act of worship, Beattie dismissed them.

One only he called to him from the farthest end of the hall—one who seemed to withdraw himself from the rest, as if in deep humility and shame. He had knelt, too, in the chapel, not within the choir, but in the antechapel. He had knelt on the bare marble pavement, had worn no surplice, had scarcely raised his head, or his voice, in any prayer but the Confession of Sin, had refrained from joining in the songs of thanksgiving; and, when the service was concluded, had reverently opened the door for the warden to retire through, and then had shrunk back into a nook in one corner of the antechapel. When he came up to Beattie, although Beattie addressed him with the greatest gentleness, and Villiers inquired kindly for his health, he kept his eyes fixed on the ground, as if unable to raise them in the face of another fellow-mortal. And there was an expression of sorrow and shame, and at the same time of meekness and modesty, in his countenance, which was full of touching interest. Few would have recognised in the subdued and devoted penitent the once profligate, seditious, and abandoned Cookesley.

Beattie begged him to visit the mendicant who was to be lodged within the walls that night, and to see if there was anything the matter with him —anything which would require medical advice. And when Cookesley had retired, Villiers could not help remarking on his changed character and depressed aspect. "You cannot persuade him yet," he said, "to take his position among you. And yet

his services, from his surgical knowledge, are very
valuable."

"I have scarcely endeavoured to persuade him,"
replied Beattie. "The illness which he suffered
subsequently to that disturbance at the Forest, and
which he caught during his confinement in prison,
completely sobered him. Bevan told me that he
never saw such an alteration, and that he was astonished to find how many good points of character
came out, which had been overlaid and buried under
the extravagances of a reckless youth plunged into
the dissipations of London, without home or guidance. Oh! when will our Church think of our
medical students? When will it remember that
with the healing of the body the healing of the soul
is most intimately joined; and while it raises hospitals for the bodies of the sick, when will it also
raise by their side colleges for those who attend to
them? Ever since he has been here he has exhibited such gentleness, such humility, such earnestness, that I have scarcely liked to disturb a discipline
which is productive of such good fruits. It is of
his own choice that he does not enter the chapel
during Divine service. He knows that the profligacy of his former life is a matter of public notoriety; and he feels more satisfaction himself in
openly taking his true position as a penitent than in
endeavouring to maintain himself outwardly on a
level with those who have been guiltless of such sins
as his."

"And perhaps," continued Villiers, "it may be
better for the society itself that it should not be
compromised by too soon admitting into its bosom
even the reformed and converted."

"It may be so," replied Beattie. "By being
brought into such a refuge as this, he is saved from
becoming the hardened, reckless, impenitent profli-

gate, or the fanatical, ill-directed enthusiast, which he
would have become in the world after a mis-spent
life like his.   And he here meets with so much
tenderness, and kindness, and Christian love from
all, that there is comparatively little bitterness in
his position—far less, indeed, than in that compul-
sory dissimulation, and almost hypocrisy, which is
forced on us by being placed in false situations at
variance with our real internal character.   The
early Church would have excluded him from Communion for a far longer time than I ventured to
exclude him.   And perhaps his best preparation for
Heaven is to remain in his present humbled and
anxious state. He has before him sufficient hope to
encourage him in his efforts at self-denial and improvement, and a sufficient fear to make him watchful and careful. And he seems to take such pleasure
in rendering services to any of the community, and
in performing for them even the most menial offices,
that I value his child-like humility more than any
ease and comfort which he might find in being
relieved too soon from the burthen on his conscience.   He has been saved, dear Villiers, as far as
human eyes can see — saved from utter perdition,
and by the shelter of this place. And to have saved
one soul from impenitence and hardness of heart,
and to have brought it to Heaven, under the strict
but blessed discipline of such a community as this,
is enough to repay you for all that it has cost you."

Villiers made no reply, but his eyes were moistened ; and shaking Beattie tenderly by the hand, he
bade him good night.   " You have done it," he said.
" It is your work, under Providence.   It is an easy
thing to give money, easy to build walls of brick
and stone — easy even to plan and arrange upon
paper an ideal system of perfection ; but to carry
it into operation, to govern and mould the minds of

others, to bear with all the infirmities of temper, to
endure all the hardships and privations, which in
any good form of society must fall most heavily —
not on those who are ruled, but on those who rule ;
to do all this patiently, and unweariedly, and without any hope of reward upon earth, and to sacrifice
for it, what you have sacrificed, the quietness, and
peace, and independence of your life in Oxford —
all this——. However," he continued, " these are
not subjects to be spoken of. May God bless you,
and keep you, and all around you." And with a
full, tender, tranquil sense of gratitude, hope, and
comfort blending with deep sorrow, Villiers was retiring, when Beattie affectionately stopped him.

" Pardon me," he said, " if I ask one question.
Shall you be present at the ceremony to-morrow ?"

Villiers almost started, but answered, at once,
" No. I would not willingly that private and personal feelings should mix with such a solemn act of
religion. Her mind has been shaken enough already;
and all that must take place should be conducted as
tranquilly and privately as possible. The bishop
will be at the chapel at ten o'clock, and Lady Eleanor will be with Mrs. Bevan. You have saved her,
dear Beattie. What a blessing to have restored
such a spirit from schism and error, to the communion of truth. You may witness her restoration ;
I can do nothing but rejoice in it."

Beattie saw that it was a subject on which he
dared not say more ; and the friends parted.

CHAP. XX.

If many visions of Villiers's heart had been turned
to emptiness and gall — if his home had been left
desolate — if the delight of his eyes had been
taken from him — if on that which had been the
hope of his happiest hours he now dared not even
look — if at midnight, in his dreams, in every
waking moment, one black spot hung motionless
before his eyes — the thought of his lost child, and
the agony of contemplating its almost necessary
destiny in the hands of villains — if, when he turned
over the pages of those fearful Parliamentary Reports, which have laid bare the miseries and sins
of the poor and deserted, he was obliged to close
the book in anguish (for his own child might now
be enduring the same fate) — and if, now that year
after year had passed away, recovery seemed hopeless, and the punishment of Heaven to be sealed
upon his own disobedience to his parent — yet
Villiers's existence was not without its blessings
— real, deep, substantial blessings, — and his heart
melted into thankfulness.

He reined up his horse, which seemed to know
every sound and movement of its master, and to
sympathise with his feelings; and from the brow of
the declivity which sloped down to the little brook
he looked back upon the Priory, now gleaming
calmly and beauteously in the placid moonlight. The
heavens were cloudless, and scarcely a night-breeze
waved the branches of the oaks, or stirred the feathers of the fern, which mantled round his path.

Every star appeared in its watch. There was no sound but the lulling murmur of the brook, and the faint swell of distant voices mingled with the deep tones of an organ, rising from the dim-lighted windows of the chapel; for on the evenings of festivals the inmates of the Priory were accustomed to meet in that holy building to fulfil the injunctions of the Apostle — " If any be merry, let him sing psalms ; " and there, reverently and piously, and as a devotional exercise, they indulged in the holy luxury of sacred music, without any of that levity and incongruity, which besets its performance in a theatre or a concert-room.

Villiers listened to the solemn strains as they rose up into the still night-air; and he blessed God, who had not deserted him — who had given him in the place of his child such an object for his tender care — such a home for his affections — such a hope of good to all around him — such a promise of fruit to his labours. He uttered a prayer for all within its walls; and repeating to himself the Psalm of David, " O how amiable are thy dwellings, thou Lord of Hosts " (Ps. lxxxiv.), he once more turned his horse, and rode slowly along the brow of the park.

As he passed one of the park gates, near which, on the outside, stood the blackened ruins of a miserable cottage, which had been destroyed by lightning, Villiers spurred his horse, as smitten with a sudden pang, and galloped rapidly along the green sward, as if to distract his thoughts from some painful subject. The blackened ruin had reminded him of a tale of horror within it, which had been brought before him in his very first inquiries into the state of his peasantry — a tale of poverty, of misery, of crime, of incest. And when Villiers came to examine into the condition of his

tenantry, and especially of his cottagers — when
he had visited them in their own miserable abodes,
and inquired into their habits, he had been so
shocked and appalled by the recurrence of similar
tales, that he scarcely ever dared to revert to the
subject, even in his thoughts. It was not that they
were worse than their neighbours ; this in itself
aggravated the evil. But Villiers had often dwelt,
in foreign climes, on the bold, cheerful, innocent,
contented, simple-minded [peasantry of England, as
they had been pictured to his imagination. And
when he came to look for them upon his own estate,
among those for whose happiness and goodness he
was responsible to Almighty God, he found —
what ? — families huddled together in miserable
hovels, without one protection to common decency,
and tempted, even familiarized, with the most horrible crimes. Their wages were scarcely sufficient
to maintain life at its lowest ebb, without one comfort — one superfluity — one provision for sickness
and old age — one hope of elevation from the depths
of want — one innocent domestic luxury to bind
together parents to their homes, and children to
their parents. Self-respect had vanished beneath
the crushing, chilling gripe of a relentless poverty,
— a poverty which those who should have relieved
it stigmatised and punished as a crime. Two hideous
objects stared them in the face, as awaiting them
at the close of their life — the poor-house and the
grave ; and the grave stripped of all the blessings,
which holiness and religion pour around it to the
peasant even more than to the king. They had
been deserted by their clergyman. The parish
itself was the same as that in which the town was
situated ; and if the town had been neglected, how
much more the distant and outlying scattered vil-
lages.

From that moment Villiers, to whom before the very name of a manufactory was odious, never indulged in one reproach even upon that frightful system. "Till we," he said, "till the agriculturists and landlords of England have wiped off the black blot upon our own fame — have repented of our own sins, and redressed the wrongs which we have committed by dealing with the possession of land as with an instrument for making money, and by becoming ourselves, not the rulers, the teachers, the parents, the sovereigns of our tenantry, but their taskmasters, and master-manufacturers — manufacturers of corn — manufacturers, with the same spirit of avarice, the same selfishness, the same mercenary calculations, the same gambling speculation, the same neglect of those who toil to make us rich, as the manufacturers of silks and cottons — till we have done this, we are in no condition to censure others."

And his first thought had been to effect this — not by acts of parliament (Villiers smiled in melancholy scorn at the name of acts of parliament), but by example, by self-sacrifice. Once more he reined up his horse, and looked down upon a hamlet, or more than hamlet, which had sprung up in one corner of the park, near to the restored Priory. He had chosen a spot where the lofty ridges of the park retired, and left a wide, open vale, surrounded with gentle undulations, green with grass, and tufted with trees. The little Hawkstone brook, crossed by more than one simple bridge, ran foaming through the middle of the vale; and hanging by its side, and about the declivities, there rose a number of white thatched cottages, not ranged in rows (Villiers knew that geometrical lines have little connection with the sympathies and prejudices of home affections), but scattered here and there, as if by accident, each having some little peculiarity, a tree, or knoll, or jutting mass of rock, to mark it to the occupant as his own home. "Man," repeated Villiers to Bevan, "never can be made what he should be till he possesses property—something that may belong exclusively to himself, something which distinguishes him from others by some mark more binding to his affections than the chequer No. 1. or No. 2."

Each cottage also had its garden ; and the gardener at the great house was in daily communication with their inmates, teaching them the proper cultivation of vegetables, and supplying them, as required, with the most useful grafts of fruit-trees, and even with the finest flowers which could be grown in the open air.

"Flowers," said Villiers to Bevan, " are the innocent luxury of nature — the triumph of that exquisite art, which the poor are as capable of enjoying as the rich. No cottage of mine shall be without its flower-garden."

Villiers did not give them at once any extent of ground beyond what might enable them to keep their pig, and, if they manifested sufficient habits of improvement, their cow. He did not think that to convert the labourer into a small farmer—a farmer without either capital or skill, to extract from the earth its proper amount of fertility, was consistent either with sound morals, or sound economy, or sound politics. But he did take care that even the labourer should have the means, not only of subsistence, but of improvement. Mr. Atkinson, in calculating their wages, had recommended a certain sum as the rate most usual in the neighbourhood. He feared that by exceeding it on one estate discontent would be produced on others. But Villiers authoritatively, and almost sternly, rebuked him.

"Calculate," he said, "not what others give, or what the labourer, driven to desperation, will consent to receive rather than perish by starvation, but what he ought to have—what a Christian should give to his brother. Ensure to him a subsistence, simple and frugal, but plentiful and wholesome. It is with his body that he labours, and his body we must nurture. Provide for him some innocent indulgencies. Let him have his little feast-days, even his occasional luxuries. What is the weary monotony of life without some recreation? And he who toils with his body must be recreated in his body. Calculate for accidents, for sickness, for old age. Teach him prudence, by giving him wherewithal to be prudent — something to lay by against the winter's day. Provide also for the rearing of a family. They whose minds are enlarged, and their enjoyments varied, may endure life in comparative solitude, and make a home for themselves in their studies or imaginations; but for the poor and uneducated a home is necessary. And let us take care that the fulfilment of a command from Heaven —'increase and multiply'— does not generate misery instead of happiness, hatred instead of love, crime instead of goodness, by coupling it with the embitterments of poverty and the dread of destitution. The peasant must educate his children. He should have the means of sending them out into the world—not in a vain effort to rise into a higher sphere than that in which nature has placed them, but to gain their bread by honest labour. Lastly, he must have the means of being merciful and charitable himself, and of casting even his mite into the treasury of the House of God. These are the calculations to be made when we are estimating the rate of wages to the labourer; and

with nothing short of this ought a Christian landlord to be content."

Mr. Atkinson heard him, and looked up with
amazement, and even doubted whether these new
Oxford notions had not turned Villiers's head; and
one day he even went so far as to consult with
Mrs. Atkinson on the propriety of remonstrating
against such extravagance, which must utterly ruin
the estate. But, after the trial of three years, he
found that instead of being ruined the estate was
increased in value: and at last even the Conservative principles of the cool, calculating, wary, and
practical agent gave way to the energy and loftiness of Villiers's theory.

Nor had Villiers forgotten their recreation. In
the centre of the hamlet he had marked out the
village green, with its tall elm-trees grouped about
it, its cricket-ground, its maypole—every thing that
could recall a second Auburn. He had encouraged
the villagers to form a little band of music, which
played in the summer evenings on the green, while
the old women sat with their spinning-wheels at the
doors of their houses, and the younger men practised
all kinds of athletic games, Villiers himself often
standing by and looking on, and with him Charles
Bevan; for Bevan also he had been enabled to fix
in the parish of Hawkstone, and to give him the
living, vacant by the death of Dr. Grant; and in
this little outlying hamlet resided one of his curates,
in that neat thatched cottage embowered in honey-
suckles and roses, which nestled close to the lowly
but reverend village church.

And with Bevan there often came a lady—simple,
gentle, sensible, and refined, and clinging to his arm
with affectionate reverence. And the same delicate
and amiable Mary Vincent, who could not go to a
ball to dance over the sufferings of her fellow-

creatures, now, as Bevan's wife, became his chief
aider and almoner in ministering to the wants of
his poor. And this hamlet was in an especial
manner their favourite resort, for here Villiers was
first trying the experiment of transplanting the
better part of that population of the town, which,
having been created by the sudden rise of its manufactures, had been thrown out of employment by
their as sudden fall. When Mr. Smith's foreign
speculations had failed, and his foreign correspondents, having once experienced that the commodities which he had furnished them were made
up out of rotten materials, had abandoned all connection with him, Villiers found that the bank-
ruptcy of the manufacturers had thrown upon the
poor-rates of the parish a vast body ·of indigent
workmen reduced to starvation; and this was the
great problem which occupied his thoughts, and perplexed him with almost insurmountable difficulties.
On a small scale he was called on to solve the
same problem, which England is called on to solve
upon a vast one, and which, however it may be
staved off for a time by some temporary revival of
trade, or by the sacrifice of the agricultural interest,
must ultimately stare us in the face, and be solved
at the peril of our life, as soon as other countries
have learnt, as they rapidly are learning, that they
need not depend for manufactures on any but their
own resources.

One mode, indeed, was offered to Villiers, not of
removing the evil, but of postponing it, with the
certainty of bringing it ultimately upon him, aggravated beyond all hope of remedy. The Messrs.
Silkem came to him, and informed him that, being
nearly, if not wholly, ruined by their past manufacturing speculations, they must stop payment, and
throw out of employment all their workmen, unless

Villiers could supply them the means of taking
Mr. Smith's vacant factory, and, by demanding no
rent for it, could enable them to carry on their speculations on a more extended scale.   And they supported their petition by the irrefragable argument
that manufacturers were the very heart's-blood of
the British empire, and that Villiers, as an agriculturist, must therefore be content to be sacrificed
in their support : nor could they at all understand
the reasoning by which Villiers calmly replied to
them — that he had claims upon him for his money
as well as they had for theirs ; that especially the
Church depended upon him for its support, which
there was no probability of its receiving from the
manufacturers ; that the surrender of his claim to
rent would only enable and tempt them to reduce
the wages of the workmen, who would in no degree
be relieved by it ; and that if ruin hitherto had
been the consequence of past speculation, future
and more extended speculation could only end in
an aggravation of the same evil.   Villiers stated
this, and much more ; but Messrs. Silkem had been
to London, and had attended a meeting of the Anti-
Corn-Law League at Covent Garden Theatre, and
they were wholly unable to comprehend his arguments.   Villiers, however, was immoveable ; and
he astonished them even more by informing them
that it was not his intention to allow Mr. Smith's
factory to be again occupied in that manner, under
any circumstances, or at any rent.   He did not
think that any amount of wealth which it might
enable Mr. Smith to accumulate for himself was at
all a compensation for the evils inflicted on a place
by bringing together a manufacturing population,
exposed to all the temptations of such a life, and
fluctuating daily between the extremes of destitution
and of self-indulgence.

The Messrs. Silkem and all the other political economists of the town opened their eyes widely at this announcement, uttered sundry profound, and not complimentary exclamations on the subject of Oxford opinions, and prophesied that Hawkstone would be ruined, and that Mr. Villiers must go to gaol. But Hawkstone had been ruined already, and Villiers did not go to gaol. He reduced his own personal expenditure to the lowest possible amount, confined his establishment to necessary servants, with the addition of a number of young boys whom he took from the schools, and caused to be trained up under his own roof, and under the eye of an experienced, well-principled, religious house-steward, and the instruction of a chaplain, that they might be fitted for various domestic situations as they grew up. And though no one was more alive to the duty and expediency of maintaining in those who are called to govern an exterior aspect of dignity, he thought that, in a crisis like the present, even this was to be sacrificed to the more pressing necessity of providing for the poor. " The Church," he would say to Bevan, " rather than that the poor should starve, would sell even the vessels of the altar."

But in the meanwhile there lay before him the large, unmanageable, destitute population of the town ; and how were they to be provided for ? Happily he was enabled to employ the assistance of Bevan, as the rector of the parish, and Bevan was not single-handed. His first thought and plan had been to gather round him a small body of clergy as his curates, who might live under the same roof, at the same table, and might govern the parish, large as it was, effectually by their united labour. And he found no difficulty in accomplishing his purpose. Oxford—the maligned, suspected Oxford—supplied

him with a number of young men, some already in
holy orders, some preparing to enter them, who
were rejoiced after taking their degree to place
themselves under his guidance, and, directed by
him in their course of reading, to pursue their
studies together, while they took a part in attending
the schools, visiting the poor and sick, and cele-
brating divine service.

At eight o'clock every morning, Bevan himself,
with his seven curates, went in a little procession
to the parish church; at four o'clock in the afternoon the same spectacle was seen: and though the
cold sneered, and the profligate mocked, and the
ignorant and self-willed declared that to worship
the Almighty twice a day, as the church of their fathers prescribed and commanded, was mere popery,
the better spirits — the poor, whose only comfort
could be found in religion, and even the earnest,
sincere Dissenters, confessed that the act was
good; and many of them came also. Bevan was an
admirable musician; and in the evenings of week-
days, with the assistance of an able teacher, he
gathered round him a little choir, and soon, very
soon, he was enabled to introduce into the solemnities of divine worship as much music as gave to it
its due outward charms, without sacrificing the realities of internal devotion to the pleasure of the ear.
And strange as it may seem to hear of a body of
seven curates employed in a living of scarcely more
than seven hundred a-year, yet the blessing of
heaven seemed to descend upon Bevan's means, as
on the widow's cruise.

He also, like Villiers, reduced his establishment
and personal expenditure to bare necessaries. Instead
of furnishing the rectory-house as modern refinement would require, he gave up all but two or three
rooms to his curates. Villiers enabled him to build on

to it, not a large drawing-room and a best bed-room, but two simple, ancient-looking apartments, with open arched roof and latticed windows, one for a little dining-hall, the other for a library ; and until means could be procured for furnishing this with books, Villiers removed into it the theological portion of his own collection. There was a charm in the community of labour and study, in the association of charity, in the regular services of the Church, in the order and decency of the system of life, in the religious and tranquil tone that pervaded the whole little community, which made a curacy of Hawkstone an object of desire and ambition to many a young man. And Bevan soon found that, instead of being required to pay eighty pounds a-year to each of his curates, he could command as many as he wanted, who were satisfied to devote their labours to him as an exercise for their profession with scarcely any remuneration whatever, and whose private means even enabled them to contribute considerably to the funds of the little association. One of them died under Bevan's roof—a young man of rank and private fortune, whom Bevan had rescued from much evil at Oxford, and had watched over with the greatest care. And, to the surprise of all, it was found that he had left a considerable sum for the permanent foundation and endowment of a body of seven clergymen in Hawkstone, to be placed under the control of the rector, and employed by him in his parochial ministrations.

Even from the first Bevan never had despaired. Beattie, and Villiers, and himself were in daily communication ; and they comforted, strengthened, and supported each other.

" Let us plan and commence," said Villiers, " what is needed for the Church, what is right, what is good. Even though it seem gigantic in idea and

desperate in execution, Heaven will provide the
means. Heaven never failed a mighty work conceived in faith and nurtured with prayer."

And it was with this little body of clergy that
Bevan and Villiers proposed to grapple with the mass
of indigence and misery now left in the streets of
Hawkstone, as shapeless rocks and fragments of
ruin are left in the bed of a torrent, when the waters
are exhausted, or the current turned.

The first refuge which presented itself for the
most destitute was the Union poor-house.   But
this Villiers steadily repudiated.   " While I have
bread to spare," he said, " no poor member of
Christ's body, no starving child of the Church in
this place, shall ever enter the poor-house. If their
poverty be a crime, the result of their own fault, and
the poor-house is to be the gaol and place of correction,
in which they are to be brought to repentance, a system and place of correction, of which the Church is
not the soul, is not fit to receive them. And if their
poverty be a visitation from heaven upon innocent
beings, far less shall they be doomed for it to the
ignominy, the privation, the confinement, and the
hopelessness of a gaol.   No, Bevan," he exclaimed,
indignantly, " let others provide as they may for
the poor of their own persuasion ; our children, the
children of the Church, must be fed and comforted
in their afflictions, at whatever cost, by the Church
herself.

He selected the families in which he could discern sufficient seeds of good, and transplanted them
into the hamlet, which has been mentioned already ;
and three other little settlements he proposed to
form in other portions of the park.   And when Mr.
Atkinson remonstrated faintly against breaking up
the pasture, and killing down the deer, Villiers took
him to the highest ridge of the park, and bade him

look down upon the famishing families of Hawkstone, which Mr. Atkinson knew were crowded into its ruin-smitten streets, and then he pointed to a herd of deer, which bounded gracefully along the green grassy glades, and Villiers asked which in the sight of heaven was most precious, and for which a Christian ought soonest to provide food? Some families also there were, who, having saved a little capital, were anxious to seek for employment in the colonies, and Villiers willingly aided them to depart. But he did not send them forth with only money in their pocket; he opened a communication with more than one of those devoted men, who have recently gone forth as bishops of the Church into our distant settlements. He provided for their reception, at their landing, into the bosom of the Church. Bevan procured for them from the bishop of his diocese recommendatory letters, attesting their church-membership, and entreating the assistance of the faithful for them wherever they might be. He communicated also with the captains of the ships in which they embarked, appointed an agent to receive them on their arrival at the nearest sea-port, took care that they should not be exposed during the voyage to the contamination and miseries of which he had seen too many specimens in the ordinary course of emigration. And it was with many a deep and fervent thanksgiving that he received from them repeated accounts of their arrival and prosperity, and of the blessings and mutual comforts which they had derived from clinging all together in a strange soil, and planting themselves in its unoccupied wastes as a body, not as scattered individuals. Since for this also Villiers had provided; and when he planned the sending forth of a little band of emigrants, as far as possible he selected those who were united together by bonds of blood or friendship.

He brought them together, and accustomed them to
look upon themselves as associated in a little polity.
Before they left the country he endeavoured to
provide among them for the various wants and arts
most important in an infant settlement.   One was a
mason, another a carpenter, another a blacksmith,
another a tailor.   And when he was enabled to purchase a large tract of land in one of the settlements,
he immediately remitted funds to its bishop, that he
might build upon it a church, and plant at least three
clergymen together on the spot, for whose subse-
quent support he provided by enforcing in the
terms of tenure the full payment of tithes, and for
the necessary multiplication of churches and ministers, and all the Levitical functions of the Church, by
setting apart in the most favourable positions valuable endowments of land for colleges.   He was surprised to find how little this cost.   The purchase of
one picture, the expense of one entertainment in
London, the losses of one night's gambling, even
the waste of a stable and of fox-hounds, would have
swallowed up sums, which now enabled him to diffuse blessings all around him.

And by degrees the mass of poverty and misery
melted away.   One rule—a strict, severe, almost
stern rule—he laid down to Bevan in all his ministrations of mercy.   Seek out the children of the
Church, those who have not fallen into schism, who
are not guilty of heresy.   Even those, who have,
must not be allowed to perish.   But let us take care,
while we succour their bodies, to think also of their
souls.   Let us not allow them to mistake an act of
necessary charity as toleration or indifference to
their sin.   Mark in the clearest way you can the
difference between a churchman and a dissenter;
it may awaken them to a knowledge of their guilt.
And Bevan found indeed that there was no disposi-

tion in Dissenters themselves to neglect their own poor; and that he was only adopting an exclusive principle which had long been enforced by themselves.

But there was still a large portion of the population, which could not be transferred into the hamlets; and Villiers knew that manufactures, in some proportion, were as necessary to the well-being and even existence of society as agriculture. What he had denounced and abhorred, both in its spirit and in its consequences, was the profligate extension of manufactures for the purpose of accumulating wealth in the hands of a few individuals, in a boundless fluctuating market, subject to reckless competition, tempting to every species of fraud, almost compelling the reduction of the labourers' wages to the minimum of subsistence, liable to panics, to gluts, to stagnation, to all the vicisitudes of gambling speculation, and thus hardening the hearts of one class by the idolatry of wealth, and eating like a cancer into the souls and the bodies of the other. Manufactures, with a fixed market, Villiers resolved to encourage. He therefore bound down all, over whom he had any influence, to obtain the commodities which they required from their own immediate neighbourhood. It was easy to exercise such a superintendence over the sellers that they should not convert this seeming monopoly into an occasion of fraud and extortion. And though the buyers might at times have been able to obtain a better article at a cheaper price from a distant spot, Villiers cast to the winds the miserable maxim of economists, that "the first law of prudence is to buy cheap, and to sell dear."

" The first law of God," he said to Bevan, "is to love Him, and to do His will. And among the records of his will I find no such law, nothing ap-

proaching to it,—nothing which does not seem to
hold it up to reprobation and scorn. And the second
law is to love our neighbours as ourselves, and to
do to every man as we would that he should do
unto us. Let us rather wear this coarse cloth, rather eat ill-made bread, rather live in an ill-con-
structed house for a time, bearing patiently `these
trifling vexations, than allow our brother to starve
at our doors because he has not yet acquired perfection in his art : and this perfection let us strive
to teach him; and, instead of calculating how little
we can give for the produce of others' labours, to
enable those around us to enjoy their comforts and
to improve their condition, let us rather think how
much we can give without injury to those other
interests, which Heaven has commanded us to
consult. Defraud not the hireling of his wages ;
wring not from the poor all that can be extorted in
the shape of cheap prices. You are purchasing your
own indulgences with the blood of the poor ; for
from their wages the reduction must be ultimately
extracted."

And when it was necessary to procure articles,
such as foreign commodities, from a distance, Villiers did not send, or teach others to send, to the me-
tropolis, and there purchase them by wholesale, at a
cheaper rate. He gave to the shopkeeper in Hawkstone—the grocer, or the wine-merchant, or the
bookseller—an introduction to the first wholesale
houses in London, where they might be sure of obtaining what was really good ; and through the
shopkeepers in his own native place he made all his
purchases, insisting on their receiving such an
amount of profit on their outlay as justice demanded,
and insisting also that the same quality of article
which he required himself should be supplied to
the poor at the same price.

But what Villiers was most anxious to encourage

was a system of domestic manufactures — the spinning, knitting — every thing which could be carried
on round the family fire-side. He loved to see the
old women sunning themselves with their wheels
before the doors, and the younger females within
employed in works of the kind under the eye of
their parents. And, in cases where this could not
be accomplished, he proceeded to establish a manufactory of his own in Mr. Smith's deserted building — but a manufactory on very opposite principles
to those which have made nearly one-sixth of England a sink of misery and vice. Villiers's object
was not to accumulate money for himself, but to
provide necessary comforts for others, and in doing
this to discover, not how little might be given to
the labourer, but how much consistently with the
object in view. Having calculated the extent of
his market in his own immediate neighbourhood,
he limited also the amount of his production. He
estimated the price set upon it, not by the extreme
point to which competition — often dishonest and
desperate competition — might be able to drive it
down, but by the cost of the raw material, and machinery, and capital, and by that amount of wages,
which, as a Christian, he felt due to the labourer.
And so far as he could restrict his consumers to
his own market, he could command from them this
price, which, though higher than that of neighbouring districts, was fully compensated by its
enabling the workmen to give a higher price reciprocally for the produce of the soil. The terms
were higher, but the proportion was scarcely altered, and the money all circulated in the neighbourhood. And in the wages due to the workmen
Villiers calculated much which an economist would
have rejected with disdain. He dealt with him as
with the agricultural labourer. He provided for

him instruction, hours and means of relaxation,
opportunities of worship, holidays — the holidays of
the Church, enjoyments of various kinds.   Mr.
Smith's factory, instead of glaring with lights at
midnight, and sounding with wheels both day and
night, now enjoyed its hours of nightly repose, its
intervals of daily rest, its Sabbaths, and its sports.
All was carried on under the direction of Bevan
and his curates.   The strictest discipline was maintained in preventing the evils of indiscriminate
association ; the greatest care was taken in encouraging industry, the firmest severity exercised
in chastising vice.   Villiers did not indeed make a
fortune by it, but he made others good and happy ;
and he knew no other use of money.   The economists looked on and smiled in scorn, and proved by
the irrefragable arguments of figures that a system
of restrictions and of confined markets must be
ruinous ; and that in the nineteenth century it was
madness even to argue against free trade, and its
necessary consequence, competition : but Villiers
was not ruined, and at the end of each year he found
his income increasing.   Heaven had given the promise, and nature, he knew not how, realised it.

Such had been some of the economical theories
and acts of Villiers in relation to the unhappy town
of Hawkstone ; and, seconded by Bevan and his co-
adjutors, he soon had the satisfaction of finding a
very considerable impression made upon its population.   From a turbulent, factious, schismatic, irreligious, profligate place, it became quiet, orderly,
decent, and religious.   Two new churches sprang
up, and the old venerable church, reseated and repaired, was converted, by the zeal of the inhabitants,
almost into a little cathedral.   The alms increased,
the irregular associations of voluntary and rash zeal
were laid aside for more ecclesiastical operations

expressly sanctioned by the bishop. One after another the schismatic chapels became empty; and notwithstanding the outcry first raised under the watchword of Popery, at last Bevan, prudent and cautious in his zeal, and never seeking to restore a form till he had created the spirit, with the support of his bishop triumphed over all opposition. Even Mr. O'Foggarty, baffled and disappointed, was compelled to make arrangements for abandoning his mission as a hopeless work. When the true image of the Church in all its beauty was exhibited to poor as well as rich, and its true principles were distinctly enunciated and enforced, not by an individual, but by a body, few could close their eyes, or withhold their obedience, but the ignorant and self-willed; the rest returned to the fold from which they had strayed, and Hawkstone was comparatively at unity with itself.

Again and again, penetrated with all which Villiers had done for them, the inhabitants entreated him to add one more obligation, and to become their member. And they did indeed expel Mr. Marmaduke Brook both from his seat in Parliament, and from his 1500*l.* a-year commissionership. But Villiers would not enter the House of Commons. He felt that his first duties lay immediately around him; and until he could accomplish his work near to his own home, he refused to be distracted from it for nearly half the year by the necessity of living in London. And he had other reasons besides.

He could not join in any act which might restore to power avowed subverters of order, loyalty. and religion — men whose principles, if not their practice, involved the overthrow of the monarchy and the corruption and suppression of the Christian faith. Villiers abhorred Liberalism. But neither

could he lift his hand to maintain in power an opposite party whose conduct might no less threaten
the insensible subversion of all that was holy and
venerable.

At the very thought of one theory of government then prevalent, he sickened and turned away
with disgust. He who recognised as the first law of
his being, as the first treasure of human knowledge,
as the palladium of states, and the salt of the earth,
divine truth, the truth of the divine nature as revealed by the Divine Being himself—he who, instead
of asking, with Pilate, "What is truth?" had examined and found it enshrined in a Catholic Church
—he who, having once recognised that Church as
the creature and minister of God, would allow neither
heresy nor schism to tamper with or persecute it—
he who knew that in divine truth, and divine commands, and divine promises, there is a power eternal
and omnipotent, and that if man will only boldly
witness to them, and reverently obey them, even the
madness of the people must be powerless against
them—he whose whole conduct was based and shaped
upon the highest of all principles, and who never
acted without a principle wiser than all expediency,
and safer than any cowardice — such a man might
well shrink, with as much pain and aversion as a
Christian sinner may feel towards brother sinners,
from that miserable, compromising, vacillating, unprincipled policy, which now, under a specious
name, had been elevated to the rule of the British empire. Villiers did not often trust himself
to converse on it, for he bore before him the injunction "not to speak evil of dignities;" and he was
humble and gentle in himself, and knew that he had
sins of his own to answer for. But about this time
he wrote a letter in answer to an application for his
vote and interest in favour of a government candi-

date; and as it has fallen into our hands we may as well communicate it to our readers.

" DEAR SIR,

" I am unwilling to omit a duty, which the constitution imposes on me, or to decline to give a vote in the ensuing election. But, in the present aspect of affairs, I can scarcely exercise this privilege without lending my support to men, and principles, and measures, which, whether on one side or on the other, would seem to be offensive to the great Ruler of all things, and full of injury to the country. If you would offer yourself to the electors of the county, as resolved to resist the further aggressions of democracy upon the church and the throne, and to aid in maintaining the true principles both of religion and of loyalty, though you should be compelled to stand almost solitary in the House of Commons, and could do little more than witness to truth, like the prophets of old, in the midst of contempt and unbelief, still you would ultimately effect, under a blessing from Heaven, no little good; and, whatever still remains in the heart of England of reverence, and faith, and courage, would gladly catch at such a voice, and cease at least to despair of their parliament and their country. To such professions as this I would willingly give my support ; but to any one who identifies his political opinions with the course hitherto pursued by Conservative governments, I must decline offering any assistance.

" After painful, but careful consideration, I am compelled to believe that nothing can inflict on the constitution and welfare of the British empire more fatal and deadly injuries than the policy now called Conservative.

" I have no doubt of the personal honesty, or of the good intentions of individuals; but neither of

these can atone for the absence of elevated principles and true wisdom. Prudence in the government of nations cannot be separated from wisdom,
nor practical expediency from deep philosophy,
without ultimate destruction to both; and no worldly
talent, no industry, no financial ingenuity, no dexterity in managing a party, can atone for that
avowed and resolute abandonment of all high principle, which is now held to be a necessary condition
of any (so called) government. To have asserted and
introduced this principle as an axiom of government
is in itself a blow to all sound views of political
society, from which it can scarcely recover. Individuals may have sinned in it before; but till recent days and trials it has been carefully excluded
from sight, and never boldly avowed, except in the
worst periods of the democracies of Greece.

"In attributing to this particular policy in particular hands the serious degree of mischief which
has been expressed above, I wish to speak coolly
and deliberately, and without the slightest tendency
to exaggeration. And the statement is grounded
upon this fact, that great truths can never be destroyed by enemies; they can only be betrayed by
professed friends. An armed force cannot annihilate my right to a property; but one rash concession of my own will extinguish it for ever.
And the true and elevated principles which raised
and preserved the British empire, however cast out
and trampled on for a time under the predominance
of a democratical power, might yet remain in themselves untouched and secured by a protest, as a standard of truth, to which the better part of the nation
might still appeal, and round which they might
hope to rally, and ultimately restore them to power.
But if those who are charged with their maintenance corrupt, and adulterate, and deny them, and

no further protest is raised in their behalf, they will perish from the face of our laws, and from the eyes of the people, and must be lost, it may be, for ever.

" Upon these grounds the Conservatives of England, and not any democratical party, if the British Empire be destroyed, must be its destroyers.

" And already much has been done towards it. By one act it has been established that, even where the Church and the truth of Christ are concerned, governments may yield to fear even what they confess to be full of peril. And that, where evil is inevitable, it may be perpetrated by those who believe it to be evil, rather than that power should be given into the hands of opponents. By another, the great maxim of our constitution, and the only safeguard of our representative system, that the representative should not be the echo and the tool of his constituents, but a counsellor and adviser for the whole empire, was surrendered, when the present leader of the Conservatives, courteously, but with no far prospective wisdom, retired from the representation of his University. It is the very keystone of society, and the pervading law of all progress in the British constitution, that no changes in it shall be made, but only developments. And yet, even in contradiction of the authors of the Reform Act, Conservatives have declared that act to be a revolution, and yet have themselves consented to take a part in the establishment of that revolution, and in carrying out its principles. To the House of Commons was virtually surrendered the right of the crown to appoint its ministers, when it was declared that since the Reform Act, no minister should hold office without the approbation of the Commons. The appointment of ambassadors was abandoned when one whom the crown had chosen was permitted to retire from his post at

the command of the Commons. The very height
and essence of all democratical tyranny has been
maintained, by defending the omnipotence of the
Commons against the laws and judges of the realm.
An Ecclesiastical Commission has been created,
which has broken up the outward system of the
Church, violated its oaths, tampered with its independence, destroyed the rights of private property,
dried up the sources of individual endowments,
mutilated those cathedral corporations which should
have been restored and revivified to become the
chief arms of its strength, and annihilated Epis-
copates for money. And when the Church,
awakened from her trance, has called out for redress
and mercy, her voice has been listened to with
indifference. The defence of the Church has been
rested, not upon its divine institution and authority, but upon vile and worthless titles, which may
be shattered and cast to the winds by the first
impugner, upon compact, upon expediency, upon
private opinions of its morality and goodness. And
in this statesmen have acted as an advocate who,
when charged with maintaining a title to property,
should suppress and stifle the true deeds, and should
put forward only forgeries — weak pleas, which a
breath would blow to atoms, and which no defence
can clear from treachery but the apology of ignorance. It has been resolved to maintain and propagate a scheme of education which is emptied of all
religious truths, in which the teacher, and the State
in his person, stands before the pupil as either too
ignorant to decide on divine truth amidst contending
falsehoods, or too indifferent to assert it. And it is
proposed now, it is said, to sanction the extension of
such a system to the upper as to the lower classes;
and at the same time to introduce it into one of the
strongholds of the Church, even into an ancient

university of the empire, as it has already been
insisted on in founding colleges in our colonies.
And the great maxim of the English law, that endowments shall not be guarded, or even permitted,
by the State, unless they are devoted to definite
ends of goodness and wisdom, has been destroyed
by a voluntary offer to perpetuate possessions left
by men without any fixed creed, in the hands of
others, whose creed is heresy and blasphemy.
These are but some of the principles which a policy,
compelled by external pressure openly to repudiate
the assertion of any principle but expediency, to
shrink from truth and from law as from an abo-
minable thing, to refuse to tie itself up by any bold
assertion of truth, which might warn or instruct
the people, to guard always some loophole for sub-
terfuge and evasion, and to profess but one rule of
action — the succumbing to circumstances under
pressure, has admitted into the practice of men
pledged nominally to be the guardians of all the
highest interests of the empire, and which have even
been stamped upon our statute books.

" If I cannot look upon such acts, and upon such
principles, except with reprobation — if I dread the
responsibility of contributing by any voice of mine
to the continuance of power which such policy must
abuse, and of trusts which it must betray — and if, in
the absence of any higher spirit, at present, to protest against these deeds and maxims, I see no course
left but to stand aloof from the administration of
public affairs, and to endeavour in a more private
and humble sphere to remedy the evils of that portion of society which is immediately placed under
my care, you must neither charge me with calum-
niating the character of men respectable in the
eyes of the world, nor with shrinking from my
duty.

" The spirit of the people must be first changed, and then the spirit of their representatives may be changed likewise; that is, if Providence has not set his seal to the condemnation of England, and devoted it finally to destruction.

" I beg you to believe me, sir,

" Your obedient faithful servant,

" ERNEST VILLIERS."

CHAP. XXI.

WE left Villiers slowly riding home, by moonlight, along the brow of the park. His heart was full—many other thoughts were crowding on him besides the recollections which we have just recalled. And abandoning himself to them, he allowed his horse to pursue the path most familiar to him, till the steed brought its master, not to the gateway of the house, but to the old oak bench, which commanded a view of Hawkstone, and to the silvery beech, whose trunk, inscribed with initials not yet obliterated, had arrested Villiers's step the first day of his return to the seat of his ancestors. Under that beech the horse stopped — it had been long his master's custom so to do : and through the thick tangled underwood, which clothed the brow of the steep declivity, an opening had been cleared away, through which the eye could rest, not on the windings of the river, or on the grey tower of Hawkstone Church, but on the distant white colonnade of Lord Claremont's house, embosomed in its grove of stately oaks. And Villiers gazed on it mournfully, and yet affectionately and reverently.

" To-morrow! " he thought within himself, " to-morrow ! " And the reins dropped from his hand ; and while the tears gushed from his eyes, he clasped his hands in prayer.

And at the same hour what was passing with the usual inmates of that pile on which Villiers was gazing ? One, who had once been its inmate, the hand of death had already smitten. Lord Clare-

mont lay mouldering in the vault of his ancestors,
within the chapel of the restored Priory. But Lady
Eleanor was still living; and at that moment where
was she? She was not in her own mansion, but
in a small, simple, but solemn-looking chamber, the
latticed oriel of which looked out upon the grey
tower of Hawkstone Church, and the green meadow,
and tall clustered elms, and gently-flowing river,
which nearly encircled the old, once-ruined hospice
of the Béguinage of Hawkstone. Ruined it was
no longer. Its simple gables, its humble wooden
cloister, roughly but quaintly carved, its clustered
chimneys, its buttressed gateway, which shut it out
from the too near vicinity of the town, its dim-
lighted refectory marked by the large square-headed
windows, and not left without their little emblazon-
ments of heraldry and scrolls of texts,—even the
little chapel, no longer a stabling for cows, had all
been restored—all touched and finished with that
exquisite delicacy of feeling, that taste for severe
truth which pervaded every work of Villiers, and
which no mere technical skill, nothing but a deep
philosophy and a Christian spirit, can ever attain
in art.

And in that chamber, before an open Bible, her
long beautiful hair let down over her face, her eyes
upturned to Heaven, her hands clasped in intense
anguish, her cheeks wet with tears, Lady Eleanor
was kneeling in prayer. She was praying for light,
for strength, for guidance, for support, now when
the hour of trial was approaching. " To-morrow,"
she murmured, like Villiers, " to-morrow!" and
then, shuddering and shrinking, she bowed down
her head upon the holy volume, and nearly drooped
to the ground. " To-morrow !" — that day of
awe !

So absorbed was she in the contemplation that

she did not hear a gentle voice at the door, or, when
no answer was given, the gentle foot which entered
the room. It was a lady, attired, like Lady Eleanor,
in black, but seemingly not as the garb of mourning.
Her dress was simple, and not uncommon ; and
yet there was something in it—perhaps it was the
plain cap, perhaps the broad collar of purest white—
which distinguished its wearer from the ordinary
world. Age had stamped her features with an
impress of gravity and dignity, chastened by a mild
resignation. Though her hair, plainly banded
across her forehead, was nearly grey, her manner
and movements still retained activity and strength.
She paused, as on entering the room she saw Lady
Eleanor, and gazed on her with a deep look of
sympathy and affection. But Lady Eleanor heard
her move, and looked round. She did not rise from
her knees, but stretched out her hands to her in
silence, and besought her with piteous looks to take
her seat where Lady Eleanor herself was kneeling.
And Mrs. Bevan did so. And bending down over
the drooping figure, she clasped Lady Eleanor in
her arms, laid her head upon her own bosom, and,
without speaking, allowed her own tears to fall
thick upon her face.

" My friend! my mother! my more than
mother ! " faltered Lady Eleanor, " pray for me,
for I am in a great strait. I thought the bitterness
of the struggle was past, but it has come upon me
again — an hour of darkness—now in the last moment. Pray for me ! "

Mrs. Bevan made no reply, except by stooping
down and pressing her affectionately to her bosom.
At last she said, " I cannot wonder at it. Hardly
would the tempter leave you without one more
conflict. But will you not see some one— some one
who could comfort and enlighten you more than I

could? My son is here. Or shall I send for Mr.
Beattie?"

" No," replied Lady Eleanor, " it is too late —
not at this hour of night—not for me. And yet—
O my mother! is it not a fearful, an awful thing to
turn aside from the faith of our fathers!"

Mrs. Bevan gently disengaged herself from the
almost convulsive embrace of the suffering convert.
And in a few minutes Bevan, who was in an adjoining room, despatched a note to Beattie, at his
mother's request, begging that even at so late an
hour he would come into Hawkstone. It was
Beattie, who under Providence had been the means,
not of exciting, but of deciding those doubts respecting the truth of the Romish Church, which
had been raised in Lady Eleanor's mind chiefly by
the mistaken conduct of O'Foggarty. To Beattie,
ever since those doubts had arisen, and chiefly since
Lord Claremont's death, she had been induced to
apply more and more frequently, and to look up
to him almost as a parent ; and under his judicious
and wise instruction she had at length conscientiously resolved on taking that solemn step which
was contemplated the day following, and requesting
the Bishop of the diocese to admit her into the communion of the Catholic Church in England.

And Beattie lost no time in following the messenger into Hawkstone. He had witnessed in the
delicate, elevated, pure mind of Lady Eleanor so
much of intense suffering during the conflict through
which she had passed, that he was prepared to find
it recur with even increased violence now when
the trying hour was approaching. And though he
trusted much to the judicious and affectionate support of Mrs. Bevan, with whom Lady Eleanor had
been domesticated for the last month, he knew that
her acute understanding might suggest doubts and

temptations which could only be counteracted by
one more experienced in the controversy. Beattie
had studied it deeply; and having studied it deeply,
he did not despise it—did not think light of its
difficulties—did not presume, as so many now presume, to despatch it with a light word and a bold
laugh.

On his arrival at the Béguinage he found Lady
Eleanor more calm. The paroxysm was past; but
the deep and fervent gratitude with which she
clasped her hands, when he entered the room, satisfied him that his presence was needed. He took
her hands in his own, uttered a blessing upon her,
beneath which she bowed down her head reverently and humbly, and then he led her to a seat
by him. She would have fallen on her knees before
him, so intense was her feeling, so deep her reverence for him; but he entreated her to be composed.

"Dear Lady Eleanor," he said, "these feelings
are natural, and almost necessary—in some sense
they may be even right. And yet in all that you
have thought and done, and resolved to do, you
have proposed to yourself but one object—truth,
the truth of Heaven; and ought we to admit of any
other? But excited feeling of any kind is scarcely
a fit preparation for clearly discerning truth, least
of all in a moment of temptation; and it may be,
that this agony into which you have fallen, this
renewed darkness and perplexity, is the work—the
last work — of the tempter."

Lady Eleanor only replied by a deep groan.

"You have prayed," said Beattie — "prayed to
Heaven for light and aid. Let us pray together."
And, kneeling down by her side, he led up her
thoughts to the great source of all truth, and entreated comfort for her affliction, enlightenment for

her doubts, support in her weakness, and wisdom
for his own ministrations. "And now," he said,
when they rose from their knees, "tell me in what
thoughts and suggestions has originated this return
of doubts, which I had thought were long since
dispelled."

"I know not," replied Lady Eleanor, faintly.
"A cloud of darkness, of bewilderment, came over
me, as if there were nothing in the world true or
certain—as if all religion was a delusion, when the
best and wisest of men so differ in their views.
And then came the memory of my father, and of
her who was to me in my childhood even more than
a mother—that saint in heaven, Lady Esther. And
I thought within myself, how could I meet them
beyond the grave—a traitor, a renegade to the faith
of my fathers? Oh, Mr. Beattie! if you are deceiving
me—or rather (I meant not that), if you are deceived yourself! Where is the truth? and how
can we find it? Were it not better to remain where
Providence has placed us at our birth, than to
plunge into the dark gulph, with only the light of
our own blinded eyes?"

"It were indeed," answered Beattie, "it were
better, far better to remain patiently under any
system, however faulty, in which Providence has
placed us, than to attempt escape solely by the light
of our own eyes. Others have fled from Romanism
in this way, and their end has for the most part
been destruction. But you are not thus deluded.
Heaven, in making us Christians, as in making us
men, has willed that we should live, and that in all
our deeds we should act, not as individuals, but in
society, under rulers, as members of a body, as
children of a family. Think not, that, in abandoning the false system and the usurping rulers
under which you have so long lived, you are to be

left without a shelter or a guide. You are not deciding upon truth and falsehood, right and wrong, by its accordance with your own notions, without any thought of an authority by which it is to be decided for you : rather you are placing yourself under authority, and submitting yourself to your rightful ruler instead of an usurper."

"I know it," replied Lady Eleanor. "I have not forgotten what you have urged so often ; and yet when the hour approaches I tremble and doubt. Am I—am I fit to distinguish between the false prophet and the true, the false usurper and the lawful sovereign, any more than between falsehood and truth, good and evil, in themselves? Must not the dimness of my own eyes and the defilement of my own heart mix with and pervert my judgment in each case alike?"

"They may," replied Beattie, "and they must do so. But this is the trial placed before us all by Heaven, and from which we cannot be exempted. This is that exercise of our private judgment respecting which, whether it be a right or a duty, we need not ask; all that we know is, that we cannot escape from it. As reasoning beings we must persevere in it. And we are so far safe from the evils and sins of the licence of human will and of human reason when, in determining our course, we resolve to inquire, not which path seems best to ourselves, but who is the proper guide for us to follow—not what we shall adopt, but whom we shall obey."

"And yet," said Lady Eleanor, "alas ! all this I have heard from you before. But you must tell me it again. Tell it to me, and I will listen humbly."

"I would remind you," said Beattie, "of that great rule which we laid down for the right exercise of this choice. I warned you often and earnestly against looking for the test of a true commission from Heaven — for the seal of your rightful rulers in the Church — to any of those deceitful marks which are too commonly appealed to in this day. Look not for it to anything within yourself, or within the minds of others. It is an outward mark. Deem not that sanctity — such sanctity as most attracts the eye of man, or purity, or self-denial, or asceticism, or much praying, or much fasting, or much almsgiving, even if they really exist, are a test of truth. They may be found, and they have been found, in the authors of many a heresy and schism, and of revolt even from the moral laws of God, coupled with those hidden seeds of wilfulness, obstinacy, presumption, and pride, which are crimes no less than sensuality. Talent, learning, eloquence, you would not yourself look to. Providence, who knows our weakness, has not thus left us to the temptations of our own follies — has not trusted the criterion of truth to these inward marks, of which so many cannot be fully discerned, and so many must be liable to be mistaken by corrupt men: rather, he has sealed and marked his appointed servants with an external commission; and for this we must search. In judging this we are not liable to be deceived by our own prejudices, or by a morbid conscience. And now recall to your mind what has so often been urged to you on the comparative external commission of Romanism, and of the Church in England."

"And yet," said Lady Eleanor, "sanctity and truth cannot be separated."

"Not real sanctity," said Beattie, "not real truth. But Heaven has not confined the appointment of its ministers to holy men. Balaam prophesied, and Judas preached and wrought miracles;

and Scribes and Pharisees may sit in Moses' seat, and we may be bound to receive what they teach, though we may not do after their work. Such is the whole system of Providence. I wave the question now, whether the Romish Church be more holy than the English—whether those unhappy men within the English Church, to whom you appeal, and who, while they remain in the bosom of their mother, are treacherously reviling and betraying her, are marked by such signs of sanctity —that is, of humility, let us say—self-distrust, meekness, charity, as would constitute them safe guides of opinion. Whatever be the sanctity of such a communion, or of such men, it is no infallible test of a divine commission, as it would give no authority to preach, or to administer the Sacraments, without an outward call. O Lady Eleanor, let us not be deceived by this false plea, which has already torn the Church into sects, and is the very badge of that rationalism and dissent against which she must so earnestly strive."

"And yet," said Lady Eleanor, "even you have not blamed me, when I confessed that what I have seen myself in Hawkstone—the sanctity of this house for instance, the self-devotion and charity of its inmates, the dedication to religion of all the learning, and wealth, and labour, by which your own community has been restored and supported, and under the influence of which heresy and schism are vanishing from your neighbourhood—that all this has weighed deeply with me, and compelled me to think of the English Church in a light which it never wore, where I saw it only secularised and paralysed, and impotent for any great work of Christian love. I thought it could not bear such fruits as those which it bears here. Are not these marks of its truth?"

"They are marks, assuredly," said Beattie. "We may rest on them jointly with others. They are great comforts, and consolations, and supports. But let us first rest our allegiance on a visible external commission. Even if the Church of England could exhibit no such fruits—even if it remained for ever maimed and mutilated in its most important organs, it might be still the duty of her children to remain in her bosom, or to return to her from a state of schism, and to endeavour to perfect her organisation, while they reverently acknowledged her authority, even in her state of weakness. Her deficiencies are the deficiencies of individuals; they are not parts of her system. As well might we estimate the authority of our Creator by, the viciousness of men, who are his creatures, as the authority of a church by the sins of its members, so long as both Heaven and the Church, in all the formal promulgations of their law, protest against evil, and command holiness."

Lady Eleanor remained silent, and Beattie continued.

"And now," he said, "call to mind that in all this fearful conflict between truth and falsehood, still upon grand fundamental principles the whole of apostolical Christendom — the Eastern Church as well as the Romish, the Romish as well as the English—are solemnly agreed. All with one voice proclaim that Christ has founded one, and one Church only — all, that this Church is founded on the Apostles and Prophets—all, that with divine revelation man may not dare to mix any thing that is human — all, that the Church, from the first day to the end of the world, must be governed by externally-commissioned rulers, preaching because they are sent, and preaching only what they receive—all, that without the pale of the Church there is no promise of salvation, and that they who separate from it are guilty of a deadly sin, measured and punished in the sight of Heaven, like all other sins, by the degrees of light against which it has been committed. With these great truths acknowledged, a Christian, even in the midst of heresy and schism, cannot become an infidel. All that he has to guard against is the falling into either heresy or schism by departing from the apostolical doctrine, or from the apostolical polity of the Church. Thus far I am only stating the very principles under which you have been nurtured in Romanism. As you value your own soul, and the safety of the Church and of Divine truth, never abandon them. They are as valid and as true in the English as in the Romish Communion. The unity of the Church, the extinction of heresy, the suppression of schism, are objects not less dear to us, nay, dearer, than to any upholder of the papacy. And it is to save you from the guilt of schism, from helping to rend asunder the one unseamed garment of the Lord of Peace, that you are now called on to acknowledge the paramount claim of the English Church to your allegiance in this land.

" For the guilt of heresy I will for the present wave. I will lay aside all consideration of what, as an individual, I believe to be in the Romish system fearful corruptions of truth, criminal tamperings with the Divine ordinances—if not amounting wholly to formally declared heresy, at least filled with such a presumptuous and unevangelical spirit as to justify the name of Antichristian. Even though supported by the declarations of our own English Church, and by that of the East, and of all the reformed Episcopal communions, it is not necessary for us to sit in judgment on the sins of a sister church. If we were living in Rome, or in a

land where there was no Apostolical Church law-
fully constituted and perpetuated, but one which
acknowledged the Romish supremacy, I should
argue very differently. Then it would be necessary to examine the question of heresy — to
consider what was corrupt and vicious in the doctrines and practice of that Romish Church of which
Providence had made us members ; to endeavour,
by lawful, humble, and peaceful means, to change
the hearts of our rulers, and to bring them to correct what was amiss ; to obey them still in all things
lawful ; to refuse obedience only where our conscience, not leaning on itself, but supported by the
external testimony of the primitive and other
churches, denounced the act as criminal ; and to
submit without a murmur to any punishment which
might be inflicted on us. This would be our
course of proceeding if we were inhabitants of
Rome.

"But in England the case is wholly different.
Your first duty is to detach yourself from a state of
schism, to place yourself under your lawful rulers,
just as it is the first duty of a citizen, who has been
seduced into rebellion, not to cavil at or criticise
the laws, but to acknowledge the authority of his
lawful sovereign. When this has been done, then
we may proceed to examine what requires to be
improved, and take legitimate means to improve it.
And by what outward marks we know the English
Church to be our lawful mother and mistress in
this land you have often heard."

Lady Eleanor answered, faintly, "Yes ;" but she
drew her hands over her eyes, as if a mist were
hanging upon them, and sighed bitterly.

Beattie was deeply touched, and even alarmed.
He almost proposed to himself to postpone the
solemn ceremony for which he had so long been

training her mind, and which she had so earnestly
coveted. The sudden vacillation and misgiving
struck him at first as inexplicable. But he reflected how fearful is the shock which unsettles our
religious faith, especially one which uproots a
system so deeply entwined as Romanism with the
very life-strings of human nature. And Beattie
also knew that near to us and about us are tempters,
whom we cannot see, and to whom power may be
permitted for a time to perplex and disturb the
minds even of saints. He once more knelt down
with her in prayer ; for prayer is, he knew, the first
and best (if not the only) solution of all doubts.
And as he reached the close, touched by an affecting allusion, which brought before her the
image of her Saviour mourning over the rending
to pieces of his Church, she melted into tears, and
a weight seemed to pass from her heart. She looked
up, with her hands clasped fervently, her eyes
lifted up to Heaven with intense devotion and gratitude. And as Beattie would have raised her from
her knees, she shook her head, and bowed it upon
her breast.

" No," she said, " it is gone — it is past. Blessed
be His holy name! the dark hour is over. Strange
that it should ever have visited me. But it is gone
like a cloud. Alas! that I have sinned in doubt.
Pray for me that I may be forgiven !"

And Beattie did pray. And at last, calmed and
composed, Lady Eleanor rose from her knees, and
meekly and humbly she asked Beattie if she might
go over with him once more the grounds and reasons
which had fortified her resolution to ask admission
into the English Church.

" I am weak," she said ; " and such hours as I
have just passed (they are not the first) make me
tremble when I am left alone. They seem to come

from without, as if some inward light was suddenly withdrawn, and a black cloud permitted to settle on me; and then it rises up and floats away, and all seems bright, and peaceable, and clear as ever."

" They are permitted," replied Beattie, " to visit even the most favoured servants of Heaven; and prayer is our only protection and refuge against them, and in our moments of calm and quiet to dwell again and again upon those truths and facts, which are the reasonable foundation of our conduct. Remember what has so often been proved, that man may not dare to disturb either the doctrine or the ecclesiastical polity which has been positively established by an authority evidently Divine—that it was an acknowledged principle of ecclesiastical polity in the primitive ages, founded, if not upon direct apostolical injunctions, at least upon the practice of the universal Church, as well as upon sound reason, that one bishop should not interfere with the diocese of another, or one patriarch with another's patriarchate. The œcumenical councils are full of intimations to this purpose. The supremacy which the Pope claims over all other bishops, and on which alone he rests his title to interfere with your lawful bishops and to withdraw your obedience, is confessed by his own adherents to have been no part of the primitive system of the Church for the first four centuries at least. It was not recognised by one half of Christendom, the Eastern Church, nor by the ancient British Church, nor by the ancient Irish Church; it was repudiated even by early popes as a badge and sign of Antichrist. It rests on no evidence, no commission,—on nothing but the assumption of Rome herself. Its gradual reception by the Western Churches can be traced step by step to motives and acts of human policy and short-sighted expediency. It made its way in an age of darkness, in minds corrupted and deceived, when the criteria of historical truth were confessedly unknown and unpractised. Even then it encountered on all sides perpetual opposition and denial, especially in England, by which protests its rightfulness was contested, and even the title of modern prescription precluded. It is made by Rome an essential article of faith, but it is not found in any creed of the ancient Church, or in any part of the Bible, except as extracted from it by metaphors which might deduce anything from anything. It is enforced upon the mind, without having ever been defined, so as to become fixed and intelligible. Its extent is disputed even among Romanists themselves. It varies in different countries. It is made paramount to all questions of Divine truth. And if the power of human ministers of Heaven be recognised, Romanism cares little either for articles of doctrine or uniformity of worship. Rome would have sanctioned our Liturgy, if we would have acknowledged the supremacy.

"It has been from the beginning the fertile, essential, unceasing cause of rebellion and bloodshed. It originated the schism of one half of Christendom from the other, by compelling the Eastern Church to protest against a claim which went to invalidate the very foundations of the Christian faith. It resisted every attempt to reform the Church in the fifteenth century, and thus is justly chargeable with the heresies and blasphemies which followed the Reformation. Instead of unity, it has produced division; instead of peace, discord; instead of purity of doctrine, corruptions of the truth, which are known to be corruptions from having no sanction, either in apostolical tradition, or in the Scriptures, or in the analogy of faith. And thus it stands upon no ground whatever, either of apostolical institution, or of primitive antiquity, or of expediency. And if we might then venture to examine it by the light of reason, it is contrary to the analogy of the Divine nature and operations, and exhibits rather a retrogression in the development of His revelations than an advance. It is virtually a restoration of Judaism. It wants every mark which our blessed Lord set upon His own divine commission and ministry; and the only pretended titles, which even itself exhibits, are the abuse of figurative language, historical falsehoods, and exploded forgeries.

" These proofs you have had set before you, as far as you have been capable of following them, and far enough to satisfy your mind that these assertions are deserving of confidence. But if Rome has no title to your allegiance, no ministers of the Church can have but those who derive their authority from an apostolical source. Once more revert to the historical proof that the bishops of England, at this day, are the regular legitimate successors of those to whom the Apostles committed the power of ordaining ministers in each church. The chain was not broken at the Reformation. In casting off the Romish yoke, and many superstitious practices which had crept in with it, they only exercised an undoubted right; they did not sever themselves from the Church, for to the ancient Catholic Church they reverted for the confirmation of their doctrine, and from it they derived their authority. They did not violate any positive institutions of Heaven: rather, in abjuring the papacy, and asserting the due independence of national churches, they restored the positive institutions of the Almighty, and once more secured the framework which he had created for the preservation of the truth, and which Rome had broken up and destroyed. Even

if, in the doctrines and practices which they then
rejected, they had cast off any rashly, or introduced
any erroneously, unless these errors were such as to
destroy the essence of the Anglican Church as a
branch of the Catholic Church, still our duty would
be to remain within it, and to endeavour to correct
what was amiss by legitimate efforts, rather than to
throw ourselves into a schismatical body ; just as we
may not join the standard of an usurper because
our lawful sovereign may, in some points, have
abused his authority. But when you search for the
changes which the English Church did make at the
Reformation, can you find any which there touches
its essence as a church, or any which, if then fatal,
are not found even more flagrantly to have been
practised in the Romish Church? Has not the
English Church the creeds, the Scriptures, the Sacraments, the ministerial succession in all essential
points, the same as the primitive Church? If the
Reformation did in any way touch the chain of
apostolical succession in the appointment of bishops,
Rome has done the same in her interferences with
their appointment. If it departed in any point
from the primitive ministration of the holy Eucharist,
Rome has departed farther. If the Reformation
was attended by acts of extortion and robbery,
what was the secular course of the Reformation
itself but the avarice of Rome? If it was effected
by evil men in the laity, what has been the character of popes? If it was furthered by the interference of the civil arm, what has been the history
of Rome but a perpetual remonstrance and a
struggle against the same interference? If in any
way it encumbered the simplicity of the apostolic
faith by the addition of dogmatic statements, what
are the decrees of Trent and the creed of Pope
Pius? If it has been followed by heresy and schism,

what is the very Reformation in the eyes of the Romish Church but a heresy and schism from itself? If it has left the English Church comparatively mutilated and weak, what is Rome herself compared with her former grandeur? If its system as a whole be a change from that of apostolical ages, what is the system of Rome? And if the motives of this change, as avowed by ecclesiastical authority, and therefore chargeable upon the Church as a church, be compared with the motives of Rome, is it better and more holy to struggle for the purification of a corrupted faith, or for the aggrandisement of worldly power? If England has sinned, she has sinned to release others from bondage; Rome to enslave others to herself."

Beattie paused. He had spoken slowly, deliberately, and calmly; and Lady Eleanor, with her eyes fixed on the ground, had drank in his words with almost suspended breath. They were only the repetition of what she had often heard from him before. And now that the strange paroxysm under which she had laboured had passed away, they restored the whole tone of her mind; and she even wondered that any cloud of doubt should ever have come between her and the truth.

She thanked him fervently and reverently. And he then led her on to speak on her future plans, reminding her especially of the perils which attend a departure from one faith to another, where any self-indulgence is allowed to interfere as a motive, or to follow in its train.

" I know it," she said ; " and my future course of life is fixed. We cannot suffer deeply and sharply without tearing up the ties which bind us to earth, whether they be memories or hopes. All that is bright in life is now to me dead and dull. And calm, and retirement, and hours for prayer, and in-

terests of Christian usefulness, are all that I now
long for. For the future this will be my home.
They have promised to receive me among them
into this blessed and holy shelter. Whatever worldly
advantages Providence has vouchsafed to me cannot be better employed than in ministering to their
wants and extending the sphere of their duties.
And He——" But here she stopped, almost choked
with her emotions. "Alas!" she resumed, after a
pause, "lacerated and bleeding hearts, which have
been passed through frightful ordeals of suffering
and fear, are not made for happiness hereafter upon
earth. Peace is all which they can hope for; and
solitude, and silence, and tranquil communion with
Heaven, all which they should covet."

Beattie could not refrain from uttering a blessing
over her head. "There is another," he said, "who
feels as you do, and rejoices that even in this you
sympathise with himself. Even though separate on
earth, hearts and souls, and lives may be joined in
communion in Heaven. Blessed are you both, that
no doubt or reviving thought of self mingles with
the anxious pains of such a moment as the present—
that you are fixed and steadfast in devoting all that
Providence has given you to others, not to yourselves—that you would rather withdraw yourselves
from each other in this life, to be united more closely
in another, than risk the loss of peace of conscience,
of Heaven itself, by rivetting again those earthly
chains which Providence itself seems to have broken
from you."

"I could not," said Lady Eleanor, "have done
otherwise. I could not take the step on which I
have resolved without making with it such a sacrifice as would prove to my own conscience that I
was not acting from a motive of self-indulgence.
Even the opinion of the world it would have been

hard to face; but there is that within which it is harder still to brave. No, let such an act as this be at least clear even from the suspicion of self-interest and self-deceit before both Heaven and man."

Once more Beattie gave her his blessing, and prepared to take his leave, promising to be with her the next day, some little time before the bishop would arrive at the Béguinage, in the little chapel of which he had promised to admit Lady Eleanor into the communion of the Church, at the same time that he administered the rite of confirmation to some of the younger females, who were dwelling within its walls, partly under its shelter from the world, and partly as receiving education from its inmates. As he left the room he met upon the stairs one of the Sisters, who was coming out of a little suite of rooms appropriated to an infirmary for poor women. It was one whom we have long lost sight of, but not forgotten — our good friend Mabel,—active, energetic, devoted, unselfish as ever, but now quiet, regular, self-disciplined, trained in habits of obedience and order, and reaping the fruits of a well-directed enthusiasm in the affectionate respect of all the inmates of the house, who owed to her zealous co-operation with Mrs. Bevan no small a portion of their happiness and comfort. She was followed by a female, in a dress not unlike her own, but slightly distinguished from it. And as her pale, care-worn, but still beautiful face looked up at Beattie with eyes in which at times there seemed to wander some strange memories of past scenes, some fitful glances of a disturbed reason, Beattie stopped to address her. He called her by her name, Margaret, inquired for her health kindly; and poor Margaret, colouring and abashed, yet grateful for his notice, answered him with reverence. She had been received into the house only a few weeks since, on the recovery of her reason, and on her removal from the asylum in which she had been placed. An outcast upon the world, destitute of all friends, of all means of support, scarcely recovered from the shock of her long illness, her intellect still weak, her feelings lacerated, she was driven by necessity out of the shelter of the asylum, to die of starvation. Mrs. Bevan had found her seated under the little archway of the Béguinage, one bitterly cold evening—sitting there without speaking, without asking for help, afraid to make her name known lest the sad memory of one sin, long since repented of, should still steel the hearts and shut the doors of her fellows against her. And when her story was known, she had been admitted into the shelter of the holy house, there to make perfect her repentance, and to become, as penitents should become, the servant and menial of those who had not sinned as she had.

Beattie was still speaking to her, when a violent knocking was heard at the gate, and a demand followed for immediate admission from a rude voice, agitated apparently by passion, yet affecting composure and gentleness.

CHAP. XXII.

BEFORE we can explain the cause of the rude knocking at the gate of the Béguinage, we must return
once more to the little green gate in the lane of
Hawkstone, which conducted into the garden of the
Reverend P. O'Foggarty, and we must enter even
into that gentleman's study. He was sitting there
in company with the mendicant, whom we left last in
the chapel of the Priory. There were words and
expostulations of harsh and angry import, fierce
recriminations, mutual charges, violence of gesture
—every thing which could imply a meeting between
men engaged in some deep plot, and disappointed of
their object by the awkwardness or mismanagement
of one of the parties.

Awkwardness and mismanagement, indeed, there
had been on the part of Mr. O'Foggarty. Notwithstanding his general blandness of demeanour,
which indicated acquaintance with the world, he
possessed little of that real knowledge of human
nature for which Pearce was so remarkable. And
in particular, he had been totally unable to understand or appreciate, and still more unable to direct,
a mind of such exquisite delicacy and refinement as
Lady Eleanor's. He had scarcely undertaken the
office of her spiritual adviser, and established himself at Lord Claremont's in the place of the good
Abbé St. Maur, than she perceived the difference
between them, and penetrated through the veil of
assumed courteousness and liberality, which he had
thought it politic to assume. St. Maur, in all his

ministrations and reasonings, had exhibited the
Catholic rather than the Romanist. His holiness,
his simplicity, his charity, true copies of many a
noble and saintly character reared in the bosom of
the Gallican Church, and preserved as by an atmosphere of personal piety from the contagion of
the evil system of papacy, had prevented the intrusion of a single doubt into Lady Eleanor's mind.
She contrasted his self-devotion, his obedience to
his Church, his fasts, his alms, his prayers, his
reverence for antiquity, the firm and unwavering
character of his belief, his recognition of authority
and guidance in all his opinions and ministrations,
with the selfishness, the individualism, the indulgence, the secularity, the bustle, the modern frivolity, the lawless speculations and arrogant presumption which prevailed in all that she saw of the
religious world of Protestantism. For into the deeper
recesses of the Church of England she was not able
to penetrate. Its real saints, its noblest children,
shrink from the public eye. They do not appear upon
platforms, or congregate at meetings, or talk loudly,
or write boldly. And of that which was obtruded
upon her sight, even in the Church of England, too
much partook of a tone which jarred upon her
delicacy, and, to speak most gently, failed to satisfy
her yearnings for a calm, lofty, ethereal spirit of
unworldliness and devotion. Moreover, all the
harsher and more dubious points of the Romish
system, St. Maur had softened down and veiled
from her eyes—not artfully, not hypocritically, but
by the innocence of his own mind. Its intrusive,
intriguing proselytism became, in his hands, zeal
for the propagation of the faith; its stern, sanguinary despotism, firmness in defence of the truth;
its idolatry, a healthy stimulus of a fervent adoration; its blasphemous worship of the blessed Virgin,

a holy and reverent affection towards an image of purity and bliss, transcendant above all human imaginations; its bold tampering with the creeds and the Sacraments, and the polity of the Apostles, an economy of prudence and necessity; and its rationalism and presumption in speaking above what is written, a reverent care to extinguish controversies and satisfy doubts. So it is with those who see only the one side, the illuminated phase of the Papacy.

But O'Foggarty's was a different mind. Worldly, and unchastened in heart, he had been drilled into the Popish system under hands which cared for little but the preservation of an exterior, and for a prudent policy. He had been taught controversy in that cold, hard, unspiritual form, which it assumes in the polemics of men, whose object is not truth, but conquest. And, instead of that single eye, which, looking outward, sees all things inward by a faculty of instinctive wisdom, they had initiated him in a theory of policy and of human nature, carefully constructed upon technical rules, in which the heart had no place — nothing was left to the full course and impulse of good affections — all was calculated — all artificial — all full of self-consciousness and self-interest. With him, even the worst features of papacy, however dissembled before others, came out, and were enforced in his private communications as parts of the system, all bound together by the one stern bond of infallibility and supremacy. And the most delicate and perilous of all his religious ministrations, that in which art and system can have the least place, and in which no technical skill can atone for the want of a chastened heart and singleness of mind — the confessional — assumed, in his hands, a form so utterly repulsive, that Lady Eleanor was compelled to retire from it.

O'Foggarty saw his mistake, and, instead of enforcing her obedience, succumbed to her resistance,
and offered to accommodate himself to her wishes.
From that moment the spell of his authority was
broken. Only a few days afterwards Charles Bevan,
as rector of the parish, had visited Lord Claremont.
He had seen both the Earl and Lady Eleanor, and
without hesitation or circumlocution he had reminded
them of his own spiritual authority over them as
their legitimate parish priest; had warned them
against the sin of schism; had offered to lay before
them the titles on which his claim was rested; and
had also, on a second visit, declared his determination, with the consent of his bishop, deliberately
to sever from the Church, by the act of the Church,
all those within the parish who obstinately and
wilfully should refuse to submit to instruction, and
should continue in schism, and to proceed to a
formal excommunication.

It was a bold, and many would have thought it a
rash step. But Bevan was well advised. He had
resolved that he would not remain in the painful
position, in which many of his brethren had been
placed, by being compelled to recognise as children
of the Church, and to perform the most solemn
offices of the Church for those who were in open
rebellion against her. He felt acutely the mockery
and ridicule thus cast on the most awful ministrations of the Church; the contempt thus poured
upon the clergy; the blindness and hardness of
heart in respect to the guilt of schism, which was
thus encouraged in the ignorant and weak; and the
total confusion and destruction which was threatened
to the very nature and being of a Church. His
bishop had promised to support him; and after a
formal and distinct endeavour to obtain a hearing
for his· instruction, those whose minds appeared ob-

stinate and incorrigible, he resolved solemnly to excommunicate.

The effect of this boldness upon Lady Eleanor,
as upon nearly all other schismatics in the parish,
was startling. It made them reflect. It was the
assertion of an authority, of which they had never
dreamed. It was the appearance of the Church of
England in a wholly new light, invested with privileges which could only belong to an ambassador
of Heaven, and the very claim of which, boldly
and unhesitatingly made, was in itself an evidence of
their truth. O'Foggarty met the menace with laugh-
ter and ridicule. But Bevan's calmness, firmness,
solemnity, and depth of thought strongly impressed
Lady Eleanor. She did not refuse to see him again.
Lord Claremont fell into his last sickness; and she
was left more at liberty to think and to study.
And though in her rare communications with Villiers he studiously avoided the subject, she could
not but see in him an example and image of the
Church, to which she recurred in every doubt, and
which attracted her reverence, while Bevan's arguments acted on her reason. Neither was she
without another image of the English Church, another proof of the energy which it could develope,
and the holiness which it could generate in the two
religious communities, now rising into maturity
under her own eye. Little had she supposed that
the English Church could ever create societies for
prayers, for alms-giving, for fasting, for meditation.
She visited frequently the little sisterhood of the
Béguinage; and there, at her own request, Mrs.
Bevan placed her in communication with Beattie,
whose age was greater, and his learning deeper, and
his character more formed than Bevan's; and the
work was accomplished. O'Foggarty retired in
despair.

" And this, then," said the mendicant to him, " is the end of your soft ways and delicate words." And as he spoke his lips curled upwards with a bitter sneer.

O'Foggarty was silent.

" You have lost him," continued Pearce, " and estranged her. And your chapel is unfinished, and your school deserted, and you yourself driven to quit the place from mere lack of support. Did I not tell you it would be so ?"

O'Foggarty still sat silent, with a vexed and angry air.

" You have ruined every thing," said Pearce. " Why did you not join the new Union Anti-religious Distinction School, the one on the Irish plan, that the Government has set up ? That would have done something for us."

" I did," replied O'Foggarty ; " I joined it from the first, and was one of the petitioners for it."

" And why did not you make use of it, then ?" said Pearce.

" I did," answered the other. " I got one of our own Catholics appointed to the mastership; and every thing was going on well; only Villiers found out that I said mass in the schoolroom, and had brought over two of the young heretics to come to chapel. I got the school built close by the gate for that very reason ; and he complained, and the board were obliged to dismiss the man."

" And then you gave it up ?" asked Pearce, contemptuously.

" I did not," replied the other, in anger ; " I sent all my boys there, and drilled them thoroughly, and taught them how to attack the young heretics in play-hours, and what to say ; and several of them came over to us in consequence. And I watched every word the new schoolmaster said; and if he uttered a syllable about religion, or any thing connected with the church, I threatened to bring him before the commissioners, so that he was frightened, and shut up his mouth. One day, when our bishop, the Bishop of Eliopolis, came to look at the school, one of the Protestant boys asked the master which was the true bishop, the bishop who confirmed him, or the bishop of Eliopolis; and the master had the impudence to say it was the bishop who confirmed him. I had him up before the commissioners instantly, and he got soundly reprimanded for introducing peculiar doctrines; and was ordered to tell the boys that he did not know, and that he had been under a mistake ; and that both were the right bishops. But this could not last long ; for the boys went on asking him questions — what they were to think about this, and about that; and he was obliged to tell them he did not know any thing about it, that the manuscripts differed, or rather that he knew very well, but the government did not know, or had not made up their mind, and would not allow him to tell them. At last there came a hot-headed curate, and he began drilling his boys in controversy, as I did mine, as the only way of saving them from corruption. And then the young ones used to fight and abuse each other all play-hours, notwithstanding the fine exhortation to love and peace, as papists and heretics, and I know not what. At last Bevan came to the living, and he took away all his boys at once, and would not allow one of them to go near the place ; so it was not my fault that the school did not answer for us."

Pearce sat moodily, with his hands before his eyes. "And to-morrow, you say," he exclaimed, "she is to apostatise formally?"

"Yes," answered O'Foggarty, "in the chapel of that Protestant Béguinage."

"It cannot be, it never shall be!" exclaimed the mendicant, striking the table with his clenched hand; "she does it that she may marry *him*. Who would trust a woman's faith, or care for a woman's doctrine? She is resolved to marry him at last, and that is why she apostatises. But I have sworn that they never shall be one; I have that which can stop it even now."

And he rose up passionately, seized his hat, and scarcely wishing O'Foggarty good night, he hurried into the street.

The cold wind howled round him as he reached the open air, but the infuriated man felt it not upon his burning forehead. A man was standing at a little distance, who had apparently been waiting for him. And Pearce made a sign for him to approach. It was Connell. Even in the paroxysm of passion, the cool calculating mind of the mendicant had prepared for the worst. He had brought Connell with him, as a tool always ready in his hand, and whose testimony he might require, and who had learnt in his own country to care little for the solemnity of an oath when he could evade it by some vain form, or stifle conscience by a plea of serving his Church. And now he bade the wretched man follow him, and watch what might happen. If he should be detained — if any sign of mischief should appear, Connell had his instructions ready. Pearce had prepared against this during the few hours which he had spent up in the Forest, in that mysterious house surrounded by high dead walls, to which he had conducted his young fellow-traveller, and in which that fellow-traveller was now immured, and almost kept prisoner against his will, till the time for action should arrive. Once more Pearce had assumed the direction of a deep-laid, long-plotted, insurrectionary movement among the

turbulent population of the district. The trains
had all been laid, and all was ready for explosion
at a given moment.

"Follow me," he said to Connell; "wait a little
distance off. If I am detained — if you see any
sign of policemen, ascertain what they are about;
and if I am in danger, hasten off to the Forest."
Connell withdrew a little way; and Pearce, once
more abandoning himself to the full tide of his
passion, hurried on.

He strode along the pavement, and nearly threw
down a miserable old woman who was crawling
home with a few sticks, which she had picked up to
light a cheerless momentary blaze in her wretched
hovel. Pearce only answered her cry of fear with
a ferocious curse. He came in front of the house
where he lodged before; and as he passed, though
it was dark, he slouched his hat over his face.
The unfinished pinnacles of the Romish chapel
caught his eye, and once more he uttered a dreadful
imprecation. Then he stopped, and felt in a secret
pocket for a packet of papers; and by the light of a
gas-lamp he looked over them, and saw that they
were right.

"It can be prevented," he muttered to himself,
"even now. Here is the certificate of the marriage: I can swear — swear that she is still alive,
and then there can be no other marriage. They
swear in the House of Commons, and do not mind
it. I can get those who will face it out. It does
not signify — a mere oath. O'Connell swore that
he would not hurt the Church; they all swear the
same; and then they vote for its destruction. No
one dares to call it perjury. What is perjury but a
name? and it is all for the good of the faith. She
will not change, if she cannot marry — I know that;
and she cannot marry, if the first wife is alive."

And the mendicant drew up his figure, and stood for a moment exultingly, as if recovered from his defeat, and sure of victory. But a sudden chill, he knew not how, fell upon him — a dreary blank, as if all was in vain; and something of a mysterious, superstitious horror, as if a cloud of vengeance long overcharged above his head were about to burst upon him. He staggered, and leaned against the lamp-post. And at that moment two men came round the corner, bearing something upon their shoulders; it was black, oblong, hollow — and Pearce saw that it was a coffin. He shrunk back as it passed, lest it should touch him; and then, to recover himself from a shock which it had given him, he hurried on.

"I can swear," he muttered to himself, "that she is still living — in Italy or Naples. It will take time, at least, to clear it up; and in time something else may happen. If she will only listen to me — will but put it off. I can make up a story that he deserted her — was cruel to her — that she ran away from him — and then that he pretended she was dead to deceive his father. Anything will do — anything for the present. I can swear."

And as he uttered the last word he reached the arched gateway of the Béguinage; he stopped. Hardened as he was, almost blinded with the wild struggle of baffled and desperate revenge, he yet felt one last expiring pang of remorse and fear — a fear undefined and superstitious, but which made him shudder. The churchyard lay before him; its wan tombstones gleaming like spectres in the pale light of a waning moon. And amongst them he saw a figure watching steadfastly, silently, moving not, but with a shadowy hand lifted up as if ready to seize him. Was it a vision of his fevered blood? He rubbed his eyes, but in vain; the figure was still there. He had forgotten Connell. Almost maddened with a conflict of passions, he rang the bell furiously. Then he recovered himself sufficiently to request admittance to see Lady Eleanor, on the most urgent business; and he assumed a voice of feigned composure and gentleness. The wicket gate was opened after a little delay to allow Beattie to pass out, while Pearce himself was admitted to wait in the little lodge, until Lady Eleanor's pleasure could be known. But scarcely had he passed through the gate, and the lamp which burnt within had flashed upon his face, than the female who had opened the wicket uttered a loud shriek, and called him by his name. It was the voice of poor Margaret; and Margaret had recognised him — recognised the man whom she had always regarded in her mind as the tempter and destroyer of her husband.

"Stop him!" she cried to Beattie. "That is the man — seize him!" And before Pearce could make a movement, Beattie had closed the wicket, and seized the key. There was no escape.

CHAP. XXIII.

THERE stands at one angle of the north side of the cloister of Hawkstone Priory a square projecting tower adjoining the chapel, and apparently communicating with some of those secret passages with which its walls are perforated. Traditions were rife in the neighbourhood of subterraneous openings into vaults and crypts below; and a legend is still current of a tale of blighted affection, in which one of the ancient inmates of the Priory was supposed to have retired into its shelter after the loss of a dear-loved wife, a member of the Villiers family, and to have built this tower adjoining to her last resting-place in the Villiers vault, that he might solace himself with her memory, and even, as it was said, might pass, unperceived, his hours of prayer and nightly vigils close to her remains, even in the vault itself. Only one or two persons were supposed to be acquainted with the secret of these mysterious passages, which were hidden in the face of the wall by large slabs of stone, turning upon pivots, and opening by secret springs. And the secret had been turned to account by the insurrectionary agents, who had planned the disturbances in the Forest, and who had thus been enabled to deposit securely the arms which they were preparing and collecting. When Villiers had restored the Priory, he had allowed this tower, as well as every other part which he could retain, to stand untouched.

But the low vaulted chamber, which formed its

lowest portion, had scarcely ever been occupied. It was gloomy, chilly, lighted only by two narrow lancet windows perforated in the thickest part of the wall. And even when a sunbeam penetrated into it, and fell upon the rough stone floor, it seemed as if it had lost its way, and would fain have struggled back into the outer air.

The Priory clock had just tolled twelve that night, and all but a few inmates of the Priory were asleep, when a light glimmered at the end of the cloisters, and five figures appeared. Two of them were officers of justice, and they led between them a third, habited like a mendicant. He was not handcuffed, or chained, but his every movement was watched lest he should attempt an escape; and his dogged, gloomy, ferocious, but desperate expression of countenance showed that he had abandoned all hopes of it. Those who bore the lanterns were Beattie himself and Cookesley. The low arched door of the tower, ribbed with strong oak, and massive with nails, was opened. The miserable prisoner was led into the chamber; a dreary, cheerless fire was kindled on the unused hearth; a single candle placed on a rude table in the middle, and a bed having been made up for him in one corner, Pearce was left to himself. The door was double-locked on the outside, and the officers took up their post for the night at the entrance of the prisoner's chamber.

As the massive door slammed heavily, and rang through the vaulted room, the wretched man sank down upon a chair before the fire. His hat fell from his head, and his hands dropped loosely by his side. He was seemingly paralysed. Up to the present moment all his plots and intrigues had been permitted, by a forbearing, long-suffering Providence, to work almost without obstruction; his calculations had all succeeded; he had become almost careless and rash from repeated success. That he should now have fallen into a snare, blind-folded — that, within walls where he conceived no one could have known him, he should have been instantly recognised — that seeming accident should have brought together Beattie and Bevan, at the moment when it was necessary to give orders for his detention — and that Cookesley himself should be at hand to identify him, and connect him with the previous outbreak, which he had been suspected of contriving, and for which warrants at the time had been issued for his apprehension,— all this was so startling and surprising to him, that it seemed as if the hand of vengeance were suddenly bared to smite him, and a cloud were rolled away, revealing to him his past crimes, and his approaching punish-ment. One o'clock struck, two o'clock, and three o'clock, still he sat in the same position, motionless. At last the fire was dying out, and a cold chill compelled him to move and trim it; and the movement in some degree broke his stupor, and restored him to reason. He looked round the low room to see if there was any means of escape, but on each side was a solid wall. The narrow lancets prohibited all egress, and even they were barred. He climbed up to them, on a wooden settle, but could see nothing without; but just as he was de-scending from the one which looked into the outer side of the cloister, and hung over the little brook, he was startled by hearing a tap on the glass. He stopped breathless. The tap was repeated, and though superstitiously terrified at first, he moved, as by a species of fascination, to the window. A small pane in the lattice was shaken and moved. Presently it was carefully taken out, and a hand was thrust in, holding a note.

"Is that you, Connell?" whispered Pearce.

"It is I, sir," was the answer. "But hush, for they are watching in the cloister."

"How did you find me out?" whispered Pearce.

"I watched the lights in the rooms all out, and when this one remained burning, I thought it might be you, and so I crept round, and climbed up to look in. I have sent up to the forest; they will be here as soon as they can. The man has just come back." Pearce took the note, and tore it open. And once more his countenance lighted up, and his energy seemed to revive. "As soon as they can," he muttered. "It must be at once. They have their men ready. To-morrow I may be sent anywhere. Go back," he said to Connell; "go back, instantly. Tell them where I am. Let there be no delay, or all will be lost. Let them come with all their strength. If I am not rescued in a few hours they will be ruined." He had spoken incautiously loud, and the step of one of the policeman moved to the door. Pearce made signs to Connell to retire; and throwing himself once more upon the chair, he gave himself up to thought. "All may be saved still," he muttered. "We have escaped from worse things even than this. They must be here to-morrow — to-morrow by noon at farthest." And, as if his mind was relieved, he threw himself on the bed. But he was unable to sleep. He tossed and started in an agony of alarm at every sound, till the daylight had pierced into the room. At last, worn out and exhausted, he took from his pocket a strong opiate, which of late years he always carried about him, and sank into a profound sleep. He dreamt that he was standing on a rock, which looked down upon a blue expanse of sea, fringed with a line of marble palaces, and crowned with a smoke-wreathed mountain. He saw a boat floating upon

the waters, and in it two forms, radiant with youth,
and loveliness, and happiness. And as he turned
from the sight he saw, standing by his side, a black
and demon figure, at the very sight of whom the
bitterness of envy and malice gushed into his heart.
He thought that the Evil Being lifted him up by the
hair of his head, and bore him over the waters, following in the wake of that little boat which danced
gladly along the silver ripple. The arms of that
angel pair were circled round each other, and
together they bent them over a sleeping babe,
dropping even tears of joy upon its innocent and
slumbering face.

Suddenly the Evil Being swooped down upon
them like a vulture, and tore the child from their
arms; and the boat sank under the eddying water,
with a hollow shriek. But the child was now lying
in the hands of the dreamer; and, as he looked on
it, its features changed, its eye-balls became distorted, its colour livid, its hands matted with hair,
and armed with claws; and it sprang up and clasped
him round the neck, and dragged him down—down
— down — an infinite depth — a depth of darkness
and horror; and the waves of the sea surged up
with hollow roars to catch him as he fell: they
closed over him—they boomed above his head. He
would have shrieked out, but the horrible monster
clung round his neck, and choked and strangled
him. Down—down—lower and lower, deeper and
deeper—they sank together! And he gasped in
agony; but still the monster grappled him, and lay
with his grim ghastly eyes staring fiercely into his.
There was a roaring around him, as of innumerable
torrents, shrieks and screams, the thundering of
many waters, the hiss of ocean serpents, the wild
unearthly cries of demons in agony calling to him
by name, and bidding him welcome to their place

of torture. He sprang up — every hair upon his head standing erect with terror, and the sweat ready to drop from his forehead. Was it all a dream, or was it real? There were the noises still — the fearful sounds, shrieks, and screams, and cries of terror, and voices like those of fiends calling on him by name; and his head swam, and he sank back upon his pillow. But again he sprang up in terror. There was thundering at the door of the tower; and once more he heard his own name re-peated: and he leaped from the bed, and remem-bered where he was, and all that had passed. He looked round, and saw faces leaping, and climbing up at the narrow windows; and a cheer of triumph rose up when Connell tore away the glass, and they could see Pearce himself. "Make haste, sir," he cried, "make haste; there is no time to lose—we are here—we have got possession of the place — but they are coming—the yeomanry will be here in a few minutes. You must come out at once, or it will be too late."

"Break open the door," exclaimed Pearce; "how can I get out without this?"·

"We cannot," said Connell; "it is locked. The policemen are killed; and we cannot find the keys: they are battering it now." And at the same mo-ment the massive oaken door, rivetted with iron, and imbedded deeply on its ponderous hinges, shook from top to bottom with a tremendous crash.

"Cannot you get out here?" asked a voice at the window; and a rough hand endeavoured, at the same time, to tear away the iron stanchions. But they defied the effort even of the gigantic muscular gripe which essayed to move them. Pearce an-swered by a laugh of derision and impatience. "Break down the door," he said; "it is all that you can do." And once more the door tottered, and

bent inward beneath another shock. Again and
again the battery was brought to bear upon the
massive oak ; one of the solid pannels was split from
top to bottom, and light could be seen through it ;
and one of the hinges had been forced more than
an inch from its bed in the solid stone : a few more
blows would accomplish its destruction. And Pearce,
in an agony of impatience, now by oaths and ex-
ecrations, and now with entreaties, was urging the
clamorous throng without to bring to bear upon it
the whole of their strength, ignorant that only a
few hands at a time could be employed in battering
the door, and that the narrowness of the cloister
embarrassed their efforts. Still there was little
more to be done. Another crash was heard, and
the upper staple was all but forced from the wall,
when a loud cheer was heard on the outside of the
Priory, responded to by a wild, irregular, confused
cry, partly of fear and partly of defiance, from the
party within the walls. And to Pearce's terror and
dismay, he heard the cry ring through the cloisters
—" The yeomanry are come ; save yourselves !" And
the next moment a heavy weight fell upon the stone
pavement ; and the sound of flying feet was followed
by a dead silence at the door.

"They have abandoned me," he cried. " Traitors ! cowards ! villains ! they have left me to my
fate. Fool that I was to depend upon such cowards !" And he rushed to the door, and endeavoured
with a convulsive effort to tear it from its hinges,
but it resisted all his attempts. Then he laid his
face to the key-hole, and tried to see what was
passing without ; but the cloister, one whole side of
which was commanded by the door, was empty.
Beyond it there were cries and clamours, as of a
deadly conflict. Shots were fired — shrieks and
screams of the wounded mingled with cheers of

triumph; but which side was victorious he could not know. Then along the other end of the cloister came dropping back, one by one, a few of the rioters, wounded, bleeding — some of them mutilated — more than one lying down to die on the stone pavement. There was another cheer, and the rear, as it were, of a dense body appeared at the farthest end, retreating, fighting as it were, their ground inch by inch. They wavered, gave way, fell into confusion; at last the whole mass turned, and fled precipitately in every direction. And the bayonets of soldiers, and the glittering of the yeomanry equipments, flashed through the vaulted cloister.

Once more the insurgents rallied on the open green sward round which the cloister ran, and which was not built up towards the south. They formed themselves into a dense body, seemingly under the marshalling and direction of one leader. He was young, fair-haired, his features delicately formed, his bearing full of grace and spirit, his eye lighted up with animation; and, but for the lines of premature vice and profligacy deeply engraven on his countenance, his face would have formed a study for a painter. He it was who rallied the routed fugitives; and, armed with a sabre which he had wrested from one of the yeomanry, whom he had dragged from his horse to the ground, and left dead with two gashes upon his head, he defied the advancing military. The next moment, round the south side of the cloister, was heard the charge of the yeomanry. They halted, reined up their horses in front of the rallied party, and their commander, a tall and noble figure, with a voice of thunder, summoned the insurgents to lay down their arms, and surrender themselves prisoners.

"Never!" cried the youth, "never, while we have life!" and he sprang up and seized the bridle of Villiers's charger with one hand, while with the other he aimed at Villiers himself a deadly and tremendous blow. At that moment, if any eye could have penetrated into the vaulted room, and have beheld Pearce as he gazed through the fractured crevices, they would have seen his face for one moment turn white as ashes. Every particle of blood seemed to have forsaken it; every movement and pulse of life to be suspended. His eyeballs were fixed. His hands grasped convulsively the iron ring of the door, as if they would have bitten into the metal. Then he sprang up with a cry of madness. Villiers had swayed himself to avoid the blow, and with one stroke dashing his assailant's weapon from his hand, he raised himself in his stirrups, and his sword whirled round like lightning, and descended upon a head, which it clove asunder, and covered the horse and its rider with blood and brains.

It was the head, not of the youthful assailant, but of a haggard, savage, bloated, yet miserable-looking ruffian, who had thrown himself in the way, that he might ward off the blow from the head of his foster-child. Irishmen never forget their children. And he had even inflicted a severe wound upon the horseman himself. But his body fell to the ground; and at the same moment Villiers recovered himself, and once more grasping his sword, prepared to prostrate his young antagonist, who had only retired a few paces to renew the combat more fiercely from the loss of the miserable Connell. But at that moment the oak-ribbed door of the vaulted room, already half torn from its hinges, fell with a crash. The prisoner within it had thrown himself upon it with the desperation and strength of a maniac. He tore it from its staples, plunged across it with a cry that made even the combatants turn round.

But at the next spring, which he made into the cloister, he fell back, staggering against the wall, and the blood gushed from his body. The order to fire had been given to the soldiers, and amidst the thunder of the discharge, the volumes of smoke and tongues of flame, a ball, irregularly aimed, had glanced from the stone-work of the cloister, and struck him to the ground. It was an accident— such an accident as Providence usually employs in executing his justest vengeance.

CHAP. XXIV.

THREE weeks had passed from that fearful day. It was midnight. And in that vaulted cell, stretched upon a bed of torture, racked with his wound, pale, haggard, his beard uncut, his hair matted, his eyes bloodshot and full of a malignant fire, while his lips quivered with fear at every sound, the miserable Pearce was lying. His senses had now returned after a long delirium of fever, during which he had made the hair of his attendants stand on end, and many of them refuse to remain with him at night, by the horrible phantasms and spectres which haunted his maddened brain. He imagined himself already in the place of torment; and even the water with which they endeavoured to assuage his burning thirst seemed to him as molten lead, administered to him by the hands of demons. Unable to be moved to prison, he had been watched over by the inmates of the Priory with the tenderest care. And by the skill of Cookesley himself his life had been saved. But it had been wholly impossible to extract from him any information, or even to question him, on any matters which might exasperate or alarm him. Beattie and Bevan alone had been awakened to some suspicion that he was implicated not only in the insurrectionary movements of the Forest, but also, in some mysterious way, with the disappearance of Villiers's child. But Villiers himself had received a most serious wound, which confined him to his room. The rioters had been driven off before they could effect

their purpose of setting fire to the Priory, especially
to the chapel, as Pearce had carefully suggested.
Within the chapel all had been gathered who could
not join in the defence, and not a hair of their
heads had been injured. But Villiers himself, while
in the act of levelling his sabre upon the bare head
of his young assailant, had suddenly swooned with
loss of blood, and had ever since been lying under
the same roof within a few yards of that chamber
of agony, in which the destroyer of his peace and of
his child was suffering the tortures of the damned.

Pearce had just awakened from a terrifying dream,
and, to his consternation, he found that the cell was
in darkness. Darkness to him was as a hell; and
again and again he had besought his nurse never to
leave him: but now, during his sleep, she had
been called away; and after sitting up in dismay
and terror, he sank back upon his pillow, almost
doubting where he was. He was endeavouring to
stare through the darkness, and recognise the place,
when his eye was rivetted by a sound, and by the
appearance of a slender thread of blue light on the
wall immediately facing him. It widened, became
more vivid, and, to his inexpressible horror, he saw
the wall itself open, and a bright light pour in
through it, behind which, almost senseless as he
was with terror, he could discern a dark, shapeless,
shadowy figure advancing to him. He uttered a
hideous shriek, and would have buried himself in
his bed-clothes; but the figure moved to his side,
and called him by his name. It was a voice which
he knew.

"Silence," it said, "or you will ruin all. What
are you afraid of? It is only I, O'Foggarty."

Pearce could not recover his breath. His heart
beat as if it would suffocate him, and his lips quivered, so that he could not articulate.

"Why, I should never have thought," said his nocturnal visitant, "that you of all men were afraid of ghosts." And he laughed scornfully.

"I have been ill," faltered Pearce. "But what do you want? How did you get here?"

"You," answered the other—"you of all men not to know how I got here! You not to be acquainted with all these old secret passages which have been useful to you before this in some of your former proceedings, as they will be useful to you now. Who are such proper persons to know all the contrivances of these old places as the persons to whom they once belonged, and to whom they must belong again? I have only just got the clue from abroad, and I have found you out without difficulty. Do you remember that hollow in the rock, by the bank of the brook, just by the great Wyche-elm, where the thorn-bushes are so thick. There is a regular passage cut under ground, from this room into the Villiers vault, and through that out into the open air. Only you must understand the springs, and how to move the stones in the walls."

"Then I can escape," cried Pearce, springing up in the bed with recovered energy, and resuming all his vigour of mind—"and at once?"

"At once," said O'Foggarty. "Slip on your clothes, take my arm; there is a horse waiting for you out by the Prior's oak in the wood; and in two hours you will be in the Forest, safe. And we shall be safe too; for it would not be very pleasant to have you in their hands—with the prospect of your telling all you know." And O'Foggarty's sneer indicated how little confidence he reposed in the honour of his confederate.

"And what of Villiers?" asked Pearce, impatiently. "Is he alive? They would tell me nothing; and I have told them nothing. Where is he? Has he found out any thing? Did he——" and the wretch hesitated—"Was any one killed?"

O'Foggarty shrank back, as horror-struck. At last he said, with a low voice, "You have had your revenge. It is all over,—but not with his sword."

Pearce sank back on his pillow, and gasped convulsively.

"How was it?" he muttered. "Tell me all. Let me know all. Revenge is sweet. Tell it me all. I can bear it; and yet I have lost what was mine— all but mine. I should have had his money."

"He is not dead yet," said O'Foggarty. "He dies to-morrow. As I came out of Broughton they were erecting the gallows. Villiers has killed him."

"How — how?" exclaimed Pearce, greedily. "Does he know it? He shall know it — know it when it is too late. And my foot shall be set upon his neck. Oh, what a triumph!" And his eyes glared like a demon's. "But tell me all—tell me this minute." And he clutched O'Foggarty's hand, who seemed afraid to move under his grasp, so completely had Pearce obtained a fascination over all who had once been brought under his influence.

"I will," said O'Foggarty. "But do not crush me so hard; you will make the blood come."

"Ay, blood—blood!" muttered Pearce. "But tell me."

"He was brought up for trial this day," said O'Foggarty. I was in court at Broughton all the time. There was no evidence scarcely against him. They did not know where he came from,—could not identify him,—did not know his name scarcely, for he had been as silent as you have been ever since he had been taken, and would not utter a word. He behaved like a man, nobly. Oh, Mr.

Pearce, have you not ruined a spirit which in other hands would have been——"

"Silence!" exclaimed Pearce, fiercely. "How dare you speak to me of what I choose to do, as much for the good of the Church as for my own revenge? Go on at once,—tell me all."

And O'Foggarty proceeded. "The judge talked of stopping the trial — said that the evidence was not enough; and the poor fellow looked up then at last, as if he had not been really so indifferent about it as he affected to be. And I do believe there were many in the court besides myself who would have been glad of his escape. He looked worn and haggard. But he has a noble face, Pearce. What a man he might have made!"

"Go on," cried Pearce, exasperated.

"I will," replied the other. "But had you not better keep quiet. Your nails have cut your hands."

"Go on," repeated Pearce.

And O'Foggarty proceeded. "We all thought he was safe, when the Attorney-General, who was for the prosecution, rose and said, that if the evidence was not sufficient, they must then be under the painful necessity of calling another witness, who had been interested in the criminal, when a boy, from having saved his life in a fire, and who had therefore entreated to be spared from appearing if his evidence was not absolutely necessary."

"He did not know it all, then!" exclaimed Pearce, impatiently. "How did he find out about the fire?"

"The gaoler had learnt it," said O'Foggarty. "And Villiers, though confined with his wound, had wanted to see the poor fellow in prison; but the poor fellow himself refused to admit any one."

" Go on," again repeated Pearce. " Why do not you make haste?"

" We all looked round," continued O'Foggarty, " and saw the clerk administering the oath to Villiers himself, who was sitting at the left hand of the judge, looking pale as death from his wound. And, I do not know how it was, he seemed to be shuddering all over, and looked more like a spectre than a man, as if he had seen something."

" And did he give his evidence?" cried Pearce.

" Yes," replied O'Foggarty, " quite distinctly. He had seen the poor fellow cut down one of the yeomanry with his own hand. And then he described how he had been at the head of the mob in the cloister, and had attacked Villiers himself. It was clear as day. The poor fellow had no counsel; and he refused to make any defence. Only he said that he had been neglected from his childhood—left without father or mother—and that he had been doing rightly, fighting against the oppressors of the poor, and the enemies of the faith. I saw Villiers's face when he talked of being left without father or mother. It was horrid to see it."

" Go on," repeated Pearce, exultingly.

" And then the judge summed up, and told the jury that they could have no doubt — that Villiers's evidence must hang him—and that whatever might be done with the others, here murder had been committed, and the law must take its course."

" Is that all?" asked Pearce.

" I do not know any more," replied the other. " For there was a bustle in the court. Villiers had fallen down, and they were taking him out. And I came off as quick as possible, for it is full twenty miles from here. And I only had the letter to-day about the secret passage, and orders to get you out without delay. And there is no time to lose. Get

up, and dress directly. Hark! there is some one
coming!"

And at that moment footsteps were heard approaching along the cloister. And O'Foggarty,
hastily closing his dark lantern, paused, and then,
as they came nearer, retreated hastily into the passage in the wall, turned the huge stone softly in its
pivot, and, with the clicking of a spring, Pearce felt
himself once more left in darkness.

But the door of his cell opened, and another light
appeared. It was Beattie.

No one knew what passed at that interview. The
deep-toned bell of the Priory told out one, two, three,
four, five, and Beattie did not come out of the cell;
and the relentless, remorseless, hardened wretch,
even under this last trial and attempt to soften him
on the part of a long-suffering Providence, counted
the strokes with a greedy ear, as if waiting for a
certain time to elapse before he acted. And meanwhile he listened doggedly and with a sullen triumph
to Beattie, whose suspicions had been roused by
some communication with Cookesley, and who now
with entreaties, and now with solemn adjurations,
endeavoured to ascertain if the dreadful surmise
which had flashed across his mind had any foundation. Pearce relentlessly remained silent. He mut-
terred to himself—"Twenty miles!—it must take at
least two hours. It will be all over at eight o'clock."
And then he looked at his watch.

At last, as it struck a quarter to six, the door of
the cell opened, and Beattie, horror-struck, but full
of terrified impatience, was rushing into the cloister.
The voice of the prisoner called him back. "Remember," he said, "the terms." I will tell it to none
but Villiers. He shall come here himself. He shall
beseech me to do it. He shall kneel down at my feet.
I will put my heel upon his accursed neck. He shall

swear to me never to take notice of what I tell him,
so as to involve me in any difficulty. He shall sign
a bond, here, upon the spot, to pay me five thousand
pounds, and then I will tell him where he may find
his son. Are you agreed?"

" And if he find not his son ? " said Beattie.

" It shall be void," cried the other, with a hoarse
chuckle of exultation.

   *   *   *   *   *

We will not pass again into that dark chamber with
Beattie and with Villiers. ·What Pearce had demanded, what he had thirsted for, laboured for during
years—what he had purchased at the expense of his
soul, he enjoyed. Providence granted him his heart's
desire — not figuratively, but really. Villiers knelt
down at his feet—not figuratively, but really. The
wretch who had been his menial set his foot upon his
master's neck, and almost spurned him; and Villiers
bore it all. He remembered the curse of undutifulness, to be made a servant of servants. He only
looked up imploringly, for his heart was nearly
broken with a frightful apprehension of he knew not
what. He made the promise; he signed the bond.
And when Pearce had snatched it ferociously from
him, he waited as one powerless, crushed, all but
annihilated, to hear the announcement so longed for,
yet now so dreaded.

Pearce looked once more at his watch, and at that
moment it struck six. " It is twenty miles," he
said, coolly, " is it not, to Broughton ? It will take
you at least two hours to get there, half-an-hour
to start. Take it !" he exclaimed, and he threw a
packet of paper, tied and sealed with black, into
Villiers's hands. " Go to the prison at Broughton ;
you will find your son — on the scaffold."

They were the last words Pearce uttered in that
cell. Villiers had no sooner staggered from the

room than he disappeared, with a triumphant laugh, within the secret passage, where his accomplice had been waiting for him to escape.

*   *   *   *   *

Seven o'clock struck at the turnpike gate of St. Columb's, about fourteen miles from Broughton, as a carriage and four drove at full gallop through it — the horses dropping with sweat — the postilions whirling their whips, and spurring them till the blood flowed—the servants behind standing up and waving their hats to warn every thing in the way from obstructing the passage. The blinds were drawn. At one point a trace broke, and a face full of agony was thrust from the window, imploring,—oh, with what anguish—that they should not delay. It was Beattie. Another figure was in the inside, kneeling on the bottom of the carriage, motionless—speechless. Not twenty-four hours afterwards his hair, which had been of a glossy black, had turned white with the agony of those two hours. Beattie endeavoured once to speak to him, to lift him up, to make him rest his head in his own arms; but the look of piteous entreaty that he might be left to himself was so earnest, so full of woe, that Beattie dared not repeat the effort. There are states of mental torture when we dread even a touch and movement as much as if the body were all one ulcer.

Eight o'clock struck as the carriage whirled round the corner of the narrow street at the entrance into Broughton. There was an enormous crowd. The postilions, ready to drop with exhaustion, were compelled to walk their horses. In vain, Beattie spoke from the windows—entreated—besought the people to make way. They were laughing, shouting, hurrying forward in joyous confusion to the market-place, where the prison stood, to see an execution; for to Englishmen an execution is a spectacle as entertaining as a farce. Two men contrived to get, one on each side of the carriage. One was singing a vulgar ribald song about Ernest some-one — the name could not be heard — who had killed a yeomanry soldier. The other was crying his last dying speech and confession, and thrust it into the windows. Villiers looked up, and asked if to advance was impossible—if they could not walk; but at that moment the great bell of the prison began to toll, and he knew that it was too late now to reach the spot before all would be over. He rose up, seated himself in his seat, quietly drew down the blind which Beattie had drawn up in the vain attempt to urge the crowd to make way for the carriage, begged Beattie to tell the postilions to take care not to drive over any one, and, closing his eyes, composed himself to resignation. Beattie was astonished, and unable to account for his calmness, till he remembered David. It was the tranquillity, not of despair, but of certainty. Any state was more endurable than doubt. Any dispensation of Heaven, once sealed, was to be accepted with patience and submission.

Beattie now ventured to propose that they should not go at once to the prison, but to the house of the clergyman of the town, whom they both knew. But just then there was a stir and movement in the crowd, which he could not account for. He looked out. The carriage had reached the market-place. In front stood the dark, gaunt, eyeless wall of the county prison, and over the gateway was the gloomy erection, towards which Beattie dared not look. The crowd seemed angry, disappointed; they were separating, pushing away, with oaths and imprecations, from the point of attraction. A sudden movement of the carriage, as it became entangled among the struggling and fighting mob, brought Beattie's

eyes unwillingly to the point which he had so
dreaded facing; but, to his surprise, the fearful
object which he had expected to behold was not
there. The bell had ceased to toll; and yet the
scaffold was unoccupied. Loud voices began to be
heard. "Is it a reprieve?" asked a woman close
to the carriage-window. "No, I fancy not," was
the answer. "Then, why do they not bring him
out?" asked another. "Why do they keep us
waiting here all this blessed day?" Beattie's heart
beat till his breath was nearly gone. A policeman
was standing in the crowd, who recognised the Villiers livery, and endeavoured to make way for the
carriage. Beattie beckoned to him. He scarcely
dared to speak; but the policeman recommended
that they should turn into a bye street. "The
people are coming away, sir," he said. "There is
to be no execution this morning."

"Is there a reprieve?" cried Beattie.

"No, sir," answered the policeman, "not that;
but I fancy something is the matter."

"Drive on, drive on," cried Beattie to the postilions, "to the prison."

The crowd made way; there was nothing any
longer to attract them. The carriage stopped. The
line of constables cleared a passage to the dark
portal of the prison; the servants opened the door;
and the mob, with that vulgar unfeeling curiosity
which is characteristic of England in the nineteenth
century, pressed and jostled forward to see what
new shape of misery was approaching the place of
punishment.

"Can you walk?" asked Beattie, tenderly; and
to his surprise Villiers, as if nerved and composed,
rose steadily, descended from the carriage, and, only
clinging twice to the iron railing of the stairs, followed one of the jailers to the condemned cell.

Beattie said a few words to the chaplain, who was standing at the door; the cell was cleared of all but the physician, who was watching the effect of some medicine on a livid corpse-like figure which lay stretched upon the straw pallet, its face distorted with the effect of poison. Villiers knelt down by the bed, took his son's hand in his own — his cold, clammy, death-like hand — bowed his head upon it, but did not weep. He was dreaming of another place — of a blue sea, a seat scooped in the living rock, a trellised vine-covered cottage. His mind seemed wandering. And then there rose up before him a fair, pensive, exquisitely beautiful face; and then it changed, as in his dreams it often had changed, into that ghastly, awful face which he had seen on his father's death-bed. It seemed strange, but his heart felt light. Anything is better than doubt. He had found his son, — and his son was dead. All seemed over.

But all was not over. Villiers started, almost in terror; for the hand which had lain dead and motionless in his own stirred with a convulsive spasm. Beattie stooped over the face. The physician held a glass to its lips; and then, with a look of hope and joy, he motioned to Beattie to draw Villiers quietly from the room. He held his finger to his mouth, to indicate the necessity of silence; and Villiers, bewildered, unresisting, as one who had lost all power of thought and action, suffered Beattie to lead him away like a child.

* * * * *

An awful feeling thrilled through the hearts of every inmate of the Priory, when, about ten days afterwards, in the solemn service of the chapel, the prayers of the congregation were desired for a person, within their own walls, dangerously ill. No eye, but many thoughts, were turned to Vil-

liers himself, who, kneeling in his usual place, at
the right hand of Beattie—so crushed with suffering that his head lay like lead upon his cushion, so
altered with the agony which he had undergone
that his dearest friend would not have known him—
moved, indeed, his lips to join the deep and fervent
Amen of the whole congregation, but could utter
nothing. From the chapel he passed to a chamber,
where, recovered to life and consciousness, but
smitten with the slow and lingering hand of death,
lay his lost treasure—his pardoned son. The physicians had ordered that nothing should be said or
done which might disturb him; and Villiers therefore sat at a distance, out of sight, or knelt behind
the bed, only drawing the curtain aside when a
fitful sleep stole upon the fevered brow of his boy,
and he could gaze on that face, so beautiful, and
now so easily recognised, without being seen.
Others often were kneeling with him, and among
them Bentley, himself in sickness; and from many
a heart, as from many a lip, morning and evening,
in public and in private, prayers rose within those
holy walls, that some token of good might still be
showed upon him who had showed, under Heaven,
so many such tokens to themselves. And at times
even faint hopes sprang up that these prayers would
be answered by the restoration of the sick to health
and strength. His mind gradually returned. His
vigour was so far recovered that he was enabled to
be removed into the open air; and, placed in a
wheel-chair, his head propped with pillows, he was
drawn backwards and forwards along the broad
terrace which ran in front of the cloisters, while
Villiers himself walked at his side, now stopping to
wipe the moisture from the pale forehead of the
sick youth, now arranging the pillows with a hand
of tenderness, and at times stooping over his face

till he almost touched it with his lips. And then
he checked himself, for still the physician forbade
that anything should be said or done to cause the
least excitement. And meanwhile Ernest looked
on wondering, but softened almost to tears by the
tenderness which watched over him. His eye had
lost its fierceness; pain and suffering had obliterated from his beautiful face all the harsher lines of
intemperance. It seemed as if a noble spirit within
him was struggling to throw off a fearful and unnatural load of sin, which some hand from without
had cast upon a generous nature. More than once
he endeavoured to speak — to say something to Villiers which might show his gratitude. More than
once, with a feeble hand, he laid bare a scar upon
his breast, which had been there ever since the
days of his boyhood — ever since Villiers had saved
him from the fire; and pointing to it, he indicated
that he knew who it was that had then rescued him,
and was now tending him. And then he would
take Villiers's hand, and press it to his parched lips;
and while the tears streamed from Villiers's face
his own eyes were suffused also. And once — oh,
how Villiers's heart melted within him at that act
— when Villiers was taking leave of him for the
night, he made signs for him to kneel down by the
bed-side. And Villiers prayed for his son, not yet
wholly lost. And he saw the lips of the sick moving
at every petition, and his eyes upturned to heaven.
And when Villiers rose from his knees the youth
raised his head faintly from the pillow, and stretched
out his hands to embrace him, and whispered, " If
God had given me such a father, I should never
have been what I am !"

The next day Beattie sat by his bed-side, and
found him able to bear conversation; and the day
after, as the same hour approached, more than once

Ernest inquired when Mr. Beattie would come; for the words which he had heard had sunk into his heart, and he longed to hear them again. And day after day it was still the same. And as Villiers listened to the accounts which Beattie gave him of these interviews, his eyes became blinded with tears; but they were tears of gratitude and hope. His son was a penitent.

Weeks passed, and though the Angel of Death still hung over the bed of the sufferer, and the last hour was only delayed, while the body was slowly breaking up, the soul within seemed purifying itself, and strengthening, and coming out, as the moon from a mass of clouds. And after the terrible sharp agonies of remorse were past, and some degree of calmness was restored, a change came over the whole nature of that troubled spirit. It became gentle, and humble, and tranquil; and at last permission was given, and Villiers laid the head of his sobbing boy upon his own breast, and whispered to him, that he had a father upon earth as well as in Heaven.

And then there was a solemn, awful, but blessed rite in that sick chamber. And then the room was closed up—closed to all but one person, who passed the days and the nights in prayer, kneeling by the lifeless form of his lost yet recovered son. The day approached when he was to part for ever with all that remained of him upon earth. The evening before, leaning on the arm of Beattie, Villiers desired to see himself the place where those dear relics would be deposited. The masons, who were opening the vault, had not been warned of his approach in time, and they were vainly endeavouring to conceal from him some object of horror which they had found on entering the catacomb. But Beattie caught sight of it, and Villiers too. It was a body

all but devoured by rats. A lantern, with the
candle burnt out, lay in one corner. All over the
pavement were traces of blood, as if the wretched
man had fled from place to place before his ferocious
assailants; and there were marks of bloody hands
upon the walls, on one place especially, where the
stones were convulsively scrabbled over with gory
fingers, and a spring was found within the stone,
but which had closed from the other side, and could
not be opened. The extremities were wholly gone.
The vitals must have been attacked last. A hat
lay at some distance from the body, and in it was a
name; and Villiers read it. It was the destroyer
of his child.

*   *   *   *   *

"O Beattie!" Villiers used to say, as, many years
after, evening after evening, accompanied by Bentley, they paced together the cloisters of the Priory,
calm and sorrowing, yet not without gratitude and
hope, for all the manifold increasing blessings of
that holy abode, "will not the vengeance of Heaven, sooner or later, in some frightful shape, fall
upon those miserable men, who, under the name
and in the garb of religion, are rending asunder, in
this country, ties which God has joined, and tearing
the children of this empire from their Father in the
State and in the Church, as my child was torn
from me!"

THE END.

LONDON:
Printed by A. SPOTTISWOODE,
New-Street-Square.